The House of Baric

Part Two:

A Brother's Defense

A novel by

Jillian Bald

HILLWALKER PUBLISHING

The House of Baric Part Two: A Brother's Defense
Copyright © 2016, 2018, 2022 Jillian Bald
Published by Hillwalker Publishing 2022
Cover design © 2022 Jillian Bald

THIRD REV. EDITION
The author edited some exposition and dialogue in this revised edition, correcting grammatical and typographical errors, adding an author's note, and renumbering chapters.

Fonts were used with permission and/or licensed: Garamond 11pt, HOPFER HORNBOOK, Centaur, and *Antiquarian Scribe* (3ip.com).

This is a work of fiction. The names, characters, events, and dialogue come from the author's imagination; they are not real. Any resemblance to actual persons, living or dead, is entirely coincidental. Historical incidences are intended to provide a sense of time and authenticity and are used fictitiously.

BISAC subject codes relevant for this book series: FIC027370, FIC043000, FIC027230, FIC071000, FIC045010, FIC045020, FIC008000, FIC032000

Paperback ISBN: 978-1-943594-16-0
Ebook ISBN: 978-1-943594-19-1

This publication was printed on demand.

A NOTE FROM THE AUTHOR

Hello, Reader! I am glad you are back for the next book in the Barics' saga. I know I left you hanging at the end of *Shields Down*, but it seemed a good place to make a cut.

Part two of *The House of Baric* picks right up where we left off: Patrik and his gang are waiting in the castle courtyard for Mauro and Resi to return from the seaside. Will it be a good reunion? You will soon learn this and other answers to questions left unresolved in part one.

If you forgot who was who and who did what, I added a 'Glossary of Characters' to refresh your memory. I know it is a long list, but many of the names there are merely people mentioned in the first book, although many still have a role to play in the following books.

If you need to be reminded of more than just the names, the online synopsis of book one can be found at: www.JillianBald.com/synopsis. But don't look ahead to book two's summary because it's filled with spoilers.

A Brother's Defense is the longest of the three novels in the trilogy, maybe because the mercenaries ended up playing a bigger role in the story than I first intended. I liked this rag-tag group of sellswords, and as I wrote the draft, I wondered what their backstories might be and how they got to this point in their lives. You'll have to trust that their talk about wives, daughters, and even horses isn't random name-dropping to fill the pages. Along with the sellswords, these newly mentioned women will get more page-time in the trilogy's final book, *Widows and Weddings*, so feel free to root for them as much as I do.

For now, let's meet these mercenaries and join the Barics and their friends as the gate opens for them in *Part Two: A Brother's Defense*.

~*~

GLOSSARY OF CHARACTERS

The Croatian Nobility

BARIC

Mauro/ Mauritius Radovan Baric: born 1624, Solgrad, Croatia. Fostered at Toth Castle from age 11. Well-traveled, careered army officer. Second son and reluctant heir to the Baric's barony. Forced marriage in 1648 to:
Resi/Terese Helena (Kokkinos): born 1628 in Thessaloniki. Unexpectedly likable, beautiful, well-read daughter of a Greek sea trader.

Mateo (Matej): 1621-1636. Mauro's half-brother who drowned in the sea.

Lorenc: 1594-1647. Second son of Fredrik. Baron of Baric 1614-1647. Mauro's misunderstood father. Died at age 53 of an undetermined illness (or possibly murder). Married twice: in 1614 and again in 1623.
Margaret: 1595-1622. Beautiful, amusing, beloved first wife of Lorenc. Died with their three children in a plague.
Johanna: 1601-1648. Mauro's mother. Sister to Renata Toth. Second wife to Lorenc. Unhappy, with a personality disorder. Died suddenly at age 47.

Fredrik: 1567-1614 in a hunting accident. Mauro's grandfather. Politically caught up in Venice. Savvy trader. Generous patron. Widower. Married in 1590 to his beloved:
Anica: 1570-1601. Sons: Vladimir and Lorenc. Died birthing twin girls.

TOTH

Vladimir (Baric): Born 1592. Mauro's uncle. Regional governor, army general, titled count in 1613 after an advantageous marriage in 1612 to:
Renata: Countess. Lady Johanna's sister. Kind and generous to Mauro.
Petar: born 1616. Eldest of Renata's four children. Heir to Toth County. Traveled with Mauro as a youth. Mauro's least favorite cousin.
Dominik: Mauro's maternal grandfather. Influential Count. Died 1613.

LEOPOLD

Neven: Nearest neighbor to the south. Mateo's childhood friend. Mauro's newest confident. Navy occupies his port town. Married to:
Nikolina: Resi's aristocratic friend. Gossipy. Expecting her fourth child.
Eleonora: Neven's widow mother. Dowager. Smart and well-informed.
Karloff: Eleonora's husband. Neven's father. Killed by bandits in 1634.
Cedomir: 1570-1639. Neven's grandfather. Didn't get along with Fredrik.

DUBOVIC

Sebastijan: Mauro's neighbor to the north. Landlord of an much over-sized barony. Scheming widower with two married daughters.

RANERI

Lord and Lady Raneri: Aristocratic landholder south of Leopold's estate. Attended the ball.

MARQUIS

Lord Marquis: Nobleman. Influential with the Venetian Navy. Landholder bordering the Republic of Ragusa. Attended the ball.

The Croatian Commoners

The Castle Servants

Idita	nanny and family nurse since 1593
Nestor (Silvijo)	steward to Lorenc, Mauro's advisor, widower
Jero	Mauro's childhood playmate/valet and steward
Alberto	stable master for over 30 years, father of six
Geoff	orphan, Verica's younger brother, stable groom
Verica	orphaned, raised at the castle, Resi's lady's maid
Natalija	Lady Johanna's lady's maid, tanner's daughter
Davor	Mauro's young valet/personal groom
Nela "Cook"	head cook, servant since 1601, aging spinster
Franja	baker, assistant to Nela, Simeon's lover
Danica	kitchen gardener, wife of Krsto
Krsto	head gardener, husband of Danica, Jero's friend
Ranko	assistant gardener to Krsto
Tin (Martin)	servant to Keep residents, Milan's oldest son
Lazar	servant to Keep residents, Milan's son
Suzana	temporary head cook after Lorenc's death
Ana	bathhouse attendant
Karl	castle blacksmith
Josip	stable groom, Alberto's eldest son
Aron	water boy, hall servant, Alberto's youngest son
Brigita	kitchen maid

Ivana	kitchen maid
Marija	kitchen maid, sister to Natalija
Louisa	house maid

Villagers

Dino Radic	village constable
Anton	new bailiff after Grgur died
Signor Sandrigo	temporary village surgeon, apothecary
Signor Martini	long-time village surgeon, deceased
Andrea	'Green Goose' proprietor, Tatjana's mother
Tatjana	barmaid, young widow, Mauro's lover
Elizabeta	Radic's third wife
Darijo	Tanner and saddle maker, Natalija's father
Luka	Natalija's brother, tanner's son, Verica's love interest
Jakov Kuzjak	salt mine supervisor, patriarch of ship's crew
Branislav Tomsic	newest Baric ship captain, Ivanoslav's son
Ivanoslav Tomsic	retired Baric ship captain, Branislav's father

The Croatian Soldiers

Mauro's New Guard:

Fabian	best friend, artillery captain in Toth Army
Stephan	second best friend, squad leader in Toth Army
Simeon	seasoned soldier from Toth Army, widower
Vilim	favorite Toth cousin, squad leader in Toth Army
Hugo	youngest, commoner, former Toth Army scout
Eduard	seasoned carry-over from Lorenc's Guard
Daniel	young carry-over with a stuttering problem

Other Named Guardsmen:

Vik	scout, soldier
Denis	scout, soldier
Teodor	scout, soldier
Adrijan	scout, soldier
Henrik	scout, soldier
Bartol	scout, soldier
Neno	scout, soldier
Latif	scout, soldier

Injured, Retired Soldiers Employed in the Keep:

Milan   Keep cook. Father to Tin and Lazar
Drazen   Keep cook
Andro   Keep cook

Lorenc's Old Guard Officers:

Tomas   poisoned with Lord Lorenc
Bruno   poisoned with Lord Lorenc
Grgur   Guard captain, later the bailiff

Other Characters:

Signor Rosso   Venetian Republic tax collector
Andrej   Baric crewman
Signor Donati   shopkeeper in Rijeka
Danko   courier/messenger for Radic
Captain Marko   Lord Dubovic's guardsman

The Venetians

Meister Uberti: Baric sons' childhood tutor.

Lieutenant D'Alessandro: Commands the navy patrolling Croatian waters. Stationed in Leopold's port town. Gambler who beds only virgins.
Captain Pasini: Second in command to D'Alessandro.
Orlando: navy clerk and assistant to D'Alessandro.

Roberto Carrera: Fabian's father. Titled lord, councilman, wealthy silk merchant. Long-time friend of Lorenc and Vladimir.
Carrera Siblings in Venice:
    Gabriel: born 1620. Married to **Perla**. Heir to the family fortune.
    Michele: born 1622 Newly married. Runs the family fabric business.
    Fabian Carrera: born 1624. Army Captain. Mauro's friend since 17.
    Cristina: born 1626. Married and a new mother. Isabella's friend.
    Caterina Carrera: born 1630. Engaged to Hungarian Viscount.
    Bianca: born 1633. Youngest. Newly introduced to society.

Paolo: Carrera guardsman. Caterina's secret lover.
Gino: Carrera guardsman.

Stephan Padovi: born 1625. Son of a prominent Venetian aristocrat. Army captain and childhood friend of Fabian. Madly in love with Mira.
Mira: young wealthy fiancée to Stephan.

Isabella Valli: born 1625. Daughter to a powerful Venetian politician. Caterina's traveling companion. Childhood friend to the Carrera siblings.
Alfonzo Valli: Isabella's only sibling. Heir to the Valli family fortune.

Lady Rosella: Noblewoman, socialite, and Mauro's former lover.

Lord Marcellis: mentioned in a seduction trick with a Duchess.

Ottomans and Foreigners

Demetrius Kokkinos: Resi's father. Thessalonian ship captain, trader, Baric's broker. Imprisoned six years for stealing from Lord Lorenc.
Celine Kokkinos: Resi's Catholic mother, who met Demetrius while he traded in her native Kingdom of France.
Kokkinos Siblings in Thessaloniki:
>**Castor**: born 1619. Sea captain for his father's fleet. Lives at the family estate in Thessaloniki with his wife and their three children.
>**Alexis**: Castor's wife.
>**Patricius/Patrik**: born 1626. A mercenary sellsword since age 18.
>**Terese/Resi**: born 1628. Married Mauro to pay a family debt.
>**Hector**: born 1638
>**Lander**: born 1641
>**Phyllis**: born 1646

Ruby (Rhoda) Spiros: born 1630. Greek friend and companion to Resi.
Angelos Spiros: Ruby's father. Sea captain. Friend of Demetrius.

Salar Nassim: Born 1614. Persian sellsword and mercenary gang leader. Wives: Hafza in Rhodes and Emine in Athens. Daughter, Shirin, is 16.
Bem (Emilio Chidubem Tavares): born 1625. Ethiopian/Portuguese raised by Jesuits, horse trainer, mercenary soldier, missing his wife Fatina.
Soren: born 1623. Mercenary soldier. Danish orphan traveling the world with his brother since age 17.
Niels: Soren's identical twin, killed October, 1648 in a battle in Prague.
Cyro (Cyrano Duarte): born 1626, Genoese nobleman turned mercenary, hiding from his future responsibilities.

Bartal Soltesz: Hungarian Viscount. Contracted to marry Caterina.

This Book Is Dedicated To Brothers:

The ones we were born to
And the ones we have found ourselves.

A Brother's Defense

Part Two of

The House of Baric

Chapter 1

The House of Baric had been thrown into a bit of turmoil for such a fine June day. The maids had been given three days alone to put the manor house in order after the baron's successful ball. It should have been enough time to rearrange the great hall again, re-stuff the many mattresses in all the bed chambers, launder the piles of linens, and wash the stacks of dishes. The servants had not counted on the Barics' early return from their outing to the seashore. The five strangers sitting on war horses within their walls did not help the anxious mood of the castle, either.

~*~

Verica and Natalija were standing at the window in Caterina and Isabella's chamber when Idita came looking for them. "There you are, girls. I thought you were done with this room," said Idita from the doorway. She walked over to the window to see what they were staring at. It had a view of the courtyard and the baroness's visitors waiting there. "Hurry up, now. The baron will be home shortly, and you will be needed to help the ladies when they arrive," she said in a motherly way.

"How can they just sit there for hours?" Natalija wondered aloud, still leaning on the windowsill to get a full view.

Idita replied, "The same way you can stand there for hours watching them."

Verica left the window to put fresh flowers in a vase Idita had brought her. "Why won't they get off their horses, Idita?" she asked.

"I guess they do not trust the baron's guards. They are being defensive by staying mounted."

Natalija asked, "How can that be defensive, stuck on your horse?"

"A soldier is always safer on his horse than off. He is faster, and the horse fights with him," explained Idita. "It is like two against one."

"Will they be fighting the baron today?" fretted Natalija.

"No, child," Idita assured her soothingly. "The baron would not allow them inside the walls if they were dangerous. One of them is the baroness's brother."

Verica said, "I bet he is the one with the tall, red boots. He looks like her, don't you think?"

"They all look very different to me. Are they bad men, Idita?" asked Natalija with concern.

"Why would Lady Baric bring them here if they were bad?" said Verica, wanting to believe her own words.

Idita explained, "They are not bad men, just bad soldiers. They are mercenaries, sellswords. They are soldiers without an allegiance."

Natalija stared out the window again while Verica took care of the last chores in the room. "Do you think they like to kill?" she asked worriedly.

"I do not think any man likes to kill, but I cannot say what motivates a man to do what he does. It was their job, but now it seems they are done. For the baroness's sake we will give them a chance to show us they are good men," said Idita. She looked around the room. "Have you turned the mattress and remade the bed for the baroness?" she asked the girls more cheerfully.

"We have, Idita. The baroness's chamber is ready for her," replied Verica.

"Good. Then I suggest you go put on a fresh apron and then see if Cook has your lunch ready. There will not be time for you to eat when the ladies arrive."

The maids left, but Idita lingered in the room a few moments longer and watched the mercenaries out the window from a distance. She had been trying to quell Natalija's worries, but the waiting visitors were indeed fearsome to behold.

~ * ~

Cook had laid out a light lunch to feed the house staff as they came and went about their urgent chores. Jero and Nestor had eaten in the kitchen with the housemaids and then filled the next hour closing out the account books for June. Jero took time to wash up and change out of his traveling clothes with nothing else pressing while they waited for the baron to return.

Refreshed but fidgeting in his small room, Jero went back to the study. Nestor was pacing there, looking out the window, also nervously anticipating the Barics' arrival. The Baric guards had pretended to go about their business as usual. Still, Nestor could see that they, too, were waiting impatiently for something to happen.

"Why are they still on their horses?" asked Jero, finally breaking the silence at the study window. "The baroness invited them with Lord Baric's blessing. Do they not understand that they are welcome here?"

"They are stubborn and prideful. They take our generosity as a trick of some sort," said Nestor. He continued to watch the scene outside. "Let them stay mounted in this heat. I do not pity them, only their horses. We did our duty and offered them hospitality, but they snubbed their noses at us. Lady Terese is a gentle woman. I hope they will not shame her by continuing to behave in such an ungrateful manner."

Jero turned from the window and hurriedly took his waistcoat from the chairback to put it on. "Well, Nestor, we will soon find out," he said excitedly. "They are opening the gate for the baron's wagon."

Chapter 2

The castle road was in full view from the ramparts after the last bend at the practice fields. The guards would open the gate for the baron's wagon long before Mauro would have to slow down. It had already been a tedious morning and a long ride from Leopolds' beach. After the scouts had found the Baric party at their seaside retreat, the mood of the travelers was tense. Resi was eager to see her brother after so many years, but Mauro was dreading that his wife would be disappointed with her reunion.

"Why are they not opening the gate for us?" Resi asked her husband.

"I am not sure," he mumbled.

Mauro halted the horses, and Fabian rode up alongside him. Ruby stopped her horse behind the wagon, where Isabella and Caterina were sitting on the remaining hay. The Venetian ladies watched Ruby's face for any clue of what was happening at the gate while Ruby watched the baron.

"Hello, Eduard," Mauro called over to the gatehouse. "Is there a problem with the chain?"

"Not with the chain, no, but there is a problem you need to know about in the courtyard," replied Captain Eduard.

Fabian gave Mauro a look of disapproval, but Mauro remained optimistic. He hopped off the wagon bench and asked more quietly, "Have the visitors arrived?"

Eduard's voice sounded strained when he answered, "Yes, sir, they have. They arrived a few hours ago, but they will not dismount."

"What do you mean?"

"Jero escorted them from the crossroad to the castle. Nestor invited them to unload their horses and wait in comfort on the terrace. They refused. They are on their horses, fully armed, waiting for you, sir."

"Thank you for the warning, Eduard. Now open the gate."

Mauro looked over at his wife with a faint smile as he retook the reins. He squeezed her hand affectionately and leaned over to explain, "I think somehow we have already gotten off to an awkward start. Your brother forgot that in order to visit *you*, he has to come into *my* guarded walls."

"Is there trouble?" she asked.

"No, my dear," he replied, "but I want you to promise me you will stay by the wagon until I take you to greet Patricius. Can I count on you to wait?"

She quelled her nervousness and answered confidently, "Of course, Mauro."

Mauro drove the wagon slowly past the high wall's entrance toward the stables and the row of strangers waiting for them on horseback. The grand terrace steps were filling with the arrival of Jero, Nestor, Idita, the cooks, and every house and garden servant on duty that day. Mauro stopped the wagon and gave the reins to Geoff, who had come running out of the stables.

Seeing her brother, Resi wanted to jump down and run to Patricius. Their eyes met, and she smiled, but her brother did not return the greeting. Stubborn man, she thought.

Mauro jumped down and then lifted Resi off the bench seat. He gave her a stern look while his back was turned to the new guests, and she faintly nodded that she would keep her word to him.

Fabian had already dismounted and went to help his sister and Isabella from the wagon. There would be no protest or argument this time. With his gallant assistance, they looked like they climbed out of the back of wagons every day of their aristocratic lives.

Before the ride home, Fabian had tied a fashionable neck scarf over the collar of his tailored shirt. Matching blue ribbons held up his pale blue stockings, and his black buckled shoes still gleamed under the light layer of road dust from a buffing before their departure. His wide-brimmed hat, decorated with a white feather plume that came close to matching Isabella's in size, covered his tied-back hair.

Before the scouts had packed away the tent that morning, the ladies had changed from their linen and gauze gowns back into their corseted silk ones. When the wagon had stopped at the closed gate, they had repositioned their elegant hats over their elaborately pinned locks. The fuss they had made to dress properly before leaving had caused the delay in their departure. With a haughty regalness, the three aristocrats now took their places next to the baron and baroness.

Alberto came over to help Ruby down from her horse. Her cheeks were rosy from the sun and wind of her ride.

Patrik's eyes were on Ruby before his gaze moved back to his sister. At Resi's side, the baron unbelted his sword and placed it on the ground. Mauro's guardsmen put their weapons down as well. Patrik looked up at the ramparts, and the soldiers there lowered their bows out of sight.

Satisfied, Patrik swung his tired leg over his saddle and dismounted to the cobbled ground. He unbelted his weapon, placed it next to him, and waited for his host to approach. The other four riders followed his lead.

Mauro held out his hand in greeting with the poise of someone in charge, but he could not quite manage a smile.

Patrik shook his offered hand, looking his host over with a steady glare. Baron Baric had the stately presence of a wealthy man in his dark, masculine riding ensemble and matching brimmed hat. Today, the baron's penetrating green eyes held no threat to him. Patrik would mind his manners.

His companions let him speak for them as they cautiously watched the reunion.

He bowed to the baron and said with as much sincerity as he could muster, "Lord Baric, we are grateful for your invitation."

"I hope you have not been inconvenienced by our delay," said Mauro, attempting to sound pleasant. "You and your friends are welcome here. My wife, especially, has been looking forward to your visit."

He turned and walked the few steps to take Resi's hand. Mauro passed her to her brother and then stepped back.

The siblings embraced each other with obvious delight. He held her outstretched arms and looked at her with pleasure. She wore the Thessalonian riding clothes that suited her so well. Her stylish Venetian hat, the one Isabella had lent her for the ride home, was all that gave her status as a baroness away. She was otherwise the same, he thought, and he smiled with relief.

Resi touched Patrik's face and frowned. Then, in their native Greek, she blurted out, "You look half-starved, Brother!" She sounded just like their mother, and he loved her for it.

"I won't lie to you. We have had a tough journey the last few months."

"I want to hear all about it, later, when we have time to talk. You know you are welcome here. Why did you make such a scene, Patricius? I am ashamed of you," she scolded.

He looked over at her husband, who was watching the siblings closely. "There were twenty men with swords and arrows pointed at us, dear sister. The welcome did not appear to be friendly."

"Well, it is friendly now," she said. "Take our offer to stay and relax, for my sake. Will you?"

She took his gloved hand in hers and squeezed it. Then her happy expression faded.

Sensing her panic, he assured her, "There are worse things that could have happened since we last saw each other. I didn't need that finger anyway."

Salar Nassim and Soren stepped forward at this time. Resi smiled at them and said, "I am very glad to see God has kept you safe."

The Persian bowed low and kissed her outstretched hand before he answered her with what seemed to be a prayer of sorts.

Resi smiled with understanding and spoke to him in her own language.

Mauro watched their familiarity with noticeable discomfort.

Patrik introduced his other companions, "Resi, these are my friends Bem and Cyro. They have been with us for about two years now."

The men stepped forward and bowed to the baroness.

"I am pleased you have such fine traveling companions, Patricius. Do you remember mine?" She turned and waved Ruby over.

Patrik's expression brightened, and he became momentarily boyish. He embraced Ruby like family and then kissed her on each cheek, which sent a rumble of uneasiness through the crowd of soldiers sworn to protect the baroness's friend.

Patrik ignored his audience. "You are a lovely sight, dear Ruby. Imagine meeting you here! Have you been watching my sister for me?"

"I have, and she is very well. You should not worry," Ruby assured him.

He searched her eyes and asked, "And how has your time here been? Do you like living with the Venetians?"

After her wonderful outing, she had only one answer: "Yes, Patricius, I am happy here."

Mauro decided the family reunion had gone on long enough. The mercenaries' icy façade had temporarily melted, and their visit might be tolerable for a time. He stepped up to Resi and asked, "Will you introduce your brother and his companions to our other guests?"

"With pleasure, Mauro."

She took Patrik's hand and led him to the Venetians. "Patricius, these are our visitors from Venice. Lady Caterina is the sister of Captain Carrera." She waved her hand toward Fabian, standing next to Caterina. "And Lady Isabella Valli is Caterina's companion," she added. "We've had a lovely time together this past week."

"It is a pleasure to meet you. Please, call me Patrik." He turned back to his friends and motioned, "These are my companions: Soren, Salar Nassim, Cyro, and Bem."

The ladies nodded politely and mumbled their salutations.

Impatient with the formalities, Mauro announced, "You and your friends will be lodged in our Keep tower, Patrik, if that is to your liking."

He looked around for who might best take the men to their chamber. Mauro decided they would not trust Eduard or Simeon again so soon. He called over to his steward on the terrace: "Jero!"

Jero dutifully hurried across the courtyard.

"Can you show our guests to their accommodations?" ordered Mauro.

Resi tugged on her husband's sleeve and asked, "May I have a word with Jero first?"

He granted her request, and she walked with Jero a few paces from the others to whisper something.

Mauro continued his instructions to his brother-in-law. "My servants will assist you in bringing your equipment up to your chamber. The stable groom can show you where you can keep your horses."

"Thank you, Lord Baric," said Patrik halfheartedly. "Bem takes care of our horses. He will go with the boy."

Bem nodded and led the two unsaddled stallions toward the stables.

When Resi returned to Mauro's side, he quietly instructed her to wait in their chamber. The other three women followed the baroness across the courtyard and through the terrace doors.

Mauro watched them go and then went to the stables to talk to Alberto about accommodating the extra seven horses. Geoff was already driving the baron's wagon away to the back of the manor house to unload. The remaining four mercenaries were unfastening their gear from their saddles.

~*~

Fabian had not needed an introduction by the baroness. He and the mercenaries had met before: once when they were fighting for the same side, and once when they were not. Fabian had not been particularly fond of their company at the time and doubted much had changed. So when he approached them in the courtyard, Fabian spoke directly to Patrik. The others would understand that Fabian was cautioning them as well.

"Just so everything is clear, Patrik, my sister Caterina is under my protection," he began. "She is betrothed to a Hungarian nobleman and is to be married soon."

Fabian looked around at the guarded faces and added, "Her companion, Lady Isabella, can be a charming woman. She is off-limits. If you so much as touch a skirt, I will cut off your prick. Have I made myself clear?"

The men remained expressionless when Patrik answered, "You will have no worries on our account, Captain Carrera. My men know how to treat women, especially friends of my sister. They will be under our protection, as well."

Fabian seemed pleased with himself that he had put them in their place. He bowed in acknowledgment of their easy acceptance and then walked to the Keep's entrance.

Once he was out of sight, the four men snickered.

Jero had been waiting off to the side. He had not heard what Fabian had said to the foreigners but was more at ease when he thought he saw them smiling. He announced to the visitors, "Tin and Lazar will help bring your things upstairs. Lord Baric has given you his private chamber in the Keep."

The men stopped their task unloading their supplies and urgently huddled together to confer.

Patrik told Jero, "We will not inconvenience Baron Baric. We will camp outside the walls, if that is all the same to you."

It was all the same to Jero, but he could not let them insult the baron by rejecting Mauro's offer of hospitality.

"I assure you, Lord Baric is not inconvenienced. I should have clarified that the Barics reside in the manor house, not in the Keep. Everything has been arranged. I will show you the way." Jero began to walk toward the stairs.

The four gathered their gear. With no more objections, the mercenaries slung what they could carry over their shoulders and then followed the steward to the tower.

At the top of the outside stairs, Jero informed them, "Lady Terese has one specific request, gentlemen." He pointed across the expansive flower garden below them. "The baroness's bathhouse is at the far end of that path. Supplies are laid out, and her ladyship asks that you visit it before attending the evening meal. You can leave any garments there that you would like laundered. The servants will retrieve them to wash for you."

Patrik gave his own appearance a quick look-over and shrugged. "Well, perhaps we could use a good washing. You may tell my sister that we will, as always, obey her wishes."

They followed Jero through the doorway, laughing for the first time in weeks. But their laughter was short-lived. They walked through the dining hall to the cold stares of the Baric guardsmen lounging there, waiting for the mercenaries to come through. Sellswords were not well-liked by the Venetian soldiers.

Jero hurried them along to the stairs. "There are four stairwells, but only this one goes to the officers' quarters. That is where your chamber is," he explained.

They came to the second-floor landing, which opened into the common room for the baron's six officers. Vilim and Simeon were seated at the long table there, awaiting their arrival.

Jero made the introductions. "Gentlemen, these are two of Lord Baric's officers, Vilim and Simeon. Their chambers are across from yours."

Vilim and Simeon tipped their hats and looked the four over rudely.

Jero ignored their unfriendly manner and walked past them. The heavy oak door to the Baric's chamber was closed but not locked, and he lifted the latch to a rush of memories. Jero and Mauro had played in this room as boys, sneaking up when Lord Lorenc's soldiers were away. It had the biggest bed Jero had ever seen at the time, and it was still immense, he thought. He shook off his hesitation and strode into the room, followed by the guests.

"It looks like two extra cots have been brought in for you. The bed will sleep three men comfortably." He continued, "As you can see, there is plenty of room for all of your equipment and supplies to be stored in here during your stay."

Jero noticed that pitchers and basins had been placed on the two grooming tables. "It looks like water has already been brought up to the room. The Keep, as we call the tower, has warm running water down on the first floor for washing, and there are toilets just around the corner of the stairwell. I think you will find the arrangements adequate for your needs."

Jero dutifully stood with his hands crossed behind his back and waited for any questions.

The men were speechless. It was all more than adequate; it was luxurious compared to how they had slept the last few years.

Salar Nassim spoke for all of them when he said, "We are humbled that Baron Baric has honored us with such accommodations. We will be very comfortable. Thank you."

Tin and Lazar came to the door carrying several saddlebags, and Bem was behind them with his arms full of their weapons.

Jero smiled and nodded at the boys to give them the courage to enter the room among the strange men.

"This is Tin," said Jero. "He is the officers' groom here, along with his brother, Lazar. If you need anything, you may call on them any time."

The boys set their loads down, quietly bowed to the new men, and then hurried off to gather the last of their gear.

"Just out of curiosity, Jero, what do men do for entertainment in such a fortress as this?" asked Patrik.

Jero thought for a moment. He himself did nothing for entertainment away from the castle. He knew Mauro provided ale and allowed music in the tower, but he did not think that was what Patrik had meant.

"I do not reside in the Keep and do not have much leisure time myself," Jero said frankly. "I would have to ask the others for you."

The chamber door was open, and Vilim and Simeon were still sitting at the long table. They had overheard the conversation.

Simeon walked to the doorway, eager to give them his advice. "I suppose you want to know where to find female companionship. Well, I don't blame you, but it isn't easy around here," he said with a glint in his eyes. "There is a tavern in the village called the Green Goose. They have drink, music, and tasty food. When the good folks of Solgrad have gone home for the night, there are a handful of attractive women willing to join you in one of the empty rooms for a price," explained Simeon.

Vilim came to Simeon's side and added, "There is only one ale house on Baric land, but about an hour to the north is a village with a few more choices. Another half hour beyond that is a bigger town our men like to visit on their day off. To the south, there is nothing but a few small settlements, until you get to Leopold's port town. There is more entertainment there, but it is a good two-hour ride."

Simeon clarified, "The baron does not want us to live like monks, but he has laid down some ground rules. We call them 'fairy laws'."

The visitors looked at each other curiously, wondering if they had misunderstood.

During their excursion together to Rijeka, Jero had learned the hard way that Vilim and Simeon liked to exaggerate facts for a laugh. This time, though, the two soldiers were mostly truthful. Mauro had indeed set rules to maintain a standard of morality among his guardsmen.

Vilim explained the rules: "If you bring a woman to your bed, she is not to be seen or heard by anyone but you. She must come willingly, and she is to be gone before sunrise."

"She would have to be a fucking fairy to do that," said Simeon, and then nudged Vilim. They enjoyed a good chuckle.

Jero did not join in their laughter. All the residents knew that women were not allowed in the tower, not even mythical ones. However, Jero did not realize that the soldiers used the unoccupied quarters on the floor above to bend this rule from time to time.

"Since you will all share this one room," Vilim went on to explain, "a woman would be seen by the others. Do you see how the fairy law works?"

Cyro spoke for the first time since arriving, "You have been extremely informative, gentlemen. Thank you for your sound advice. We will consider your recommendations."

Vilim and Simeon had heard their share of accents, and both now stared at the well-spoken man. They had not met Cyro during their encounter with Patrik Kokkinos's gang a year ago. They puzzled over how the European man came to be part of such a motley group of mercenaries.

Jero interrupted the awkward silence, "Shall I escort you now, as her ladyship requested? Dinner will be in just a few hours."

"Yes, Jero, we will take that offer now," said Patrik.

He and the others found their satchels with their change of clothes and left Vilim and Simeon alone in the corridor without a glance back.

"I will bet you five lire that this Cyro is a Frenchman," Simeon told Vilim.

"He is a Spaniard—short and dark, arrogant as hell," replied Vilim, turning to shake Simeon's hand to seal the bet. "We will find out at dinner tonight. Have your coins ready."

Chapter 3

The Venetians left Resi and Ruby at the top of the stairs to go to their own chamber after the introductions in the courtyard. The ladies would have welcomed a refreshing pot of hot tea, but in the flurry of activity caused by the new arrivals, Natalija had entirely forgotten about it. When they did not see the teacups in their room, Isabella rang the bell for their maid.

"Can you believe Mauritius sent Lady Terese to her chamber as if she were a child? She was having a wonderful reunion with her brother, and Mauritius dismissed her," said Isabella, fuming.

Caterina peeled off her gloves and sat down to unlace her high shoes. "Do not be so harsh on Mauritius, Isabella. Even I could see Lady Terese was exhausted." A mischievous smile formed on her rouged lips, and she asked, "What you think of her brother and his gang? They looked as though they had not slept under a roof in weeks—so wild and strangely clothed, too."

Isabella considered her appraisal. "I suppose we would have looked the same after a few more days at the seaside."

Isabella set her hat on the side table and took a linen cloth from the stack there. She wet it in the basin to wipe the perspiration from her face and neck. It had been a hot and dusty ride in the wagon bed. Feeling cooler and refreshed, she reflected, "They cannot be as uncivilized as they appear, Cat. Even though the blond one looks like he is straight from a gallery painting of a Viking warrior, they could all speak several languages. That takes some learning. And they had fine horses and numerous weapons. They must have some wealth to afford all of that."

"Yes," agreed Caterina, "and Lady Terese said the Persian man plays music and cards. One must be intelligent to do that. Maybe we will see a different side of them once they dress for dinner."

Isabella turned side to side in front of the looking glass. "We are almost as dirty from just sitting in that filthy wagon. I am trying to decide if I should change before our tea or wait until after."

Caterina stood next to her friend and examined the state of her own attire in the mirror. "I will wait to change. I will need help from Natalija, if she ever comes. Did you ring the bell?"

"I did."

Isabella glanced out the window and saw the colorful men walk down the garden path toward the bathhouse. She contemplated the visitors as they disappeared under the rose arbor.

"Caterina, what do you make of Lady Ruby and Patrik's embrace? Do you think they were once lovers?"

"She is too young to have had him as a lover, if he has been away all those years. That would have made her no more than fifteen." Caterina immediately found fault in her own argument. She herself had been introduced at court at fifteen. "I suppose they could have been once, if they were childhood friends, like you and Fabian."

"Yes, but Fabian and I were never lovers," said Isabella.

"I do not know why you keep denying it, Isabella. There were years when you talked nonstop about my brother. Cristina once told me she caught the two of you in a dark corner of our villa and your bodice was practically unlaced." Caterina raised her eyebrows to tempt her to refute it.

"This conversation is not about me, Caterina, it is about Lady Ruby," Isabella said with irritation. "I would not blame her for having an adolescent flirtation with Patrik. He is rather handsome, like his sister. He has those same fantastic bluish eyes and wavy hair. He looks exotic, even dangerous. I think I shall have nightmares tonight about the whole group of them."

Caterina plopped down on the bed. She gave her friend a coy look from her nest in the pillows. "You do not fool me, Isabella. Your dreams tonight will make you tremble but not from fear."

Isabella conceded, "I did find the whole introduction quite exciting, with the weapons being surrendered and the tension between the soldiers. Then Lady Terese welcomed them, hardly noticing the drama they had caused."

She began to pour a glass of water from the pitcher on the table, then decided against it.

"It is too bad I will not be here long enough to enjoy the full benefit of their visit," Isabella concluded.

Caterina sat up from the bed and said, "Which would get you into more trouble."

"Trouble no longer concerns me, Caterina. I am feeling adventurous."

Isabella walked away from the table and rang the bell a third time. "And I am dying for a drink of tea. Shall we go down to the kitchen to see if we can have something brought out onto the terrace? I would not mind a little more fresh air."

~*~

The ladies had never been to the kitchen but knew it was somewhere behind the staircase. They began opening doors at the end of the foyer.

Nela and her maids stopped their work when the two ladies entered the bustling room. "Lady Carrera, Lady Valli," Nela said as she came forward and curtsied to them. "What can I help you with?"

Isabella looked around for Natalija but did not recognize any of the women working there. "Our maid neglected to bring our tea to our room. Perhaps you could arrange for refreshments out on the terrace for us?"

"I beg your pardon for your inconvenience, my ladies. We have two maids out ill today. I will have tea brought to you directly," Nela assured them.

Franja had overheard their request and was already getting a tray set. She whispered to Brigita to fetch Natalija from the vegetable garden.

Satisfied at having resolved their problem, the Venetians said a polite thank-you and left out the door they had come through.

~*~

Natalija came with the tray to their small table in the shade of the canopy a few minutes later.

"There you are, Natalija," said Caterina in a friendly manner. "We thought you might have been one of the maids taken ill that your cook told us about."

"I am so sorry, my ladies. I lost track of time. I was out helping pick the greens for dinner. Cook asked me to pick some figs for dessert, too." She poured the tea and served them biscuits on their porcelain plates. "I will lay out your dinner gowns before I go back to the garden."

"Where are these fig trees, Natalija?" asked Isabella curiously.

"At the end of this path by the bathhouse, madam. You cannot mistake them. They are quite full of figs."

Natalija finished topping off the tea in their delicate cups, but she was eager to get back to her other pressing chores.

Isabella pondered. "By the bathhouse, you say?"

"Yes, my lady. There are two trees on each side."

"If you bring us a basket, we shall pick your figs, Natalija," proposed Isabella out of the blue. "Then you can organize our dinner wardrobes without disappointing the cook."

It did not occur to the servant girl to talk the gentlewoman out of such folly. Natalija eagerly accepted before Caterina was able to protest.

"Cook said I should get about forty figs. That should not take two people very long," said the maid. "Thank you, my ladies! I will hurry back with the baskets." Natalija left them to finish their tea.

Caterina wondered at the absurdity of her friend's offer. "Well, Isabella. Making coffee in the morning and climbing fig trees in the afternoon. What has come over you? Is this a part of your new adventure? Will you be washing our stockings next?"

"I have a reason to be climbing fig trees, but you might find my motive wicked when you hear it."

Caterina cocked her head. "Go on."

"Earlier, when I was standing at the window, I watched Jero and the warriors walk toward the bathhouse. I only get one day to flirt with these foreign men, and I am betting we will have a chance encounter there. Do you mind joining me in my foolishness?"

"Your motives are mischievous, Isabella, but not entirely shocking. It will be a complete bore when you are gone, you know."

~ * ~

After leaving the mercenaries in Jero's hands, Mauro went into the stables with Josip, who led two of the visitors' horses ahead of him. Several wooden panels on the walls had been removed to let air circulate in the summer heat, and the late afternoon light streamed into the large holding area. Most of the Baric horses were out in the open corral today. The building held their musky smell, mixed with the aromas of hay and oiled leather from the many bridles and harnesses that hung on pegs along the walls.

A section of the sprawling building was set aside for visiting horses, and Alberto had shown Bem to these stalls. Mauro trusted Alberto with the new arrivals. Still, he wanted to know firsthand what kind of men he was dealing with. The best way to see a man's character, Mauro had learned, was by how he treated his horse.

Mauro had never met the African soldier who was the visitors' horse master. He was glad to see that Alberto overlooked the color of his skin and was courteously conversing with him. Black-skinned men were a rare sight in this part of the Republic. In the cities, most were indentured servants, even slaves. This freeman spoke fluent Latin and seemed experienced in the care of animals. Maybe he would share his unusual story with the baron if he stayed long enough.

The baron walked along with Josip between the horses he was leading. He instinctively put a firm hand on each horse's rump. They did not startle. Both beasts were tired and undernourished, like their riders, but there were no whip marks or spur scars that showed they were overworked or forced while in battle.

These two horses still carried their ornate Ottoman cavalry saddles on woven blankets fringed with colorful threads of red and gold. The saddle frames were small but padded and skillfully made. The mercenaries had already unloaded the weapons outside. Still, Mauro could see where the rider could practically hold the sword, shield, and quiver with arrows. He would look at the details more closely when the saddles were off.

Alberto was talking to Bem when Mauro approached the two.

"There is no need for you to stay, sir," Alberto told Bem. "Our grooms will rub your horses down and feed them. They will be well-treated."

Bem turned to Mauro and said, "I usually care for our horses myself, Lord Baric. I will not insult your men by refusing their assistance, but I do have one extra request."

"What would that be?" asked Mauro.

"Every shoe on every horse has about worn down. I see you have a blacksmith at your castle. Could we use his services?"

"Our smith is called Karl. If you have any specific requirements, you can discuss them directly with him. Alberto can instruct him to get right on it."

Alberto nodded and said, "Karl will be sure your horses are fit for when you leave again."

Mauro then pointed out, "Your saddles can be stored here near the stalls for you to come and go as you please. The grooms will take good care of your things."

"You are very generous, Lord Baric. Thank you," said Bem with a respectful bow.

Before Bem turned to walk away, he gave one of the horses an extra pat on its snout and a rub between the ears. The horse made a soft sound of gratitude.

Mauro did not remember whether it was the horse the man had been sitting on when he had arrived, but she was a beautiful mare. Bem seemed to hesitate to leave its care to someone else.

Josip had returned, leading two of their remaining horses, and Geoff was back with the third.

Bem took the bags and bundles from its back. As a last thought, he turned directly to Alberto and said, "They will need extra grain. Horses were impossible to come by after the last battle. We did the best we could for them along the journey back, but we could not lighten their load until we were nearly to Vienna. We acquired the two extra ones there."

Mauro watched the two men converse. Alberto loved horses more than he loved his children, Mauro sometimes thought. His stable master would look animals over and pass judgment on the owners. Mauro sensed Bem knew this, and he wanted Alberto to think better of him. With that, Mauro decided he could trust the African. So did Alberto.

"The grooms will give them extra oats until they are fit," Alberto assured him kindly.

~*~

When Bem had gone, Josip and Geoff unburdened the horses with a rush of excitement. The saddles were different from any Venetian saddle they had cared for. Each had unique decorations and embossing, making them works of art.

Mauro lifted one that Josip had set on the saddle stand and examined its light frame. "I want the tanner to have a look at this design," he said to Alberto, who was busy in the stall unbridling Bem's mare.

"You want an Ottoman saddle made, my lord? Darijo is an excellent saddlemaker, but I don't think he has the flair for such elaborate detail."

"I do not care for the ornate embellishing so much, Alberto, but I am not too proud to acknowledge the superior design. The horses take well to the saddles' positioning on their backs, and the weapons are held very practically on the frame."

Mauro examined another saddle; this one had a higher ridge to the seat. "The Ottomans may be a plague to us, but there is no denying they have a superior cavalry. Why not consider it for the next saddle if it lets us match them in horsemanship?"

"Excellent point, Lord Baric. Darijo is making a delivery this week. I will be sure to show him these."

Mauro was startled from his focused inspection of the saddles when Fabian came around the corner of the stall.

"I thought you might be with the horses," cried Fabian. "Your valet has been looking for you, Mauritius. Letters from Stephan arrived. I also received one."

Davor had been standing behind Fabian and came forward to hand the baron a sealed parchment.

Mauro pried the wax off as he walked out into the daylight of the courtyard. He quickly read his friend's letter, then held it out to Fabian. "Stephan writes mostly about his arrival and pending wedding. Do you want to read it?"

Mauro stopped at the well and took a drink from the dipper while Fabian finished reading the letter.

Fabian turned and complained, "There has been no letter from my father, yet Stephan was already at his family's villa when he wrote this. Something is wrong, and I cannot stand the suspense."

He gave the parchment back to Mauro, and Mauro held it out for Davor.

"There is a ferry leaving at ten tomorrow, and I think I will be on it," Fabian announced.

"Will you go with Isabella then?"

"I was sending her back because I can no longer tolerate her company. But if I am leaving, then her departure is unnecessary. I will tell her she is free to stay a little while longer. That is, if you agree to have her here."

"I do not share your complaint about her company, and my wife seems to like her very much. She may stay."

From where they stood at the well, Mauro faced the garden, where he saw the colorful dresses of Caterina and Isabella.

Mauro pointed to the path that led down to the bathhouse. "It seems the girls are taking air in the garden. Go tell them your decision."

"Thank you for understanding, Mauritius. I will make it up to you." Fabian hurried down the garden path to find Isabella.

~*~

Davor was still waiting off to the side, and Mauro waved him on to come with him to the house.

"Have you seen Jero this afternoon?" Mauro asked.

"He was leaving the Keep with the new guests when I came to deliver Lord Fabian's letter. I don't know where he went after that. Shall I find him for you, my lord?"

Mauro did not have anything urgent for Jero, but the thought of talking to him seemed somehow reassuring. "It isn't pressing. I will be in my chamber if you do see him."

They walked together through the front door and into the quiet foyer. The study door was ajar, and Mauro looked in and said, "Nestor might need some assistance for the evening arrangements. He is at his desk."

Davor bowed and disappeared through the threshold.

Mauro took the steps two at a time up the stairway and went to his bedroom. He was pleased his wife was awake. She sat in front of her grooming table, with Verica poised behind her.

"Hello, Resi. Did you already take your bath?"

She had told him about how she longed to soak in her warm pool to wash the drying salt off her skin on their ride home. "I asked Jero to take my brother and his friends to the bathhouse instead. They need it more than I do today."

"That was kind of you, my dear. I am sure Ana will be cleaning the pool all night after they are done." Mauro winked teasingly at her. Resi had not thought of the mess five dirty men would make in her tidy bathing pool.

Chuckling at her anxious expression, he went to the far side of the room to open his trunk. He absently looked through it, not in the mood to make another decision today, no matter how trivial.

Verica watched the baron pick through the wardrobe chest. "If I may interrupt—your evening clothes are laid out on the chair for you, Lord Baric, if that is to your liking. Aron came with warm water for her ladyship, and there is plenty left behind the screen. I will leave you now, sir."

"Stay, Verica. I can see you have already started something lovely with my wife's hair. I will return later to dress." Mauro was hot and dirty from the long day and longed to wash up, but they still had an hour before dinner.

"You stay, Mauro, and dress behind the screen," suggested Resi. "I wanted to talk to you."

Mauro did want to hear what she thought of the welcome, so he sat down, slipped off his shoes and stockings, and then stepped behind the screen to undress fully.

"I was just telling Verica how beautiful our camping spot was and about our boat trip to the island," said Resi. "It was the best adventure I have had in so long."

Mauro asked Verica through the partition, "Did your mistress tell you that she sailed the little sailboat herself?"

"No, my lord, my mistress did not share that with me," Verica answered as she finished the last twist of hair and secured it with the feathered comb.

Mauro washed the dust and sweat from his bare torso with the soapy linen cloth. "The baroness is an extraordinary woman, Verica," he said.

Standing behind her, Verica looked at her mistress in the reflection and replied, "She is, my lord."

He kicked off his breeches into the room and finished washing in the shallow tub with the last of the water. "What is most remarkable," he continued to say, "is the baroness's knack for languages. I am impressed at how she has mastered Croatian in this one short year. Do you not agree, Verica?" He wiped off the dampness and hastily dressed so he could carry on the conversation while looking at his wife's smiling face.

"Yes, sir, I do. The baroness is very clever with languages."

Resi blushed at being spoken about as if she were not right there. She pointed out, "It took several years, really. I memorized most of the words from a book while back in Thessaloniki. I don't know how I would have learned to truly speak Croatian without Verica's help, though. Her patience has been quite a gift."

"It has indeed," agreed Mauro. "Perhaps, Verica, you might think of something my wife can gift to you. You are very deserving of one."

"Lady Baric has already been more than generous by teaching me to read, my lord."

From her mistress's expression reflected in the mirror, Verica realized this should have been kept secret. Verica was a servant. There was no reason she would need to read or write.

Mauro noticed the women's odd silence. He stepped out from behind the screen with clean breeches on and tucked in his lacy shirt. He gave his wife a puzzled look.

"Are you teaching her to read, Resi?"

"I am," she admitted. "I am sorry that I did not ask you first. The maids enjoy listening to the stories I read to them, and I began pointing out how the words are written in the books. Please, do not be angry, Mauro."

He took his waistcoat from the chair back and put his arms through the sleeves, tugging at the lace to fall freely over his fingers.

The women watched with noticeable nervousness—most men disapproved of educating women, especially female servants.

Mauro looked up at them, having thought it through, and at last replied, "You did right, Resi. Verica is a clever girl, and she should know how to read her own books."

Verica was flushed with embarrassment to have caused any conflict between the two. "Thank you, Lord Baric." She finished the last touches on the baroness's hair and set the brush down, ready to be excused.

"If you are such a good teacher, Resi, I was thinking it is time I learned to speak Greek with you."

His wife turned to him with a startled expression.

"Why do you look so surprised?" he asked.

"I never thought it was important to you. Did it bother you that you didn't know what I was saying to my brother?"

Mauro shot a glance at Verica, who looked down at her feet. This conversation should have been private, but he answered anyway.

"I do like to know what is being said. Like when you and Salar Nassim spoke. What did you say to each other?"

"Your hair is finished, my lady," interrupted Verica. She curtsied and went to the door to leave.

"Your mistress will need help with her dress. She will wear a Venetian gown tonight." Although Mauro was talking to Verica, he looked only at his wife. "I would like to see her in the yellow one she wore for my homecoming party. It is very becoming," he said, still studying his wife at the grooming table. She was watching him in the mirror. "It could use more lace along the shoulders. I would like it a bit more modest tonight."

He then turned to Verica and added, "I will knock on your door shortly."

The maid closed the Baric's door quietly behind her.

Mauro sat on the chair, pulled a stocking over his calf, and tied it with a matching red ribbon. "I am interested to hear what Nassim needed to say in Turkish."

Resi sensed Mauro's simmering jealousy. "I am keeping no secrets from you, Mauro, if that is your worry," she assured him. "It was an old poem in Farsi, very similar to one in Turkish. I don't think I can repeat it in Latin."

"You seemed to understand the meaning quite well earlier."

Mauro finished tying his second stocking and waited for her to explain.

She sighed. "Alright, Mauro. Let me think. It translates something like how God wanted him to be where he finds himself to be, and he is glowing with wanting, and—"

She stopped when she saw him scowl disapprovingly.

"The wanting? The glowing? Persian poems are known to be overtly inappropriate for a man to tell a lady," asserted Mauro.

Resi laughed in surprise that he would care that much. "It is not at all what you are thinking. It is a nice poem, more about a general wanting in life, not him wanting me. I told you, it does not translate very well."

She came to his side by the chair. "Mauro," she said with a frown, "it was all very innocent. I did compliment him in Turkish that the poem was lovely. That is all that was said. Nothing more. He has two wives, and I have one husband."

"Yes, you do." He took her hand in his and kissed it lightly, then added, "Thank you for explaining."

Then he remembered what he came to the room to share with her in the first place. "I have some news about Fabian and Isabella you will want to hear."

Beaming, she replied, "I wanted to talk to you about them, too. I wish you had been there this morning. You missed their dancing at breakfast. It was beautiful, Mauro. I am hopeful they can be friends again."

Mauro was sorry to disappoint her. "Fabian is leaving tomorrow, Resi. He will not be here to rekindle any friendship with Isabella."

"She isn't going with him?" Resi sat down on the unmade bed as she contemplated the news.

"No, Isabella will stay on with us after all. Fabian is cancelling her escort and is taking the ferry back himself tomorrow."

"Why can't Fabian wait?"

"He has waited longer than he can tolerate, I suppose. He feels he has to settle his sister's affair in person."

She sat in silence, looking unhappy for her friends and their new situation. Mauro wanted to comfort her, but a different desire grew as he watched her sitting on their bed. He had not touched her since handing her to her brother, and he had an overwhelming urge to do that and more.

"Did I tell you how beautiful you look today?"

He stretched out his hands for her to take in his. She stood in front of him, and he gently touched her styled hair, pinned high on her head. "I will be careful not to make more work for Verica when she returns. But I can help Verica now by undressing you myself."

He went behind her, nuzzling her neck, breathing her in. He gently slipped her light jacket from her shoulders.

"But, Mauro," she protested meekly, "you are already dressed for dinner."

He kissed the nape of her neck and said, "I do not plan to undress."

He continued his objective and unfastened the embroidered sash around her waist. It dropped to the floor. She stood still as he untied the laces holding her tunic closed and eased the light fabric off her arms. He lifted the bottom of her gauzy underdress carefully over her curled hair. She was dressed only in her shift now, the pretty one she had worn on the island. He undid the tie on its bodice. The satin straps slipped from her shoulders, and the shift fell onto the colorful pile of fabric at her feet.

Mauro stepped back to look at her. Resi remained motionless, unashamed that she was gazed upon so wantingly. She wore only her gold necklaces and the dangling hoops in her ears. Mauro thought he was the luckiest man in the Empire. He yearned to kiss her, to mark her as his, before displaying her to the others at dinner.

"I have to have you, Resi." He slid his belt buckle free.

"Undress, Mauro," she whispered, "so I can have all of you, too."

"Later. I promise." He wrapped his arms around her naked hips and lifted her to his own. "This, I must do now."

Chapter 4

Fabian had not been happy to receive a letter from Stephan before hearing news from his father. Something was amiss.

Stephan wrote that he and the Carrera escorts had arrived in Venice with no troubles and had gone directly to the Carrera villa. His letter explained that Roberto Carrera had just received a message from Viscount Soltesz. It seems the viscount had been tracking Caterina's carriage and had objected to her delay. Stephan mentioned that Paolo was blamed for their detour and was 'dealt with.' The rest of the letter was about Mira, their happy reunion, and his wedding plans for September. It revealed nothing about what Fabian's father wanted him to do.

Fabian had seldom been back to Venice in recent years. A return visit would force him to discuss his own marriage plans, and his father's silence was the bait meant to draw Fabian back across the Adriatic. Fabian considered all of this, and he was still sure of his decision.

~*~

Fabian had neared the end of the path when he saw Caterina and Isabella. His sister was next to the kitchen garden's fence, and she was eating figs out of a basket. She waved at him as he approached.

"What are you doing?" he asked her with an amused smile. "Mauritius told me I could find you here, but I did not believe him. Are you in charge of dinner tonight?"

Caterina had stuffed her mouth with figs, and she only nodded with a grin.

"Part of it, at least," replied Isabella for her friend. She was at the tree across the path. She reached up into the branches and dropped the plump, purple produce into her basket. "We wanted to be helpful, so we are picking fruit for dessert tonight."

"They are so delicious," Caterina told him.

She handed her brother one of the fat figs from her basket. Fabian bit it in half and grinned in agreement. Then he looked into his sister's container and saw only five figs remained. Isabella's was almost as empty.

"How long have you been out here?"

"Too long, and the kitchen needs forty figs for the dessert tray," moaned Caterina.

"How many have you eaten?" asked Fabian.

"Enough to not need dinner tonight," conceded Caterina.

Isabella asked, "What did you come to tell us, Fabian? It cannot be time to come to the table. You have not yet dressed."

Fabian frowned at Isabella's criticism. He thought he would wear exactly this outfit to dinner. "I have news to tell you."

"Father has written?" Caterina guessed with excitement.

"No, but there was a letter from Stephan. He arrived well in Venice, with your guardsmen. There were no instructions for you from Father," Fabian said, "so I have decided I will leave in the morning and settle this myself."

"To Venice? With me?" asked Isabella cautiously.

"Not with you, Isabella. That is my news," he said. "You may stay at Baric Castle with Caterina."

Isabella let out a distinct sigh of relief. "Thank you, Fabian," she said.

"Was there news of Paolo?" asked Caterina hopefully.

Fabian would rather let his sister worry over her lover's fate for a few more weeks than tell her the truth. "Stephan did not mention Paolo in his letter."

Caterina nodded, then her solemn expression brightened, and she asked, "Why not just stay and wait with us, Fabian? We were beginning to enjoy ourselves with the Barics. We had such an amusing time at the seaside, did we not?"

"Father's silence is a clear message to me, Cat. He wants me home. I forgot to mention, Stephan also wrote that your beloved Viscount Soltesz already knows you changed route and did not continue on to Hungary. A messenger from him arrived the same time Stephan arrived. A resolution will have been made by now."

He studied his sister's face at this news and found only determination there. It was better than the anguish she had shown when she first arrived at Baric Castle. Either way this played out, Caterina would be alright.

Shaking off the glum mood, Fabian looked at the baskets on the ground and remembered why the girls were there in the first place. He picked up one and dumped its contents into the other.

"I know how to finish faster," he said in a happier tone, leaving them to venture into the kitchen garden.

Growing along the garden fence in the summer sunshine were vines of small melons. He leaned down and smelled one of the striped, round fruit that hung there among the green foliage.

The women watched with curiosity, and he turned to smile at them. "These are ready," he called over. He took out his knife and cut several free, then carried them back with a smug grin.

"But, Fabian, Natalija said the cook asked for figs," maintained Caterina.

"I do not think anyone will object to fresh melon garnished with your little figs. I will bring them to the kitchen, and you can go dress for dinner."

Fabian picked up both filled baskets and started toward the manor house.

"We wanted to wait—" Caterina began to explain, but Isabella urgently shook her head.

Fabian turned and asked, "Is something wrong, Cat?"

Isabella took Caterina's hand and pulled her along. "Nothing is wrong, Fabian. Everything is just perfect," Isabella answered for her friend.

It was indeed, now that Isabella was staying at Baric Castle.

~*~

In the kitchen, Fabian set the baskets down on the corner of the center table.

"What have you brought there, my lord?" asked Cook cheerfully.

"Figs for the dessert tray, as requested, Nela. My sister and Lady Isabella ate more than they collected, so I brought you a few melons to add to it."

Nela realized what this implied. "Oh, Lord Fabian, I hope you do not think I would ask the gentle ladies to pick figs for me. One of the maids was given that task. I will give a strong talking to her."

"My sister and Lady Isabella can be very insistent if they set their minds to do something. They wanted to help, so they did. Not very well, I am afraid." He tipped the basket to show her and chuckled. "But I think they enjoyed it."

Fabian lingered in the kitchen. "I have a request, Nela," he said at last. "Tomorrow is Lady Isabella's birthday."

"How wonderful! Then we shall prepare a grand meal for her ladyship."

"Thank you, but, um, I was wondering if it would be possible for Franja to make a special cake for tomorrow's dessert."

Upon hearing her name, Franja came over to the table. "Do you have a preference, my lord?"

"I will not be here to enjoy it myself. I must leave for Venice in the morning. But there is one particular cake you make that is especially delicious," he said with a charm that would melt butter.

"Anything, sir," said Franja.

"Is it possible to make your marzipan cake for tomorrow?" he asked hopefully.

"Oh, well, that is indeed a lovely cake, but it takes some time to prepare," said Franja before Nela could interrupt her.

"Yes, Lord Fabian, it takes a little more work than others, but it will be a pleasure to make one for Lady Isabella," Nela assured him. "Safe travels to you, sir. Franja will have it ready for the birthday dinner."

"Thank you, Nela. Thank you, Franja."

He bowed in the graceful way that always made the maids' knees weak and then headed back to the stables. Fabian had just enough time to ride to the village before dinner and secure a place on the boat for tomorrow.

Back in the kitchen, Franja looked stunned. "Nela, how will I make his cake? It will use all the sugar in the pantry."

Franja thought for a moment, then added, "I could make the marzipan with honey. I have plenty of that."

"It is to be a proper marzipan, and Lord Baric will not mind us ordering extra sugar for his friends," Nela told her as she unpacked the melons from the basket.

Franja continued to fret. "I can bake the cakes tonight, but I will need all morning to grind the almonds and roll out the paste."

"You don't have to feed a hundred people like you did for Lord Baric's celebration," Nela reminded her. "It will be just for the Baric household and his lordship's guests."

"But, Nela, it is normally a wedding cake. Won't the lady find it an unusual choice for her birthday?"

"Are you dense, Franja? Can't you see what Lord Fabian is telling the lady with his choice? We will make the cake he wants."

Franja considered this. "But he is leaving. Lady Isabella won't even get to thank him."

"He will be back, and she will remember," Nela assured her.

The foyer door opened, and that made the women start. Jero came into the room smiling.

"I am at your service, Nela. What can I do first?"

Nela held out the apron she had set aside for Jero. "For starters, you can fetch ten eggs and a pound of butter from the cellar. Franja has a cake to bake."

Chapter 5

Four of Mauro's officers—along with Jero, Nestor, Idita, and Ruby—joined the Barics and their seven guests for the evening festivities. If the ill-clad sellswords were uncomfortable sitting at the banquet table with the elegant Venetians in their formal finery, they did not show it.

The women sat in awe of how the mercenaries consumed all the platters put before them. Mauro and his soldiers didn't notice since they ate hungrily along with them. Resi had wanted to talk with her brother finally, but the soldiers dominated the dinner conversation, and they nearly ignored the ladies once the meal began.

As dinner ended, the conversation turned to the topic of war. The Baric soldiers encouraged Patrik's gang to share the details of the battle in Prague last autumn and to recount their journey back from Bohemia to Vienna in the spring, after having survived the harsh winter in the desolated region.

The communal meal had not changed the Baric men's opinions of the sellswords. They still disapproved of how they hired their services out to the Barics' enemies, but they could not deny the visitors' apparent courage and resolve. Moreover, they were admittedly impressed with Patrik's harrowing account. The potent ale had loosened their tongues, making the new guests willing to answer the Croats' many questions. The other three let Salar Nassim and Patrik describe the fighting in their accented Latin.

Resi might have been engrossed in the tales if they had not been stories of actual people and their real agony. The terrible things the men recounted were what her own brother had lived through, and hearing the details of it was unsettling to her.

Patrik told how they joined the fight against the Swedes in Bohemia. Soren and his brother had wanted their revenge to honor their parents, who had been killed in the Swedish invasion in their homeland six years earlier.

It grieved Resi to learn that Soren's twin brother, Niels, had met his death in the last battle near Prague. Soren listened with a blank stare as Patrik narrated the events. Patrik did not tell them the exact circumstances of Niels's death, only that it had been quick and tragic.

The other soldiers around the table were quiet. Resi wondered how they could react with only a grunt or murmur in disgust. She did not notice that their breathing had changed, their jaws were clenched, and the beads of sweat on their foreheads were not from the evening heat—the guardsmen had connected with these foreigners and their shared experiences.

Jero and Nestor were as absorbed in the retelling as the warriors, though neither had fought in a battle. Idita had stitched up wounded men for too long, and she listened to Patrik's tale with sadness. Caterina, Isabella, and Ruby were ashen with horror while listening. The ladies excused themselves from the table before Patrik had finished, and Idita excused herself with them to retire for the evening in her room upstairs.

~*~

Resi followed Mauro's earlier suggestion that the party withdraw to the smaller sitting room after the meal, and she escorted the women there. It was more intimate than the great hall, and a breeze came through in the evening. Ruby's and Resi's musical instruments were kept in the sitting room, as were the games and cards for quiet gatherings.

Ruby found her small lute and began to strum it softly. "Will the men be joining us?" she asked.

"Yes, shall we plan to play cards tonight?" asked Caterina expectantly.

Resi's mood was already lighter, and she cheerfully replied, "I think this would be a good occasion for a card game or two, Lady Caterina. I hear my husband's officers are partial to dice, though. Those are kept in that little ivory box on the shelf."

Isabella found the box for her and set it on one of the two game tables.

"Tomorrow, ladies, maybe we can take an outing," Resi said as she set out the cards. "I think the soldiers will be practicing in the fields again, but there should be someone available to escort us."

"We could go to the river if the weather holds," said Ruby hopefully. She had enjoyed their swim in the sea, and the river below the castle had a nice swimming hole.

To Resi's surprise, Isabella suggested, "Perhaps we could go riding tomorrow. Since I will not be leaving for Venice, I was thinking I could learn to ride with Lady Ruby."

The men had come into the sitting room through the foyer door. Resi was just about to ask Isabella how she had convinced Fabian to let her stay when Mauro was suddenly behind her and saying, "I will talk to Alberto tomorrow, Isabella, and have him saddle my wife's horse for you."

"Yes, Mauro, and when Lady Isabella is feeling confident on the saddle, she can chaperone Ruby on the trails," remarked Resi, with the hope of an easy approval again.

Fabian had arrived with Mauro and had overheard Isabella's conversation as well.

"I do not think she will get to that point in a week, Lady Terese," said Fabian. "Riding out on the open trails requires practice and training. I will only be gone ten days, at most. I am not sure Alberto has so much time to devote to lessons."

"No one said you must hurry back, Fabian," replied Isabella.

Bem was at Fabian's side and offered, "I can have the lady ready to ride with a few days of training. My mare needs little prompting from a new rider if I am by her side."

"That must be an extraordinary horse," said Fabian.

"She is," Bem agreed. "I could teach Lady Isabella how to ride in place of your stable master." Bem looked at Mauro for permission.

Mauro seemed to contemplate what it would mean to say yes. Alberto had a lot to manage with the extra horses in the stables and the soldiers training each morning. He looked to Fabian—his friend's expression showed he was against it.

Resi quickly maintained, "If Lady Isabella does learn to ride on Bem's horse, then Ruby can ride Ophelia on the trails with her."

Like Fabian, Mauro did not believe Isabella would make it out of the practice enclosure to ride alone. But to appease his wife, he agreed.

"Very well, Bem, if your mare is up to it. You said she needed to be shod first."

"Yes, Lord Baric. She does," Bem acknowledged.

"Karl can look at your horse first thing in the morning. Lady Isabella can meet you at the paddock after her breakfast."

Bem was a soldier and was up at first light. "Will that give Karl enough time?" he asked.

"Venetian ladies start their day very late," said Fabian with a laugh. "Your horse will be ready in time."

Mauro told Isabella, "If you can be at the stables by midmorning, then you shall have your riding lesson."

"You have given your guest the wrong impression of me, Mauritius. Of course, I can be ready. I am most appreciative to have this lesson." She looked at Bem with a coy smile and added, "Thank you, sir, for your generous offer."

Bem held her stare. "Riding can be very pleasurable," he said. "I will be happy to teach you, madam."

Cyro had been looking at the baron's fine collection of swords when he first came into the sitting room but joined Bem's side just as the conversation about riding lessons concluded. Even though Bem considered himself a married man, he had a naturally flirtatious personality. Cyro would be sure to fill him in on Fabian's warning before getting himself into trouble over the beautiful Lady Isabella.

~*~

Having resolved Isabella's riding arrangements, the small gathering began to mingle.

Ruby's lute playing drew Salar Nassim to the window seat. He picked up Resi's small guitar and began to strum along with her. They soon found a song they both knew and played softly for the room.

Davor was the groom serving that evening, and he brought out a tray of small glasses for the bottle of brandy Mauro had just opened. The first round of drinks warmed their dispositions, and the atmosphere was not so strained after the glasses were emptied and refilled.

Mauro answered Bem's and Cyro's questions about the history of the many weapons on display. Patrik and Soren were enticed to join Hugo, Vilim, and Simeon for a game of dice. And the two Venetian ladies shuffled the cards at the small table next to them.

Fabian was alone near the terrace door, holding his half-full brandy glass, watching the room of people.

Resi approached him and asked, "Do you not play dice, Fabian?"

"I do, my lady, but I must hold onto my coins for my trip tomorrow. Hugo is a good player. I have never won against him," said Fabian.

Resi regarded the game across the room. "He will have a challenge with my brother."

Fabian turned to look at her. "It does not surprise me that your brother would be a challenge."

He had not meant to denounce her brother's character, but Resi could have easily interpreted it that way. She was not offended. Either way, Fabian was right.

"Will you be gone long to Venice?" she asked.

"Only as long as it takes, my lady."

There was sadness in his voice, and she sensed his melancholy for the first time. "I know you've said you do not care for Venice anymore. But aren't you glad to go back for a little while? It must be very provincial for you here."

His eyes twinkled with his characteristic exuberance again. "At least life in the provinces is real. The capital is like a grand painting, Lady Terese—an illusion."

"Illusion? What do you mean, Fabian?"

"Oh, well, the masters flatter us in their portraits of Venetian life. The people depicted on the canvas seem to relish living in our perfect world, and one is envious to be a part of it. Those illusions of opulence and gaiety hang in the galleries, and we begin to believe them. In reality, the life portrayed is as flat as a painting itself."

Resi considered his criticism. "I have never seen the grand paintings you and your sister talk of, depicting parties and the enticement of society. The only real paintings I have seen are here in the manor house and in the chapel. I have not been so drawn to those, but I would like to see the ones that you described."

"One day your husband will take you to Venice, and I hope you see it differently than I do now."

Their talk of paintings put an idea in his head. Fabian took the baroness's hand and kissed it with a bow. Then he quickly apologized, "If you will excuse me, Lady Terese, I just remembered an urgent errand."

He walked hurriedly away, passing Mauro on his way out with hardly a glance toward his inquiring friend.

"Lady Terese?" Caterina jolted Resi back to the present. "We need one more player for our game. Would you like to join us?"

Resi saw Isabella and Salar Nassim already seated together. Ruby was sitting on the window seat, looking content playing her songs for their entertainment. Patrik seemed occupied with his dice game at the next table. Mauro, Jero, Nestor, and the other soldiers had settled into small groups, conversing with each other.

"Yes, I would like that," she agreed, glad to have a new distraction.

At the table, Caterina and Salar Nassim decided on a game and began to deal the cards.

~*~

Across the room, the friendly dice game had quickly turned to betting, and there was a small pile of coins in the middle of the table. The adversaries were in good moods, and the conversation flowed informally.

"So, Patrik," said Vilim, "your father and brother are both sea captains. Why did you become a mercenary soldier instead of a sailor?"

It had been Hugo's turn to roll, and Patrik was watching what the dice showed. It was a good roll. He turned to Vilim and replied, "The sea does not call everyone. Perhaps she passed me by. As for soldiering, I did not want to fight for the Turks, so I left to sell my sword to fight against them."

"No one can blame you for that," said Simeon. "Does the Ottoman Army still require tributes from Greek families?"

Patrik answered, "Not until the fifth son."

Hugo claimed the small pile of coins and passed the dice to Soren. "The baroness said there are four brothers in your family. You are lucky you could choose sides so freely."

Hugo's comment was meant to be a friendly one, just continuing the line of conversation Vilim had begun, but it was unknowingly a sore topic for Patrik.

Soren shot Patrik a warning glare before rolling the dice, but Patrik did not heed his friend's quiet counsel. "My parents have Count Toth to thank for having only the four," Patrik replied.

Hugo laughed good-naturedly and asked, "Did Count Toth take your family tribute instead of the Ottomans?"

Soren's and Patrik's eyes met across the table, and Soren shook his head to tell him not to continue.

Patrik chose otherwise and said loudly, "My sister was our tribute to Count Toth, Hugo. Her potential as a future beauty was ransom enough to let my father out of the count's dungeon after he was rotting there for six years."

Ruby stopped playing her lute, and the others in the room quieted.

Then Patrik concluded, "My family can never thank Terese enough for paying my father's debt to the Barics."

Patrik looked over at his sister. She was still sitting in her chair but was visibly livid.

He turned back to the men at his game table and added in a quieter voice, "It all worked out in the end. Lord Baric and Count Toth returned my father, my mother had three more children, and my sister gets to live in a fucking castle a thousand miles away from her family."

Patrik threw a coin into the new pile and took the dice for his turn to roll.

Resi did not notice Isabella's and Caterina's unspoken empathy across the table just before she stood from her seat and slammed her cards down in front of her.

The group watched her walk to the glass terrace door. The crisp swishing of her satin gown drowned the silence. She turned and flashed a piercing glare at her brother, then left the room without a word.

Salar Nassim turned to Patrik at the next table and told him in Greek, "Go make it right with her."

Patrik looked around the room of stunned faces, stopping on the unreadable face of Baron Baric. Patrik could not care less what the man thought. He only worried that he had unintentionally hurt his sister. He followed the same path out of the room and met her under the torchlight of the small terrace.

All eyes were now on Mauro. He went to the closed door and stood watching the dim outlines of his wife and her brother standing together. Ruby was suddenly next to him and touching his sleeve. He looked down at her, and she told him, "I have known Patricius my whole life, Lord Baric. He adores his sister and wants her to be happy. He will know how to comfort her." She looked up at him and waited.

That was the most Ruby had said directly to him since coming here, Mauro thought. If she were brave enough to defend her friends, then he would trust her insight. "Thank you, Ruby," he said.

Mauro turned away from the door and rejoined Jero, Nestor, and the two guests. He poured himself another glass of brandy and offered the bottle to Cyro and Bem. "You have quite a lively traveling companion," he told them.

Cyro took it upon himself to explain Patrik's outburst. "There is an old proverb: 'He who wants the rose must respect the thorn'. We all expected this would be difficult for Patrik, as it is assuredly difficult for you to have him here, Lord Baric. He has been waiting a long time to see his sister again. Let them talk it through."

Mauro held Cyro's stare. He was right, of course.

Mauro filled the men's glasses with the remaining brandy in the bottle and begrudgingly toasted: "To thorns!"

~*~

At that moment, Salar Nassim called over to Bem from the card table. Bem excused himself from the baron and went to see what Salar Nassim wanted from him.

"We are in need of a fourth player," Nassim explained, "and the ladies have requested you."

Isabella and Caterina each gave him an enchanting smile. The evening was getting interesting, he thought. He took Resi's empty seat across from Isabella.

"Bem is an unusual name. Is it short for something?" asked Isabella after the cards had been reshuffled and dealt.

He answered coyly, "Yes, my lady, it is."

Isabella prodded further. "Are you African, sir?" she asked with a playful smile.

Caterina looked up from her cards at the odd question. "Do not offend the man, Isabella. He is not that black," she declared, then played her turn.

Salar Nassim chuckled with amusement as he considered the card she had played. Western women often asked such questions.

Bem sorted his hand for his first play, then said to his partner, "I am not as dark as most would expect, coming from Ethiopia. My father's skin was white, and my mother's was black. This is the result."

He waved his hand in front of him as if the ladies needed the obvious pointed out.

Isabella sat contemplating him. "Your mother must have been beautiful."

"For my father to want to marry her?"

"You favor her looks," Isabella clarified.

Bem raised his brows at her flirtatious remark.

"Isabella!" exclaimed Caterina. "We are trying to play a card game here, and you are distracting your partner. It is your turn to lay down a card, Bem." She smiled at him sweetly.

Bem was intrigued by his new partner. It was a shame he had to play the card game at the same time, especially since Salar Nassim had not told him which one they were playing when he took the baroness's spot.

"I am not familiar with this game," said Bem.

"Show me your hand, and I will tell you which card to play next," offered Isabella, reaching across the table for him to hand her his cards.

Bem instead walked around the table and leaned discreetly over Isabella's shoulder to let her look at his cards without the others seeing. She took her time surveying his options.

"You have a good hand, Bem. You can play this one, but this one is not a bad choice either." She touched his fingers holding the cards and looked up at his handsome face.

"You seem to know what you are doing," he told her.

The two openly considered each other.

"Bem, play your hand and then bring Cyro to the table, if you will," said Salar Nassim to him in Latin. "She is not to be seduced," he quietly added in Arabic.

Salar Nassim was their commander on and off the battlefield. Bem did not question his order, and it was an order. Instead, Bem played the card Isabella had suggested and then said, "If you will excuse me, ladies."

Across the room, Cyro was still sitting with Mauro and his stewards.

"Cyro, may I interrupt?" Bem said.

Cyro came to Bem's side a few feet from the sofa. "You are to replace me to partner with Lady Isabella. She was being flirtatious, and it offended Nassim."

Cyro smirked at the news. "Not Nassim. It offends Fabian Carrera. You were in the stables when he warned us that Lady Isabella is his woman. Carrera said touch a skirt and you will lose your cock, or something to that effect. Nassim is just helping you keep your favorite asset, my friend."

Bem beamed with understanding. "Enjoy your card game then, Cyro."

He patted his friend on the back, and Cyro went to try his luck in the unlucky seat.

Bem looked beyond the ladies and took Patrik's empty seat at the dice table to try his luck there. The three captains were talking among themselves while Soren absently rubbed two coins together and studied the rolled points. Soren seemed to be winning, but the mood at his table was still cordial.

~ * ~

On the terrace, Patrik noticed Mauro walk away from the door. He was glad not to have to defend himself to both his sister and his new brother-in-law. Patrik did not know what he would say to Resi, but he needed some time alone with her.

Resi knew what she wanted to say to her brother, and it was not pleasant. "How dare you bring that up again after I warned you? It was rude and ill-mannered and uncalled for. My husband will not allow you to stay if you cannot control your tongue."

"This tongue has gotten me out of more trouble than in," he argued, then saw her hurt expression. He pulled her in close and said, "I am sorry, Resi, but it just came flooding out. I hate the Barics. I cannot help it."

"You will have to help it. No one in that room is responsible for what happened to Papa. What is done is done, and I can live with it. Mauro has been good to me, Patricius. Put your grudge aside."

His expression softened when he asked, "Are you done yelling at me?"

He made her smile again.

"Yelling, yes, but there is something I have not told you . . . I am pregnant."

Patrik stepped back to look at her wholly. Her pleated gown hid her swelling middle, and the lacy fabric over her bodice concealed her fuller breasts.

"You wrote me that you'd lost the child."

She laughed for the first time and told him, "This is a new baby. I am halfway along and am feeling perfect this time."

Still, he could not share her joy. "And then you will seal the alliance for our families and give the Barics their heir."

"I don't think of it that way," she said. Disappointment came through in her voice. "I am trying to make this my new home, and these people are now family, Patricius."

Patrik tried to be happy for her. He took a deep breath. "Do you love him, your new prince?"

"Yes, I love him. When I wrote to you before, I was not so sure. I did not know a baron could have so many other burdens, and there were always battles he was called away to. We did not spend much time together in the beginning. But we do now, and we are good together. He likes me, Patricius."

"He *likes* you?" Patrik threw up his hands and laughed with contempt. "Of course, he must like you, Resi—perfumed and in pretty gowns, with jewels in your hair." Patrik looked at her changed appearance again. "You are a stunning woman, Sister, but I need to know that he loves you, like you deserve to be loved."

She looked down at her feet, and Patrik tilted her chin so that their eyes would meet again.

"Does your husband not return your love? Has he not told you so?"

She held his gaze this time. "He is a complicated man, Patricius. I think he returns my love, but he is not a man who professes such things. I am content that he will find the words in his own time."

Patrik could not let it go. "What is the matter with him? The man is a cold-hearted bastard, Resi."

"And you are hotheaded!" She was angry again. "Mauro did not protest when I asked if you could visit. That was generous and warm-hearted. But if you are to stay here, and I truly want you to, then you will need to watch your words. You and the others can rest and regain your strength, but Mauro will not tolerate you here if you appear to be a threat."

Patrik took a deep breath to calm himself.

"I will not make another scene like tonight," he promised her. "I came to see you and to be able to tell Ma and Papa that you are safe and well. I can see that you are, and I will be content with that, lovely sister."

"I will be content, too."

Forgiven and humbled, Patrik added, "I neglected to tell you just now, but I am very happy to be an uncle again."

The siblings embraced and held each other tightly for a long moment. Then Resi stepped back from him and wiped away her fresh tears of happiness.

"We should go back to the party," she said. "We can talk again tomorrow morning. Mauro is going to the village if you want to meet me while he is gone. I have a surprise for you."

"A surprise? And the husband must be away? This sounds promising."

Resi feigned annoyance at his teasing, but she missed her favorite brother's playfulness. "Next to my bathhouse is a small meadow that leads to the cesspool and—"

"Do you plan to throw me in for my bad manners tonight?"

"That was not my plan—yet," she warned, grinning again. "I want to meet alone, and the rampart is not guarded in that corner of the wall. I will send a groom to your chamber after breakfast when I am ready. Meet me by the big pine in the meadow there. We can talk more tomorrow."

~ * ~

Jero had leisurely conversed with all of the guests, but what he wanted most was to spend time alone with Ruby. She had been chatting with the company, as well, and now sat alone on the window seat.

"Mauro, would you mind if I sat with Ruby for a while? She wanted to show me how to play some chords."

Sometimes Mauro forgot that Jero was his servant, and as one, he had to ask permission to take personal time to flirt with pretty girls. Mauro looked over at Ruby. It was apparent she was tempting his steward to join her.

"That sounds useful. Yes, Jero, take your time," he answered jovially.

Jero hurried from the couch and crossed the room to Ruby's side.

"Where have you been?" Mauro asked Fabian when he came to take Jero's place on the long sofa.

"I had forgotten to get something for my trip," replied Fabian.

Mauro did not press him to explain.

Fabian looked around the room at the others enjoying themselves. "Where are your wife and her brother?" Fabian had seen no one else in the corridors.

"Here they are now," Mauro was able to tell him without going into the story of Patrik's outburst.

Patrik and Resi were coming through the terrace door, holding hands.

Chapter 6

The Venetian women had been immediately fascinated by the Persian when they first sat down together. He looked to be older than the others, with slight wrinkles on the corners of his wide, black eyes and a few gray hairs beginning to show in his trimmed black beard. Isabella had already asked Salar Nassim to tell them about himself while Resi had been at the table. He had answered all of their questions with charm, amused at the unexpected interest they showed. They had never met a man with two wives—perhaps one wife and a mistress, but not two marriages. It made him more mysterious and intriguing to the curious women.

"Is divorce forbidden by Muslims, like in the Catholic faith?" asked Isabella. "Is that why you kept both wives?"

"Divorce is not forbidden in my religion, but it is not encouraged either. Cyro, it is your turn to deal next," said Salar Nassim, changing the topic.

Cyro had played three hands with the Venetians while their focus had been directed at Salar Nassim. As he was dealing the fourth hand, his luck had run out. It was Cyro's turn to be interrogated.

"Where am I from?" Cyro repeated Isabella's question as he gave Caterina the two cards she required for her play. "I am from . . ."

Cyro looked over at Salar Nassim for help but found none, only his amused smirk.

"Cairo," Cyro finally answered.

Salar Nassim nodded that he had chosen his answer well.

"Cairo, in Egypt? With the pyramids?" asked Caterina.

She seemed to doubt that Cyro had the Oriental look that one expected from an Egyptian. Sure, he had dark wavy hair and dark lashes shading his nutmeg eyes. But his skin was too fair, and his accent was not right. She continued to regard him skeptically.

Cyro attempted to subdue any further questions. "I was not born there, my lady, but that is where Bem and I met a few years ago." That was the truth, at least.

Caterina was satisfied that she had been correct in her assessment and went on to declare, "We learned about the pyramids from our tutor, my sisters and I. I would love to see them in person. Did you see them, Cyro?"

"Why, yes. I went there purposely to study them."

"What is there to study?" asked Isabella, not caring much for what she thought were stacks of old stones. She liked paintings but had little interest in the buildings that housed them. "The pyramids seem rather simple to understand without needing to travel such a distance in person."

She played her card and focused her attention on Salar Nassim, whose turn was next. Salar Nassim was focused on his friend, who seemed unsure of how he should explain himself.

Caterina unwittingly came to Cyro's rescue. "Think about it, Isabella. I had to study the mosaics of San Marco's Basilica as a part of my art lessons. Granted, I did not have to travel across the sea, but I did spend all day there. It was far better to see the tiles up close than to only hear them described. It must have been the same for you, right, Cyro?"

"Yes, Lady Caterina, it was exactly like that. I, too, had tutors in my youth. One of them was fascinated by ancient Egyptian artifacts, and that is what he taught during my art lessons at home. I could not miss the chance to see the pyramids up close, to walk among them, to climb their steps after so much book learning."

Isabella asked the unlikely sellsword, "And how did you get from wandering the pyramids to fighting wars with Salar Nassim?"

Salar Nassim explained for him this time. "I came across Cyro and Bem at the port in Athens. I was looking for a few more recruits to travel north with us at that time. They were interested in our line of work."

"So were you always a soldier, Cyro?" asked Isabella.

Cyro admitted, "Actually, I only became a soldier just a short time before arriving in Athens. I was traveling there following my stay in Cairo, but our ship ended up stranded on an island after we were pirated."

"Pirated? That sounds frightening," exclaimed Caterina. "But if it was a Venetian island you sailed to, it could not have been so uncivilized that you couldn't have gotten a ship back to the mainland."

"You are right, Lady Caterina. Indeed, it was a Venetian outpost, but it was not civilized. They are warring there, the Venetians against the Ottomans. Bem and I signed on as mercenaries for the Venetian Army to stay fed until we could get off." He laughed lightly at the memory of their fateful choice. "It took several months until we eventually made our way off the island to Athens."

"What was waiting for you in Athens?" asked Isabella.

He replied, "Nothing, really. It may sound odd, but I had always wanted to go there just to marvel at the monuments." Cyro stopped himself short of telling them that he had studied Greek architecture at the university.

Seemingly pleased to have found a common thread, Caterina asked, "Do you enjoy art and architecture, Cyro?"

He smiled and nodded in reply.

"So do I!" she exclaimed. "Isabella and I were planning a trip to Rome to see the great galleries this summer until we were, um . . . Well, there was a change of plans," she said reluctantly.

Isabella interjected, "They will hear our sorrowful story soon enough, Caterina, so there is no need to be coy."

"I don't know how to explain it," said Caterina sadly.

The men listened with interest as Isabella clarified, "It is somewhat complicated. Instead of traveling to Rome, we were sent off to marry total strangers in Hungary. On our journey, we convinced our escorts to divert us here, to the Barics. I think we have made quite a mess of everything, though. Fabian is returning to Venice tomorrow to learn what has become of our betrothals."

"You are not yet betrothed, Isabella. Only I—"

Caterina stopped midsentence when she noticed the winning hand Salar Nassim had laid down on the table.

"How did you do that again?" she demanded.

Salar Nassim laughed. "What did I do again, dear Lady Caterina?"

"You won, and I think you cheated, too."

Salar Nassim remained unaffected by her accusation, but Cyro could barely contain his amusement at her expression. It was a mixture of anger, surprise, and lovely innocence.

"He is the Barics' guest, Caterina. Why would you call him a cheater?" asked Isabella, with a sudden embarrassment for her friend.

"Because I cheated, and he still won. I want you to teach me how to play like that," Caterina said to Salar Nassim.

He shook his head. "I cannot teach you to cheat, dear lady."

"Then I want you to show me how you won," she said.

He studied the delicate noblewoman across from him. "Is this so important to you?" he asked. "Winning is not everything, is it?"

She did not answer, but her expression confirmed that it was.

There was something about her youthful innocence and competitive determination that drew Salar Nassim in, and he irrationally accepted her challenge. "Shall we begin tomorrow?"

Caterina flashed him a victorious smile, but Isabella simply shook her head.

"You will have to play without me tomorrow, Caterina. I have had enough of cards for a few days," said Isabella, trying to hide her yawn. "You should have your card-cheating lessons while I have my horse-riding lessons."

"I am not going to learn to cheat, Isabella. That would be wrong," clarified Caterina. "But you do have a point. Could we meet in the morning while Isabella is out riding, Salar Nassim?"

The time was late, and he stood up to leave. "If that is what you wish, Lady Caterina. We can meet in here again when Bem and the lady are with the horses."

"No, this room will require a chaperone," she said abruptly. "If we met on the front terrace, then I would not have to impose on Lady Terese or Lady Ruby to sit with us."

The Persian nodded his understanding. "I look forward to it, Lady Caterina. I will find you on the terrace."

Salar Nassim now looked to his companion and said, "Cyro, I think we are not used to such late evenings any longer. Thank you for your company, dear ladies."

They nodded politely back.

Cyro bowed to each of the noblewomen, and his stare lingered on Caterina.

The two mercenaries watched Hugo and Soren play out the last few rolls. Simeon and Vilim had lost the last of their purses. Bem still had coins in play, but he was ready to forfeit them and retire for the night.

"I have lost enough for one evening," said Bem.

Soren exchanged a look of satisfaction with Hugo. He put his winnings into his pouch and rose to leave with the others.

Patrik had been avoiding his new brother-in-law by talking to Ruby and Jero at the window. He saw Salar Nassim bid the baron and baroness a good night. When his friend left for the door, Patrik followed him and the others out, flashing a smile in his sister's direction.

Mauro's captains gave the mercenaries a few paces head start toward the Keep, then left the manor house with a short bow to each of their hosts. Mauro had already instructed them that training with the new recruits would begin again in the morning. Dawn would come early for everyone after the entertaining evening. Only Fabian lingered.

~*~

The tired women were leaving to go upstairs to bed when Fabian touched Isabella's arm to stop her.

"May I have a word with you?" he asked.

Caterina gave Isabella a sympathetic glance of encouragement as she left with the Greek ladies.

Mauro had overheard Fabian's request to Isabella, so he asked Davor to leave the last candles burning. Mauro led him and Jero out of the room, stopping only to tell Fabian, "I will ride with you to the village in the morning."

Fabian nodded and shut the sitting room door after them.

Alone now, Fabian turned to Isabella. "I have been thinking that I may not return from Venice to see you again, Isabella. I wanted to tell you that I am glad we had this one last chance to meet."

Isabella was nervous now. Not from being alone with Fabian in the dimly lit room, but nervous that she would not say the right thing in the end, if this was the end. There was too much left unspoken.

"I know you would not go back to Venice if it were not for your sister's sake. You are a good man, Fabian, and a good brother. I have always thought so."

"I do not believe you have always thought so well of me. I am glad that you do now, though."

He had remained in front of the door, and she walked toward him.

"Fabian, we cannot keep dancing around what could have been. Let us part as friends, shall we?" She stopped in front of him, thinking he would step aside and open the door for her.

"I just need to know one thing, Isabella."

She sensed with dread what was coming. Years ago, she had walked away from Fabian after this same question. There was no escaping tonight when he asked, "Why did you not choose me, Isabella?"

"Why do you have to make everything so hard, Fabian?" she whispered her frustration.

"It is an easy question, Isabella. I will spend the rest of my life asking it if you do not give me an honest reply for once."

She saw that he was determined this time and would indeed not let her go.

"Very well," she conceded. "I will tell you something that I have never told anyone and then you will finally understand why some things are better left unasked."

"Tell me then."

His gaze was intense, and she looked away for courage. Her heart was pounding when she told Fabian, "I only became friends with your sisters in order to be paraded in front of Gabriel. He was my mother's first choice as a match until he decided against joining the Senate. She thought that a man of commerce was too ordinary for a son-in-law, and you and Michele would not inherit a title or wealth. Impressing either of you was not in her plan for me."

Fabian knew her mother was bent on finding the perfect husband for her only daughter. Gabriel was only seven years older than Isabella, and he would inherit the Carrera fortune. Gabriel had finally chosen the beautiful Perla from Florence three years ago. They had a happy marriage together and already had a son.

"If your mother had changed her mind, why did you spend so much time at my home after that?"

She replied unflinchingly, "I needed attractive friends to attend parties with, so I continued to visit your house to be with your sisters."

Fabian drew in a jagged breath through his clenched teeth. "Your mother was using you to seduce my brother and then used my sisters to make pretty bookends for you? Did you ever want to be with us?"

Isabella was ashamed of what she had admitted to him, but she could not change the past. She took a step away from him to regain her nerve to defend herself. "I grew to love your sisters like my own," she told him, "even though gaining their friendship was not my desire in the beginning."

Fabian clutched her arm so she would not move farther away, and he tilted her chin, making her look up at him again. "And me, Isabella?" he asked. "For what gain were you using my friendship? Or was that all just pretending, too?"

"Why are you doing this?" she pleaded.

"I want to hear it from you."

"All of it?"

He nodded, and she obliged him.

"You were not good enough, Fabian. You are not even the second-born, and you know what that means for a marriage. But you were a good flirt, and I used your friendship to tempt the other men to notice me, to make them jealous."

He still had her in his grip when he asked, "Did you not enjoy my company at all, Isabella? Was I not tempting enough for you?"

"We had some fun together. You know that is true. I told you—it was not my choice."

He let her arm go but did not walk away. He was agitated and finally raised his voice in his frustration. "Did I help you get Sergio? Was he your mother's next choice after Gabriel?"

"He was," she admitted feebly.

"How could she choose him?" he shouted. "Sergio was a prick and a drunk. He did not love you. He did not appreciate you. He was fucking other women and telling the men at the club about it while he courted you."

Isabella was not shocked by Fabian's harsh description of her former fiancé. She knew of Sergio's blatant lying and other affairs, but she would have married him anyway.

"Yes, he was a disaster as a suitor, but he was filthy rich," she shouted back. "He had already inherited a huge estate. Sergio was good husband material, Fabian. Do you not get it?"

"Too bad you could not seal that marriage before he fell drunk into the canal and drowned. You think you lost a big fish, but you should consider yourself spared. In fact, you were spared twice, were you not?"

Neither truly wanted to argue on their last evening together, but there was no turning back.

"How was I spared twice?" she asked, fuming.

"You would be stuck with Gianni if he had not gotten himself blown up in battle. He had the promise of his father's title, but he was so timid we all thought he was a mute. What did you even talk about with him? Ah, but you did more than talk, didn't you, Isabella?"

"Do not speak of him like that," she hissed. "We talked about all sorts of things you cannot even appreciate. And so what if we did more than talk?

Gianni was a good man, Fabian, and I could have been happy with him. I did love him once. He did not deserve a death like that."

"I am sorry," he told her, no longer shouting. "I am stupid to have asked you to explain. You are right. I am wrong. I have always been wrong with you." Fabian walked the length of the room, his fingers pressed against his temples.

Isabella said nothing as she watched Fabian compose himself. He was like a chameleon that could change his mood at will, and he did, right in front of her.

Fabian stood before her again, far enough away that he would not follow his impulse to hold her.

"You have always been beyond my reach, Isabella, yet I keep grasping for you every time I see you again. I will leave you now and not think these thoughts any longer. I wish you well with whomever you are matched. He will be a lucky man."

He had meant for that to be his goodbye. They gazed at each other for a moment in the flickering light, and then he gave into his aching need to touch her. He pulled Isabella to his chest and kissed her once on her mouth tenderly and with yearning.

Isabella did not draw back or protest. They had embraced at parties over their years of friendship, and his kisses had always held a fiery passion. This kiss held sadness.

He released her, and she bowed her head. She could not look him in the eyes after he had bared his heart. It still hurt her to her core.

Fabian walked quickly out of the room, leaving her alone. She was no longer a part of his future, and he had finally faced that. She had accepted this fact long ago.

Isabella had wanted to walk out this door for the last ten minutes, but now she was glad it was closed. She needed time to let the tears she had been holding back finally fall. Caterina would ask her what had been said between them, and she needed to be able to lie convincingly.

Isabella sobbed alone in the dark room. When she ran out of tears, she dried her eyes on the lace of her wrap, took the last lit candle, and then made her way back through the quiet house to her chamber.

~ * ~

Mauro arrived at his chamber a few moments after his wife. "Can I help you out of your gown, Resi? Then you will not need to wake Verica," he said.

She stood in front of him, and he undid the tight laces that held the bodice closed in the back.

"I know you said you like this gown, Mauro, but I will have to pack it away until after the baby comes. It is a relief to have it unlaced," she said.

He slipped the top from her shoulders and began to unfasten the skirt.

"I could ask Fabian to bring you a few bolts of pretty fabric from his brother's warehouse. His mother could recommend a seamstress to design something that will leave you more room to grow."

Mauro could not see her face as he undressed her, but he could feel her body tense.

"You do not have to have a Venetian seamstress sew your gown, Resi. Perhaps Verica can make you one again. I liked how she mixed your traditional style of dress with the Venetian style."

Resi stepped out of the skirts, and Mauro picked them up off the floor and draped them on her trunk. She went to the looking glass and began to pull the feathered combs from her hair.

"I like your idea, Mauro. Verica is talented with dresses. I had her move the stitches in the waist of the blue one your aunt sent. I will wear that one for you tomorrow," she chattered, wanting to please him.

"I know you are more comfortable in your robes. I do like them on you. But sometimes I like to see you across the room looking like the regal baroness that you are now. That is why I asked you to wear the gown tonight," he said, standing behind her at her grooming table.

He kissed her softly on the nape of her neck and then went to his own grooming table. Once washed and undressed, Mauro opened the shutters to the room like he did each night. The bright light of the moon glowed around him at the window.

"I promised you something tonight," he said in a low voice, looking out into the night sky.

Resi had already slid under the covers. "I believe you promised me all of you tonight," she said. Her words meant more than the nude figure standing at the window, although she was sure she still wanted that.

He turned back toward her and smiled sheepishly. "I think the day has caught up with me. This morning I was at the naval port with my ship. This afternoon we welcomed five unlikely houseguests. This evening, well—at least no one drew swords."

She sat propped on the pillows, waiting for him. "So much has happened in the past few days," she agreed quietly.

He came to bed and blew out the candle. The moon gave enough light to see his wife by.

"Tell me what happened tonight, Resi. I am worried your brother's visit was not a good idea."

Resi had expected this and had rehearsed her apology. "I am sorry about our behavior, Mauro. We are siblings, and our emotions got the best of us. Patricius is a passionate man, and now you know that I can be, too. Something said at the dice table set him off, I guess. It is all settled now. I hope you can forgive him."

"That kind of passion in the wrong house gets a man killed."

Mauro had not meant it to sound so threatening, but Resi understood his warning. "He did not mean to cause any tension between you and him. They were tired, Mauro." She slid down in the bed and wrapped the cover around her. She was tired, too.

"It is forgotten then. I will talk to him, convince him that you are safe and cared for."

"Thank you, Mauro."

"I do not have to leave again for a while, so maybe I can get to know your brother like you know him. There is a council meeting in July, but I do not expect anything else will take me away from here until then."

He pulled her close, his hands resting on her middle. She sank her back into her favorite spot against his chest and hoped he would be rewarded with a kick or a turn from the baby, but it seemed the baby was already sleeping.

"When you go to the village tomorrow, can you ask about Elizabeta? Her baby is due any day now."

"I will ask Radic for you."

"I was thinking, Mauro. Elizabeta has been quite unhappy in confinement these last weeks. She is restricted to her chamber in the summer heat. Will you let me roam freely until the day comes, like we do in Greece? I do not want to be stuck in bed, like she is."

Mauro knew little of the rules of confinement, except that his mother had not followed them, and she had given birth alone in the chapel.

"I am told it is the midwife who decides these things. She knows best. And it will not be summer when your confinement time comes, so you may not mind staying indoors."

"Just the same, I don't want Elizabeta's midwife. Will it be all right to find a different one?"

"You shall have Idita with you, Resi. She is a healing woman and a midwife. She delivered all of the Baric children, so she will deliver ours, too."

Resi trusted the old nanny but wondered, "Do you think Idita remembers what is needed? That was a long time ago, and that was only two children."

Mauro chuckled. "She and Cook have helped deliver all of the castle's children over the years, as well as the five Baric children."

"*Five* Baric children, Mauro? Did you have more siblings? You never told me about them."

"Mateo was my half-brother, remember? My father was married to Margaret for many years, and she had given him four children. I don't know what they looked like. My mother took the painting with Margaret's children down, and I have yet to find where she hid it."

Mauro wrapped her in his arms again, and the baby kicked for him. He shut his eyes with satisfaction.

When it was apparent that Mauro was not going to say anything more, Resi asked, "What happened to all of them?"

He groggily said, "A plague, Resi. Margaret died, along with three of her children. Only Mateo survived. My father was away at the time. He came back to the news that they were all dead and laid to rest."

She stroked his hand resting across her. "That must have been devastating for your father."

After a moment, he replied in a whisper, "He loved them."

Resi thought that was the first time Mauro had spoken about love when he talked of his father.

"A man always loves his wife and children," she said.

But Mauro didn't hear her. He was already breathing deeply against her shoulder.

~ * ~

The mercenaries had drawn straws to see who would sleep on the big canopied bed. Cyro and Salar Nassim drew the short straws and took the stuffed pallet on the floor.

All were settled in their new beds when Cyro told the quiet room, "I think I have found my future bride."

Bem was nearly asleep, stretched out in the oversized feather bed with Patrik and Soren next to him. "Is this going to be a guessing game," asked Bem drowsily, "or will you tell us which of the women you are in love with?"

Patrik protested, "You cannot marry any of the women, Cyro, so don't get your hopes up." He rolled over to look at Cyro across the room. "Your first obvious choice would be my sister, but she is already married. Your second choice should be Ruby, but I will not allow you to marry her. She is too good for you! Your third and fourth choices are just as restricted—the little one is matched to a Hungarian blue blood, and Fabian Carrera will challenge you for the tall one."

"Thank you for your advice, Patrik, but my choice is made. The Hungarian has not yet claimed Caterina, so I will convince her and her father to allow me to marry her instead."

Bem considered Cyro's remarks as earnestly as Cyro had meant them. "What did you see in this woman that made you decide she is the one?" He had preferred her companion.

Cyro lay on his back, looking up at the timbered ceiling. It reminded him of his own room in his family's home. "I cannot say exactly what it is I love about her, except that I do. I found her to be perfect for me," he said dreamily.

"That is the mystery of love. There is no questioning why," said Salar Nassim poetically.

Bem's advice turned earnest. "You know, Cyro, you will only have a chance for her hand if you return to what you have run from. She will not marry a sellsword, but she will marry you for your fortune and title."

"I think I am ready to go back to my old life, but I do not want her to marry me just because of my wealth. She must not know what I really am until she loves me for me."

"Will your old life even be waiting for you? Your family thinks you are dead. Much could have changed," Patrik reminded him.

"I do not know. I have no brothers to take my inheritance, so I think my parents would be happy if I came back from the dead. Either way, I have decided I will return home. I would like to take Caterina with me."

When the laughter died down, Salar Nassim declared, "Then I will help you in your quest. When I meet the lady tomorrow, I will put your little bride to the same test I gave you when you came to us a spoiled nobleman. This will help you see her true character beyond her lace and silks."

"I do want to get to know her and make her fall in love with me. Your test is the perfect solution. Thank you, Salar Nassim."

"We can talk more of our plans in the morning, Cyro. Now we should thank Patrik for being the new brother of a nobleman who has offered us the best beds we have slept on in years," Salar Nassim said to the group.

They all mumbled their appreciation to Patrik, and Cyro blew out the last candle.

~ * ~

Down the hall from the mercenaries, Fabian was undressed for bed in his chamber. Before he extinguished the light, he went to his packed bag on the chair and opened it again. Fabian had taken a drawing from Isabella's sketchbook and brought it to his room while the others played their games. He took the carefully rolled paper from the bag and set it with the other important scrolls on his desk shelf. He would leave it here with the rest of his memories.

He sat down on his soft bed and blew out the candles on the table. The shutters were open, and the sea air drifted in through the window. Fabian looked out at the stars in the black sky. Two nights from now, he would be back at his family home, sleeping under this same sky but in a different world. Would he be allowed to choose which world he wanted to stay in? Maybe he would be better off in Venice. Fabian would let fate decide.

Chapter 7

Fabian was outside the stables tying his two satchels onto Bacchus's saddle when Mauro rode through the gate. The soldiers and castle servants were busy at their assigned duties before the day got too hot, and the courtyard was empty.

"Am I late?" hollered Mauro as he rode up next to him.

Fabian tilted his broad hat to see his friend better. "Did you have trouble on the fields?"

"No, no," Mauro answered, catching his breath from his hard ride. "You chose a good group of men for me to work with. I just lost track of time, is all."

"I am ready if you are." He patted the last bag to see that it was steady and then mounted Bacchus.

Mauro looked at the laden horse. "Why have you packed so much?" he asked. "I thought you were only going for a week. You have not raided my wine cellar, have you?"

Fabian laughed. He was known to help himself to his father's fine bottles of wine from their family cellar. "How could I? Jero never lets me have his key," Fabian told him.

"Have you asked him before?" Mauro laughed at the thought. "Is my best brandy in the sitting room not enough for you?"

Fabian brushed off the deserved accusation of the disappearing brandy bottles. "I will tell you my change in plans when we are through the gate."

The two rode their horses past the Baric guards and out the gate in silence. They slowed when they were on the empty castle road, and Mauro asked, "You are not coming back, are you?"

"Not in a fortnight, like I had first intended," Fabian replied with certainty. "I have been thinking for a while about what it might mean to go back to Venice. I even prayed to ask God for a sign."

"And God sent you your sign?" asked Mauro doubtfully.

Fabian thought about Isabella's confession. "Yes, last night, as a matter of fact. My father is right, you know. I am turning twenty-five soon and need to begin my life. Maybe I will give his offer a try for a year or two. Either way, I will be back again. If I am happy with my new arrangements, I will come back to organize my things to be sent to Venice. If I am unhappy, I will beg you for my humble chamber and promise to be the doting uncle to all your spoiled children."

"I can actually picture that. But you should plan on being a father yourself one day and spoil your own children," said Mauro encouragingly.

They were coming around the bend that flanked the shooting fields, and Fabian waved to the men training there.

Mauro asked him, "What is it about my little part of the empire that you like so much, Fabian? You have such low opinions of every other territory beyond Venice."

"I admit I do have some prejudices, but there is something about your village that is particularly delightful—as long as I do not have to suffer learning the local language," Fabian teased.

Mauro told him in Croatian, "You are too lazy to try, you Venetian snob."

"See, I love how even insults get stuck in your throat. Croatian just does not flow as nicely as Venetian. And I am not a snob," Fabian declared.

"Ha! At least you know the important words. My wife and Ruby have learned Venetian, and they manage in Croatian as well. I think you may have a mental deficiency, old friend."

Fabian laughed along with him. "I have learned enough in the years of living here to know what is being said. But I prefer to hear it all in Venetian."

The two had talked about this before. Latin was the official language throughout the Serene Republic of Venice. Still, the citizens in Croatia taught their children to speak the old dialect of the Croats. The residents of Baric Castle were no different.

"Fortunately for you, we can all choke out our words in Venetian to suit your delicate ears."

"Speaking of delicate ears, what do you make of your Genoese guest?"

"Do you mean Cyro? Did he say he was from Genoa? He told us little about himself," said Mauro.

"I did not have to ask him. They have a particular accent that is hard to hide from other Italians, and he was being very vague about his whole background. He would know the Venetians hate the Genoese."

"I have heard your list, Fabian, and I know your opinion of them. But he obviously left there for a reason, so perhaps he shares your view. He seems like a decent man. I have only known him one day, and I am not ready to pass judgment."

"It is your house to welcome whomever you please, Mauritius. But I am suspicious of visitors who avoid giving their full names. I just hope he is not more trouble for you."

They had reached the crossroads, and the highway was busy with carts and people on foot coming and going to the village. Several of the travelers respectfully greeted the baron and Fabian.

When they were alone again on the street, Mauro assured Fabian, "Cyro will not make any trouble. It is the others I am worried about. But I will write you since you will expect the worst until you hear otherwise."

"And I will write to you when I have a definitive answer for the fate of my sister. The girls must continue on with the carriage one way or the other. I will let you know when to expect the escorts."

They had meandered their way through the carts being pushed along the small lanes until they got to the village square. Most mornings were busy like this, and Mauro was pleased the merchants made a vigorous trade. The constable's office was where Mauro had planned his first errand, and they stopped in the alley next to the building.

"Are you sure you do not want to take Bacchus with you?" asked Mauro.

Fabian gave his favorite horse a pat on his glistening neck, and Bacchus acknowledged him with a flick of his head.

"He would not be happy as a city horse. He is not used to too much confinement."

The temperamental horse would be extra work for the stable grooms to exercise, so Mauro offered, "I could assign Bacchus to one of the soldiers to ride while you are gone. Do you have a preference?"

Fabian smiled as he decided on his answer. "Bacchus has taken well to Jero. He can ride him."

Mauro was surprised by the rare show of trust in his steward. "Yes, I think Jero is a good choice," he agreed.

They both dismounted, and Fabian untied his luggage. He set the bags on the ground and hugged Mauro tightly when he said, "I owe you, dear friend. How can I ever repay you for all that you have done for me?"

Mauro patted Fabian on the shoulder for good measure when they stepped apart. "I know how you may repay me," he told him. "My wife has a request for something from Venice."

"Anything for your beautiful wife," said Fabian, and then suddenly looked at Mauro with wide-eyed panic. "Shit!" he exclaimed. "There was something I needed to tell you, but there has not been a chance. I wanted you to hear it from me, Mauro, and not from your wife."

Mauro did not like Fabian's tone of guilt. "Go ahead," he said.

"While you were collecting your ship, I was fishing for our breakfast. Your wife came and sat with me on the dock for a time and began questioning me on politics, of all things. I have never talked politics with a young woman, and I have to say your wife is well-read on government."

Mauro frowned at the odd confession, and Fabian went on to explain, "That is not my disclosure. After our heartfelt conversation, and catching two fish, she asked me something."

Fabian paused for emphasis, as he always did when telling a story.

"Fabian, you will miss your boat to the ferry if you do not hurry and just tell me."

"She asked me to call her Terese—Resi, even. She thinks we are friends, Mauro. It was really quite charming."

"Was that really all you were talking about? That seems like an odd request after discussing politics."

Fabian smiled, thinking of the pleasant morning on the dock just yesterday. "Yes, well, we spoke of government and what my father's role in the Senate was. I was surprised that she took such an interest in it. The fish were biting, and I was enjoying her company. Then she caught me off guard with her request. I may have offended her with my answer."

"What did you say to offend her? She did not grow up as nobility, Fabian. The rules of etiquette are not so easy for her to understand," he said defensively.

"I know you are protective of her, so I just wanted to mention that we had this conversation. I blamed you for our formality, actually." Fabian watched Mauro consider his confession and then added, "I felt a bit insecure after our conversation ended. I was being my usual, alluring self and she was not distracted in the least."

"It is refreshing to know that you have no effect on my wife. Perhaps it is time you marry, before you lose your charms of seduction altogether."

Fabian shook his head with alarm. "I think you might be right, Mauritius. I am losing it—my fucking memory! How could I have forgotten this?"

"What is it, Fabian?"

"It is about your neighbor." Fabian looked up and down the shadowed alley to be sure they were alone. "Your wife told me that Dubovic had a conversation with her at the ball."

Mauro thought about that night, not even a week ago. "Yes, I noticed the two talking together before they danced."

"Well, he mentioned to her that he was courting your mother after your father died. Dubovic was considering *marrying* her."

"Marry my mother? That is outrageous." Mauro began pacing the narrow alleyway. "How could he even visit my mother without my knowing it?" He stopped in front of Fabian again. "How would this even come into conversation with Terese?"

"That is exactly what I thought. You will have to ask your wife to retell what was said."

Mauro's agitated thoughts raced back to the circumstances at the castle last year. "There was much trouble on the Habsburg border between my father's death and my mother's. We were gone for weeks at a time, were we not?"

"Yes, and your mother would have been alone in the house with only your servants. Nestor and Jero might know if the baron visited her and how often."

Mauro surmised, "Natalija was with her constantly. She would have witnessed everything."

Fabian wanted to stay and work this out with Mauro, but this could not be solved in a few minutes. His time was short. Instead, he reminded Mauro, "Before I go, you still need to tell me your wife's request."

Mauro nodded to his friend and said soberly, "It seems trivial now, but she would like a new gown made. I was thinking you could pick out a few bolts of fabric from your brother's warehouse." He tried to be cheerful again and managed a smile.

Fabian smiled back. "That is an easy request. Your lovely wife can wear any color beautifully, so I cannot disappoint her."

Then Fabian gave his glum friend one last piece of advice: "You need to let others compliment your beautiful wife without becoming jealous every time. It does not suit you to look so sour, Mauritius. She loves you. That is clear to everyone but you. Take care of her. She will be your new lucky charm."

Fabian had always joked that he was Mauro's lucky charm. Trouble happened to him without Fabian around, and Mauro still could not believe that they were saying goodbye.

"I will take care of her, Fabian. Godspeed for a safe crossing."

Fabian tipped his velvet hat. Without another word, he picked up his bags, walked out into the street, and crossed the lively village square.

Mauro watched him disappear into the crowd. He looked up at the midmorning sky, where a band of clouds darkened the western horizon. A storm was developing over the Adriatic, and Mauro shook off the sudden panic. Fabian's ship would be fine.

~*~

Mauro left the cobbled alleyway where the horses were secured in the shade of the buildings and climbed the broad, sunny steps of the constable's office. The constable's door was open wide to let the morning air circulate in the cluttered office.

Mauro saw someone seated at the desk studying a scroll unrolled in front of him. Mauro called over, "Constable Radic?"

Radic looked up sternly from his concentration, but then his mouth formed a toothy grin when he saw it was the baron. He stood and removed his hat to bow respectfully.

"Good day to you, Lord Baric. Come in, come in," said Radic.

"I was not sure I would find you here today. I was told your wife was near her time. I thought maybe you would be at your home."

"Yes, she is ready to burst at any moment. I will warn you, sir, it is nerve-racking when the end of the wait is near." He ran his fingers through his thick, graying hair and set his hat back on his head. "She is my third wife, you know. I have gone through this before, but it doesn't get any easier. So I try to keep myself busy until they call for me."

"Then I have a task for you to work on while you wait." Mauro went to the desk and sat on the stool across from the constable.

Radic rolled up the scroll he had been studying and asked, "How can I be of service, my lord?"

"First, I needed to look at the village registry."

Radic went to the shelves along the wall between the holding cell doors. "There have not been many changes since your arrival, Lord Baric."

Mauro saw from his place at the desk that there were several volumes with dates printed on the bindings. "I need the ledger for the years 1638 to 1639. I am not sure of the exact date."

"Oh? Anything in particular I can help you locate?"

Mauro trusted Radic to keep this confidential. "I want to know where the Tomsic family came from."

"Your ship's captain,?"

"Yes. It would be recorded in the registry, would it not?"

Radic pulled down a dusty leather volume. "All the information is recorded, including which jurisdiction they were under before coming here. We have to notify that landlord that they are taken off his tax registry."

"Were you constable back then, Radic?"

"No, sir, they arrived before I became constable, so that would be before April of '39. Yes, here we are, my lord. Ivanoslav Tomsic arrived with his wife and four sons on the eighteenth of June, 1638."

"And is it written where they moved from?"

Radic brought the log to the table and turned it around so the baron could see for himself.

"Venice," Radic read aloud.

"That is not what I expected. I thought they were from the territories, not the capital."

"Old Ivanoslav's sister lives in the territories. Maybe that is what you are thinking of, sir. She's Lord Dubovic's tenant. Ivanoslav is living at her cottage while he recovers."

"Do you know why Ivanoslav is living with his sister, and not with one of his sons?"

"Her husband has been dead for several years now, I believe. Maybe she wanted her brother to keep her company. As for his sons, they were sailors, probably captains now, like Branislav. I don't know who they took up with after they left here, but they have not been back. They could be dead, for all I know."

"One brother is still alive. Branislav was helping him with some extra work while my ship was held those two weeks."

Mauro reread the entry, wishing for more details, but there was only one line. "What do you think of Branislav?" he asked the constable.

"Your ship's captain? I think he is a good man. His crew likes him well enough, and so does Jakov. Why do you ask, sir? Is he giving you trouble?"

"I am not troubled by his work for me. But he may have gotten involved in something illegal outside of his duties."

"Illegal? Do you want him arrested, my lord?"

"No, I want him cleared," said Mauro with an uncomfortable laugh. "I do not know where I will find a captain as good as he is for the job required. Can you check around whether there is talk of cargo missing coming from Venice, or worse?"

"Do you suspect him of pirating? That is serious, my lord."

"It is only serious if you have pirated from someone who will press charges. If no one complains, then there is no crime. I am interested in knowing of any murmurs of that, too," Mauro said. "I do not think Branislav would have helped his brother with his scheme if he was not assured that there would be no risk. Insurance fraud will be investigated but only superficially. There is bound to be talk among the sailors."

Radic pondered for a moment. "I understand where you are going with this, sir. Sometimes a merchant will insure a vessel and arrange to have it stolen for the insurance payment."

Mauro did not bother to insure his ordinary cargo, but many merchants did that for their valuable glass, textiles, and gold coming out of Venice.

"I have heard this sort of desperate profit taking through insurance claims is more common lately, even at the high cost of insuring a shipment."

Radic nodded. "I will find out what I can, sir. The Venetian Navy will know the most details about any lost ship in the Adriatic. I will ask my contacts there, too."

Mauro was ready to return the registry to the constable when the breeze gusted from the open door and flipped the light parchment. His eyes wandered to an entry at the top of the new page. The dateline read 3 September, 1627: Jero Kasun, age four. Residence: Baric Castle. Mother: Sonja Kasun, deceased. Father: unknown. Prior residence: Dubovic Castle. The third of September was the date they celebrated as Jero's birthday. Now Mauro knew it was the day Jero had been registered to Baric Castle.

Radic was suddenly concerned. "My lord, are you alright? You look as pale as a ghost. Can I get you a drink?"

"I am fine."

Mauro looked up from the yellowed document. "It is recorded here that Jero came from Lord Dubovic's residence," he said. "Would that be correct?"

Mauro turned the ledger around, and Radic leaned over and read where Mauro pointed.

"It seems so, sir. No living mother, no father. Lord Dubovic takes in orphan boys for his service from time to time."

"But he was only four years old. Why would he already be a servant for Baron Dubovic?"

Radic looked at the entry again. "Well, some say Lord Dubovic is charitable to take in boys no matter how young. That would make sense if Jero lost his mother and some relative sold him, rather than taking on the care of another child."

Mauro frowned at the thought of Jero living at Dubovic Castle. "How many in his service were orphans?"

"Hard to say, sir. I believe he picks his house grooms from the orphans as the boys grow. Those he likes stay, but some say those are not the lucky ones. I do not want to talk ill of his lordship."

"I have heard bits and pieces of what you mention already. Now I want to hear what you know, and what you think of the man. Ill or not, you may speak freely."

"Well, Lord Baric, I have heard that he misuses the boys. He has one with him day and night. It seems unnatural, if you know what I mean. If they fall out of favor—become disloyal, if you will—he sells them to other noble houses as indentured servants to repay their debt to him. I am friends with Lord Dubovic's new constable, and that is the truth of it. Jero may have just been lucky to be discarded so young to your family. He was probably too young to know himself how he ended up at Baric Castle."

"Jero has said he has no memory of his life before coming to us." Mauro closed the ledger and said, "Tell me, Radic. I have recently heard that Lord Dubovic was a frequent guest at my castle after my father's death. Do you remember his visits while my mother was still alive?"

"Now that you mention it, sir, he would come and go through your land regularly for a time. His daughter also married a man from the south in that same year. But whether Lord Dubovic turned off to visit your mother, I cannot say for certain. I leave the comings and goings along your castle road to your own guardsmen."

"Like I said, it is recent news to me. I will ask my soldiers myself. Thank you, Radic. You have been very helpful. If you can get back to me on Branislav's activities, then that would be more helpful."

"I will follow through on that right away, sir."

Mauro stood up to leave, and Radic followed him.

"While you are here, my lord, I did have something personal I wanted to discuss with you."

"Yes, Radic?" The baron waited.

"After my new child is born, and all goes speedily with my wife's recovery, I would like to host a baptismal celebration."

"I would expect you to," agreed Mauro.

"Yes, sir, but it seems the entire village is wanting to wish us well," he said with a chuckle. "I would like to host a party at my house, but there would never be room."

When the constable hesitated, Mauro asked, "Do you want to use the castle grounds?"

"No, no, my lord, I ask nothing as charitable as that," exclaimed Radic. "It's just . . . I have talked to the priest, and he would not be against having the celebration in front of the church, with food tables and dancing in the square. It would essentially close the village down, though."

Mauro grinned at the budding suggestion. The village had not had a community celebration in a long time.

"Radic, that is a wonderful solution. If Father David agreed to it, then you may hold your party in the church square. We would all be delighted to celebrate with you."

Radic shook the baron's hand. "Thank you, Lord Baric. You honor me greatly."

"My wife will be especially pleased to hear when Elizabeta has the child. Send word to the castle, will you? I will leave you now to your work."

"I will send word, my lord. Thank you again, sir."

Mauro went out into the bright sunshine. From the constable's steps, Mauro admired the village square. The statue of his grandfather stood prominently in the center of it. He took a deep breath and smiled. As Fabian had pointed out, it was a particularly delightful place.

Chapter 8

Verica hastily pulled out all the possible choices for riding clothes from the baroness's wardrobe. If Isabella could find a solution to her billowing skirts, then she would have her riding lesson. Ruby had already looked through her own limited selection. Lady Isabella was a few inches taller than Ruby, and her shorter leggings did not meet the requirement that Lady Isabella's calves be modestly covered. The baroness was nearly as tall as the Venetian aristocrat, and she was her last resort.

~*~

Earlier that morning, Isabella had arrived on time at the stable yards to find Alberto and Bem disagreeing over the saddle she was to use. Alberto insisted a lady should learn to ride like a lady, and he argued that Lady Isabella should be seated on Lady Johanna's sidesaddle.

Bem refused to saddle his mare with the boxy contraption. He argued that such a saddle was not good for the horse's back, or the lady's.

When Isabella arrived in her favorite satin gown with the layers of lacy underskirts, it complicated the discussion even more.

"Lady Isabella will not be subjected to the indecency of riding astride in a gown," asserted Alberto. "There are standards of decency in this land. We shall saddle another horse with the baroness's sidesaddle."

"So it is now the dress of the lady that determines how she rides?" asked Bem impatiently.

Alberto pointed out with equal irritation, "You can see, sir, that the lady's dress is the main drawback."

Bem turned to Ruby, who had come to the paddock with Isabella to watch her first lesson.

"I noticed yesterday, Ruby, that you rode your horse without such a lady's sidesaddle. Might you have appropriate riding clothes to lend to Lady Isabella for her lesson today?"

Bem then glared at Alberto, who frowned back at Bem's show of defiance.

Ruby sensed that her answer was pivotal. "I can see if my riding garments would fit Lady Isabella. If not, the baroness would certainly have something for her to wear."

"Must I have a special gown to ride in? I am quite comfortable how I am," protested Isabella.

Alberto explained to her, "Your teacher wants you to ride on his horse with his saddle, my lady. There is a question of covering your legs with your skirts while you ride. It is inevitable that a beautiful gown such as yours will not stay down unless you sit on the box seat. But the man will not allow his horse to carry you with it."

"Well, I prefer to learn as my instructor recommends," Isabella stated simply. "You will saddle his horse as he prefers, and I shall return with my legs appropriately covered. Come, Lady Ruby."

~*~

Verica had been straightening the baroness's room when Ruby and Isabella entered. Resi had already left to meet her brother in the meadow by the bathhouse. Ruby was sure Resi would not object to lending Lady Isabella anything that she needed for her lesson.

Verica unpacked the baroness's riding ensemble from her trunk, and Isabella hastily tried it on.

Ruby sighed with disappointment. Even Resi's flowing leggings would not be long enough to satisfy Alberto's strict standards.

"This will not do either," fretted Isabella. "Your old stable master was very adamant that no leg be showing." Desperate, she suggested, "Perhaps I could wear some of the baron's breeches."

"I have an idea, my lady," said Verica, near-bursting with renewed enthusiasm.

Verica went to her mistress's armoire and searched through the clothes Countess Toth had sent her earlier that month. She pulled out the rose-colored breeches and matching floral jacket that the baron had forbidden his wife to wear. Verica held them out for Isabella, who took the silky garments from the maid with a wide grin.

"These are lovely. Do you think the baroness will mind me wearing them? They look absolutely precious."

Ruby laughed. "She will not be able to fit into them until after the baby is born, and even then her husband finds them to be, um, too pretty."

"Hmm. Yes, they are indeed pretty. All the more reason I will wear them."

Isabella held the breeches to her corseted waist in front of the looking glass. They went down to her shoes. She smiled happily.

Verica went to work, lacing them on her. Verica found the baroness's green tunic to wear under the long open jacket for an extra layer of modesty. Ten minutes later, Isabella was back at the stables, fully outfitted to ride astride.

Bem patted Alberto on the back as the two watched the women coming toward them across the courtyard.

"Yes, this change in dress is much better, wouldn't you say, Alberto? It is a good thing we are both married men." Bem chuckled at the old stable master's scowl.

Isabella joined the men with the self-confidence to match that of the countess who had provided the scandalous ensemble. Her legs were covered, yet outlined like narrow petals of a pink lily held upside down, with the pale green of the belted tunic flowing above the flowery leggings.

Alberto delicately helped her onto Bem's saddled horse for her first riding lesson. Not a word more was spoken about her attire.

~ * ~

Caterina went downstairs for her card lesson shortly after Isabella had left for the stables. She was surprised to find Cyro sitting with the Persian at a table under the canopy on the terrace.

Both men stood up to greet her with formal bows. She took her place at the table, and they sat down again across from her.

Salar Nassim spoke first. "I beg your permission to allow my friend to join us, Lady Caterina. I think he can play a helpful role in expediting your lessons," he said.

Cyro smiled at Caterina as she turned her focus to him.

"I did not find you to be much of a card player last night. Do you have some tricks to offer me?" she asked disapprovingly.

Cyro was not discouraged by her criticism. He told her, "I will not be joining you at your card game, my lady."

Caterina raised her brows with curiosity.

Salar Nassim clarified, "There is more to winning a game than learning how to manipulate the cards. You must also be able to manipulate your opponents. Cyro will show you how to do that."

Caterina openly contemplated the young Italian. There was something about him that she did not trust and something that she was drawn to. His gold tooth gleamed in his otherwise white smile as he regarded her hopefully across the table. She took exception to his velvet cap, but his unfashionable clothes seemed to suit his carefree nature. He was harmless enough.

"All right," she said, "I will hear what Signor Cyro has to say. Where do we start today?"

Salar Nassim smiled slyly at his private victory. "Today, my lady, we will play one game of your choice."

He pulled a well-used deck of cards from his jacket pocket. Caterina set a crisp deck of cards she had brought in her pocket next to his on the table.

Salar Nassim turned to his companion and said, "Cyro, you may leave us." He continued to tell the surprised Caterina, "Cyro will find you later to show you what you will need to bring for your lesson tomorrow."

Cyro quietly stood up and bowed to Caterina before he walked away, back to the Keep.

~ * ~

Soren had parted company with Patrik at the path to the bathhouse and walked along the back castle wall, looking for his washed shirt among the many others drying on the line. The rows of white fabric that blew in the warm breeze reminded Soren of the sails on the ship that he and Niels had taken when they first left Denmark.

"If you're looking for your clothes, they are down here," a feminine voice called out.

Soren looked over to where the voice had come from and then followed Natalija to the end of the row. He examined the line of shirts and found the one he was looking for.

Soren removed his soiled shirt and put the freshly laundered one on. He was annoyed at himself for not removing it earlier that morning when he was cleaning his weapons. Soren was down to two shirts, and this one would be ruined, too, if the oil set too long.

"Your shirt was just washed, sir. I don't think it is dry," the maid said cautiously. Natalija should not be speaking to the guest at all.

"It will dry on me," he replied bluntly in his thickly-accented Latin.

She took a few steps closer and held out her hand. "Give me the dirty one, my lord, and I will wash it before we empty the cauldron."

He handed it to her, grateful for the easy solution to his earlier mistake, and then corrected her mistake. "I am not a lord," he said.

She lingered by him, holding the musky shirt tightly in her arms. "My mistress said you are from Denmark." She took no notice of his blatant stare.

"Yes," he answered.

She chattered on, "I heard they have lots of kings and noblemen there. I did not expect a man from Denmark to look so kind, though. You are not frightening at all."

Soren finished tucking his damp shirt into his belted breeches. He looked up at the wall and saw that they were being watched from the ramparts. Soren could have thanked her and walked away, but he was curious and asked, "How is it that you have such a poor opinion of Danish noblemen? Has one been unkind to you?"

"I have never met anyone from so far north, but Lady Baric read us a story about Denmark. It is a dark place, and the people are very unhappy. I did not imagine them looking like you. I imagined them darker and, well, angry."

Soren was intrigued. Either this girl was very brave or very innocent.

"I do not frighten you then?"

"No. I can tell you are not angry. You actually remind me of my oldest brother. He does not have light hair, but he is tall and strong, like you are."

"Do you have many brothers?" Soren immediately regretted asking. He did not want to talk about brothers.

"Luka works with my father in the village, but Janko, the oldest, went to work for a tanner in Zadar. I have four sisters, too, which is why my mother sent me to work for Lord Baric. Our house is small for all of us. So now I live here, in the castle."

"Can you visit them?" Soren was curious to know how normal people lived.

"Lord Baric lets me spend Sundays with them after Mass. But I didn't get to go home this past Sunday because there was too much work to finish. The baron just had a ball, you see. With all the guest rooms occupied, they left a mountain of laundry for us."

Natalija began to ramble, and Soren listened patiently to her trivial news. He had not heard a woman talk of anything but death and misery for at least a year. He was somehow stunned that life could still be ordinary. War had not touched this girl's life, just the piles of dirty linen.

"I am a lady's maid really," she clarified, "but two of the wash girls are sick today, so I was asked to help the house servants get caught up on the linens. Well, Louisa isn't really ill," she told him. "She has her time of the month for the first time, and Idita cannot convince her she isn't dying. Her mother didn't tell her what was to come. Still, she won't stop crying over her misfortune. Idita told her to stay in bed until the week is over and then Louisa will see that we are right. Oh, dear." She giggled with embarrassment. "You have the same look my brother has when someone talks about woman problems. You must not have any sisters."

"No," he said, shaking his head.

"And you aren't married?" she asked.

"I am not," he replied.

"Well, then you cannot know what I am talking about," she cheerfully concluded.

"I suppose not," Soren answered her with a rare smile.

Another girl's voice from among the drying sheets called out Natalija's name.

"Coming," Natalija called back. "I must go. I will wash your shirt and hang it out with the rest," she told him, grinning, and then ran off down the long row of limp shirts with his clutched in her arms.

Soren watched her disappear, then turned to walk the short distance back to the Keep.

Hugo approached Soren as he neared the steps to the tower. They had played a friendly game of dice last night, but Hugo had gone out of his way to be unfriendly when they crossed paths at breakfast that morning. His expression was stern when he told Soren, "Leave the girl alone."

Hugo was not the one Soren had noticed on the ramparts, so news traveled fast among the guards.

Soren matched his hostile tone. "I did not know she was your girl."

"All the women here are under my protection. Do not forget that," Hugo warned.

Soren raised a brow and asked, "And they are not allowed to talk to anyone but you?"

"Just those they know," asserted Hugo.

"She knew my shirt on the line, and now she knows me," Soren replied coolly.

"The servants are not to be bothered. Consider this a warning."

Soren resented the underlying accusation. "I only wanted my shirt. If I did want to bother her, it would not be in full view of your guards." Soren was unarmed, but a clear challenge came across in his voice.

Hugo seemed to decide he had made his point without drawing swords, and he turned to walk back to the guardhouse.

Cyro was just coming from the terrace. He watched the confrontation without the benefit of hearing what was said. Soren had been watching Hugo leave and was startled by Cyro's sudden presence.

"What was that all about?" Cyro asked Soren.

"I went to the laundry line for my shirt and somehow broke a Baric rule of morality by talking to the wash maid."

Cyro was sympathetic. He had been with Soren at breakfast and recognized the guard from the encounter.

"He is a cocky one. Pay him no regard," Cyro said.

They climbed the stairs together.

"How long do you think we will stay?" asked Soren. "I can be packed in an hour."

Cyro thought about the urgency of his new obsession. "I plan to stay until I can convince Lady Caterina to marry me. I do not think she even likes me yet. I will need a few more days here," he declared.

Soren considered his friend's dilemma. "Very well," he told Cyro. "I will stay the four days we promised Patrik. If you cannot convince her in that time, then she is not worth taking home."

"Agreed," said Cyro.

Chapter 9

Resi had been asleep when Mauro rose early for his duty at the training fields that morning. Verica woke the baroness at her usual time, but Resi did not take her offer to help her dress in the blue gown Verica had laid out for her mistress.

While picking at her uneaten breakfast, Resi asked, "Will you tell Geoff to come to my chamber when Fabian leaves for the village?"

"And then I will be back directly to fix your hair, Lady Baric."

"I won't be needing your help this morning, Verica. I will see you after my bath."

Verica seemed reluctant to leave her fidgeting mistress alone, but she curtsied obediently and left to find her brother in the stables.

Once Resi sent Geoff away with the message for Patrik, she dressed with care for her rendezvous. She wore her long kaftan over the breeches she had taken from Mauro's trunk. With a belt, they were a better fit than she expected.

She wrapped the cumbersome sword case in one of her scarves and carried it through the sitting room and out the small terrace door. The morning was already warm, but a band of gray clouds to the west promised a change in weather.

In the small meadow, Patrik sat relaxed in the shade of the tree where Resi had instructed him to meet her. He was absently tossing cones he had found beneath the ancient pine when she came around the corner unnoticed. Patrik wore European breeches and a vest over his open-collared shirt today, not the Ottoman dress he had arrived in. He looked older than his twenty-two years, but he was still the brother she remembered.

Resi watched him playfully juggle a prickly ball before she interrupted his trick.

"You would have been better off joining a theater troupe. You were always fond of illusions."

Grinning, he looked around and picked up two more of the fat cones and then began to juggle them above his head. He let each hang in the air before catching them, one after the other, in the opening of his shirt.

Resi clapped and laughed. "Ah, that is very good, Patricius. Or should I call you Patrik?"

"Do you object to my new name?"

"What is wrong with your old one? Patricius is a good Greek name."

"It is Venetian as well. Patrik sounds stronger, don't you think?"

"No, I don't. I think I will never get used to it. But, if that is what you prefer to be called now, then I will try."

He saw she was awkwardly carrying something and asked, "Is this your secret?" He pointed to the wrapped case.

She set the scarf off to the side and put the box down.

Patrik knew what would be inside such an elegant case. Noblemen were very particular about protecting their best weapons. "What are you doing with swords, Resi?"

She opened the latch. "They are not sharp. I have been practicing with them. I want a rematch."

Patrik let out a laugh. "I am not going to fight you, Resi. I have had enough fighting to last a lifetime. Besides, you told me last night that you are pregnant."

"I am only a little pregnant. I can still move about quite well, as you can see. You challenged me the last time we saw each other and then you left before making good on your promise."

Patrik took out one of the swords and held it in his hand, feeling the weight. He smiled. "Did your husband give you these? They are quite finely made."

"Mauro doesn't know I have them. Jero gave them to me."

Patrik gave her a questioning look.

"Well, I suppose they belong to the Barics and not Jero himself," she affirmed. "I asked him to give me a real sword, and he gave me the set of sparring swords instead. At least I think it was him. The case appeared in my chamber, and I have kept my practicing a secret."

He put the first sword back and took out the second. "I like this Jero already. Is he your lover?" Patrik asked casually.

"Don't be ridiculous. Jero is our steward. He is here to look out for me, not to seduce me."

"It isn't so ridiculous. Jero is a young, handsome man at your beck and call. Your husband is gone for months at a time. It happens quite naturally often enough." Her brother was never one to shy away from frank opinions.

"I do like Jero, and I think of him as a friend, really, not as a servant," she maintained. "But that is not why he gave me the sword case. Besides, he is in love with someone else."

"Ah, well, I am glad for his sake to hear that he has romantic opportunities. It seems there are far too few women to go around for all the men here."

"I brought the opportunity," she said with a chuckle. "Jero admires Ruby."

"My Ruby?" asked Patrik.

Resi laughed at his shocked expression. "She is not *your* Ruby. If anything, she is *my* Ruby. She has been a dear companion to me and my best friend. She thinks she loves him, though."

"Then why didn't she tell me that when I teased her about finding a husband in the castle?"

"Jero doesn't know that Ruby loves him, and he has not directly said that he loves her."

"Is that how love affairs work at Baric Castle? No one tells the other their feelings?"

"I told you Jero is a servant. He is not a good match for Ruby. He has nothing of his own and has little to offer her," Resi repeated the reasons she had already given Ruby.

"Has Ruby decided she must marry a baron, too?"

"Of course not, but her father is particular. You should know that," Resi reminded him.

"It was suggested once that I should marry Ruby Spiros, and I had nothing to offer her."

"But Angelos Spiros knows that our father would give you an occupation and a home. Ruby would want for nothing as a Kokkinos wife."

"Could she not live in your castle as Jero's wife, and Jero continue in his role as a married man? She would be cared for and could still keep you company," Patrik argued.

Resi picked at the grass next to her. "It doesn't work like that with the aristocracy."

"Yes, I know. The greedy noblemen have to have everything for themselves. If you are some distant, blue-blooded relative, you get your own castle. If you are not, you get a corner in the stables. I have seen too much of the aristocracy to have any desire to live in their world."

He had been waving his hand for emphasis, and Resi reached out to take it.

"Let me see your hand, Patricius."

He did as she asked.

Resi examined the neat scar that was the only mark to show that a fourth finger had been there. "Tell me now how you lost it."

He took a deep breath in and then out again. "I was climbing a wall, and a few loose stones began to give away. My finger got caught, crushed in fact, and it couldn't be set again."

She released his hand. "The scar is very smooth. Who stitched this for you?"

"Niels did. He took the bones out, then cut it clean to the knuckle."

Patrik looked at the hand again, thinking of the pain it had given him before his friend amputated it. "He was the surgeon of our group. Blood never bothered him," he said.

"What happened to Niels, Patricius?"

He leaned back against the old tree and picked at the cones again in front of him. Patrik had never talked about the whole story. He took a second to think how best to explain the events of that terrible day.

"It was awful, Resi," he began.

"How did he die, Patricius?" she asked, and he wanted to let the memories out, once and for all.

"It was a long battle, Resi. We were armored in breast mail and thick leather, and we had all come through unharmed. We were regrouping. Niels and Soren were walking toward our horses, stepping over bodies. You cannot imagine it. The ground was littered with dying men."

He leaned back and shut his eyes, then said, "We don't know what happened. Niels might have kicked that soldier, or stepped on him, it is hard to know, but the dying man reached up and put a dagger in Niels's thigh as he crossed over him."

He heard his sister gasp, but Patrik did not look at her when he said, "We had to pull the dagger out, and when we did, the wound would not stop bleeding. We tied Niels's leg off tight with a rope and a stick, knowing he would lose it, but the blood didn't stop flowing. The wound was too deep."

Patrik was uncharacteristically solemn when he told her, "I will never forget that feeling of helplessness, Resi. We were frantically pushing on his leg, begging God to stop the bleeding. Niels was the one worried about not going to heaven when he died. At one point he told us it did not feel like he was heading toward hell because he was so cold. Then he was dead."

Tears slid freely down Resi's cheeks.

Patrik had run out of tears long ago. His eyes were dry when he told Resi, "Soren went almost mad with grief and then settled into a silent acceptance, which was even worse. He is coming around, but I don't know if Soren will ever be the same man. After that, he and I made the decision that we would not fight any more. That is when I wrote to you."

"Are you going home, Patricius?"

He shrugged. "Thessaloniki is no longer my home, but we will go there and visit before making our way south to Athens. Bem's wife might be there. We promised Bem we would help him learn his wife's fate before parting."

"Bem left a wife behind?"

"Yes, but it is complicated. I will tell you the story another time."

Patrik stood up abruptly and took the sword in his hand, testing its weight. He flashed a strained smile. "Now, dear sister, I would like to play with your lovely toys."

Resi rose to her feet as well and removed her kaftan. He gave her a renewed look of surprise when he saw she was wearing a man's shirt and breeches.

"Does the baron know you wear his clothes? They suit you well."

Resi lightheartedly replied, "I would be at a disadvantage in a gown. Besides, Mauro has many clothes. He won't notice these missing."

"I do not like the upper class, but they do have many unused things that come in handy." He handed her the second sword from the case.

"Like extra clothes?" she asked.

They stood formally across from each other and touched swords, and then they began their play-fighting.

"If clothing is what you need, yes. Or silver, fine horses, and expensive weapons like these."

"Did you steal their things?" asked Resi.

"Steal? No! When a man is dead, he does not have use for worldly possessions. They are free for the taking while he is burning in hell."

Resi blocked his blade and stepped to the side when he retaliated.

"Mauro works very hard for all that he has, Patricius. He works from dawn till dark to keep his people fed and his castle protected."

"I will take your word that he lives up to his grand title. While he is fulfilling his noble duties, what do you pursue, your ladyship?" Patrik asked mockingly.

Resi took a swipe at his leg that made him yelp in protest.

"Nothing is required of me, but I do find things to keep me occupied. This week the kitchen is making fruit preserves and pickling the vegetables. There is much to do in summer to prepare for the winter needs, and I don't mind lending a hand."

As he had taught her, Resi blocked her brother's quick thrusts before she added, "My favorite job is to gather the eggs in the afternoon."

"They let the baroness collect the eggs? Isn't that rather dirty work, foraging in a chicken coop?"

"You sound like Mauro," she said with a laugh. "I like to visit the chickens, and I might as well take a basket with me."

He looked for an advantage after they clashed swords again. His sister was quicker than he remembered. "I expected you to be running the house by now."

"Jero runs the house so efficiently that there is not much else that needs to be done. It gives me time to do other projects. Ruby and I make all the soaps. I have time to read books and play music. I do sleep more now, being pregnant."

"It all sounds perfect for you, Resi. The more time I spend with you, the happier I am for your future here."

She lowered her sword.

"Have you thought about the future for yourself, Brother?"

"What do you mean? Like a wife and a family? I am only twenty-two, Resi."

She walked around him, the blunt tip pointed in his direction. She jabbed him with the sword and with her words, "You do want to marry someday, don't you?"

"I like the company of women if that is what you really wanted to ask. But, first, I will help my friends solve their complicated wife problems. Then, when my bones get too tired from riding all over the empires, I will look for that perfect woman to settle down with. She will be someone pretty and adventurous, like you, Sister."

Resi set her sword down. "I am glad," she said with satisfaction, "but I think I am done with this adventure, Patricius. You have worn me out."

They sat together against the tree, catching their breath.

"You challenged me this time, so does that mean I have won?" Patrik asked smugly. "I usually did win when we were younger, didn't I?"

"Why did you let me play with you and your friends?" she asked with a new seriousness.

He shrugged, thinking back on the days he took guardianship of his sister. "It wasn't really my choice. After Ma confined you to the house for kissing that boy—what was his name?"

Resi had not thought of that in a long time, and she smiled at the memory.

"Eugene was his name. And you were the one who got me into confinement by telling Mama."

"Yes, well, anyway," he acknowledged with a chuckle. "After a while, Ma thought you needed company. You were becoming too serious alone with your books all day. She told me I had to sit with you and keep you entertained."

Resi laughed. "In the house? How did you get out of that?"

"I convinced her that I could keep you out of trouble with the boys if you stayed with me."

She considered this. "That was very charitable of you to sacrifice your playtime. Thank you, Brother."

"I thank you, Sister. Because of you, Ma convinced Papa that I was needed to keep you occupied instead of working on the ship. I would be a sea captain now if not for you."

"So I held you back? Did you never want to be a sailor?"

"Papa still taught me everything about his ships, and I do miss the sea. But I am not captain material, like Castor is."

"I suppose not," she readily agreed.

Patrik finished his confession, "Eventually, Ma told me she would find other things for you to fill your day in the house—girlish things that you needed to know as a wife. But I still asked you to come along with me."

"Why?" she asked.

He regarded his sister affectionately. "Because you were good at everything you did, and everything I did. And the other boys still hoped to try their luck with you for a spare kiss, so I always had friends who wanted to join me."

He winked playfully.

"Ah, this is the brother I remember. You had your own selfish reasons then."

"Perhaps."

"And have you outgrown your preference for male companionship?" she asked bluntly.

He shrugged. "Men ask less of me for the same gratification. I don't like to be needed so much, Resi."

"Not all women are demanding," she said disapprovingly. "You should try a little harder to find love."

He returned her frown.

"Love that leads to marriage?" he asked. "You will be happy to know, Sister, that I do find women to be pleasurable company, although I don't think I will ever understand their complexities."

She was thoughtful for a moment, then said, "I must disagree with your logic, Brother. The castle men are confounding, my husband being the most difficult to understand."

"Did you consider that they might have felt the same about you, their new mistress? You came into their male world, and they had to change. That is exactly my point about women. You require extra pampering that men don't— a different speech, gentleness, especially with your baroness status. The castle men may not have understood what your expectations of them were."

"My brother, the philosopher," she said. "I had not thought of it like that."

"You weren't the only one reading books, you know. Philosophy was my favorite subject. My insight got me out of a tight spot on several occasions," he boasted.

Resi stood up with some effort and brushed herself off.

"Tell me, Enlightened One," she said with a chuckle, "do I look presentable enough to sneak back into the house? It must be almost lunchtime, and the servants will be in all the hallways."

"To be honest, I think you look enchanting. Your face is smudged, your shirt is dirty, and you are wearing a man's breeches. In my opinion, you are quite presentable," he teased.

As he began to pack up her swords, he suggested, "Why don't you go to your bathhouse and clean up a bit? I will find your maid and have some proper lady's clothing brought to you."

"That is a good idea. Do you want to come and wash up as well? You have smudges of dirt across your face."

He brushed his sleeve across his cheek.

"You've made it worse," she said.

"Your tower seems to have an endless supply of water. I will wash up there. Besides, the others are probably waiting for me. We are riding out to have a look at your village and have our meal at the tavern recommended to us."

She nodded. "Very well. Ask in the house for Verica, she will know what to bring me."

He handed her the case and kissed her on her forehead. "I will look for your Verica. If I cannot find her, I will bring the fresh clothes myself."

They walked together to the domed building. He opened the door for her.

"Thank you for fighting with me, Patricius," she said.

"Thank you for giving me a reason to laugh again. Enjoy your bath, Resi."

Chapter 10

The foyer doors to the great hall were open, and Mauro was alone there looking at the wall of portraits. After returning from his visit with Radic, he needed time to think about what he had discovered in the ledger.

Jero interrupted his quiet contemplation. "May I have a word, please?"

Mauro turned and recognized his father's eyes.

"I am sorry to disturb you," Jero quickly apologized.

Mauro shook off the alarm and tried to smile. "You are not disturbing me. I was just, um—what do you need, Jero?"

"There is a problem in the kitchen you need to know about."

Mauro was suddenly concerned. Nela was in the kitchen from dawn until well after dinner, and she was getting on in age. "Is Cook all right?"

"She is in one of her moods, but she is well," Jero assured him cheerfully. "It seems we will need to hire a temporary kitchen maid, perhaps two. Danica is pregnant."

Mauro genuinely smiled at the news. "That is a good problem to have, I would think. Krsto and Danica have been married for how long—a year now?"

"Yes, congratulations are in order, but she seems to be quite ill with it, like your wife was in her first pregnancy. She was not able to work the past few mornings. Danica is usually in charge of the early harvest in the garden, and the crop is abundant."

A year ago, Mauro would have answered differently, but today he told Jero, "Tell Krsto that Danica will be given the time she needs to rest."

Jero nodded. "I will tell him, Mauro. But there are not enough hands to manage the garden now. The carrots and onions are ready to be cleaned for storage. Cook said she would like two new servants to fill in. Danica tried to do the onion braiding, but so far the smell has made her sick."

Mauro thought for a moment. "I have seen Verica do very quick braiding. Have her help during the day when my wife does not need her."

"Cook wanted to ask your wife and Ruby if they could help with the pickling again," said Jero.

Mauro frowned.

"Ah, well, I can see from your face, Mauro, that you were not home during the first harvest last summer. I suppose you did not know that her ladyship worked with the servants. I will tell Cook not to ask her."

"You know it does not matter whether I give my permission or not. If my wife wants to help, she has her own will. Tell Cook she may ask her. In the meantime, Ruby can make herself useful until we can find two new maids from the village. Does that settle it?"

"There is one more thing. Um, I just learned a small feast has been arranged for Lady Isabella tonight. Today is her birthday," Jero informed him.

"Is it? My wife did not mention anything about birthdays. How did this arrangement come about?"

Jero suppressed a laugh. "Fabian left instructions yesterday for a cake to be made and a nice dinner to be served. He asked for a marzipan cake for her."

"Of course, he did," Mauro said, shaking his head with a smile. "Fabian is very good at organizing extravagant celebrations at the last minute. He is also good at keeping these details secret."

Mauro walked away from the portrait gallery, and Jero followed him.

"All right," Mauro said finally. "We will celebrate appropriately. When you see my wife, tell her we should make a special night of it."

"I have not seen Lady Terese at all today. As a matter of fact, I have not seen any of the ladies," Jero told him.

"I will find my wife and tell her myself. We will have lunch together." Mauro stopped on the staircase. "And, Jero?"

Jero turned back, awaiting instructions.

"Thank you," said the baron. He climbed the steps.

~*~

Mauro rounded the landing corner and saw his wife's maid going into her small room adjacent to the Barics.

"Verica," he called out.

She opened her door again and stood in front of it, waiting for the baron's instructions.

"Where is the baroness?"

"I am not sure exactly, my lord. Lady Baric wanted to meet her brother earlier, but she has not come back yet. Shall I find her for you?"

"No, I will find her myself. Where was she meeting him?"

Verica hesitated. "Geoff said they were by the bathhouse, my lord."

"Good. Oh, and your help will be needed in the kitchen until Cook can get an extra maid started."

"Will I be cooking, Lord Baric?"

Her panicked reaction amused the baron. Verica had proved to be a competent lady's maid and an excellent companion to his wife, but she had not enjoyed her time working in the kitchen before that.

Mauro told her kindly, "You might already know this, but Danica is not feeling well. She is pregnant."

Verica's face lit up at this news.

"Until she can work again, they are shorthanded for the summer preserving. Cook could use your talent braiding onions."

"Yes, of course, sir. I will go talk to Cook right away."

She shut her door and curtsied before hurrying away, down the hall to the servants' staircase.

~*~

The quickest way out was to follow Verica. The servants' stairs took Mauro directly to the house's back entrance, where the gravel path ran alongside the kitchen garden. He was just coming along the final turn to the bathhouse when Patrik came toward him on the pathway.

Mauro greeted his brother-in-law cheerfully, "Ah, Patrik. Good day to you. I was looking for my wife and was told she was meeting you here earlier."

Patrik was in a good mood after spending time with his sister. "Yes, Lord Baric, I just left her. We had a nice, um, little talk."

Patrik's shirt collar was open, and beads of sweat glistened on his chest and forehead. There were crumpled pine needles and specks of dirt on his breeches where he had knelt to pack the sword case when Resi and he had finished sparring.

"You look a bit disheveled for a talk. What else were you doing?" Mauro asked doubtfully.

Patrik pondered his remark with a smirk. "Why don't you ask Resi? She is in her bathhouse now, washing herself." He strolled away, grinning.

Mauro watched him turn the corner of the path until he was out of sight. Mauro found it hard to like his new brother-in-law.

At the bathhouse, Mauro stopped in the small foyer with the cold water fountain. He took a quick drink from the cascading spring and then entered the main room.

Resi had not heard him from the pool. She was standing in the warm water and lathering the creamy soap over her half-exposed body.

She looked up, startled to see him. "Mauro," she exclaimed, "I thought you went to the village."

"I did, but I settled my errands quickly. Are you all right, Resi? I just ran into your brother outside."

"Oh, yes, everything is fine," she said happily. "I wanted some private time with Patricius, so we met under the old tree, where it is quiet. But the sun is very hot this morning, so I decided I would freshen up a bit before lunch. Did you need me for something?"

"No, nothing specifically. The ride back was dusty, and I thought I would take a bath to clean up."

She did not believe him. He could wash up in five minutes with a bucket of water in their chamber. There was something else he wanted.

Mauro stepped around the pile of his own clothes lying on the tiled floor. He saw her kaftan folded neatly on the bench but did not notice the black case hidden under it.

"What have you really been up to?" he asked quietly.

"I told you, we were talking."

With the toe of his boot, Mauro lifted his crumpled shirt from the floor to show his wife he had not overlooked it.

"Oh, and settling an old bet, is all."

She sank back down into the water. The suds formed a ring around her as she came up again in the deep middle of the pool. "Don't you have pressing duties, Mauro?"

"Duties, yes, but not pressing."

She leaned back and floated in the water. There was a comfortable silence between them as Mauro sat on the bench and slipped off his boots and stockings.

"Mauro, I have always wanted to ask you something," said Resi dreamily.

"You can ask me anything."

"What made you think I would want a bathhouse? What if you had built this, and I never went in? Some people think that bathing can cause illness, you know."

He unbuckled his riding doublet and hung it neatly on a peg. He was pleased with her question and answered her honestly, "Nestor suggested I give you a wedding gift that was special, just your own. I had no clue what you would want, or what you were even like. Stephan came up with the idea when we were in Hungary. There are many bathhouses in Ottoman lands, and he thought you might miss that when living here."

"That was kind of Stephan," she said, distracted by her husband's firm muscles flexing along his back as he pulled his shirt over his head and hung it next to his vest.

"What were you doing in Hungary?" she asked.

He turned back around. "We were called in to support my uncle at a siege taking place deep inside the Habsburg border. We took refuge at a bathhouse one day. I recall we were more interested in warming up than cleaning up. To make a long story short, everyone agreed a bathhouse would work very well here, with the hot springs in the mountain behind us."

He took off the last of his clothes and came to sit on the edge of the pool, getting used to the heat of the water.

"I do love your gift, Mauro, but wouldn't a husband give jewelry or a special token to his bride? A whole building is very extravagant."

He smiled at her, and she back at him.

"I am glad you think so, my dear. But, in case you have forgotten, I also gave you a fine horse and my grandmother's emerald ring."

"I have not forgotten," she said shyly.

Mauro scooted down and sat on the step in the water and finished his story, "Anyway, once I decided on having this made, my uncle put me in contact with a builder in Budapest while we were still there. The hardest part would have been the water for the bath, but the spring has always flowed unused behind the wall since anyone can remember. It was not so hard for the designer to pipe it in. I am glad they convinced me to decorate it with the mosaics."

They never spoke of money, but even a baron could not afford to pay for every possible pleasure. "It is a beautiful room. I don't know how much things cost, Mauro, but I am sure it was too much."

"The builder and I agreed upon a trade for his payment, so it was not as extravagant as it seems. It is a gift to me that you find pleasure in it."

Mauro stepped down from where he was sitting and onto the lower platform. He stepped back up and stood near the edge, then leaned against it.

Resi laughed at the sight of him. "What are you doing?"

"The builder took measurements of my height. I am testing a theory. Come over to me."

He had a devilish look of mischief in his eyes that was uncharacteristic for her earnest husband. Resi did as he asked.

"If I stand on this platform," he said, "we are exactly hip to hip, perfect for coupling. And if I step down to this level, we are on the perfect level for something else."

"Oh," cried Resi as he lifted her by her waist and set her on the ledge of the pool in front of him.

"Are you too cold sitting there?" he asked.

"No," she breathlessly told him.

He leaned in and whispered, "Good."

He took a step back, contemplating her like a canvas he would paint. Her calves dangled in the water, and he began stroking them slowly and deliberately. Then he made his way higher to the tops of her thighs and then slowly back down again. He spread her legs to stand between them and repeated the same long, magical strokes along the inside.

She sat still, bewildered by his calculated seduction.

"Lean back," Mauro told her.

She did so without question and propped herself on her elbows, letting the sensations wash over her as he began kissing her where he had caressed her with his fingers.

Mauro brushed his lips over every freckle, every curve of her smooth skin. He had kissed her like this in their bed before, but hastily, in the middle of a hot passion. He had not lingered, like now.

Resi had read about this sort of lovemaking and was full of anticipation of what he would do next. Mauro did not disappoint her.

After he wrapped her legs around his broad shoulders, his mouth found its way to the top of her thighs. This time he stayed, teasing her, seeing what pleased her most with his tongue.

She shut her eyes and tilted her head back. She forgot her worry that she would sink him with her pressure while he coaxed her to such a height of pleasure that she thought she would break.

They did not hear the knock on the bathhouse door.

When she called out for him to stop his magical manipulation, he released his intimate hold on her and sank into the warm water.

Mauro swam to the other side of the pool. He found it erotically satisfying and was pleased with her.

Breathless from the intense gratification, she finally sat up and saw him sitting on the pool's edge. "Are you getting out?" she asked, puzzled that he would so soon.

"I thought you might want to finish your bath in peace."

Her sudden laugh echoed in the domed room. She did not want to be alone right now. She wanted more of him.

Resi stepped back into the deep water, dunked her head for a moment, then came up for air with a question that surprised Mauro, "Do I have Lady Rosella to thank for that?"

It was Mauro who laughed this time. "I suppose you do," he admitted. "I think that was lesson number three. She liked bathing but never alone. I am convinced that is why they make baths so big."

"I wasn't even in the bath," Resi reminded him.

He slid off the edge and back into the water, but he kept his distance. "I wanted to give you a special pleasure."

"You are a very gratifying lover even without a pool, but you can try that again anytime."

He flashed a satisfied smile but made no advances. He was toying with her, she thought, and Resi wanted to keep playing.

"While you were sinfully kissing Lady Rosella, I was learning to kiss with a boy named Eugene."

Mauro had not expected such a statement since his wife had already told him how she was kept from potential suitors.

"Is that right?" he asked.

"I was just reminiscing with Patricius about how that first kiss got me confined to our house."

She picked up the pot of soap from the ledge and crossed the pool to her husband. She set it down next to him.

"I was thirteen," she said. "There were more boys than girls in our neighborhood, so even a tall, skinny girl was desirable to practice with, you know."

She dabbed some soap on Mauro's chest and began to lather it over his silky hair. She explained, "Eugene gave me his favorite polished stone to persuade me to kiss him."

Unable to look away from her lips, Mauro asked, "And was he a good kisser?"

"He was only fourteen, so I would say no, not really," she admitted with a laugh. "But, at the time, I thought kissing him was the most wonderful feeling."

She massaged the suds over his shoulders and down his ribs.

Mauro took her hands in his to stop her from moving any lower. "And did you and Eugene kiss only once?" He pressed her hand to his lips.

"Twice," she replied. "The second time he asked, I told him he should bring me one of his favorite shells in exchange."

"Ah, my wife, the prostitute," declared Mauro with a chuckle.

She laughed and splashed the suds away from his shoulders. "That could have been the beginning, but Eugene told Patricius what we were doing, and Patricius told my mother."

These new revelations about his virtuous wife fascinated Mauro. "And what did your mother say?"

"She was angry, of course. I did not get to leave our house for a time. I was angry at my brother for betraying me. Just today he told me it was his doing that got me out of my confinement. He convinced our mother that he could watch over me just as well outside our courtyard. The two of us became very close after that."

Mauro had no sisters to compare her to, but he asserted, "Most girls would want to spend time with their mother."

"I did spend time with her. She showed me things the other girls were learning from their mothers—or at least tried to. My mother was certain I would have a cook and a maid here, so instead of baking and sewing, she focused on the skills she thought I might need for my new life with you."

He floated her back to the seat built into the pool wall. Pulling her to him, Mauro set her on his knees.

"What kind of skills did she think you needed?" he asked with genuine interest.

Resi thought for a moment, then said, "She did her best to teach me to be a lady, to be devout to God, and to be obedient to my husband."

Mauro raised his brows at the last skill, and Resi laughed.

"So, when I failed miserably at all of those, Mother bought me my first real storybook. She thought if I read about ladies in castles, I might learn something useful."

"I imagine your mother did not read those books herself. There are not many stories where the princess is being obedient and ladylike. She is usually troublesome, and only when the princess finds true love does she begin to come around to the obedient part," declared Mauro.

She studied his face for a moment. He was always able to surprise her.

"I thought you didn't read romantic stories," Resi said.

"I was told many bedtime stories about princes and princesses like the ones in those books you like to read."

Being so close on his lap was distracting, and her thoughts wandered.

At last, Resi conceded, "You are right about my mother. She was busy with my baby brothers and never had time to read books herself. She would not have given me those stories had she known how silly they were." She was suddenly bashful.

"I hope you were not disappointed coming here," Mauro told her. "I am not a prince. I do not even live in a real castle."

"And I am just an ordinary girl from Thessaloniki," she reminded him.

Mauro didn't care if she were ordinary or a queen. He had never felt this aching love before, not for Lady Rosella or any of the lovers he'd had over the years.

He moved her off his lap. "As you might have noticed, Resi my dear, I have a bit of a dilemma. In my mind, I was happy to just let you have your pleasure. But another part of my body is telling me otherwise now."

"I think you should listen to it," she replied, taking a step toward him in the pool.

Her braid hung down over her bare shoulder, heavy from the water. Mauro moved it out of the way and gently cupped her breasts in his hands.

Resi responded with a low moan.

Mauro did not need more prompting than that. His caresses became urgent. Then he lifted her in the water and held her next to him. She wrapped her legs around his waist as she clung to his neck and lowered herself down onto him.

There was no question that Resi knew how to kiss, and Mauro melted in the heat of it as he rocked her to an unheard rhythm in the center of the pool. He thought he would smother her as they moved together as one, but she was not breathless from that. His climax did not take long once he felt her relax against him.

When the two finally untwined, Mauro broke the lovers' spell with an everyday problem.

"I was expected at the Keep earlier. I think I will be missed by now. I should get dressed."

She smiled dreamily in the warm pool water and asked, "When I am an old woman like Lady Rosella, and you are too preoccupied to satisfy me, can I take young lovers to my bath, too?"

Mauro laughed at her innocent request.

He hopped energetically out of the pool and took a linen towel from the clean stack. "What makes you think Lady Rosella is old?"

No one had mentioned her age to Resi, only that she was in an unhappy marriage and took fresh, young newcomers to her bed.

"How old is she then?" Resi asked.

Mauro finished drying his legs and reached for his breeches to put them on. "When I first met her, she was just a year or two older than you are now," he said.

Her jaw dropped in surprise.

"The ladies did not tell you that?" asked Mauro.

Resi shook her head.

"Well, Rosella's husband was indeed older, probably in his forties then. He got more than he had bargained for from his new young wife. At eighteen, Rosella already had quite an appetite in bed, and her husband could not satisfy it. Maybe it was true, or maybe he did not bother trying."

"I don't know why I thought she was old and preying on young men," Resi admitted, still trying to get the image of a motherly figure out of her head.

"Oh, she preyed on young men, all right. I met her at a party given in her honor. She was celebrating her twenty-first birthday. She was charming and outgoing and very affectionate—which I mistook for something else. Rosella already had one child, but that had not diminished her beautiful figure, and she liked to show it off. As a matter of fact, she loved taking baths. We had most of our encounters there."

Mauro pulled on his boots, not affected by his wife's shocked expression.

He casually added, "Rosella's husband knew about her affairs. He was not worried about his wife falling in love with another man. I heard he was more worried about her giving him syphilis, really. So, at his request, she only took virgins as lovers to ensure they were free of anything that he might catch from her later."

"Wasn't he jealous of the affairs? Didn't he love her?" Resi asked.

"Maybe he loved her, or maybe he found her to be too demanding and childish. Rosella had a craving for society that he did not share, and she needed to be the center of attention. Either way, it seemed they had an understanding. She promised her husband that she would not flaunt her lovers in public, and she made good on that. My mistake was that I asked her to the opera. The next time I called on her, she had a new lover."

He fastened his doublet and then took the towel to his damp hair one last time.

Resi was stunned at his casual statement. "Lady Rosella must have had some feelings for you."

He stood by the pool again, ready to leave.

"Rosella did not love the way you love, Resi. Back then, I was a naïve seventeen-year-old, and I took her carefree affection for me the wrong way. I realized soon enough, though, that what I felt when I was with her was not love, either. It was purely physical, like the adrenaline rush in battle, and I did not mistake the two again," he said bluntly.

She looked at the man who had just given her such a rush of physical pleasure. She was sure until that moment that it had come from love, but perhaps it had only been another game to him.

Mauro seemed oblivious to her distress. He was upbeat when he said, "I came to have lunch with you today, Resi. Do you want to get dressed now and join me? I will do my errand at the Keep as quickly as I can and then meet you on the terrace."

Resi would have to put on Mauro's clothes again, and the kaftan she had worn leaving the house was hiding the sword case.

"Well, um, Verica was going to bring my robes to change into. Maybe you can send her to me?" she awkwardly asked.

Mauro walked around the pool and kissed her on her forehead.

"Promise me I will never see you wearing men's clothes again."

She looked up and nodded pitifully.

As he went to the door to leave, Mauro saw Resi's clean robes stacked on the floor next to the fountain. Smiling, he brought the pile of clothes to a bench.

"It seems Verica got your message," he said. "Hurry along, my dear. I am famished."

He left the bathhouse fully satisfied.

~ * ~

Verica had helped all afternoon in the cellar, sorting the baskets of newly dug onions. They had cured nicely on the dry earth of the garden and needed to be tied into bundles for winter storage or pickled in crocks by the maids.

Verica was distracted by the heavy onion scent on her hands while she stood behind her mistress, styling her long locks.

"I am sorry I was not here to comb out the braid before it dried, Lady Baric," Verica grumbled. She was more particular about the baroness's hair than the baroness was.

"It doesn't matter, Verica," Resi said absently. "You can leave it braided."

Verica thought the baroness was unusually preoccupied after her bath. Her mistress had spent the afternoon in her bedchamber reading and napping. The young maid felt she needed to make an extra effort to cheer her up.

"Did you hear all the good news today, Lady Baric? Word came while I was downstairs that Elizabeta Radic had her baby. Jero read us the note from the courier. It all went very quickly, once the pains began. She had a little girl, and both are doing fine."

"Verica, how could you have kept this from me for so long?" Resi scolded her with a grin. "A girl?"

"A girl," repeated Verica.

They knew what it meant to Elizabeta. She had prayed every day for a boy.

"I hope Radic is not too disappointed. That is his fourth daughter. We will have to go visit her as soon as possible."

Verica nodded her agreement in the looking glass as she finished up.

"What is the other news, Verica?"

"Well, you heard that Danica is with child now. She could be as much as two months along, but Cook was not sure."

"That is such a blessing for her. They have been married longer than I have."

"Danica would be happier if she were not feeling so ill. I will be helping in the kitchen sometimes until Cook finds another maid to do Danica's work. At least I will hear all the gossip to pass on to you, my lady."

"Have I missed anything else?" asked Resi, seemingly more cheerful now.

"There is one last bit of news that is somewhat related. Geoff found a litter of kittens in the stables this morning. There are six of them, all different colors." Verica knew her mistress would want to know about that.

"Tell Geoff to move them before Alberto gets someone to drown them. He doesn't like too many cats in the barn, but we haven't had kittens in a long while."

"Geoff already has, my lady," Verica assured her.

The women both turned toward the window at the sudden flash of light. The wind blew the shutters closed with a bang.

Verica went to latch them shut and to close the glass on the beginning rain.

"I am afraid the rainstorm will spoil Lady Isabella's party," said Resi disappointedly. "Now we will have to be indoors."

Verica added a satin ribbon to Resi's smoothed-out hair. "Dinner is not for another hour, madam. Perhaps it will pass quickly."

Chapter 11

The afternoon storm did pass. By the end of the meal, the sky had cleared just in time for the party to witness a colorful sunset of brilliant pink and orange over the castle walls. The air was fresh and comfortable now, so torches were lit, and the festivities moved outside.

Along with the houseguests, Mauro's officers had joined them again that evening. The maids, too, were invited to the terrace to share Isabella's delectable birthday cake. Davor uncorked a house-made port to accompany the elaborate dessert, and the familiar company mingled informally.

Isabella approached her host at the serving table and exclaimed, "The calamari was the best I have ever had, and the cake is just delicious, Mauritius. You should not have gone to so much trouble."

Mauro turned to her. Each evening Isabella dressed regally at dinner, but Mauro thought she looked exceptionally captivating in her splendid pink crepe gown tonight. A gold chain with amethyst jewels was draped around her bare neck, and more gems dangled from her ears.

Mauro matched Isabella's rouged smile when he replied, "I would like to take credit for all of it, Isabella, but I cannot. It was our friend Fabian who arranged all of this before he left. He is to blame for this wonderful evening."

It took her a moment to find her comeback.

"Fabian is always full of surprises. I must admit to you, Mauritius—we had an argument last night. I am not so sure Fabian intended that I deserved all of this."

Mauro, too, was at a loss for words. "I am sure all of this is his apology," he finally said.

She accepted his answer with a nod, and he smoothly changed the subject.

"You have had a full day on your birthday, Isabella. How did your riding lesson go?"

She brightened. "Better than I expected. Did Bem not talk to you? Perhaps he has not had the chance. He would like to have Lady Ruby ride with me tomorrow."

"Oh? Will you be going on the trails?" Mauro was surprised Isabella was ready to ride a horse out of the enclosure.

"No, no," she said with a flick of her fan. "I did not make that much progress. We will stay in the paddock. Bem thinks it would be helpful for Lady Ruby to be next to me while he explains what to do, though."

To show Isabella maneuvers, Bem would have to hold on to her, which he did not have permission to do. Mauro appreciated the African's good judgment.

"Will Ruby ride behind you then?"

"Do you think that is a good idea?"

"I think that is an excellent idea, Isabella. Unfortunately, Ruby is needed in the morning for a special task with my wife."

Mauro did not think now was the time to tell Isabella that his wife and Ruby would be barreling pickles.

"Perhaps you can have your riding lesson after lunch," Mauro suggested.

She shut her fan with confidence. "That seems just as agreeable. If you will excuse me, Mauritius, I will go talk to Bem now to tell him of the change in plans."

Mauro watched Bem's face light up as Isabella approached him across the terrace. But Isabella was not Mauro's responsibility. Caterina was, though, and he needed to uphold his promise to Fabian.

He saw Salar Nassim sitting next to Ruby on a bench with their small guitars. Mauro went to talk to them.

"Ruby, if I may," Mauro said. "I wanted to tell you that Lady Isabella will ride later, in the afternoon, instead of in the morning. Perhaps you should discuss the new riding time. Lady Isabella went to talk to Bem about it." He pointed to the two, chatting below the terrace steps.

"Thank you, Lord Baric." She turned to her partner and said regretfully, "Excuse me, Salar Nassim." Ruby put her instrument on the bench and left the two men.

Mauro sat in her place next to the Persian soldier. The mercenary must have been an intimidating man in action, but here Mauro noticed his black eyes seemed kinder, and his rigid jawline relaxed into a friendly smile of greeting.

"Salar Nassim, we have not had a chance to talk alone," said Mauro politely.

Salar Nassim set his lute down against the bench. "I am most appreciative for your warm hospitality, Lord Baric."

"You are very welcome here, you and your friends. I have enjoyed your conversation at the dinner table, but I wanted to ask you about something else. Privately."

"Of course, Lord Baric," he replied cautiously. "I am at your service."

"If I heard correctly, you met Caterina Carrera earlier today."

"Yes, Lord Baric, right here on the terrace."

"And what would be your motive to meet the young lady, like you did this morning? Alone."

A smile curled across the sellsword's face.

"We were not alone," Nassim stated matter-of-factly. "Your servants were working around us, here and there, during our card lesson."

Mauro did not smile. "Card lesson? Do you expect me to believe that is your only motivation to sit with the young lady?" the baron asked.

"Lady Caterina requested that I teach her what I know—short of cheating, of course. She is quite talented, so I do not mind playing cards with her. And if I am honest with myself, I do miss sitting in the company of women."

Mauro raised his brow at Nassim's confession.

"But I do not intend to seduce the young lady if that is your concern, Lord Baric."

"It is my concern. She is under my protection."

"As a father to a daughter, I understand your worry. Therefore, I will be frank with you, Lord Baric."

Mauro waited impatiently as Salar Nassim took his time to choose his words.

"My companion Cyro does intend to seduce the lady. I am providing a reason to spend time with her."

Mauro could not mask his surprise at the admission. "Then it is Cyro that I will give my warning to."

Mauro stood up and scanned the terrace to find him.

Salar Nassim quickly added, "The young lady is not in danger in his company. Cyro should give you no cause for concern. He is a gentleman, through and through."

Mauro sat back down on the bench. "A gentleman, you say?"

"I have met many noblemen of the Western world, and there are few who I trust. The exceptions would be you, Lord Baric, and Cyro."

The silky words of the mercenary soothed Mauro, but he didn't trust him. "Who is he?"

"Cyro is no one of great importance, but he is a man of status. If Cyro succeeds in capturing the lady's heart, he will come clean with his identity. If he does not woo the lady, then he will leave here as he came—a simple sellsword."

"You are speaking in riddles," said Mauro. "Is the man of nobility? Is that what he can offer?"

"If that is important to know, then yes, he is." Salar Nassim said. "I suppose you can understand how titles and wealth can sway a woman's heart. Cyro wants to make her fall in love with the man, not the aristocrat. Will you allow him one week to try?"

"So you propose that I let a rogue aristocrat of unknown origin seduce an innocent young lady, who is perhaps already betrothed and heading home to marry, without any interference on my part? I should allow his game to just . . . evolve?"

"It is indeed an odd request, but it is not a game to him. She has captured his heart, as love does for unexplained reasons. She will be chaperoned according to your protocol. If she finds him acceptable as a suitor, then he could match any future husband her father could arrange."

"And is this why you have married twice, Salar Nassim? Am I to believe you are a hopeless romantic?"

Salar Nassim leaned back on the bench, laughing softly. "I have been called many things but never that. I welcome the new accusation. After too many years of fighting, I can admit that I prefer love."

Mauro stood up again and said quietly, "Fabian Carrera does not trust your friend Cyro, but I happen to disagree with him. It may be foolish, but I will give the man until the end of the week. Lady Caterina will be chaperoned, and he shall remain a true gentleman, or I shall deal with him myself."

"You are a fair man, Lord Baric. I will tell Cyro that you are in agreement."

"It seems Cyro is proceeding without my permission," said Mauro.

The men watched as Cyro strolled toward Caterina, who was walking along the garden pathway.

~ * ~

"May I join you, Lady Caterina?" Cyro asked when he approached her.

"Ah, it is the master manipulator. I was just going to finish a tour of the garden. Have you come for our first lesson?"

"I have," he replied. "May I join you on your garden tour?"

They were soon out of view from the terrace, and Cyro began his awkward attempt to win Caterina's heart.

"I must defend myself against my friend's misrepresentation of me, Lady Caterina. My part in helping you master your card game is an honorable one."

"I judged that the Persian would trick me more easily than you might, Cyro. But I am interested to hear why he chose you to advise me. I get enough of that already."

"I am sorry that you have any troubles that require guidance. A lady should have no worries."

She sighed. "I do have many worries, today especially. I apologize if I am not good company on our walk. I was expecting to hear something from Paolo."

"Is Paolo your betrothed?" Cyro was curious to know his competition.

"I am to marry Viscount Soltesz, but Paolo is my only true love."

The trellis arches were still dripping with rainwater, so they left the path under the roses to walk along the open flower beds. Cyro took his chance to steer the conversation.

He asserted, "True love must be an amazing feeling, Lady Caterina. I have always wondered what makes a love true. I have yet to experience it."

"Well, I have only been truly in love once myself, and Paolo is the one and only for me. The way he looks at me, and the things he says to me—there is no feeling like it."

"Have you known Paolo long?"

"I have known him four months, ever since he was placed on my Guard."

"He is your guardsman?"

Cyro could not hide his disapproval, but Caterina did not seem to notice.

"He is. But with love that does not matter."

"As your personal guard, I imagine he would say kind words of admiration because he must."

"Do you doubt his true love for me?"

"Forgive me. I just know men better than you might, my lady."

"But you just said you have never been in love," she reminded him. "I do not think you can judge him then."

"Oh, Lady Caterina, I do apologize. I must have misspoke," said Cyro confidently. "I have never found my true love, but I have been in love before. I was even unsuccessfully betrothed once. Perhaps you can tell me what to look for next time."

She stopped her stroll and looked him in the eye when she told him what to expect. "If you are truly in love, you will feel like you need no food or sleep since love will sustain you. And you cannot part from the other without suffering."

He returned her intense stare and said, "I like to eat, and especially sleep. What else should I be aware of when truly in love?"

She flipped open the fan she was carrying and looked at him from behind the lace.

"The rest is too intimate to share," she said.

"Paolo has not been by your side for how long? One week? Two weeks? I have seen you eat, and I imagine you slept last night, all without his words or even his presence. That is encouraging, Lady Caterina."

She flicked her fan shut and protested, "Why are you set on mocking me, Cyro?"

His nutmeg eyes were convincingly pleading. "I beg your pardon, Lady Caterina. I am too forward by nature. It has always been a fault of mine."

She was warming to his rolling Italian accent and his charming smile with its flash of gold. She did seem to forgive him.

"Was this my first lesson?" she asked.

"No, Lady Caterina. Your lesson will not be about love but about beauty. I am to help you find one thing of beauty to bring to Salar Nassim tomorrow."

She took the path back through the flowered arches.

"That should not be so difficult. I could bring my jeweled bracelet with me to the lesson. It is my favorite thing of beauty."

She held up her wrist for him to see. He took her hand in his to admire it.

"That is indeed lovely, but that is not the beauty Salar Nassim wants to see. Here, for example."

Cyro picked a flower from the vine next to them and held it out for her.

"This is an unusual blossom. It reminds me of a lady dressed for a night out. The showy outer petals are like a pink gown cloaking a slender flower inside that is delicate and pure. Now that I see it for what it is, I find it very beautiful."

She examined the flower he was holding.

"Am I to bring just the one flower to my lesson?"

"Salar Nassim would like you to ask a different person for something beautiful to bring to each lesson. I can be your first, if you like. Please, my lady, I offer you this thing of beauty."

He bowed with such practiced formality that Caterina was taken aback. She accepted the delicate flower from his outstretched hand with a gracious nod, then she took out a handkerchief from her gown pocket and carefully wrapped the blossom in it.

The archway of matching pink flowers concealed them from the rest of the garden. Caterina took a step back from Cyro's closeness and said, "I will be missed by now."

"Let me walk you back to the terrace."

He offered his arm to guide her, and she took it. Cyro had laid the seed he had wanted. Now he had three days to make it grow.

~ * ~

Resi was standing alone, eating her last bite of the delicious birthday cake. Patrik sneaked up behind her and whispered over her shoulder, "How was your bath? You smell divine."

She turned to him and tried to smile.

Patrik looked at her with concern. "What is bothering you, Sister? You were in such good spirits this morning."

She sat on the marble bench and set the empty plate down beside her. "I have puzzled over something all afternoon, Patricius. Perhaps I should ask you," she said.

"This sounds serious." He moved her plate to sit down next to her.

"It's just—can someone make tender love to you and not love you at the same time?" she blurted out. "You either love someone or not, isn't that how it works?"

Patrik considered her question. "Is your husband this someone, Resi?"

"Well, yes."

He lifted her chin to look into her eyes. There were fresh tears in them. "You should be asking him, instead of me."

"I have tried."

The siblings were seated by the fountain. The flowing water distorted their conversation, and they could speak privately.

"All right then," Patrik said with confidence. "Yes is the answer to your question."

Her shoulders slumped with disappointment.

"Sexual attraction is a force, Resi, and men react to it differently from women. We can't help it," he said with a shrug. "What follows is not necessarily lovemaking. Intercourse is just as satisfying for a man without the love part."

Resi was never shocked by Patrik's counsel. He had always been brutally honest.

"We have been married a year now. I want more from Mauro than reacting."

"You deserve more," he told her. "Try again to ask your husband. Corner him, if you must. I know you are good at that." He nudged her playfully.

She smiled for his sake. "I am glad you are here, Patricius."

He became solemn. "We won't be staying, Resi. We have decided to leave at the end of the week."

"Why so soon?"

Patrik pointed toward the Baric officers across the terrace. "We do not feel welcome here."

Resi nodded. "I could see the divide at dinner. I will ask Mauro to move you into the manor house."

He shook his head. "I have come to see that you are taken care of and I am satisfied. Even if it isn't perfect, I can see that you are happy here."

"But I want you to stay, Patricius."

"I am not leaving tonight," he assured her with a hug. "We will see each other tomorrow, and the next day, and the day after that."

A yawn came over her as she slumped against his shoulder.

"You should go up to bed, Resi. You've had a full day of fighting and bathing and whatever else it is that you do."

"I am exhausted," she admitted, then put her hand across her round middle. "The curious thing is that the baby always seems to come awake when I am ready to go to sleep."

"I never imagined my little sister as a mother, but you will be great at it. Here, let me help you."

He stood up and took her hand.

She gave him a coy smile and said, "I am not an invalid, Patricius."

"I know, but can't I be a gentleman?"

She kissed him on the cheek, and he squeezed her hand before he let it go. "Good night, Patricius."

Resi had forgotten to ask Mauro for an escort to visit the Radic baby tomorrow, but she was too tired to interrupt him now. She would try to catch him in the morning before he left.

~ * ~

Natalija was near the serving table when Soren came through the double doors onto the terrace. She watched him bow to her mistress as the baroness went through the same doorway to retire upstairs for the night.

Soren seemed to be looking around the crowd for a friendly face when the young maid approached him.

"I was able to get the grease out of the shirt you gave me today," she said.

He walked a little closer so he did not have to raise his voice to be heard.

"That is kind of you," he replied.

"I kept it out, though. Idita said we should mend any tears in the clothes we launder."

"You don't have to do that. I can mend my own shirts. I just haven't had the time until now."

"You know how to sew?" she asked with interest. Even the Baric soldiers had the servants do their mending for them.

"I learned as a sailor on a Dutch trading ship. We spent months at sea and met with many storms that ripped and tore at our sails."

She took a step closer. "Why were you on a ship for so long? Did you sail to the end of the world?"

He chuckled with rare amusement. "It felt like it at the time. We traveled to a place called the West Indies. You go nearly to the end of the world, and then you turn right. Once you arrive, though, it is like paradise."

"If it is paradise, why would you come back then?"

Soren didn't want her to stop talking. He found her ordinary questions to be extraordinarily rewarding.

"We did stay," he answered. "We found work rigging ships, getting them seaworthy again. I was with my brother. After about a year, he convinced me to return to Europe. Niels didn't like the West Indies as much as I did."

"Did it take as long to sail home, or did you find a shorter way?"

Soren cocked his head, considering her question. "We came back the same way we went, but it was shorter. We knew more what to expect, and we had the winds helping to speed us home."

She regarded him with continued curiosity. "I have never met a sailor. What do you do on such a long voyage?"

"The same things you do anywhere else, except you cannot leave. You eat and sleep and work. Most of the time is spent keeping the ship afloat. When the sailing was calm, though, we would make things from little pieces of wood or bone. We played a lot of dice, too."

Natalija told him, "My mother said respectable men don't play dice."

"Your mother is right, but I have not met a man who does not play. So what does that tell you about men?"

All the Baric soldiers played dice. She reconsidered her mother's warning.

A voice called out, "Natalija."

Idita was standing by the servants' entrance waiting for her.

"I must be going," said Natalija hastily. "Good night." She curtsied and turned to go into the house.

~*~

"Did you see that, Mauro?" asked Eduard. He and the others were across the terrace from Soren.

"What should I have seen?"

Mauro looked to where Eduard gestured, and he saw Soren. Natalija had just walked away toward the kitchen entrance with Idita.

"He was flirting with her again," Hugo said to Mauro.

Mauro had noticed the two talking, but it had not distracted him.

"The Dane was standing two strides from Natalija with his arms crossed. I have seen better flirting between you and Eduard, Hugo. Find something else to occupy yourselves, something other than our guests. That is an order."

Mauro walked away to refill his port glass. From the corner of his eye, he saw Patrik go to Soren's side.

~*~

Patrik handed Soren a glass and said quietly, "You are being watched, Soren."

"Let them watch. I am doing no harm," Soren answered.

Patrik stood close in front of his friend and said, "That is twice now. What do you want with the girl?"

"Nothing," Soren said, avoiding Patrik's stare.

"Why are you seeking her out then?"

"I don't know," Soren said. "She somehow gives me peace."

If this girl could bring his friend peace, Patrik wanted to know her secret. "What does the girl say that makes you feel better?"

Soren shrugged. "Everything. She has not starved, not seen her friends murdered in front of her, or had her home burned to the ground. She is innocent. She has two brothers and three sisters and two parents—all alive, and she visits them after church every Sunday! She does not have to beg to launder my shirts for money to feed her bastard baby." He sighed deeply, then said, "I like talking to someone who isn't messed up."

Guilt swallowed Patrik whole. He had not been able to help Soren cope after Niels's death, and he continued to fail his friend.

"All right, Soren. Talk to the maid, but stay in the open, in plain sight, will you?"

"I don't desire anything more from her," declared Soren.

"I know that, but be careful. We are back in the land of rules and propriety."

Soren smiled an exceptional smile.

"I can get used to that again."

"Yes, so can I."

Patrik was hopeful but also dead tired. The sun had set a while ago, and the men still rose before dawn out of habit. They went to tell the others they were leaving.

The mercenaries headed back to their room in the tower. Caterina and Isabella had left the gathering with Ruby shortly after Resi had gone up to bed. The Baric officers said their goodnights after the mercenaries had gone, and Mauro and Jero left to walk through the great hall together.

The torches from the open foyer doors illuminated the shiny marble of the expansive great hall. Mauro and Jero could have easily crossed this room in the black of night, and they had once or twice together as boys.

Neither spoke as they climbed the stairs together. Now would be the time for Mauro to tell Jero what he had discovered today in Radic's office. His father's portrait in the gallery confirmed what Mauro had felt in his heart for years, but he was at a loss about what to do next.

Mauro and Jero had lived more than twenty years as master and servant, and a few more days would not change anything.

Chapter 12

Mauro had taken his early breakfast with Nela instead of in the Keep. Cook worked long hours in the kitchen and would not have asked for extra hands unless the maids were truly overwhelmed. He wanted to tell Nela personally that she would have more help beginning today.

Remembering that he had left his jacket and hat on the chair in the foyer on his way to breakfast, Mauro went to retrieve them. Davor was walking toward the sitting room with a long ebony case that Mauro did not recognize.

"What do you have there, Davor?" Mauro asked.

"This was left in the bathhouse. Ana brought it in this morning, sir. I thought it belonged with your swords displayed in the sitting room. Would you like it kept somewhere else, my lord?"

"Bring it over here."

Davor set it on the table next to the stairs.

Mauro examined the outside of the polished sword case. "This is not mine," he said.

Davor pointed out, "It has the Baric crest on the inlay, my lord, and there are swords inside."

Mauro opened it and looked in awe at the handsome matching blades.

"I have never seen these," mumbled Mauro. He took one out and held it. "You say Ana brought them from the bathhouse?"

"Yes, my lord. Just now," his valet confirmed.

Mauro put the sword back in its place and turned to Davor with a stern expression. "Do you know if Patrik Kokkinos is about this morning?"

Mauro reasoned his brother-in-law must have found the sparing swords in the Barics' chamber in the Keep and brought them to Resi. That was what they were doing in the back meadow yesterday, he realized.

Davor replied, "It is still early, sir. He and the others are probably just now having their breakfast in the Keep."

"I will look for him there."

Mauro left the case and walked out the front door.

Davor closed the lid again and watched his master stride across the empty courtyard before he shut the entrance door.

Mauro's guardsmen were eating breakfast when Mauro stormed into the dining room and hurried wordlessly past them to the stairwell. His officers were sitting together at one table. They turned to each other with surprised expressions but continued their breakfast with no second thought to the matter.

The mercenaries were still dressing in their room when Mauro opened the door and shouted, "I will have a word with you, Patrik!"

They looked at their angry host and then back at Patrik, who was just as surprised as they were at the baron's early morning intrusion.

"Leave us," Mauro instructed the others.

Patrik nodded to his friends, and they filed out of the room half-dressed. Patrik crossed his arms and waited for Mauro to explain.

"You were sword-fighting with my wife!" Mauro shouted.

Patrik replied with a smug smirk, "Is that it, Lord Baric? You are bothered by a little sword play? That's better than molesting her, like you first assumed."

"I would not put anything past you, Patrik Kokkinos."

Patrik let the insult slide. "I did not intend to duel with Resi, but she brought the swords and the challenge."

Mauro crossed the room and leaned over Patrik at the table, where he sat. "You lie!"

"If you truly knew my sister, you would know it is not a lie. But I compliment you on your excellent taste. It is quite an elegant case for practice swords—ebony with pearl inlay."

"Where did you find it?" Mauro hissed.

"The swords did not come from me, Lord Baric. Your man Jero gave them to Resi."

Mauro could not hide his surprise, and his first thought slipped from his lips, "Jero?"

"Ah, so you did not know. Maybe it was a lover's gift, huh? They are friends. My sister told me so."

Mauro's anger flared. "She is pregnant! You could have hurt her, you idiot."

"I agreed to her little dare because I knew she would not be hurt. She is quite good with a sword."

Patrik walked around the wide table. The weapons were lined up there. Mauro said nothing, gave nothing away this time. Patrik taunted him anyway.

"What do you even know about your wife, Lord Baric? You are never home to ask her. You are away fighting your wars like a good baron."

"They are same wars you fight, if for different reasons."

"Yes, you are a lord, and you fight to keep your wealth and your fancy castles."

"I fight because I am told to!" Mauro practically spat the words. "Why do you fight, Patrik?"

"I fought once for duty, for my ancestors. But, now, I fight like all the rest—for money."

Patrik picked up his sword from the table and held it in front of him. His expression hardened, and he waved the sharp tip of his weapon in the air. The honed blade flashed in the sunbeam streaming through the window.

"Put your sword away, Patrik. We have no fight here."

"Don't we, Lord Baric?"

Patrik had the same eyes as his sister. Mauro saw her in them for a brief moment. "Why have you come here?" Mauro demanded.

The mercenary walked around the baron, his sword in hand. "I had once hoped that you would die in battle, Lord Baric. Maybe I would even get the chance to kill you myself. Then a letter from my sister found me four months ago, and I came to convince myself that you are still the cold-hearted brute that I thought you to be. Do you know what was in that letter?"

Mauro did not know. He knew very little about his wife and what was in her thoughts.

"It was not pleasant to read," Patrik maintained. "She was ignored, alone, and unloved. My sister, the most deserving girl I know, who is missed every day by her family, is married to the most undeserving man." He pointed the sword at Mauro. "You, Lord Baric."

Mauro did not flinch when the blade touched his shoulder. "I will not fight you."

Patrik looked the baron up and down. "Oh, you aren't the worst of men, I suppose. You give my sister pretty things while you keep her waiting for you, ready to be fucked when it suits you. You are a cold bastard, like your father was."

This was the Patrik that Mauro had met over a year ago, the one who pointed this same sword at him in a crowded ale house in Hungary. Mauro did not fight him then, but he wanted to now.

"Shut up, Patrik," growled Mauro as he surveyed the swords on the table, contemplating the four choices.

"Take it," demanded Patrik. "Draw a weapon, you coward!"

Mauro chose a sword and pulled it from its sheath. Patrik was ready and met his blade.

Upon hearing the clash of steel, Vilim, who was in his chamber next door, ran to the doorway. "Mauro!" he exclaimed.

"Leave us, Vilim!" Mauro shouted and kicked the door shut, flipping the bolt.

Vilim shook the locked door, unable to open it.

Mauro turned to defend against the next blow. "Your sister will not want me to hurt you, Patrik."

Their swords clashed again.

"She won't have to worry about that!"

Patrik kicked the chair out of his way and into Mauro's path. Mauro quickly stepped around it but was backed into the corner. "What did I ever do to you?" Mauro demanded.

"You are a Baric, and the Barics ruined my family. What did we do to you? Steal some fucking salt?"

Patrik lashed out at him, and Mauro could only duck to avoid the heavy blade.

"You took my father and then you took my sister," Patrik yelled while swinging.

Mauro saw his chance and rolled over the wide bed to the other side of the room. "I was just a little boy, like you, Patrik."

Patrik followed him over the bed, catching the bed's curtain with his sword. He pulled to free himself and ripped it down.

Mauro was ready for him by the window, and they clashed metal again. "Your father did not steal just salt," grunted Mauro, fighting Patrik back, "he stole secrets. Did you not know that? Baric secrets! That was his crime."

Mauro backed Patrik into the corner now. He shoved a table between them and lowered his tired arm.

"Your sister was a payment for your father's freedom, but so was I," said Mauro. "You got your father back."

In a rage, Patrik leaned across the table and shouted, "We got him back six years later! Do you know how that nearly destroyed our family?"

Patrik had exposed his true anguish, and Mauro felt sympathy for the man and pity for himself. "My father ruined my life, too. He sold me, too. If I had a choice, I would have left Resi in Thessaloniki."

"You had a choice, you selfish bastard!"

Patrik came wildly at him, and they crossed swords in the open. "My sister was held prisoner in her own home, waiting for word from you. She waited years."

"What would you have wanted from me? That I sent for Resi and then left her a widow?"

"You could have released her. She could have been happily married to another man."

They were both tiring, but neither would give in first.

"Resi is happy here!" Mauro cried, attempting to appease his opponent.

Patrik glared from across the table. He had a staggering expression of clarity.

"You are a fucking idiot," said Patrik. "You think she is happy? She isn't happy! She told me just last night she is certain you do not love her. Even if you don't love her, but only love the smell of her, the taste of her, you have to say the fucking words, you bastard. Even I know that is what a woman needs to hear."

"You are wrong, Patrik."

Mauro came around the table and threw down his sword in front of the mercenary. Then he threw his fist at Patrik's smirking face. The mercenary's nose spurted blood across the carpet.

"Ah, shit! What the hell was that for?" yelled Patrik. "I am just repeating what she told me." He stomped away, holding his bleeding face.

Mauro ignored Patrik's agony. "How could she say that I do not love her? Of course, I do! She is the best thing that has happened to me."

"God!" Patrik pounded his fist against the table, leaning over in pain. "Damn!"

Mauro saw a dagger on the table and used it to cut Patrik's sleeve free from the shirt he was wearing. Mauro then pulled Patrik up by his collar to look at his nose.

"Move your hand so I can see if it is broken."

Patrik did as he was asked, biting his lip in pain as Mauro swabbed the dripping blood with the ripped sleeve. "I can fix it, but it is going to hurt a little."

Patrik groaned and sat on the wooden chair facing the baron.

Mauro put the knotted cloth into Patrik's mouth to catch the running blood and give him something to bite down on. "I did this with Fabian's broken nose, and it worked. Hold still."

Patrik braced himself, holding onto the seat as Mauro manipulated the injury with his palms. Patrik blanched and swayed when Mauro put his fingers into his nostrils for the final adjustment.

Mauro pulled the cloth from Patrik's mouth and asked, "Are you alright?"

"I am going to vomit now," he said weakly.

Mauro grabbed the basin off the table and put it under Patrik's chin in time to catch the regurgitated blood.

Patrik wiped his fouled mouth with his shirt. "I feel much better."

Mauro wiped his bloody hands on his own shirt. "Your nose was not broken, just out of place. Does it still hurt?"

Patrik gingerly felt around his nose. "I can bear it now." Blood was dripping from his nostrils, and Patrik's eyes were beginning to swell.

Mauro found a towel to dip into the water pitcher. He put the cool cloth over Patrik's nose and said, "Stay or go, I do not care one way or the other. But, if you are to stay, I cannot be walking around my own halls wondering if you will put a dagger in my back."

Patrik seemed to consider what was said.

Mauro went on to say, "Most of what you said is actually true, but I cannot change the past. I imagine your sister was unhappy, but Resi is my whole life now. I love her like I could not have imagined possible. And I will be sure she knows that."

Patrik looked like a defeated man when he raised his head and said, "I have hated the Barics for a long time. It will not be easy to forget that."

"I do not expect you to. I do not hate you like you hate me, but I will not forget you tried to kill me once."

Patrik dabbed his swollen nose. "Yes, um, I am sorry about that. I suppose I should thank you for not having me arrested and thrown in jail."

Mauro sat down on the chair across from him. "I could have, you know."

Patrik had always wanted to know why Mauro had defended him. "Why didn't you?"

Mauro said, "I had already written to your father to send Resi to marry me, so I could not agree to imprison his son just before the wedding, even if you were not invited."

Patrik managed a small smile.

"And I did understand why you hated me then. But you are in my home here, Patrik, and in my world. Leave, if you still hate me."

Patrik nodded that Mauro's ultimatum was clear. He made no attempt to move.

Mauro leaned over and picked up the sword he had used. He held it in his hands a moment before he slid it back into the sheath. "This is a good blade, light and balanced. I could have easily killed you with it."

Patrik moved the cloth from his nose and winced as he said, "When you picked up Nassim's sword, I regretted telling you to take a weapon. He honed it last night."

"You are out of practice, you know. We train every morning at full light outside the walls. You and your friends can join us. If you keep a cold cloth on your nose, you should be able to breathe through it tomorrow," said Mauro.

Patrik tried not to laugh. "I will do that. I like to breathe."

Despite Patrik's lack of enthusiasm at his offer, Mauro considered him to be in agreement.

"Good!" replied Mauro. "You will need a sixth man. I will have Daniel partner with one of you. He is a good swordsman but not too good."

Patrik set the vomit-filled basin aside and poured water into an empty one to splash his face.

"I'll partner with Jero," he said finally.

Mauro shook his head. "Jero is not a soldier. He is my steward. He does not train with us."

"Well, he should. How long has he had that pretty sword case he gave my sister? Don't you want to see what he can do with a real sword?"

Mauro did not take the bait. "I will give you Daniel."

As he went to unbolt the door, he looked around the room. "You owe me a curtain, Patrik."

"You owe me a shirt."

"I will send one over," Mauro said kindly. "And do not bleed all over my carpet, either."

Smirking, Patrik folded the cloth again and put it under his nose.

Mauro lifted the bolt and opened the door to a sea of faces. Simeon, Vilim, and Hugo were all armed with swords. Wide-eyed, Lazar poked his head in between the men. Mauro should have expected it, but it took him a second to decide what he would say to the anxious men.

The four mercenaries pushed their way into the room without waiting. They were certain Patrik had not come through unharmed if the baron was standing in the doorway covered in blood and soaked with sweat.

Idita had been brought to the Keep by Vilim, who was sure someone would need to be sewed back together. She shook her head at Mauro and walked past him into the chamber carrying her medicine basket.

Mauro found his voice. "There is nothing more to see here. Lazar, go find Davor and tell him to bring me two clean shirts. Two, mind you."

Lazar pushed through the pack of soldiers to the stairwell.

Simeon checked his friend for cuts that might need patching. "You look awful, Mauro. Are you hurt?"

Mauro looked down at his bloody hands. "No, I do not think so." He was beginning to shiver from the damp shirt and loss of adrenaline.

"Come with me," said Simeon. "Hugo, fetch some hot water for the baron."

Hugo nodded and ran down the stairs.

Vilim led Mauro to Simeon's chamber, just across from the Barics' chamber. Its window faced north, and the air was chilly in the morning.

Vilim pulled off Mauro's ruined shirt, and Simeon wrapped the cover from his bed around Mauro's shoulders.

Mauro sat down on the feather mattress and pulled the blanket tight against him.

"What the hell was that all about?" Simeon asked when Mauro finally stopped shivering.

"It was nothing, and you should not hold it against the visitors. Patrik and I have a bad history, and we settled our grudges today. It had to happen, and it ended well. I broke his nose, is all."

The men could not suppress their laughter at the news. Mauro managed a weak smile, too.

Hugo was just coming into the room with the filled bucket, wondering what he had missed.

Mauro set the blanket on the bed and rinsed his arms and face directly in the pail.

Simeon gave him a rag and a pot of soap, and Mauro used it to remove the last streaks of dried blood. Finally, he felt better and told his men, "Go ahead and start without me this morning. I will be there shortly."

They looked skeptically at each other, wondering if they should talk him out of it.

"I am fine, really," Mauro promised.

Idita came to Simeon's chamber and waited at the threshold. His officers each patted Mauro on his back for encouragement as they walked out and left Idita alone with him.

Mauro sat down on the bed and took up the blanket again.

Idita moved the stool from Simeon's table behind the door and then sat down facing Mauro.

"You did a good job on the nose," she said.

He wasn't sure if it was a compliment or not. "Breaking it or fixing it?"

"Fixing it. He will be bruised for a week but will still be handsome."

Mauro chuckled at the nanny's remark. "Patrik will be glad to hear you think so."

"Do you want to know what else I think?" Mauro knew what she would say, and she said it, "I think you could have killed each other."

"We didn't," he told her.

She leaned in and said quietly, "Those were not wooden swords, Mauritius, and you are not a little boy playing in your grandfather's bedchamber. If you are so set on dying, wait at least to see if your wife gives you a son. Remember, you are the last of the House of Baric."

As he nodded obligingly, it occurred to Mauro that the old nanny had more memories of the House of Baric than anyone alive, and he asked her, "Who was Sonja Kasun?"

Idita seemed to steel herself. "Where did you hear that name?"

"I read it in the registry in the constable's office yesterday. She was Jero's mother. There was no father listed. Jero is my brother, isn't he?"

Idita frowned and shook her head. "I do not know who Jero's father was. He was an orphan when Lorenc found him."

"Found him? So my father knew he was out there. He was looking for his son."

"Mauro, I am not the one to explain it. Please, do not ask that of me."

"Idita, you are the only one who can explain now. The dead cannot speak, and I need to know."

She pleaded, "Jero is happy here as your steward, Mauritius. Some things are better left alone." But she could not sway him.

"Not this, Idita. Tell me everything. Please."

She smoothed her apron, covering her lap with her wrinkled hands. "All right, Mauritius. If that is your wish," she said finally. "Where would you like me to start?"

"Who was Sonja Kasun?" he asked again.

"Sonja was the cooper's wife and Mateo's wet nurse. Sadly, her husband and baby boy had died in the same plague as Margaret, so she came to live in the nursery with baby Mateo. I recall that your father was not even at home when Nestor hired Sonja. He came back a few weeks later and was grief-stricken when he learned that they had all perished.

"It was difficult for your father. Sonja would bring Mateo to Lorenc to comfort him. Mateo was almost a year old by then and wanted to move about and play, but Lorenc just held him tight. Sonja stayed in the nursery while Lorenc had him. He did not even notice her at first, I think, but after a while he began to trust her with Mateo, and he would stay and watch the two playing together."

"Did my father fall in love with her?"

She shook her head. "Not right away, no. Vladimir pressed his brother to get away from his troubles and back into the fighting. That is when Lorenc was introduced to your mother as a potential bride."

Mauro had never heard any of this, and he was absorbed in her story as she explained, "Your aunt Renata thought your father needed to marry again. Lorenc had known Johanna for years, of course, but he refused to consider marrying her. It was too soon, I think.

"When he came back to Solgrad after another month away, Lorenc *was* better. He seemed to be happier and more relaxed. Mateo was getting bigger and stronger, and it was decided that he had outgrown the need for a wet nurse. I had always been the children's caretaker once they were weaned, but your father gave Sonja that role for Mateo."

Mauro looked at Idita with concern. "Was that hurtful to you?"

"No, Mauro, your father was generous and made me feel needed. There was still no mistress to run the household, so he gave me that role. Moreover, little Mateo was very attached to Sonja."

"What happened then?"

"It was autumn, I think, and Lorenc spent more time at home as the weather turned bad. I do not know when he fell in love with her, but Sonja brought joy back into his daily life. He openly sought out her company, but if they were lovers, then he was careful about keeping it hidden."

"And she became pregnant."

Idita smiled as she recalled, "I do not think Sonja knew she was pregnant when she left."

"Why did she leave, Idita?"

The nurse leaned back in her chair and took her time sorting through the memory.

"Well, Mauro, that is what I am not sure of. There was a rumor at the castle that your father intended to take Sonja as his new wife. Your uncle would have been against it. Lorenc needed to marry well again, and the countess was still set on matching Lorenc with her sister.

"The rest is speculation," explained Idita. "Toth soldiers came to Baric Castle while your father was out on a mission, and Sonja left with them without saying goodbye. She was well-loved by all of the servants here, and we were concerned for her."

"What did my father do when he returned?"

"He was furious, of course. He looked high and low all across the countryside, and when he could not find her, Lorenc went to confront his brother at Toth Castle. He was gone for several months, and when he came back, your mother came with him. They had married, and he brought your mother home to stay."

Mauro had only known bits and pieces about his parents' courtship. Idita made it all sound sudden. "He could not have loved my mother, then, if he was still in love with Sonja."

"I think they tried to make their marriage work, Mauritius. Your father was very attentive to Lady Johanna at first, but she complained that life was too dull here. You know how grand Toth Castle is, with visiting dignitaries and elegant parties. Her two lady companions added little amusement to her day. Lady Johanna wanted the same glamorous life here."

"Why did she not leave him, Idita? Many wives lead separate lives from their husbands."

She nodded. "That is true, Mauro, and she almost did leave when she discovered that Lorenc was still searching for Sonja. Your father agreed and began looking for a villa in Venice, where your mother could live the social life she wanted. Then they discovered she was pregnant with you, and she stayed."

Mauro stared ahead blankly. His mother would have been happy in Venice, but, because of him, she was miserable.

Idita saw how this news affected him. "I am sorry, Mauro. I told you, some things are better left unsaid. It is a painful story for you to hear and painful for me to tell you."

Mauro shook off the sentiment and said, "Tell me how Jero was found."

Idita shifted uncomfortably on her hard chair but answered directly, "It was by sheer luck, really. It seems Sonja had gone to stay with a sister-in-law to have the baby. She must have told her family that a local baron had fathered Jero but not given them the name. We never learned how Sonja died, but this relation of hers wrote to ask for money for the boy shortly thereafter. We think Sonja's family wrote to all of the barons in Croatia."

There were at least twenty baronies in the territories. Mauro thought about who would have gotten the letters.

He almost missed Idita explaining, "It took months for Lorenc to learn who the relative had sold Jero to. It was Lord Dubovic who had paid for Jero, and Lorenc bought him back."

"He bought him? I do not understand. Why did my father not accept him as his bastard son? Why keep Jero a secret?"

Idita took a deep breath and let it out. "I think we should stop now, Mauro. You are tired. I will finish the story later."

"I am not tired. I need to know all of it."

Idita stretched her arms and fidgeted on her seat, but she continued as asked, "Alright then. What I know is your mother found out what was happening, and she told Vladimir. Vladimir then convinced Lorenc that Sonja had probably gotten pregnant by another man after leaving, which no one could verify. Lorenc already had two legitimate sons that he needed to put first.

"But Lorenc could not stand the thought of Sonja's boy being a servant for Baron Dubovic, even if Jero was not of his blood. So he bought the boy and registered him as his indentured servant. That made Jero bonded to the Barics until he was a man. My belief is that Lorenc hoped one day he could find a way to tell you and Mateo about Jero's true parentage."

"But my mother got in the way," said Mauro guiltily, as though he were to blame.

"Lady Johanna was a devoted mother to you, Mauritius, but she was not prepared to mother two other sons from women your father still loved and mourned. Can you understand that?"

He bowed his head. Mauro was indeed exhausted from all that had transpired. Idita moved to the side of the bed to sit next to him.

Mauro looked up at her and asked, "What am I to do about Jero, Idita? He was meant for more in this world. What should I tell him?"

She wrapped her thin arms around her favorite boy and stroked his blanketed shoulders with love. "I do not know what to tell you, Mauritius. It is all up to you now."

Chapter 13

The three kitchen maids greeted Jero in unison when the baron's steward walked up to their work table under the arbor in the garden.

Even though it was an open secret that Jero had his eye on Ruby, he was still an eligible bachelor until he made his intentions known to her. Unfortunately, Ruby arrived in the garden just after Jero and spoiled the maids' chances for his attention once again.

Jero sensed the uncomfortable silence among the women. So, mustering his best aristocratic Venetian, Jero asked, "What delightful activities have you envisioned for your amusement today, my ladies?"

They laughed at his playful mockery.

Brigita answered in their ordinary Croatian, "Ranka and I are topping carrots for Krsto to bring into the root cellar."

Ivana smiled at Jero sweetly and added, "I am to wipe down the cucumbers for pickling tomorrow."

"How can I best be of help?" asked Jero as he took a seat at the table.

"You and Lady Ruby could help us prune the carrot tops," suggested Ranka. "We have plenty of those to do."

Jero saw only one basket and thought the work would be quickly managed. Then Krsto came around the corner with Tadija, who was pushing a cart with more colorful carrots.

"Oh dear. I think we will be here for a while," said Ruby when she saw the filled cart.

"These are just the ones we will store for the fall, Lady Ruby. We will plant a second crop to leave in the ground for winter. Nela cannot have too many carrots," replied Krsto.

"I hope Franja makes us carrot cakes tomorrow," exclaimed Ranka.

"Cook makes such delicious carrot custard. I like it when she uses the red ones," said Ivana. "It is so festive at Christmas time."

"You are making me hungry," exclaimed Jero with a laugh.

"Oh! Hello, Jero. I didn't notice you there," said Krsto.

Jero greeted him cheerfully, "Hello, Krsto."

Krsto had begun working at Baric Castle a few years ago, and the two became friends right away. He was Jero's age but looked years older. Toiling long hours in the sun and wind had weathered his handsome face.

"How is your wife today?" asked Jero.

"Well, Danica is up and down with a bucket near her side. She will be here later, if she can. I never thought such a tiny baby could make so much trouble already." He finally noticed that Jero was wearing an apron over his waistcoat. "Are you doing women's work today, Jero?" teased Krsto.

"Gladly," said Jero, looking around the table. "My other choice was to fill in ledgers while sitting across from Nestor. I like this company better."

The maids next to him giggled at his remark. Although they understood he was there to spend time with Ruby, Jero never ignored them.

"Here are the last of them," announced Krsto. "You can put the topped carrots into these baskets. Tadija and I will carry them down to stack in the cellar later. You can join us for that, too, if you like, Jero."

"Well, I may not have enough time today, Krsto," he said with a laugh.

"Suit yourself," he replied with a friendly shrug and a wink to the maids. Krsto would not have accepted Jero's help anyway. Such work was below his station as a steward.

Krsto gave Jero a cordial pat farewell with his dusty hand before he and his assistant went back into the garden.

The group had begun to work quietly again when Ruby asked, "May I take some of these greens for the horses? I will be riding with Lady Isabella this afternoon."

Jero knew riding was what Ruby enjoyed most. "Where are you going?" he asked her.

"Nowhere," she told him bluntly. "Lady Isabella did not make much progress on her first day, so we will stay in the paddock." Ruby added more quietly, "She fell off twice."

Jero looked sympathetic when he said, "I am sorry to hear that."

"I watched her lesson yesterday. Bem was very patient with her, but Lady Isabella doesn't understand how to move with the animal. I am going to sit behind her on the horse today. Bem cannot help her like that, of course."

"Of course," agreed Jero. "That is kind of you to help her, Ruby."

"It is selfish, really."

The maids all looked up from their work, surprised to hear Ruby admit this sin in front of Jero.

Ruby did not notice their shocked expressions and went on to explain, "I need a chaperone, you know. I would like Lady Isabella to ride well enough to come on the trails with me."

"You would need at least two escorts," Jero pointed out as he continued cutting the green tops, one after another.

Ruby sighed. "I don't agree with the baron's silly rules. His soldiers aren't going to ravage me if I am alone with one of them."

The maids whispered to each other that Ruby would dare talk so openly about such an indecent act.

"Did I say something wrong?" They were speaking Croatian, and Ruby was still unsure of her words.

"No," said Jero, "you said nothing wrong." He looked sternly at Brigita, who was still snickering over it. "The baron is very protective of you, as he should be. Sometimes he cannot spare two soldiers to take you riding, with or without another lady."

Ruby considered this. "I wish he could." She had given up on the tedious carrots and began inspecting the basket of cucumbers for spots. Then she remarked, "Maybe you could be one of my escorts, Jero, along with a soldier, of course. Perhaps Hugo?"

Jero did not want to compete with Hugo for Ruby's attention. "Or Daniel," he suggested.

"Or Daniel," Ruby agreed with a grin, clearly understanding his choice.

"I will ask Lord Baric. Now that the baron is here to manage more things himself, I have some time free."

"For topping carrots?" asked Ruby. She had that playful expression on her face that Jero found so endearing.

"Exactly," he said, "when it helps a friend."

As he spoke, something odd caught Jero's attention. He had a clear view of the Keep from where he sat at the table, and he watched the baroness as she chased Davor across the cobbled courtyard.

"Wasn't Lady Baric planning to help us this morning?" Jero asked.

"Yes, she will be here shortly," said Ruby offhandedly.

"Perhaps not," replied Jero. "I see her running up the Keep's stairs. Should I go have a look?"

The maids had been listening, and they shared his concern. Indeed, there were rules against women in the Keep.

Ruby turned to see what Jero saw, then said, "She is Baroness Baric. Is it not her Keep, as well?"

Jero grinned at Ruby's defiant reasoning. "Indeed it is."

~ * ~

Resi had just finished her breakfast when Verica rushed into her chamber.

"Lazar said the baron has blood all over his shirt, and your brother is crouched in the corner. They had a sword fight, my lady! I am to find two shirts for Lazar to bring back," she breathlessly exclaimed.

"Two shirts? Wait, what?" It took a moment for Resi to register what Verica had said. "Patrik and Mauro are fighting! Oh, dear God," cried Resi. "Are they in the field?"

"No, Lady Baric, in the Keep," she stammered.

"In the Keep? Good. Give me the shirts, Verica. I will go myself."

Resi did not take time to change out of her house slippers before she ran down the steps. She met Davor at the bottom of the stairs.

"Tell me what has happened!"

He was just as shocked and said, "I don't know, Lady Baric. I just heard the news myself."

Resi saw the black sword case sitting on the side table next to the clock. Frantic, she asked, "Where did that come from?"

Davor looked at the case, then at his mistress. He seemed to understand now whose case it had been.

"Ana brought it in this morning, Lady Baric, and I gave it to the baron by mistake. I thought it was his. I am sorry if it caused any trouble."

"I am certain it did, but it is not your fault," she assured him. "Take me to my husband!"

The baroness had trouble keeping up with Davor in her slip-on shoes, so she kicked them off and ran in her stockings. They hurried to the stairs that led into the dining hall.

Mauro's captains had made good on their promise to the baron and had taken the soldiers to the field already, so the large hall was empty. Resi wanted to take it all in, but there was no time to look around just then. It was like Fabian had said, not gloomy and cold as it looked from the outside. It was a welcoming room, filled with the smells of what had been a savory breakfast. No wonder Mauro came here in the mornings.

"It is this way, Lady Baric." Davor led her up the wide, winding stairs to the second-floor landing.

Lazar was already there and told his mistress, "The baron is in Simeon's room right over here. The Baric chamber is this one." The boy pointed across the hallway, proud that he was helpful.

Resi went to Simeon's room first. If Mauro was injured, maybe Simeon was tending to him.

The door was cracked open, and she looked in. Resi was surprised that Idita was with Mauro, not Simeon. The old nanny was sitting next to him on the bed. A wool blanket was wrapped around Mauro's tall frame, and Idita had her arms around him. Resi could not see Mauro's face, but she could see Idita's. The nanny looked sad and pensive as she sat holding him. Resi stepped away.

Davor and Lazar were standing to the side of the door, their hands folded behind their backs as the servants waited dutifully for further instructions. They did not ask their mistress what she had seen in the room or why she looked so frightened; it was not their place.

Resi's heart was racing as she crossed the wide hallway and reluctantly opened the door to the Baric chamber—her chamber, which she had never been in.

There was no panic, no hysteria of tending to a dying man. It felt surreal to Resi to see the normal movements of its occupants and hear their masculine voices talking casually. Patrik was not crouched in a corner but sat on a wooden chair next to a large table with basins and pitchers. Soren was wringing out a linen cloth in one of them, but Resi could see that the water was red with blood. Cyro, Bem, and Salar Nassim were buttoning vests and jackets; they had finally finished dressing.

Patrik was the first to see her standing at the doorway. "Resi, come in," he said with visible discomfort at moving his jaw.

Resi hurried to her brother's side, clutching the folded shirts to her chest. "What happened here?"

He lowered the cloth to show her his bruised face. She gently touched his swollen nose. "Does it hurt?"

He winced.

Bem told her, "Your healing woman left Patrik some powder for the pain, but he'll need a little food first. Your husband broke his nose, but he also fixed it."

"Is that all, Patricius? Mauro just came in here and broke your nose?" Her sympathy had been short-lived. She was livid again. "What did you say to deserve that? What did you break of his?"

Salar Nassim came to her side. "The baron came out unscathed, Terese," he reported calmly. "We were locked out for a good amount of time while the two fought with swords, so just one bloodied nose is not a bad outcome."

"You fought in here with swords!" she shouted in Greek. "Are you insane?"

She looked around the furnished room. It was bigger than her chamber in the manor house but crowded with the two extra pallets and bags of gear on the floor. The large bed looked trampled, and one of the canopy curtains was ripped.

She said to the men, "Can you leave us for a moment, please?"

Soren handed Patrik the fresh cloth. She watched Soren silently dump the basin with the bloody water into the one with the vomit. Patrik nodded his thanks before his friend carried it out to empty it down the toilet chute. The others silently followed Soren out of the room.

Resi noticed Patrik's torn and bloodied shirt, and she spoke softly this time, "I suppose one of these shirts is meant for you. I will put it here for later."

She sat down on the chair next to him and said, "I know Mauro found the swords. Is that what you fought about?"

He nodded and told her bit by bit, "That was part. I challenged him. For Father. He did not want to fight. But did. I said he was an idiot. For not loving you. He punched me." Patrik chuckled, then gritted his teeth in pain. "It seems he does," he managed to finish telling her.

She took the cloth away to study his face again. "You got what you deserved, you know. I hope you can finally be at peace with Papa's imprisonment. Papa is."

He nodded and shrugged.

"I think Mauro feels bad that he hurt you. I looked in on him across the hall. He was talking to Idita. You should apologize to him." He nodded again. "Did he really say that he loved me?"

Patrik smiled a lopsided grin.

"Will you still leave in a few days?"

He nodded once more that they would.

She poured fresh water into the empty basin and dropped the cloth into it. There was no new blood in it this time. She wrung it out and handed it back to Patrik.

"Did all of this happen before your breakfast?"

Patrik nodded.

"Then I will go find you something to eat." She leaned over and kissed Patrik's forehead. "You are a stupid man, but I love you, Brother."

She went out into the hall, and Mauro was just closing the door to Simeon's room. Idita was no longer there. She had left while Resi was talking to Patrik.

"What are you doing here, Resi?" He was not expecting to see her.

"There was quite a commotion in the manor house. How could I resist seeing who had killed whom?" She laughed nervously, even though it could have been a realistic outcome for the two stubborn men. "I left your shirt in the other room. Patricius is in there. He has something to tell you."

Mauro reached for her hand before she could walk away. "Is he alright?"

She touched her husband's face with her other hand. Mauro seemed uninjured, and she was glad for it. "I think so. He needs food to take with the powder Idita left. I was going to go find him a bowl of something downstairs."

He took Resi in his arms and held her close. His bare skin felt warm, having just left the blanket behind.

"I am sorry, Resi. I should not have hit him."

"Patricius is pigheaded and was bent on making you angry, Mauro. You probably knew that anyway. Let him apologize to you."

He let go of her, and she left down the stairwell.

~*~

Patrik was in front of the looking glass, wiping the red streaks from his throat when Mauro came into the room.

"You will have a good bruise between your eyes for a few days, but it will make you look more dangerous when dueling tomorrow," Mauro said from the doorway.

Patrik turned around. "I never should have challenged you, Lord Baric. I am sorry. I let my anger take over. I was out of line."

Mauro could not help but smile at Patrik's rehearsed speech.

"You were out of line," said Mauro, "and I accept your apology. We do not have to be friends, Patrik, but I hope we can at least be civil."

"I can do that, Lord Baric."

Mauro offered Patrik a true flag of truce. "Lord Baric is very formal for family. I would like you to call me by my given name: Mauritius. We are brothers now, and my brother called me Mauro. You may call me either one if you like."

Patrik found smiles hurt less now, and he managed one. "I will do that. Thank you. Mauro."

Mauro looked around. "My wife said she left me a shirt in here."

"There, on the table," Patrik said, and Mauro picked his favorite of the two.

In a friendlier tone, Mauro told Patrik, "I am expected to join my soldiers shortly. I will tell them our misunderstanding has been cleared up. If there is any lingering resentment toward you because of it, let me know, alright?"

Then Mauro's expression became stern when he said, "But draw a sword on me again in my own house, Patrik, and it will be you who needs protecting."

"Understood," he replied solemnly.

Mauro slipped the shirt over his head and went toward the door.

Patrik offered one last commentary, "I want you to know that my father never spoke of what happened to anyone. He kept your Baric secrets."

"I believe you," the baron said, and then he left the room.

Davor and Lazar were still outside the chamber, waiting for the baron near the stairwell.

"Lazar," Mauro said, "you need to find your brother. Take the curtain down for the maids to mend and see what can be done for the stains on the carpet."

Lazar bowed and ran down the stairs to find Tin.

"And Davor."

The valet stepped forward.

"I left without my hat and jacket. Could you bring those to the stables while I get my horse? I will not be back at the manor house until dinner."

Mauro went down the stairwell and continued all the way to the armory, where he found the person he was looking for.

"Eduard, can I have a word?"

Eduard was sorting the shields left behind that morning and looked up. "Good morning, sir. Did you need me to keep an eye on the troublemakers?"

"There is no trouble here, Eduard. It was a family argument, and it has been resolved. I wanted to talk to you about training the servants, though. The men should know how to wield a sword for their own protection."

"That is a fair suggestion," agreed Eduard.

"I will talk to them myself and will set a schedule, beginning next week."

"Very good, sir."

When Mauro lingered, Eduard asked, "Is there something else you needed from me?"

"There is," said Mauro casually. "Do you know if Jero has any training?"

Eduard visibly perked up when he answered, "It has been several years, but I sparred with him myself. Jero was a good swordsman at one time. Your father trained him. Did Jero not tell you that?"

"Yes, I thought as much," Mauro lied smoothly. It made sense now. His father had taken Jero under his wing while Mauro had been away.

Mauro changed his mind about pairing Daniel with Patrik and told Eduard, "That is why Jero will come to the training fields tomorrow. The mercenaries will also join us, and the odd man needs a partner."

Eduard raised his brows in question, but he did not argue with the baron over his choice.

"Make sure you pick out a good weapon for Jero, one that he can wield well. I want him to make a good impression on my brother-in-law."

Eduard seemed to like the sound of that. "You can count on it, Mauro."

The baron left the armory and walked out into the bright sunshine to what he hoped would be a less eventful rest of the day.

Chapter 14

Isabella stood at her bedroom window early that morning and watched the young maids carry the table planks out to the garden below. She was not thinking about the industrious servants but about her lounging friend.

"Caterina, I have decided I cannot allow you to be alone with this foreign man. He is too suave. He will seduce you."

Curled up under the covers, Caterina was not ready to surrender to the morning or her friend's wishes.

She said from her pile of pillows, "Salar Nassim is old, Isabella. He could admittedly be my father."

"How many older men have you seen seduce girls like you? Too many! I do not trust him."

"We will only spend one hour together, and I want no disruptions from a chaperone." Caterina put a pillow over her capped head and sunk deeper into her blankets to make it clear that the topic was closed.

Isabella turned from the window and came over to their breakfast table across from the bed. She took a drink from the glass of sweet wine she had brought upstairs with her last night.

Still frustrated with her friend's imprudence, Isabella asked, "Has he already seduced you? He has those wonderful mysterious eyes that are hard to avoid looking into."

Caterina gave in and sat up in bed. "He has two wives already, Isabella. He does not want a third. Do not fight me on this."

"I feel responsible for you, Caterina, now that Fabian is gone. You must have your lesson in the open, not at the table behind the bushes."

"We were not behind any bushes! Why can I not be trusted?" she said and pouted.

"Men do not have your best interests in mind when they are alone with you. I do, Caterina."

Isabella finished the wine. The two stared at each other in silence for a long moment, then Caterina acquiesced. "Very well, Isabella. Join us this morning and see for yourself, but you must leave me alone for the lesson."

"Agreed," said Isabella.

She leisurely went back to the window and looked out. Ruby was walking down the path and disappeared beneath the foliage of the grape arbor. "I wonder what Lady Ruby is doing so early this morning."

Caterina slid back down under her covers. "I am wondering the same thing about you, Isabella. Why are you up so early, Isabella?"

"I am just excited to start the day. I cannot wait to try riding again. It was so freeing yesterday, sitting astride on a horse."

"Promise me that you will ask Lady Terese if you can use her bathhouse. You smelled so strongly of horses it made me have wild dreams about Paolo. He always smelled of horses. But do you know what the funny thing was?"

"Hmm?" Isabella was staring inattentively out the window.

"The funny thing was," Caterina repeated pensively, "I do not think the man in my dream was Paolo. I could not see any details of his face. He was shadowed because of the veil I wore. He held me in a romantic embrace, and when he lifted the veil to kiss me, I woke up."

Isabella came back to the bedside. "Did he have black eyes, a trimmed beard, and a turban over his sleek hair?" she asked playfully.

Caterina threw the pillow at her.

"Dream on if you like, Cat. I am going to ring the bell for my breakfast."

~ * ~

After the heart-pounding start to their day—a bloody duel in their shared chamber—Cyro, Soren, and Salar Nassim went together to the calm of the manor house. The baroness had earlier offered them use of the library, and Soren and Cyro planned to look through the books while Salar Nassim held his lesson with Lady Caterina. They had left Bem to look after Patrik, who was knocked out from the potion Idita had given him for the pain.

They greeted Isabella and Caterina on the large terrace, and then Salar Nassim asked, "Will you be joining our game today, Lady Isabella?"

"No, sir, I will not be playing any games, but I will be watching with my sketch pad."

"Delightful," replied Salar Nassim, brushing off her warning.

"Will the others be playing?" asked Caterina with concern.

"No, Lady Caterina. My friends are in search of entertainment in the literary form this morning."

Soren and Cyro bowed their departure and continued into the great hall without comment.

The ladies followed them through the open double doors with a swoosh of their full skirts.

"Shall we sit inside, ladies, near the window?" offered the Persian.

"Isabella will not be sitting with us," said Caterina a little too sharply.

Isabella understood her friend's prompt and clarified, "I will sit by the hearth. The light is so much better there for capturing your lesson."

Isabella crossed the room, took a seat in one of the stuffed chairs, and then opened her notebook to a clean page. She waited for inspiration to come over her.

Caterina was eager to begin their private session. She pulled out a little box from her skirt pocket and set it on the table in front of her teacher. The box was beautifully enameled with a delicate gold design. "I brought what Cyro asked me to show you."

Salar Nassim had not seen the snuff box in Cyro's possession before, so he knew it was not the thing of beauty Cyro had given her. He waited for Caterina to open it and show him what was inside. Caterina took out the limp blossom and carefully handed it to her teacher. Salar Nassim was impressed with the showy flower, despite its wilted state.

"Did Cyro tell you why he chose this flower?"

Caterina thought again about her conversation yesterday under the arches and told him, "He said it reminded him of a lady at a ball. The pink petals are like a fine gown she might wear, and the delicate blossom hidden inside is the lady herself."

Salar Nassim smiled, seemingly impressed with Cyro's description. He gently turned the precious flower over in his hand to examine it.

"I can imagine the lady now. It is a true thing of beauty, this little blossom. Thank you for bringing it."

He handed it back to her, and Caterina put it into her box again, then into her pocket.

"Is this how it will be each day?" she asked. "When you are done toying with me, will we play cards?"

"You asked me to teach you, and I will. Playing cards should be amusing, though," he said.

"Are you amused, Salar Nassim?"

He looked at her serenely and said, "May I ask you something?"

"You are the teacher," she said, watching him thoughtfully choose his words.

"Why do you play cards, Lady Caterina?"

"To win," she answered without reflection.

"And why do you think your opponent—let's say, your friend Lady Isabella—might play cards? Is it for the same reason?" he asked.

"I suppose so," Caterina replied with an impatient shrug.

"Card games are meant to entertain, so I suspect your friend would play for her amusement. Cards provide a social way to help you forget your troubles and enjoy frivolous time with others. Would you not agree, Lady Caterina?"

"I had not thought of it that way. Isabella does play cards often, even though she rarely wins."

"At the card table the other evening, I had the sense that you played differently from your friend. That is why I will play a second game with you."

She cocked her head in confusion.

Salar Nassim went on to explain, "There is more to a card game than playing your hand well. You should find enjoyment in the company at the table. The best card players are also pleasant partners, Lady Caterina. I will teach you how to be one."

"Do you mean to insult me, Salar Nassim? Am I not a pleasant partner?"

"A teacher must tell the truth, and some truths come from observation. I win at cards because I observe my opponents. Can you say the same?"

She found he was right. "I watch the cards, but I will admit that I do not watch the people. Is that wrong then?"

He leaned in when he told her, "Very wrong. By paying attention to what your opponents give away, you will discover their weaknesses. You must watch how the others at the table will react when a card is played. Even the best players will give something away. Like Cyro did yesterday."

"Cyro? Does the flower have something to do with his weakness?"

Salar Nassim sat back in his chair at the window and smiled across the table at her. "Exactly! Cyro unwittingly told you his weakness when he told you why he liked the flower. He gave you an opening, something to talk about, and you now have a way to distract him."

Caterina was drawn in by his soothing voice and handsome looks as they spoke across the small table.

Then the memory of Isabella's warning made her shutter, and she asked, "Are you trying to seduce me, Salar Nassim?"

He chuckled in surprise. The innocent cock of her head, styled with glossy curls and satin ribbons, and the slight pout on her rouged lips were indeed alluring to any man.

"Would you be disappointed if I said no, Lady Caterina? I will play cards with you, as you wished, but I do not plan to seduce you." Then he added, "But should I ask the same question of you?"

Her eyes widened at the suggestion. "Me, seduce you, sir?"

He laughed softly. "Is that not done in your land, a younger woman choosing to openly charm an older man?"

She smiled shyly and admitted, "Yes, I suppose it happens."

"Are your intentions pure, Lady Caterina?" he asked with an intense stare across the table.

She became bashful even though her intentions were indeed pure. "Yes, Salar Nassim, I will just play cards with you," she assured him.

He took out his cards from the pouch on his belt. "Now that we understand each other, shall we take a look?"

His honesty was inviting. Caterina relaxed against her chair and said, "I am ready to play your game."

Isabella had watched the interaction across the great hall without the benefit of hearing their conversation. Something had changed, and they set a beautiful scene that she could not wait to put down on her paper. She picked up her pencil to sketch them.

~ * ~

Natalija was bringing the ladies' breakfast tray back to the kitchen when she noticed Soren and Cyro through the open door of the sitting room. She left the stacked tray on a side table under the stairs and dared to enter the room.

"My lords," she said and curtsied, as was expected of her. "I have finished the mending I promised you. I will give your shirt to Tin."

Soren turned around. "I told you I am not a lord. My name is Soren."

Cyro was at the bookshelf with Soren. He flashed Natalija a friendly smile before turning back to hunt for the perfect afternoon read.

Natalija walked farther into the sitting room and pointed toward a high shelf. "The book about Denmark is that red one there," she said.

"Can you read?" asked Soren. He sat down casually on the arm of the sofa and gave her his full attention.

"No, sir, but I know what the book looks like. Her ladyship read it to us this past winter. She told us it is a play, and she used different voices when she read it."

Cyro pulled the red book off the shelf and read the title. "*Hamlet,* is that the book?" He handed it over to his friend.

"Yes, sir, that is the one," Natalija answered nervously.

"I will read this on your recommendation," Soren told her, setting it off to the side.

Natalija awkwardly lingered while Soren went back to his browsing.

"I am going to visit my family tomorrow afternoon," Natalija said unexpectedly.

"That is nice for you," replied Soren indifferently.

"My sisters would be happy to hear about your adventures in this Indies place," she went on to tell him.

Soren turned in surprise. "Are you inviting me to meet them?"

She seemed embarrassed now and glanced in Cyro's direction. He appeared engrossed in the first pages of a book, so she took a step closer to Soren and whispered, "If you have time, that is. I usually walk, but since the baroness will have an escort to visit her friend, I will ride along in the wagon. My parents live next to our tanning shop in the center of town."

Soren thought it might be a good excuse to get out from the confines of the walls again. "Very well, I will join you tomorrow, as long as your father won't mind a visitor."

"No, my lord, he won't mind at all."

He shook his head at her before she realized her mistake.

"Soren, I mean. The baroness has not told me exactly when we will leave. But, since you are friends with her, I suppose you can talk to the baroness directly."

"I will ask her," agreed Soren.

She curtsied, backed out of the room, and disappeared down the hall with her trays.

Cyro looked up from his book with a grin. "Meeting the sisters? This is getting serious, Soren."

"I see no harm in it," Soren muttered. "I have fond memories of my time in the West Indies and do not mind retelling those stories. Besides, we will be back on the road before she asks for my hand in marriage."

Cyro looked pleased to hear Soren joke again. Still, he took the red book from Soren's hand and put it back on the shelf.

"I have read *Hamlet* and do not recommend it. It is engaging enough, but only because it is about death and madness." Cyro handed him a different volume.

Soren read the front cover aloud, "*The Ingenious Gentleman Don Quixote of La Mancha*. That is your recommendation?"

"Yes, I liked this book very much," said Cyro. "I read it in Spanish, my mother's native tongue. I am sure this translation is acceptable."

Soren seemed puzzled. "When did you have so much time to read so many stories?" he asked.

"I spent a good part of my adolescence at my grandparents' castle on Corsica. It was a long boat trip from Genoa for a boy, so I read books to pass the time."

"Then you may have read most of the baron's collection."

"For a soldiering man, Baron Baric has an exceptional variety of books in his library. I see a few new titles that pique my interest." Cyro browsed through another row of novels on a shelf. "Will you stay in the sitting room to read, Soren?"

Soren picked up the book Cyro had offered. "No, I will take this back with me. Bem wanted to check on the horses in the stables, but someone needs to stay in the chamber with Patrik."

Cyro nodded and said, "I am going to linger here a while. I will see you for lunch."

~ * ~

Cyro remained captivatingly mysterious to the Venetian ladies. He had a unique quality to his personality that held their attention, although his appearance could be considered quite ordinary. He was the shortest of the strangers, and thin might best describe his slight build. His mismatched, well-worn attire highlighted his impoverished circumstances. It was apparent, though, that he took special care with his long hair under his velvet cap, and he skillfully trimmed his beard each day. The ladies accepted him as presented despite his guarded past. Cyro was an unremarkable mercenary soldier traveling with the baroness's brother.

Isabella smiled politely at Cyro as he crossed the great hall to sit in the chair next to hers.

"Am I disturbing you, Lady Isabella?" he asked graciously.

She held up her hand to quiet him. "I am almost finished. I just need to add a few more touches."

He looked across the room at the card players. They seemed to be in deep concentration at their lesson. Cyro opened his book and gave Isabella the time she needed.

Natalija came into the great hall and set a tray with tea on the small table between them. She silently poured the steaming liquid into the pretty porcelain cups, then curtsied and left again.

Isabella set her drawing pad down and smiled at her new companion. "You must intimidate her, Cyro. She usually talks up a storm when she brings me tea."

"Maybe she understood that an artist cannot be disturbed. May I see what you have captured on your paper, madam?"

Isabella drew for herself and rarely showed others what she sketched. She handed him the notebook and then picked up her cup of tea. She blew over the rim to cool it while he studied the picture, and she studied him.

"You drew this just now?" he asked.

She nodded.

"You are a very talented artist, Lady Isabella. It is exceptional," he said.

She set her cup down to take the sketchbook back, but he held onto it.

"May I see what else is in your book?"

He began to turn back the pages before she could stop him. He silently flipped through her drawings of landscapes, the sea, the view of the Keep, and then the people. There was a sketch of almost everyone in the house, including himself with Caterina.

He glanced at Isabella out of the corner of his eye. She noticed, uncomfortable that he might think poorly of her interpretation of the two together. He didn't.

Cyro continued on to the back of the collection and found drawings of people he did not recognize, except for one. At the end of the notebook were sketches of Fabian. Cyro closed the cover and gave it back to her, smiling charmingly.

"I envy you," he said.

She cocked her head doubtfully. "Do you? Why is that?"

"I would love to be able to record memories, especially of those I love. God has given you a wonderful gift."

"God tortures me with it," she heard herself answer.

He picked up the delicate teacup and drank from it. "Why would you say that?" he then asked.

Isabella sensed that Cyro had lived in her world once before and might understand her restrained position as an aristocratic woman. She leaned in, like she was sharing a secret, although they were entirely alone in their corner of the great hall.

"I want to paint," she confided, "but my mother will not allow it. She says it is too dirty. It will stain my hands and make me smell of chemicals."

"She is right about that," Cyro agreed without hesitation.

Isabella was about to argue, but he shook his head and added, "I am not defending your mother. That is a terrible reason to subdue such talent as yours. A man will overlook blue fingers on the woman he loves. And any man not interested in art is not worth your time, my lady."

"The men I have encountered are interested in art, but only art made by men. I do not know any ladies who paint."

"You seem like an independent woman, Lady Isabella. There are ways around everything if you put your mind to it."

Her frown told him she did not share his optimism.

"Put a man's name on your art if that is all that is holding you back," he said.

He took another drink of his tea as she puzzled over the idea.

"Do you mean, use a pseudonym? Is that really done?"

"It is, and more often than you know. And when you find yourself with paint and a canvas, I will be your first patron," he said with certainty.

She chuckled. "You are comical, Cyro. Will you pay me with your delightful conversation, or will you become a bandit and fund me with the spoils?"

"Indeed!" He saw now how absurd that must have sounded to her. "I will sponsor you after the second plunder. I will need the first fortune to find an appropriate home to hang your paintings in."

They both laughed a little too loudly at that, and Caterina and Salar Nassim turned from their card game to look at them.

"I will leave you to your pleasure now, Lady Isabella."

Cyro stood up and retrieved the book he had set down. He bowed gracefully to her before he crossed the room and stopped at the card table, where he whispered something to Salar Nassim. Isabella watched him walk away and out the terrace door.

Outside, the maids were setting out a lunch for the four ladies. This was Caterina's cue that her time was over. She stood up to say her goodbye to her teacher.

While waiting for Caterina, Isabella opened her notebook again and flipped through the pages, reliving the memory of each. She smiled to herself as she thought of a man's name she would paint under.

Isabella was near the end of her collection when she realized that one was missing. It was her favorite drawing of the beach and the sailboat, with everyone pictured. She had even drawn herself into this sketch. She went back through the sheets of paper, looking for it, and saw the small remnants of where a page had been torn from her book.

Isabella closed her notebook with irritation as Caterina approached her, already chatting about her new assignment.

Chapter 15

Isabella picked at her lunch. She was too nervous about her second riding lesson to eat. Bem had assured her yesterday that it had been a good start, but she knew otherwise. Bem had been patient with her, walking her all around the paddock on his gentle mare, telling her kind words of encouragement. Isabella found she was looking forward to seeing him just as much as she was looking forward to riding the horse. After their meal, the four ladies had hurried back upstairs to change clothes.

Ruby came to the Venetians' room dressed for riding as Isabella was putting on her broad-brimmed hat in front of the looking glass. Isabella wore the rose-printed riding breeches again with the matching floral jacket, but she had chosen a distinctly shorter tunic from the baroness's wardrobe today. Her shapely legs were no more covered than a man's would be when she rode. The baron would disapprove if he came by to watch her lesson, but Isabella was beyond caring.

Caterina noticed Ruby's expression and remarked, "She looks scandalous, doesn't she, Lady Ruby? I told her she cannot go out while dressed so indecently."

"This is a beautiful ensemble, Cat, and you know it," answered Isabella instead.

Caterina shook her head with disapproval. "What would Fabian say? And Mauritius!"

"Why should I care what Fabian thinks? He disagrees with everything I do. And Mauritius's own aunt wrote that the French ladies are wearing this same ensemble on the riding fields of Paris, so why not in the woods of Croatia? Come, Lady Ruby, I am ready. Are you coming too, Caterina?"

"Later, with Lady Terese. She wanted to lie down for a short nap. I had such an early start to the day, Isabella, so I decided I will take one, too."

"Fine, but do not be surprised if we have already moved outside the walls by that time. I think I will succeed quickly today."

Isabella picked up her gloves from the trunk, and she and Ruby went through the quiet house and out the front door to the small arena near the stables.

~*~

Bem waited with his saddled horse at the paddock. Alberto did not entirely trust the foreign man to be with the women unsupervised, so he assigned Geoff to help Bem with the horses. They had bridled Ophelia for Ruby to use and one of the baron's horses, should Bem want to ride next to the ladies.

When Bem had offered to teach Isabella to ride, he had not expected it would bring back the aching memory of his wife, Fatina. Bem missed the feminine conversation he had enjoyed yesterday with Isabella. The Venetian was as different from Fatina as two women could be, but she was unquestionably appealing, and she fascinated him. Bem saw something in her that had first attracted him to his wife—an untamed spirit.

Geoff found himself staring at the unusually spirited lady and had to look at his feet when he brought Bem's horse around to Lady Isabella.

Bem did not comment on either of the women's chosen riding attire, but he thought about Fatina and how she would like these feisty women.

With little greeting, Bem said, "We'll get right to work if that is all right. I will help you up, Lady Isabella, and Ruby can ride behind you on the rump of the horse." He quickly lifted the two women onto his mare.

Ruby settled in close to the saddle and held Isabella around the waist. Isabella turned back and asked, "You won't slide off, will you, Lady Ruby?"

"Only if you do, Lady Isabella." Ruby winked at Bem, who had overheard her. He was still holding the reins as the women settled in.

He handed control of the horse over to Isabella and said, "Remember what I showed you yesterday. I just want you to walk her along the rails and get a feel for the horse's movement."

Bem made a clicking noise with his mouth, spoke a few commands to the mare, and then the horse began to move at a slow trot.

Ruby gave instructions from behind, encouraging Isabella to relax and not think so much about what she or the horse was doing.

The ladies went around the exercise yard once, and then Bem stopped Isabella to ask, "How did that feel to you?"

"I am not sure I can stay seated on this," she fretted. "I feel like I am in a broken boat instead of on a horse. I am rocking forward one minute and falling back the next."

That was precisely what Bem thought she looked like—a drunken sailor. "When you learn early in life, you catch on faster how a horse moves, and you are less fearful of sitting up high on an animal. Fabian Carrera was right when he warned that it would take some time."

"Because I am so old?" Isabella cautioned him with her practiced glare.

"Not at all," he assured her with a chuckle. "You are not too old, you are just afraid."

"I am not afraid! Maybe I need a different saddle, is all."

Bem looked the saddle over again and checked the straps over the blanket. "This is a well-made saddle, and it fits you nicely."

Geoff interjected, "Maybe the lady would be better without one, like Lady Ruby."

Bem considered that. "Come, let me help you down," he said with no further explanation.

Isabella gracefully swung her leg over the back of the horse's neck.

Bem held her by her waist and set her on the ground. Then he did the same for Ruby. He began unbuckling the saddle, and Geoff hurried over to lift it away.

"Up you go, Ruby," commanded Bem. He gave her a foot up with little effort. "Ruby will have the reins this time. You will be in back, Lady Isabella."

Bem then helped Isabella onto the horse the same way. "Hold on tightly to Ruby's waist or you will fall. Do you understand?"

Isabella nodded unhappily but did not protest.

"Ruby," he said to get her attention, then spoke to her quietly in the Ottoman language they both understood: "I am going to have the horse run. If you ride by feeling, the lady will feel it, too. I want you to move with the horse, and she will move, too. Don't hold back, alright?"

Ruby nodded that she wouldn't and then took the reins from Bem.

Isabella wrapped her arms around Ruby's waist and held tight, unaware of what Bem had said in secret.

Bem whistled sharply, and the horse began to gallop around the large enclosure.

Ruby leaned into the curves of the paddock fencing as the horse ran around in a wide circle. She double-backed, steering the swift mare in a different direction.

Isabella bravely held on, leaning into Ruby in the curves, following her instinct to stay seated on the back of the beast despite the bouncing and jostling. Her long hair flew behind her.

After a few minutes of watching them gallop back and forth, Bem whistled again, and the mare came trotting back to him. He patted Fatina on the curve of her strong neck.

Bem looked at the riders and asked, "Are you still afraid, Lady Isabella?"

Isabella's cheeks were flush, and her eyes beamed with excitement. "No, Bem, that was fantastic. I am not afraid any longer."

~*~

Caterina had been more tired than she thought and woke from her nap panicked that she had missed her friend's lesson. She hurried to put on her shoes and hat and then headed down the corridor.

Verica was coming out of the baroness's chamber as Caterina approached. "Is Lady Baric awake now? We were going to go together to the stables," Caterina said hopefully.

"Oh, I am sorry, my lady. Natalija told my mistress that you were sleeping, so Lady Baric went to visit the hens. Shall I take you there to find her?"

"I have seen the henhouse along the path, and I can find my way. Thank you, Verica."

Caterina had never collected eggs before. What an adventure that would be, she thought.

Caterina's wish was not fulfilled, though. Resi was coming down the path just outside the manor house. She had already filled her basket with nearly a dozen eggs and was bringing them to the kitchen.

"Hello, Lady Caterina. I saw the horses are still in the arena, so we are not too late. I'll just leave these here for now, and we can walk over together."

Resi set the eggs down in the shade on the nearby bench, and Caterina looked into the woven basket.

"Lady Terese, why do you collect the eggs if I may be so bold to ask?"

"I like to," said Resi thoughtfully. "The kitchen maids collect the bulk of them when they feed the hens. There is never more than a handful to gather in the afternoon, but I look in each nest anyway. There is something especially divine about finding a warm egg."

Caterina remembered she was to find another item of beauty for tomorrow and asked, "May I see?"

Resi opened the cloth covering the basket and took out an egg nestled in the middle. "It is still warm," she said. She handed it to Caterina with a smile.

Caterina held it cupped in her hand and studied the tan egg for a moment. The shell was smooth and fit perfectly into the palm of her hand. "May I keep it?"

Resi chuckled at Caterina's strange request. "Yes, of course. But what will you do with it?"

"I must bring it to my card lesson tomorrow," she replied as if that was all the answer the baroness needed. "I will leave it here."

Now kindred spirits, Caterina and Resi linked their arms, and the two friends walked across the courtyard together to cheer on Isabella.

~*~

When Caterina and the baroness arrived at the paddock, they found that Isabella's riding lesson had attracted several spectators. Grooms and soldiers stood at the fence watching Ruby on Ophelia, Bem on the saddled Baric horse, and Isabella bareback on Bem's mare, riding between the two in unison. Caterina stood on the bottom fence rail to get a better view.

Geoff came to the baroness's side at the railing. He described the events she had missed and how he thought for sure Lady Isabella was going to fall off again but didn't. He seemed proud that he had a share in her success that day.

Mauro had also been watching from his horse before taking it to the stables. He handed Janus's reins to Josip and walked across the courtyard. He would not interfere with the spectacle today but would be sure his soldiers never ogled the ladies in the future.

At the well, Jero was talking to Danko, who delivered the post and other official messages from the constable to the Barics. Mauro saw them shake hands in parting, and then the courier left on his horse, back out the gate to the village.

"Anything important?" Mauro asked Jero as the steward came closer.

Jero held two envelopes, one small and one large. "Lady Caterina got a letter with the post."

"From her family?" asked Mauro.

"It does not show the sender, but it does not look like a Carrera seal." Then Jero handed the baron the larger envelope, sealed with embossed wax and official stamps. "You received something from the Venetian Authority."

Mauro opened it. "It says my complaint against the navy will be reviewed at a future date." He handed the envelope back to Jero.

"Should I have Nestor send a reply that it has been settled?"

Mauro took the cup hanging from the well and dipped it in for a drink. "No, I think I will keep this active until my next shipment is successful. You never know if the lieutenant will have too much time on his hands again and follow my ship for his own perverse pleasure."

Mauro splashed his face with the cool water and then wiped it with his sleeve.

"Are you coming from the salt fields?" Jero asked.

"Yes. I was able to get the manifest signed off after the navy inventoried the cargo themselves. Well, the cargo that is on board now. We are all set for Friday."

"Excellent news. I'll take this letter to Natalija now to give to Lady Caterina if there is nothing else you need."

"There is. I have some more news you will want to hear." Mauro's lips curled into a mischievous grin when he told Jero, "The mercenaries will join in our sparring practice tomorrow, and Patrik specifically asked for you to be his dueling partner."

"Me?" Jero was stunned. "Why would he ask for me?"

"They are in need of one, and I think Patrik does not like any of my soldiers," replied Mauro.

"Mauro, you know that I—"

"You will do fine, Jero. I asked Eduard what he thought of the matchup. He said you were once quite good. You have hidden that from me," Mauro said with a laugh.

"I could fight well enough years ago. But to spar with Patrik? He's quite intimidating."

"Patrik is at a disadvantage—he cannot breathe," Mauro reminded him and then said, "Be ready at first light. We will have breakfast together in the Keep. Oh, and Fabian has granted you quite a prize before he left."

Jero frowned. "A prize from Fabian?"

Mauro could not help but laugh when he said, "You are to ride Bacchus while he is away."

"That is no prize! The horse has a reputation for throwing anyone but Fabian."

Mauro replied, "I saw Geoff ride him once. I suppose we will find out tomorrow."

Jero suddenly turned to walk away, and Mauro called out, "Where are you going?"

"To the stables," Jero called back. "I want to introduce myself to the fickle beast again before I strap my gear on and he rejects me."

Mauro shook his head in amusement. It was a good possibility that Bacchus would.

The castle seemed preoccupied at the stables, and Mauro would have time for one more task before dressing for dinner. He walked the short distance to the chapel.

~*~

Bem decided the lesson was over for the day and took the reins of Isabella's horse to guide her to the gate.

Alberto had come to watch what the African had managed in a day without him. When he saw the gawking crowd along the fence, Alberto hollered, "Off you go, the lot of you. If you don't have enough work, I've got something for you to do."

The audience of soldiers hurriedly left, laughing and muttering to themselves, while Alberto went into the paddock to help Isabella down from her horse.

Ruby rode up next to them, and Geoff took her reins. She put her finger to her lips to warn the groom not to tell as she slid off the horse unassisted.

Bem took the reins of his mare and spoke softly to it after Isabella was off.

Ruby asked him, "What language are you speaking to her?"

"It is Portuguese, the language of my father," Bem said proudly.

"Do you think it is easier for the horse to understand?" Ruby asked.

"It is not for my mare but for me that I use Portuguese. I don't want to forget how to speak it."

"Even though she cannot talk back," Ruby pointed out with a laugh.

"But she does," replied Bem mischievously. "In my mind, I decide what she would answer in Portuguese. It sounds a bit mad, but that keeps the language alive for me."

"I think I understand how that would be. I might be doing the same if I could not speak Greek with Resi."

Isabella had been dusting off her silks and had overheard what Bem had told Ruby. "How did a Portuguese man end up in Ethiopia?" she asked.

Bem hesitated. He hadn't talked about his family in years, but the women were an encouraging audience.

"My father was a part of the Jesuit group that came to my country," he began. "He was not a priest but was one of their escorts. He had been in the country a few years already when he met my mother. They fell in love, and they married."

Isabella pressed him, "Why did you leave your home country?"

He took a breath and let it out again, seeming to decide how candid he would be.

"I went to find my father," he said finally. "My mother died giving birth to my sister when I was five, so my father raised me. When the unrest against the foreigners began, he knew there was no future for us in Ethiopia. He left me in the care of the Jesuits while he sailed back to Portugal to secure a new home for us. I never heard from him again. I was eleven."

Ruby and Isabella exchanged shocked glances.

"That is heartbreaking," said Ruby.

He shifted uncomfortably at their outpour of sentiment and said, "That was almost a lifetime ago, ladies, so do not be sorry for me. I was raised by the Jesuits after that, and they treated me kindly. They schooled me with the other children, and I took care of their donkeys and horses in return. Those skills have served me well."

"You said you went to find your father. When was that?" Isabella wanted to know.

"I was sixteen when I finally made my way to Portugal. It was a long, difficult trip. It took almost a year. But, when I found the village he was from, I was told he had never made it back all those years ago. So, I returned to the port city he would have arrived at. That was where I learned the ship he had taken was recorded as lost at sea."

"So what did you do?" asked Ruby.

"I stayed at the port and found work as a dock hand. There, I also found that to be a black man was a dangerous existence. I barely escaped abduction once."

Isabella covered her mouth with alarm. "Abduction!"

"In Portugal, I could have been sold into servitude, slavery actually, just for the color of my skin. So I left."

"To where, if you were so young and all alone?" asked Isabella.

Her sympathetic brown eyes were enough to entice him to continue explaining, "I was good with the horses working on the docks, and I could speak Arabic. A Spanish horse trader unwittingly came to my rescue. He was sailing to Libya to buy Arabian breeding horses and needed a translator. I got on the ship with him the next day."

Over the heads of his captivated audience, Bem noticed the other two ladies were approaching. Caterina called over, "Isabella! I saw you riding so beautifully. We were watching from the other side of the pen."

"Yes, Caterina, I am glad you came to watch. Bem was just telling us a story about horses. Did you want to finish your tale, Bem?"

Bem already regretted opening that complicated chapter of his past and felt fortunate for the well-timed interruption.

"Another time, perhaps," he said with a respectful bow, then clicked his tongue to signal his horse to move again.

Geoff followed behind him, leading the two Baric horses back to the stables. Having listened to Bem's narrative, the stable boy now had a new respect for the unfortunate African.

Isabella watched Bem go until he was lost to the shadows of the building. She then turned her attention to her friend again.

"I must tell you, Caterina, that my ride was nothing less than marvelous. I could have stayed on the horse all day!"

"Oh, Isabella, you must be exhausted." Caterina rambled on with concern, "Are you not overheated from the sun? Your hat nearly blew away. Look at you, dear Isabella—you are covered in dust. Lady Terese already said you may freshen up in her bathhouse. Perhaps Lady Ruby would like to come, too?" Caterina hooked her arm in Isabella's and began to lead her away.

Ruby patted her leggings with her gloved hands, and a cloud of dust rose around her. "A bath might feel good just now. I am quite hot. Do you want to join us, Resi?"

After her reviving nap, Resi was not in the mood to soak with the ladies. She had something else in mind.

"I need to talk to Geoff first. I will join you later."

Ruby nodded and ran to catch up with the ladies.

Resi went alone into the stables to find the stable boy. She returned a friendly smile from Bem as she approached the far stalls. He was humming a familiar tune while he rubbed down his horse. Geoff and Josip were tending to the two Baric horses next to Bem.

"Geoff, can I see you for a moment?" asked Resi.

The boy looked up at his mistress, suddenly worried about what new errand she might impose.

Resi motioned for him to follow her to the other side of the stables. She asked in a hushed voice, "Where can I find the kittens? Verica told me you hid the new litter before Alberto could take them."

Geoff looked over at Josip, who was watching them with curiosity, then turned back and whispered, "I put the kittens in a box in the barn. The mama cat can get to them, but they cannot crawl away. Should I show you where they are?"

It felt wrong to pull the boy from his chores. She had gotten him into trouble several times already for that in the past. "Can I find this box myself?" she asked.

"If you have been in the hay barn, then I can explain where to go."

She had, and he did.

Resi walked to the next building, went to the far corner where the extra tools were kept, and found the open box with the six sleeping kittens. The mother cat was nowhere to be seen. Resi picked one kitten up, and it squeaked a meow in protest.

"You are adorable, all of you," she told the newborn kittens before she picked up another. Then she heard voices coming from outside the plank walls. "I will take you somewhere cool and quiet where we can get to know each other." She tucked the two small bundles of fur into the crook of her arm and walked across the cobbled yard to the chapel.

Chapter 16

An angel guarded the chapel's small foyer. The smooth marble sculpture held a basin of holy water blessed by Father David. Resi touched her finger to the water and crossed herself while she clutched the squirming kittens.

The single door leading into the cheery sanctuary was closed. Resi did not expect to see anyone when she opened it. The other castle residents reserved their public prayers for Sunday Mass in the village church, the one place in Solgrad Resi had not yet visited.

The first bench, in front of the statue of Saint Mary, was Resi's favorite. The flattened cushion there marked her spot. Once seated, Resi put the helpless kittens down on her lap and gently examined them. One was black and white, and the other had brown flecks in its mostly white fur. She turned them over to check if she was holding boy or girl kittens. Both were girls. Alberto would drown them for sure, she thought.

A sudden sound in the front corner made her jump. A door creaked open, and a current of cold air stirred around her. Resi had never noticed that the dark paneling behind the altar hid a doorway, and she braced herself to meet whoever was coming out from behind it.

"Mauritius Baric, I almost went through the roof," she shouted before she realized she was yelling in the chapel and then lowered her voice. She clutched the frightened kittens.

Mauro was just as startled by her unexpected presence.

"Resi! What are you doing here?"

He sat down next to her on the bench and was immediately distracted by what she was holding. "Where did you get those?" he asked.

"One of the barn cats had babies," Resi replied, stroking the soft fluff-balls.

"I can see that, but why do you have them in the chapel?"

"Well, it was hot in the barn, and the chapel is the closest building that would be cool," she replied.

Mauro took one from her lap, and she nervously asked, "You aren't going to kill them, are you?"

He looked at her with surprise. "No, why would I do that?"

She eyed his kitten with maternal protectiveness. "Geoff said Alberto takes the kittens and drowns them because there are too many cats in the barn."

"Cats are useful. Alberto brings mother cats and their babies out among the cottages to keep the mice down. He would not kill them."

His smile comforted her, and Resi accepted his explanation as fact.

"Speaking of babies," she said, "I have been meaning to ask your permission for something but was too distracted with all the visitors."

"What do you need my permission for, Resi?" Mauro asked.

"Elizabeta had her baby," she said abruptly.

"So I heard."

"Well, we wanted to go visit her tomorrow—Ruby and the ladies. At the same time, Natalija can ask her mother if her younger sister might work in the kitchen until Danica is well again. Verica asked to go with her."

"That is a sound suggestion. Yes, you may all go."

Mauro thought for a moment how his wife would be escorted. "I will have Alberto hitch up the Carrera carriage. Six women are too many to ride comfortably in the wagon."

Resi had not expected it to be so complicated. The grand carriage driving through the streets of Solgrad would surely be a spectacle.

"It is only a few miles, Mauro. There is no need for a carriage."

"Will you walk then?"

She was about to say yes, but then he leaned over and firmly added, "You will not."

"I have an idea, Mauro. Ruby and Lady Isabella can ride on horseback, and Verica and Natalija can sit in the wagon bed. The maids do not mind. They think it is a treat. And Lady Caterina and I will sit with the driver."

Mauro considered her suggestion. "Is Lady Isabella up to it?"

Resi nodded. "Didn't you see her? She was riding by herself quite well."

"Riding in an enclosure is different from riding through the village streets with other horses and people around you," Mauro reminded her.

Resi would not be deterred. "It will take longer for Geoff to saddle her horse than for Lady Isabella to ride into the village. Please, Mauro."

He sighed. There was no reason to be against it, except for one. "Isabella cannot wear the riding breeches she had on today."

Resi raised her brows. "So you did see her riding?"

"I did not say otherwise," he defended himself. "I only watched as she was finishing her lesson."

"I will find her something more appropriate to ride in," Resi promised.

"Something that covers her completely," said Mauro.

"I know just what will fit her," Resi assured him.

"Very well. I will arrange the wagon and soldiers for you tomorrow afternoon. Will that be a good time to visit the Radic house?"

"No time is better or worse with a new baby. Did you know that Elizabeta had a baby girl?"

Mauro saw the worry in his wife's eyes. "I heard Radic is very happy and cannot wait to celebrate his new daughter. There is a big party planned for the baptism in another week. Everyone will go, including us." He had said the right thing to put her at ease again.

Mauro then stood up and held out one hand for her, cradling his fluffy baby cat against him. "Have the kittens cooled off enough? Shall we go now?"

Resi stood up with her own baby cat in hand and asked, "What is behind that paneled door?"

He cocked his head in surprise. "Have you never been in the crypt?"

"No, I had no idea the entrance was there. Is it big?"

"Come, I will take you down to see it." He reached out and said, "Let me have the other kitten."

She did as he asked but worried that Mauro would leave them on the floor. Instead, he tucked both deep into the opening of his doublet. Then he took her hand in his.

"What were you looking for in the crypt?" she asked as he opened the heavy door again.

"Answers," he said.

The torch he had left in its iron holder on the stone wall was still flickering. Mauro took it with his free hand, and they made their way into the earth below the sanctuary.

When the stairs ended, Resi saw that they were in a long passageway with large alcoves cut into the cavern walls. Marble and granite tombs neatly filled the spaces. It was eerily quiet.

Mauro walked past the first alcoves, moving dusty cobwebs from Resi's path. After a few more paces, he stopped in front of a small room and lit a second torch, illuminating the stone wall and the crypts there.

"Each Baron of Baric has his own tomb. This is where my father's family was laid to rest."

Resi stood beside Mauro and read at the names and dates engraved on the tarnished plaque.

Mauro pointed to his father's grave. "His four children and his two wives are entombed with him. This vault is complete," he explained.

They walked to the next alcove, where his grandfather Fredrik was interred with his wife, Anica. Mauro pointed out the two girl names engraved there and explained, "His twin daughters died with my grandmother in childbirth."

Mauro lit the torches along the dark passageway as they walked back in time to one more room. He quietly contemplated the names on his great-grandfather's inscription.

Resi waited for Mauro to explain this generation of Barics, but he didn't. She finally asked, "What kind of answers were you searching for, Mauro?"

He looked at her with a scowl of continued concentration. "The Barics have a particular name pattern. I found that we really only use the same dozen names over and over," he quietly said. "You can see some are biblical and others honored a favorite ancestor. The Empire requests that Venetian noblemen give their children Latin or Venetian names, but my family christened their sons with Croatian spellings of those names. I was the exception among the Baric men. My names are not here," he said.

Resi asked, "Who were you named for?"

"I was told I am named for my mother's relations and not any of my father's. My father conceded that much to her when I was born."

Resi took a torch and walked from tomb to tomb, reading all the names of the male forefathers and their children over the centuries. Each had second and third names as well. Here was another Matej; there a few Fredriks. Resi counted one Vladimir, one more Lorenc, two Jeronims, and a couple of Petars, along with several other repeating favorites.

"Who was Mauritius Radovan on your mother's side?" asked Resi when she met him back in Lorenc's alcove.

"I was named for each of my mother's grandfathers," he said.

"And will we name our first son after you, or after your Baric forefathers?"

He answered her with a stern seriousness, "My son will be given Baric names."

Resi reassured him, "Your mother must have loved her grandfathers if she named you after them. There is nothing wrong with that."

Mauro's expression showed he disagreed.

Resi fixated on the names again. The children's names on the tombstone— one girl and three boys—followed the pattern. Mateo's given name was written as the Croatian Matej. Her father-in-law's full name was Lorenc Jeronim Fredrik Baric. Resi reflected on a name for their baby and studied the girls' names, just in case.

Mauro broke the silence when he said, "Come, Resi, you are shivering from the cold down here. I have these warm kittens against me, you do not."

He offered his hand again, and they ascended the stairs, snuffing the torches as they went. The heavy panel creaked loudly again as Mauro shut the door against the blackness.

The whitewashed chapel seemed warm and inviting after the cold of the crypt. They sat down on the padded bench, and Mauro pulled the two sleeping fur balls from his leather doublet. He put the kittens back onto Resi's lap.

"May I tell you a story before we leave?" he asked out of the blue.

"Yes," she said with anticipation of what he might share.

He looked out to the statue of the Virgin Mary and seemed to hesitate under her watchful eyes. He finally began, "When I was a little boy, Idita would tell me a story each night. I still wonder if she can read since she never had a book with her. She knew many stories, though, and she would retell my favorites, word for word, whenever I asked her."

Resi smiled, thinking of a little Mauro lying in bed, listening to his nanny.

"Mateo and I shared a room. Ours was the blue room." He turned to her to ask, "Do you know why it is called the blue room?"

She stroked the kittens and answered, "Because the furniture is blue?"

He laughed. "Yes. Blue is the Toth banner color. My father wanted his boys to have a green room, the Baric color, but my mother ordered blue fabric for our coverlets and cushions."

"Was he angry at her for that?"

Mauro nodded. "He was angry at her for everything, and she at him." He did not linger on those thoughts but went on with his story.

"When Mateo was about eleven, he decided he was too grown up for Idita's stories." Mauro paused at the memory, then said, "One evening, when Mateo was off somewhere and I had been sent to bed, Idita sat across from me on his blue coverlet. She had just finished one of my favorite tales of knights and battles. The prince won the kingdom and became king, taking a princess as his bride, of course, because they had fallen in love."

Mauro stared at the altar and said, "I loved Idita as a boy, and that evening I asked her if she loved me. I can still see the look on her face, and I understand now why the question was difficult for her."

"What did she say?"

"She told me that love was something I would share with someone special, like a parent. She explained that one day I would find my own princess, marry her, and love her like my parents loved me. Idita gave me a tight squeeze and kissed me on my forehead goodnight after that, but she never answered my one question."

Resi took his hand in hers and said, "She answered it beautifully, Mauro."

When Mauro finally looked at his wife again, his eyes were full of doubt. "You don't understand, Resi. I was just a child, but her response changed my life in a regrettable way. I decided if what my parents shared was love, then I did not want it. If what regard they showed to me was truly love, then love was not like in the bedtime stories."

Mauro searched Resi's eyes to see if she understood, and then he told her, "I know it is just a word, Resi, but it is not one that I have used since. I did not want a marriage like my parents had. They were placed together, but they never grew together. They never loved each other." He touched Resi's cheek and smiled when he said, "But I love you, Resi, like the prince in those stories. I think I loved you from the day we were married in this little chapel. You put on a brave face that day, much braver than I would have after arriving in a foreign land and marrying a stranger on your second day here. I was very proud of you, and I thought you were the most interesting young woman I had ever met."

She laughed through her tears of joy. "Interesting, Mauro?"

He laughed, too. "Maybe that is not the best description, although it is true. I also thought you were so very pretty. I liked the way you dressed and the way you spoke. I liked your bright eyes and soft hair, your laugh and your shy smile. I thought I must be the luckiest man to have been given you as my wife. But I was afraid to love you."

Mauro caressed her cheek and tenderly wiped a tear away with his fingers. "Idita pointed out not too long ago something that I had not considered. She said I treated you like a precious gift, one that I put on a shelf to only admire. I think she was right about that. I should have tried harder to know you."

She stopped him. "It is alright, Mauro."

"No, Resi, it is not." He held her hands in his when he said, "We never had a courtship. I wish now that I had given you more time to know me before our first night together. It was not romantic, like in your poems. I wanted it to be better. I am sorry if our wedding felt more like duty than love."

Resi stared at her regretful husband, searching for the words to let him know he had nothing to worry about. "I think you have made up for our missing courtship, Mauro. You have made up for everything."

Mauro wanted to believe her. Through his wet lashes, he saw tears trickle down the corners of her mesmerizing eyes, and he ached to hold her.

"Do you love me, Resi?"

She wiped her eyes with the back of her hand. "This is all so unexpected, Mauro. Did I only imagine it, or did you say you love me?"

His shoulders slumped with humility. "I can command a hundred men with confidence, but something happens to me when I talk about love." Then Mauro took a breath and said, "I love you, Terese Helena Baric. I have wanted to tell you all of this for so long, and today I knew I must."

She wrapped her arms around him and promised, "And I love you, Mauritius Radovan Baric."

There, seated in front of his patron saint in the little sanctuary where he was born, Mauro understood his world had changed. She loved him, and he loved her.

Blinking back his tears, Mauro reached down to pick up the helpless kittens by their scruffs. Neither Mauro nor Resi had noticed they had slid onto the floor and were searching blindly for their mother.

Mauro put one baby cat gently into Resi's hands and held onto the other.

"Shall we go now, Resi? These little ones are hungry for their dinner, and I have a feeling that we are late for our own."

Chapter 17

It had been an eventful day, and the two Venetians retired to their chamber just after sunset. Natalija helped the ladies undress for bed.

Isabella was at their cluttered breakfast table, dabbing her hands with her favorite concoction, as she absently said, "It is a shame the baroness's brother will have two black eyes."

"It spoils his looks," Caterina replied. She was at the grooming table where Natalija silently brushed out the Venetian's long locks. "I wonder why Mauritius fought him. Did you hear the reason?"

"No, I never did," said Isabella, "and they seemed to have forgotten the reason themselves. The two were laughing on the terrace together after dinner. Oh, but you were not there, Caterina," Isabella said accusingly. "What were you doing in the garden?"

Her friend sat up straighter. "I went for a stroll, as I do every evening."

Isabella set her little pot of cream down and turned to her friend. "Were you unchaperoned with Cyro again?"

"He was in the garden, yes," replied Caterina.

"He always seems to turn up when you are alone. What did he want from you?"

The usually even-tempered lady did not mask her annoyance and snapped, "Why are you interrogating me like my mother? Cyro is a perfect gentleman in my company. He only wanted to ask what I had found to bring to my lesson tomorrow."

Isabella frowned with suspicion. "You have to bring something to the lesson? Why did you not tell me about that?"

Natalija was securing Caterina's sleeping cap in front of the looking glass, and Isabella could not see her friend make a sour face in the reflection.

"I thought I told you about Salar Nassim's request. He asked that I bring something of beauty each day."

Isabella was genuinely interested now. "What did you bring today?" she asked.

Caterina turned in her chair and pointed to the table where Isabella sat. "It is there, in the little snuff box."

Isabella opened it and took out the droopy flower. "This?"

"It was beautiful yesterday," maintained Caterina.

"Hmm. They are pretty along the path."

Isabella set the flower down and pulled out her handkerchief from her sleeve. She wiped the pink stain of the disintegrating petals from her fingers. A smile formed on her rouged lips as an idea crossed her mind. "And what will you bring tomorrow? More flowers?" Isabella asked.

"I am bringing an egg, there on the scarf," Caterina said from the grooming table.

Natalija had finished at the grooming table and was picking up the ladies' loose underskirts scattered around the room to put back into the wardrobe. She walked by the table to see what Lady Caterina had brought. She saw a silk scarf was piled like a nest, and an egg was indeed in the center of it.

Isabella picked it up. "This is just a hen's egg."

"Lady Terese gave it to me when it was still warm from the mother hen. It is like holding birth, Isabella."

"You will be lucky to birth something as small as this egg," Isabella said with a smirk.

Caterina held her head high when she declared, "You do not understand beauty."

Isabella contemplated the little oval marvel and confided, "Your admirer Cyro seems to think I do. I had a little chat with him today. He says I have talent and thinks I should be a painter."

"A painter! Why would he suggest something like that? I do wonder, Isabella . . . do you think Cyro is truly, well, sane? He says some outrageous things."

"Men always do," replied Isabella with a casual wave of her hand. "I thought he was an odd character at first, but he is growing on me. When he sat with me for tea, he suggested I paint under a man's name."

Caterina leaned in as if sharing a secret. "See, that is what I mean. Is that even truly done?"

"That is what I asked, and he assured me it is, often. What I found charming was that Cyro said he will be my first customer."

Caterina's eyes widened with surprise. "How could he seriously suggest something like that—being your patron? His speech may be convincing and his demeanor polite, but then when I look at him—well, I know he is probably making it all up, like some theater actor."

Isabella serenely twirled the little flower in front of her and declared, "Theater or not, talking to Cyro has given me hope. When I get back to Venice, I will buy some paints and canvas and give it a try."

"Will they let you paint in the nunnery? You might not even be returning to Venice," Caterina reminded her.

Isabella dropped the crumbling flower. "Well, if the priest is convinced that my paintings are divinely inspired, he will put a man's name on my work and sell it to profit the Church. As long as I can paint and sketch like a man, it is all the same to me," she said dreamily.

Caterina looked at her friend with pity. "And what about riding like a man, Isabella? You seemed to enjoy your new hobby today."

"I did immensely, which is why I will use my freedom while I have it. It will take weeks for the escorts to return from Venice. You should enjoy this holiday, too."

Natalija had finished tidying up and interrupted the momentary lull in the conversation. "Will that be all, my ladies?"

Isabella looked up from her contemplation. "Yes, Natalija, that will be all. In the morning, though, I will need a bouquet of flowers—some of these pink ones, some yellow, and something red." Isabella then asked no one in particular, "Daisies have black centers, do they not? And make sure the flowers have lots of pollen," she added to Natalija.

Natalija repeated, "Pink, yellow, red, daisies, and lots of pollen. Yes, my lady. I will bring what you require in the morning."

The young maid wasn't sure what her new mistress meant by all of that, but she would ask Krsto to help her find the pollen. She left the room and climbed the stairs to her shared chamber without remembering that Lady Caterina's envelope given to her earlier was still in her apron pocket.

When the servant had gone, Caterina said to Isabella, "That was an odd request you made."

"Indeed, an odd idea has come to me, Caterina. I have decided that you may have your lesson without me tomorrow. I have something important I need to do."

Isabella stood up and took off her dressing robe. She draped it across the bed and climbed in under the covers.

Caterina got into bed next to Isabella and blew out the last candle, remembering to tell her friend, "My lesson will be an hour later tomorrow. Salar Nassim is going with Mauritius to his battlefields in the morning. Maybe you will be done by then and want to join me."

"No, I expect I will be occupied until lunch with what I have to do," Isabella said through a yawn. "Good night, Caterina."

"Good night, Isabella."

Isabella looked up at the moonlit ceiling and thought about what she would create in the morning. She had visited many museums and had seen that artists did not always use oil paints. Her planned experiment would surely stain her manicured fingers, but there was no one here who would be judging her hands. With those images floating through her mind, she drowsily curled up next to Caterina and fell into a peaceful sleep.

Chapter 18

Mauro brought Jero to the Keep for an early meal before their sparring practice. At the fire, the two loaded their platters with generous portions of roasted ham, boiled apples, and toasted black bread. While searching the room for a seat, Mauro was disappointed when he saw the divide still lingered between his guests and his loyal men in the dining room. The mercenaries were sitting well apart from Mauro's officers and guardsmen. The baron could not order his soldiers to get along with the visitors, but he would show them how.

Mauro cheerfully greeted his men as he walked past each table before setting his plate on the table in front of Patrik. His brother-in-law's face looked worse than it did last night at dinner. The swelling was down, but shades of blue and purple encircled his eyes, and the bridge of his nose was puffy and bruised.

Mauro was about to apologize once again for his temper, but Patrik stopped him and said, "I don't know what magical pain potion your healing woman left for me, but I feel better than I look. I can see, and I can breathe. As long as I can hold a sword, I will be fine."

Jero came to the table, balancing his platter and two slopping mugs of ale Drazen had poured for them. He sat down on the empty stool next to Patrik.

Surprised, but honored, to see the baron and his steward at their table, the sellswords greeted them in good humor despite the ongoing chilly reception from the rest of the room. Then they continued to feast on their breakfasts.

"What happened to your man Daniel, Mauro?" asked Patrik as he took a bite from his platter. Although it hurt his face, Patrik managed to smile when he turned and asked, "Are we to be partners, Jero?"

Jero nodded his reply with a full mouth.

Mauro explained as he picked up his knife to eat, "Daniel will be nearby to partner with if Jero is too good for you, Patrik. You can decide as you practice."

Patrik chuckled at his brother-in-law's obvious taunt and gave Jero's shoulder a quick pat. "I will try to keep up with your steward."

Mauro told Patrik, "I wanted to let you know that we are delivering some cargo to your father's ship at the end of the week. My captain would not object if you wanted to sail with my crew. I know you have all of your equipment and horses, but at least you could go visit your brother and give him any news before coming back." He glanced around the table at the other four. "All of you are welcome."

Patrik looked hopefully at his companions and said, "That is an interesting offer, Mauro. How long does your crew sail to meet the Kokkinos ship?"

"It takes five days, sometimes a week round trip, depending on the winds. The ships meet just outside Venetian waters."

The mercenaries discussed the proposal in low voices while Mauro and Jero hungrily ate.

"Your offer is generous, Mauro, but a second week's delay will not fit into our plans," relayed Patrik. "We would be grateful, however, if your ship's captain could give our letters to my brother. That way, our messages to our families will arrive more quickly."

"That is easily done," agreed Mauro. "You should come to the docks with me on Friday and tour my ship and salt flats—all of you. You can bring your correspondence then."

Salar Nassim answered for the group this time, "We will gladly come to see your ship. Thank you for the opportunity, Lord Baric."

Mauro saw the other guests nod their agreement. "Excellent," he said and stood up to leave. The sun was shining into the tall windows. "Shall we ride out?"

~*~

The training that day was focused on blade-handling skills. The newest recruits would use blunt swords the baron provided. Hay-stuffed dummies had been assembled to help keep the less-experienced fighters from hurting anyone. Seasoned soldiers would practice against each other with their battle swords. Mauro assigned the scouts and soldiers to each of his officers and then took a small group of his recruits to work with individually.

Bem and Cyro had little formal fencing instruction and fought mostly by instinct. They joined Mauro's practice group to watch how the well-trained baron taught his soldiers to wield a sword defensively.

Salar Nassim took the opportunity to help Soren with his blade work. The Dane had been primarily a pikeman in battle and could still improve on his swordplay.

Patrik and Jero followed Salar Nassim and Soren, but they practiced separately, one-on-one. Their pairing was a convenient arrangement that would allow for a private conversation, and it seemed each was interested in gaining information from the other.

The two were using sharpened blades, which could open real wounds. To protect themselves from a slip-up, they wore leather jackets with gloves to their elbows. Patrik wore riding boots that covered his legs up to his thighs. Jero had on thick leather breeches and knee boots to guard against errant swipes of the blade.

They touched sword tips and began a slow dance of smooth swings and blocked clashes. Jero was already sweating in the morning sun as their deliberate movements became more energetic. Patrik was a strong adversary despite his shorter stature and recent injury.

"Your technique is good. Who taught you?" Patrik asked as the steel clashed.

"Mauro's father, the late Lord Baric, worked with me," Jero explained, stepping side to side with his partner.

"Did you ever go into battle with the baron's army?"

Jero fought off Patrik's advance, remembering the footing he had been taught. He took a moment to catch his breath, then answered, "No, I never did. I was brought here as a servant, not as a soldier. I was Lord Lorenc's valet when he died."

"Soldiers are just as much servants to the man in charge as a valet is," Patrik reflected.

"I think a good valet is harder to find than a good soldier, and the baron did not want to risk losing me."

Their swords met again, but Patrik's quicker forward jabs had Jero cornered against a tree. Face-to-face, he told Jero, "My sister and Ruby said good things about you, but they did not tell me you were funny."

Patrik bowed to the valet and claimed that round. They touched blades to begin the next.

Jero moved in a more relaxed manner now, having gotten used to Patrik's style and technique. Salar Nassim and Soren were clashing swords nearby, but out of earshot, so he dared broach the subject he was most interested in.

"I suppose you have known Ruby a long time, Patrik. The baroness said you grew up together."

Between swings, Patrik explained, "Indeed. Our families have been close my whole life. Her father took us in while mine was, um, away. I'd not seen Ruby since leaving Thessaloniki, but I still care a great deal about her, Jero. I would do anything to protect her." Stopping momentarily, he added, "I love Ruby like a sister."

"Like a sister," Jero repeated, winded from the swift movement. "That is good. You have brotherly concerns for her well-being. That is very honorable."

Patrik set his sword down and reached for his water pouch. He took a drink and passed it to Jero, studying him critically.

"Tell me, Jero. Would you do anything to protect Ruby?"

Jero took a long gulp, then said, "I never had a sister, but I suppose I would."

"That's not what I mean. Would you protect her like the woman you loved?"

Jero froze at the seriousness of Patrik's tone.

"I am not in competition with you, Jero. If I were, you would have felt this blade already. You like her, though, don't you?" His puffy eyes and purple bruises made Patrik's expression impossible to read.

Jero cautiously answered, "I do like her. I like her very much."

Satisfied, Patrik picked up his sword again, and Jero followed his lead. The men stood close with their blade tips touching to begin the next round, and Patrik continued to chatter.

"You probably find Ruby different from your Venetian women here. She has many hidden qualities. If you have gotten to know her, Jero, then you understand what I am referring to."

Jero's cheeks turned scarlet, and it wasn't because of the heat.

"Are you blushing, Jero?" asked Patrik with rude laughter. "Her feminine attributes are not the qualities I was talking about. Perhaps you have been sheltered too long behind your Baric walls."

"I have been out of the walls a few times," Jero said defensively. He swung his sword at Patrik for emphasis, but his opponent was ready for him.

"Let's hear it, Jero. Where have you gone?" Patrik would get to the heart of the man's history now.

Jero lunged and jabbed and recounted, "Hungary was my first trip. I was still sixteen. I spent two months in Florence after that. I also went to Venice a few times, and here and there through Croatia by road."

"That is a fair amount of traveling for a young man."

They circled each other.

"Is Florence worth the trip? I have never been there," said Patrik breathlessly.

They clashed steel.

"Florence was my favorite place. The city is grandly built. It is a marvel to walk through its streets."

The sun was warm, and so were their jackets. Beads of sweat trickled down their temples under their wide-brimmed hats, the only shade they enjoyed.

Jero advanced again. "I have always lived near the sea, but I like the countryside of Tuscany. Lord Lorenc did not find it as agreeable. He thought the company he kept in Florence was too academic."

"Was he not a learned man, the old Baron Baric?" Patrik asked as the two walked in a circle, panting. He swung his blade at Jero.

Jero retaliated as he answered the Greek's question, "Lord Lorenc was educated. Still, the baron preferred the company of merchants and politicians over scholars and clergymen. He became bored."

"He must have liked Venice, then. It is a lively city, to be sure. I was there once, for Carnival. The outrageous people never slept."

After that brisk round, they lowered their tired arms. Jero wiped his brow and said, "I was in Venice one Carnival season, too, although I remember little of it. I was only eighteen—a good age to be initiated into something like that."

Patrik noticed a revealing smile crossed Jero's lips before he took another drink from the pouch, and the sellsword asked, "Then you aren't a virgin?"

Jero coughed and choked on his water. "What?"

Patrik hit him between the shoulders to clear his sputtering.

When Jero was no longer red in the face, Patrik explained, "You are a discreet man of manners, Jero, so you might find me overly frank. I happen to believe a man of a certain age should know a few things before he considers marriage. I was worried you might not have had the opportunity, is all."

"Soldiers might be forthright with such questions, but I am not used to discussing my, um . . . experiences." Jero straightened his hat and handed the water back to Patrik.

The sellsword reflected, "I've never had a conversation with a house servant, so you'll have to forgive me for that. Military men have this relentless need to make sure those fighting with them have been acquainted with the female anatomy before they die. I am only curious whether you were initiated the same way in Venice."

Patrik took a long drink but did not seem to be in a hurry to pick up his sword again.

Jero was at ease with his partner now. The Baric soldiers had worried over the same fate for him, and it no longer seemed shameful after hearing Patrik's reasoning. Jero found himself admitting, "I was not initiated in Venice, but in Hungary."

Patrik sat up a little taller. "Hungary? I knew there was a story. Let's hear it!"

Trusting that Patrik would not scoff at the memory, Jero divulged, "The first time I traveled with the Baric soldiers, they would not let me go to my chamber until they were sure I had gone to a room with a woman."

Patrik chuckled in solidarity, not ridicule. "They never worry that the young man doesn't know what to do once he is alone with her."

"Well, in my case, the Baric soldiers felt obligated to pick a woman they thought would help a young man out. She was older, that I remember, but soft and pretty. They did later ask," Jero said modestly.

"And?" Patrik asked.

Jero stood up. "That is my story."

Patrik grinned at Jero's restraint. "House servants are a different breed from soldiers, to be sure. Don't you have any torrid escapades you'd like to brag about? I like to be amused while I am fighting."

Jero was not corruptible. He shrugged and said, "I do not know what would especially amuse you."

"Ha! Well played! You are a discreet and considerate man, Jero, and I think you would be an excellent choice for Ruby. I give you my blessing."

"Now *you* are amusing, Patrik." Jero vigorously shook his head when he said, "I do not plan to marry Ruby. She is a fine woman and I admire her greatly, but we could never be matched together."

"Why not, Jero? You love her. Ruby will tell her father that she loves you. Angelos Spiros trusts my opinion, and I will tell him that I approve. He will have to allow it," Patrik concluded.

Jero stared blankly, stunned that Patrik had given his permission to pursue the woman of his dreams. How could he not ask for Ruby's hand?

Jero talked himself out of it. "It is not that simple," he said.

"It is that simple, Jero. She loves you, you love her, her father says yes, and you can marry."

Patrik thought Jero should be happy with this news, but the servant still had an odd expression on his face. "What is wrong, Jero?"

Jero reached into his pocket, took out a folded kerchief, and said, "Your nose is bleeding onto your shirt, Patrik. Here, you can use this."

Patrik had met few men with clean handkerchiefs in their pockets. He accepted it gladly and dabbed his dripping nostril.

"Well, Jero," Patrik said as the warm blood soaked the white linen, "you've convinced me you are perfect."

~*~

Salar Nassim and Soren took Jero into their little group while Patrik sat against a tree on the edge of the woods to nurse his nosebleed. With the Persian's encouragement, Jero continued to improve quickly. Like Patrik, they were excellent fighters. Jero did not win a duel, but he held his own and came away unscathed. The mercenaries worked with him for another hour until Mauro called it a day for the fencing practice.

Tired and sweating, the fifty-odd men noisily made their way back from the outlying fields to the castle on foot and horseback, laughing and talking about their successes and failures that morning. At least no one was hurt.

Jero felt especially tall in the saddle on the powerful warhorse after the compliments Salar Nassim and Patrik had given him about his swordplay. They insisted that he would have made an excellent warrior, had Jero's lot in life been different.

The baron's steward had never done anything else but serve at Baric Castle. He grew up alongside Mauro and Mateo and played with the Baric sons at their whim, but he was given none of the young lords' privileges. At the same time, Jero knew all the servants' and soldiers' children by name, but he did not play with them in front of their cottages. Jero existed between the two worlds, and he had always yearned for more.

When Jero was little, he could not understand that he was different. As a boy, Jero thought Mauro had a job at the castle, like Jero. Mauro worked to be a future lord, and his mornings were spent learning with tutors. When Mauro wanted to get away from his books, he called on Jero to explore with him. Jero was supposed to do whatever the boys asked.

The first time he could remember leaving the castle walls was when Mateo showed him and Mauro the secret tunnel that led out the old well and into the eastern woods. That had been the spark that flamed Mauro and Jero's future clandestine adventures together. Mauro had wanted to know all of the secret places in the castle. Jero remembered Mauro told him that it would be Mateo's castle one day, and Mauro would have to build his own castle, so he needed to learn every part of it. Jero had asked if he, too, would need a castle when he grew to be a man. Mauro had said he didn't think so because Jero did not have a father who lived in one already. Jero had accepted that as fact. He had accepted everything Mauro said.

Mauro rode up alongside Bacchus before they came to the castle wall and jolted Jero from his contemplation.

"Patrik told me you fought well, Jero. He said you bloodied his nose again."

Jero recovered quickly from his daydream and laughed. "The man bloodied his own nose, probably from talking so much."

"The Kokkinos men are indeed chattier than the Barics. Patrik's company takes some getting used to, I think. But tell me, did you enjoy your time on the field?"

Mauro held Jero's stare as they rode through the gate, side by side.

"Very much so. Patrik was actually a good partner, and I learned a lot. Thank you, Mauro."

"I am going to have Davor and Krsto join us next week, and the other servants will be on a schedule after them. You will be given time to practice again too, Jero." Mauro gave him an encouraging smile when he said, "There are no conflicts now, but war can start again at any time. I want to be sure that you can protect yourself and those you love. It has been my duty, and it will be yours."

Chapter 19

Isabella sat on the bed and leaned over Caterina's sprawled figure. She patted her back and continued to try to soothe her. "Stop crying, Caterina. You cannot bring him back. He is lost to you now. It is for the best."

Hidden in her billowing gown, Caterina covered her head with her lacy sleeves. She had not stopped wailing since reading the letter that Natalija had brought at breakfast.

As the bearer of bad news, the young maid felt it was somehow her fault that Lady Caterina's lover had moved on, and Isabella had to send her away when she began crying, as well.

Isabella read the letter that Caterina had dropped on the floor when the dejected romantic flung herself onto her bed in her misery. It was two pages of scrolled excuses why her lover could no longer be with her. It seemed Paolo was taking a post in Verona, but the letter did not say with whom or for how long. Isabella was sure Roberto Carrera had made those arrangements for the handsome officer to keep him away from his daughter.

Paolo spoke of his love for Caterina, but unconvincingly, Isabella thought. He would miss her bright smile and her doe eyes, he wrote. Isabella read between the lines that he would miss the ample dowry he expected to gain, the promotion to more stature, and the respect that his new father-in-law would provide after marrying a Carrera daughter. The suave Paolo had tried his luck, licked his wounds, and had moved on to greener pastures in Verona.

After a while, Natalija came to the door again and stood quietly at the entrance.

"Yes?" Isabella said, looking up from her project she had spread over the window ledge.

"The foreign gentleman is waiting downstairs for Lady Caterina's lesson. What should I tell him, madam?"

Caterina moaned through her pillows, "Tell him that I am ill, Natalija. Tell him that I shall never recover and will probably die of this broken heart."

Natalija looked to Lady Isabella for instructions, but the sensible Venetian merely shook her head. "Paolo has made his choice, and you have had a good cry over it, Caterina. Now go play your game," Isabella said.

Caterina finally sat up. She wiped her wet nose and whimpered, "How could he say it was not destined? How could he say he would love me forever and then not fight for my hand? We made such a wonderful match."

"Yes, my dear Cat, you made a handsome pair, but someone else will come along and steal your heart again. Dry your tears, sweet Caterina. Salar Nassim is waiting for you."

Isabella had run out of charity for her overly dramatic friend. She had wanted to mix her colors in peace this morning.

She turned back to the maid and instructed, "Tell Salar Nassim that she will be down shortly. And then bring me some tea, if you will. I will also need four cups."

"Yes, my lady," the maid answered quietly, then curtsied before she hurried out the door to deliver the message and bring the tea.

Isabella went to her friend on the bed once again. "You have not spoken of Paolo since we returned from the seaside, Caterina. You are not troubled that you have lost your true love. You are troubled that you have lost the idea of true love."

Caterina took a deep, sobbing breath and nodded.

"We will find love again, both of us," Isabella promised her. "Maybe not this year or next, but we will wait for it. And in the meantime, we will have our fun. Now, dry your eyes and think about your cards for an hour. It will do you good."

"Oh Isabella, I am truly sad over Paolo. Of all people, you should understand that. He was so handsome and charming, and he cherished me. But maybe I was wrong. Maybe *he* was wrong. I will never know for sure."

Caterina blew her nose in her damp handkerchief and asked, "Do I look a mess?"

"You do, Caterina," Isabella said with a soft laugh. "But I think your Persian partner will not judge you for that. Have a sip of wine and take your little egg of beauty to him. He will probably take time off your hour for being late, so do not keep him waiting too long."

Caterina had not thought of that. Salar Nassim said he would give her one hour each day, and Isabella was surely right that he had begun counting the time already. She checked her hair in the looking glass, made the adjustments to the pins, and then slipped on her shoes and hurried out of the room.

Isabella went back to the window and the flowers she had set out on its ledge. She had organized the petals by color and thought she had most of the shades she would need. Unfortunately, she only had one stem of blue and would have to think of something to paint that did not require much of that.

Natalija came into the room and set the tea tray with the four cups down on the center table. "Shall I pour all four?" she asked.

"No, I do not want any. You may leave them on the table," Isabella told her distractedly.

The maid did not ask if she required anything else and left the room before being told to bring more unwanted things.

When she was alone again, Isabella took the cups and saucers and set to work trying to extract the colors from the petals using the hot tea water. After much trial and error, Isabella had a mess of crushed flowers and a colorfully stained apron. She also had four cups filled with deep tints to use on her paper.

Isabella looked out the window at the bright blue sky with the green treetops waving gently in the Adriatic breeze. She would not be able to paint the sky, she thought. Or could she?

Their room had one window to the east that overlooked the mountain. Isabella pushed the smaller table in front of that window and set up her painting station there. She put saucers over the tint-filled cups, satisfied with her final decision. She had never been awake to see dawn breaking here, and she hoped it would be inspiring.

~ * ~

Brigita had brought Salar Nassim a pot of tea. Caterina saw him set his cup down when she came into the great hall. He was alone today, waiting at their usual table by the window where they could be seen, but remain unchaperoned.

He stood up when he heard the clicking of her heels on the marble floor, and he waited for her to cross the open room to his side. She offered her hand in greeting, and Salar Nassim bowed over it, brushing his lip to her skin. He looked up and studied her tear-stained face but asked for no explanation.

Caterina thought she had her emotions under control, but a fresh tear slid down the corner of one eye. She wiped it inconspicuously away with her knuckle and caught the musky smell of the scented oil her teacher had used to groom his glossy beard. It lingered on her hand from his kiss—fresh and masculine. It was different from Paolo's scent, but it reminded her of him just the same.

She sniffled. "Salar Nassim, I am afraid I will not be able to play cards today. I have taken ill, but I wanted to tell you in person. Tomorrow, I will be better."

Her sad look reminded him of the girl he had left at home. He wanted to solve her troubles as any father would. "Perhaps you should tell me what your illness is. I may know a remedy," he replied soothingly.

She plopped down on her usual chair, not caring to smooth her pink satin skirt that bunched and crinkled in her lap.

Salar Nassim sat down across from her without acknowledging her distress. He simply took out his cards and shuffled them methodically over and over. The lady would not have stayed if she did not want to talk about it. She would speak when she was ready, and he had time to wait for her to calm her thoughts.

He dealt the cards as he would for a game, flipped each of the four hands over to see what they would have played, then collected the cards and reshuffled them.

Caterina watched the cards dealt and shuffled as though in a trance. After a few rounds, she said, "I received a letter from my . . . Paolo. He says we may never meet again. He is going away, leaving Venice, probably forever. I love him."

Salar Nassim continued to shuffle and deal as though she had just spoken of the weather.

"Of course, it is love," he told her at last. "You are like a beautiful magnet, and love cannot help but be attracted to you."

He stopped shuffling and put the deck down when she finally looked up at him. Her eyes were dry again. "Do not be discouraged. Love will find you again," he concluded.

"I do not want to be in love again. It is too painful."

He told her, "I am afraid you do not have a choice, Lady Caterina. Love will turn up in a place you may not expect, so there is no shutting it out."

"What makes you such an expert, Salar Nassim? Because you have married twice? Is that what qualifies you?"

Salar Nassim understood she was angry, but he knew it was not directed at him. "I did not go looking for a second wife, but I have stayed true to both."

"How can you love two wives at once?"

Her voice resonated with doubt. Many had asked this question before, and Salar Nassim had an easy answer ready. "In your land, I might have a wife and a mistress. My religion allows me to take the mistress as a wife. Her life is better as a married woman, whereas a mistress's fate is not."

Caterina asserted, "You have not answered my question. Do you love both wives equally?"

"Well, to understand my answer, you need a little more experience with love."

She furrowed her brow at his patronizing. "Try me."

"I would tell you that I love both equally, but there are different kinds of love. Sometimes love begins as a romantic feeling, then fades to a platonic one.

But it is still love. That is my love for Hafza. And if God wills it, the romantic love stays forever. Emine has proved that to me."

Caterina pondered his words and said, "I have had a question in my mind for a while now. Perhaps you can answer it."

"Ask, and I will try."

She sat up tall with determination and asked, "Why is it that a man gets to decide how many women he can love at once, and a woman cannot?"

The Persian held her glare. "Are we speaking of love or lust now?"

Caterina shifted in her chair. "I am asking about love and marriage. Why did you stop at two wives? Why not four or six, if it is allowed?"

He answered, "Marriage brings a responsibility. I do not want to watch over six wives, or even three. Love is different, though. A woman I want to be with does not have to become my wife. Sometimes a fleeting romance is preferable."

"Love is skewed toward men," she snapped.

"You are right, Lady Caterina. Men have chosen the rules of love and marriage, but do not let that stop you. My first wife, Hafza, married me by choice when she was very young. I was young, too. We knew nothing about lasting love. Our passion faded when our daughter arrived. Hafza is a good mother and a kind, gentle woman. I love her because of that."

"Did you search for a new wife because the passion was gone with Hafza?"

"I was already a sellsword then and had to leave one family behind. I was not thinking of making a second family wait for me," he explained. "It happened that I did fall in love with Emine, and she with me. Emine chose to marry me despite being the second wife. Hafza is a part of my past that I must keep, but Emine is the woman I go home to for almost ten years now."

Salar Nassim's story had struck a nerve, and Caterina asked, "How can they get along together, knowing that?"

"They have never met," he told her bluntly. "Before Emine married me, she made me promise to let her live a separate life back in Athens. I have kept that promise, and that is where she is now. Hafza is content in Rhodes, where her family comes from. Her parents live with her and our daughter."

Caterina should have expected him to have children, but it still surprised her. "How old is your daughter?"

The guilt he felt thinking about her caught him off guard. He crossed his hands on the table and held his emotions in check.

"Shirin is sixteen now. I was only nineteen when she was born, and she is the true love of my life."

"She will be of marrying age soon," Caterina reasoned. "Will you tell Shirin the same things you are telling me? Will you tell her to wait, to believe that love will find her? Or will you arrange a marriage for her, as all fathers do in the end?"

Caterina did not hide her bitterness, and the Persian felt it.

"That is a dilemma I have yet to face. I must keep her future interests in mind, not just her heart. I believe your father has done the same for you."

Before she could protest again, he added, "If Shirin does tell me she loves someone already, I will consider her wishes and choose the husband she wants. But one must try to marry well, Lady Caterina."

Caterina noticed for the first time that his gold earrings had tiny jewels in them. Although the blue silk shirt showing above his mended red jacket was faded, both were well-tailored, with finely embroidered details.

"Did you marry well, Salar Nassim?" It was an accusation.

Salar Nassim smiled for the first time since Caterina had sat down. His whole life had been about finding ways to obtain more money, but that was before he had met Emine.

"If I had Emine's money, I would not be selling my sword all over Europe. She was a widow with her own means, and I a struggling sellsword, but she chose me anyway. In that sense, I married well."

Caterina studied the man in front of her, so calm with his hands perched on his deck of cards. The two intricate rings on his fingers distracted her now. Were they for each of his marriages?

She smiled warmly again and said, "I do not know why your story of two wives who have never met has lifted my spirits, but it has."

"If my pitiful love story has done that, then I am happy to be pathetic for you."

She finally laughed. "You are not pathetic, but I thank you. Do we have time to play a game still?"

He looked out the window. The servants had finished setting the table under the awning for the ladies of the house.

"I am afraid we have used all our time. We can play again tomorrow if you like." He stood up and pocketed his cards in his belted jacket.

"Wait, I have not shown you what I brought for you today."

Caterina carefully pulled out the silky bundle from her dress pocket. She set the padded nest with its fragile contents on the table. "It is an egg," she announced.

Salar Nassim regarded the scarf's contents. "This is an interesting choice, Lady Caterina. Who gave this to you?" he asked, still the teacher.

"The baroness did. She had collected several from the henhouse. She goes herself because she likes the birds. She let me have this one while it was warm from the mother sitting on it," Caterina proudly explained.

He held the egg between his thumb and first finger, moving it in the light from the window.

"Simple and perfectly made by its mother. It is a thing of beauty. Thank you for bringing it." He handed it back to her. "Life gives us life, Lady Caterina. You should take this to the kitchen so it will not go to waste."

When she looked at him blankly, he chuckled and said, "Or have your lady's maid return it for you."

She stood up and smoothed her hopelessly wrinkled skirt. "You look at me as though I would not know where the kitchen is. I have been there, so I can find my way."

"I am certain you can." Salar Nassim bowed his goodbye and left out the terrace door.

~*~

Caterina walked down the foyer and looked for the kitchen door again. She opened it to the surprised looks of the busy kitchen staff.

Nela came over to her and asked, "Can I be of service, Lady Caterina?"

Caterina smiled confidently and held out the egg. "This is from the basket the baroness collected yesterday. I wanted to return it."

Nela fought the urge to laugh when she took the egg from Caterina's open hand.

"Thank you, my lady," Cook said. "We will put it with the others."

Ivana hurried to Nela's side and took the egg to the pantry.

Caterina was pleased, and she would tell Salar Nassim so at dinner. When Caterina turned to leave, she noticed Aron in the corner. Seeing him made her think that she wanted to wash her tear-stained face before lunch.

She came over to where he was sitting and said, "I will need some warm water brought to my room shortly."

Aron scrambled to stand up properly for the lady. The boy had been holding an unusual gray ball. Aron carefully set the strange object on the window ledge near where he had crouched against the wall and picked up his pail. He was about to leave with it through the servants' door when Caterina stopped him.

"Show me what you have there, boy," she said.

"I, um," Aron began. He was scared to talk directly to the fancy lady visitor. He set his bucket down again and picked up the little thing to give to her.

Nela noticed the two standing together, and she walked over to Caterina to see what trouble Aron had caused.

"Dear God," she whispered to herself. He was handing the lady a hornet's nest. Nela hoped nothing would begin to fly out.

Caterina marveled at it. "It is almost like holding air. What is it?"

"It is a nest, madam. My brother Josip took it from the barn and let me have it. The wasps eat the wood and use their spit to make it. It was filled last year, but the wasps have all gone."

"Can I keep this until tomorrow?" Caterina asked him sweetly.

Nela saw the hesitation on Aron's face. His arms were outstretched, ready to take his new treasure back. Cook urgently nodded her head *yes* behind Caterina, and Aron moved his head in the same direction. Caterina was thrilled that he had agreed.

"I will be very careful with it," she promised. "I will take it up to my room now, and you can bring the water." The Venetian had found her item of beauty for tomorrow. She walked back out the door she had come through.

Aron stood stunned at how he had just lost his little prize only a few minutes after he had gotten it from Josip.

"She will break it," he told Nela sadly.

Nela leaned down and said, "The lady will not break it. Hurry now and bring her a pail of warm water and you can look around the room for yourself. She will have put it nicely away. When you come back, you can have your lunch."

She handed him an almond-stuffed date from the dessert tray she had arranged for the ladies' table. "Take this to keep you going until then."

He popped the plump treat into his mouth, grinning, and then rushed out the door.

Chapter 20

The Dane walked his horse over to where the wagon was being hitched for the ride into the village. The ladies had not yet arrived, and Bem was still in the stables, readying his horse for Isabella. Daniel and Teodor were lining up two horses to the wagon's halter. A few soldiers were crossing the courtyard for the change of guard duty. They slowed when they heard Eduard's stern tone.

"Can I be of assistance?" Eduard asked Soren.

"I need no assistance," Soren told him, not wanting to talk to the gruff soldier.

"Then you should wait someplace else," Eduard said too harshly.

"I am going with Natalija," Soren informed him.

Eduard pressed the issue. "Did the baron give you permission to chaperone her?"

"I am not chaperoning her. She invited me," Soren said. "It is not your business what she does when she leaves here."

Eduard crossed his thick arms over his barrel chest and declared, "It is my business. The castle women are under my protection, and that includes protecting them from you."

"Do I look like I would harm her?" asked Soren, moving directly in front of his accuser.

"You sellswords are all known to be rapists and thieves," Eduard snarled. "I would not trust you within twenty feet of her." He slid his hand to his sword handle at his waist.

Soren had not brought his sword with him; there would be no reason to wear it going the few miles to the village. He regretted it now.

Daniel and Teodor had overheard the conversation and went to stand loyally by Eduard's side.

Soren was outnumbered. Frustrated, he tied his horse to a nearby post and stomped off to the Keep.

Salar Nassim was coming down the winding stairwell and heard Soren cursing in Danish as he came up. With outstretched arms, Salar Nassim blocked his passage.

"I thought you were going to the village," Salar Nassim said with calm restraint.

"I need my sword." Soren shouldered past him, up to the second floor.

Salar Nassim watched him go and then followed him back to their room.

Soren belted on his weapon and added his dagger that was on the bedside table.

Salar Nassim knew that blank look of hate and acted swiftly to stop his friend. "Soren, look at me," Salar Nassim called out.

When Soren began to leave again, Salar Nassim grabbed his friend's arm with force to stop him.

"Talk to me, Soren. What is going on?"

"That bastard Eduard called me a rapist. I am not a rapist! After I cut off his tiny balls, he won't get the chance either."

"The Baric captain is an idiot! He was just trying to get under your skin. We will be leaving soon. Why do you care what he thinks?"

Soren jerked his arm to free himself from his commander's hold and growled, "I care what she thinks."

Salar Nassim understood the complication now. Soren was out to prove something, if only to himself.

"Listen, Soren. She is just a servant girl. You don't have to see her again. Come, let's go for a ride! We will go to the sparring fields. You can cut the balls off the stuffed soldiers there."

"And their fucking heads, too."

Salar Nassim gave Soren a sideways glance and belted on his own sword. Their stay was becoming risky—first Patrik, now Soren. They would be on their way sooner than the end of the week, Salar Nassim decided.

~*~

The two mercenaries went first to the stables to saddle Salar Nassim's stallion and then retrieved Soren's horse from the hitching post near the armory door. Bem was waiting near the wagon with his bridled mare, and the ladies were crossing the courtyard with their arms full of baskets of gifts when Soren and Salar Nassim rode out through the gate with no explanation.

Natalija watched Soren ride away; her shoulders slumped with disappointment.

Bem watched Eduard pointing at the two riders and laughing with the small group of soldiers. Bem wondered what had happened. He would find out soon enough.

Simeon and Hugo came into the courtyard from the stables with Mauro. The baron had assigned them to escort the women that day. One would drive the wagon, and the other would trot alongside it on horseback for protection. The baron's soldiers found the conversations with the women so entertaining that they usually flipped a coin to see who would get to drive the wagon. Simeon won the right to sit on the bench seat with the ladies today.

Their escorts took the packages from Natalija's and Verica's arms and loaded them into the wagon's bed. Then, the two maids climbed in and sat on the open end of the wagon so their skirts could hang down nicely without showing their stockings.

As they waited for the wagon to roll, Natalija asked Verica, "Where do you think Soren went? I was sure he wanted to come with me today."

Verica reassured her with a pat on her knee. "It looked like something unexpected came up since he was riding away with his friend. I wouldn't worry. He would have come if he could."

Natalija nodded and settled in for the short ride to the village. She had not had a chance to tell her sisters anyway, so she did not worry about disappointing them. She had looked forward to hearing the stories herself, though.

Watching Isabella walk across the courtyard brought back memories Bem thought were hidden away. The Venetian wore a more modest riding outfit today, one that had a distinct Ottoman flair to it. His wife would have approved of the flowing trousers and choice of jacket. Fatina loved bright colors.

Isabella nodded hello, and Bem helped her onto the saddle, holding her corseted waist a little longer than he should have.

Isabella looked down at him and smiled coyly, noticing the brazen mistake.

"Be confident," he told her. "I will not be there to instruct your horse today."

A sudden panic washed over her powdered face. "But I do not know Portuguese," she fretted.

He assured her, "My mare came to me from another rider, and probably another before him. She seems to understand Latin, Venetian even. I don't know for certain. But I do know that she understands what to do when given directions. You are the rider, and you are in charge." Bem handed her the reins.

Isabella situated herself on the horse's back. "I think we will get along fine," she said, "but you never told me your horse's name."

Bem rubbed his horse under the fringe of hair above its big brown eyes and said, "I call her Fatina." He kissed the mare's muzzle, and the horse whinnied at him.

"All right, dear Fatina, we are partners now." Isabella rubbed her gloved hand over the crest of the mare's neck, smoothing the long mane that lay lightly there. She then turned the horse and lined up next to Ruby.

While the women were being helped onto their horses and into the back of the wagon, Mauro had taken Resi aside. He was still floating high from their tender conversation in the chapel yesterday and the passionate evening together afterward.

Mauro held his wife by the waist. She was wearing a fetching Venetian gown, which he preferred for a public outing, but the many layers of skirts kept him from closely touching her.

"Did you bring your parasol? The sun is strong this afternoon. You do not want to exhaust yourself," he reminded her.

Resi took his hand in hers and squeezed it in gratitude. "I like that you worry about me, Mauro, but I have this enormous hat your aunt gave to me. I think that will shade me and Simeon, both."

She looked over at the wagon where Simeon was helping Caterina onto the front bench seat. Resi would sit between them.

"I will send Elizabeta your best wishes, Mauro. We will be home for dinner. I don't want to intrude on her too long."

"Until dinner, then," Mauro said, then leaned in to kiss her goodbye. His embrace lingered longer than usual in the very public courtyard, where a kiss most certainly would be a spectacle. But she was his wife, and he loved her. He did not care anymore about concealing his affection for her.

Resi stepped back from the farewell kiss, breathless and smiling with satisfaction.

Mauro walked his wife to the wagon and helped her up onto the seat. He nodded to Simeon, who winked in return, assuring him with that small gesture that he would protect the baron's wife.

Simeon then climbed up to sit next to the baroness as Resi adjusted the folds of her billowing skirts to make room for him. Simeon flicked the reins, and the horses took them out the open gate to see the new Radic baby.

Chapter 21

Elizabeta had been napping when the ladies arrived. They were let into her darkened bedroom by Elizabeta's mother, who was staying with her while she recovered.

The new mother welcomed them in with a sleepy wave of her hand. "I knew you would be here any time, but I was so tired from my first night with the baby. I hope you will forgive me for greeting you in my bedchamber, Lady Baric."

"Do not worry yourself, Elizabeta," said Resi as she came to her bedside. "We came to gaze at your new little girl, not at you in your nightclothes."

Elizabeta proudly pointed to the cradle next to her bed. "Well, there she is. My little baby girl."

"She is precious, Elizabeta," exclaimed Ruby as she picked up the swaddled bundle.

"It is very dark in here," Resi said.

The window shutters in the room were closed, and Resi opened them to let in the warm sea breeze and afternoon light.

"The midwife said the baby should not take too much air."

"The air is for us, Elizabeta. Ruby is holding your little girl so tightly she will never get any air anyway."

Ruby's three sisters came staggered into the family within two years of each other, and Ruby had been caring for babies since she was a small girl. She sat on the foot of the new mother's bed and put the bundle down in the middle of the covers for all of them to admire.

"May I unwrap her?" Ruby asked, already untucking the corner of the knitted wool blanket and opening the folds.

The ladies all leaned over to look at the pink little person hidden in the tightly wound blanket.

"She is so tiny," said Isabella.

"She has so much dark hair," Caterina pointed out.

"She is perfect," Resi told the protective mother with a smile.

"I haven't really looked at her yet," said Elizabeta. "My mother has kept her swaddled. She told me it soothes the baby, but I will hold her now and see if she wants to suckle."

Ruby wrapped the little girl loosely in her blanket again and put her into her mother's arms.

Elizabeta unlaced her bodice and leaned against her pillows to put the tiny baby to her breast.

"My milk has not come in yet, but my mother said to try every few hours anyway."

While Elizabeta occupied herself trying to nurse the infant, Resi and Ruby took the two chairs from the small table where they had set their gifts and brought them over to the bedside for the Venetians to sit in.

"Elizabeta, I think you have not met our guests. This is Lady Caterina Carrera, Lord Fabian's sister. And this is Lady Isabella Valli, her companion from Venice."

In the fogginess of waking from her nap and introducing her new baby to the baroness, Elizabeta had not fully noticed the other two women in the background.

They sat gracefully on the chairs Resi had set out and nodded their greetings at the flustered young woman.

"Oh, my ladies, you are most welcome. The sister of Captain Fabian! My, this is a pleasure. Your brother is so charming." Elizabeta giggled nervously, then added, "If I had known we would have company from Venice, I would have had some tea and cakes prepared."

"We brought cakes and cider for the occasion," Ruby told her. "Nela even bottled up some lemonade for us from the last of the winter lemons."

She went to the table and began unpacking their treats. Nela had not packed any cups in the basket, so Ruby went to the kitchen to find some.

"I understand the baptism is already planned for next week. Will you be able to go to the celebration?" Resi asked Elizabeta.

"Dino wants to have the baby named and blessed as soon as possible, but I will have to be churched first. The midwife told me the baby slid out like a greased pig, so there is not much healing needed. I feel quite fine, really. Just a bit sore and puffy in the middle," she said with a giggle again.

"You look very well, and not even half the size you were before, Elizabeta. I am sure you take comfort in having it all behind you now," Resi said.

"It was not so bad, Lady Baric. I am already hopeful to try again for a boy as soon as I can." She looked down at the baby latched onto her breast and said, "My husband loves his new little girl, but he has three daughters already. The midwife said I have good hips to be able to give him lots of sons in the coming years."

Isabella spoke up and advised, "Then you should find a good nurse and let your milk dry up. That is the quickest way to become pregnant again."

"Yes," Caterina agreed. "All of my friends immediately gave their babe over to a wet nurse, and they were pregnant again after only a few months."

Elizabeta touched the baby's cheek. "Is that the only way? I don't think I could send her away."

"If it is important to try for a boy, it is the quickest way to the next baby," Isabella continued to recommend. "But you are very young, my dear, and you have plenty of time to give your husband a houseful of boys." Isabella studied the maternal scene on the bed with an artist's eye and contemplated the lovely sketch it would make.

Ruby came into the room again with the filled glasses. She handed Lady Isabella cider and a plate of honey cake, interrupting her thoughts.

Caterina stood up with her lemonade and went to the window of the small bedroom. She had never been inside a cottage before. The detached stone house was like most of those in Solgrad, perhaps a little grander, though, because it belonged to the village constable. The Venetian noted it was clean and comfortably appointed, with a kitchen garden and a henhouse in the back. She watched the milk goat wandering the walled yard outside the window.

"You have a pretty little house here," she told her hostess. "The view of the sea is enchanting."

The new mother moved the baby from her breast and turned it over her shoulder. She rocked the little bundle and explained, "The view from upstairs is even nicer if you want to have a look. My sister has taken the girls to her house for a few days until I am ready to climb the stairs to take care of them again. I am so glad to be able to move about and get back to the way things were." She chuckled and said, "Dino has been sleeping on a cot in the sitting room for the past few months. He can't wait, either."

The Venetians politely smiled when she seemed to be finished speaking.

Resi commented, "You were very round at the end, Elizabeta. We all thought you would have twins."

"I was afraid of that myself. Dino does have twins in his family." She looked at the baroness's figure and remarked kindly, "It will go quickly now for you, Lady Baric. Soon, you will be as round as I was."

Resi stroked her middle absently and said, "I feel wonderful now, but I expect it will get harder in the end."

"The middle was the hardest part of being pregnant for me, actually—when everything felt good and normal, but you still had to, you know, stop with your husband." Elizabeta set her empty mug and her baby down next to her. She laced up her bodice again and then continued her gossipy chatter, "I know he isn't much to look at, but my Dino is very good under the covers, having had two wives already. I will be glad to have him back in my bed again," she said with a girlish grin.

"Well," said Caterina, "being pregnant can be an advantage in that respect. I had a friend who told her husband every other month that she was pregnant just to keep him out of her way. She was not pregnant, of course, so she would have to let him bed her once in a while to keep the charade going."

"And he believed her?" Elizabeta asked, finding the Venetian's story amusing.

"Oh yes! Some men are very naïve about how it all works—the timing of your courses and all."

"Indeed," interjected Isabella.

Caterina then added, "Some women are just as ignorant, I suppose. I knew a lady who did not understand why she could not lace up her gowns any longer, even though she had stopped eating altogether to try to fit back into them. Then a physician told her it was because she was carrying a child. She had the baby only two months later. Imagine that!"

Isabella nodded, knowing exactly who she was referring to.

Elizabeta admitted, "The midwife told me I was almost halfway through my pregnancy before I realized what was going on. I'd only had my monthlies a short time before marrying, so I did not know there was something wrong when they suddenly stopped. Father David only gave me a small penance of nightly prayer because he said I was not deliberately disobeying God. Dino had to fast with only bread and water for a month! Father David thought that after two wives and three children he should have seen the signs and stopped coming to me."

Caterina shook her head solemnly. "Our priest in Venice gives light penances, too," she said. "He understands the temptations we face every day in this sinful world. You can always pray for forgiveness to make it right again."

Off to the side of the room, Resi had been silent. Isabella noticed the odd expression on the baroness's face and quickly grasped why. Isabella was born into her Catholic faith, and she imagined the baroness had only recently converted to make it possible for her to marry the baron in the Church. Isabella doubted that anyone had explained to her all the ways one could sin in a marriage. She turned to the baroness and acknowledged, "The flesh is weak, especially with such a handsome husband."

Elizabeta seemed to think Isabella was talking about her. "Oh, my Dino is not so handsome, really. He is like a big, hairy bear. But he pleases me and takes good care of me and the girls."

She touched her sleeping baby's cheek, then noticed the baroness wobble and sway. "Lady Baric, you look so pale. Are you unwell?"

Ruby anxiously went to her friend. "Sit down, Resi. Did the cider not agree with you?"

Resi was not ill from the cider but from clarity. She understood what the good Catholic women were talking about now, and she was mortified. Her mother had tried in vain to teach her how to be a good Catholic and a dutiful wife. She should have listened better. She should have studied the doctrine her mother gave her. She should have known better before she told Mauro that she wanted him to touch her. She had practically begged for it! What must he think of her blatant wickedness? She sat down as the ladies gathered around her.

"I just have a bit of a sudden headache. Perhaps it was the drink," Resi told the alarmed women.

"You should not take any chances that it isn't something more serious, my lady," Elizabeta said warily. She did not want a plague in her house, but she could not send the baron's wife away, either.

To Elizabeta's relief, Ruby suggested, "Maybe we should leave now, before you feel worse." Ruby put the baby back into its cradle and turned back to its mother. "We will leave our gifts here for you to open later. Perhaps we can visit again when the baroness is feeling better."

Caterina and Isabella seemed eager to go and delicately shook the hostess's hand in parting.

"It was so lovely to see your new baby," said Caterina.

Isabella added, "Perhaps we will still be here when you have your party. I do so love a celebration."

Elizabeta touched her capped head, looking suddenly self-conscious next to the elegant aristocrats. "I hope you will be able to attend, my ladies. I should be more presentable then." She waved to them as they left her in her bed.

~*~

Their escorts had not expected the women to be ready to return to the castle so soon. Simeon and Hugo had gone to the alehouse around the corner for refreshments while they passed the time. Only Daniel was sitting under the shady tree outside the low wall when the ladies came out of the cottage.

"Daniel, where are the others?" asked Resi.

He scrambled to his feet and came to open the little gate for her. "Uh, th-th-they w-went f-for a d-d-drink," he stuttered.

The two Venetians were not used to his clumsy speech and openly stared at the young officer.

"Run and tell them that we are ready to ride home now," Resi said impatiently.

"Bu-bu-but who w-will g-guard you if-f-f I am g-g-gone?"

It was a reasonable question that Resi knew her husband would also ask when he found out later. She assured Daniel convincingly, "No one will bother us here for a few minutes. We are at the constable's house."

Daniel did as she asked and ran down the street to retrieve Simeon and Hugo.

Resi put her hands on her hips in frustration. Now that they had said their goodbyes over her feigned illness, she could not impose on Elizabeta to sit in her house while they waited for the men to return. She walked over to the wagon, and the other women quietly followed her.

Caterina took her fan from her deep pocket and opened it to cool herself in the humid air. After a moment of silent fidgeting, she asked, "Has Isabella told you she is going to be a painter?"

Ruby brightened at the news. "That is wonderful, Lady Isabella."

"What inspired you to decide on this?" Resi asked, momentarily forgetting her troubles.

At first, Isabella seemed embarrassed by Caterina's boldness to share her secret, but she quickly reconsidered the power of letting secrets out.

"It is just a whim of mine. I have never actually painted before. If I am any good, Cyro suggested I do my art under a fictitious man's name."

Caterina said as she batted her fan, "Imagine the scandal it would create if it were known."

"There would be no scandal, Cat. Women pretend to be men in the arts all the time," Isabella declared. "Actors are always listed as men on the bill, but if you look closely, there are occasionally women who dress as men on the stage. It should be possible as a painter, too."

Resi had an idea to help her new friend get started and told her, "Mauro is searching for a portrait artist. You draw such beautiful sketches, Lady Isabella. When you are ready, I would trust you completely to paint a true likeness of me."

Isabella beamed at the suggestion. "If I am not sent to a nunnery for my poor behavior, I will paint you, Lady Terese."

Resi's expression became sullen again at the mention of the nunnery.

"What is the matter now?" Ruby asked with worry. "You seem to be hot and cold with emotion today."

Resi looked from face to face. "It is a silly worry, really. I could just confess, but I feel rather stupid now to confess all of this to Father David after it has gone on for so long, but Mauro did not tell me otherwise."

Ruby was puzzled. "Tell you what?"

Isabella came to her rescue and explained, "I think the baroness had her first realization that marriage is more complicated than one would expect. It is not so tragic to sin sometimes, Lady Terese," said Isabella sympathetically. "Mauritius does not seem to be so distraught at his lack of self-control. Perhaps he has already confessed to your priest."

Caterina now understood that the conversation was about sex and considered the baroness's predicament.

"Pride is also a sin, Lady Terese, so you must put that aside and make your peace with God," she said frankly. "But I would not worry one way or the other. The priest will judge it as your husband forcing you to be a dutiful wife. There is no shame in that—it is what God wishes, really."

Ruby was looking beyond the ladies, and they turned to see Daniel running back up the lane with Simeon and Hugo jogging along behind him.

~ * ~

They left the tanner's house with Verica, Natalija, and her sister Marija in the back of the wagon. Simeon directed the horses through the cobbled streets and onto the trade road, back to Baric Castle, and the other four riders trotted along on their horses behind them. Caterina and Resi had been sitting quietly during that time, lost in their own thoughts.

Caterina finally said, "You know, Lady Terese, I was thinking again about your confession to the priest."

"Shhh," Resi whispered, turning to Caterina. "My husband's captain will overhear you."

Caterina chuckled softly. "The driver? Oh, Lady Terese. Escorts never listen to women. They have their duty and cannot be bothered to follow a conversation. Watch, I will show you." She imagined what a real distraction to her would be and then exclaimed, "Look at that nasty insect! It is crawling on the collar of the driver!"

Simeon did not flinch.

"See what I mean, Lady Terese?" The Venetian continued, "As I was saying, I am not the scholar that you are, but I was required to read the Bible cover to cover, and my mother personally instructed us girls in our catechism. She was very busy attending to the affairs of our household, but she said it was her job to pass on our Catholic faith. That was the most time she spent with us, so we knew it was important to pay attention."

Caterina frowned and concluded, "I am sorry to say that I do remember the passages regarding fornication. What Elizabeta said earlier is correct. Sex is only sanctioned for making God's children, not for our pleasure."

Resi stared ahead. "That is why I feel so terrible now. I am worried that Father David will think I am a depraved, wanton sinner when I say my sacrament for the first time."

Caterina looked confused when she asked, "For the first time, Lady Terese? Did you not make your confession to this same priest before your wedding ceremony?"

"Well, I tried to," Resi explained quietly. "I had only arrived the day before, and I was a bit nervous and flustered about the whole ritual of confession and marriage. In the end, Father David excused me from the sacrament. He said that I must be coming to them with no sins to confess, being that I was so sheltered in Thessaloniki. And I do believe he was right at the time. I did not have any sins of consequence in the beginning."

Caterina shrugged off the baroness's worry and said with confidence, "We were all born to sin, Lady Terese. It is our natural weakness here on earth. Your Father David will not think you are depraved. He will assume that you were being an obedient wife to your husband's desires. Those are rules," she said, repeating what had been taught to her.

"I cannot lie to Father David. In Mauro's defense, it is I who wanted—"

Caterina held up her hand to stop the baroness's confession.

"The priest does not need to know that, Lady Terese. As a matter of fact, you should say as little as possible. Priests generally disapprove of women speaking about their desires. You are the baroness, and he will not ask such intimate details. You can explain them in your prayer to God when you do your penance. That is all that counts."

"Do you really think so, Lady Caterina?"

"I do."

Caterina thought of her conversation with Salar Nassim earlier that morning. She understood now what he had meant and shared his words of wisdom with the baroness.

"Yours is a romantic love, Lady Terese. We cannot stifle that sort of love when it finds us. Mauritius is your husband, so I do not think lust is your sin. You must find a way to avoid him, though. Perhaps, go to bed early and pretend to be asleep when he comes to you. Or do what Elizabeta and her husband did—have separate sleeping rooms until the baby arrives."

"I had not thought of all of this," Resi said, now more troubled by what she must consider.

Caterina did not notice. She folded her hands on her lap with satisfaction and said, "I am glad I have solved that for you. Make peace with God and then keep your husband at arm's length, Lady Terese."

They were coming up to the gate, and Simeon reined the horses to a halt. He looked over at the baroness next to him on the bench seat, and she smiled back at him. The Baric captain was sworn to keep her private conversations just that: private. It had never been a problem because the Greek women always spoke in their native language when they had something personal to discuss. After listening to her unexpected conversation with Lady Caterina, Simeon thought that Mauro might want to make an exception to his rule. Simeon would keep that confidence for now. Maybe the baroness would clear this up with her husband herself.

Chapter 22

The baron watched Resi and the others disappear out the gate to visit the constable's wife. With his pressing duties for the day settled, he would use the quiet afternoon to go over the renovations planned at his small villa. It was where Mauro would have resided if Mateo had lived to become the baron of Baric. It was situated at the eastern edge of the barony, away from the village and the salt fields. Not an ideal distance for dealing with the daily business of the House of Baric, but it was an idyllic location for a second son to prosper in his own right. It had gone unused for years, and Mauro now knew the perfect use for it.

"Davor said you wanted to speak to me?" Jero asked from the doorway.

The baron was at his writing desk and waved him over. "Yes. Come in, Jero. You can leave the door open."

Jero strode across the room and stood next to the desk. The baron had an old scroll laid out in front of him, and Jero leaned over his shoulder to have a look. "What plans are those, Mauro?"

"This is the old villa," Mauro told Jero quietly. "When I was in the village yesterday, I talked to Signor Bernardo about renovating it. He is leaving for Venice on Monday, but he can ride out tomorrow to walk through the house and go over ideas for updates. The timing works well since he can order what is needed from Venice while he is there."

"Why are you renovating it now?" Jero asked.

The villa had not been occupied by a Baric since Mauro's great aunt died almost twenty years ago. Mauro had not thought of a clever reason if Jero were to ask. He quickly invented one.

"I was looking over the account books. I have a good sum of money available now and am home to supervise the renovations, finally. Nestor told me that the last time the inside was redecorated was nearly forty years ago. I like to keep up appearances, you know."

Jero scratched his head with doubt but did not contradict him. "Are you updating just the furnishings?"

"That, and maybe a few more improvements. The house is sound, but it can be modernized." Mauro then pointed to the parchment unrolled across the desk. "The stairway is awkward, and the sitting room is too small. I am considering changing those."

Jero scanned the scroll. "It is interesting to look at it on paper—how the rooms were designed, and the two levels balanced."

"I am glad you think so. I was to meet Bernardo tomorrow, but now I am going to take Patrik and the others to the salt flats. I cannot be in both places at once."

Mauro looked up from his scrutiny of the plans and said, "I would like for you to go instead. Take the scroll and make some notes of what Signor Bernardo suggests, and then we can go over it before he leaves."

Mauro forced an encouraging smile, hoping Jero would accept the assignment without question, and the steward did.

"It is a nice ride out there, Mauro. I will gladly go in your place. May I ask a favor, though?"

"Yes, ask," Mauro answered quickly, rolling up the scrolls to put back in the leather cases.

"May I take Ruby with me?"

Mauro frowned as he considered it. He wanted to tell his brother yes, that Jero could take the woman he loved out riding, but instead, he said, "I don't know, Jero . . ."

"I will need an escort anyway," Jero hastily began. "And I thought that Lady Isabella might enjoy the next challenge on the open trail, and—"

"It is nearly five miles! Lady Isabella cannot already ride so far on the open road," Mauro protested.

"It is only half that distance if we take the trail by the lake through the valley. We do not need to take the wagon road for just the horses. She can ride that far. She seems rather determined. And if not, then we will stop at the lake to rest. It is halfway." Jero added, "Ruby would be so pleased."

Mauro stared at his hopeful expression. "I know she would be pleased. My wife has already asked that I take Ruby out again on the open fields, but I have not had the time."

He let out a sigh and made his decision.

"The ladies are in the village now," Mauro said. "When they return, we will know if Isabella is up to a longer ride after her going to the constable's house. If she is, I will allow Isabella to be Ruby's chaperone."

Jero grinned. "Thank you, Mauro."

"There is no need to thank me," Mauro replied. "Now that I think about it, it is safer to take the lake trail. I will have Eduard alert Neno and Latif that you will be riding that route. They are patrolling my border this week."

"Should I ask Eduard for an escort?"

"Unfortunately, I have plans for most of the men tomorrow." Mauro considered another option. "What do you make of Bem?"

Jero shrugged. "I like Bem well enough. Do you want him to come?"

"Isabella seems to feel confident with him nearby, and I would like her to succeed in her lessons. I will ask him if he would not mind joining you," said Mauro.

At that moment, the front door slammed, and Patrik came rushing through the empty foyer.

"Mauritius Baric, I need to speak to you," Patrik shouted up the staircase.

Mauro hurried out the open study door to meet his brother-in-law before Patrik disturbed the whole house.

"There is no need to yell. What is the problem?" Mauro motioned him into the room and shut the door.

"The problem is with your Captain Eduard! Your officers are set on insulting us every chance they get. You said we are welcome here, Mauro, but we are not. We will be packing our bags today."

Mauro squeezed his temples. "Sit down, Patrik."

He got the wine bottle from the end of the table and poured a glass for Patrik.

Patrik drank the glass empty and then sat down at the other end of the long table.

"I meant what I said earlier. Tell me what has happened, and I will deal with it," Mauro assured him.

Patrik took a deep breath to check his anger, then said, "Eduard is a lying bastard, and he needs to apologize."

Mauro and Jero exchanged glances.

"What did he say?" Mauro asked.

"He called Soren a rapist in front of your soldiers and said he would not trust Soren within twenty feet of your wash maid, or any woman here."

Mauro shifted uneasily, hearing his account.

Patrik gritted his teeth to tell him more calmly, "He accused a decent man of a wretched crime. Maybe Eduard has to force a woman to lie next to his ugly pocked face, but Soren does not."

Mauro had to walk a fine line between defending his men's actions and being fair to Patrik's complaint.

"I agree with you. Eduard should not use accusations so lightly. But Hugo told me he had a few cross words with Soren over Natalija. Is she the maid you are talking about? Hugo said they were alone in the wash yard."

"Alone in plain sight, Mauro! Did Hugo not tell you that? Soren was just talking to her. You do not accuse a man of rape for talking to a girl!"

Jero nodded sympathetically.

Mauro was not so quick to agree. "They were following my orders, Patrik. The castle women are under my Guard's watch. A man alone with a young woman usually wants something more than conversation."

"If you judge all men from that perspective, then you are not the nobleman I thought you to be. Am I to assume you would molest your servant women if no one was watching over you?"

Mauro understood his point but remained faithful to his officers. "We are not talking about me, and I am looking at it from the soldiers' perspective. What does Soren want from her?"

Patrik ran his hands through his unbound hair in frustration. "He wants her normality. Is that a crime?" he asked. "It is the first time in a year he stumbled upon someone unaffected by war—a girl who talks only about the washing and visiting her family after church. The man held his twin brother as he died, Mauro, and then rode through a hellish landscape, leaving him behind. Soren is a bit fucked up right now, and I want my friend to be whole again. If he is finding comfort in talking to the girl, then that is a favor I will gladly repay ten times over."

Patrik poured his own wine this time and took another drink before shouting, "If he touches her, then he will face your consequences! But he won't! Soren has not taken comfort from a woman's touch since Niels's death. I don't think he is going to start with your little lady's maid. Do you understand what I am saying, Mauro?"

Mauro understood. "What are you asking that I do, Patrik?"

"Tell Captain Eduard and your other warriors to give us some peace. We are not welcome in your tower, and they have made that clear. But they don't need to be questioning our every move."

Mauro shut his eyes, rubbing his brow. When he opened them a moment later, Patrik was still staring at him.

"Alright," Mauro said. "I will talk to Eduard and the rest of them. Eduard will apologize to Soren, but I cannot make my guardsmen trust you. They have fought bravely with me in sieges and skirmishes on our borders, but my men have not experienced the sort of hell you came through."

Patrik emptied his glass and got up abruptly.

Mauro held up his hand to stop him from leaving. "One more thing, Patrik. I can understand what Soren sees in Natalija's innocence, but her innocence is the problem. She is only seventeen and is quite impressionable. Soren is, as Terese once described, a handsome man."

Patrik raised his eyebrows, not disagreeing with his sister.

"My point is, Soren may be trusted with her, but Natalija may not be trusted with him. She is very easy with her friendships and has not always shown the best judgment. Do you understand my dilemma?"

"Yes, all right. Soren will stay away from her," Patrik agreed. "But I want Eduard to back off."

"Consider it done."

Chapter 23

Mauro wanted to show his guests more personal hospitality before they left, without the strain of the conflicting personalities at the table. After dressing for dinner, Mauro went to the Keep.

The baron found his captains together in the dining hall, enjoying their savory pasta and roasted pork. Vilim and Simeon had arrived earlier from their duties, and their platters were almost empty. The other three's hearty meals were nearly untouched yet. They looked over in surprise when they saw their elegantly dressed commander coming toward their table.

Vilim was the first to greet him. "Are you joining us for dinner tonight?"

"No," Mauro said, sitting down, "I just came to ask something."

They stopped talking and gave him their attention.

His glance rested on each man around the table. Then he said, "I have been thinking lately about all we have been through together, and I am grateful to have had you by my side."

They nodded and mumbled their appreciation for his compliment.

Mauro turned to Simeon and said, "You have seen the heavy loss of life the infantry endures and the brutality of hand-to-hand combat."

Simeon acknowledged with a solemn nod that he had.

The baron addressed Vilim and Hugo next, "You fought with my uncle's army in full battle formations with thousands of soldiers flanking each side. Cannons shooting over your heads. Walls exploding apart beside you. It was a hellish experience, but we survived that together, didn't we?"

They exchanged glances and nodded to the baron.

Mauro directed his next question to Eduard, "Did my father ever take his men into a full battle, or was he required to mostly hold the borders?"

"Mainly border skirmishes, but it was a bloody way to die just the same," replied Eduard grimly.

"Yes, there are many bloody ways to die." Mauro then looked to his youngest officer and asked, "Have you ever seen a pike man in battle, Daniel?"

"N-n-no, my lord," Daniel answered.

Mauro shook his head. "I did not imagine you had."

He singled out Eduard again and asked, "Did you ever witness a troop of two hundred pikemen clash with two hundred opposing pikemen—no shield to protect you and no horse to get you away? Face-to-face with the enemy, a pikeman's job is to force them back, or kill them before they kill you. It is you or them, and the pike handlers are trained to think of it that way."

"No, Mauro, I cannot say that I would like to see that," Eduard reflected quietly.

"No, nor would I. But that is what our guest Soren did in battle. His brother fought by his side before bleeding to death in his arms. A man needs time to recover from these horrors, and my guests are here to recover their strength of will, not just of body. They still have a long journey home, and I have offered them respite. They have not found it here, and it troubles me."

Mauro would now give his order, and he commanded their attention, their platters going uneaten in front of them.

"All of you will show my guests respect for their right to be within these walls. If you cannot offer them hospitality, you will at least not offend and insult them. You will be sure every man under you knows that this request comes directly from me. And, Eduard, you will take the earliest opportunity to apologize to Soren for calling him a rapist."

The others turned to Eduard, who stammered, "He was, um . . ."

"He was doing nothing," Mauro said, challenging him. "He was riding unarmed with my *armed* escorts to the tanner's house. Soren was asked to tell stories to Natalija's sisters about the voyages he took before he became a soldier. Let me remind you, gentlemen, Natalija is not your daughter, and you cannot forbid her choice of company on her own time outside the castle."

Eduard protested, "But we are under your orders to protect the maids en route to the village, sir."

"The three escorts today were assigned that duty—until Natalija is home. Then her father may decide who will come into his house, not you."

"Of course, Mauro," Eduard acknowledged.

"The mercenaries will not be here long, but they are here at the baroness's wishes and mine, do you understand?"

"Yes, sir," said all five men in unison.

Mauro's words carried throughout the dining hall when he said, "We will start back on a normal training schedule tomorrow, and our guests will join us at their pleasure. You will let them come and go in peace, and you will keep your sentiments to yourself. Have I made my orders perfectly clear?"

"Yes, sir," all of them repeated loudly.

Mauro stood up and nodded to the group. "I will join you tomorrow for breakfast. I bid you a good evening."

When Mauro crossed the room to the stairwell to descend to the armory, he met Patrik on the landing. The other four stood on the steps above him.

They were coming from their chamber, having dressed in clean clothes for dinner at the manor house.

Patrik grinned at his brother-in-law with satisfaction, and Mauro gave him a brief nod before going down the stairs without further comment.

At the captains' table, Simeon asked, "Now, why did you have to pick a fight with the Dane, Eduard?"

"I don't like the look of him," Eduard answered curtly.

"You didn't like the look of me at first, and here we are sitting together," Simeon said through the last bites of his cold dinner.

"Yeah, and I still don't like the look of you," said Eduard, chuckling.

Simeon laughed good-naturedly along with him. They got on well after working side by side for two years.

Hugo pointed out, "Soren asked me if Natalija was my girl. I already warned him two days ago to keep away from her."

Vilim gathered his empty plate and mug and stood up to leave. "Give the Dane a break, gentlemen," he said. "It is not a sin to talk to a maiden when you collect a shirt from the wash line."

Vilim saw the subjects of their conversation coming into the dining room. He tipped his hat in greeting to them. Patrik and Bem made the same cordial gesture as they passed.

Salar Nassim was carrying his lute, and Cyro had a small drum under his arm.

"Will you play tonight?" Vilim asked the two in a friendly tone, as ordered by the baron.

"We will," said Cyro, reciprocating Vilim's smile with his own diplomatic one.

"I look forward to it," Vilim said. He passed Soren with a friendly nod before going up the stairs to his chamber.

Eduard then stood up and awkwardly approached the Dane, who had come into the dining hall last.

Soren halted in front of the Baric soldier while the others continued out the door near the fireplace. Soren was a head taller and fifteen years younger than the stern soldier. He looked down at the man in front of him.

"I wish to express my apology for my words earlier," Eduard stated flatly.

"Apology accepted," Soren said briskly in his accented Latin. He then continued after his friends and left the Keep.

Simeon burst out laughing. "I didn't know you could apologize. You did not explode into flames or anything. I will have to remember that!"

Hugo covered his mouth to suppress his laughter, and Eduard reminded him, "You should count yourself lucky the baron did not tell you to apologize too, Hugo. You had some words with the Dane."

"Yes, tell us what that was about, Hugo," Simeon said teasingly. "Are you sweet on Natalija? Is she your girl?"

Hugo began to choke on his bite of bread, and Simeon hit him hard on the back to help him recover.

"No," he coughed his reply and then took a drink of ale to regain his voice. "It was Daniel who was on duty and saw them from the ramparts. I just did the talking for Daniel."

Simeon saw that Daniel was blushing and directed his teasing at the young officer. "That is a match made in heaven, wouldn't you agree, Eduard? Daniel will never have to say another word. He'll just let Natalija do all the talking for the two of them."

Daniel looked to Hugo for help, but Hugo just shrugged.

"I l-l-like her. Is th-th-that a c-c-crime?" Daniel managed to say. He took another bite from his supper to avoid being asked to explain more.

"It depends," Eduard said with a wink to Simeon. "Now we will be watching you at the wash line, Daniel."

Chapter 24

Cyro and the baroness walked side by side on the path by the greenhouses after dinner.

Cyro reflected, "You have a magnificent garden here, Lady Baric. So expertly laid out around your manor house. I surmise, it is beautiful in any season."

"Yes, it seems my mother-in-law had quite a vision. She is the one who designed the gardens and had the greenhouses built. She cultivated many of these exotic plants that would not survive the cool winters otherwise."

They stopped to open the door to one of the glasshouses, and Cyro looked in. "Your gardener was kind enough to show me your greenhouses earlier today. I am sure they must be invaluable in the winter."

"You sound like you have experience with gardens, Cyro. Was that your occupation before you left to fight wars?"

"No, no," he said with a chuckle. "My grandparents have a large garden at their home. I spent much of my childhood there." He did not say that they, too, lived in a fortified villa surrounded by gardens of exotic plants on the island of Corsica.

They strolled past the glasshouse in the direction of the terrace, and Cyro remarked, "Your mother-in-law was Lady Toth before she became a Baric, if I heard correctly."

Cyro's comment surprised Resi. "Yes. Did you know her?"

"Not your mother-in-law, no," Cyro answered vaguely.

Resi was curious and asked, "Do you know the Toths?"

"Indirectly. I know who Count and Countess Toth are. I, um, fought in a battle that he commanded. He is an outstanding general. We won that siege."

"My husband's uncle has been praised many times, but I must admit I have never met him. Have you met the countess, too?"

To answer her honestly, Cyro would have to explain more than he cared to. He found a way out. "Ah, there is Lady Caterina by the fountain. Would you mind terribly if I excused myself for a moment, Lady Baric? I have something urgent I needed to ask Lady Caterina before her lesson tomorrow."

Resi politely granted him leave. "Not at all, Cyro. I look forward to our little concert later."

He bowed and hurried off in Caterina's direction.

~*~

"Oh, hello, Cyro," Caterina said when he came toward her. She presented her hand, and he bowed over it, kissing it lightly. "I am glad to meet you like this. I wanted to tell you that I have come up with another item of beauty by myself."

Cyro had not expected that she would play the game so eagerly. "How very clever of you, my lady. What did you choose for tomorrow?"

"It is a wasps' nest," she told him proudly.

"You are very inventive, Lady Caterina. Will you bring the wasps, too?" he asked in a manner that did not please her in the least.

"No, of course not. The little water boy was given it quite empty, and he let me have it until tomorrow. You would have to see it to understand its true beauty."

"Describe it to me," he said.

If Caterina had looked into his eyes, they would have betrayed his true feelings for her as he struggled to play coy.

She pondered what the water boy had told her and then explained, "It is made from paper that the wasps make themselves by chewing up wood, yet it is as light as air. Is that not remarkable?"

"It is very remarkable, and an excellent choice," he finally said emphatically. "The water boy who gave this to you, does he have a name?"

Caterina seemed puzzled by such an inquiry. "I am sure he does. Everyone has a name, Cyro."

"Salar Nassim will want to know his name when you explain who the nest belongs to. He is very particular about those details," Cyro warned her.

She thought for a moment but could not come up with it.

Irritated, she asked, "How would I know his name, anyway? There are many servants at Baric Castle. I cannot call them all by name."

Cyro had once shared this reasoning, but had since understood the importance of such a small gesture. He had not enjoyed being called 'you there' or 'him' as he worked as a nameless hired-hand during his descent from aristocrat to mercenary soldier.

"Was he not introduced to you once?"

"I suppose Lady Terese told me his name once, but I must admit that I am not good with names."

"Then ask her again tonight," Cyro suggested kindly. "Then you will know it for tomorrow."

"Is it so important?"

"Yes, Lady Caterina, I think it is," he said confidently. "And when you return the boy's wasp nest, you can call him by his name."

She cocked her head and smiled charmingly, like a girl who had been scolded and wanted to be forgiven. "Why are you talking to me so severely tonight? Sometimes I think you have exceptional manners for a soldier, and then at times like this, you contradict yourself and have no manners at all."

He stood close enough where he could speak softly and still be heard over the splashing of the fountain. "I did not mean to make you upset, Lady Caterina."

She took a step back as though stung. "Upset, you say? I suppose Salar Nassim told you about our session this morning."

Cyro did not try to hide from her that he had, and she turned away to the fountain to avoid his intense stare.

Her tinted lips quivered when telling him, "I did receive some painful news from my, um—" She faltered.

"From your lover?" Cyro hid his disdain for the man in his voice, although Caterina would have seen it in his face had she not been looking at the water.

"Yes, that is the word I cannot manage to say. Paolo is no longer my lover. I will never see him again."

Finally, she turned and said, "I am quite unattached now."

Cyro sensed this was his last chance to win the lady's heart. His friends were set on leaving soon, and he had little time left to make the impression. He held out his hand to lead Caterina to a stone bench a few steps from the fountain.

Seated there next to her, he tried his luck and told the truth, "I was attached not long ago. She moved on quite quickly."

"Oh, Cyro! Why did she abandon you?"

Cyro answered plainly, "She thought I was dead, my lady."

Her eyes widened with bewilderment. "Dear God! What made her think that?"

"It is a long story, but I will tell you, if you like."

She nodded kindly. "Sometimes it is better to talk about it."

"Alright, then." Cyro began to explain, "I was meant to be on a ship that sank in the Mediterranean. I was on my way to see my beloved, but I missed that sailing. All those aboard perished, so she had every reason to believe I was dead. I was actually on the ship that sailed the next day, and when I arrived in the port, I learned that she and my family were mourning my death."

Caterina looked at Cyro in dismay. The solution seemed so obvious to her, and she wondered, "Why didn't you clear up the mistake right away? You should have gone to the authorities, right there at the port, and told them who you were."

Cyro bowed his head in shame and admitted, "I have no excuse, except I was selfish and stupid. It was a life-changing decision I made on that fateful day, but it set me on the path to you, and that was also fated. I will go back and try to make amends for all of the trouble I know I have caused my family, but I do not regret where that choice has led me."

"You are perplexing, Cyro. You are thought to be dead by your family, you have lost your betrothed, and you have no regrets?"

Caterina had not heard what he was truly saying. She saw him as a man who needed her counsel, and so she asked, "How can you be sure you still cannot marry your fiancée?"

"I was on Candia several months later. There, I read an announcement in an Italian newspaper. It was reported that she had just married."

"Only aristocratic families announce their daughters' marriages in newspapers," she thought out loud. "How can that be that you could ruin an important match to a noble family?"

But then, a more puzzling question came to Caterina. "When were you on Candia?" she asked.

Cyro was losing her.

"It is not important now where I was, or that Felicia married someone else. It was providence that I was taken off the ship. I was not meant to die that day, but she was not meant to be my wife, either. And because of that divine intervention, I found someone that I could truly be happy marrying in her place."

The Venetian sympathized with the poor soldier's plight. "You must realize your story is incredibly romantic, Cyro. When you leave here, will you go to this other woman? Does she know you are alive? Is she waiting for you?" Caterina was in suspense, wanting to know all the details.

"She knows I am alive, but she does not know yet that I will ask for her hand."

Caterina imagined she had found the perfect fairytale ending. "But you must! You will go to her straight away and tell her that you love her."

Cyro jolted Caterina out of her spell. "I thought I would go home first and ask my father's permission. It will take some time to explain, but once they are over the shock that I am alive, I will then go straight away to ask her father's permission."

"No, Cyro. That will not do. Fathers do not like surprise proposals from undeserving matches."

"I am certain her father will find me a poor match, but I will beg and plead if I must. I will marry her."

Caterina seemed to celebrate his perfect ending. She wanted this for him. "When she sees such devotion, she will have to marry you, Cyro. Salar Nassim said true love cannot be shut out."

He watched her with tender admiration. "If true love does conquer, I pray that she will accept me and say yes."

Caterina shut her eyes, imagining his joy. "She will say yes."

<h1 style="text-align:center">Chapter 25</h1>

Resi couldn't hear what Cyro was saying to Caterina at the fountain to make her look so lovesick. The water's splashing cloaked their conversation. Cyro's intentions were becoming serious. It was clear to everyone that Cyro sought Caterina out each evening. Whether she realized he was courting her or not, she made the opportunity easy for him.

Resi went over to where Patrik was talking to Bem and Jero near the steps to the terrace. Patrik would tell her what game Cyro was playing.

"May I steal my brother away for a moment?" she asked the two sweetly.

Patrik followed her onto the terrace, and they sat down together on a bench where the siblings could not be overheard. The sun was sinking behind the castle wall and casting a soft light over them.

"You look beautiful tonight, as usual, Sister," Patrik complimented her.

"I am glad to see you look happier, Patricius. Mauro told me what happened today. Is everything cleared up?"

Discovering that his new brother-in-law was a fair man had not changed their decision.

"I am worried for Soren, but he is doing better," Patrik said in an optimistic tone. "We have finalized our departure. Cyro insists on attending Mass on Sunday, so we will leave on Monday. He is the only Catholic among us, but we will honor his request."

Resi frowned when she said, "You are Catholic, Patricius."

He pointed out, "Mother is the Catholic in the family. She only baptized us so we would have a chance to make it into heaven with her. I will take my chances in the afterlife without the pressure of the Church," he said with a chuckle. "If I were truly a Catholic, then I would be guaranteed a place in hell for my sins."

"Oh, don't talk to me about going to hell today. I just discovered that I have committed real sins since marrying Mauro. I didn't even know I was sinning, and now I will have to make my confession. It will be awkward, I am afraid."

"What is so awkward about talking to a curtain?" asked Patrik.

"It is not so anonymous," she said with a groan. "I have been here a year and don't even know the local priest, but he will know my voice, and then he will know what an immoral woman I am."

"Is that why you have called me aside, to practice your confession?" Patrik asked, trying to ease her distress with his humor. "Immorality is my specialty, you know. Go ahead, Resi. Tell me all the shocking details and I will tell you what you should confess to your priest and what not to worry about."

She bit her lip and shook her head. "I know you too well, Patricius, and I do not intend to share any details you can hold against me in the future."

He feigned disappointment. "No confessions, then?"

"I did want to ask what you think about Cyro."

He perked up. "Is this your scandal, Sister? Has Cyro done something immoral with you?"

"Will you behave? I am being serious now," she said. "What kind of a man is he, Patricius?"

Patrik pondered a moment and then began to rattle off his friend's perceived qualities.

"Cyro is a good soldier," Patrik began. "He doesn't complain. Nassim had to show him how to fight dirty, but Cyro is otherwise skilled with a sword. And he is stronger than he looks. Cyro was the one who pulled the rock off me when the wall gave way onto my hand."

"No, Brother," she interrupted with a chuckle, "I don't want to know what kind of a soldier he is, but what kind of a person. He has been spending a lot of time with Lady Caterina, and I find his intentions confusing."

"Confusion is not a good state of mind, Resi."

"Neither is frustration, Patricius. Can you not give me an answer?"

Patrik had sworn to keep Cyro's true intention secret, but he wanted to appease his sister's curiosity, too.

After a thoughtful moment, he said, "All right, Resi. I think Cyro is confusing you because his outward appearance does not match the person he truly is. I find him to be smart, well-spoken, educated, funny —"

"Does he have a wife?" Resi interjected.

Patrik shook his head. "He told us he has never married."

She continued her interrogation, "Does he have a profession to go back to?"

Patrik shook his head again. "No, I am afraid he has no skills except those I have already mentioned."

She sighed. "Then he would make a terrible match for Lady Caterina if I am correct that he is courting her. Am I correct?" She raised her brows, wanting Patrik to confirm her guess.

"I am not so sure he would make a terrible match. I have just described your husband, and you say you are happy with your marriage."

"What you described could also be you, Patricius!"

"But I am not a wealthy man like Mauro, and that seems to be the critical difference."

"Neither is Cyro," said Resi.

"Is that Cyro's flaw? That he is not rich? I understand Lady Caterina was just in love with the captain of her Guard, and I assume he is not wealthy."

A serene smile formed across Resi's lips as she visualized Paolo. Patrik had his answer.

"By the look on your face, Terese Kokkinos Baric, I can see that he did have one quality of importance. Was this guardsman especially handsome?" he asked knowingly.

"He was practically beautiful, even after Fabian bruised his face," she replied.

Patrik shrugged. "Then Cyro has no chance with the lady unless he can change his looks or—"

Patrik stopped mid-sentence when a flash of green caught his eye. Resi had moved her hands in her lap as they sat side by side, and he noticed the emerald ring on his sister's finger.

"Jewels might help Cyro entice the lady, don't you think? Let me see your hand, Resi," he said.

She laid her hand on his knee, and Patrik slid the ring off his sister's finger and appraised it.

"It was Mauro's grandmother's ring. He gave it to me for our first wedding anniversary," she said, suddenly bashful.

He slid the ring back onto her finger and then studied the intricate gold band on her other hand. "Lovely," he said.

"I wish you would just tell me about Cyro and not be so distracted."

He held her hand and said, "What if I were to tell you that Cyro believes Lady Caterina is not as shallow as you think her to be? He is not the most handsome of men, but he is a man of good character and solid conviction. He is the moral compass of our little gang, if you will, and he is trying to make her see that."

"I like Cyro, but he does not have a chance for her hand, so it doesn't matter in the end whether he is a good soldier of moral character or knows how to make amiable conversation."

Patrik was uncommonly earnest when he told her, "Cyro understands the rules of the marriage game, Resi. If the lady is becoming interested in Cyro's company tonight, then there is a chance for him to win her."

She shook her head in disagreement. "I don't think Lady Caterina is even aware that he is making advances toward her."

Patrik glanced over at the two, still talking innocently together at the fountain. He then turned his attention back to his sister.

"Why don't you just let this play out, Resi? Of all of my descriptions, I forgot to mention that Cyro is a gentleman. He will not hurt her feelings, but he is willing to put his own on the line. Let him."

He patted her hand affectionately before he released it and stood up.

She nodded, knowing now what she wanted to learn.

~ * ~

Mauro poured Isabella a glass of wine as they stood together near the abandoned dinner table. "How was your ride into the village today?" Mauro asked her. "Hugo mentioned that he thought you did a fine job managing the horse."

She took a drink from the delicate glass and laughed softly. "I appreciate his compliment, even if I do not find him entirely genuine. That Hugo is a flirt, Mauritius, just so you know to warn your future female guests."

"So I have been told," Mauro said with amusement. "My wife and Ruby usually request him as their escort for that reason. He is quite harmless, though."

She finished her glass and set it down. She enjoyed a flirtation herself, and married men were safe entertainment for her. She hooked her arm in Mauro's own and began to walk with him.

Mauro did not mind being used in this way. He understood Isabella's innocent intentions, strolling with him, and he indulged her need for company. This also gave him a private moment to ask her to escort Ruby.

"Do you think you will want to ride again soon? An outing could be arranged for tomorrow if you like."

Isabella considered the unexpected offer from the baron. "I must admit, my backside feels bruised from the short excursion. I may need a few days to recover."

"The best way to recover from a sore bottom is to keep on riding," he replied cheerfully.

"Is that why you men are always on your horses?" Isabella asked playfully.

"If you are up to it, I am sending Jero out to my villa in the valley on an errand, and he asked to take Ruby along."

Isabella looked at him suspiciously. "Ah, and she needs a chaperone, is that it? I would not worry about those two getting into trouble, Mauritius."

"Just the same, I am obligated to provide her with one. Jero is talking to Bem right now about it. It would be just the four of you. Should I have any worries about that?"

She stopped and held his stare. "That is what I have always liked about you, Mauritius. You talk convincingly of following the rules of protocol, but you really do not concern yourself with them, do you? We have that in common."

He said nothing to contradict her as she considered the offer for a moment.

She initiated their stroll along the patio path again, her stiff skirts swooshing as she moved. "I will escort Ruby, and I promise to behave myself," she finally agreed with a shy smile.

"Thank you, Isabella," he said, happy to have this arranged. "It is not very far. Jero wants to take the mountain trail instead of the wagon road. That is a shorter ride, but it can get steep in parts. Jero thinks you are determined."

She laughed and replied, "I am glad Jero is paying attention. You should feel lucky to have such a steward. What will he be doing at this villa of yours?"

"I had arranged to meet with a local architect to go over some renovation details, and he will go in my place. I am going to update the house—bring in new furnishings, modernize the kitchen, maybe open one of the walls in the sitting room."

"How wonderful, I love such things! I will tell you everything that needs to be changed, Mauritius," she teased him. "It will be a pleasurable outing in all respects then."

They had made the small loop around the kitchen garden and were back at the terrace when Isabella said, "Here comes Caterina with Cyro. Do you not find it odd, Mauritius? Cyro always seems to be in conversation with her. What do you make of that?"

Mauro noticed Caterina looked at ease in Cyro's company.

"The mercenaries are leaving on Monday already, Isabella. I do not think anything unusual will evolve by then if that is your worry."

"You are right," Isabella agreed. "He will be gone before he falls in love with her, or something awkward like that."

She watched Cyro as he took a seat on the first of the four chairs placed in the corner of the terrace. Salar Nassim sat down next to him with his instrument.

"Is there to be music?" Isabella asked hopefully.

Mauro's expression brightened. "I believe my wife and Ruby are going to sing with Salar Nassim and Cyro. Shall we sit together and listen?"

~ * ~

Vilim and Simeon came to enjoy the music just as the sun fell below the castle walls. The maids were at the terrace doors, listening to the impromptu concert as well.

Soren walked behind the small audience that was randomly seated in front of the four musicians. He stopped near Natalija at the double doors for a moment. Patrik had warned Soren not to talk to her again, but Soren felt compelled to explain why he had left so suddenly that afternoon. He caught her eye and gestured with his head before he went inside.

Natalija waited at the door for a count of ten, then followed him into the great hall. Soren had taken a seat on one of the stuffed chairs near the hearth. The maid crossed the open space and sat down on the stool next to him.

Soren did not waste valuable time. "I am sorry for leaving without explaining," he said quietly. "I intended to ride into the village until just a few minutes before you arrived."

She picked at the folds of her apron and replied, "I understand you had more important things to do."

"That was not the reason," Soren said. "I have been reminded that men and women cannot just meet freely and talk as friends. I should have known that and could have gotten you into trouble with your father."

"It was my fault for talking to you and getting you into trouble. The guardsmen watch over us closely." Then she said shyly, "I heard you are leaving soon."

He looked down at his folded hands between his long legs when he replied, "We have a long journey ahead of us, and we want to get started."

"Where will you go next?" She was curious about the outside world that she would never see.

"South," he said, "to the baroness's family home and then to Athens."

"Is the war over, then?" she asked. "Are you done fighting?"

His companions had not openly discussed whether they were done fighting, but he had a clear answer for her, "Wars are never over, but we will not fight any more. We have an errand to do for our friend Bem. Then I might leave Europe for a while, maybe sail again to the West Indies. I did enjoy that life."

The sun had faded outside, and the great hall was deep in shadows. A house groom entered with a torch to light the many sconces.

Natalija immediately stood up. Servants were not supposed to be sitting here. Looking around, she hastily said, "I would still like to hear a story about your adventures on the sea if you have time."

They could be packed in less than an hour. He had time, Soren thought. He turned to the girl and said, "If the baron allows it, then I will tell you some tales before I leave. Go back to the others now before they notice you are gone. I don't want any more trouble."

She curtsied to him, as she was trained to do, and went back out onto the terrace to stand near Verica again.

Soren was alone in the great hall now. The flickering lights cast shadows on the stone walls that seemed to dance to the music outside. He listened to the singing coming through the open doors. It was a Greek song he had heard before, a complicated tale of love and triumph, and the two women sang it well.

Soren took a deep breath and smiled to himself. He had never said out loud what he wanted to do next. Now that he had, the Dane felt a surge of longing for better days to come. If he could convince Patrik to join him, Soren would sail away and leave the old, hurtful memories behind him forever.

~ * ~

Mauro blew out the candle on the bedside table. The day seemed to have been exceptionally long, although they had left the gathering on the terrace just after full dark. He slid up next to Resi under the cover and held her around her middle. Her fresh rosewater scent was delicious.

Resi was nearly asleep when Mauro came into bed. Feeling his touch, she relaxed against him until she felt his hand slide up her shift along her leg.

"Mauro, I can't tonight," she said too urgently.

He left his hand where it was against her warm skin, but he searched no further. "We have both had a long day," he said quietly, not sensing her tenseness. He lifted her heavy braid and kissed her neck. "Good night, my dearest. Sleep well."

She felt him loosen his grip as he began to fall asleep quickly. "Good night, Mauro," she whispered.

Resi lay awake in the darkness, unable to let the day go as easily as her husband could. Her new predicament was gnawing at her. She would not be able to deny him each night without an explanation. But she could not bear to have him fall out of love with her after she had waited so long to be in love. She would have to find a way around it.

Chapter 26

Isabella looked at the three watercolors now drying on the stone floor and was satisfied. She felt energized, despite her restless night of lying half-awake, thinking she would miss the dawn.

Last night, Isabella had asked Natalija to wake her just before the first light. When the servant tip-toed toward the bed, Isabella was already sitting in front of the east window. Isabella had waved her away so she would not wake Caterina by mistake. Isabella wanted no disruptions.

She only had three linen sheets of paper to work with. Without a paintbrush, the Venetian had improvised, using torn bits of her bathing sponge and feathers from ink quills. Then she used a linen handkerchief to blot the excess liquid.

Her first try in the dawning light had been a runny mess of color. She'd had too much water in her sponge when dipping it in the petal extracts.

The second try was better, and she had hurriedly painted the pale pink sun as it rose in the gray sky over the granite mountain. She sketched in the hillside blocking its way, but it wasn't quite right.

On her third attempt, the sun had broken to almost full light, and she captured the contrast of the dark mountain and the multicolored sky before the illusion was lost. The yellow ball illuminated her room quickly after that.

Isabella put her pile of tinted linen scraps and bits of sponges aside and then lined up her colorful papers on the floor before her. She would draw in the details with her charcoal stick later. Isabella had never painted anything before, but it all felt right. This was what she wanted to do.

At the grooming table, she washed the colors from her fingers in her basin. They smelled nice of fermenting flowers, as if dipped in a homemade perfume. The receding colors left the tips of her fingers a dull brown instead of the vibrant yellows, reds, and pinks on the paper. She did not mind.

In the quiet, Isabella noticed for the first time how the house came alive in the early hours outside her solid chamber door. There was a faint clicking of many shoes on the marble floor in the hallway, probably the baron and his servants going to the stairs to start their day, or perhaps the maids beginning their cleaning duties.

She looked over at Caterina, sound asleep under the light summer coverlet. Isabella usually slept well into the morning with no real reason to rise early.

Today she had a reason. She still had an exciting day ahead of her, and she looked forward to the horse ride out to the countryside and to the baron's old villa.

While she waited for Natalija to return, Isabella untwisted her long braid and began to brush out the wavy locks. She would ask Verica to do something special with her hair today. Isabella wanted to look nice for her outing. She stared into the looking glass and let out a sigh. There were no parties to look forward to, no theater dates scheduled, nor any celebrated concerts to attend, yet Isabella found she was not bored. She never thought it would be possible, but she was becoming happy here.

~ * ~

Caterina had slept late that morning, and Isabella was long gone on her outing for the day. She dressed and went downstairs to meet Salar Nassim. She was surprised that she was on time, even a little early. As planned, Salar Nassim had been to the practice fields, but he had stopped at the Keep to clean up before their lesson. Caterina was at their usual table by the window when her teacher came striding into the great hall.

The young Venetian had not considered before their last meeting how handsome the mercenary looked in his belted red jacket and turban; today he wore a white one instead of the black headdress he preferred. Caterina noticed he never wore a cravat with his collarless shirt, and the olive skin of his throat was deeply tanned. The orange-colored one he wore today was attractive against his dark features. Yesterday it had been a blue shirt, and on the first day, the Persian had worn a green one. Caterina wondered if he owned a shirt in every color of the rainbow. She smiled as she made a bet with herself that tomorrow he would wear yellow.

Salar Nassim returned her bright smile and sat down in his usual chair across from her.

"I hope I have not kept you waiting too long, Lady Caterina," he said in his smooth Persian accent.

Caterina poured him a cup of tea from the pot the maid had left next to the table. Salar Nassim usually waited for her and enjoyed the sweet drink until Caterina arrived for her lesson.

"I thought I would show you what I have brought today while you have your tea," she said.

He accepted the porcelain cup with a nod and noticed the small gray ball on the table for the first time.

"Your idea of beauty has evolved, Lady Caterina," he said in his straightforward way.

"Do you know what it is, Salar Nassim?" Caterina asked.

"I have encountered hornets' nests before. Who gave it to you?"

He drank the last gulp of his tea and watched her pretty face light up as she explained her rehearsed facts.

"I was told it was a wasps' nest. The little water boy, *Aron*," she said with emphasis, "got it from the stable groom. He said it was found in the barn. Did you know that wasps bite bits of wood from walls and use that to form a nest?"

She held it by the top, so the sun reflected against it through the window. "It looks heavy, but it is as light as air. It is paper, really. You may hold it if you want."

Salar Nassim took the apple-sized nest carefully in his hands. It was just as she had said, fragile yet strong.

When he gave it back to her, Caterina confided, "I told Aron I would return it unharmed, but I am curious to look inside it. There is only a small opening, so I cannot see in without ruining it. Can you imagine how many wasps crowded into this small home? Shall we poke a little hole and take a peek?"

The mercenary could not help but see the darker side of her innocent remarks. How many walls had Salar Nassim helped break and bring down in his years of warring? How many homes had been destroyed because of that?

"You should stifle your curiosity, Lady Caterina, and return it to Aron undisturbed. Those wasps worked tirelessly to build a beautiful nest. The inside can be left to your imagination. Thank you for bringing it today."

She set the nest aside and nodded, pleased with herself. Then she handed him her deck of cards, but he gave them back to her across the table.

"Shuffle the cards like I taught you," he said directly, the teacher again.

She did as she was told and set them in front of her.

"Now, what is the bottom card on the deck?"

She answered correctly, without looking at the deck.

"If you needed that card, how do you move it to the top?"

She impressed him with her skill as she repeated the trick he had showed her.

"Now, explain how you hold back a card if you think your opponent needs it to win."

She did so beautifully.

Salar Nassim took the cards from her hands finally and said, "You are an excellent student, Lady Caterina. You have learned all my tricks, but there is one piece of advice I still need to impress upon you."

Salar Nassim chose his words thoughtfully, "I don't have to remind you that there are expectations placed on you, a lady of the aristocracy, that are not placed on a simple sellsword like me."

Caterina raised her brows at his statement. "And your advice?"

"Don't use the tricks I taught you."

Her smile faded, and her frustration was telling in the pitch of her voice. "Why have I wasted all of this time practicing then?"

"It has not been a waste. On the contrary, I think you are a better card player because of it. You are a competitor, Lady Caterina, and a skilled opponent without the tricks and cheating."

She rolled her eyes. "So I get no advantage because I am a lady?"

He contemplated her complaint as he contemplated the lady.

"I believe you have long understood your innate advantage, Lady Caterina. You don't need the tricks I taught you to manipulate a gentleman at a card table. He may even find it amusing if he catches you cheating, but he would not say anything to embarrass you. Those rules are in your favor."

Caterina nodded that he had made his point. She went on to say, "I did play with a naval lieutenant at the Baric ball not too long ago. He considered himself a gentleman, but he accused me of cheating at cards in front of the others. He was very drunk, though, so it may have been the brandy talking."

Salar Nassim folded his hands on the table and added to his counsel, "Being sober with drunken players is a distinct advantage. That is why I never drink," he said.

Caterina looked at him curiously. She knew little about other religions, except the few odd facts that the Venetians found worth ridiculing.

"I thought Muslims did not drink alcohol. Is it not forbidden in your faith?"

"This is true," he said, without acknowledging that gambling was also forbidden. "But my counsel comes from years of observation, not Islam's doctrine. Any serious task should be done with a clear head."

"I have never been drunk," she told him.

He picked up the deck of cards and absently sorted them as he continued, "It pleases me to hear that, but your soberness will never be tested. As I said, you will never be invited to join in a wagering game. A man will ask you for your feminine company to win you over, not to win at cards."

Her temper flared. Defiant again, she asked, "Why bother to teach me at all if I am not worthy of being a partner? Or did you just want my feminine company, like you say?"

He set down the cards and looked at her kindly when he said, "I told you, I am not here to seduce you."

"I will consider your advice if I ever play at a table of men. Do you have anything more to warn me about?"

He chuckled. "I do, as a matter of fact."

"Very well, Teacher. What have you neglected?"

"That cards are a game of chance," he said. "Every now and then, the cards will not be in your favor. When this happens, you must know to cut your losses and accept defeat."

He reached over and touched her pouting chin. "Accept defeat humbly," he reminded her with a smile.

She almost smiled back, but was too stubborn. "Should I not play to win, though?"

"Always remember, there is no skill in wagering on a losing hand. In war, a good commander does not put his soldiers into the fight to be massacred; he keeps them for a better time to gamble their lives. As a sellsword, I choose the battles I will wager my life on. I look for the advantage one side has over the other, and I am alive because I pick the winning side. But sometimes I will choose not to fight at all and walk away."

Caterina looked into his intense, black eyes. "Have you always been a sellsword?" she asked cautiously, wondering what made a man do what Salar Nassim did in life.

"I have been a mercenary for ten years now, a lifetime of moving from one place to another," he said.

"Ten years is a long time. God must smile down on you."

He nodded, but his thoughts were not at the table just then.

"What was your profession before that?" asked Caterina. "Were you a soldier in your homeland?"

"No, I had a different profession," he said. "I was more of a problem solver back then."

"I do not know what that means. Were you an advisor of some sort?"

"You could call it that," he replied. "My services were sought by politicians and men of commerce, someone like your father, perhaps—busy men with many affairs to manage. I was assigned to fix delicate problems with customers or colleagues that they could not resolve themselves."

"Why would you leave such an important job to do something as dangerous as being a mercenary soldier?"

He wanted to laugh, but there was nothing funny about his past, only about her question. He could not tell her that he solved the problems of the affluent class in Persia through silencing witnesses or stealing evidence that might implicate these wealthy men in their own corruption.

"Perhaps I like danger," he finally said.

She cocked her head and pursed her lips with doubt. "You contradict yourself, Salar Nassim. You just told me you would not gamble your life, yet you choose to risk it over and over as a mercenary, rather than taking a safe profession at home with your wives and daughter. Is there something more you are not telling me?"

The mercenary did laugh now.

She waited patiently for his answer, unaffected by the servants outside who glanced toward them through the glass.

"Some stories take too long to tell, Lady Caterina. Mine is best left for another day."

He leaned back in his chair next to the window. He could not help but admire Caterina's spirit, hidden in the pretty silk and lace package of a well-dressed lady.

"You are right," he added. "Maybe it is time to find different employment when I return to Athens. Maybe I will put my sword away and stay at home. Do you think that is a better choice?"

Caterina beamed with satisfaction. "Very much so," she replied, believing she had helped him finally decide on a better path.

Salar Nassim looked at her young face full of innocence, and he knew that she had.

Chapter 27

Bem had not joined his four companions on the training field that morning but had lingered in the Keep. Jero had told him last night that the Venetians were late risers, so their departure time would be up to Lady Isabella. In the meantime, Bem took note of needed supplies as he repacked his gear for the long ride home.

Lazar knocked on Bem's door only two hours past daybreak to announce the Baric party was waiting. Isabella had surprised them all when she was ready hours before planned.

Bem hastily found his hat, donned his jacket, and although he didn't expect any danger, he belted on his sword and tucked in his pistol beside it.

He found Jero to be an amiable man, and Ruby seemed to be a self-sufficient woman, the kind he enjoyed. She was the kind of woman Jero seemed to enjoy as well, he thought. He chuckled to himself as he descended the two flights of stairs. Bem understood the four were to chaperone each other, but he would try to give the Baric's steward a chance to be alone with the woman he was plainly pining for.

At the stables, Bem insisted Isabella continue to ride Fatina, even though Isabella wondered why he wouldn't want to ride his own horse.

"Cairo will be happy to have me take him out today," he argued. "I don't think you would like his temperament, but he and I get along well."

Finally, having sorted out the horses with the riders, Jero strapped the lunch baskets onto the two men's saddles, and the four companions headed out the gate at a steady gallop.

They took the road to the cottages and then followed it toward the orchards. This frontage road was well-used by the baron's tenants and was wide and smooth enough for horses and wagons alike. They were not in any hurry with the extra early start, so they slowed their pace once the road narrowed beyond the orchards.

Jero and Ruby were content to take the lead since they knew the way, and Bem and Isabella fell into a private conversation as they followed them.

"I have been trying to figure out what Bem could be short for," Isabella said flirtatiously. "Is it an African name?"

"It is the name my mother gave to me," Bem replied in the same flirtatious tone, still not giving up the information she demanded.

"She named you just Bem, not something more? Does it have a meaning?" Isabella persisted as their horses rode steadily together.

"All right, my lady. If you are truly interested, Bem is short for Chidubem, an old family name," he explained. "It has been a lucky name, and my mother wanted me to have it. My father named me from his family as well."

"Chidubem. I like it. And what is your other name?" she asked.

"It is Emilio, Emilio Chidubem Tavares. But I prefer just Bem. I am a simple man, and it is a simple name," he told her kindly, hoping that would satisfy her curiosity.

They rode a few moments in silence, and then Isabella reflected, "You picked interesting names for your horses, Bem. Or were they already named?"

He patted his small gelding with affection, then replied, "I gave them their names. We found this one abandoned earlier this year when we most needed an extra horse to get us back. I call him Cairo because my luck changed for the better in Cairo once, and he changed our luck again."

"And Fatina? Is that a lucky name?" Isabella asked pleasantly.

Even though this would be the opening for more questions, Bem told her the truth, "Fatina is named for my wife."

Isabella had considered that Bem was probably near her age, but she had not expected that he would have already left a wife somewhere.

"For your wife? Was she a beautiful Arabian like your mare?" she asked, trying to play down her surprise and her disappointment.

"She was Libyan, actually. She *is*, I should say," Bem corrected himself. "That is my hope, at least. She was taken from me, and I could not get her back."

Isabella did not hide her shock this time. "That is terrible! Was she kidnapped?"

"Yes, something like that," he said calmly. Bem was long over the despair he had felt in the months after her disappearance. He explained, "My employer's daughter took Fatina back to Athens with her while I was in Cairo. That much I know. When I first learned of it, I signed on with the crew of the first ship leaving for Athens. That was a lifetime ago." Bem sadly smiled as he tried to recall Fatina's face again.

Isabella watched him as her horse plodded along after Jero and Ruby. "Did you find her in Athens?"

"No. Without money to buy information, I could not track her down. That is why I became a mercenary soldier—it pays well. If I can find out where her mistress is living now, someone there will know Fatina's fate."

His story noticeably shook her. "Then how is Cairo a good memory if that is where your wife was taken from you?"

"Cairo was not where we were living, but that is where I met Cyro. Meeting him changed my fate and gave me hope when I thought all was lost."

Isabella was beginning to warm to Cyro, although she still could not place what bothered her about him. "Cyro told us he was in Egypt studying the pyramids. Were you on the pirated ship with him?"

"We were on the same ship, but Cyro was a passenger, and I was a deckhand. When the pirates took all of our food, water, and valuables, they left us afloat but stranded in dire straits. Our captain made for the nearest shore, which was the island of Candia."

"I know of this island. The Venetians are fighting the Ottomans there. It cannot be totally desolate."

"It was a war zone, and the port catered to naval ships, not merchant boats like ours. Our captain didn't have any credit with the port there, so he could not purchase supplies to continue on. I thought that was where it all ended for me, but Cyro was not so pessimistic. He convinced me to venture out together to earn money so we could get back on our way."

"That was clever of him," insisted Isabella.

"Indeed. Cyro was also clever enough to hide some coins in the lining of his jacket that the pirates did not find. We took a chance and gambled his silver in a dice game. Together, we made enough to buy two decent swords and proper boots, and then we hired out our services to the Venetians."

Isabella was fascinated. "That is a remarkable tale, but you and Cyro seem an unlikely pair," she told him.

Bem chuckled "I suppose we are. Most Europeans of his, um, background would never have befriended a man like me. But he looked beyond my poor situation and my skin color, and we became fast friends."

"Cyro seems to be more of a talker than a fighter, though." She could not hide her suspicious tone, and Bem understood why.

"He may not give the impression, now in the comforts of Baric Castle, but Cyro is a serious and focused man. He can keep his mouth shut."

"He does not seem to show that restraint with Caterina."

"I think he likes your friend," Bem said with a wink.

Isabella replied with a frown, "So I have noticed."

~*~

Farther up ahead, Jero and Ruby were lost in their own conversation. Ruby was looking up at the sky when she said, "Sometimes I would lie in the open field and pick out animals in the funny shapes. The ones stretched across the sky there look like sheets blowing on a sailing ship."

Jero pointed and asked, "And that one, over there?"

"I see a wave rolling over the sea," Ruby remarked, studying the sky as the horses plodded along the path without the riders' guidance.

Besides the streaks of windblown clouds, the sky was bright and blue that day. A sliver of the waning moon looked down on them.

"Why do you think the moon comes out in the daytime?" Jero asked Ruby, who was still happily contemplating the sky.

She answered, "That makes me think of my two little cousins I cared for. They were always up and down at bedtime. I would have to sing them songs to get them to fall asleep again. Maybe the moon is like a little child who should be in bed, but sneaks out to see what everyone is doing at night. For the moon, though, it is the daytime it misses."

"It sounds like you had a wonderful life there before coming here, Ruby. I am sure you are missing it."

Ruby's hold tightened on the reins, and she turned her attention from the shifting clouds to the road ahead of her. "I imagined I would live my whole life next to my parents and sisters and cousins, who had done the same for generations," she told Jero. "But when I saw the sea so close by, and these mountains with their tall green trees, I realized I could make a home here, too."

Hearing her answer, Jero was hopeful that she would.

~*~

A comfortable quiet had fallen over the riders. While Bem was content to ride in silence, Isabella wanted to hear the rest of his tale.

"So you made it off Candia, Bem. Where did you go from there?"

"Do you really want to hear more?" he asked.

"Yes," she insisted.

He indulged her curiosity as they trotted along. "Well, where did I leave off?"

"You gambled Cyro's money to buy swords."

"Yes, it took us several months of soldiering to have enough money to pay for our passage off the island. By chance, the next ship sailing from the port was the one I had crewed from Cairo. It had been stranded at the harbor the whole time and was finally resupplied. The captain took us both on as crewmates, so we were able to save our hard-won silver. Once we arrived in Athens, Cyro tried to help me find Fatina, but we found Salar Nassim instead."

Jero slowed his horse to trot next to Bem, interrupting his story. "We are going to take this trail along the hillside," he said. "We will have to ride in a single line for the first part."

"Lead the way, Jero," said Bem.

Jero did, with Ruby following him, Isabella following her, and Bem bringing up the rear. It was slow going at first. Pushing the drooping branches aside, they managed the narrow section where the trail hugged the side of the mountain.

Ruby turned to ask Isabella as they rode, "How has the ride been so far today, Lady Isabella?"

Isabella flashed her new friend a bright smile and said, "My horse seems to know the way, even if she has never been here before. I am enjoying it immensely."

The group concentrated on the rocky trek for the next few minutes until they descended into a clearing around the bend. They crossed over a shallow stream and stayed at the water's edge to offer their horses a drink.

"This is a lovely meadow," Isabella remarked.

Jero told the group, "Long ago, this was once an arm of the river that flows through the village. A family of beavers dammed it to make this pond."

"Are there still beavers living here?" Ruby asked, looking around at the strands of beech trees growing along the edge of the water and the hardy pines shading the denser forest beyond.

Jero replied, "The former Lord Baric liked to hunt here. From the size of the trees along the bank, it seems the beavers might be long gone."

"What is making that awful noise?" asked Isabella suddenly, looking around perplexed.

Jero laughed. "Those are frogs, Lady Isabella. They must own the lake now."

"Frogs and beavers! What other wildlife shall we encounter? Snakes and bears?"

Isabella was too distracted with these thoughts to notice the abundance of waterfowl that had claimed the wetland. Birds could be seen nesting in the shallow reeds and circling in the sky overhead.

"I am sure there are snakes in the grass, but bears would not be about the lake at this time of day," Jero tried to assure Isabella.

Bem added, "I wouldn't worry. If there are bears nearby, the horses will sense them and rear up to tell you."

Isabella gripped the reins tighter.

Ruby loved the woods and would not have minded watching a bear forage on the edge of the lake. She turned to ask, "Is it far to this dam, Jero? I would love to see it up close."

"If I remember, it would be at the other end of the lake. We can stop on our way back if you like. Signor Bernardo might be waiting for us, and we are not far now from the villa."

"Let's ride on then," Bem suggested. He was not interested in picking through the underbrush in search of beavers.

~*~

Leaving the lake behind, they unexpectedly came alongside a gang of men cutting and stacking wood. Two wagons were being loaded on the road to haul to Baric Castle for its winter needs. The riders stopped for a brief exchange of boisterous greetings and handshakes between Jero and the four men at the wagons, the urgency of meeting Signor Bernardo forgotten.

When they rode on a few minutes later, Jero explained, "Those are the Copic brothers. They lived in one of the castle cottages when I was a boy. The brothers share a tenant farm out here now and work for the baron."

The wagon road took them out of the forest and away from the swampy meadow. After a short distance, the four riders approached a different setting—a pastoral one, with straight lines of manicured trees and low-fenced fields. The nearby tenant farmers tended the orchards of walnuts and almonds. Several people could be seen working in the distance, pruning and tying the grapevines for the fruit to ripen in the summer sunshine. In the middle of this ancient landscape was the large stone manor house, rising above its mossy fortified wall and rimmed with a marshy moat. They had reached their destination.

Their horses halted at the crest of the hill, where they took in the beauty of their surroundings. Isabella remarked, "This would make for a lovely picture."

They descended slowly to the main road while Jero explained what he knew about the villa's history.

"The house has belonged to the Barics for many generations, used as the residence for the baron's siblings or close relations. The last person to live here was Lady Teodora. I believe she was the Lord Baric's grandfather's sister. She had no living children when she died, and the house has sat vacant ever since. Two caretakers and their wives live on the estate, but no one occupies the villa itself."

The drawbridge over the murky water was lowered for their arrival, and the gate in front of the tall stone wall was open. Perched tall on her horse, Isabella took it all in.

"It is a lovely place," she said, "What does the baron plan to do with it?"

"It seems the former Baron Baric put it off these twenty-odd years, and Lord Baric has the time now to focus on its renovation. I am eager to have a look inside and see how neglected it really is."

Looking around, Bem wondered, "Where is the boundary with the Habsburg territory from here, Jero?"

"We are it," Jero said with a chuckle. "I am told the tenants live peacefully with the Habsburgs. The neighboring families are used to each other and the line between us. There are few conflicts unless their lord asks them to fight for him."

Bem looked back at the ancient rampart. It would never withstand a modern siege. The moat-protected walls defended the residents from bandits and thieves, not from cannons and battering rams.

They rode across the small courtyard to the stables. An older man came toward them out of the barn, grinning and waving at Jero. He called over as he approached, "It is good to see you again, Jero. The baron sent a message with the change of plans."

Jero halted Bacchus and dismounted to greet the caretaker. "Good to see you, too, Ervin. Has Signor Bernardo arrived?" Jero looked around for signs of a visitor.

"Not yet. I see Nela made up a basket for you. Will you be staying the night?"

"Just until the afternoon. Is the house open?" Jero asked the old servant politely.

"Yes, Jero. I didn't take off the furniture coverings, but that is easily done if you wish to see everything."

Jero understood how much work that would make for the elderly couple. "No, we will just peek under if we need to look. There is no need to bother with uncovering everything."

Bem helped the ladies dismount from their horses, and they stretched their stiff legs and wandered slowly to the front door.

Bem had not followed Jero's conversation with Ervin to know how long their outing would be. "Will we be riding again soon?" he asked Jero.

"We will be here at least a few hours. We can unsaddle the horses."

The men left their animals in the care of Ervin's son and joined the women at the front steps. Jero opened the heavy oak door to the front foyer.

"After you, my ladies," Jero said with a formal wave of his hand, and they all went inside.

Chapter 28

A message came from the constable while the baron had been at the training fields that morning. In it, Radic spelled out what he had learned about the stolen ship. He confirmed it belonged to Lord Dubovic and had high-value cargo on board. The investigators had implicated Ivanoslav's eldest son, but Branislav was not named—yet. Whether his brother would rat him out was another possibility. Radic wrote in his message that it was rumored another high-value ship in the Adriatic would be targeted next.

Mauro handed the note to Nestor to read. "What do you make of it, Nestor? Is that typical, that the pirates would take the ship and crew as well?"

"Those are not normal acts of thieving on the Adriatic. Most pirates only take the cargo that they can sell quickly on the black market. A ship is marked and is not easy to disguise to sell, but I have heard it is done on the Mediterranean."

"I am heading out to the salt flats shortly and will let Branislav know that I expect he meets the Kokkinos ship at the end of the week, not his brother's."

"Should I put the word out that you are looking to hire a new captain for your ship?"

"No, Branislav has not crossed me yet. I think we can resolve this today," Mauro said. "I will see you later, Nestor."

Mauro left the old advisor at the writing desk. From the study door, he saw the bright colors of his wife's gown disappear into the sitting room. He followed her there.

"Hello, my dear. I thought you would be having lunch with Caterina on the terrace," he said from the threshold.

"Oh, hello, Mauro," Resi said with surprise. "She will be down soon. I am just looking for a book."

Mauro noticed she was standing in front of the shelf with the old Baric volumes. "Are you looking for works on religion and ancient history today? No poems or adventures this time?" he inquired playfully.

In truth, his wife was looking for a copy of the Holy Bible, or perhaps a book of the catechism lessons used by the Baric children. Resi thought she remembered seeing one shelved somewhere with the old collection.

"Won't you be late for your outing?" she asked more coolly than she intended.

"There is always time to say hello to my wife."

He came across the room and to the bookshelf. He leaned in to kiss Resi's mouth, but his lips met her cheek as she turned her head.

Unaffected by her shun, Mauro told his wife, "When I return from the salt fields, I am sure I will be dusty and hot. Would you like to take your bath with me then?"

"Um, well, I, um," stammered Resi. She would quickly have to find a good reason not to join him. Lady Caterina came first to mind.

"That sounds wonderful, but I promised Lady Caterina that we would soak in the bathhouse this afternoon. Lady Isabella is gone all day, so I thought that would be a nice activity for us."

Mauro did not quibble. "You are a good hostess, Resi. Enjoy your afternoon, then."

He held her cheeks with his hands this time and kissed her lips. When she failed to return his warm affection, he asked, "Is everything alright? You seem distracted."

"Do I? I was just, um, perhaps I am just a little tired."

Her mind was in a panic, standing there next to him. He seemed so concerned. Should she take this chance to tell him what kind of a woman he was married to? That it was her laziness that had kept her from being a good Catholic and a good wife.

"You should be going, Mauro. They will be expecting you," she finally answered instead.

His men would wait all day if he commanded, and she knew it.

Mauro did not press the point. "I will see you later, Resi. Maybe you should lie down after lunch, if you are not feeling well." He kissed her lightly on her forehead and left through the terrace door.

~*~

On the path by the servants' entrance, Mauro met up with Simeon, who was just coming from the kitchen.

"It seems like you are taking an unusual number of meals in my kitchen, Simeon. Is there something you want to tell me?"

"All right, Mauro, I will make my confession," Simeon replied with a chuckle. "The women eat better in the kitchen than we do in the Keep, and that is the honest truth of it."

Mauro agreed with a laugh, and the two continued on the path to the courtyard together. "So, is it just the tasty food that attracts you to dine with my maids? Not one girl in particular, perhaps? You know the night watch reports any comings and goings."

"It is good to know they keep alert in the early morning hours," Simeon said sheepishly.

"You should do the right thing, Simeon, and ask Franja to marry you before you cause a scandal in my house."

They stopped at the well. The guards were rotating shifts, and Simeon was to replace one at the gatehouse, but he lingered to answer Mauro's question.

"I have thought long and hard about it, and, to be honest, I am not sure what to do, Mauro. Things were simpler with my first wife. We lived together with Elise's parents not much differently than the way she had lived before marrying me. Marrying Franja would be different."

"Does she make you happy, Simeon?" Mauro asked.

"She does, yes. I would marry her if she would have me. I just don't want to hear her say no."

"Why would she reject your offer? If you let her think the choice is hers, I believe she will agree to marry you. I know she would like to continue in the kitchen, and we would all miss her contribution to the house, but every woman wants a husband," Mauro reasoned.

Simeon saw Hugo waving at him from the gatehouse. Simeon waved back to signal that he understood, but instead of going to his shift, he stayed at the well.

"And your wife, Mauro—how is Lady Baric today?" asked Simeon. "Is she well?"

Simeon was a disciplined guardsman, and it was not like him to linger in conversation when duty called. Mauro looked at him suspiciously and said, "We were talking about a wife for you, Simeon. Why this sudden interest in mine?"

Simeon's cheerful expression hardened when he said, "I have taken an oath to keep your wife's conversations confidential. And until today, I promise you that I have not broken it."

"Did something happen yesterday in the village? I give you permission to answer honestly," Mauro said with concern.

Simeon continued to be vague, "So, your wife has not confided in you? She said she might."

Mauro impatiently shifted his feet. He had left his hat in the study, and the high noon sun baked the cobblestones where they stood.

"No riddles, Simeon. If you think there is something important to tell me, I am listening." Mauro pulled the dipper from the water bucket and helped himself to a drink.

"Very well, Mauro," said Simeon. "You know that, um, the baroness and Lady Ruby talk at times in Greek during their wagon rides, so no one understands personal matters being said between them."

Mauro nodded. "That makes your oath easier to keep, I suppose."

A smile brightened Simeon's serious expression. "Right, but yesterday in the wagon, your lady sat with Fabian's sister, and Lady Caterina convinced your wife that I was not listening while driving."

"I see. And what could they have possibly said that concerns me, Simeon?"

Simeon cleared his throat awkwardly and said, "It seems the baroness thinks she has committed some grave sins. From their conversation, I imagine it was revealed when she was visiting Radic's wife."

"That had to be a remarkable conversation. What kind of grave sins could my wife be worried about?" Mauro asked with a laugh. "Terese is a fine and decent woman."

Simeon looked around uncomfortably to be sure they were alone and replied, "The baroness is indeed a fine lady, but, well, she mentioned a few sins you might have committed together."

"Together?" Mauro thought for a moment as to what that could mean.

Mauro met his captain's eyes, and there was a playful twinkle in them. "The ladies discussed our marriage bed in front of you?" he asked.

Simeon nodded, still managing to keep his smile in check, then added, "My wife was never pregnant, so we did not face your dilemma. I can imagine the wait is long without some level of sin together. The flesh is weak," Simeon said, repeating what the ladies had concluded on the wagon ride home.

Mauro's thoughts went to Resi in the sitting room just a short while ago—searching through the old volumes and refusing to kiss him on the lips.

"Did my wife say she needed to ask for penance for this, um, sinning?"

Simeon let his guard down and chuckled when he said, "Penance was the main topic, Mauro. Lady Baric's worry was how to tell Father David of these sins. The baroness told Lady Caterina that she has corrupted you and that she wants to take responsibility for your, um, participation."

"She is worried about my corruption?"

Mauro rubbed his temples while he paced the length of the well. Looking up again, Mauro could not help but find Simeon's grin contagious.

"Just so you know," Mauro declared, "my wife need not be concerned about going to Hell. It is because she is such a good person that she is troubled about it at all. It was right of you to tell me, Simeon, and I will keep your confidence."

Simeon patted Mauro's shoulder in sympathy and then sauntered off to relieve Hugo at the guardhouse.

Somehow, Mauro would need to confront his wife about her perceived plight without revealing that Simeon had broken her confidence. He hoped he would find inspiration in the course of the busy day to come up with a solution. For now, he would have his late lunch in the Keep.

~ * ~

The empty dishes were being cleared from the kitchen table, and Nela reminded the chatting maids, "We still have the baroness and Lady Caterina to feed. Ivana, make a nice platter of those fried sardines. Include the peas and boiled eggs in aspic from the pantry. The baroness likes that dish, but put it on a bed of garden greens. If there is any of the carrot cake left, that might please Lord Fabian's sister to eat a little more at her lunch—the lady eats like a sparrow. Brigita, fetch a fresh pitcher of water to put on their table."

The maids were one step ahead of her, and they went about the tasks before Cook had finished her orders.

As Nela organized the younger servants into action, Franja slipped out the back door to follow Danica. She hurried to catch up with her friend.

Franja called out, "I am happy you are feeling better today, Danica."

"I think I am over the worst of it," replied Danica as they continued on the path toward the vegetable garden together. "I still cannot stomach even looking at the sardines, but I think I will be able to keep the rest down. Krsto is tired of emptying my bucket by the bed. He asked me to let him know when I am heading to the cottage. I hope to see you in the morning, Franja."

Danica began to walk at a quicker tempo down the path to meet up with her husband, and Franja summoned her nerve to follow through on what she had wanted to ask.

"Wait, Danica! I was wondering something." Franja hesitated.

Danica came back to her side.

"Do women always feel so sick when they are first pregnant? I mean, can you be pregnant and not, well, be ill at every meal?" Franja asked.

Danica thought about it a moment. "Everyone is different, I suppose. Remember how the baroness was retching every morning before she lost her first baby? Then with this one, she didn't believe she could really be with child again until after the second month passed. She said she felt very well from the start," Danica reminded her.

"That is what I was afraid of," mumbled Franja.

"You're a little old to be meeting boys in haystacks," Danica teased. Then she saw the stricken look on her friend's face. "Oh, I am sorry, Franja. You are serious, aren't you?"

"I am over three weeks late, Danica, and I am never late. I have not been sick, but something feels different."

Danica's guess of Franja meeting a lover in the barn was not too farfetched. "Is Simeon the father? How did you manage any time alone with him?" she asked.

With downcast eyes, Franja replied, "It's not that I am lustful or anything. It wasn't planned that way. We only wanted to have a private conversation for once, to learn more about each other. So we went upstairs, and it just happened that I slept there all night with him."

"In the Keep? Franja!" Danica scolded.

She looked up and down the path after her outburst. Krsto, who was across the fence in the vegetable patch, looked up from his work.

Franja lowered her voice, "We were very careful. Simeon told me as long as no one saw me, it was not forbidden."

"That is not what I heard," Danica hissed. "There are others just across the hallway."

"No, we went to a room on the top floor, where no one lives. I went there twice and never saw anyone."

"Twice!" Danica blurted out.

Franja panicked and covered her mouth. She had not intended to mention the second night.

Danica recovered from her shock and said more kindly, "Oh dear. Then you are pregnant. Have you told him?"

Franja shook her head. "I wanted to be sure before I say anything. I started bleeding a little a few days back, but it stopped that same day, and then I began to wonder."

"Well, don't wonder too long or the priest will be calling it a bastard child. You can say the baby is born early, but only by a month or so. By the time you get married, it will be that long."

Franja took a crumpled handkerchief from her apron pocket and began to sob. "I have been so tired, and my back hurts from being on my feet so long. There has been extra baking to do, and I have been working earlier and earlier, trying to get it all done." She blew her nose and added, "Then I began hoping I would maybe lose it."

Danica held her friend squarely by the shoulders and looked her in the eyes. "You cannot think that, Franja, let alone say it out loud. A baby is a gift from God."

"I know it is a sin, but I am not thinking straight. I am not ready for all of this."

"Look at me, Franja."

Franja wiped her tears and took a deep breath to calm herself.

Danica assured her, "Simeon obviously likes you, or he would not come around every day. He may even love you. Have you thought of that?"

Franja stared at her blankly.

"You wouldn't be the first house servant to get married in a rush," Danica said with a chuckle, trying to find the humor in it for Franja's sake. "We have been to weddings where the bride was secretly a month or two along, haven't we?"

Franja did not smile along with her friend. "But those girls wanted to marry. I don't know if I want to marry Simeon," she confessed quietly.

Danica slumped in frustration. "Simeon is a good match," she reminded her friend. "Why would you let him bed you if you don't like him enough to marry him?"

Franja began to sob again. "I don't want to be a wife in a cottage, Danica. I don't want a baby."

Danica shook her head with pity that her friend was so miserable over something Danica was glad to have herself. Danica wrapped her arms around Franja to comfort her.

"Oh, Franja, it is too late now. You will have to marry."

"But they need me in the kitchen."

"Nela will manage," Danica assured her.

"The baron will be upset," insisted Franja.

"No one will be upset. Your time to marry is long overdue."

"I want to bake, Danica." Franja's tears flowed freely down her cheeks again.

"Simeon will let you work in the kitchen when you are married. I still work in the garden, doing what I like to do."

Franja would not be comforted. "Yes, but for how long?" she groaned. "Once your first baby is here, Krsto will have you making the second. That is always how it happens."

Danica squeezed her friend tightly against her and whispered, "You cannot keep this secret from Simeon. You will feel better after you tell him, but make it soon."

Franja cried onto Danica's sympathetic shoulder and nodded that she would.

Chapter 29

The architect arrived just as Ervin's wife had set out Nela's packed lunch on the patio table. The man was brimming with words of apology for his delay, but the stress of wrong turns and backtracking on the forested trails had fueled Signor Bernardo's hunger, and he gratefully joined the four at their lunch table.

Bernardo held out his glass as Jero offered the wine bottle in his direction once again. "You were most generous to invite me to your luncheon, Signor Jero. It was an unexpected pleasure," the architect said, putting down the wishbone he was sucking on from his third piece of chicken.

"I am happy we could go over the plans during lunch, Signor Bernardo. Should we walk through the house now?" asked Jero.

"With pleasure. The message from Baron Baric said that I am to shop for your choices of fabrics and furnishings. I will send the baron a price list from Venice."

"Yes, Signor Bernardo," Jero confirmed, "that is what the baron wishes."

The architect then turned to Isabella and said with a greasy smile, "I will take great pleasure in hearing your refined suggestions, Signorina Valli. You must find Lord Baric's villa rather provincial."

"I find it exceedingly charming, but I do have a few ideas," Isabella answered.

The Baric party had already explored the villa from cellar to attic before lunch while waiting for their guest. The four had speculated what changes they would make if it were their home being renovated with the baron's money. Bem had made it clear that his opinions would be of little value, and Ruby had offered to keep him company while Jero and Isabella discussed the plans with the designer.

Jero suggested politely, "Shall we start upstairs?"

The wooden stools scraped against the granite flagstone as the three rose and excused themselves to conclude the baron's assignment. Bem and Ruby were left alone on the patio.

Bem poured another glass of wine for himself, enjoying the unaccustomed leisure time.

"I have never personally known anyone who has an extra house that he has no use for."

Ruby said, "I never even had my own room before coming to live with the Barics. One does get used to such luxuries, though."

"What is your favorite part about living with the Venetians?" Bem asked, setting his glass down to give her his full attention across the table.

Looking at the platters and crocks laid out in front of them, she replied, "I like their food, but that could be because Nela and Franja are fantastic cooks. Oh, and," she said but then hesitated, shaking her head and chuckling.

Bem prodded her arm playfully. "You can tell me, Ruby. What else should I envy?"

She held his steady stare and said, "This might sound vain, but I like their looking glasses."

Bem raised his brows with surprise.

"Well, I never had one before. Resi told me I can take the one in my room with me when I go back."

"That is an especially Venetian commodity, and very expensive." He waved his hand at the paned windows above them and added, "Like the glass in the window openings. I have never had anything but shutters or skins over my mine."

"Nor have I," she agreed.

Bem dipped a piece of bread in the sauce on his plate and then declared, "The Venetian food is tasty, but it is still too bland for my preference. I think I would trade your looking glass for a feast of spicy couscous."

Ruby knew this dish. It was a staple in the southern lands, like pasta was to the Venetians.

She cocked her head and asked, "Of all the foods to choose from, isn't that a rather simple request?"

He swallowed his bite and proclaimed, "It is not a simple request at all. Couscous reminds me of home, but to the Austrians, it reminds them of their Ottoman enemy. You do not find it served anywhere in Habsburg territories."

"Was it your mother's specialty?" Ruby asked.

"My mother died when I was young. It was my wife's specialty, actually. She is Libyan. She liked to serve it with young goat, or sometimes lamb, with a spicy sauce mixed with sweet raisins." He smacked his lips for emphasis.

His off-handed remark caught Ruby off guard. She had witnessed Bem overtly flirting with Lady Isabella, and he gave Ruby herself such focused consideration while they conversed that she was nearly drawn into his charms as well. But Bem had a wife.

Ruby warily asked, "You must miss your wife dearly. When did you last see her?"

"It has been two years. I will see her soon, though, when we return to Greece," he said confidently.

Ruby studied his attractive young face, not yet lined from the traumatic ordeals of his short life. She asked, "How old were you when you married, Bem? You cannot be older than Patricius, and I could not imagine him ready to settle down with a wife."

"Nor could I," Bem said with a laugh, "but I fell madly in love. I was twenty-one, only a little older than my wife. Come to think of it, Fatina was your age when we married. I expect that you plan to marry soon."

"I am afraid it will not be my choice how old I am when I marry."

"But if you fall in love, Ruby, you must try to hold on to it," Bem asserted. "It took two months of asking to get permission to marry Fatina, but I knew I wanted her as my wife. We were so happy together."

Ruby stood up and began packing the remaining food into the two baskets. "For one so lovesick, you are a patient man to wait two years to go back to her," she told him.

 Bem looked up at her from his seat at the table. "I think those who are truly in love are the most patient. Would you not agree?"

His tone was playful but held a challenge. Bem had seen firsthand that Ruby seemed as in love with Jero as Jero was in love with her.

"Yes, I see your point," she replied coyly.

He turned his focus to the stables across from the patio and asked, "How did a seaman's daughter become such a good horseman? Did Alberto teach you to ride?"

"No, my grandfather taught me."

"He owns a horse in Thessaloniki?"

"No, he lives in the hills. My grandfather is a horse trainer, and so are my uncles. I lived with one of those uncles for a time. I helped his wife with her small children when she became pregnant again. I ended up staying almost a year with them on their farm until I was called away to travel here with Resi. But while I was there, he taught me to ride."

Bem's expression grew serious as he listened, and his question to her was jarring. "Are you a Muslim, Ruby?"

Ruby shook the crumbs from the basket's cloth cover with a crisp snap. She then tucked it around the packed crocks and answered firmly, "I am not."

She sat back down again across from him, and an awkward moment passed.

"I am confused, then." Bem continued, "I spent several years in Libya, and the Ottoman rules are clear. Only Muslims can ride horses or own their own land, especially as horse breeders. Even Patrik never learned to ride before coming to Athens."

Ruby held his stare and said, "My grandfather converted to Islam to save our ancestral farm. Horses were in his heart, and he could not leave that life behind. Even in Libya, you might have noticed that not all Muslims practice their faith earnestly, especially those forced into it."

"Your father wasn't forced, like your grandfather and uncles?"

"My uncles were only children at the time, but my father was already a young man. When he refused to become a Turk, my grandfather pushed him out and made him leave, so he went to Thessaloniki to find work. They eventually reconciled, but it took years."

"I understand your grandfather's dilemma. And are horses in your heart too, Ruby?" Bem asked.

She let out a sad sigh. "I have been spoiled here this past year. My fear is that I can no longer live without both. I love horses and the sea."

"Then why not stay here?"

She shook her head at the simplicity of his advice. "I cannot just stay as I wish and be a guest forever," replied Ruby. "I am not a servant, and I am not a lady from their society. I just take up space and cost Lord Baric money."

Bem laughed at her logic. "Lord Baric has plenty of rooms, and I saw you eat—it should not cost him too much to feed you," Bem teased. "But if you don't want to burden the baron, you should find a husband and make your life here with him. Your father would not have let you leave in the first place if he was so protective of your future arrangements."

"I was asked by Demetrius Kokkinos to come as a sort of assurance, and my father agreed. I was to keep Resi from running away, if you want to know the truth of it."

"Are your services still required?"

She grinned and said, "You can see for yourself that my job is done. I write home often to say both Resi and I are truly content here, but my father does not trust the Venetians or the Barics. He probably thinks I am forced to write that."

Bem scoffed. "Patrik did not trust Lord Baric, either. That is why he had to come see for himself that his sister was being treated well. He is satisfied and has just written to Demetrius to say so."

"I hope it will be enough to convince my father that I have more reason to stay than to go home now."

Bem's expression brightened, and he was playful again. "A pretty girl like you must have left a sweetheart behind."

She blushed. "There were a few boys I liked in Thessaloniki, but I am not sure I would want to meet them now."

"Those boys will be grown men when you return. Do not already count them out as being unsuitable. You are young and time is on your side, Ruby."

Then he stood up, and a look of mischief crossed Bem's face when he said, "What shall we do with our time this afternoon?"

Ruby looked around at the appealing neglect of the villa house grounds. They would have at least an hour to entertain themselves before Jero finished his business with Signor Bernardo.

"Do you want to walk around the wall while we wait? Maybe have a look at the moat?" Ruby suggested.

Bem sized up the young Greek, comfortably dressed in her practical Ottoman riding trousers and sturdy short boots. "Why don't we walk *on* the wall? I am sure there is a way to get onto the ramparts. Are you willing?"

Her face lit up with excitement, and he was pleased he had chosen correctly. They left the patio and crossed the small courtyard that led to the open drawbridge.

"Do you think anyone will mind us climbing up?" asked Ruby, hurrying along to keep up with Bem's long strides. "The guardsmen at Baric Castle would not let me on the ramparts. These walls look even more ancient. They are probably guarded by the spirits of old soldiers."

"There is no one here who would mind us exploring a little, except maybe those old ghosts. Look, Ruby, there is a ladder. Let's go find them."

Chapter 30

At the salt fields, the group of riders tied their horses to the railing. The mercenaries took in the view of the entire mining operation from the upper cliffs before descending on horseback to the dock.

"This is impressive, Lord Baric. I had no idea your tidal flats yielded such a production," said Cyro.

The baron replied, "The Barics have been mining this inlet of the sea for hundreds of years. I have little to do with its operations, except to supervise that the salt gets harvested and sold so that more can be harvested and sold."

"Spoken like a true man of commerce," Patrik said under his breath.

Soren remarked, "Yours looks like a modern ship, Lord Baric. I would have expected you to use a galley on the Adriatic."

"We have reliable winds, so my father switched to the new sailing ships many years ago. In a pinch, there are oar locks, and the sailors can row the ship in tight spaces. As a Dane, you probably have more knowledge of my ship than I."

"I might. I grew up surrounded by water and sailing craft of all kinds. I captained my first little sailboat around the island I grew up on at the age of eight." Soren looked over at Patrik when he said, "I am trying to get Patrik to sail with me. I am sure there is much I can learn from him. He captained his first little boat at seven."

"Why would you not join Soren in a sailing expedition?" Mauro asked.

Patrik laughed when he explained, "Soren is not telling the whole story. He's not talking about the North Sea, he wants to sail to a place called Brazil— a six month journey! Just because the Kokkinos men have saltwater in their blood doesn't mean I want to go to the end of the world."

"Suit yourself," mumbled Soren.

Mauro sensed this was part of a private argument they had not yet concluded.

"My ship only goes as far as the Greek shoreline," Mauro told Soren. "Shall we go down to the pier, and you can have a look at it? They are almost finished loading it for tomorrow's departure."

The baron and his four visitors went along the weathered boardwalk that led out across the edge of the salt flats to the open body of water where the ship was docked.

Patrik told his brother-in-law, "Before I forget, Mauro, I have a few letters to give to Castor. Salar Nassim also wrote to his family in Athens and Rhodes. My brother can courier them from Thessaloniki."

Mauro took the small bundle of sealed papers Patrik held out for him. "I wish I had thought of that when I posted my last letter to Ruby's father. I have not yet heard back from him."

"One of these letters is to Ruby's father. I wrote him that I think Ruby would have a good life here with the most suitable husband that I could recommend for her."

Mauro raised his brows in surprise. "That was kind of you to do that for Jero."

"Jero? I was talking about Eduard," said Patrik, but could not quite manage to hide his smile.

Mauro laughed at the unexpected joke. When he wasn't trying to irritate Mauro, Patrik could be good company.

Mauro humbly said, "Thank you for that gesture. Your sister will miss Ruby if she must go back to Thessaloniki. She has become a part of our family here, and I would like her to stay."

Patrik shook his head and shrugged at his comment. "I never expected you to be such a generous man," he said. "I may want to stay myself."

They continued down the creaking walkway side by side; the others were now well ahead of them.

Mauro reflected, "I noticed Soren has only said but a few words before today. I was surprised when he joined the conversation just a while ago."

Patrik looked down the path at Soren with Cyro and Salar Nassim. They were chatting contentedly at the bottom of the gangway that led onto the Baric's ship.

"Indeed. Soren is finally looking ahead, instead of mourning the past. He is coming out of his shell, now that he's had a little peace."

Mauro stopped and asked, "And how are my soldiers behaving in the Keep?"

"They are civil enough. We might be getting drunk with some of them in the tavern tonight. We are going there for dinner, and to see what else goes on after dark at your Green Goose. Vilim invited us, actually. He is a relation of yours, isn't he?"

"He is a cousin on the Toth side. His mother was my mother's cousin. He comes from unfortunate circumstances, though."

"Your cousin doesn't seem too underprivileged."

"Vilim should be living as a lord, like all the Toth cousins, but his mother married a commoner."

Patrik scoffed. "Isn't it funny how this whole bloodline thing works? My sister marries you, and she has jewels at her throat and on her fingers. If she had been the baroness and you a Greek sailor's son, your children would get none of her father's wealth."

"Vilim was not without some support, I suppose. He was tutored and trained to become an officer, the same as I, but not given a home or a title," Mauro clarified.

"I think you should first prove you are truly a noble person and then be given the title, not the other way around. I could tell Vilim had a different upbringing from your other captains, though. He has a certain something about him."

"Nobility?" Mauro suggested with a grin.

Patrik rolled his eyes. "What I mean is, he comes across as a decent man."

Mauro nodded. "Vilim has moral character. My cousin Petar, for example, will inherit the title of count from my uncle and the entire Toth estate. He is the eldest of three brothers and the least deserving. But birth order does not determine character."

They stopped just before the gangway up to the ship's deck. The others were already on board, being greeted by Mauro's crew.

One sailor motioned to the baron across the ship's deck with a questioning gesture, and Mauro nodded to the sailor to give the newcomers a full tour.

Patrik waited with Mauro, pensively regarding his brother-in-law, a man who seemed to have everything one needed in life. He then said thoughtfully, "We are both second-born, Mauro. Even if I were the better captain and savvier negotiator, my brother would still inherit my father's ships and his customers. I was encouraged to learn the family business, but only to assist in Castor's fortune. That is the way of it. I will always be second in line."

Mauro was not even second-born if he counted Jero, but it had all fallen to him in the end.

"So, you just walked away from your brother, is that what happened, Patrik?"

"I was not needed. My father took Castor under his wing and focused on making my brother succeed, not me."

Mauro saw things differently now. "It is a family business with several ships. Maybe your brother wants you to be a part of it, perhaps even as an equal."

Patrik considered that scenario before admitting, "I was young when I left Thessaloniki for the first time. It seemed Castor was taking the helm of not just the ships, but of the Kokkinos family. He married and was starting a family in my father's home—my home. I did not see a place for me in his shadow. I had to get out of there."

Mauro listened to Patrik's sentiments while he watched Cyro and Soren disappear into the ship's hold. Salar Nassim leaned against the mast, watching the comings and goings up the gangway. The baron and Patrik should have joined them, but Mauro was more interested in hearing this story.

He asked quietly, "Is that when you enlisted in the Ottoman Army? Resi said that you wanted to be the family tribute before a brother could be taken later."

"She told you that?" Patrik chuckled. "Well, I guess no one corrected the story for her then."

"What is the real story?" demanded Mauro. His stern gaze required an answer.

"There is nothing to hide," Patrik finally said. "I went to Athens, intending to join up. That part is true. I wanted to be someplace anonymous, not a soldier in Thessaloniki, policing my own friends and family. I had the enlistment date and arrived a day early in the city. I figured the army would take everything I showed up with, so I went to spend the money left in my purse."

Mauro listened with interest as Patrik continued to explain, "I went to one of the bigger bathhouses in Athens—a grand one. I had lunch and wine and a massage. I was feeling quite good about my last day as a free man when I noticed Soren and Niels across the pool. They were hard to miss, with their matching blond hair in a sea of black-haired men. I was already drunk from the wine and the heat of the room, so I went to find out what these Northerners were doing in Athens."

"That was brave of you. The two must have been a fearsome-looking pair together," Mauro remarked.

"They were also nearly naked and half drunk—different from the brothers on the battlefield!" Patrik chuckled at the memory.

He continued, "That was a fateful day for me, meeting the two of them. We shared some more wine while they told me about their recent return from the New World and how they had just met Salar Nassim at the docks. He was recruiting men for his gang and had convinced them that the real adventure was in mercenary soldiering, not in expeditions. Nassim had Jonas and Alex soldiering with him at the time, which would seem like enough riders with the addition of the Danes. But Salar Nassim has a lucky number: six. He needed another man to ride with them to make that lucky combination. Since he was eager to be on his way, he agreed to give me a try."

"So you did not show up for your registration," Mauro said expectantly.

"No, and we left for the North the following week."

"Why wouldn't the Ottoman Army hunt you down? I understand they do not like men changing their minds."

Patrik asserted, "I was not a designated tribute and had not officially signed on, so I was not bound to the Ottoman Army yet. My father did say they came looking for me, but everyone agreed I must have met with some mishap along the way to Athens. I felt sort of bad about that."

"How long did they think you were dead?" Mauro asked.

"I wrote to them right before I left, so as long as the courier took to bring my letter. My father didn't like me being a mercenary soldier, but he agreed it was better than joining the Empire's army. It wasn't until we came back through Thessaloniki almost two years later that my sister must have thought I went from one line of soldiering to the other. We had just lost Alex and Jonas, so we were taking a break from the fighting up north."

Mauro nodded. He knew that next part of the story.

Soren and Cyro were back on deck from their tour below, and Mauro asked, "Does Salar Nassim not like ships? He didn't go with the others."

Patrik looked across the deck. "That wouldn't bother Salar Nassim. He seems to be more interested in your operation. He observes everything, takes in the details of every place he goes. Remnants of his former clandestine life, I suppose."

"I know of his past," Mauro said, still watching the Persian. "Men love to point out a dangerous man, once he is exposed."

"Occupations do not make men dangerous, just like your aristocratic titles do not make men noble. Salar Nassim is no more dangerous than you, Mauro," Patrik said smoothly.

The baron was reputed to be calculating, cunning, and a respected commander.

"Are you saying that I am a dangerous man?" Mauro replied.

"Salar Nassim has never broken my face, so there is some proof."

Mauro could not deny it, staring now at the damage he had done to his brother-in-law's nose.

"Your face is healing nicely. In a few days you might look normal again," Mauro said sympathetically, then added, "But I think it was you who started our fight."

Patrik gave him a sideways smile of guilt.

On deck, Branislav was being introduced to the visitors by one of the crewmates.

Mauro noticed that and said with a new urgency, "Let us join the others. I need to have a word with my ship's captain before we head back. It will only take a few minutes. That will give you time to have a look around."

The two continued up the gangway onto the crowded deck. Mauro's crew stopped their work to acknowledge his arrival, and Branislav came over to greet him.

"Branislav, good day," Mauro said to the sea captain. "Might we go over something in private?"

Mauro left Patrik with the others and then disappeared through the salt-stained door of his captain's quarters. He removed his wide hat to keep the feathers from bumping into the low ceiling beams, and he looked around the small room.

Mauro had never been in Branislav's residence. It was as tidy as the rest of the ship. Branislav's narrow bunk was covered with a clean blanket, and scrolls of maps and charts were tucked away on the rack above the empty table situated along one wall. There was an iron stove for heat and a narrow writing desk with more scrolls, an inkpot, and a few cups and bottles.

Branislav motioned to one of the two stools at the little table. He took two of the cups and the bottle of wine and then poured the baron a drink and a generous portion for himself.

Mauro accepted it and asked, "Do you foresee good sailing conditions tomorrow?"

Branislav sat down on the stool across from his employer and answered the trivial question, "It is hard to tell this time of year, sir. We can go weeks with fair weather, and then there can be a sudden storm over the water."

Branislav drank a gulp of the wine.

Mauro took his time to introduce his accusation. He tilted his cup and watched the red liquid swirl.

"I have always found a man's motivations interesting," the baron said, looking into the wine like a fortune-teller looks into their cup of tea leaves. "I have known rich men who are still motivated by money, and I have met destitute men motivated solely by risk and the addictive rush it gives them. You have been loyal to the Barics. Do you think I have been a fair employer to you?"

Mauro looked directly at the young sailor now.

Branislav answered unflinchingly, "Yes, my lord, you have."

Mauro continued to query the captain, "Is it enough for you, or is there something lacking? More money, more adventure?"

Branislav somehow remained steady under the stern Baric stare.

"What are you suggesting, Lord Baric?" he asked.

Mauro leaned in across the low table. "I know your brother has been charged with pirating. You were gone two weeks ago when it happened. I want to be sure that you are not putting my ship and my crew in harm's way."

The closed cabin was stuffy, and a bead of sweat rolled down the sailor's temple as he reflected on his answer.

"I only went once, my lord, as a favor. I would never betray you or put the crew in danger."

"But you would betray the neighboring lord?"

Branislav said firmly, "We did not betray him, sir."

"Is that so? Your brother stole Lord Dubovic's ship and cargo, and you helped him. How is that not a betrayal, and a crime?"

"I cannot say," the captain answered too quickly.

Mauro was not in the mood for word games and raised his voice in anger, "You will say, or you will be off my land before the day is over."

Branislav emptied his cup with one last gulp. He nodded to his guilt and confessed, "It was a job, not thieving. The baron himself paid my brother to take his ship and make it look like it was stolen. We delivered it to Lord Dubovic's buyer."

Mauro did not like his neighbor. He did not trust him, either, but this was a serious accusation Branislav had made.

"His buyer? Are you saying it was a scam of Lord Dubovic's own making?"

"I am telling you the truth, sir. Lord Dubovic's ship is somewhere in the Mediterranean under new paint and new sails. He sold it at a loss, but he profited from the insurance money and the sale of the cargo it held. He paid us for delivering it—that is all we did."

Mauro remained seated but was ready to pounce. "And do I pay you so little that you would risk everything to commit this crime for Lord Dubovic?"

"If you must know, we did it for my father, Lord Baric. My aunt is looking after him while he recovers, but he is wasting away in the countryside. We will use the money to build him a little house to look out over the Adriatic again."

Mauro swallowed the wine, and his stern features softened. "Despite your motives, your brother is facing difficult charges, and you could be next. How will your father stand the news that his sons are in prison, just for some house on the sea?"

"Lord Dubovic assured us we would not be caught."

"Did you really think the Venetian Navy would not hunt down pirates in their waters? Lord Dubovic is not just a merchant, he is a nobleman of the Empire, and he knows the navy is bound to protect his investment. He lied to you," Mauro hissed.

"Yes, sir. I know that now."

Mauro stood up and grabbed his hat. "Look, Branislav," he said more quietly, "I will see what I can do for your father, and possibly your brother. But if you put my ship and crew in danger for a few coins of silver, I will personally see that you are hanged for your crime. Have I made myself clear?"

"Yes, Lord Baric. Thank you. I will not let you down."

Mauro reached into his jacket pocket and set the tied bundle of mail on the table. "You are to give these to Castor," he said. "They are from his brother. Tell him that Patrik is on his way home."

"Yes, my lord. I will, without fail, sir."

Mauro pulled the latch to open the door. A rush of salty air swirled in the dank cabin.

"We will leave you to finish readying the ship. I wish you a safe voyage and a swift return, Captain Tomsic."

Mauro did not wait for a reply. He left Branislav sitting at the table as he went through the low doorway and back into the bright afternoon sunshine.

Chapter 31

Signor Bernardo rolled up his parchment. "Well, I think I have all the notes I need for Lord Baric. Will you inform him what we agreed upon, Signor Jero?"

"I will, Signor Bernardo. Thank you for coming out today. Will you be alright riding back alone, or do you want to wait to join us on our return?"

The architect shook his head and waved his lacy-sleeved arms against the offer. "It was a silly detour that caused my delay earlier," he said. "I think I can find my way back now. And I have my pistol, just in case."

Jero hoped Bernardo would not mistakenly shoot himself in an encounter, but he did not insist that he joined them, either. Jero wanted to ride back through the woods by the lake again, not along the wagon road.

The architect turned to Isabella, waiting with them in the sitting room. "It has been a delightful afternoon in your company, Signorina Valli. I thank you for your helpful suggestions. You do know the current fashion," he cooed.

She offered her hand, and he kissed it lightly, looking up with a smile. He was as old as her father, and she seemed to find no harm in his exaggerated friendliness. She flattered him with a demure cock of her head and a sweet smile in reply.

When Signor Bernardo finally departed and the two were alone, Isabella asked Jero, "Do you think the baron will be in agreement with the changes?"

"The baron will have the final say, of course, but he trusts our instincts. The kitchen needs renovating. That is clear. And he wanted a brighter sitting room, so it makes perfect sense to have this wall come out," Jero said, touching the solid plaster.

"I know we are not in agreement about the dark paneling in the study. It is rather medieval," Isabella pointed out.

"It would be costly to remove it, and the baron likes the dark wood in his own study."

Isabella went to the narrow staircase, looked up, and reminded him, "The sleeping chambers are rather small, and there are no real guest rooms. What will you suggest to the baron?"

"This is meant to be a guest house, my lady. The two larger chambers are plenty large, and a bed and a dressing table fit into the smaller chambers with reasonable space around them. I think that is enough for any visiting family."

"Signor Bernardo did say it would cost a small fortune to expand the top floor. Is the baron a very wealthy man, Jero?"

Money matters were generally not discussed around women like Isabella. She knew what her own things cost when she shopped, but she had no education in how noblemen earned their money to pay for all the conveniences of a household.

Jero had seen the Baric's accounts and the enormous sums collected and spent each year. Mauro had inherited a profitable business and sizable wealth from Lord Lorenc, but Jero was uncertain whether this was usual for a baron or not. He replied, "I do not have much reference to judge one way or another, my lady."

Isabella pursed her red lips and maintained, "The baron and I are old friends, you know, but I suppose there are limits to what you can divulge about his income as his steward."

Jero considered her point and her feminine naïveté. "I think the baron would not object to your curiosity, my lady," he said, finally. "Lord Baric is a lesser nobleman, so in that respect the Empire does not expect him to have significant holdings for his rank. Lord Baric's income is tied to many things, and he has a great deal of expenses as a landlord and village patron. He does not spend lavishly on himself, and you have seen that he has many servants and guardsmen to house and clothe, as well as the salt workers to pay, and the tenant farmers to support when the crops do not carry them through."

Isabella nodded her understanding as Jero listed Baric Castle's many burdens. "I had no idea," she said in solidarity.

Then, with a broad smile, Jero confided to her, "I am not concerned for the baron, my lady, and you should not be either. If Lord Baric wanted to expand this house, rebuild it even, he could easily pay for it."

The Venetian ran her hand down the velvet drapes as they stood by the window in the sitting room again. Isabella chuckled to herself when she thought how she had let a rich catch slip away so many years ago. But she'd had other ideas about life back then. "That is what I had hoped to hear," she said.

Jero was eager to be on the road again, so he suggested, "If you would like to wait here, I will go find Bem and Ruby and let them know we are ready to leave."

Isabella, who had been facing the glass, told Jero, "I think I have found them. Come look out the window."

He began to laugh as he watched the two climb down the rungs of the tall ladder leaning against the old stone wall.

"You find that amusing, Jero? Lady Ruby will fall to her death!" declared Isabella.

"I was worried they would not keep themselves occupied while waiting for us, but it seems the two have been busy."

Isabella saw how Bem helped Ruby on the last few steps of the ladder. He held her a little too closely when he caught her before the last broken rung.

"Are you not a little jealous, Jero?" Isabella asked.

"Of Bem, you mean? No, I am grateful to him. Lady Ruby has asked to walk the ramparts before, and the baron would not let her. I am glad she got her chance. She is very capable," he said.

Through the glass, Isabella saw their flushed faces and suggested to Jero, "Perhaps we should have a refreshment before we are on our way again."

"Yes, of course," agreed Jero.

He left Isabella by the window and went out the front door, intending to find Ervin.

~*~

"Do you want a cool drink before we leave?" Isabella asked when Ruby came into the sitting room. Her cheeks were rosy, and the front of her jacket was streaked with a mossy coating of dust.

"We drank our fill at the well before Jero found us. He and Bem are going to saddle the horses."

"Did you enjoy your time with Bem? I saw you on the wall," said Isabella with a questioning cock of her feathered hat.

"I am certain there is some sort of rule against it, but Bem and I could not resist. You can see the whole valley from the top."

"Is that right?" Isabella smiled at a sudden thought. "I had no idea there would be such inspiration here. I prefer modern villas to these old musty ones, but this is far more interesting to sketch."

Ruby had sat down on an upholstered chair to retie the loose laces on her boots. She looked over and asked, "Have you always drawn, Lady Isabella?"

Isabella thought about the lost years without her outlet. "I was always doodling something when I was younger, but my mother made me put my sketchbook away when I came of age. She said it was too solitary. I would not attract conversation sitting by myself with my sketchpad."

"When did you decide to begin again?" Ruby asked.

A shadow of sadness crossed Isabella's face. "Gianni gave me the sketchbook I have now. He was my fiancé at the time. He understood art and convinced me to start drawing again."

"Your fiancé?" Ruby stammered with noticeable surprise. "Why did you not marry him, Lady Isabella?"

"He died last year, just a few weeks before our wedding day, fighting in some bloody battle. He was all wrong for soldiering, but he wanted to make his father proud. He wanted to follow in his father's footsteps."

"Was his father an officer?"

"Oh yes, a decorated commander, but he was also a brute. Gianni was so intimidated by him that he could hardly talk in his presence."

Ruby dared to ask, "Did you want to marry him?"

Isabella was quiet for a moment and then went on to reflect, "I had never given it much thought in the beginning, whether I wanted to marry him or not. It was something that I was required to do. Gianni's family is very rich, but my married friends pitied me. They warned me that such a bashful husband could never satisfy me in our marriage. After a while, their comments began to worry me, so I let him come to my bed before he left again. I needed to know for sure."

Isabella continued as though in a trance, "Gianni was painfully shy in public but was a different man when we were alone that night. He was open and romantic and attentive. I actually looked forward to our wedding after that. I think he might have loved me."

Ruby took Isabella's hand and patted it for comfort. "Of course, he loved you, Lady Isabella. How could he not? Did you love him after that?"

Isabella returned a pitiful look. She had asked herself this same question, wondering why she was so numb when word had come of Gianni's death. She had not understood what the loss of a lover truly felt like until she killed that love herself only a few nights ago. Isabella had mourned Gianni's lost love and left those memories buried in Venice months ago. She would do the same with Fabian's.

Ruby regarded her with concern and said in a hushed voice, "Here come the men with the horses, Lady Isabella. Do you want my handkerchief to dry your eyes?"

Isabella had not realized she was crying. She shook her head and pulled a folded cloth from her own pocket. "I am better already," she assured Ruby and quickly dabbed the last of her sorrow away. She could have no regrets if she were to carry on, and carry on she would.

Chapter 32

Halfway through their ride home, the four stopped to find the beaver dam at the end of the lake. This side trip not only fulfilled Jero's promise to Ruby, but also rewarded their desire to be alone with their chosen companion.

Jero and Ruby left their horses in the clearing with Bem and Isabella, who insisted they go alone. Isabella made the excuse of worrying she would tear the baroness's riding clothes on the scruffy underbrush, but she really just wanted some unchaperoned time to flirt with Bem.

What remained of a path around the lake was overgrown with shrubs and saplings. Jero helped Ruby climb over a fallen tree that blocked their way. She still wore her riding gloves, but the act of holding her hand made him remember their dance lessons and his bad luck of not getting to dance with her at the ball. Jero had thought he'd never seen her more beautiful than that night. But seeing her now in this idyllic setting, with a rosy blush and windblown hair, made him change his mind.

A few loose strands of her auburn hair clung to her cheek. Jero reached over and stroked her face, setting them free again in the breeze.

Ruby smiled shyly at his gesture and asked, "How much farther until we are there?"

"This would be it," replied Jero, pointing to the mound of mud and sticks in front of them. "The beavers built the dam across what was long ago a stream. It does not look like much from the outside. Most of it is underwater."

"Do you think we can look in?" Ruby asked excitedly.

"The entrance is underwater, too. It keeps predators from entering."

Ruby walked across the hardened mud and said, "It looks massive for just a few small animals."

"Whole families can live here. They have room to raise their young, and the beavers add on rooms when the in-laws come to live with them."

"Just like people do," Ruby said, chuckling. "What would happen if the baron took the dam apart? Would the lake empty?"

Jero had asked the same question years ago, and he repeated what had been explained to him, "Eventually, the landscape would go back to how it was. Lord Lorenc liked the lake, though, so he left it dammed."

"Was the old baron a nature lover?"

"Mostly for his table! The lake attracts many kinds of ducks and geese. Lord Lorenc would come here to hunt them on occasion. I came once or twice with him," Jero recalled.

"I suppose even if no beavers returned, the birds need a good home."

The two continued their slow tour around the lake, alongside the marshy reeds.

"Speaking of homes," Jero said cheerfully, "did you hear that the baron is renovating the end cottage?"

Ruby and Resi had talked about this vacant cottage. It was along the row of tenant houses situated below the castle walls.

"It has been empty for a while, hasn't it?" she asked.

"A few months, I think. Tomas's widow lived there until she moved to be closer to her family."

"Geoff told us about Tomas. He died with Lord Lorenc, didn't he?"

Jero nodded somberly. "He was a good soldier, but Tomas was not very skilled in fixing leaking roofs and chimneys. The masons had a lot of repairs to do, but it should be ready any time now."

"Who will move in?" asked Ruby.

Jero shrugged and said, "Whoever needs it."

She smiled slyly and speculated, "So, if I were to marry someone at the castle, like Hugo perhaps, would the baron offer us the cottage to live in?"

Jero frowned at a scenario that included Hugo. Mauro's youngest captain was a distinct challenger for Ruby's affection.

"If you had a lapse of judgment and married Hugo, then yes, you would probably move into the cottage to start your family. Would you like that?" Jero's wide eyes expressed his hope, even as he tried not to be so obvious that he meant for Ruby to marry him instead.

Ruby pulled at a cattail near the trail as she thought about it. "I am a bit ashamed to admit this," she said, "but I am afraid I would make a useless wife, Jero." She let the little pieces of stuffing from the cattail fall onto the shiny mud.

"I doubt that very much," said Jero with a shake of his head.

"It is true. My mother imagined her daughters would have a house with a cook and a maid, like she had. I did not learn any domestic chores from her. I only know how to mind children, not grow cabbages and bake bread."

She watched his eyes to know whether she had disappointed him with her declaration, but his brilliant green eyes seemed to glow with admiration.

Jero insisted, "That is already a good start for a wife since you might want children right away. Besides, if you married a man who served at the castle, he could take his meals with the men in the Keep. You wouldn't have to cook at all."

"And what shall I eat?" she retorted with a laugh.

"I hadn't thought about that."

They hiked on, and Ruby pondered out loud, "And what about when my husband's clothes need mending? Would he annul the marriage when he runs out of stockings with no holes?"

Jero said, "I think your husband would still consider himself the luckiest man in the world to have a wife with so many other charms and talents."

Ruby blushed at his bold compliment.

He added, "Most of the soldiers can mend their own clothes, anyway."

"Can they?" Ruby asked with surprise. "Can you sew, Jero?"

His eyes twinkled when he said, "Yes, of course I can. I have not mended anything recently, but I had to learn when I was a boy. I was always tearing some part of a shirt or breeches when I worked in the stables, and I only had one other set of proper clothes to my name. I think it was Alberto who taught me to thread a needle and make straight stitches."

"That is impressive, and something for me to consider in a husband. But even if Hugo had such mending skills, I don't think I could marry him or any other man without first kissing him."

Jero was taken aback by her playful yet daring admission and nearly gasped.

Ruby laughed out loud. "It is something the baroness talked of before meeting the baron. She told me she would be very disappointed if her new husband had rotten teeth or ate onions all day. It got me thinking about my own situation."

Jero cleared his throat and surmised, "I think it worked out for the baroness. The baron is very particular about his teeth and rarely eats onions."

Ruby turned her back, playing coy again. "Yes, she is satisfied with how it all turned out, but is it not a valid concern? Kissing is something married people do quite often. It should be pleasurable, don't you think?"

Jero absently picked up a rock from the path and threw it low across the lake. He watched it skip on the surface and then sink.

Jero turned and replied, "I have kissed a few times and have always found it pleasurable. But what if you did not like the kiss? Would you not marry the man?"

Ruby shrugged meekly and paced the water's edge.

"You should have a plan," asserted Jero.

She came back to his side. "I suppose we could always practice a few more times and see if there is improvement. The trouble is, I am never alone with a man long enough to even have that first kiss."

Her penetrating gaze sent a shiver of apprehension through Jero. It was clear she had opened the door for him to kiss her, but etiquette ran too deep in him.

He took a step back. "A man should not take advantage of a lady's vulnerability when they are alone."

She met his gaze and said, "If I found myself alone with a man that I knew and trusted, I would not call it taking advantage."

Jero reached out and touched Ruby's sleeve, running his hand lightly down its length, and then he closed the last space between them.

"We are very much alone here," he said softly. "May I kiss you, Ruby?"

She nodded and shut her eyes, anticipating what was to come.

He stroked her cheek with the back of his fingers, hesitating. His heart pounded as he fought the urge to pull her tightly to him. "You have put enormous pressure on me to get this right, Ruby," he whispered.

She opened her eyes again and smiled. "I will give you a second chance if you get it wrong."

With her enticement, Jero leaned down and touched his lips to hers, his love welling up inside him.

Ruby seemed to swoon at his tender exploration, and then began to kiss him in return, holding him when he finally took her into his arms.

After what seemed like only seconds, but could have been an eternity, Jero stepped back from their embrace. He was puzzled by the stunned look on Ruby's face and knew he must say something to break the awkward silence.

He apologized, "Was that not good?"

Ruby cleared her throat and said, "I think we should go back to the horses now."

Jero slumped in disappointment as she turned to leave. "But what about my second chance?" he called out.

Looking over her shoulder, she hollered back, "If I give you a second chance, then I will want a third and a fourth, too. The next time you kiss me, you will have to marry me!"

Jero could only stare, bewildered, as he watched her leave down the muddy trail. She was already halfway back to the horses by the time he realized what she had revealed. Ruby Spiros wanted to marry him!

Whoop!

Jero let out such a shout of glee that it startled the lounging birds along the shallow shore. The underbrush came alive in one sudden upward motion as roosting waterfowl took to the sky.

Ruby turned back to see Jero in the middle of the rush of wings. She covered her mouth to keep from laughing at the sight.

~ * ~

Bem hobbled the horses after Jero and Ruby left. The animals were content to nibble on the juicy grass growing in the clearing. He joined Isabella on the downed tree when he finished with the last holding strap.

"Are you sure you don't want to look for the dam, Lady Isabella?"

"No, I am fine waiting here in the sunshine."

"As am I," he agreed.

After a moment, Bem said, "I was thinking, would you like to try riding with a saddle again?"

"Do you mean right now?" she said with surprise. Isabella had other flirtatious plans in mind while they waited.

"Why not? Cairo is not used to novice riders, but I can put my saddle on Fatina."

Isabella considered this. "I used Lady Baric's saddle before. Will a man's saddle even fit me?"

"I am sure it will. You are almost as tall as I am," Bem said kindly.

She frowned in displeasure.

With a wink, he added, "I like tall women."

Yesterday Isabella would have taken his comment as an opening for playful flirtation, but the terms of their game had changed.

"Is your wife a tall woman?" she asked from her place on the log.

"No, she is petite, like Lady Caterina, but I like small women, too," he said with a mischievous grin.

Isabella did not know what to make of him, but she knew she liked him. She leaned back and let the sun in under her wide-brimmed hat, posing, while Bem finished tightening the saddle straps.

Bem held out his hand. "Here, Lady Isabella. Let me help you onto the saddle."

She let Bem help her find her footing. Once seated, Isabella stroked the horse's pretty mane and asked, "What made you fall in love with your wife, Bem? Is she beautiful?"

He stepped back from his mare and answered, "Very beautiful. My wife has the spirit of a lioness packaged into a gentle kitten. That attracted me most when we first met. There, how does that feel?" he asked, referring to the saddle.

The horse began to walk with Isabella seated on its back. "It feels fine, actually."

Bem explained, "A saddle is important to give you something to grip when the riding gets rough. It helps the horse, too. It distributes your weight when you move."

"Why would I move?"

Bem laughed at her remark. "You might have to reach for your water pouch without stopping, or unsheathe your sword, or lean over to stab a man fleeing on foot." He waved his arms dramatically as he mimed the last bit.

Isabella's eyes widened. "What a gruesome picture you have put into my mind!"

"That is war," Bem reminded her in a more serious tone. "Your horse is an extension of yourself in battle. For whatever reason, sometimes you need your hands free. A good horseman is able to ride without holding the reins, and a well-trained horse will still know what the rider wants him to do without pulling on them."

Isabella knew she would never be such an expert, but the possibility thrilled her. "Can you do that?"

"My job before I met up with Salar Nassim was exactly that. I picked out horses with the right disposition and then trained them for the officers. Not all horses can be warhorses."

Isabella wondered, "How do you steer without the reins? Could you teach me?"

"Ride back to me, and I will show you," Bem offered.

She turned the horse and stopped at his side again. He took the reins from her hand and said, "You push your leg against your horse on one side or the other, just like you would pull on the leather reins to guide her."

While walking alongside Isabella, Bem pressed and released her thigh against the beast. The horse turned each time. He said a few words, and Fatina stopped. "See how easy that is?"

She looked down. Bem's hand still rested on her leg. "I do see. I bet you were good at your job, and at many other things."

Realizing his mistake, Bem let his hand drop and gave her back the reins.

When it was apparent her lesson was over, Isabella swung her leg across the front of the saddle and reached her arms out. She looked like a child who was begging to be picked up.

Bem smiled to himself as he took hold of her. Bem could smell Isabella's flowery scent as they stood face to face.

Feeling emboldened, Isabella said, "I admire you for being so faithful to your wife."

"I am devoted to Fatina, but faithfulness is harder to achieve. It is one of my admitted flaws."

She licked her dry lips and cooed, "Then we have something in common."

Her feet were on the ground, but Bem had not released her. Isabella was game for testing the boundaries. She guessed at how much time they had before Jero and Ruby would return and brazenly slid her arms around Bem's waist. She could feel her heart beating, or was it his?

"Do you want to kiss me?" she asked.

He cocked his head and bit his lower lip at the invitation. Bem had met his match. "I want to," he told her, "but I won't."

"I will not bite," she said.

His pulse quickened at her comment. "I would not mind if you did, Lady Isabella, but I won't be kissing you." He let his hands slide off her and took a conscious step back.

Her lips pursed into a pout, like a spoiled child's would when denied a treat. "How disappointing," she said. "Soon I will wed a decrepit duke and be doomed to wait out the Hungarian winter in his icy castle as I dream of one last kiss from a handsome horseman."

Bem moved a step closer again. His fingers stroked her shoulder and then down the sleeve of her summer jacket as he reflected, "I have been to Hungary and know the winters there are cold and the castles icy. But I imagine you will be lounging before a warm hearth, wrapped in furs and velvet. Who is to say it won't be a handsome young duke who gets to join you by the fire?"

Isabella touched his hand on her arm and imagined out loud, "My fate may be bleaker. What if I told you I may end up in a nunnery, weaving shrouds for the dead. Would that make me pitiful?"

He could not keep his eyes off her rouged lips when he said, "You could never be pitiful."

She shrugged and took her hand away, toying with him yet again. "I had hoped to charm you, have a little fun, but you are a very married man, Emilio Chidubem Tavares." Isabella held her breath, waiting for him to take the lead in her game, finally. He did not disappoint her.

"You have charmed me more than I would like to admit. I am a married man, but I am not without desires. I think I would like that kiss now."

He held her again, but this time his hands slid down her hips. He gently pulled her against his body as a blast of noise split the air.

Whoosh!

Hundreds of birds at the water's edge took flight in one screeching, cawing mass of wings. The lovers' trance was broken, and their kiss was abandoned.

Bem saw Ruby come out of the underbrush in the distance. He exchanged a glance of regret with Isabella and then released her, straightening his jacket to cover his mistake. He walked away to replace the saddle for the journey home.

Isabella's heart was still racing when Ruby approached. "Where is Jero?" Isabella breathlessly asked.

Ruby was flushed and had mud on her trousers from slipping in the muck. She tried to wipe the dirt from her gloves before she pointed in the direction of the path. "Jero is behind me somewhere," she said. "He will be along shortly."

In a sudden panic, Isabella realized that she had neglected her one duty. "Are you alright, Lady Ruby? Did something happen at the lake between you two?" She leaned in to see Ruby's honest reaction.

"No, nothing at all," Ruby insisted, although she could not hold Isabella's stare. "I just came back more quickly than Jero did."

Bem rejoined the two, leading their horses to them. He seemed to find Ruby's happy expression contagious and grinned despite his disappointment a minute ago. "Did you find what you were looking for?" he asked her.

Ruby took Ophelia's reins and heaved herself onto her mare's back. She gave the horse a friendly pat and said to Bem, "I did, and I am ready to go home now."

Jero's arrival just then, hurried and separate from Ruby's, was awkward for everyone.

Bem handed over Bacchus's reins to Jero with a questioning squint. Isabella was less discrete with her accusing glare. She commented, "Ruby is in a rush to leave, Jero. She wishes to get back home."

Jero put his foot into his stirrup and was quickly tall and confident in the saddle. Smiling from ear to ear, he directed his answer to Ruby, "I will happily grant her wish—any wish at all."

Isabella vowed she would get to the bottom of this. She told Jero, "You and Bem may lead the way. Ruby and I will ride together this time."

Chapter 33

That afternoon, Resi and Caterina had the quiet house to themselves. Nestor was working on the accounts in the study, Idita had gone with Nela and Franja to the village, and the house servants took their hour of personal time after their noon meal.

Resi found that a nap each afternoon was the only way to stay awake while hosting so many guests each evening. She excused herself to do just that. Caterina had wanted to finish the baby gown she had taken over for the baroness, and she happily lounged on her own soft bed with her sewing.

A few hours later, Brigita brought a hot pot of tea and a platter of little almond pastries to the women when they met up again in the sitting room.

"It has cooled off nicely outside. Should we move to the terrace, Lady Caterina?" Resi suggested.

"Yes, I believe the fresh air will do me good. I am sure Isabella has enjoyed more fresh air this one day than she has all week." Caterina added with worry, "I hope she did not fall off her horse."

"She will be just fine on Bem's gentle mare. It is a short ride to the villa," Resi assured her.

The maid opened the door to the terrace and unpacked the teacups on the table there. Caterina's light skirts lifted in the afternoon breeze as she followed the baroness outside to the cushioned chairs. Clouds were blowing in from the north.

"It had been such a lovely start to the day," said Resi when a motion of color in the room caught her attention. It was Cyro at the bookshelf.

Resi went to the door and asked cheerily, "Are all the men back already?"

"Oh! Lady Baric! I did not think anyone was in here," he apologized politely. "The baron had some errands in the village, but the rest of us are back from our tour. I was just returning this book to the shelf. I did not mean to disturb you."

Caterina came to the doorway and said, "You must join us for tea, Cyro. We have not even taken a sip."

"Yes, join us," said Resi. "Brigita, will you bring us one more cup and another plate? I am sure our guest is hungry after his excursion." Resi then turned back to Cyro and said, "Come sit with us on the terrace and tell us about your outing."

Within a few minutes, tea was being poured for all three, and the ladies were enjoying Cyro's entertaining conversation.

Cyro was saying, "I know little of commerce, but I can tell that your husband is a man of many talents, Lady Baric. I know for a fact he is an excellent soldier, and his salt operation appears quite successful. His ship is surprisingly modern and his crew exceptionally industrious. I can see that you have an interesting life on your estate."

"I am pleased you find it so," replied Resi. She did not want to admit that she had never seen the salt mines in operation or been on the Baric's ship. But she wanted to know more and inquired, "Did you ever serve under my husband? You have such a good opinion of his soldiering skills."

Cyro set his steaming cup down. "I met your husband twice before coming to Baric Castle. Well, *met* is an overstatement. I was assigned to his division for a battle. He probably did not even notice me, but I remember him. We were in a dangerous spot, hidden before our attack. As the muskets fired around us, he and his men waited for the enemy to be within range. I was impressed how his soldiers trusted him unflinchingly and how well they fought. We all came back alive that day," Cyro said with a nod, picking up his teacup once again.

"We are all very glad for it," Resi told him, then asked, "But are you quitting the mercenary work? My brother said you will not be traveling south with them."

"I will be returning home, my lady," said Cyro.

Caterina chirped, "You must be happy to go home, Cyro. Your family will be thrilled to see that you are alive." She then turned to the baroness and informed her, "Cyro let his family believe that he drowned in a shipwreck."

Resi dropped the little pastry she was dunking in her tea and looked over in surprise.

"Do not fear, Lady Baric. I have made amends to my family," said Cyro. "They know that I am alive."

Caterina looked disappointed that he had not earlier explained this twist in his story. "You did not tell me that," she said.

"Oh, well, I may have neglected this last detail, Lady Caterina. I could spend hours sharing all that has happened since leaving home, but there has not been time."

Caterina insisted, "Tell us now, Cyro. We have all afternoon."

If there was one thing Resi knew about the young Venetian, it was that her attention to one topic wavered quickly. Still, Resi agreed it would be delightful entertainment, not to mention a generous gesture on her part, chaperoning the mismatched pair as they went about their unwitting courtship.

Cyro set his plate of cakes down and asked, "Where shall I begin?"

"From the shipwreck," said Caterina. "Why did you wait so long to tell your parents? Won't they be angry at you?" she wondered.

"I am sure of it, but I believe I explained my reasoning thoroughly enough in my letter to them. I did beg their forgiveness and their understanding."

Caterina asked, "How did you meet up with the mercenaries? You said you were on Candia. Is that where Salar Nassim and the others were fighting?"

"No, Lady Caterina. That came later, after I went to Athens."

Resi was puzzled. "How did you get from Corsica to Athens?"

He took another sip of tea. "For that, I suppose I should go back to the beginning," he said.

Caterina set her cup down. "Tell us about the shipwreck."

"I should have been on one ship, but instead was on another, the ship that had left the following day." Cyro had already told Caterina the next part, but he explained for the baroness's sake, "When my ship arrived on Corsica a day later, the port was in turmoil. I still cannot explain it, but something came over me as I stood there unnoticed. I had my bags and some money with me, and I decided right then that I could disappear, so to speak. There was another ship in the harbor, leaving for Alexandria, in Egypt, and I bought passage on it."

"That is adventurous," agreed Resi.

"It was a long voyage, but once there, I traveled all over seeing the ancient sights. I was living my dream of adventure, but began to feel guilty about choosing to fake my death. I was in Cairo at this point and went to check the shipping schedule. I would have sailed back to Italy, back to my family and my old life, if not for the ship in the harbor leaving for Athens the next day. Having already come more than halfway, I could not resist the temptation to see the monuments in Greece. I decided a few more weeks away were not going to make such a difference."

Resi thought of the adventures she was never granted as a girl and remarked, "I lived my whole life in Greece and never traveled to the Acropolis. Why such an interest in Greek culture, Cyro?"

Forgetting that the women considered him an underprivileged soldier, Cyro replied, "I studied ancient sculptures at the university. My father sent me to study law, but I secretly attended art classes. He was unhappy with me when he found out. He wants me to follow his decided path, not one of my own making."

"Is your father also involved in politics? Mine wants Fabian to follow in his footsteps, too."

Cyro leaned back in his chair, composed and confident. "It is actually my grandfather who is politically connected, and I am to follow in his footsteps.

My father travels often, and I was raised more by my grandfather than my father."

"Where was your mother?" Caterina asked. "Was she not there to raise you?" She imagined a sad little boy, tragically motherless, taken to live with the only relations who would have him.

"Oh, yes, my mother was very much a part of my youth," Cyro said buoyantly. "She is an excellent mother, really. I could not ask for a better one, but she is unusually independent for a woman. My mother travels at times with my father. He lets her come and go at her will."

"Were you not sent to be fostered as a part of your education?" Caterina inquired.

"No, my mother was against that. I was educated at my grandparents' house. I am afraid I had more training in what they thought was interesting for a boy, meaning less athletic endeavors and more of an artistic focus."

"How could you become a soldier then?" Caterina wondered.

"I was not formally trained like the baron and your brother, but I could ride and spar well enough. I will admit soldiering was never an undertaking I had foreseen doing on my voyage."

Cyro spoke rather quickly at times, and Resi lost track of the storyline somewhere after he described his life with his grandparents. "I thought you took the ship to Athens to see the monuments," she said.

"Ah, yes. It is a rather complicated tale. Do you want to hear it?"

"Yes," the ladies said in unison.

"Well, I left Cairo that next day, as I already mentioned. It would have been a fairly short voyage to Athens, but we were boarded by pirates in the middle of the journey. Ours was a merchant ship, and the pirates stole everything."

Caterina exclaimed, "That must have been frightening."

Cyro chuckled and said, "It was, actually. But most worrisome was being stranded with no food or fresh water, and there was no land in sight. The closest place on the captain's map was the island of Candia."

"Is that where you met Bem?" asked Caterina.

"Bem was a part of the ship's crew," Cyro explained. "He was working for his passage to Athens to find his wife."

Caterina's eyes widened, caught off guard by his casual comment. "Bem is married?" Patrik had already told Resi this.

"Indeed. I could hardly believe it when he told me. Do you want to hear what happened to her?"

"Yes," they both answered, laughing awkwardly at their shared enthusiasm.

Cyro became animated again when he explained, "Before I met Bem, he was a horse trainer in Libya for a wealthy Ottoman general. This general had one daughter, whom he spoiled like a princess. Hmm, what was her name?" Cyro paused to think.

Caterina interrupted him, "And Bem fell in love with her?"

Cyro laughed. "No, he fell in love with her handmaiden. You see, this daughter was to have a new horse, and her father sent her to Bem to help her pick one out from the herd. The daughter would come each day to try one of the possible matches. She would ride with her escorts while her handmaiden stayed behind. Bem became enchanted with this servant girl and would stay at the stables to talk with her. Ah!" Cyro said unexpectedly. "Now I remember. Fatina was his wife, and Alimah was the general's daughter."

"I think Fatina is the name of Bem's mare," Caterina corrected him.

"Yes," he said with a chuckle, "Bem loves his wife, and he loves his horse, so they share the same name. As the story goes, Alimah finally did choose a horse and then her visits ended. By this time, Bem was in love with Fatina and decided he had to marry her. He tried for weeks just to talk to her again, but it was impossible. In the end, the general received orders for a transfer to a new post in Egypt. He wanted Bem to come with him and continue to train his horses there. Since Bem was not bound to the army, he refused the offer. But the general knew Bem was in love with Fatina, so he promised to release her from her servitude to marry Bem if Bem would agree to come."

"That is so romantic," Caterina cooed. "So, he married her?"

"He did, and luckily for Bem, she was happy to marry him. Bem worked for the general in Egypt, as promised, and Fatina became a free woman. Until the tragic day Fatina disappeared, of course."

Both women gasped.

"What happened to Fatina, Cyro?" Caterina asked.

Cyro continued to explain, "It seems Alimah was not happy that her father had released her favorite servant. She herself was destined to marry a military man in Athens. The story goes that she asked Fatina to help her pack for her voyage. Fatina loved her former mistress and agreed to help her prepare for the move. When Fatina did not come home after two days with the general's daughter, Bem went looking for her. But Alimah had left that morning and had taken his wife on the ship with her."

"That cannot be true," Resi quietly protested.

Cyro shrugged and said, "It was indeed true. When Bem learned what had happened, he complained to the general that Fatina was his wife, which means she was his, well, property of a sort. The general's daughter could not just take her."

Caterina and Resi nodded to each other in agreement.

"Of course, the father did not like that his daughter was being accused of kidnapping, so the easiest solution for the general was to arrest Bem."

"No!" Both women reacted with the same shock.

"Poor Bem," Resi added.

"Yes, poor Bem," Cyro agreed. "They put him in shackles and held him in jail until the army left for their new assignment. It was luck that his jailers were not with the army and were sympathetic to his plight. After a few weeks, they let him go free, and he went straight away to find the first ship out of Egypt to Athens. Leaving so hastily, though, Bem did not have the means with him to pay for the passage. That is why he signed on with the crew. That leads me back to our pirated ship, where I left off."

Caterina said, "Your story gets better from there, I hope."

"It depends on whether you think a better story is fraught with turmoil or concludes with an easy ending. Mine does not."

"You did make it to land safely, didn't you?" asked Resi.

"We made it to the island, yes, but since it was a war zone, we were stuck, and the pirates had stolen everything of value. The good turn in my story is when I remembered I had a little money hidden in the lining of my jacket, and Bem and I were able to double it in a dice game."

Caterina was fond of gambling, but she found the choice reckless and scolded, "You bet all your money! What if you had lost, Cyro?"

"I agree that it was a gamble in all respects, my lady, but it paid off. In our recklessness, we found we gave each other courage," said Cyro thoughtfully. "Still, we were hungry, and the best way to feed ourselves was to join one of the armies. It was easy to choose the Venetians after what had happened to Bem in Egypt."

"And that is how you became a mercenary soldier?" Caterina asked again.

Cyro smiled brightly and said, "That was the beginning, yes, Lady Caterina. We fought for the Venetian Army a few months and then managed to make our way off the island. By then, Alimah was no longer in Athens, but someone gave us Salar Nassim's name as one who might be able to provide more information about her husband. Alas, it turned out he was no longer in the information business, but in the mercenary business. At the time, he was looking for two more men to join his gang, and he offered us those spots. Bem needed the money to find Fatina, and I joined with him, thinking I would make my way back home. We have been together ever since." Cyro sat up straight in his chair and took a drink of his cold tea.

Both women sat in silence.

"That is a remarkable story," Resi finally said. "You have had quite an adventure, haven't you?"

"I have, Lady Baric. I would dearly love to help Bem find his wife after all of this, but I am determined to return to the reality of my own destiny. You see, the expectations for me at the time were more than I felt I could measure up to. I am ready now to follow the path my family has set for me."

Caterina's smile expressed admiration for the modest man. But she wondered aloud, "What if your path is no longer there, Cyro? What if your brother has been given your role instead?"

"I have no living siblings, Lady Caterina, but I do have one close cousin that I met up with in Vienna before coming to Baric Castle. He was shocked to see me alive, of course, but he is my nearest relation who might have been given my, uh, family role. He told me that nothing had been decided within the family, even after these two years. My grandfather is still a strong, healthy man. There was no reason to designate a new heir."

Cyro had gone from subject to subject, but still, there were holes in his story that Caterina wanted to have filled.

"What are you an heir to, Cyro?" she asked.

He laughed uncomfortably. "I apologize, my lady. I do speak in circles at times. It is one of my many faults," he said, trying to explain his ambiguity away. "I mentioned earlier that I am to follow in my grandfather's footsteps, and so I shall, after he accepts me back into the family. I am sure there will be many questions to answer first. Mostly, they will think I had some bout of insanity," Cyro said with a laugh. "Even more so when I tell them I have chosen a bride. They had arranged one for me, but they will come to accept my choice, I am certain."

Resi cocked her head suspiciously. Now he must tell the truth, she thought. "First, we learn Bem is married, and now you tell us that you have found a wife, Cyro?"

"I found her, but there is much to do before I can marry her." Cyro's eyes lingered on Caterina as he stood up and said, "I thank you for the tea, Lady Baric. It was most delicious and very kind of you. You are delightful company."

He left the table without another word, went down the terrace steps, and rounded the corner of the house.

Resi sighed and asked, "Have you had enough, Lady Caterina?"

Caterina was too puzzled by Cyro's sudden departure to focus. "Enough, Lady Terese?" she mumbled.

"Enough tea? Ours has become cold," Resi clarified. "Brigita can bring a hot pot if you like."

"I am quite content," said Caterina. She absently watched Resi stand up and straighten her skirts, seemingly lost in her thoughts.

Resi rang the little bell on the table and smiled down at her troubled friend. "I will send Brigita to find Verica. We can go ahead to the bathhouse without her. I think we have much to talk about."

~*~

Resi closed the pipes to the cool spring water, and the hot taps filled her bathing pool to the edge. She poured her favorite rose oil into the water while Verica helped Caterina unpin her elaborately twisted hair. The room fogged with the fragrant steam coming off the surface.

It was a luxury for Verica to be asked to join her mistress in the pool, but today there was no usual chattiness between the ladies. Both were pensive and quiet while they washed and soaked in the warm water.

Caterina finally broke the steamy silence, "I was thinking about our tea with Cyro earlier."

Resi had been waiting for her to bring up the topic. She had been thinking about nothing else. "What do you think of him? He seems to be quite at ease in your company, Lady Caterina."

"I find I enjoy his conversation and his company more and more. Lately, whenever he leaves, I want him to come back. But he made it clear today that he is in love with someone and will be marrying her, once he gets permission from her father."

"I agree he made it clear that he is in love, but he was very vague about who she is," Resi pointed out.

Verica looked from her mistress to the Venetian as she quietly washed her hair. Their conversation was like a story the baroness would read to the maids on a winter's evening, and she hung on every word.

"Strangely," reflected Caterina, "I found myself envious of Cyro's lover after he spoke so compellingly. He deserves to find true love, even if his family does not approve of his choice."

"Lady Caterina, I suspect that the woman he wants to marry is you," Resi finally declared.

Verica dropped the pot of soap and scrambled to fish it out of the water.

Caterina sputtered, "Me? How can he want to marry me, Lady Terese? We have done no more than talk."

"If you think about it, Cyro may have talked about his love for you indirectly." Resi tried to be delicate in her wording since she herself still doubted the obvious.

"But he is leaving on Monday, Lady Terese. Our lives will never cross paths again. I am to be sent to Hungary. He is going to Corsica," Caterina argued.

Resi said cautiously, "He seems to adore you."

Caterina stared across the watery expanse, scowling at the tiled wall as she thought about their walks through the garden together. "Cyro never mentioned my beauty or wanting me. He has not tried to kiss me. I do not recall him even taking my hand. This notion of marriage is ridiculous, Lady Terese."

"Think about your circumstances. Cyro had little choice but to be discreet, courting you in front of a crowd of onlookers."

"But you can see, Lady Terese, it would be impossible for him to marry me. He is a wandering soldier. His dress shows he has nothing to his name. He may not even be accepted back into his family, whoever they are. My father would never agree to such a match," she argued feebly.

"I heard something different in his story today. He is to follow in his grandfather's footsteps in politics, a profession for gentlemen. He has been tutored and educated at the university. He had money to book passages on ships. He is heir to whatever family is waiting for him to return, and he will fulfill the role that was planned for him. Not as a carpenter or a blacksmith. He is more than the poor soldier he pretends to be."

"Dear God, you are right, Lady Terese. He was supposed to marry a noblewoman. He saw the announcement for her wedding in a newspaper after he deserted his former life."

Caterina shook her head and frowned hopelessly. It seemed new despair came to her mind. "I know what sort of a man would have close relatives in Vienna and Corsica. If what he says is so, then Cyro is an enemy to my family."

Resi said unconvincingly, "It no longer matters, Lady Caterina. The war is over. Why should anyone care now about these connections?"

"My father will care. Fabian will care. Cyro has not been honest with me," Caterina moaned.

"He has been vague, but he has not lied. Patricius considers him to be an honest man. He called Cyro the moral fiber of their gang. That is good, isn't it?"

The three women were sunk down in the warm water, seemingly thinking about what this would mean for Caterina.

The Venetian was the first to speak again, "I cannot believe that I am this future bride he was talking about. Cyro must be out of his mind. I am spoken for, and he must know that."

Resi asked, "Could you love him, Lady Caterina?"

Caterina leaned against the pool's edge, her long black hair floating in the water around her. Her voice echoed in the domed room when she answered, "Men have courted me since I was fifteen. I know when someone wants to marry me, Lady Terese. And yet, I am drawn to him more than I have been to any of my other suitors." She smiled at the baroness and admitted, "There is something about Cyro I had not considered in that way until today, but I think I could love him."

A rush of fresh air stirred their steamy atmosphere. All three women turned toward the entrance, not knowing who to expect.

"Are you ladies taking a steam bath today? I can hardly find you."

The sight of Isabella and Ruby at the archway pulled Caterina out of her melancholy. "Is it so late, or are you back early, Isabella?" she asked.

"We are right on time and will join you if that is all right," Isabella replied happily. "We had the most delightful outing, did we not, Lady Ruby?"

"It was truly a day I will remember," Ruby agreed. She plopped down on the bench. She unbuckled her muddy boots and began pulling off her stockings.

Resi's pensive mood was already lifting in their cheerful company. "And what was so memorable about it, Ruby dear?" Resi asked.

"I have been dying to hear the answer to that myself," Isabella said.

Ruby turned back from hanging her jacket on a wall peg and saw their curious eyes focused on her.

"Were you not together?" asked Caterina.

"Not entirely," answered Isabella. "While Jero and I toured the house, Lady Ruby was climbing the villa ramparts in a most unladylike way with Bem and then may have gotten herself into a difficult situation in the swamp with a certain steward. She would not confirm or deny it on our ride back home."

Undressed now, Isabella stepped into the water next to Caterina while Ruby chose her words carefully.

"I had a wonderful adventure at the villa," Ruby told them. "Bem and I did walk the top of the wall, but there was nothing perilous about it. Bem was good company, and he told me all about his life with the Jesuits as a boy, about looking for his father in Portugal, and about couscous being his favorite dish." She pulled her tunic off and asked Isabella, "Did you know Bem is married?"

"Bem did tell me, yes. He gave his horse his wife's name, which isn't entirely unromantic," she remarked with noticeable irritation. "He must love Fatina because I tried very hard to get him to kiss me while we were alone. Did you succeed with Jero, Lady Ruby?"

"Isabella!" Caterina chided her. "Just because you seduce every man you are alone with for five minutes does not mean others are so inclined."

Ruby's cheeks went bright pink, although it could have been from the steamy room.

Resi gave Ruby a suspicious look and asked, "Where did you and Jero go?"

Ruby told her an abridged version, "We went to see how the lake was made by the beaver dam. Jero took my hand to help me over some logs, but there is nothing to tell beyond that. I don't know why Lady Isabella is so worried. Jero is a gentleman. He would never want to cause a scandal." Ruby then plunged into the water.

Isabella gave her one last skeptical glance as she moved along the pool wall to reach the soap. "And did you, ladies, have a good afternoon without us?" she asked.

Caterina answered before the baroness could say the wrong thing, "We were just discussing our interesting day, Isabella. I had my last lesson with Salar Nassim, and Cyro met us for tea. I am looking forward to dinner actually. I have something to ask each of them."

Isabella smoothed her wet hair from her face and reported, "I do not think Cyro and Salar Nassim will be joining us this evening. Bem said something about going to the village with the soldiers tonight for dinner and gambling." Isabella noticed Caterina's smile drooped. "You look so disappointed. Are you upset that they will be playing cards without you?"

"I am not disappointed, Isabella. Men do not gamble with women anyway," she remarked a little too sharply. "I think I have been in the bathhouse too long, is all."

Verica stepped out of the pool as if on cue and began to dry off and dress in her simple twill uniform. Caterina would need her to help fasten her intricate gown.

"But we have just arrived, Caterina," Isabella said. "Let Verica comb out your hair, and I will tell you all about our fantastic outing."

Chapter 34

Mauro left his guests to make their way back to the castle without him after touring the salt fields. He needed to meet with the priest to discuss the final details for the communal party on the church square a week from tomorrow. The Barics owned the church and most of the village, but Mauro wanted the priest's blessing in using the sacred space.

Father David had been in Solgrad for Mauro's entire life. The priest had baptized Mauro when he was born, and he knew all of the young man's pains and pleasures through the confessional. Father David had a broad education in life, beginning in his early years as a pilgrim doing missionary work for the Catholic Church. He had wanted to see the world around him, and in his twenty years of wandering, he went from Catalonia to the Holy Lands and back to Venice, where he then asked to be assigned a steady parish to minister. Father David took Father Enrique's place when the latter died of the same plague that killed Lady Margaret Baric and her three children.

Despite his age, Father David still had a keen sense of hearing, and he listened to Mauro's unscheduled confession after they went over the party plans with Radic. Mauro had last visited the priest after his wife's miscarriage in the winter; it had affected the baron enough to ask for guidance then. The priest had counseled the baron on the benefits of asking God more often for forgiveness for his sins. Disappointingly, Mauro had not taken the sacrament since.

The Baric family had been good to Father David, and he knew enough about human nature to not expect to revolutionize the way of life of the ruling class. He wisely accepted the baron's apprehensive faith in the Church. The priest guessed that something profound must have happened to cause the baron to seek God's forgiveness today, but he didn't ask to hear more than what the troubled nobleman offered to reconcile.

"I absolve you of your sins, my son, in the name of the Father, the Son, and the Holy Spirit," Father David said through the ornate wall of the confessional booth. "Give thanks to God, for He is good, and He is a merciful God. As penance for the sins you have confessed today, and to restore the grace in your soul, you will need to do three good works."

"No prayers, Father?" Mauro asked quietly across the barrier.

"No, my son, but the Church is in need of communion wine. Three casks should be enough until your next confession. Also, Constable Radic is not a rich man, and he can ill afford to feed and quench the thirst of the entire village." The priest let the statement hang in the air.

"Yes, Father. I will send supplies for the party this week. And the third good work?" Mauro asked, impatient to be on his way.

"That will be a deed of your choice, Lord Baric, but it should be outside your normal caretaking. There are many who need your charity, and I will leave it to you to seek one out," Father David advised.

"Thanks be to God," Mauro recited after receiving this third assignment and then crossed himself before stepping away from the booth.

The village priest came out from behind the curtain and smiled kindly at the baron.

"I have a request, Father David," Mauro said. "Is it possible for you to come hear the confessions of my household tomorrow?"

"Has the Spirit of the Lord moved you so fully today, Lord Baric?" the priest inquired, chuckling. "Do you feel obliged to have your servants' sins absolved as well?"

Mauro did not want to explain that it was only his wife's sins he was concerned about, but he acknowledged the irony with a laugh.

Father David asserted, "I see most of your House regularly at Mass. I am not at liberty to say who comes to the confessional, but a visit to your castle tomorrow could be a valuable service to them."

"Come for lunch, Father David, and then you can hear confessions individually in the chapel afterward."

"I will be pleased to do so, Lord Baric. Until tomorrow then, God go with you," Father David blessed him.

Mauro left the church in a good mood. His sins were forgiven, and his wife's unnecessary guilt would be lifted tomorrow as well. He rode back directly to the castle.

~*~

Geoff ran up to the baron outside the stable entrance and took the reins of his horse.

Mauro had not noticed before how fast Geoff was growing. He could almost look eye to eye with the young man. He would have to include Geoff in the sword training, too, he thought.

"Is the traveling party back from the villa?" asked Mauro.

Geoff held Janus steady and replied, "Jero and the others arrived back a short time ago, my lord. I just finished rubbing down their horses."

Mauro nodded, and Geoff patted the baron's horse to get it moving to the stables.

Mauro wanted to find Jero. If he had only just returned home, as Geoff said, then he was bound to be in his room changing out of his riding clothes. Having shed his sins in confession, Mauro thought this would be the right time to lift the last weight that God alone could not. Only telling the truth to Jero could unburden the baron.

The house was reliably quiet in the late afternoon. Mauro first went to his room to freshen up, expecting to find Resi enjoying her afternoon nap there. But the room was empty. She must be in the bathhouse with Caterina, he thought.

He left his room again without taking the time to change for dinner. Mauro did not want to miss finding Jero alone. His boots clicked with each step on the stone floor of the silent corridor. He stood in front of Jero's door, remembering the last time he had intruded on his brother's homecoming and finding him asleep on his bed. Mauro knocked. A few seconds later, Jero came to the door, already dressed in his evening clothes.

"Mauro," Jero said with surprise.

"Yes," Mauro replied, standing in front of him.

"Did you knock?" Jero asked lightly.

Mauro realized that he had for the very first time. "I did. May I come in?"

"Of course."

Flustered at the formality, Jero opened the door wide for his master. He then shut it again and waited while Mauro crossed the room.

"How did it go with Bernardo?" Mauro asked briskly.

"It went well, Mauro. I think we covered all the possible changes. He will check prices and samples in Venice once he hears from you," said Jero. "Lady Isabella and Ruby seemed to enjoy the outing, and Bem was good company."

"Good to hear. Thank you for taking care of the tour with the architect. We will go over your suggestions tomorrow."

Mauro was staring out Jero's window. The sunlight was gone from this side of the building, but the manor house cast interesting shadows on the hillside. It distracted Mauro as he decided what he would say next.

Mauro turned to Jero and said in a businesslike tone, "There are two things I wanted to tell you about. Have a seat if you like."

Jero sat on his bed, seemingly bracing for whatever Mauro needed to tell him.

Mauro smiled, trying to ease Jero's noticeable discomfort, and began, "I still need your help moving the two chests from the tunnel. I have decided where to keep them, and tonight would be a good time. Vilim is taking the mercenaries to the Green Goose for some entertainment, so we will have a quiet evening here. I thought we could carry the chests out after the servants go to bed."

"Will you not join them tonight, Mauro?" asked Jero.

Mauro shook his head. "No, I promised my wife I would not seek any more entertainment there."

Jero nodded sympathetically.

Then Mauro considered for the first time that Jero might want an evening out at the Green Goose, too. "But you are welcome to join them," Mauro added unexpectedly.

Jero thought on it a moment. "Thank you, Mauro, but I will stay in for the evening as well. I will feel better when the gems are hidden again."

Mauro could see how Jero had put his duty over pleasure, and he felt an odd pang of guilt for assigning this chore tonight. He nodded his agreement.

Jero stayed seated on the bed and waited for more instructions, but Mauro just looked at him. Jero finally asked, "Did you say there were two things you needed?"

"Yes."

Mauro regained his focus and said, "I have also been thinking the baroness is ready for more responsibilities. She is smart and capable, and I would like her to begin to supervise the household. I would like you to show her how to manage the staff and the kitchen purchases. She understands mathematics, and you can show her the ledgers and such. If Cook or the other maids have any concerns, they are to go to my wife now. Can you tell them that?"

Jero could not hide his displeasure as he objected, "That is half of my duties, Mauro. Nestor manages the finances and paperwork with the Empire. I will only have your shipments to manage."

Mauro pulled up a chair from the table and sat across from Jero on the bed. "Only?" he said. "You work from dawn until night every day, Jero. I would like to offer you time to ride and spar, and maybe even have a drink with the men at the Green Goose. Would you not enjoy that?"

"I just thought . . ."

"Yes, Jero?"

"I am sorry I questioned your decision. I did not realize at first that you were just being generous, Mauro."

"Did you think I am pushing you away, Jero? This house runs very well without me, but not without you."

"That is not true," said Jero. "You also work from dawn until night, and more."

Mauro leaned in when he said, "I think we work well together, Jero."

He held Jero's stare. It was as if his father were looking meekly back at him. Mauro wanted to finally tell him what he came to his room to explain, but words failed him.

Jero was staring at Mauro for a different reason. "Mauro," he said, hesitating.

Mauro asked patiently, "Yes, Jero?"

"I need to tell you something before you hear it from the baroness. Ruby might confide the whole story to her, so I will tell you myself."

"I am listening," Mauro said uneasily.

"I know it was wrong, but I, well . . ." He blurted out, "I took advantage of her."

"Of Ruby?"

Jero nodded.

Mauro rose abruptly from his chair and demanded, "At the villa?"

Jero hung his head. "We were at the lake. We got off the horses and walked to the end of it, just the two of us. I knew we could not be seen by Bem and Lady Isabella. That is when I kissed her."

"And then what happened?" Mauro waited for the confession.

"Then she walked away."

A flash of confusion crossed Mauro's face.

Jero shrugged and said, "It was wrong of me, Mauro."

Mauro smiled at the innocence of it. "I was prepared to hear much worse than stealing a kiss and being rejected," he said.

Jero's expression remained somber, and Mauro stopped smiling.

"What is the matter, Jero? What else happened?"

"Ruby said she was walking away because she wanted more. If she had not thought to leave me just then, there might have been more to confess." Jero took a deep breath and told the baron, "I want to marry her, Mauro. I love her."

Mauro sat down next to him without a word.

"I suppose you already knew that," said Jero quietly.

"Yes, I knew that. You hid it well enough, but my wife told me a while ago that Ruby had confided in her. She said she thought Ruby loved you."

Jero let out a long sigh. "Ruby told the baroness that?"

Mauro nodded and said, "You *can* marry her. She just needs her father to agree to let her stay. I did not tell you before, but I have written to Angelos Spiros."

Jero was taken aback by this news. "About me and Ruby?"

"I thought if you knew Angelos Spiros would let her stay in Croatia, then you could tell Ruby how you felt. Or if you knew she must go back, you could save yourself the heartache."

Jero seemed uplifted and exclaimed, "This is great news, Mauro! Have you received a reply?"

"You know the post takes a long time, Jero. I expect it will still be a few weeks. Can you be patient and not say anything to Ruby?"

"I, I . . . ," he stammered, "I don't know what to say. Yes, of course, I can wait. A few weeks is nothing, now that I know she loves me, too."

But then Jero panicked. "What if he says no, Mauro?"

"I could not imagine why he would, but let us not worry about that until he does." Mauro patted Jero on the shoulder and then went to the window again and looked out.

Jero watched him and asked, "Why are you helping me, Mauro?"

Mauro willed himself to tell Jero the truth, to say it was because they were brothers, and brothers helped each other.

He turned back to Jero and heard himself say, "I want you to be happy."

"But this will change everything," said Jero.

"Some change is good, Jero."

Mauro crossed the room to the door, then turned to add, "I will give you a house when you marry. I would like for you and Ruby to live nearby."

"The widow's cottage would be perfect."

Jero had no idea of Mauro's true plans, but Jero thanked him and said, "This has been a wonderful day, Mauro. I will be downstairs shortly if you need me."

Mauro left and went back down the hall to his empty chamber to dress for dinner. He would carry the weight of his secret a little longer.

Chapter 35

Simeon and Hugo had reluctantly joined Vilim for a night out at the Green Goose with the mercenaries. When the soldiers left their horses at the stables, the black clouds made good on their threat and dumped a deluge of rain. The men raised their capes and made a quick dash around the corner to the tavern.

The Baric captains warmed to the foreigners after their meal together. Boisterously, the group then moved to an open table near the bar for a few rounds of dice. Vilim ordered pitchers of ale for the room, and servants brought more lanterns, and the tavern locals began placing side bets as the game progressed. Even the losers were in good humor after mugs of the house ale were drained.

Andrea was thrilled that the Baric soldiers had brought these newcomers to her establishment. She watched their serious faces as the soldiers tossed coins into a pile on the table. The barkeeper would need more women in the room to keep the patrons lively and drinking. She sent a kitchen maid to wake the extra serving girls sleeping in their attic chamber. Andrea ran a reputable alehouse and rented rooms to travelers by the night. But if a customer ended up needing a room for an hour for his relaxation, Andrea did not object. Patrik had taken a curvy brunette upstairs already.

"I heard Patrik was not so eager for the ladies," said Hugo when Patrik left the winning game to play a private one upstairs.

Salar Nassim upped his wager and shook the dice. He offered a round-about explanation as he rolled his turn: "I do not fault a man who is true to himself. Most men would not easily admit they prefer the life of a hedonist. When women are available, he seeks them out. If Patrik is anything, he is an honest man."

Simeon scoffed at the remark and shot Hugo a cynical glance.

Noticing that, Salar Nassim went on to say, "I have learned to leave it to God to judge men. What I care about is whether a man would risk his life to save mine. I have fought beside Patrik for four years now. He has proved himself worthy of my respect and has earned my loyalty over and over. I do not judge what he does for pleasure."

"When I look for pleasure, it doesn't include another man's cock," Simeon righteously declared. "Two large breasts are what I need, and I see a pair coming down the stairs that I am willing to go to hell for."

The men watched Andrea's woken barmaids disperse around the room that was crowded with men.

Vilim picked up the dice and told Simeon, "Mauro said the priest is coming to hear confessions tomorrow. That seems good timing for you."

As they conversed, a barmaid sat down on Bem's knee. She had loosened her low bodice, and her ashen hair flowed around her exposed shoulders. She was already plump and full-breasted for someone so youthful, but was touching Bem in a way that told him she was not that innocent.

Bem had long ago decided that bedding a willing barmaid was not a betrayal to his wife. There was no chase, no seduction, like his averted pursuit of Lady Isabella. He had been saved from his near-blunder today by a flock of birds. Bem still longed to taste Isabella's lips instead of the blonde's on his knee. She would do for tonight, though.

Pursuing the topic of confessions, Bem turned to Simeon and asked, "Are you a man of faith then?"

Simeon chuckled. "I fear God as much as the devil and his burning hell." Looking around, he added, "I guess that makes me a good Catholic, like the rest of these men."

The locals nodded and laughed in agreement.

"And you, Bem?" inquired Simeon jovially. "Coming from Africa, you have your own pagan religion, I suppose."

Vilim handed Simeon the dice for his turn.

Bem watched the numbers rolled before answering, "I was raised by Jesuit priests and have kept their religion close. The fear of your Catholic damnation has helped me through the years."

The girl on his lap stirred when Bem discreetly slipped his free hand under her skirts. She nuzzled his neck in response, distracting him.

Hugo set his newly filled mug down on the round table with a slosh. "I saw you on the roof from the ramparts yesterday," he said to the Muslim. "Now, that is devotion—to rise before the sun without someone yelling at you to get up."

Salar Nassim did not seem to take offense, and he laughed along with the rest of the players before explaining, "I have not been so faithful these last years, but I say my prayers when I can. If my religion allowed it, I would prefer to stay in bed, like you."

Simeon directed the round of inquiries to the Dane. "I suppose you are a Protestant," he said.

Soren answered, "That's right. I have no need for your Catholic threat of damnation. It cannot be worse than what we have lived through here on earth."

"I raise my mug to that," exclaimed Vilim, a reluctant Catholic like his cousin Mauro.

Everyone drank a toast to Hell, including the olive-skinned brunette at Soren's side. He had shrugged off the other hopefuls, but she had a quiet seductiveness that sparked something in him. Soren had let this one stay at his side.

Tatjana leaned on the bar across from the men at their table. She dried the washed mugs as she watched the game, catching Vilim's eye now and then. Since the baron no longer patronized the tavern, Vilim had become her regular patron.

Vilim stood suddenly and proclaimed, "I double my bet! I want to lose the rest while I am sober enough to walk up the stairs."

The men cheered as it became clear Vilim got his wish.

Vilim shook out his purse and took a bow before he stumbled to the bar, grabbed Tatjana's hand, and pulled her along with him, not looking back at the laughing men as he clumsily climbed the stairs.

Bem was next to leave the game. He lifted the eager girl off his lap and put his arm around her to steady himself as he rose from his chair. He, too, had drunk one mug too many. Bem let the pretty blonde lead the way, tipping his hat to Soren and Salar Nassim with a crooked grin.

As the evening wore into the night, all the men at the gambling table would find a pretty partner to take them upstairs. And when the soldiers finally rode home, alone or in pairs in the predawn hours, each was satisfied with their night out at the Green Goose.

Chapter 36

Cyro had not joined the escapade to let loose at the Green Goose that night. He had said it would be dishonorable to propose marriage to a woman the morning after sleeping with a whore. His friends tried to convince him that Lady Caterina would not be the wiser.

Cyro stayed at Baric Castle that evening, dined alone in the Keep, and then returned to his room to repack the few items he wanted to take back with him. Once done sorting and discarding the worn but memorable things from his pack, Cyro lay down on his cot and went over the details in his mind of the Adriatic crossing and beyond. It would only be a matter of weeks before he would be back home. Home! The thought filled him with longing and apprehension.

Sleep eluded Cyro, so he got dressed again. He unpacked his neatly folded cape from his bag and went out into the cool night. It had rained hard after sunset, and the trees were still dripping from the heavy showers that had crossed the sky that evening. The courtyard seemed empty, but the occasional footsteps from the ramparts above echoed against the stone.

Cyro crossed the torch-lit expanse to the chapel. Its small windows glowed brightly, and he took it as a sign. After shutting the foyer door, Cyro dipped his fingers into the holy water and then cautiously opened the second door to the baron's chapel. Cyro had not asked if he could use it, but he was sure he would not be intruding at this late hour.

The small sanctuary, with its whitewashed walls and cushioned benches, was cool but welcoming, and Cyro felt an immediate sense of peace. He took a seat on the first bench and bowed his head in his hands to ask God for guidance.

While deep in prayer, Cyro became aware of an odd creaking noise. He looked up and saw two cloaked men coming from behind a door in the paneling. He gasped!

Mauro jumped. "Cyro!"

When Cyro realized the two cloaked figures emerging from the wall were not demons, but only the baron and his steward, he admitted with a laugh, "I am as startled as you are, Lord Baric."

"Are you back early from the tavern?" asked Mauro, regaining his composure.

"I was not in the right frame of mind for the evening my friends had planned." Cyro added, "I had pressing things to do."

"Ah," said Mauro, nodding with understanding.

Jero then interrupted, "Lord Baric, if you do not need me for anything else, I will be going back to my chamber, sir."

Earlier, the brothers had brought two chests and several small canvas bags with Lord Fredrik's remaining wealth to the crypt for safekeeping. Mauro had determined he had enough raw and cut gemstones to last more than his lifetime. If anything were to happen to him, Resi would find the treasure in his tomb when she laid his body to rest there, and she and his child would want for nothing. Only five people alive knew of the precious emeralds his grandfather and father had mined in a deep mountain cave: the baron, Jero, Nestor, Count Toth, and Demetrius Kokkinos. The secret emerald mine would remain secret.

"Yes, of course, Jero. Good night."

Jero bowed to both men and left without another word.

Cyro watched Jero close the sanctuary door and wondered what errand the Baric's steward had been helping with at this late hour. He regarded the baron's tired face and dusty clothes and said, "I apologize, Lord Baric. I did not know I was intruding."

Mauro put on his pleasant host smile and assured his guest, "The chapel is not private, Cyro. I will leave you to your prayers. Good night."

Cyro took a chance and cried, "Wait, Lord Baric. I know it is late, but if you would not mind staying a moment, I wanted to ask you about something."

Others would have found Cyro's direct speech disrespectful, but Mauro seemed unbothered and sat down on the bench next to Cyro.

"I am listening," Mauro said with the same directness.

Cyro nodded. "I am conflicted," he began to tell the baron, "and sharing a room with four men does not offer the solitude needed for meditation. I came in here to reflect on my choices."

"And you are welcome to." Mauro managed to add a smile.

"Patrik has told me a little about you and your situation: about how you came to your title through unfortunate turns of events, your brother's early passing, your father's unexpected death, and your mother's death that followed. We have a few circumstances in common."

"Oh?" Mauro's curiosity was piqued.

"I am to inherit a title, but I am afraid I have made quite a mess of it," Cyro said matter-of-factly. "My family believed I was dead. Becoming undead will affect many people and many plans. But I want to go back."

Mauro did not smirk as one might, or mock the absurdity of the man's confession, but simply asked, "Is that your conflict? Whether to come back from the grave or remain a dead man?"

"Indeed, it is."

Cyro smiled to himself when he explained, "This week at Baric Castle has made me realize I have been groomed for bigger things, Lord Baric. You see, I, too, am the only remaining son of a dying House. I have second cousins who might fight each other for the title, but no one is left to directly inherit my grandfather's estate and all that goes with it. Just me."

Mauro locked eyes with the stranger next to him and asked, "Who are you?"

A shrug escaped his tired figure. "I am Cyrano Duarte, from the Republic of Genoa. My father is Lord Eduardo Duarte, head of the Genoese Banking Council, advisor to the Doge. My mother's father is Viscount Santino Flores, from the island of Corsica. He is of Spanish nobility a few generations back but considers himself Genoese. I was named his heir after the deaths of my older brother and my uncles."

"Well, Lord Duarte, that is quite an inheritance to walk away from."

"I know that now, but at the time, I did not know who Cyrano was. I had never been allowed to make decisions, to think for myself, to be myself. When I let everyone believe I had drowned in that shipwreck, I was freed."

The stark white room was cool, and so was Mauro's voice when he asked, "Can you be Cyrano Duarte again?"

Cyro could not help but laugh. "That has been my question and my struggle. Indeed, living as a common man has been humbling on every level, Lord Baric. I have calluses on my hands and holes in the soles of my boots. My friends and I have ridden this continent up and down, frozen and starved together, killed and looted to survive. But it was real living, with no advisor or council planning each detail of my life. I would not trade that experience for anything. But through it all, I realized I have a duty to others, too, and not merely to myself. Someone must govern. I am ready to do that now."

Mauro frowned as he considered Cyro's dilemma. "If you tell your family you were lost, it would be the truth, you know. I suppose we do have that in common. I, myself, had always planned to stay far from Baric Castle. I understand now how that would have been a mistake. It wasn't until my father's death that I realized I could be the next Baron Baric and still be myself, not forced into being the man my father wanted. I suppose I am still coming to terms with that."

Cyro nodded that he understood all too well. "I have a cousin in Vienna, and I surprised him when we stopped there last month. With his seal as proof, I wrote a letter to my family confessing what I had done."

"If you decided this in Vienna, why did you not simply go home from there?"

Cyro said, "You are right, of course. I guess I was afraid to face the trouble I had made. My cousin already gave me quite an earful when we met."

"Was he not happy you were alive?"

Cyro chuckled, thinking about his cousin's overt disappointment. "It did not seem that way at first. He is third in line for my grandfather's title."

"I see."

Cyro leaned in when he added, "There was another reason I stayed on with my friends. I was curious to come here and meet Lady Baric."

"You wanted to meet my wife?" Mauro asked, puzzled at such a bold admission.

"Well, and you too, actually, Lord Baric. I had met you in passing before, but Patrik had woven such a story about his sister's arranged marriage and your horrible family—well, I had to see how it all turned out."

Mauro laughed. "I am sure Patrik had nothing good to say about me. You probably expected to find my wife locked in her room, and you yourself only offered bread and water. I imagine that was why you did not accept my offer to stay in the Keep at first. I hope you were not disappointed."

"There was enough drama to make it interesting at the beginning," Cyro joked. "But I am glad Patrik's worries were unwarranted. I have had an enjoyable week here, Lord Baric."

"It pleases me to hear that. Tell me, Lord Duarte, how much do your companions know of your ancestry?"

Cyro explained, "Bem introduced me as a runaway nobleman's son from the start. Salar Nassim does not have a good opinion of our privileged class, but he liked Bem straight away, so he took me into the group on Bem's promise that I would not make trouble for them. I had already been a soldier and had sailed as a deckhand with Bem. He was the one who taught me how to keep my head low and my mouth shut. I passed Salar Nassim's test, and here I am today."

"I believe there is one more person that needs to know your secret," said Mauro.

"You mean Lady Caterina? Yes, well, I have been trying to make her fall in love with me first, but she is still mourning her old lover. I fear I am not handsome enough to sway her, and my charms have failed me miserably."

Mauro pointed out, "You have not taken all the players into account. Are you aware of who her father is?"

"I know who Roberto Carrera is, but I do not care about the old politics, and I did not think Lady Caterina would either."

"And your father? Will he approve? There is a long history of hatred between the Venetians and the Genoese."

"And a need for new alliances, Lord Baric!"

His voice reverberated in the sanctuary, and he lowered it when he said, "I know what card to play when I tell my father about Caterina. I will be sure he will find some gain in my marriage with a Venetian."

"Do you plan to leave here without telling Caterina your intentions?"

Cyro shrugged sheepishly. "Possibly."

Mauro shook his head. "I know the Carrera family as well as my own, so let me give you some advice. You will not succeed in gaining Lord Carrera's permission to wed Caterina without her influence. You need to be clear with her, and soon. If she wants you, she will do your bidding with her father."

"That is also why I am on my knees asking for God's guidance tonight. After all the battles and victories, perhaps I am still a coward. I do not know how to tell her I love her."

Mauro spoke from his own experience now. "You must summon your courage and tell her the truth. If she does not love you after that, then you will never convince her father, and you should plan to find another woman to love."

Mauro stood up from the bench and stretched his stiff back. "It is late, Cyro. I will leave you to finish your prayers."

"You have been extremely helpful, Lord Baric. Thank you. I will take your advice to heart."

"I am glad to have helped you. Good night, Cyro."

Mauro gave the man one last, long look. He had seen something promising in Cyro from the start, but hearing his story tonight made it clear that the young nobleman was a determined and deserving man.

Cyro watched the baron go. Once alone again, Cyro felt suddenly tired. He bowed his head and thanked God for sending Lord Baric to him tonight. Then Cyro left the little chapel and crossed the dark courtyard to his empty chamber in the Keep. He was at peace for whatever was to come tomorrow, and not even the rustling of his drunken friends crawling into bed soon thereafter could wake him.

Chapter 37

One candle still burned by the bedside. Mauro lit a second to bring behind the screen, where he hastily undressed and washed before sliding under the blanket. His old catechism book lay open on the bed where Resi had dropped it when she fell asleep. He set it on the side table by the candle.

Resi still wore her dressing gown over her shift. It looked twisted around her full waist, so Mauro reached over to untie the sash and slip it open. She looked peaceful lying there now. He kissed her on her cheek, and a smile formed on her lips. She sighed softly in her sleep.

"Good night, my darling," he whispered. He leaned down and kissed her again.

Her eyes opened, and her smile faded as a startled expression took its place.

Mauro laughed. "Were you expecting someone else to kiss you awake?"

She blinked twice, still in a fog of sleep. "No, I … I thought maybe I was dreaming."

"I think you were. You had such a sweet smile on your lips that I had the overwhelming urge to kiss them."

He picked up his book on the bedside table and flipped through the pages. "Is this what you were reading tonight? This book usually gave me bad dreams. Father David made us memorize most of it."

"Did you read it in bed?"

"Oh yes. I would check the rules every night to know whether I had done something to anger God that day."

"How old were you then?" she asked sleepily.

He shrugged and said, "Ten, or maybe eleven. Idita finally convinced me not to worry about making God angry. She told me boys are naturally corrupted, and life without sin is impossible. We are doomed to disobey. We must continually pray and ask for forgiveness because of it. At least that is what good Catholics can agree upon. But I am not a good Catholic."

Resi lightly stroked his arm next to hers, puzzling over his admission. She asked, "What do you mean, Mauro? You do not agree, or you do not pray for forgiveness?"

"Both," he mumbled.

"And yet you are patron to a grand church and chapel."

"And, for that reason, I have never forsaken my faith altogether. Which reminds me," he added with forced cheerfulness, despite his sleepiness, "Radic and I made our final plans for his party."

"It will be a nice party. I am looking forward to it."

"It will indeed, since I am to provide all the drink for the festivities and a fat hog to roast. The Church also requires three casks of our wine for communion as a part of my assigned penance, along with one other benevolent work of my choice for my sins."

Resi sat up, wide awake now, even as Mauro slid down deeper under the covers to go to sleep. "But you just said you were not a good Catholic, and yet you made your confession to Father David today?"

"I also said I did not leave my faith. Father David was with Radic before our meeting. He reminded me that it had been too long since my last reconciliation with God, and he was willing to hear it today. Or he was running low on wine for Sunday's Mass and needed a way to ask for more."

"How does that work? Could you come up with sins on the spot like that?" she asked, seemingly anxious to know and not know at the same time.

"Do you want to hear all of them, Resi?"

"No," she answered too quickly.

Mauro knew she was thinking again of her own newly found-out sins, and he wanted to put her at ease.

"I could think of no grave sins from soldiering to confess this time, but when I was honest about my thoughts and actions, I found I am quite the sinner. For example—"

She put her hand over his mouth and said, "If you have been forgiven, then there is no need to tell me."

Mauro playfully took her hand away. "I am sure you were expecting a more devout and virtuous husband. You might want to know what an immoral man you married."

"Is there such a virtuous man to be had?"

He opened one eye and said, "Father David, perhaps?"

Resi chuckled as she absently stroked Mauro's hair. It was growing longer, curling around his temples. Mauro was on the verge of sleep when she asked, "Do you meet Father David often?"

"Often enough, considering I do not attend Mass," Mauro answered drowsily. "I usually visit after returning from battle to clear my conscience and make peace with what I had done. Father David reminded me it had been seven months since my last penance. The usual sins have been adding up."

"The usual ones, Mauro?"

He looked up at her again from his soft pillow. "I am sorry to say I had to mention a few sins I committed with you, since you are still so enticing with your growing curves. Father David might expect you will ask for forgiveness for the same sins, but only if it is important to you to tell him."

Resi stared ahead, quiet for a moment.

"It's not that it isn't important to me," she finally said. "I told you I was a terrible student in religion. I regret not paying attention to my mother. I don't even know all the sins I could be committing."

"That makes it easy, Resi. If you do not know you are committing a sin, then you cannot deliberately disobey God. You will be forgiven for it," Mauro explained, just as Caterina had told Resi on the wagon ride home.

"I never told you, but I could not get through the sacrament before our wedding vows. The priest thought it was because I was a nervous bride, but really I had no idea what I was supposed to say. I do not know the first thing about confessing," she fretted.

"Is that all you are worried about? Come here and let me hold you. I will tell you the words to say, and you can practice for tomorrow."

"Tomorrow?" she asked.

After she settled into her favorite spot near his shoulder, he whispered, "Father David is blessing the fresh holy water in the chapel, and he will hear confessions afterward."

She slid free from his hold and faced him again. "My confession?"

"You are not being singled out, Resi, if that is your worry."

"Oh, well, if he is coming anyway, then maybe I will meet with him."

"When you do, you should wear one of your veils. We have no screen in the chapel."

He could feel her take an anxious breath. "Alright, Mauro. And what do I say to Father David?"

"Oh, you say something like this: I confess to Almighty God and to you, Father, that I have sinned. And then you tell God when your last confession was, list the sins you have committed since then, and at the end of your confession, you ask for forgiveness."

"Maybe I should practice."

"There is no need to tell me," he whispered. "You will do just fine. And when you are done, you tell God how you detest your terrible deeds, and then you ask for His mercy to go to heaven. Father David will absolve you of your sins and tell you what penance you are to do. He usually gives me charitable duties, because he knows I can afford it. He may do the same for you, or he may just have you pray to keep your resolve."

Although his eyes were shut, Mauro could feel her penetrating gaze on him when she asked, "Did you vow to keep your resolve, Mauro?"

"That is the hardest part, Resi. Once a sinner always a sinner, but I did make a vow to try. For my sin of fornication, for example, I am not planning to sleep on a cot in my study. I have done that already, and it was not very comfortable."

"What is your plan then?"

He pulled her close to him again and said, "You are practically irresistible, Terese Baric, but I will resist temptation in my own bed. I will hold you like I am holding you now, and that will be enough for me until the baby comes."

He yawned deeply.

"Mauro, don't fall asleep yet."

"It is late."

"I need to tell you something important, something I must confess."

"Shhh. There is nothing to tell me. I know everything I need to know. You are perfectly lovely, perfectly charming, perfectly sinful, and I love you that way. You practice in your head what you will say to the priest, but I must sleep now."

She wrapped her arm around his bare waist. "Mauro," she whispered.

He groaned.

"How do you know how to make everything right, even before I can tell you what is wrong?"

"I won't always be able to, you know," he replied, his words barely crossing his lips, "but I will try."

Chapter 38

Caterina's ruffled nightcap peeked above the edge of the covers as she lingered in her dreams under the toasty blankets.

Isabella sat by the window. Since getting out of bed an hour ago, she had watched the Baric compound come to life below her. She was dressed in yesterday's gown, the one the maid had left slung over the chair.

Isabella got up to see if there was any tea in the pot from yesterday evening. Finding it empty, she replaced the porcelain lid with a clank.

Caterina woke from the jolting noise and curled the cover down. She looked around the room for her missing bedmate. "Why are you already dressed? Were you painting sunrises again?"

Isabella sat down beside her sleepy friend. "Did I wake you, Cat?"

Caterina lowered the covers further. "Not really. I feel like I did not sleep a wink. Why must love be so complicated, Isabella?"

Isabella cocked her head in confusion. "I thought you had given up on Paolo after the letter," she said.

Caterina pulled the covers tight again. She did not bother to tell her friend it was no longer Paolo filling her thoughts.

"I have something you can help me with that will put Paolo out of your mind."

"What do you propose, Isabella?" asked Caterina, curled up in bed again.

"The mercenaries are leaving soon. I think we should ask the baroness to give them a special farewell dinner tomorrow night."

"I am sure Lady Terese has already thought of that," Caterina said, seemingly unimpressed with her suggestion.

"Not a Venetian feast, Cat dear, but something unexpected. I was thinking about what Lady Ruby had said in the bathhouse. We could ask the cook to make an exotic meal of roasted goat and couscous."

A puzzled look crossed Caterina's fair face. "Why would they want goat when they can have a lovely salted sea bass, or Nela's fabulous grilled squid?"

"Because Lady Ruby told us it would remind Bem of home."

Caterina mumbled under the blankets, "Again Bem."

Isabella was not discouraged. "I am going to ring for the maid and then I will go talk to the cook myself."

~ * ~

Franja had fallen ill during the night with aches and a fever. At dawn, Idita had come to Nela's chamber as she was dressing to say that Franja should keep to her bed for at least a day, if not two. Idita told her that Franja's illness was not contagious, the first question on everyone's mind. Without Franja, though, the kitchen's schedule fell apart. The Baric's baker arrived each morning before Nela to unbank the coals, light the oven, and start the dough for the day's bread.

Nela's stiff fingers told her it would be a difficult undertaking if she had to knead and form the loaves herself. She had not had to make the bread for the castle in years. She stood at Franja's marble table and measured out the flour. If Danica was feeling better, there was hope that she could manage the loaves. Once Danica finished that, Natalija's sister, Marija, might be trusted to tend the baking bread since Nela would also need Danica's help with the lunch preparations.

As Nela mixed her flour and yeast and mulled over the morning assignments in her head, the baron stopped by the kitchen to tell Nela about Father David's visit. Lunch was usually a simple meal for the ladies, but Nela could not offer a meager plate of smoked ham with fruit compote to a guest of the baron. After Nela put the bread dough aside to rise, there would still be time to prepare a few chickens before noon. That would make a far better offering for the priest.

The maids arrived, and Nela instructed Ivana to get one of the servant boys to catch four young roosters from the chicken yard and pluck and gut them, ready to roast.

Nela drank her morning cup of tea late while waiting for the maid to bring the plucked fowl and for her second batch of yeast to bubble. To her surprise, Lady Isabella opened the door to the kitchen. She wore a silk gown that took up most of the space between the doorway and the table where the cook sat.

Nela stood up to greet the baroness's guest with a curtsey. "Did Natalija not bring your morning tray, Lady Isabella?" Cook asked with worry.

Isabella smiled sweetly and replied, "I have had my breakfast, thank you. I am here on an errand. I have a request for tomorrow's dinner."

Nela dreaded to learn what new burden would be asked of her today. "What is your pleasure, my lady?" Cook asked dutifully.

"The baroness's brother and his companions will be leaving us on Monday. I heard that they sorely miss their home cooking, and one of their favorite meals is couscous. Do you know this dish?"

Nela had been cooking for all occasions for decades, but this peasant dish had never made an appearance on the Baric's table. "I do, madam, but I am sorry to tell you, we do not make this dish here," Nela replied.

Isabella shrugged and said, "I did not expect that you do. It is really more of an Ottoman tradition, and who would want to encourage that?"

"Indeed, it is not our tradition," Nela agreed.

Isabella pressed her, "But it is a dish that you could make, is it not? Perhaps one that is spicy and sweet, with roasted lamb or goat to accompany it? It would be a grand gesture, so the men could look forward to their own homecoming."

Just like Lord Fabian, Lady Isabella had an expression that conveyed she would not take no for an answer. Nela wondered if all Venetians had such insistent glares.

Cook gritted her teeth and politely replied, "If it would please the visitors and yourself, then I shall do my best to make this Ottoman dish."

"Marvelous. Thank you, Nela," Isabella said. She turned with a whoosh of her gown and left the old cook alone in the kitchen again.

Nela sat back down on the low stool and put her head in her hands, wondering what she had done to upset God today.

"Nela, are you all right?" Danica asked when she came through the servants' entrance and saw Cook bent over the table. She rushed to her side.

Nela looked up. God was going to help her after all, she thought.

"You are a sight for sore eyes, Danica. I have a long list of things that cannot possibly be finished without you. How are you, dear? Can you work today?"

Danica looked around the kitchen. "Where is everyone? Where is Franja?"

"Franja fell ill last night with a fever and is still in bed. Poor girl, she hasn't been sick one day since she arrived here. Idita says she will recover, but she is in awful pain."

Danica thought of their conversation just yesterday and asked, "What kind of pain, Nela? Stomach pain?"

Nela realized Idita had not said. "I did not ask, now that I think of it."

"Well, I am sure Franja will rebound quickly. What is on your long list for today, Nela?"

"The baron wants a formal lunch for Father David and the Barics today. Lady Isabella wants a special Ottoman dinner for the guests tomorrow. I don't know how I will ever have time to make any couscous pasta today to be dried for tomorrow. I have not yet baked one loaf of bread, and that has not gone unnoticed in the Keep. Lazar came to say the men ran out of yesterday's bread to toast for their breakfast. The dough is ready to be rolled into loaves for a second rising, and I have started more yeast for the second batch."

Danica took an apron from the peg. "We will not waste any time then."

"Thank you, Danica. I knew I could count on you," Nela said. "But first, will you go find Jero for me?"

~ * ~

Resi had kept busy that morning so she would not have to think about her upcoming confession to Father David. She spent the last hour in the sunny sitting room penning a letter to her mother, telling her about her new happiness and good fortune. She would give it to Patrik to take with him. She then searched the bookshelf for a good story she could get lost in until lunch.

Resi was settling down with her open book when Jero came in and asked, "May I interrupt, Lady Terese?"

"Good morning, Jero. Of course, you can," she said cheerfully.

"Your husband might have mentioned that he wanted me to explain some of my duties in the household. Going forward, he said, he would like you to be in charge of these duties. He asked, too, that Nela and Franja come to you with any problems that arise in the kitchen."

"Did he?" Resi asked with surprise.

Jero hesitated. He was of two minds. He had just come from explaining to Cook that the baroness was now in charge of the household staff. Cook had insisted she did not want to bother the baroness with what she might find insignificant. Jero had assured her that the baroness would not see today's problems as trivial, and Nela would have to learn to trust her mistress to manage such situations from now on. But he could also handle this one last duty alone. "It was only yesterday that the baron suggested this to me. If you prefer to talk to him first, my lady, I will leave you to your reading."

Resi put her book back on the shelf. "If that is what he told you, then there is no need for me to talk to Mauro. It just all seems rather sudden somehow."

"I am sorry for that, my lady. It has been an unusual morning. Franja is ill in bed today, and Cook made the bread dough herself, but there will not be fresh bread ready in time for Father David's lunch visit. Also, Lady Isabella came earlier to ask that Cook make a special couscous meal for tomorrow, but the dough for that will have to be rolled from scratch and dried today. Danica is back in the kitchen, but she will take over Franja's baking duties, so dinner preparations will be falling behind, too. If you like, I could take care of this today, and we could begin with something less urgent."

"No, um . . . I see the trouble. You are right, Jero. If I am to take on this task, then there will be no better time than the present."

Jero smiled encouragingly. "If you could come to the kitchen, madam, maybe you can offer Nela a solution."

~*~

Resi frantically processed in her mind the details Jero told her while they walked the short distance to the kitchen. When he opened the door, it did not seem to be in the state of upheaval Jero had described. Nela was seasoning six birds for roasting on a spit over the fire; the kitchen girls were cleaning vegetables for the side dishes; Danica was rolling out the loaves to rise once again before baking.

The maids stopped their work and curtsied to their mistress

"Lady Baric," exclaimed Nela when she saw her. "I told Jero I did not want to disturb you with our simple troubles this morning."

Jero crossed his arms defiantly at the remark.

"Jero told me what a busy morning you have had, and I wanted to help. We never realize how important one person is until they are missed. Is Franja feeling unwell?"

"Idita says she will be fine after a day in bed, but Franja is the first one to the kitchen to light the oven and begin the baking, so we are several hours behind, my lady," said Cook.

"I understand Father David is a man of modest requirements. I am sure he will not notice the missing bread," the baroness assured her.

"But Franja is known for her bread, Lady Baric. It will surely be noticed," Nela fretted.

Resi knew this was true. She looked around the kitchen thoughtfully while Nela and Jero stood by, waiting for instructions from the baroness. Her eyes rested on Danica, forming rows of loaves to bake.

"I have an idea," Resi told Nela after a moment. "If the priest spent time in the Holy Lands, then he would know flat bread. That can be baked in a fraction of the time a loaf can. That is how we make our bread in Greece."

Danica perked up at the idea. "I know how to bake flat bread, Lady Baric. I will just need to stoke the fire, so the oven is good and hot."

Resi could not hide her sigh of relief. "Good, Danica. We will tell Father David it was especially baked in his honor. It will be a treat for me as well."

The women of the kitchen nodded to each other, pleased with her solution.

Resi interjected, "But there was one other concern for today, is that right, Nela?"

"Indeed, there is a problem with Lady Isabella's request for tomorrow's dinner. I have the right flour necessary, but the pasta would have to be made today by hand, and it is time-consuming. If I put my two maids working on that this afternoon, then dinner will be late."

"I see," replied Resi as she mulled over a solution. Then the baroness's face lit up. "If you can provide me with the supplies, Ruby and I will make the couscous pasta. I have seen it done before, and we can lay it in the sun on some cloth to dry. It may not turn out perfect, but I think our guests will appreciate our effort."

"But, my lady, the baron will object, and—" Nela began to protest why her mistress should not be doing such menial kitchen work.

Resi anticipated her argument. "The baron will not object. Especially if he is not told," she assured the worried cook. "It is a lovely day to sit outside. I could be strumming my harp in the garden, or rubbing a sieve making couscous."

Still, Cook frowned.

"Are you not in agreement?" asked Resi.

"It is just, um, there is more to her request than the pasta, my lady. I think I have all the spices required to make a true Ottoman dish, but if I do not have all the necessary pieces . . . Also, we will need a young goat roasted."

Jero offered a solution to the last concern.

"There were several young goats foraging around the cottages when we left for the villa yesterday. I will make arrangements with the owner to have one slaughtered for tomorrow. How will that be, Nela?" he asked.

Nela dropped her grip on the ends of her apron and agreed, "I think that will be just fine, Jero. I will get these chickens roasting next, and we are back on schedule."

"I will come by the kitchen after Father David leaves," Resi offered.

Beaming with relief, Nela said, "I will have everything ready for you. Thank you, Lady Baric."

Resi had been worried about confessing her sins to God, but now she was eager to give thanks for being given this new role in the house. "Thank you, Nela," she said before she walked out of her kitchen.

The last time Resi had been this nervous was on her wedding day. She had rehearsed in her head what Mauro had taught her about confession last night, but her mind went blank when she walked into the chapel.

Resi would be first to make her confession to God that afternoon. It was supposed to honor her place as baroness. She thought she would prefer to wait until the end of the day when Father David might be glad for a shorter, truncated sacrament.

Resi had enjoyed hearing the priest's stories of his journeys before he came to Solgrad during their leisurely lunch, and she had guessed right about his modesty since he seemed to relish their simple chicken meal, despite Franja's missing creations. She knew she should not be frightened—Father David was a gentle and amiable man.

She collected her courage in the foyer as she stood in front of the demure angel that held a dish of the freshly blessed holy water. Resi dipped her fingers into the basin and said a quick prayer for strength as she crossed herself. Then she lowered her dark veil over her face and went into the familiar sanctuary.

Father David had set up two chairs, back to back, in front of the altar. Resi sat down next to the already seated priest. Father David would know it was her when she began to speak, and she did her best to sound confident.

"Do you wish to confess your sins before God?" the priest asked from his place, facing the statue of the Holy Mother.

Resi faced out toward the door she had just come through. "Yes, Father David. I have sinned, and I wish to ask for forgiveness."

He waited for her to begin. When she didn't, he said, "I will hear your confession now."

Resi felt safe behind her veil, but she shut her eyes anyway when she said, "I don't know where to begin, really. I thought I was being a dutiful wife, but it turned out that what I thought was wonderful and loving was actually wicked and wrong."

He waited for her to elaborate, and when she didn't, Father David asked in his solemn way, "And for that you ask forgiveness?"

"I do wholeheartedly," she replied, eager now to explain how it wasn't her fault. "You see, my sin stems from when I was younger and did not heed my mother's advice. My mother is a good Catholic woman, and she tried to teach me what I needed to know to be devout, but I didn't understand I could be in such trouble from God for not studying his rules."

"Are you asking forgiveness for your sin of sloth, my lady?"

"Sloth?" she repeated with alarm. "Oh, I had not thought of it that way," she whispered. She spoke up again to ask, "That is a mortal sin, isn't it, Father?"

"It is," he replied in a low voice.

"Oh, dear."

She sighed unhappily. Resi had no idea that she was in such trouble with God.

"That is almost like murder or adultery," she said. "I only thought my sins to be small, like lying to my husband and disobeying what was asked of me."

"Lying is a sin, as is disobedience to your husband. You should confess those today as well."

"They are adding up, just as my husband said. Am I a terrible sinner, Father David?"

"No, my lady. God will not judge your sin of sloth to be a mortal one, unless you committed it with full knowledge that you went against Him."

"Then forcing my husband to fornicate would not be judged badly if I did not know it was against God's will?" she asked.

The priest had heard the baron's confession yesterday, and he asked, "Do you mean to say that your husband forced you to fornicate, and you were obedient to him? God will forgive you if you were coerced by another."

"It was I who pressured him," she said with conviction. "My husband tried to keep away from me when he learned I was with child—he slept on a cot each night in his study. I thought it was because he didn't love me, Father, but now I know he has loved me from the beginning." She smiled to herself, having said out loud what she knew to be the truth. Then Resi sat up tall in her chair and confirmed, "That is my confession. Yes, I am sure of it. Alright, Father, I am ready now to tell God."

She could not see him smile when he answered, "I think God has heard your sins clearly, madam. You did not have a full understanding of the severity of your acts, nor intended that they provoke someone else to sin. If you ask now for His mercy to forgive all that you have confessed today, I will absolve you."

Resi bowed her head and pleaded, "I am truly sorry for not listening to my mother, for not listening to my husband, and for wanting things that I now know went against God. I ask for God's mercy to forgive me, and I resolve to try harder." She hoped she had covered everything.

"For this and all your sins, I absolve you," Father David said with priestly composure. "As a penance for the sins you have committed and have been forgiven for, you are to pray daily for strength to keep your husband happy in a *godly* way. Second, you are to come weekly to Mass to continue your moral commitment to Him."

"No charity, Father?" she asked quietly.

"Not this time, madam."

Resi stood up and went to leave. Before opening the door, she turned and said, "God is good. Thank you, Father David. That was not so bad."

His back was still turned to her. He looked ahead at the modest altar and smiled to himself at her innocence. Yes, that was not bad at all, he thought. "God *is* good," he repeated under his breath when he heard the door close. He had finally discovered what kind of a wife God had given the young baron. She would be good for him and for the village.

Resi met Caterina in the foyer. Caterina, too, was anxious to clear her conscience with the holy man. Father David would have an enlightening afternoon, indeed.

~ * ~

Nela was in the pantry looking for the special grind of flour the baroness would need to make her Ottoman pasta. From within the small room, she heard a man's voice talking to Danica in the kitchen. Thinking it was Krsto, Nela poked her head around the pantry door to say hello, but stopped short when she heard what they were saying.

Simeon was with Danica, and he did not bother to keep his voice low in the empty kitchen. "I heard Franja was ill today. I wanted to visit her, but men are not allowed in the women's quarters."

"It is a good thing men are not allowed, but I understand you don't follow those rules in the Keep."

He met her anger with a scowl. "What are you saying, Danica?"

"I am saying Father David is still in the chapel if you want to make your confession. Franja will recover from her mistake, but you should marry her before you ask her to do something like that again."

Simeon looked stricken. "What does that have to do with her sickness?"

Danica kept her fury in , but she held her stern glare. "I won't scold you for being a man, Simeon. Franja is a grown woman, and she made her choice, too. But only yesterday, she was telling me she didn't want a baby, and today she is doubled over clutching her middle, losing it. I told her to tell you, but I guess she didn't have time."

He stared at her, finally understanding Franja's plight. "How can I see her? I need to talk to her, Danica."

The hardened soldier looked suddenly fragile and broken, and Danica felt sorry now for bringing him the hurtful news. She squeezed his hand and said more kindly, "I will take you tomorrow. It would not be fair for me to sneak you up when she is at a disadvantage, sick in bed and full of sorrow. Franja needs some time to grieve alone."

"Please, Danica. I want to tell her I will make this right and marry her. I love her."

Danica took him by the arm and walked him to the door. "Tomorrow, Simeon. Tell her that tomorrow."

Danica came back into the kitchen and slumped on the chair, filled with conflicting emotions for her two friends.

Nela came out of the pantry and set her armload of goods down on the long table.

Danica looked up. "Did you hear what was said?"

Nela sat down next to Danica and whispered, "I wish she would have told me."

Danica shook her head. "She didn't know herself until we talked yesterday. Idita is right, though; Franja will be better tomorrow. I went through this twice myself until this baby finally stayed with me. It hurts when you learn you've lost something precious, even if it was with you for just a short time."

"I heard what Simeon said, Danica, and I believe he loves that girl, like he told you."

Danica stared ahead. Her eyes filled with tears when she told Cook, "Franja doesn't love him, Nela. She loves the kitchen and her work, and she doesn't want to abandon you."

Nela wiped her cheeks with her apron and scoffed. "Franja is a fool, and I will tell her so. But first I have to organize this for the baroness." She pointed to the bag of flour, cloth, and sieves she had set down on the table. "Will you help the mistress get started in the garden, Danica? I am going upstairs to lie down for a few minutes myself."

Danica asked, "Will you talk to Franja about Simeon?"

"I will follow the advice you gave to Simeon and wait until tomorrow."

~*~

Caterina was returning to her room when she saw a glimpse of green at the end of the corridor. Just as she hoped, it was the servant boy Aron. He was the solution to her problem of getting something to the Keep.

"Aron," she called out to him.

The boy hurried to her side with his empty pail and waited wordlessly for her instructions.

"I have a message I want taken to one of the foreign men in the tower. Can you do that for me?"

"Yes, madam," he answered eagerly. He regarded her pretty face and did not look away like he did with his mistress. She had been kind to him when she gave him back his wasp nest unharmed. She had also given him a lira for letting her borrow it. He had never had a whole lira before, and he would surely do more errands for the refined lady for nothing to repay her generosity.

"Wait here. I will only be a minute," she ordered.

Caterina went to her writing desk while the boy obediently stayed outside the open door. Her time with Father David had been helpful and encouraged her to do what she was about to do.

Caterina had quickly confessed her sins in the chapel, but she lingered longer to unburden herself of her troubled feelings for Cyro and her unconventional friendship with Salar Nassim. She had explained to Father David how she and Salar Nassim met each morning and discussed things of beauty, leaving out the part about the card cheating. Father David was tolerant of other religions, and he gave her good counsel on the subject of her father-daughter friendship with the Muslim. Her story about Cyro did not go over as well with the priest. Deceit of any form was wrong, he had told her. If Cyro did not come clean with his true intentions and identity, the priest had counseled that Cyro was not an honorable man worthy of her consideration.

With the priest's advice in mind, Caterina wrote her short note and blotted it dry. Then she searched her jewelry box, looking the gift she wanted to add to it. Caterina did not have a lit candle to melt her sealing wax, so she took a ribbon from her grooming table and tied the little package closed. She brought it to Aron, who was crouched on his pail in the hallway.

"There, that did not take too long, did it?" she chirped.

He nodded and took the package she held out to him.

"This is for the Persian man with the turban. Make sure he gets it. Do not leave it with anyone else."

"I will look for him and wait if I have to, my lady."

"Good boy," she told him and then handed him a piece of hard candy from the tin Isabella had brought from Venice.

He looked at the little yellow thing with curiosity.

When Caterina realized the boy did not know what he held, she said, "It is a sweet treat for you. You suck on it."

He popped it into his mouth and immediately grinned at the citrus flavor before hurrying off with her letter and his flopping bucket.

Back in her room, Caterina plopped down on the bed. She lay looking at the ceiling while she peeled off her gloves, thinking about what she wanted to say to Cyro. Father David had tried to be diplomatic about the stranger welcomed by the Barics, but he had made his point clear about deception. She would not allow him to continue his farfetched storytelling. Cyro was playing with her, and she would not be fooled again. In fact, she planned to stay in her chamber until they left. She would see him no more.

~ * ~

Isabella did not go to the chapel with Caterina. She had no sins of significance she needed to confess to the priest. She happened to be on the stairway when Resi returned to change out of her formal gown and into something more practical for making pasta. With nothing better to do, Isabella offered to help with the problem she had created.

The two went together to find Ruby, who was already at the table Danica had set up for them in the garden.

None of the ladies had a precise recipe in mind for mixing the flour, water, and salt into workable dough, and the kitchen maids could offer little advice. At first, their fingers were coated with a gooey mess, but after some trial and error and with a lighter touch, they managed to form their first handful.

It would take nearly an hour of rubbing the coated flour balls through the sieves to make ever smaller pieces and cover their drying cloth with enough pasta.

"I had no idea this would be such work," declared Isabella.

"Back at home, women work together to dry enough pasta to last several weeks. We are only making enough for one dinner," said Ruby.

"Will we also have to butcher the beast ourselves?" asked Isabella, fully expecting that they would.

Resi chuckled at her apprehensive expression. "Jero is arranging that. If Nela had more help in the kitchen today, the maids would be making our couscous. This has been amusing, though, Lady Isabella. Would you not agree?"

"In its own way," Isabella admitted. "I have tried more new adventures in my short time at Baric Castle than all year in Venice. Some things, though, I probably will not try again."

Jero walked up the path to where the ladies were working, and Resi remarked, "Oh, look, Lady Isabella. Jero is here with the goat."

Isabella looked up from her concentrated work in alarm.

"I have no goat with me, Lady Baric, only a letter," he answered cheerfully. "The courier has come, and he brought something for Lady Ruby."

Ruby reached out and took the worn, sealed envelope from Jero. It was from her family, and she always enjoyed their long letters. This one was especially thick. She set her tray of flour mixture down to open it.

"There are two letters in here," Ruby said after unwrapping the outside parchment. "One is addressed to Patricius."

Ruby set it aside. Her smile faded as she skimmed through her own letter, and Resi went to stand behind her to read it over her shoulder.

Both Jero and Isabella watched the Greek women with concern as their expressions became gravely serious.

Ruby dropped the letter on the ground and wordlessly ran from the group back toward the house.

"Did someone die?" asked Isabella.

Jero, looking stricken, seemed to wonder the same.

Resi picked up Ruby's abandoned letter and reread the last page. "Everyone is fine, except for Ruby."

Trembling, Resi sat down again and reasoned aloud, "I guess my brother wrote to my parents that he was coming here. Her father writes that Ruby is to come home with Patricius as her escort. A marriage contract has been signed. Ruby's time here is over."

Resi folded the letter and rose from her seat without further explanation, leaving Jero alone with Lady Isabella.

Jero took the sealed envelope with Patricius's name on it from the table. "If you will excuse me, madam, I must deliver this second letter." He made a slight bow and left down the path.

Isabella was alone with the nearly finished couscous. She picked up her sieve and began rubbing the flour beads absently to make the tiny balls. She arranged the last of the moist pellets on the linens like the baroness had shown her while deep in thought about what this unwelcome news would mean for her new friends.

<h1 style="text-align:center">Chapter 40</h1>

Patrik rushed through the front door. "Where is the baron?"

Davor was in the foyer and recoiled. Patrik's bruises had healed into a pale yellow mask across his eyes, and it gave him an unnatural look.

"Lord Baric escorted the priest back to the village, sir."

"Is my sister upstairs?" Patrik demanded.

"Yes, sir. She is with Lady Ruby in her room," Davor answered politely, despite his growing anxiousness.

Patrik ran up the marble staircase, not asking which room was Ruby's.

Davor shouted up to him, "Her chamber is the third door on this side."

Resi had heard the shouting and opened Ruby's door before her brother could knock. "I was expecting you," she said.

Patrik saw Ruby lying face-down on her bed. Her long hair was a mess of tangles, and her pillows lay on the floor.

Patrik hurried to Ruby's side. "Jero said you got a letter, too. What exactly did yours say?" he asked.

She sobbed, "He promised I could stay a year, and the year is over. I knew it was coming, but I never expected the rest."

Patrik turned to his sister. "I wrote to Ma and Papa in April, when we arrived in Vienna, when I decided to take my chance to visit you."

It was just as Resi had thought, and she told him, "I still have hope, Patricius. The letter is dated from May. Father Spiros would have gotten Mauro's letter by now, and he might have reconsidered after Mauro told him about Jero."

Ruby looked up at Resi with her red, teary eyes. "The baron wrote to my father about Jero?" she asked. "How did he—"

"I am sorry I broke your confidence, Ruby. I told Mauro that I thought you loved Jero, so he wrote a letter explaining the possible marriage match for you here."

Ruby seemed stunned and whispered, "Why didn't you tell me?"

"I couldn't let you get your hopes up."

"Then I'll wait for more news. Father will surely change his mind," Ruby said.

Patrik was not so convinced. "What else was in your letter, Ruby? In mine, your father said he has arranged your marriage with Nikko Areleous. Nikko's father is an influential man in Thessaloniki. If they already agreed upon it in May, then it does not matter what the baron wrote. The contract is done. They are simply waiting for the bride."

"I won't go, Patricius!"

Patrik took pity on her but held fast to his duty to persuade her. "It won't be so bad, Ruby. I remember Nikko growing up. He was a nice boy then, and he is probably a nice man now. Do you know him?"

She sniffled loudly before answering, "I know who he is. Still, I don't want to marry him. Can't you pretend you never got the letter?"

Patrik sat down on her bed and stroked her loose hair to comfort her. "I love you like a sister, Ruby, but your father raised me like a son for six years. I cannot lie to him. I must follow his request and take you home. Salar Nassim might not be so happy to take you along, but—"

"Then I will stay," she told Patrik defiantly.

He shook his head and said, "You didn't let me finish. Salar Nassim may not be happy with the request, but I will convince him that you will not be a burden. You can ride one of our extra horses, and the baron can send your belongings to Thessaloniki."

Resi insisted, "She needs to say goodbye, Patricius. There is no way she can be ready by Monday morning. If she really must go with you, can you wait until the end of the week and let her say her farewells to everyone?"

Patrik grunted at the complication. "Soren and Bem will not be happy about it, but they will follow Salar Nassim's decision. Cyro will leave for Venice, no matter what our plans are."

"Please, Patricius," begged Resi.

"I will tell you our decision tomorrow, all right?"

Resi nodded solemnly. She would no longer argue with him.

Ruby turned away from Patrik and pulled her blanket up tight again.

Patrik bent to kiss her cheek. "I am sorry, Ruby."

Without another word, he left Ruby's room to persuade his companions to wait one more week.

~ * ~

Mauro came into the empty Great Hall through the terrace doors, then went through the quiet foyer to the study. The door was locked—Nestor had the only key—but the sitting room door was open, so he looked in. Isabella was at the writing desk in the corner.

"Hello, Isabella," he said in a friendly manner. "Where is everyone?"

She looked up from her parchment and replied, "Sulking, I am afraid." She turned back to her letter.

"Do you care to elaborate?" Mauro had only been gone for an hour and could not imagine what tragic news might have arrived in that short time to quiet the whole house.

"Yes, of course, Mauritius," she said with a forced smile.

Isabella set her quill down and turned her full attention to the baron. She then took a deep breath before she recounted the news.

"A letter arrived for Lady Ruby that set the wheels into motion. It seems her father told her to pack her bags. She has been promised to a man at home, and your brother-in-law is to escort her there. It was her lover, Jero, who presented this letter and then took a second one to Patrik. What has happened since then, I am not sure, except no one is coming out of their chambers. That would include Caterina, who has decided, after speaking to the priest, that Cyro is a fraud and has been abusing her with his false stories." Isabella turned back to her letter. "I believe that covers everyone."

Mauro was not offended by her snub; he was too bothered by the news himself to want to stay.

He strode to the stairs and took them hurriedly two by two as he thought about what exactly Angelos Spiros might have written. Letters to the Greeks had always taken weeks, sometimes months, to reach them. So it seemed this letter was not an answer to Mauro's recent correspondence.

Mauro rushed down the quiet corridor to his chamber. His wife was there alone, looking out the window, and she turned toward the door when she heard it open.

Mauro's heart sunk at her sad expression, and he came to her side at the window.

"I was hoping to find you here. I did not want to have to knock on Ruby's door looking for you," he said. "What has happened? I talked to Isabella downstairs. She told me everyone is upset about letters from Greece."

"Oh, Mauro, I have been dreading this day," Resi told him in a flood of emotion. "The letter is more than a month old. Surely, your request has arrived by now."

"I agree, my dear. This cannot be the final word. Ruby should wait here until her father confirms his decision."

"Patricius thinks otherwise. He is taking her home, Mauro."

"I will have a talk with him right now, and then we can forget there was ever a problem," Mauro promised with a forced smile.

Resi could see that he thought the solution was simple, but Mauro did not understand her brother. Still, the fight had gone out of her.

"All right, Mauro," she said quietly, then turned to look out the window again.

He left her to her tearful solitude.

~ * ~

"She cannot ride with us," Salar Nassim told Patrik for the second time.

The mercenaries were gathered around the small table in their quarters, where Patrik had read them the letter and explained what he believed was between the lines. Cyro sat off to the side of the four at the table. He was not traveling south, and the men would not count his opinion.

"You still have not given a reason why? Our first planned stop has always been Thessaloniki," argued Patrik.

Bem intervened in Ruby's defense. "Ruby is as good a rider as any man. I feel confident she can make the trip at our pace."

Salar Nassim listened to Bem's opinion but was not swayed. He looked intently at Patrik and said, "The numbers are wrong."

Patrik was very familiar with his commander's superstition. He insisted, "The numbers would be wrong with or without her."

Soren spoke up against taking her along. "It is one more week here, Patrik. We agreed to leave as soon as the horses were rested."

"We did, but you won't hear them complain about eating oats and wormy apples another week. You can lie in bed here and eat and drink your fill for another week, too, Soren. We all can. Would that be such a punishment?"

They went around the table, giving shrugs, nods, and head shakes.

Patrik gave them enough time. "She comes with us, or I will take her by myself. Angelos Spiros is like a second father to me. I cannot deny him this request."

Bem stood up. "I will ride with you," he said, looking cautiously at Salar Nassim.

Soren stood up next and said, "All right, Patrik. I will, too."

The elder of the group had always made the final decision. Salar Nassim held Patrik's stare with disappointment.

"Very well," Salar Nassim finally agreed. "But why does she need a week if she will only take what she can carry?"

"To say a proper goodbye. Ruby has grown fond of these people this past year. I think we should grant her that one consideration," Patrik answered, clearly wanting to have this concession go his way, too.

Salar Nassim looked from man to man.

They each nodded.

"Agreed," their leader said.

~ * ~

Jero dressed early for dinner. He had decided he would busy himself with any remaining duties downstairs before being called to the table. The baron was coming out of his room at the end of the hallway when Jero shut his chamber door.

"Jero," Mauro called out to him.

Mauro did not ask the question he wanted to ask. Jero's glum expression was enough of an answer.

"Come with me to the Keep, Jero. I want to talk to Patrik about these letters."

Mauro set a brisk pace, and Jero hurried to keep up with him. The fresh air revitalized him after sitting alone the past hour, thinking about how his dreams were shattered with the arrival of the post. But if anyone could change his fate, Jero guessed that Mauro could.

Jero and the baron cut through the busy dining hall, then hurried up the stairs. They found Patrik and the others together in their chamber, having concluded their meeting about Ruby.

"Good evening, gentlemen," Mauro said in greeting as he entered the room. "I would like to have a word with Patrik."

"Good evening, Lord Baric," replied Salar Nassim with a subtle bow. "We were just going for an early dinner downstairs. We will leave you to your privacy."

The other three nodded and followed the Persian out the door. Patrik was still sitting at the round table.

"Patrik, this letter that came for you today seems to have my wife and Ruby in a panic."

Patrik looked at Jero standing by the baron's side and said, "I'm sorry for your misfortune, Jero."

Mauro crossed the room and sat down at the table. "I would like Ruby to wait here until we receive clarity from her father. By now, he would have gotten my letter, and I am sure he will agree to Jero's proposal."

Patrik folded his hands in front of him and bowed his head as if to hold in some rage—or perhaps only his laughter. Then he looked up and said, "Marriage games are played just the same where we come from. I do not like to see Ruby unhappy, and I already told you I am in favor of her marriage to Jero. But Angelos Spiros would not have made this marriage contract unless it was important to him in some way. He has a profitable business, and this union between the families must be advantageous in some way. I cannot contradict his decision from here."

"I am sure there is a reason, just as you say. But I only ask that she waits with us a few more months. Surely, the wedding can be delayed long enough to know who the groom is."

Patrik got up from the table and walked to the door. "You may not think it possible that I have loyalties, but I do. Angelos Spiros wrote to me directly because he knew Ruby would tuck his letter under her pillow and not follow his will. He knew that I would. Our family owes him more than we can repay, Mauro. I will not question his request, and I ask that you not question my resolve. The others have agreed to deliver her safely home. We will give her the week to say her goodbyes. We will leave with her in seven days." Patrik opened the door and walked out.

Jero slumped down on the chair and put his head in his hands.

Mauro had never seen Jero cry, not even when they were boys, and he did not want to witness it today. He left out the open door, then hurried down the stairs, all the way to the armory, and out of the tower.

Geoff was in the stables, brushing down Janus from his master's ride to the village only a short while ago.

"I need my horse, Geoff," Mauro said in a low voice, startling the groom.

"Yes, my lord," replied Geoff, not asking why. He pulled the blanket from the rails and re-saddled the baron's horse. The groom brought it out into the courtyard.

Mauro took the reins and trotted to the gatehouse.

"Will you be out for long, Mauro?" asked Simeon as he turned the heavy chain to open the iron gate for him.

Sunset was still a few hours away. "Yes, close the gate behind me."

Mauro needed time to think. He rode along the south wall road, past the orchards and around the shoulder of the mountain. The wagon road was smooth, and Janus was free to run at full gallop. Both rider and horse were sweating and breathing hard.

After miles of riding, the villa came into view, and Mauro slowed at the wall. The entrance gate beyond the murky moat was shut, but it did not matter. He did not need to go inside. It belonged to his brother. Mauro would renovate it to Jero's suggestions, and Jero could move in—with or without a wife. Jero thought he loved Ruby, but he would find love again. Mauro would wait until then to share his secret.

Chapter 41

The conversation at dinner was strained. Even after the Barics and their guests moved the party out onto the terrace, the mood remained somber, and one by one, they retired to their chambers earlier than usual that evening.

Mauro was as restless and unhappy as everyone else. He wanted more than only to lie in his wife's arms, but he wanted her to keep the promise she had made to God during confession today. He had made a vow, too, and would keep it.

Resi was resting sleepily against his chest as she whispered, "I saw Cyro walking the gardens after dinner. I think he was waiting for Caterina to come out."

"Maybe I should talk to Caterina," said Mauro. "Cyro is leaving on Monday. He might start yelling for her under her window if she does not come out before then."

"That could be an amusing diversion for all of us," Resi said with a low chuckle.

"What about Ruby?"

"I don't think she will come out of her room, either. She doesn't want to marry Nikko. She barely knows him."

"You did not know me at all, and here you are lying naked with me in our shared bed."

"I got lucky."

He gave her a squeeze of appreciation. Then he asked, "Do you know him?"

"Not well, but I know who he is. I remember he was very short, but he may have grown since I last saw him. It has been a while. Patricius knew him better. Nikko is a year older than him."

"He cannot be so bad, can he? She will learn to love him," Mauro said with certainty.

"Ruby loves Jero," Resi replied with the same confidence.

Mauro stroked her arm absently when he said, "She thinks Jero is a perfect match for her. Who am I to say he isn't? But short of begging for her hand—like Cyro plans to do for Caterina—Jero can do nothing, now that the marriage contract has been made."

Resi looked up eagerly in the dim candlelight. "He could do that! Jero could plead his case to marry her."

Mauro disagreed with as much skepticism. "He could not! It is a long way for Jero to go to be rejected. At least Cyro is a nobleman who will inherit land and a title. Caterina's father is not a fool, and he will consider that advantage, even if Cyro is Genoese."

"What?" She sat up next to him with puzzlement. "Mauro, how do you know this?" she asked.

"I haven't had time to tell you I crossed paths with him yesterday evening, and he asked me for advice. That is when he told me the rest of his story. His grandfather is a viscount of old Spanish nobility. His father is an advisor in the Genoese banking realm. Roberto Carrera will find that connection intriguing."

A chuckle rumbled in his chest as Mauro concluded, "Fabian will be pulling out his hair at the idea of it all. He does not like the Genoese."

Settling down by her husband's side again, Resi confided, "I like Cyro. Caterina already admitted she likes him, too."

"Well, maybe you will have one match made this summer. But you need to forget about Ruby and Jero's future together, Resi. He is upset today, but Jero is a practical man. He will let her go." Then Mauro sank his head into his pillow, and his mind wandered toward sleep.

Resi gave him a little shake. "Will you come with me to Mass tomorrow?" she asked.

"That is your punishment, not mine," he replied.

"Do you think of it as a punishment? I thought it was a very light penance Father David assigned."

"I am not so sure Father David was trying to be generous to you," Mauro whispered. "Some of his assignments are for his own benefit."

Resi did not see the connection. "Like the wine needed for the church?" she asked.

"Like having you represent the face of the Barics to the village each Sunday, because he knows I will not come willingly."

"My second penance was to your advantage, not the Church's," she said playfully.

He opened his eyes and smiled at her. "Keeping me happy in a godly way? He wants to get to me through you."

"And what is so bad about going to Mass, Mauro? When was the last time you went?"

"Twelve years ago," he stated with certainty.

"Twelve years?" she exclaimed, sitting up again to see him better. "You never attended Mass while you lived with the Toths, or stayed in Venice?"

"Never," he said, not showing the remorse his wife expected. "I told you, I am a not a good Catholic."

"Come with me tomorrow," Resi insisted.

"Twelve years and one day," he said defiantly.

She leaned over him and said, "Come with me to Church, and I will give you a reason to make your next confession."

He saw the daring look in her eyes that could not be mistaken. "You are a sinful woman," he said.

He then sat up on his elbows, fully awake, and thought about her proposal. "If you make good on your offer, Resi, you too will have to confess again."

"We could let our sins pile up."

He laughed in surprise. "I won't let you draw me in like a seductress. I will be the corruptor, and you the obedient wife. It will sit better with my conscience."

"I am not obedient by nature, but I will play along." Her hand slid along his thigh, resting where it made the most impact.

He shut his eyes in response to her skillful strokes.

"Out of duty to me?" he asked breathlessly.

"Yes, this is just for you. The priest said I am to keep you happy."

She leaned over and kissed his parted lips. He allowed himself to be aroused by her, controlled by her. She rolled on top of him, poised to continue her lovemaking, but first asked, "Are you coming to Mass in the morning or not?"

"You would make a good jailer. You know how to get the answer you want."

She continued to tease him, gliding over his hips. "Make your decision, Husband."

"You are torturing me, Resi. Put me out of my misery," he moaned.

She shook her head. "I need your answer first."

He acquiesced. "I will come with you."

He sighed with satisfaction when she lowered herself onto him.

"We will do this one last time," she said before she moved against him for her own pleasure.

"One last time," he breathed out.

~ * ~

Across the courtyard, high above the ramparts, Salar Nassim was bent over his small carpet in prayer. The tower roof offered the perfect refuge for his solitary ritual.

After kneeling to praise God, Salar Nassim rose to sit on the wide ledge. He took Caterina's package from the pouch that hung from his belt and unwrapped the satin ribbon holding it closed. It was a beautiful gesture, and he wound the ribbon carefully and set it next to him. He then neatly unfolded the parchment that held a polished rock. Amused, he moved it around his hand for a moment, reflecting on how smooth and cool it was to his touch. Another thing of beauty, he thought.

The note the stone was wrapped in was written in a flowing Latin. It read: "I brought this from the shore of my home. I wanted something to remind me of my beautiful seaside while in the mountains of Hungary. I want you to have it instead, to remind you of our time together on this side of the Adriatic. I will not forget you."

She did not address it or sign it. It could have been for or from anyone. But she had still taken a risk to tell him in writing. She had thought they would not have a private moment again before he left.

The Persian touched the white oval stone to his lips and put it into his pouch, along with the neatly folded paper and the wound ribbon. He went back to his chamber, where his friends were already in bed, snoring softly. One candle had been left burning on the grooming table. He hastily washed his face and hands there before sliding into his bed that was next to Cyro's. Cyro was still awake, his hands clasped across his chest as if in prayer.

Salar Nassim quietly asked his pensive friend, "Did you decide to ask the little one to marry you?"

"Yes. I looked for her in the garden, but didn't see her. Tomorrow I will explain everything to her."

Salar Nassim nodded in the dim moonlight. "Good."

Chapter 42

Isabella had offered to join Resi for Mass that morning before Mauro was persuaded to come. The baron drove the two ladies in the wagon, Vilim and Simeon rode along as escorts, while other castle residents left on foot in small groups for the village church.

Cyro saddled his horse after the Baric riders had gone but did not try to catch up to them along the way. He went into the church alone and sat in the back, content to listen to the priest in anonymity.

A few of the villagers openly stared at the elegant stranger sitting among them, but most focused on catching a glimpse of their baron, their new baroness, and the glamorously dressed lady who sat in the front pew with them.

Father David had expected that the baroness would follow through on her resolution to attend Mass, but he had not dared hope that she could convince her husband to join her. The priest was pleased to see their village patron come through the grand doorway with his wife. But if one watched Father David closely, he would have noticed that the priest's eyes rested on the beautiful Venetian entering after them. Perhaps he wondered if she were the unfamiliar voice who had asked his advice yesterday.

In the Barics' honor, the choir sang two additional songs at the end of Father David's extra-long sermon. When the rituals finally concluded and the Baric group rose to leave, they were met along the aisle with bows, curtsies, and handshakes from the many well-wishers who were happy to greet their lord and lady in the church his grandfather had built for them. Mauro was not accustomed to such extended public attention and seemed relieved when he finally led his wife back to their horses.

Cyro was waiting with his horse by the Barics' wagon when they approached. "I thought I would ride back with you if that is all right," he said.

It took a moment for the group to recognize the mercenary soldier. Cyro had shaved his neat beard and cut his long locks, making him look exceptionally youthful in his broad felt hat covering his short curls. His elegant neck scarf and flowing sleeves under his velvet jacket elongated his short stature. He had on heels instead of boots, and his pleated breeches expertly matched his waistcoat. He wore an ancient gold band with an engraved signet on his right hand and a large ring set with a brilliant, oval ruby on the other. Cyro was barely recognizable as Cyrano Duarte.

"I did not know you were here, Cyro. You should have come and sat with us for the service," said Mauro with an irrepressible grin.

"I arrived late, and I did not see where you were sitting until the priest had already begun his prayers. I did not mind sitting in the back, though. You have a lovely church, Lord Baric."

He then turned to Isabella and asked, "Did Lady Caterina not join you today, madam?"

Isabella could hardly keep from gaping at the handsome nobleman. She found her voice and answered, "Oh, um, she was not up to it this morning. She has actually not felt well since yesterday. Perhaps she will be better when we return."

He nodded, not hiding his concern for his darling's well-being.

Vilim and Simeon waited on their steeds while the lords and ladies spoke. They had known something was unusual about the sellsword, but they had not expected him to be an aristocrat in disguise.

Cyro offered Isabella a hand up onto the bench seat while Mauro helped his wife from the other side. He ignored their blatant stares, taking pleasure in their discomfort at his unexpected transformation.

Mauro said from the driver's seat, "I have a sense that it is well past lunchtime. I am sure Nela has a delicious meal waiting for us. I would be glad if you would join us at the table, Cyro. The rest of the ladies will most likely be there as well."

"With pleasure, Lord Baric," replied Cyro, confident that the ladies he referred to included Caterina.

~ * ~

Isabella came into the Venetians' bedroom to deposit her hat and refresh herself before the noon meal. Her friend was still lounging in bed.

"Get dressed, Caterina, and come to lunch," Isabella insisted. "You cannot stay in bed all day."

Caterina put the pillow over her capped head. "I told you, Isabella, I will come out when Cyro is gone."

"Well, Cyro is gone, and a nobleman had taken over his body. He was at High Mass this morning wearing the clothing and jewels of a duke. We were right about him."

Caterina glanced up at her friend. "It is all a part of his fictional tale. He probably stole those clothes and invented another story for you."

"Yes, dear Caterina, it is all too strange to be true, but I think this might be the true Cyro. Do you not want to have a look?"

"No."

"I told Cyro you were ill, but now I will tell him you are incurable."

Isabella bent to kiss her friend's cheek in sympathy before she left again. "I will have Natalija bring you a tray."

~ * ~

Later, Caterina answered the knock on the door, believing it might be the baroness. As a kind hostess, Lady Terese would be concerned for her guest and visit after lunch.

To her surprise, Salar Nassim was at the threshold instead of the baroness. He was dressed in his usual jacket and turban but wore a pale yellow shirt today. Caterina held back the smile that threatened to cross her lips at having won her private bet of a rainbow shirt collection.

Natalija had brought her a lunch tray, then had promised to return to help the young noblewoman dress for the evening, but the maid had not found time.

At the doorway, Caterina seemed more girlish. Her long hair was pulled tight and hung straight down her back in a braid. The unadorned gown she had slipped on was missing the usual lifted underskirts and lace stomacher, and her pretty face was not yet rouged. Seeing her vulnerable like this would make it easier for Salar Nassim to speak to her.

"May I come in?" he asked.

She opened the door fully and walked away.

The Persian followed her in and shut the door, not concerned with the impropriety of it. He wanted a quiet word with her alone.

She sat down on the upholstered chair by the table, but Salar Nassim waited by the entrance.

The two stared at each other until Caterina broke their silence. "I hear you are delaying your departure," she said.

"We are, but Cyro will still be leaving in the morning."

"Why should I care?" Her voice wavered.

Salar Nassim noticed the falter and insisted, "Because you have spent much of your time this week getting to know him."

"I do not know him," she said with certainty again. "He has told me stories of his life—half stories, really. He has taken advantage of me and has wasted my time with his lies." When he did not add his commentary, she sighed and told him, "I am ill today. Please leave me."

Salar Nassim watched her, his arms casually crossed as he leaned against the sturdy door. Her rosy cheeks and bright eyes did not look to be from a fever, so he continued with his mission.

He came over to the table and sat down across from Caterina. "I will leave you after I make my confession," he said.

"Confession?"

"Our card sessions—it was to test you."

She looked puzzled. "What does that mean?"

"After Cyro met you that first evening, he told us he was in love."

She scoffed in disbelief.

"Exactly. How could he fall in love so quickly? That was my question to him. So, for him to be sure it was you he loved, and not the idea of love, I offered to challenge you the same way I challenged him when we first met in Athens."

Her expression remained unchanged. "You taught him card tricks?"

"No, Lady Caterina. I taught him to look at things differently. If he was to join my gang, he would have to see us as his peers, equal and worthy. He had grown up as a lord with servants bending to him, saying yes to whatever he wanted, foolish or not. I could not have such a spoiled man in our group, risking our lives. But he is a man of solid character, and he proved it to me. Asking you to find these things of beauty, and to explain them to me in your own words, showed me your character. That was the test."

"And you told him about our sessions? What we discussed and what you thought of me? You were playing matchmaker and spy?" she asked with increasing disgust.

"I did not tell him. He had to find that out for himself. But my test gave you a reason to talk to him."

Salar Nassim's sport was an unexpected dagger to her already wounded heart. "I trusted you," she said.

"I kept your confidence."

"Tell me, Salar Nassim—did I pass your little exam? Am I fit to be paired with a liar, or am I, too, a spoiled aristocrat?"

"I am sorry you are angry, madam. In truth, I had thought we would meet only once or twice. You did pass—beautifully—and still I met with you. If anyone is a liar, it is me. If Cyro had told you all that he wanted to, you would have thought him to be just another wealthy suitor pursuing you, not a man who loved you. Everything he said was true. All the stories were his. Cyro did not lie. He merely held his tongue. But he wants to talk to you again, Lady Caterina."

She remained resolute. "There is nothing to say. I am not free to choose a suitor, and he should know that. It is better he leaves without making this worse for himself."

"If you were free to choose, dear Lady Caterina, could you love Cyro?"

She squeezed her eyes shut, as if in pain, and answered, "Two weeks ago, I loved another man and he broke my heart."

"Perhaps your heart was broken for Cyro to find his way in. Can you consider that? A sort of fateful destiny."

He was no longer the teacher. He was the father she needed advice from.

"Why is it important to you, Salar Nassim?" she asked.

He knew this question was coming, and he tried to explain it convincingly.

"I have been with Cyro every day for two years, Lady Caterina. He has made good choices, the right choices, and his instinct was always correct. The last free choice he may have is who he will marry. He told me it will be you, and I believe he is right."

She became defiant again. "You have wasted five days of your time with your little experiment. I am not his to have and not yours to manipulate. I have been given to another already."

"How can you be so sure?"

"Because that is how it works!"

He let his guard down in that moment and his feelings showed in his eyes.

Caterina said, "You told me about your daughter. Does the father not make the matches where you come from? My father holds a list of possible mates for his daughters. He will have a husband arranged in no time if my Hungarian groom changes his mind. Cyro is not on that list."

She stood up and walked to the window. "Our lesson is over," she said to the glass.

Salar Nassim went to the door. "Cyro is waiting for you in the garden," he said and then shut the door behind him.

Caterina lingered at the window and anxiously watched for a glimpse of Cyro on the path. Frustrated, she sat down at the table again and sighed. What did it matter whether she met with him? It would change nothing.

~*~

Franja had briefly come down to help with the lunch duties but was returning to rest again. The cramping pain from yesterday had passed, and the bleeding subsided. There was no evidence left that something had been different in her life. She convinced herself that it was all for the best.

The maids were hanging up their aprons to go off to their private quarters for an hour before dinner preparations would begin. Franja hung her flour-dusted apron on a peg near the door with the others. She went out into the garden for some fresh air before she would climb the stairs to her stuffy chamber under the roof.

Simeon was sitting on a low wall at the edge of the path and got up when he saw her. "Franja, wait! I need to talk to you," he called out to her.

Franja froze. She was not ready for this. She had asked Nela to keep Simeon away today. She had not expected him to be waiting for her outside the kitchen.

"Shouldn't you be on duty this afternoon, Simeon?"

Simeon walked up to her. Had her hands not been deep in her skirt pockets, he would have taken them in his own to hold when he begged, "Why are you avoiding me like this, Franja?"

She walked away from him. Still, he followed behind her.

"I have to go, Simeon."

"I wish you would have told me, Franja."

"There was nothing to tell. You don't have to show me any special consideration."

The crunching of his footsteps stopped behind her, and she stopped, too.

"Special consideration," he said pitifully. "I would have been happy for you to be pregnant, Franja. I'd have married you right away. I still want to marry you."

She summoned her courage to turn and face him again. "Simeon, I don't—" She stopped. She couldn't say the words that would hurt him.

He lifted her chin so she could not avoid his pleading eyes. "Marry me, Franja," he begged.

"Oh, Simeon," she whimpered, "you are a good man, but—"

"No buts, Franja. We don't have to marry right away. Just tell me that you will one day. Tell me that you love me, like I love you."

She shook her head. "I would not make you a good wife."

"You would be the best wife," he whispered.

She wiped away a tear that betrayed her and took a deep breath.

"I cannot marry you, Simeon," she finally said. "I would be miserable darning your socks and milking your goat. I like to bake bread all morning and pastries all afternoon."

"I can share your baking, Franja, if you will share our home each night. You can keep working for the Barics. I have already talked to the baron."

She hung her head, and a groan slipped from her lips. "It is no good, Simeon. I can't work in the baron's kitchen with children at my feet."

"You can try," said Simeon hopefully. "Think about it, Franja. Don't tell me no."

"I will think about it," she promised him.

Then she continued down the path. Simeon did not follow her this time.

~ * ~

"I wish you had come with us, Ruby," said Resi, sitting on Ruby's bed still dressed in her Venetian gown. "I have never seen the church with so many people inside like today. The benches were filled with the merchants and farmers we know from the market. It is more ornate than I remembered. I couldn't stop looking at all beautiful paintings from the scriptures and the mosaics in the marble floor. Especially nice was the group who sang hymns on the balcony above us, and Father David told a story of deception and redemption from the Old Testament. It was quite a moving service, with more singing and prayers after his sermon."

Ruby only wanted to know, "Did Jero go?"

"I haven't seen Jero today."

"He wasn't at lunch?" asked Ruby.

Resi shook her head. "No."

"What will I say to him when I see him, Resi? The topic cannot be avoided, and I don't want to bawl like a baby again. I don't want his last memory of me to be that."

"I think he feels the same way, Ruby."

Ruby stared ahead out the window. "I do want to see him, though," she said. "I want to talk to him. To tell him it is not my choosing."

"Of course, you do. You are friends now, and you can stay friends until the last day. But the longer you stay in your room, the harder it will be. You should get dressed and come to dinner with us. Please."

Ruby nodded. "I will miss your friendship the most—you know that, don't you? I may cry right now just thinking about it."

"If you start crying, then I will, too. Let us save our tears for the last day, shall we? And then we will cry all day together. But until then I want to have happy memories."

"Yes, we will make this week one to remember."

Chapter 43

The couscous dinner was a complete surprise and duly appreciated by all of the guests. Bem could not say enough about the intense flavors Nela had put into the sauce that accompanied the delicious, roasted goat. Patrik and Salar Nassim praised the four ladies for their thoughtful efforts. Soren, Cyro, and the five Baric officers showed their agreement by clearing the last offerings from the platters onto their plates.

Without Franja's help, the kitchen girls had only managed to make a raisin pudding to cut the spiciness of the meal. The afternoon had been stormy, but the rain had moved on, so the servants brought dishes of dessert out onto the terrace for the party to enjoy in the sunshine.

Jero had spent the afternoon in his room and then avoided looking Ruby's way at the dinner table. More than anything, though, he wanted a few moments in private with her. But how?

Ruby was mingling with the baroness and her brother when Jero finally gathered up his nerve and approached her.

"Ladies, Patrik," said Jero awkwardly.

Resi seemed to understand he was not there for small talk. She saved him the effort and said, "Patricius, I forgot to show you something. Please, excuse us, Jero."

Resi took her brother's hand and led him away without a word on his part. Ruby was left alone with Jero in the middle of the terrace.

"Would you like to take a walk with me?" he asked.

Ruby didn't think she could move at all now that she faced him, but she could feel the others watching. "Yes," she replied.

They walked down the path to the greenhouses in silence. When Jero finally found the right words, he mumbled, "I am a fool, Ruby, and I am sorry. I should have known there would be men back home who would want to marry you."

"I don't even know this man, Jero. I doubt he wants to marry me any more than I want to marry him. I want to marry someone here," she dared to tell him.

The marble bench next to the greenhouse door was sheltered and dry. Jero motioned for Ruby to sit down. He sat down next to her. Her hand gripped the bench, and he laid his own over hers.

She looked up at him. He saw in her brown eyes a sadness that stung his heart, and his feelings came spilling out.

"I should have asked you sooner. If this letter had not arrived, I would be kneeling down to ask you to be my wife. I will never forget you, Ruby Spiros." His voice was low and solemn to match the tender words.

She turned away from him. "It is all so unfair," she cried. "I would have answered you yes—then, or now."

Jero wrapped his arms around her, not caring that she belonged to another man.

Ruby melted into his warm embrace and said, "I want to leave as friends, Jero. I want my last memories here to be happy ones."

She began to weep.

Jero held her and stroked her back until her sobbing stopped. He took both her hands in his and faced his lost love. There were tears in his eyes when he said, "We have one more week together, Ruby. We will make it a happy one."

~ * ~

Bem and Isabella found themselves alone together near the terrace door.

"What an unexpected end to a lovely week," Isabella remarked. "Of anyone here, I thought Jero and Ruby would have had their wishes fulfilled. But love is cruel."

Bem watched Jero and Ruby disappear down the path toward the greenhouses and then said, "Love is not cruel, Lady Isabella. Time is cruel. The timing was wrong for him. But he will love another, one day. It makes life more bearable if you try to love again," Bem concluded.

"You surprise me, Bem. Do you not hold out hope you will find Fatina again? Would you move on so quickly and not keep her love strong in your heart?"

Bem looked into the distance as he explained, "No one has taken Fatina's place in my heart. Time has stopped for me. It will begin again when I have exhausted my search for her in Athens. If I cannot find her there, then I will have to finally come to terms with losing her."

Isabella cocked her head. "Do you not mind waiting another week to begin your search? I would be frantic to be on my way."

"Another week, or two, or three—if I am meant to find Fatina, then I will. In my heart, I believe that I will succeed."

Isabella ventured to ask, "And what will you do this week to amuse yourself? Would you like to take a ride with me? We did not get a chance to finish our conversation. I would be glad to visit the lake once more. Perhaps Jero and Ruby would be willing, too.”

A smug grin crossed Bem’s face when he said, “Ruby did you a favor, arriving when she did. I have given our, um, conversation some thought since that afternoon, and I believe we should not converse alone again.”

Isabella opened her fan and shot him one of her practiced pouts. “Come, come, Bem. I think we can enjoy a little air together without compromising ourselves. How can I persuade you to ride with me tomorrow?”

Isabella noticed his eyes narrowed in thought and then sparkled again.

“You have persuaded me, dear madam. I will gladly join you for another outing and will be content with only that. I will find the baron and get his agreement.” Bem bowed to the victorious Venetian and walked away.

~ * ~

The baron excused himself from his group of officers and went over to talk to Simeon, who stood alone near the fountain. “You are quiet tonight, Simeon.”

Simeon looked up from his glass of brandy.

“Is Franja still ill? I noticed we have pudding instead of pastries,” Mauro said.

“I talked to her after lunch. She said she is feeling better,” Simeon reported.

“I am glad to hear that,” said Mauro, stalling. He wasn’t in the mood to open more lovers’ wounds, but Simeon was his friend, so Mauro owed him a chance to vent a little.

Unaware of Simeon’s recent setback in his quest to marry Franja, Mauro asked, “What is the matter, Simeon? You seem especially glum.”

“We didn’t only talk about her health today, Mauro. I asked Franja my question.”

Mauro looked around to be sure they were out of earshot of the others. “You proposed marriage, then?”

Simeon took another drink from his half-empty glass. “I did.”

“Did she turn you down?”

“Not exactly,” Simeon replied. “She said she would think on it.”

“We had talked about that possibility.” Mauro held back a grin when he added, “It is a start, Simeon. At least she did not say no right away.”

“No, she didn’t. But she wasn’t all smiles, either.”

Mauro patted him on the back, happy to hear there was some progress for his friend. “She is not going anywhere, and neither are you. Ask her again in a week or so.”

"But Mauro," Simeon began and then seemed to change his mind.

"Listen, Simeon. You should not worry too hard about this. Women are emotional creatures. She will come around."

"She was pregnant, Mauro," Simeon blurted out.

Mauro slumped at the weight of his word. "And she lost it yesterday? I am sorry, Simeon. That does change things."

"Danica was the one who told me. She said Franja didn't know until just a few days ago. I would like to be a father, Mauro. I would marry her tomorrow, you know that."

"I know. She knows that, too. But she has more on her mind than your offer today. This is hard for women. Give her some time, Simeon."

He nodded absently. He had shared his pain, but Simeon could talk no more about it. He walked away from Mauro, back toward the Keep. Mauro felt the burden pass on to him.

The baron looked around at the group on the terrace—a festive mood could not be kindled tonight. Mauro went to find his wife.

<h1 style="text-align:center">Chapter 44</h1>

Caterina had purposely sat on the same side of the table as Cyro to keep from having to look in his direction. Now that they left the great hall and mingled on the terrace, she could not avoid him, short of leaving the group altogether. Isabella had been at her side since the meal ended, but she abandoned Caterina to go talk to Bem. Caterina was momentarily alone, holding her plate of pudding. She set it down and began to walk back toward the house when Cyro touched her arm from behind.

"I do not know what I have done to anger you," he said. "I would like only a minute of your time to say goodbye."

He was changed, and her thoughts were overwhelmed with all that was different about him.

"Where did you get these clothes, Cyro?" was the accusation that rolled off her tongue. It was poor manners to ask him such a question, but she was tired of the games.

"I bought them in Vienna, when I was visiting my cousin. I did not want to look like the beggar that I normally do when I returned home."

"You did not look like a beggar." She stared openly at him. "These clothes are a remarkable change, and your hair—why have you cut it?"

"It will take me a few weeks to get home, and it is easier to care for. I will let my beard grow during the trip, as it naturally would. That is easier, too."

She looked at him oddly. Suitors don't usually share their grooming plans.

Cyro seemed to realize this mistake. He explained with a chuckle, "I have been living on the road for a long time now. From that, I know it is better to start fresh."

"Yes, well, you look very nice, Cyro," she acknowledged awkwardly.

"There is little time left and so much to say. Will you walk with me, Lady Caterina?"

"No, I do not think so."

He masked his disappointment. "I have something I wanted to tell you in private."

"You said you wanted to tell me goodbye. Can you not say that here?"

Cyro looked to see who might overhear them. "Yes, I suppose I can."

He took a deep breath to steady his nerves, then declared, "Dear Lady Caterina, I have enjoyed every minute of our time spent together. I would like to give you something to remember me by, if I may."

Cyro lifted his cravat and pulled a gold chain from the opening between the buttons on his shirt. On it hung a gold cross and a sapphire ring. He found the clasp and removed the jeweled piece.

He held the sparkling ring out to her. "I would like to give you this for safekeeping."

Caterina put out her hand, more to look at the beautiful ring than to keep it. Along with the precious blue stone, there were two perfectly cut diamonds flanking the square gem.

She left her hand outstretched and said, "I cannot accept this."

Cyro closed her fingers around the jewel and held her hand in his. "I will come back for it, and I hope you will be waiting for me. Keep it until then."

"Is it yours?"

She felt foolish as soon as the question slipped from her lips.

He released his breath and laughed. "Yes, my lady. This is the ring I was to present to my wife. It has been passed down in the family, and my mother wanted me to give it to the woman I love. I never found that woman. Well, not until this week."

Caterina looked at the beautiful ring in disbelief. "I cannot accept this," she repeated.

"You can. Keep it until I come to Venice to ask your father for your hand."

She looked up from the treasure. "Cyro, what are you saying?"

"I am saying I want to marry you, Caterina. I want to take you home with me to be my wife."

"Oh, God," she whispered. Why was this happening to her again?

"Shall we take that walk now?" he asked.

He linked her shaking arm with his and led her away from the terrace, toward the long arched walkway. It was covered in the blossoms he had given her on their first stroll together.

When they were deep in the shadows of the flowery roof, Cyro stopped and turned to ask, "Do you think you could love me, Caterina?"

Caterina saw that the man who had played Salar Nassim's game so confidently was shrouded in doubt. She recalled the abridged story of his shipwreck, and she understood why he was expecting her to say no.

"Felicia did not love you, did she?" Caterina asked with pity.

Cyro had nothing to lose by telling her the truth. "She did not. In fact, I am certain Felicia would have never loved me."

"Was she so cold-hearted? How can that be possible, Cyro?"

He shifted uncomfortably at her question. "It is not easy to ask a woman to marry you. But to talk about a failed engagement in the same breath is even harder. Why do you want to know this, Caterina? Do you think it will reveal some fault of mine that I have not already shown you?"

"I do not know," she breathed out. "Tell me and let me decide."

This was why he loved her. After this, he would know if she loved him. "Very well, Caterina."

There was a small bench a little farther down the path, and they took a seat. "Upon your wish, I will bare my soul to you, and then I will ask for your answer again."

She nodded.

"Felicia did not love me because, well, she found me to be too simple."

In her nervousness, Caterina laughed.

"See, you already knew that," Cyro said with a smile.

Caterina looked at him earnestly and said, "That is not the whole truth."

He nodded and said, "The truth is complicated. Our problems began when Felicia first believed I would follow my father's path into politics in Genoa. She wanted to be pampered, attend balls in the Italian Courts, and visit the capitals of Europe. When I told her I had changed my focus from law to ancient arts and we would live in my grandfather's villa on Corsica, she became quite upset with me."

"I have read Corsica is a perfectly lovely island. Did she not want to move there?" asked Caterina, not caring about the rest.

"Felicia lived there already. She was born there and was bored with its limitations," Cyro explained solemnly. "She said she would marry me anyway, but I was to buy her a house on the mainland. I would have to change my profession to suit her desires, or we would live separate lives. Our marriage would be on her terms."

"Did you tell your family this? Could you not convince her to live otherwise?"

"I felt helpless to say anything because everyone had gone to such care to arrange this match. Only I knew Felicia wanted to marry to get away from her dull life for a more exciting one as the wife of an important man. I was going to be neither important nor especially wealthy until my inheritance was accessible. I did not know how I would ever make her change her mind."

Caterina asked pointedly, "Do you disapprove of a woman having opinions?"

Cyro seemed to realize how his story was unhelpful in winning Caterina's love. In a panic, he asserted, "I do not mind a wife who has her own ideas. I was raised by my grandmother, who is a very opinionated woman, but also very kind and caring. Felicia was neither of those. She had been indulged and spoiled her whole life."

Cyro seemed still uncertain if he had said the right things to sway Caterina, so he continued to explain, "I do enjoy balls and parties, but not as a lifestyle. I will travel to Rome and Paris, but to visit their museums and cathedrals, to regard the fabulous paintings and murals, not to dance in palaces. Felicia found all that quite unacceptable."

Then he shrugged and added, "I might have still married her, but fate gave me a chance to get out of our mismatch by faking my death. And here we are, the two of us. And, despite being considered a poor match by a beautiful noblewoman, I will ask you what I have wanted to ask for days."

Caterina shook her head. "Don't, Cyro."

He got down on one knee anyway and pleaded, "Caterina Carrera, will you do me the greatest honor and be my bride?"

She clutched his sapphire ring in her hand, thinking about all the reasons she should say no.

"First, I must ask you something."

"Anything," he said, his chestnut eyes twinkling with hope.

"Why have you not said before that you loved me, that you adored me? Men always say things, like, how beautiful I seem, or how much you desire me. I just . . . you have not even told me your full name."

He paced the walkway, and she overheard him say, "You are a fool, Cyrano."

When he returned to her side, he sat down next to her on the bench and said, "You might ask why I did not tell you the sky was blue or the sun was warm, but you know that to be true without speaking about it. That is how I see you, my dearest Caterina, so obviously beautiful and desirable.

"I did not attend court as a young man, so I never learned how to make love to a woman with pretty words. I believed I was courting you, but I see clearly how inept I am. You wanted to hear how beautiful you are when your jewels sparkle radiantly against your smooth, pale skin? I must admit, the first thing that drew me to you was the color of your gown and the playful curls against your cheeks. The second was when you played cards and accused Salar Nassim of cheating. And then you admitted that you had cheated! I decided right then that I wanted to know the woman you are, and for you to know me without talk of our finery and titles. I may have botched the whole thing, but here I am, humbly in front of you, an aristocrat in velvet and lace that I wear with familiarity. For I am Cyrano Duarte, the last living son of Eduardo Duarte, banking advisor to the Doge of the Republic of Genoa. I will be the next Viscount Flores of Corsica when my grandfather is no more. I am also just Cyro, the soldier and man you met. With God's mercy, I survived two years of killing and war to make it here to meet you. I know I love you,

Caterina. Will you accept me as I am, Cyro and Cyrano? Will you allow me to come to you in Venice and beg your father to let me marry you?"

Caterina was speechless. No one had ever spoken with such heartfelt sincerity to her. How could she not believe him?

"Please, dearest Caterina, I need your answer."

She bowed her head and said the words, "My answer is yes, Cyro. Yes, I could love you. I may even love you already. My father will be furious, but I will not marry another. I believe that you love me, and I choose you for my husband, Cyrano Duarte of Genoa."

"Hold me, or I will float away," he cried.

Caterina placed her hands over his, and he held them tightly.

"Oh, my love, you have made me the happiest man in the world today."

"I will keep your treasured ring safe, and I will wait for you."

Cyro slid it onto her middle finger. "Until I see you again, my dearest, I wanted to ask for a token from you to remember this day by."

"What can I give you?" she asked hurriedly, drowning in the excitement of the moment. "A maiden will give a knight a ribbon from her hair, or a scarf scented with her perfume. Shall I go find you something like that?"

"You may consider this bold, but I was hoping you would grant me a kiss before I go."

"A kiss? Yes, of course, Cyro. We must seal our love for each other. Please, you may kiss me."

The next words from his lips were unexpected. "Have you kissed many men, Caterina?"

She frowned. "Will you love me less if I said that I have?"

"Of course not! I know you loved Paolo. Other men would have found you beautiful and wanted to love you, to kiss you."

"I have been kissed by a few men," she admitted, hoping not to sound wanton.

"Many?" he asked.

She smiled coyly. "Is five many?"

"Five?" He sounded surprised but took the large number in stride. "No, since that would make me number six. Six is Salar Nassim's lucky number, and it will be mine as well."

He scooted a little closer on the bench and said, "Promise me I will be the last man you will kiss."

She blushed. "I promise."

Before she realized what was happening, Cyro's lips were on hers, lingering only long enough for her to sink into his embrace. She let the tingling feeling of their kiss burn into her memory.

As if stung, he stood up and then held out his hand for her. "Shall we go back?"

She bashfully put her hand over his, and they began their silent walk back to the party. The sun was setting, and with no torchlight to guide them in that part of the garden, Cyro linked his arm in hers to keep Caterina close along the dark path.

The new couple was at ease with each other and holding hands when they came into the torchlight of the terrace.

The others turned and looked their way.

"Was that enough to remember me by, Cyro? Should we say goodbye again before you leave?" whispered Caterina.

He walked her to the foot of the terrace steps. "Will you do that for me? Will you come to see me off in the morning?"

She blushed again and said, "If you kiss me one last time, I will be there."

"I do not want to cause a scandal, embracing you in front of the others."

"We are engaged now, Cyro. One expects to see a romantic kiss at a lovers' farewell."

Still a gentleman, he bowed to Caterina and said, "May I kiss you goodnight, just on your hand?"

"Kiss me on the lips. Isabella is looking this way, and she loves to be shocked."

With a genuine tenderness, he eagerly did as she had asked.

~*~

Resi and Mauro were together near the terrace doors as witnesses. "Did you see that, Mauro?" Resi asked with a broad smile.

"I did, my dear."

Mauro took a few steps in the direction of the new lovers and asked loudly enough for all to hear, "Are congratulations in order, Lord Duarte?"

"They are, Lord Baric. I have asked Lady Caterina to marry me, and she has accepted."

As host, Mauro announced, "I would like to offer a toast to your engagement. Jero, could you fetch a few bottles of the reserved vintage my uncle sent? Davor, we will need a tray of fresh glasses to congratulate the new couple properly."

Davor bowed and hurried away on his errand.

Jero was glad for an excuse to leave. The group was relying on him to expedite the engagement toast, one he would never have.

Jero descended the cellar stairs quickly and unlocked the door to the wine chamber. He went to the rack with the Toth stock of wines and found two bottles of the vintage the baron had requested. He held one in each tight fist and threw them at the wall.

"Ahhhhh," he yelled in his anguish.

Jero leaned against the cold cellar wall and let the rage wash over him. There would be more weddings, births, and celebrations at Baric Castle. How could he be happy, watching others lead wonderful lives he no longer imagined possible in his future?

His anger turned to guilt when he looked down at the shattered glass littering the floor. He breathed deeply, in and out, and then stood tall again. He would clean it up in the morning. For now, he went to the shelf and took two more bottles down, relocked the door behind him, then hurried up the stairs and back to the party.

Jero opened the bottles at the servants' table and brought one to Mauro.

"Thank you, Jero," said Mauro, not noticing how Jero lowered his eyes in guilt. Davor held the tray, and Mauro poured the wine.

Cyro raised his glass and said to the group, "I am happy to share this moment with you, my friends. I must still ask Lord Carrera for his daughter's hand, but to know that Caterina returns my love is enough for me tonight."

Then Cyro directed his gratitude toward the baron and baroness. "Thank you, Lord and Lady Baric, for being such generous hosts. I will always remember my stay here at Baric Castle."

"Here is to your safe voyage home," toasted Isabella, holding her glass in his direction. "Where is your home, Cyro?" she added slyly.

"Genoa, madam," he replied. "I will take a boat to Venice tomorrow and then cross Italy on horseback from there."

"Then you could stop and talk to my father," Caterina said without a clear understanding of her fiancé's complicated homecoming.

"If only I could, dear Caterina. My family will first need to get used to the idea of me being alive, and then I will tell them about you, my darling."

"How long will this take, Cyro?" Caterina wondered out loud.

"Before returning to Venice? Two months," he guessed.

"Is it so far? Two months is too long," Caterina blurted out.

Mauro came to Cyro's rescue and gently explained, "It is not too long, Caterina. You yourself may not even be home in that time. It will take another week to arrange your escorts, and your carriage ride home will take ten days by the land route. That is only after you have packed your things here and said all your goodbyes. Two months will pass quickly."

She seemed to accept his reasoning.

After her concerns were soothed, Patrik and the other mercenaries stepped forward to give their well-wishes.

"Congratulations, Lady Caterina," Patrik said. "Cyro was the most noble of noblemen I could recommend, that is until I fought my brother-in-law here." He looked over at Mauro, who gave him an appreciative nod. "I wish you much joy as the future Lady Duarte."

Patrik kissed Caterina's hand in congratulations and noticed she was wearing the elegant ring Cyro had worn on the chain around his neck. He winked at Cyro, who answered back with a nod.

Salar Nassim took his turn to wish the couple well. "Dear Lady Caterina, you already know I am happy in your choice to marry our friend Cyro. I wish you a long life together with the best kind of love."

Bem and Soren each bowed, murmuring their heartfelt congratulations to the new couple.

Cyro then turned to his betrothed and said, "I do not want to leave this party, but there are still many things I must do before I can sleep tonight. Will you meet me in the courtyard in the morning, my love? We will say our farewell then."

"I will, Cyro," she said dreamily.

With that, he modestly kissed her hand, as the others had, and followed his four friends across the courtyard to the Keep.

Vilim, Hugo, Eduard, and Daniel each bowed in turn to the young lady before they, too, went back to the Keep.

Caterina declared, "I feel suddenly exhausted."

"Of course, you do, Cat, my dear. Such unexpected excitement to end this day with," said Isabella. She hooked her arm in Caterina's. "Come, I will take you upstairs."

Only the Barics and their servants were on the terrace. Mauro picked up the second bottle. "There is no sense in letting this go unfinished. Can I pour you another glass, Nestor? Jero? Davor, did you get a taste?"

Nestor and Davor held out their glasses, and Mauro filled them. Jero had barely touched his first drink.

"Resi, my dear, did you want more?"

"Not for me, Mauro. Ruby slipped away earlier, and I thought I would tell her goodnight before it gets too late."

"I will walk you, Lady Terese," Jero said.

The two crossed the great hall and were in the foyer when Jero remarked, "I am very happy for Cyro and Lady Caterina. They are both fine people."

"Yes, Jero, they are," Resi agreed, climbing the broad staircase by his side.

"Is the man Ruby will marry a good man, Lady Terese?"

"In truth, Jero, I hardly remember him." Resi then seemed to weigh her words before she added, "Ruby's father would not match her to a dishonorable man, Jero. I know that for certain."

Jero's room was on the opposite side of the corridor from Ruby's. He looked at the light under her door as he stood by his, then said, "I am glad to know that. Good night, Lady Baric."

"Good night, Jero." She watched him disappear with his flickering candle into his dark chamber.

After crossing the hallway, Resi knocked on Ruby's door and entered.

Ruby was lying on her bed, staring at the beams in her ceiling. Her eyes were red and swollen again.

"Why did you leave right when we were going to toast Lady Caterina and Cyro?"

"Oh, Resi. I am happy for Lady Caterina, but the announcement was too hard to bear. I think I will not be able to make it through the week. I have decided to ask Patrik to leave as soon as we can."

Resi sat down next to her. "Do not fret, Ruby. Cyro will be gone in the morning, and Lady Caterina will be in her room crying on her bed the rest of the week. It will be too much for her to bear as well."

"I had not thought of that."

Ruby sat up and wiped her eyes with her damp handkerchief. "Will you help me pack tomorrow?" she asked.

"Ruby, please," Resi pleaded. "Stay for Radic's party."

"I want to, I truly do. I just don't know what I can do to keep busy until then."

"You should go riding again tomorrow. You will need to get used to the horse for the long days ahead."

Ruby sniffled and nodded. "Not with Jero, though. I want to leave that memory of his kiss by the lake as the perfect outing."

"Then keep your memory well and go on an outing with Patrik instead," Resi said with fresh enthusiasm. "He will want to be sure you can ride, even though Bem defended you to Salar Nassim."

"Did he? That was kind of him. I like Bem," Ruby said more cheerfully.

"I am glad to hear that, since you will be with Bem for three weeks. And with Soren and Salar Nassim and Patricius."

Ruby plopped back on her bed. "I will be in very good company, won't I?"

Resi kissed her friend on her forehead, glad she was coping again with her unhappy situation.

"Go to sleep now, Ruby. Tomorrow things will look better."

When she left Ruby's room, Mauro was coming up the stairs, and they walked to their chamber together.

Mauro went to the window to open the glass and let in the night air. Staring out the window, he asked, "Did Jero say anything to you after you left?"

Resi thought about their conversation. "Nothing, really. He said something kind about Lady Caterina and Cyro and then asked if Nikko was a good man."

"I think I should send him on an errand, something away from here," he said suddenly. "I wish Branislav had not yet sailed. Jero has always wanted to go on a delivery."

"Do you think that is wise, to send him off? Maybe Jero wants to spend all the possible time with Ruby?"

"It is eating at him already," Mauro said. "I unwittingly rubbed it in his face when I sent him to fetch the special reserve."

"Ruby is a bit overwhelmed at the timing of Cyro's proposal, but she will be fine. I am going to keep her busy. Patrik can take her riding to get her used to the horse again. She can begin packing tomorrow, too. I will need to find an empty trunk to put her new wardrobe in to send to her."

Mauro nodded. "My mother's empty trunks were put away in the nursery. I will have Davor bring one down."

That reminded him that his mother's last trunk still sat unopened in the corner of his study. He would find some time this week to unpack it.

The couple went about their bedtime routine, each lost in their own thoughts. Resi sat down on the bed, exhausted from the day, although the baby was awake and kicking.

When Mauro finished, he sat down next to her. She leaned into him, and he wrapped his arm around her and kissed her forehead tenderly.

"I would marry you all over again if it were allowed," he said sleepily. "We would do it right this time, in the village church, and everyone would be there."

"Is there a rule against marrying someone twice?" she asked through a yawn.

"It is probably in your Catholic rules book," he said.

He got up and pulled back the blanket. Resi slid in and curled up next to him, already finding it hard to keep her eyes open.

Mauro whispered, "I was thinking this morning how lovely the church is and how beautiful you would look on the top steps in your emerald gown, a veil flowing behind you."

Shutting his eyes, he saw his vision. "So happy," he whispered.

She sighed next to him. She was already fast asleep.

Chapter 45

Natalija woke the young Venetian before sunrise to help her dress to meet Cyro one last time. Caterina chose her favorite gown, the blue and black dress with a low bodice and corseted waist. Caterina had not worn it since she arrived, so her beloved Cyro would not have seen her in it.

Resi sent Verica to her room that morning to make her hair especially pretty for a last impression. With limited time, they settled on simple curls cascading down her back and tiny ringlets next to her soft brown eyes.

Isabella had said her goodbye to Cyro yesterday and decided not to complicate their morning by also trying to get ready at the early hour. Resi would accompany Caterina, and the baroness came to Caterina's room before full light to walk with her to the courtyard.

Caterina and Resi were not the only ones who came to see Cyro off. They met Mauro, and Cyro's four companions were with him.

Cyro was dressed in his old traveling clothes, cleaned and mended by the Baric maids. He had packed his finery away to save for his arrival home. He carried only two satchels and his bedroll for the long journey, along with his lucky sword. He would travel the distance first by ship across the Adriatic, then by horseback overland. The journey by horse would be speedier than by coach, and Cyro was used to long days riding and sleeping outdoors.

Salar Nassim, the man who had taught his foster son humanity despite their brutal occupation, stepped up to his side first.

Cyro hugged his mentor for the last time. They had already said all their words of well-wishes and regrets yesterday. They exchanged no more words now except "goodbye."

Patrik walked up to him next. Cyro's energetic, strong-willed friend had shown him that it paid to take risks and follow one's instincts. Patrik's own journey had led Cyro to the Barics, and he embraced his companion for the last time with gratitude.

Soren was a head taller than the young nobleman when they embraced tightly. The Dane had taught him the strength of brotherhood and that time could heal even the most profound hurt. He would miss Soren's solid friendship and his stoic nature.

But the friendship the young nobleman would mourn the most was Bem's. Their fellowship was the hardest for Cyro to let go of. Bem had helped him figure out who Cyrano Duarte was. They had formed a bond from the first day when their futures collided, and things had looked so dire. They had spent every happy and miserable day together since. In his prayers, Cyro asked to find a way for them to meet again one day, and he believed that they would.

Cyro had given Bem his pouch of gold earned during their years of fighting, keeping only the silver he would need to get home. He wanted to help Bem find his true love again, and this was the only way Cyro could help him now. Bem would ride with him to the village and bring his horse back to the castle. Zeus was a warhorse, and where Cyro was going, such a fine warrior's steed would not be needed. Cyro would purchase a horse in Venice to finish his journey across the land to Genoa; he would leave Zeus behind to help the others on their way.

He turned now to Caterina, waiting patiently with the baron and baroness. She was his new strength and his future. She was exceptionally breathtaking this morning, and he would not miss the chance to tell her that.

He smiled at her through his tear-filled eyes, and she smiled back. "Your beauty takes my breath away, Caterina. It is burned into my memory and will sustain me until the next time I see you. I will miss you dearly," he told her.

"And I, you," was all she could manage to say in her misery.

If he did not leave now, then he would never be able to go. Cyro took his betrothed in his arms and kissed her tenderly again. It would have to be enough.

The baron wished him well for the second time and turned to let his wife say her goodbye. Resi had grown very fond of Cyro and had been overjoyed yesterday when the fairytale ending came true for her two new friends.

"You must marry in Venice," Resi told him, holding his hand in hers. "Corsica will be too far for a pregnant lady to travel, and I will not miss the occasion."

"I will look forward to seeing you again, dear Lady Baric." He looked over at his sobbing fiancée and said, "Do not let my Caterina be sad for me."

She gave his hand a squeeze before she let it go. "We will take good care of her," Resi promised.

Simeon opened the iron gate, and Cyro took that as his signal to depart the solemn crowd. He was plenty early to meet the small boat to the ferry that would take him across to Venice.

Bem mounted his horse, and Cyro did the same. He waved one last time to the new love of his life, his beloved companions, and his new friends. The two then galloped away.

The others began to disperse to their morning duties. The mercenaries had accepted Mauro's offer to train with his soldiers another week for something to do while waiting for Ruby to say her goodbyes. After lunch, Bem and Patrik would take Isabella and Ruby riding. They had no plans beyond this. Mauro, however, had a full agenda.

"Resi, I expect to be gone all day today. Will you be sure Caterina is taken care of this afternoon? Isabella will go riding with Ruby again," Mauro said as they walked back into the house with Caterina at their side.

Caterina was not listening to the couple; the strain of saying farewell had overcome her.

"We will find something to do," Resi said hopefully, although she had no idea yet what she could offer.

~*~

Later that morning, Mauro came up the cellar stairway and into the kitchen in a good mood. The kitchen staff never questioned what the baron needed to fetch himself when his attentive servants were at his beck and call to run his errands. Lord Lorenc had kept a private chamber on each floor of the manor house, and he never discussed what he kept under lock and key in each one. It was assumed his son had followed in his father's footsteps.

Mauro scanned the busy kitchen and saw Nela bent over the hearth. She was retrieving the steel pot from the fireplace.

"Good day to you, Nela. I will need three sacks put together for three lunches, and maybe a dinner, too. They must fit into saddlebags, so do not be too generous."

Nela wiped her sooty hands on her linen apron. "Are you leaving again so soon, my lord?" Her tone was disapproving, as only Cook could get away with.

"No, Nela, I am staying here. I will be having my lunch in the Keep, though. Can you have the sacks ready in an hour? Davor will come get them from you."

Satisfied that it would not be the baron who was departing, she confirmed, "I will pack up something tasty for your men right now."

Mauro noticed Franja was in the kitchen that morning. She was filling a row of tart crusts. She put her knife down and gave her master her full attention when he came to her work table.

"Simeon told me you are feeling well again, Franja. I am glad to hear it."

"I am better today, my lord. Thank you," she said with a dutiful curtsey.

"Simeon is a good man, you know," he said quietly across from her half-filled baking tins. "I have known him for years, and there is not a more dependable man. Honorable and loyal, too. It is hard to say no to a man like that."

"Yes, my lord," she replied, avoiding his steady gaze.

When she offered no further comment, the baron took a fat plum from the bowl of fruit she was cutting and began to walk away with it.

"Lord Baric," she called over when he was nearly out the door, "I have not said no to him."

He turned and said kindly, "I know that, Franja."

"Do I have to say yes, my lord?" She looked distressed, no longer able to hide her true feelings.

"Simeon told me once he would let his wife keep working in my service. I will hold him to his word if that is your only worry." For Simeon's sake, Mauro hoped he had said enough.

At the door, Mauro bit into the juicy plum. The delicious sweetness surprised him. The baron took a second one from her bowl with a boyish grin and left with his snack to his study. Breakfast was hours ago, and there was still much to do before the day got away from him.

Davor was by the staircase when Mauro came around the corner from the kitchen.

"Have you seen Jero?" Mauro asked quietly so his voice did not echo up the stairs.

Davor shook his head. "Do you want me to find him for you, my lord?"

"No, I need you to do something else for me. I need Hugo and Teodor. They are out at the shooting fields. Send Josip to get them. They are to come to my study. And I will need Eduard to find two scouts to courier a message within the hour. Tell Eduard they must be fit to ride to Zadar and be back in the morning. Come find me when he has the men arranged, and I will have my message ready."

~ * ~

When Jero did not come to breakfast with the servants, the kitchen maids put together a tray to bring to his room. Ivana knocked on his door.

Jero opened the door dressed for the day in his striped breeches and matching waistcoat. He had hoped that wearing his favorite ensemble would help lift his spirits, but it had not worked. Jero had expected the knock was the baron and was surprised to find Ivana standing there instead.

"We thought you might be feeling poorly today, Jero. Here is some tea and toast," the maid said, looking down at the generously filled tray she carried, "and a little ham and soft cheese. Franja made plum dumplings earlier, and Brigita added some honey and the marmalade she made yesterday."

Ivana straightened the little rose in the vase she had put on the tray herself. She gave him a sweet smile, and Jero took the tray from her hands. She stayed by the door as he set it on the table across the room.

He turned back to see the girl still standing there. "Thank you, Ivana. That was very kind of you."

He expected her to close the door again. When she didn't, he asked, "Was there something else?"

"Well, Lady Ruby is also still in her room. Nela said she is going to run out of trays with everyone keeping to themselves and not coming downstairs. I just wanted to let you know that we are sorry she has to leave, and we wanted to cheer you up."

In his sorrow, Jero had forgotten what faithful friends he had in the house. "You can tell Cook that I won't need a tray for lunch. I overslept is all, and I will be down soon."

She smiled again in her girlish way and shut his door.

Jero poured himself the tea and looked at the thoughtful meal with a growing appetite. If he could get through today, he could get through tomorrow and the day after that. He then hastily ate his breakfast and left the refuge of his room. He met no one on the servants' stairway to the kitchen. He would bring the tray back first.

Jero braced himself to face Nela's motherly intervention, but he heard only muffled voices coming from the pantry room as he opened the door to the kitchen. Jero was relieved to slip in and back out without having to explain his absence that morning.

In the foyer, Jero noticed Mauro's study door was open. He would not be able to avoid his employer. Looking in, he saw Mauro writing something at the desk, with Davor at his side. Jero cleared his throat to make his presence at the doorway known and said, "My lord, I expected you would be in the shooting fields this morning."

"Ah, good. I was going to send Davor to look for you. Come in. I have an errand for you, Jero."

Mauro finished sealing the letter and handed it off to Davor, who already knew his own errand. He was to give the letter to the Baric scouts to expedite it to an arms merchant in Zadar, confirming the baron had accepted his terms.

Davor nodded his greeting to Jero as he walked out the door.

When they were alone, Mauro told his brother, "Shut the door, please. I have an important task I want you to do for me."

"Of course, Mauro." Jero stood across from the baron, waiting for his instructions.

"You will need to pack an overnight bag, perhaps enough for a few nights," Mauro said while he carefully put his sealing wax away.

Jero watched him roll up the unused parchment papers and tidy his desk. The baron was anxious about something.

"Where am I going?" Jero asked cautiously.

Mauro finally looked up. "I have been working on a deal to purchase ten more muskets for my armory. I want you to go to Zadar in my place."

"To buy firearms? I do not know anything about weapons," Jero protested.

Mauro assured him, "You just need to know about contracts, and I am confident that you do. Here, you can look over my last purchase. We will have the same terms, but I will pay one extra gemstone this time."

Mauro unfolded a parchment on the desk for Jero to read the details.

Jero looked up and asked, "Why does it cost one more this time?"

"It seems that is the new price for confidentiality."

Normally, Mauro would have made the French smuggler sweat a little longer than to accept his inflated price on the first go-round—the last deal was more than fair to the Frenchman. But Mauro could think of no other reason to get Jero away from the castle this week. The extra gem payment for the firearms was worth it.

"Teodor and Hugo will go with you," Mauro continued to explain. "You can make it in a day, but there is no hurry. Here are instructions how to find the, um, merchant. He isn't expecting you until Wednesday afternoon."

Jero took the folded note and opened it. "Are you trying to get rid of me?" he asked as he skimmed the details and then put the note into his waistcoat pocket.

"No, Jero. I need to finish this deal before he finds another buyer, but with the visitors staying on, I cannot get away as planned."

Mauro set a small leather purse and a little snuff container down in front of Jero.

Jero opened the cord to the purse and looked up, surprised. "This is generous!"

"You do not have to spend it all. It is for the three of you to find decent lodgings, a few nice meals, and whatever entertainment you might like."

Jero put the pouch of Mauro's coins into his other pocket and then regarded the baron skeptically. "Do you think a whore will get Ruby out of my thoughts?"

Mauro shrugged. "Then use it to gamble, or buy expensive bottles of French wine to smash."

Mauro had seen the shattered glass on the floor when he went to retrieve the snuffbox he had just placed on the desk.

"It was an accident. I was going to clean it up today," Jero explained quietly.

"I do not care whether you get drunk from the wine or smash the bottles, it is equally satisfying sometimes. But keep this snuffbox safe."

Mauro tapped his finger on the oval container, and Jero picked it up.

Like his father, Mauro did not care for tobacco, and he encouraged his men to avoid its use. However, the Barics did have a collection of snuffboxes of various sizes and quality to last several years. His Venetian silversmith designed the unique, double-bottomed boxes without questioning the purpose.

Mauro kept them filled with tobacco and hidden where his father had, in the wine cellar under lock and key.

The small, ornate boxes were the Barics' preferred method to disguise payments when paying a merchant with lire was not an option. Offering another man snuff was common and could be done in the open without attracting undue attention. Mauro's client would be prompted to comment on how he appreciated the quality of the snuff, and then Mauro or his agent would offer the rest as a polite gift to the gentleman. The client would accept the snuffbox, and the deal was done.

Jero opened the delicately engraved silver lid and touched the fine, golden-brown powder. Jero nodded that he understood there would be a determined number of fiery emeralds under the false bottom. "You could send any of your captains to handle this transaction, Mauro. Why me?"

"You are my steward, and you will handle my purchase in my place." Mauro waited for an argument from him, but Jero seemed satisfied.

Mauro went on to say, "Hugo and Teodor have been told to check each musket before they are crated. Have the weapons sent by wagon in the same fashion as last time. They will know. See that the drivers are on their way that same evening. They will be paid when they arrive here. Once they are on the road with my purchase, you are free to stay on and do whatever you want in Zadar."

Mauro looked up from his desk chair, studying his brother's face. He could see the escape he offered Jero was finally sinking in.

"For a few days, you said?"

"If you do not want to come back until after Sunday, it is your decision. I know Hugo and Teodor would like to be home for the Radic celebration. I told them you could take all the time you needed. They will stay on as your escorts without question."

Mauro's choice of especially good-humored companions was considerate. Jero nodded that he understood. "Thank you, Mauro. I do not want to—"

Mauro cut him off. "You should leave now," Mauro said bluntly, the baron again. "The men will be waiting for you in the stables. They have already been given their instructions."

"Now? Not after lunch?"

"Now is better, Jero. Nela has made up a lunch for you."

Jero could not help but chuckle. "How long have you been working on this? You seem to have thought of everything. Have you packed my bag, too?"

Mauro finally smiled. "It has been a busy morning. When would I have had time for that?"

Mauro returned his attention to the remaining papers in front of him, and Jero left out the door to gather his things.

Chapter 46

Isabella and the baroness had lunch together on the small terrace while Caterina slept through the mealtime hour.

Afterward, Resi came with Isabella to her chamber to help her change into her riding attire for her outing with Bem and Patrik. Resi tried to convince the pouting Caterina that Cyro would want her to enjoy herself, not sulk until they met again.

Isabella primped in front of her looking glass and added, "You have your husband now, Caterina. He has given you a beautiful promise ring and is riding to tell his rich grandfather that he wants you as his bride. How much better can it get?"

"My father will say no! That is how much worse it can get," Caterina retorted.

Resi added her encouragement. "Mauro is writing to Fabian to tell him what has happened. He can convince your brother that Cyro is a fine match for you. When your father finally meets Cyro, he will already have two good opinions of him—one from my husband and one from Fabian."

"It is kind of him to persuade my father on my behalf. He does trust Mauritius," Caterina agreed. "And if I tell my father what a gentleman Cyro is, and what a bright future he has. . ."

Caterina got out of bed and walked to the open window in her wrinkled, blue gown. She was smiling once again.

Thanks to Resi's help tightening the ties on the flowery breeches, Isabella was ready to leave. "There is the optimistic Caterina I know. Get dressed in a fresh gown, dear Cat, and enjoy your afternoon," she said.

"When will you return?" Caterina asked her companion, who was putting the final touches of rouge on her lips.

"I expect to be gone all afternoon. If you are done with your little card lesson, Lady Terese has interesting ideas for the two of you."

"My lessons have ended," she answered Isabella and then asked the baroness, "What do you suggest we do to fill our day?"

Resi looked uneasy, not having anything to offer as exciting as Ruby and Isabella had planned. "There are some household chores I usually help with, but I have not had a chance until today."

Caterina frowned and repeated, "Chores?"

"Amusing things," Resi clarified. "The old nursery is on the top floor, and the maids have been bringing freshly cut herbs up there to dry. I like to tie and hang the bundles myself. It smells wonderful when we are done. We are also running low on scented soap. Ruby and I usually make pots of that for my bathhouse. Or we could do something else, if you'd rather."

An odd smile spread across Caterina's lips as she considered these matronly duties she might one day need to know about.

"I have never done any bundling before, Lady Terese. It sounds perfectly amusing. And I would like to see this old nursery. Your manor house has many interesting rooms to explore."

"It does," Resi agreed cheerfully. "I will show you the servants' quarters on that floor as well. Mauro's father built those when he became baron."

Caterina found her slippers and turned to Isabella. "You will be missing a grand afternoon, Isabella," she said. "We will see you in a few hours." She hooked her arm in Resi's and dragged the surprised hostess out of the room.

Resi waved and smiled at Isabella as she closed the door behind them.

Relieved that she no longer had to worry about Caterina, Isabella finished lacing her short boots and checked her hat in the mirror. She then went down the hallway to Ruby's room.

~ * ~

Patrik and Bem were waiting in front of the paddock when the ladies arrived for their outing.

"We talked about this, Patricius. I don't like saddles," Ruby protested when she saw the four saddled horses.

"How do you know? You've never ridden more than half a day, Ruby," Patrik pointed out. "You will need to carry your own pack, and maybe even a weapon. We will expect you to keep up when we ride fast. The saddle will make it easier for you."

"I had not thought of that," she conceded. "But they are so big and hard."

Bem took charge and said, "It is decided, Ruby. You will ride my horse, Fatina, with Cyro's saddle on the trip. It is well-padded and should fit you fine. I will ride his horse, Zeus. You and Fatina will need to get used to each other. That is why Lady Isabella will ride the baroness's horse today."

"With a saddle?" Isabella asked, joining in the conversation.

"With my sister's saddle," Patrik said, amused the women were so against the valuable equipment. "Here, let me help you up."

Isabella looked to Bem, who had turned away and busied himself with Ruby's harness. It had been planned that way. Bem was to keep from touching Isabella.

Once settled on their horses, they left the stable yard. "Where are we riding to?" Ruby asked when they halted before the rising gate.

"You choose," Patrik told her with a grin. This outing was for her pleasure.

"Let's go along the road that takes us through the tenant farms. That is a nice ride."

They nudged their horses to be on their way. Both women kept up with the two men as they galloped down the castle road and merged with the carts and pedestrians at the village crossroads. Once they were beyond the village foot traffic, they rode at a good speed again.

The landscape seemed familiar to Bem, and he said, "We came this way last week, didn't we, Patrik?"

"We did. We also went this way to the salt flats with the baron."

"I would like to see these famous salt mines I have heard so much about," Isabella shouted to be heard while keeping up with the others. "Can we stop for a look?"

"I am not sure it is allowed," Ruby warned, riding up alongside her. "The road is guarded. We would need permission."

"The mystery thickens," Isabella said playfully. "You are friends with all of the soldiers, are you not, Lady Ruby? The guards will not block your way, especially with you looking so pretty today."

Patrik chuckled at Isabella's boldness. He was beginning to see what all the fuss over her was about. He enjoyed the company of rebellious women.

"You have a point, Lady Isabella," said Patrik, "First stop: the baron's salt mine."

~*~

The entrance to the harbor road itself was inconspicuous, flanked on one side by thick pines and on the other with a massive boulder. Beyond that was a low gate guarded by two soldiers.

Adrijan stood at the gate. He was a recent recruit and had not encountered anyone besides the Baric men at the gate.

"Open the gate. We would like to ride down to see the salt fields," Patrik told Adrijan with authority.

Adrijan looked to Denis, who came out of the small guardhouse when he heard their voices.

Denis knew who Patrik was, but he wasn't sure if being the baroness's relation was enough to let him pass.

Ruby saw the dilemma on Denis's face.

"Hello, Denis," she said. "The baron has already shown these two gentlemen the docks, but Lady Isabella and I wanted to have a quick look. Will you please open the gate for us?"

Denis gave a respectful nod to Ruby and the Venetian noblewoman. "Of course, my lady, if that is what the baron wants."

Isabella cocked her head demurely and lied, "The baron insists I not leave without seeing it."

Denis glared at their escorts critically. He told Ruby in his native Croatian, "I will gladly escort you and the lady if you wish. The others can wait here."

It was a tactic Patrik often used in Greek, and he did not enjoy that the Croats could do the same to him. He shot Ruby a questioning glance, but she shrugged it off.

"Thank you, Denis, but my friends can escort us. We will only be a few minutes," Ruby replied in the same dialect.

Denis nodded to Adrijan, and the young guard lifted the gate for them.

~*~

From there, the winding road slowly backtracked to the tidal flats, the only sea harbor on the Baric estate. The docks were unoccupied. The ship and crew were at sea, and the remaining workers had already finished their duties and had gone home.

Isabella looked out over the multitude of water-covered partitions that stretched between the walkways. "Is this it?" she asked. "It is rather like a marsh, is it not?"

Patrik laughed. He had the same reaction a few days ago, so he explained what the baron had told him.

"The first harvest of salt has been collected, so they let in new seawater to evaporate in what they call fields. I'll take you to see where they have stored the harvest."

Patrik urged his horse down the steep road to the operation, and the others followed.

"Has the baron's ship gone to meet Castor?" Ruby asked Patrik.

"They sailed two days ago. The other ship docked here transports supplies for their own use, Mauro told us."

"Where are all the workers?" asked Isabella.

"They go with the ship, as its sailing crew. They tend the fields between shipments. The baron is an efficient employer," Patrik explained as he dismounted at the pier. He went to Isabella's horse and helped her to the ground.

Isabella regarded Patrik's features, with his face so close to hers. He was handsome again; the fading bruises were no longer shocking. She thought Patrik looked very much like his sister but could tell he didn't have her subtle character. He smiled confidently at her when he noticed her staring but took no interest in her charms. It was clear to Isabella that Patrik was meant to chaperone her today, and she urgently wanted to ask Bem why.

Bem led Ruby down to the storage docks near the harbor where the smaller ship was moored. Isabella and Patrik followed behind. The brisk breeze warned of a rainstorm building against the mountains, but they welcomed its cooling effect on the hot pier planks.

Patrik pointed dramatically to the open warehouse, with its piles of white salt and stacks of empty urns and crates ready to be packed.

"This is how the baron makes his fortune," Patrik declared with a mix of amusement and skepticism.

"And he sells all of it?" Isabella asked. "It is quite remarkable, really. I never knew salt was that important."

"Not everyone in Europe lives by the sea like we do. You cannot grow salt, so if you don't have it, then you must buy it," Patrik stated.

"Can I look at his ship, Patricius?" asked Ruby.

Patrik glanced over at Bem for his opinion.

Bem shrugged his indifference.

"Why don't we all take a quick look and then be on our way. Come, Lady Isabella. I will help you up the ramp," Patrik offered.

"You go on without me. I have somehow managed to get a pebble in my shoe, and it is most annoying."

Isabella sat down on a narrow bench at the end of the dock and began to unlace her boot.

Bem waved Patrik on, and Patrik went with Ruby onto the ship.

~*~

"I have never seen this type of boat in Thessaloniki," Ruby said to Patrik.

"Hmm, you may be right. It is typical of one meant to cross small seas like the Adriatic, not the open waters our families sail. It would be a nice size to captain, though."

"Do you miss the ships, Patricius? Do you not want to stay on in Thessaloniki and learn to captain one of your father's ships?"

"I cannot make any decisions beyond this week." Ruby scowled, and he added, "I will consider it after I come back from Athens."

Patrik leaned over the railing and saw Bem shake out Isabella's boot. The other two would be along soon, Patrik thought, so he led Ruby to the other side of the ship to look out onto the azure water of the shallow harbor.

Ruby broke their silence and asked, "Will I stay in Thessaloniki?"

"Nikko's family is there. Where else would you stay?"

Patrik saw her pained expression. He took her hand and said kindly, "You have to make peace with this, Ruby. The baron has sent Jero away. You need to forget him now."

Her eyes widened in alarm. "Sent away? When?"

"I saw him and two soldiers leave a few hours ago. I asked the baron where they were going. They went to Zadar. They will return on Sunday."

"Why would Jero go to Zadar without saying goodbye?"

Patrik rolled his eyes that he had to be the messenger of her worst fear. "How can Jero say goodbye, Ruby? This is better for you and for him. I think the baron knew that."

She did not try to hide her anger. "The baron had no right to send him off like that," she said, fuming. "I wanted to talk to Jero! I need to see him before I go!"

"Ruby, you will get over Jero. By the time we arrive home again, you will have forgotten him."

"Do you have no heart, Patricius? Have you never been in love?"

She stared angrily, expecting an answer, but Patrik said nothing. What could he say to save the moment? Not a thing.

"I need to ride again," Ruby told him suddenly. "I want to see if Bem's mare can keep up with Ophelia. She can run like the wind."

"Sure, let's go, then. But, Ruby," he added, "I want you to know that I do know what it feels like, and I am sorry for your pain."

She had tried to be brave, but it was a hard blow. Ruby began to cry.

Patrik had known Ruby since she was a little girl, and he held her like one. He gave her all the time she needed to let the tears out. "I don't like to see you unhappy, but this was the right thing to do, Ruby. The baron is a selfish bastard at times but not this time. And in a few days, you will believe that, too."

She breathed out one last sob, then said, "Let's get Bem and Lady Isabella now."

Patrik had been so focused on Ruby that he had neglected his role to keep the two apart. From the railing, Patrik could see that Isabella did not look happy with whatever Bem had just told her.

"Shit," he said under his breath and wondered whether Bem had gotten himself into another awkward mess. He took Ruby's hand to help her off the rocking ship's deck.

~ * ~

Bem had helped pull Isabella's boot off and shook it out. There was no pebble, and she shrugged innocently. He laced it on her foot again like he would help a child, not concerned with the indecency of holding her ankle so closely.

"Why are you ignoring me, Bem?" she asked outright.

He looked up from his task, almost done with the tie. "Why would you think that?" he asked cheerfully. He patted Isabella's foot and let her set it back on the ground.

Bem stood up and took her hand to help her to her feet. "Shall we go onto the ship?"

"I do not really care for ships," she said with a pout. "I did like our ride to the lake. I have thought about that often."

She was not ready to quit her efforts to win this game. She wanted her reward.

"I am learning so much about you, Bem, and want to know more. When we ride through the fields, I hope we will have time to pursue that privately again."

Bem held her stare. Isabella looked striking in this light, with the breeze blowing the strands of loose hair under her wide-brimmed hat. She was going to make this difficult, he thought.

"Patrik will not grant us the same convenience that Jero did. You like a little sport and so do I, but our game is over, madam. We will not be able to share anything in private. It is better that way."

"We have an entire week," she cooed. "We could go out again tomorrow. Perhaps take a picnic lunch. Maybe the baron will let you take me out alone, now that he can see that we are friends. We are friends, are we not? There is more about me that I would be willing to share."

"That is indeed tempting, Lady Isabella. I will admit I find you very alluring, but that won't be possible. You have a champion protecting you, and I don't want to test whether he will make good on his threat."

Bem saw her expression flash from flirtatious to furious.

"Did Lord Baric threaten you?"

"Lord Baric? No. He seems to trust me with you well enough. Your champion is Fabian Carrera." Bem caught her completely off-guard.

She bit her rouged lip, and her brow furrowed as she contemplated what that meant. "Fabian has been gone all week. What would he have to say about our rides together? It is none of his business."

"I think he cares enough about your virtue to have made it his business. I am sorry, but that is the impression he left on us."

"He has quite a reach from Venice to here. What did he say to you, Bem? Tell me!"

"Not to me directly, I was in the stables. On the day we arrived, he specifically warned my friends that any man touching you would, um," Bem chose his words carefully, "would have to answer to him."

"And you found that to be a threat?" Isabella shrugged and said, "Fabian is all talk. He has no authority over me, or who I choose to kiss."

"His threat was specific to a certain loss of a body part. I have seen him wield a sword, and I trust he is not all talk."

She summoned her stiff aristocratic poise again and said, "Fabian has no right to interfere with my life or my virtue, and the next time I see him, I will tell him so."

Bem closed the gap between them. He took her hands in his to soothe her. "I don't know if it makes any difference to you, but I would have done the same if I were leaving my woman behind."

She looked away when she told him, "Well, I am not his woman and never have been. I made that perfectly clear before he left."

"Your champion seems to believe you are, Lady Isabella. That is why our game is over."

She stepped away from him.

"I want to go back to the castle," Isabella announced crossly.

Bem was immediately regretful. "I am sorry I upset you," he said. "Of course, we will go back."

"You have not upset me. I am feeling suddenly unwell, is all. It must be the salty air."

Bem was relieved to see Patrik and Ruby walking toward them. "Let me help you onto your horse, Lady Isabella. Are you well enough to ride?"

Isabella needed no help, really, but she let him guide her one last time onto the saddle.

"We are riding back," Bem announced when the two were within earshot.

"Are we?" Patrik asked earnestly.

"Yes," Bem answered.

Patrik groaned. Something must have happened, a regular drawback to seducing women, Patrik surmised. He had never had the patience for such romantic entanglements like his friend.

Ruby did not know Bem as well as Patrik did, but she did understand that she would not get her wish to ride like the wind. She would not get any wishes at all today.

~*~

They rode back up the slope to the gate, said a quick goodbye to the two guardsmen who opened the way for them, and then traveled the next few miles without conversation.

When they reached the crossroads, Patrik told Bem, "You will be fine from here. Ruby and I will be back at the castle later."

Bem shook his head, not able to hide his disapproval. "You cannot take Ruby out alone. The baron forbids it."

"I am Ruby's guardian now, and we will see you later."

Ruby beamed with approval. The two turned their horses and galloped away.

Bem turned back to Isabella. She, too, had a broad smile on her face. "Now that is a champion," she said. "Where will he take her?"

He chuckled and said, "Wherever she wants. Patrik cares nothing about most people, but he will do anything for those he truly does care about."

~*~

As they trotted up the castle road, Isabella began to feel better. Her black mood seemed to lift while Bem made small talk about the things they saw in passing.

When they reached the gatehouse, Eduard was on duty. He called down to Bem, "Where are the others?"

"They will be back before dark," Bem hollered to the gruff soldier as he and Lady Isabella rode through the entrance.

"Stop," shouted Eduard, "I want to talk to you! The baron will hear about this, and he won't like it."

His words were lost. Bem was already helping Isabella from her horse at the stable door. He bowed politely as she brushed the road dust from her lovely trousers and then walked away.

Looking over her shoulder, Isabella threatened playfully, "We *will* have our picnic this week, Bem."

"And I *will* keep my manhood," Bem answered a little too loudly.

Isabella stopped suddenly.

She turned and called out, "Is that the body part Fabian would cut off?"

Bem laughed and walked a little closer. "What else would get another man's attention?"

She muttered to herself in disgust, "Well, he can choke on his for all I care."

~*~

Bem was unbridling the baroness's horse in the stables when he noticed the many blankets hanging over the railings. Each had a matching emblem.

When Josip came up to him, Bem asked, "Who has arrived?"

"Lord Fabian and five escorts from his father's house," the groom replied curtly. He still seemed in awe of the black man and nervous talking to him. He led Ophelia away.

So, the champion arrives to rescue his woman, thought Bem with a chuckle. Fabian could only be here to bring the ladies home or possibly onto Hungary.

It was for the best, he thought, as he began to unsaddle Zeus. One private picnic with Isabella would not have been a fair trade for meeting Fabian's sword.

Chapter 47

Fabian and the five Carrera escorts trotted slowly between the carts and wagons heading south toward Solgrad. He had seen the four riders depart from the castle road through the village crossroad—Ruby's colorful riding attire and Isabella's hat were unmistakable. So she had managed to learn to ride, after all, he thought. What else had she managed in a week, and where was Isabella going with the two mercenaries? These thoughts distracted him from the others that filled Fabian's mind while he was riding back up the familiar road. Baric Castle was a world apart from Venice.

~*~

It had been opportune that his father had already arranged for his sister's escorts to ride out that day. Fabian had only been home three days, but that was already two days more than he could stomach. On an impulse, he saddled a horse and left Venice in the soldiers' company without so much as an explanation.

No explanation was required, really. Once Fabian's warm homecoming welcome had worn off, his parents had laid out their decisions for his immediate future and the rest of his life. They had chosen a bride for him and a job in the Senate as well. He and his new wife would begin their union together in an apartment in the grand Carrera villa. His brother Gabriel and his wife were expecting another child, and they were renovating a new home to accommodate their growing family. Fabian would have their old one.

There was no room for discussion, no talk of compromise. Fabian was almost twenty-five, yet his parents were deciding his future as if he were a child. So he did what a child would do: he ran away.

After the long two-day journey, the Carrera group rode through the open gate and into the courtyard. Fabian dismounted and walked his horse to the stables.

"Where can I find the baron?" he asked the surprised groom.

"He is in the armory, Lord Fabian." Grinning, Geoff added, "Welcome home, sir."

Sadly, this was no longer his home. Fabian would only stay long enough to see his sister and Isabella leave with their carriage back to Venice.

~*~

Mauro had heard horses clomping by from the open armory door, but he had thought it was his men returning from shooting practice. The last person Mauro expected to see when he looked up was Fabian, walking toward him.

"What are you doing here, Fabian? You just left a week ago!"

"Yes, and what a miserable homecoming it was."

Mauro set down the weapon he was holding. "What happened?"

"I will tell you in private, or have you given my chamber to your new brother-in-law?"

Mauro dusted off his hands on his breeches and put his arm around his friend to pull him along. "Come, it is a hot day and you are obviously in need of a drink."

They took the tower stairs directly to the officers' quarters. The Keep was nearly empty, and the second-floor hall was quiet.

"I have been dying to know, how did your visitors behave?" asked Fabian.

"It was a rocky start, but we managed to iron out our differences without killing each other."

Fabian laughed, not realizing the truth in Mauro's comment.

Mauro told him, "They will be leaving soon, but as far as I am concerned, I am not pushing them out the gate. They are good men."

Fabian shot him a look of disbelief before he opened the door to his old room.

"So tell me, Fabian—what disaster did you arrive home to?"

Fabian took off his dusty hat and set it on his desk. "It was just as you thought, Mauro. Things have been decided."

"So you left?" Mauro asked.

"I came with Caterina's escorts. Her fiancé found out about her detour, and he does not want a young wife with such a will of her own. My father is already making arrangements for another suitable groom."

Mauro shook the water pitcher. Empty. He set it back down. "Did you by chance run into Cyro at the ferry harbor?"

"No," replied Fabian, "we took a private sailing so we could bring the horses. We landed farther north. Was Cyro heading to Venice?"

"Yes, and then onto his family to tell them about his engagement. Your strong-willed sister has already accepted a marriage proposal from Cyro."

Fabian threw up his hands. "That miserable piece of shit! I told you he was hiding something. What did he do to my sister?"

Calmly, Mauro said, "You might want to sit down for this."

Mauro then sat down on a chair across from Fabian and filled him in on the details, "*Lord* Cyrano Duarte has done nothing to your sister except make her fall in love with him. He has gone back to Genoa to ask his father, advisor to the Doge of the Republic of Genoa, and his grandfather, Viscount Flores of Corsica, to help him negotiate with your father."

"He is a fucking Spaniard! I knew it!"

"Is that all you got from what I just said? He is of old Spanish nobility, yes, but he impressed me and her. Yesterday, he asked for her hand, and she agreed. Once your father thinks about the advantageous ties to Genoa this will give him, he might agree to the match."

Fabian got up from the bed where he was sitting. "So you are in favor of my sister marrying this foreigner?"

"Times are changing, alliances are shifting. There are worse men you could have for a brother-in-law."

As though he had no more strength to think about these new circumstances, Fabian plopped back down on the bed and stared up at the canopy overhead.

"I have more brothers-in-law coming my way," he said. "My parents have chosen a bride for me."

Mauro breathed out an exasperated sigh. "So soon?"

"I know, that's what I asked." Fabian shook his head in his self-pity. "My mother even forbade me from attending a few parties to look at the other eligible ladies. I am a grown man, for God's sake. But it has all been decided for me, like I was some fucking, oh, I don't know . . ."

"Daughter?" Mauro finished the thought for him.

Fabian bounced upright again. "Exactly!"

"Why the hurry to marry?" Mauro wondered out loud.

"I told them just that. They have two grandsons, and it is not like we will run out of males to carry on the family name. Unlike you, Mauritius, my seed is expendable. I could become a priest, and it should not matter."

"Where is she from?" Mauro asked.

"I do not know, and I could not care less. She will be there at the end of the month for me to meet her. She does not even live in Venice."

Mauro sat down on the bed. "And you are not even curious?"

Fabian frowned and admitted, "Yes, of course, I am curious. This young lady will change my whole fucking life. I asked Cristina about her, but she said Mother is being very tight-lipped until the negotiations are finalized."

"Think about it, Fabian. She must be a desirable girl if they are going to so much trouble."

"Desirable for them! I doubt they considered whether she is desirable for me to live the rest of my life with."

Fabian sprang off the bed and went to the water pitcher Mauro had already found empty.

Mauro watched him. "So you just left?" he asked.

"My father was sending the escorts for the girls, and I saddled a horse and rode off with them."

"Without so much as a goodbye? Fabian, you are an idiot," Mauro said with a laugh.

"Yes, so you've mentioned before. This time, I suppose I have to agree." Fabian managed to smile.

"Everything settles with time, Fabian. The sooner you let it, the sooner you can start to be happy again."

Fabian shook his head. "Things are going smoothly for you now, but my life will soon be turned upside down."

"All right, Fabian. You are here now. Rest, get some food and drink. Do your men know where everything is, or shall I send Tin to them?"

"Don't trouble yourself. They are the same escorts that were here before." Then Fabian asked, "Where are all the Baric men?"

"Out on the fields, I think. Vilim had an errand in the village. Hugo and Teodor went with Jero this morning to purchase the next set of muskets."

This caught Fabian's interest. "More of the new flintlock type?"

"Yes, I like the design."

Easily distracted, Fabian replied, "Hmm, yes, so do I. But I suppose I should tell the girls to begin packing."

"Isabella isn't here. She went riding," Mauro told him.

"Then I was right. I thought I saw her from the highway."

"She can ride well now, Fabian," Mauro said more cheerfully. "She rode out to the old villa earlier this week, and they are riding into the valley this afternoon. Bem is a good teacher."

"Is he? Why is he still here? You said Cyro left today. Why did the others not leave, too?"

So much had happened in the last few days. Mauro would need time to explain. For now, he said, "Things are in a bit of turmoil here, too. A letter arrived from Greece. Ruby will be going home, and the mercenaries will escort her. She convinced Patrik to wait until after Radic's big party. You should stay, too. It is at the end of the week."

"The end of the week?" Fabian contemplated for a moment and then agreed, "Sure, why not? The men might enjoy a break before the long ride back. I will talk to the girls about it when Isabella returns."

"Caterina is in the house. My wife was going to find something to keep her entertained, but she might be in her room. You should go tell her you are here," Mauro suggested. "She is still a bit overwhelmed by Cyro's leaving. She could use a brother's shoulder today."

Fabian's mood was lighter already when he answered, "I can give her that. You are probably right, Mauro. Cyro will be a better husband for her than the old Hungarian bastard."

"I am going to finish my chore in the armory. I will find you later. I have some things I want to hear your thoughts on, but it is not pressing."

Fabian opened his trunk and pulled out a clean shirt. "I am glad to be wanted," Fabian replied. "I will see you at dinner."

~*~

After dressing in fresh clothes, and having a mug of ale in the Keep, Fabian walked up to his sister's door and knocked.

Isabella opened it. The two stood in front of each other with a mix of surprise and disbelief at meeting again across the threshold.

Isabella's stunned expression melted away, and, just as suddenly, she swung her arm and slapped Fabian across his face.

He instinctively put his hand up to his burning cheek. "What was that for?" he asked in dismay.

She walked away from him as she protested, "You are not my father. You are not my brother. And you are not my lover."

Isabella then turned back to Fabian at the open doorway and shouted, "You had no right to lay claim to me, Fabian Carrera."

Fabian shut the door. "You are hysterical. What are you talking about?"

"You forewarned the men to stay clear of me as if I were some out of control girl, open to wanton love affairs without my champion standing by, ready to cut off my lovers' body parts. How dare you paint such a picture of me? But even if I wanted to be that girl, that is my business, Fabian Carrera, not yours!"

She walked to the closed window and opened it in need of air.

Fabian thought the only way Isabella could know of his warning was if she had been in a compromising situation with one of the mercenaries. Fabian chose his words carefully.

"I gave that warning before we had our talk, before we said our goodbyes. It was not you I did not trust, Isabella, it was them. That is why I insisted they keep their distance from you."

His reasoning did not soothe her as he had hoped.

She turned back to him at the window. "You had no right."

"Why do you have to be so reckless? You should thank me for trying to protect you from yourself."

She was beside herself as she cried, "No one cares what becomes of me! I am to be tossed away like an old rag. I want to have something exciting to hold onto, something to be remorseful about in my prayers at the nunnery."

"Stop feeling sorry for yourself, Isabella. You will not be going to a nunnery," Fabian grumbled.

Isabella's mouth opened to say something, and then she shut it and bit her lip with worry. "Do you have news for me?"

Fabian joined her at the window and replied, "Your mother has not been idle. She has made a new arrangement for you. I hope for your sake, you can give yourself as freely to your new husband as you would have to the African."

She tried to strike him again for his jealous insult, but he caught her arm and held it this time. "It is still painful, and you know it," he said through gritted teeth. "And I do not mean my cheek."

She held her hostile glare before she shook her arm free. "You are exhausting, Fabian. It is always the same argument. Why did you have to come back here? I want you out of my life."

Fabian walked to the door and said, "I will grant you your wish, Isabella. I was going to escort you and Caterina overland with the carriage, but I will go home by sea instead."

"You brought escorts?"

"Pack your things. You will leave in the morning."

She recoiled. Fabian's words hit her like the slap on the face she had just given him.

"I like it here," she said, "and I will stay."

"Mauritius will not let you stay if I tell him you must leave. And I will. It is over for you, Isabella. The sooner you return, the sooner you can get on with your real life," he said, repeating the advice Mauro had given him earlier.

Defeated, she pointed to the door. "Get out!"

"I will find your maid for you. Be ready in the morning." He shut the door before she could argue.

~*~

Sometimes Verica was waiting in her chamber to be ready for her mistress. Fabian saw her door was open, and he looked in, but the room was empty. He then went to the baron's open door and knocked.

Verica opened it with wide eyes of surprise. "Lord Fabian, sir," she gasped.

He summoned a practiced smile. "Hello, Verica. I have come to take the ladies back to Venice, and they need help packing. Could you find their maid and arrange this? They will leave tomorrow morning."

"Tomorrow?" she murmured to herself before agreeing, "Yes, of course, Lord Fabian. The trunks can be quickly managed." After a polite curtsey, she hurried down the corridor toward the servants' stairway.

Then Fabian remembered his main errand, and he called out to her, "Verica, where can I find my sister?"

She pointed to the narrow wooden staircase. "The baroness and your sister are in the nursery upstairs, sir."

"Nursery?"

"My mistress is tying the herbs in there for drying. The ladies might be done by now, but that is where they were going earlier."

Verica then disappeared down the stairs, and Fabian went up.

~*~

Fabian had never been to the top floor of the manor house, but directions were not needed. He followed his nose to the open door where the fresh, fragrant scents of rosemary and thyme came from.

Looking in, he was amused to find the two noblewomen in their aprons, hanging strings onto the rods the washwomen used in the winter months for laundry.

"Hello, Caterina. Hello, Lady Terese. You make a pretty picture," he announced to the startled women.

"Fabian! You are back!" his sister cried. She ran to the doorway.

"Yes, I am back, and I bring good news."

"I am going home?"

He tried to sound upbeat as he embraced her tightly. "Your marriage to the Hungarian viscount is off. You are going to Venice."

"Well, that is a relief because I am going to marry Cyro," she told him brightly.

He forced a smile when he said, "I just heard that news from Mauritius."

"Perhaps you want to talk in private," Resi interjected. "We were just finishing up here."

She undid her apron and set it down next to the snippets of branches. "I think I will rest a bit in my chamber before dinner. I am delighted to see you back, Fabian."

"Um, Lady Terese," Fabian said awkwardly, "I just met Isabella in her chamber. You may want to check on her."

"Is Isabella back already?" asked Caterina, seeming not to notice the earnest exchange of looks between the two.

Directing his answer at the baroness, Fabian said, "She was there when I went looking for you, Caterina."

Resi nodded to Fabian that she understood the problem, and she closed the nursery door as she left.

Fabian talked as he walked the room, touching the fresh herbs as he went. "Isabella is also going back to Venice. Her mother has found her a husband, Cat. I have come with your escorts." He then stopped and turned back to her. "Paolo is gone, you know. But I guess you have already forgotten him."

She set her apron down, shoulders back, defiant again. "I have not forgotten him, Fabian, but I understand now that what we had was not true love."

Fabian had seen this stubborn expression many times before. He took her hands in his and asked, "Do you already think you love Cyro?"

"I did not plan for this, Fabian. Cyro swept me off my feet. I really like him, not just his face. And when he talks to me, it isn't about parties and people. He has opinions about everyday things. He likes art—and he is funny, too. I did not believe he could be from royalty, but he was dressed in his finery on Sunday, and he looked every bit the nobleman. But Fabian . . . he is on the wrong side of the war."

"I have been reminded that the war is over. Politics are starting over. There are no wrong sides now," Fabian conceded.

"Then are you on my side?" Caterina pleaded.

Fabian nodded. "If there is a side to choose, it will be yours, Caterina."

She wrapped her slim arms around his masculine frame. "I knew I could count on you."

She stepped back and held her hand out to her brother. "Just because he left me this ring for safe-keeping does not mean I had to say yes."

Fabian studied the sizable gem on her finger with fascination. "Well, who could turn this jewel down?"

She pulled her hand away. "I really meant it when I agreed to marry Cyro. I cannot wait to go home and tell Mother and Father. Will you write to Father, Fabian? Tell him what a gentleman Cyro is and how much he loves me?"

"I will tell him in person. I am not staying at Baric Castle. I was not supposed to come back at all."

Her smile faded.

Fabian was no longer smiling either when he told her, "Mother has found me a wife, and when the details are agreed on, I will marry her."

"I do not understand. Mother arranged a bride? Who is she, Fabian?"

He absently touched the green bits and stems on the table next to them. "I have not actually met her. The arrangement was not my choice, which is why I left in anger. Mother is probably dredging the canal for my body, as we speak."

"I am sorry, Fabian. Why would they do that to you?"

"Father wants me to start a profession. He thinks if I had a wife, she would hold me down."

"I am sure she is beautiful. How else could she convince you to stay put?" Caterina took her brother's hand in hers again and counseled, "It has been a long time since you were in love. Love is good, Fabian. You should try it again."

He shook his head and chuckled. "You are only eighteen and giving me advice on love?" He squeezed her hand and then released it, looking at his sister fondly. "I will try, Cat. But what if my wife does not feel the same affection for me?"

"How could she not love you?"

Fabian let out the breath he didn't know he had been holding. "I am glad I talked to you, Sister. We should go now. You have much packing to do."

"When will we leave?"

Fabian opened the door for her and explained, "As soon as the carriage is readied in the morning. I will be taking the ferry home."

They walked down the polished wooden steps.

Caterina wanted to be assured, "Will you help me convince Father about Cyro?"

"If that is what your heart is really telling you this time."

"It is," she said with a conviction Fabian had not seen in her before.

"Then I will," he agreed.

At her chamber door, he said, "I will see you in the morning, Caterina."

"Not at dinner?"

"I have much to do. I will have a quick meal in the Keep."

She opened her door. "All right, Brother. Good night, then."

"Good night, Caterina," he said as she closed it.

Chapter 48

Mauro had been in the Keep, talking to the three mercenaries about Patrik and Ruby. Coming from their room, he noticed Fabian's door was cracked open, and a light was burning. Mauro knocked and went in.

"Is everything alright, Fabian? You did not come to dinner."

Fabian was putting on his waistcoat. He straightened his collar in front of his looking glass before winding his cravat over it and then tying a loose knot. "I am sorry, Mauro. I should have sent Tin with a message. I was not in the right frame of mind to be good dinner company for you."

"We had no company at all. Your sister and Isabella did not come downstairs, either. What is going on?"

Sitting down on his bed, Fabian bowed his head. He took a deep breath and then looked up again. "Don't be angry, Mauro, but I have changed my mind. The girls are leaving tomorrow. I instructed Alberto to hitch the carriage in the morning. I am leaving, too."

"But you just arrived!"

Fabian nodded unhappily and told him, "I went to Caterina's room, as you suggested. She was not there, but Isabella was. We had a heated argument, and then I told her she would leave for Venice in the morning."

Mauro took a seat across from him at his small table. "What was it this time?"

"Somehow she found out I gave the mercenaries a little sermon when they arrived. Something about how she and my sister were under my protection. I may have been a little specific about her charms, and what I would do to them if they touched her."

"You didn't!" Mauro said in surprise. "Did Bem tell her about it?"

"Maybe it was Bem who told her. You would know best, Mauro. You were chaperoning her."

When Fabian went to the wardrobe, Mauro noticed it was nearly empty of his things. Mauro got up and looked in Fabian's trunk. It was full of the garments that should have been hanging in the wardrobe.

Mauro said absently, "I did allow some liberties with Isabella's confinement here."

"I do not care anymore, but when she slapped me—" Fabian began.

"She slapped you?" Mauro interjected.

Fabian slipped his cape over his shoulders in front of the mirror and then turned back to his friend and said, "Her emotions are running a little high now that she knows her fate is sealed. She is to marry some unlucky bastard back in Venice. She wants to stay at Baric Castle. I told her no, and she was a bit angry at me."

Mauro asked, "How will you manage a week on the road with her?"

"I am not going back with them," Fabian said.

"So you will stay a while?"

"I could, but I won't. You are right, Mauro. It is time I faced the inevitable. I should not have run away like a scared boy. I am a man, and I should start living like one."

Mauro pointed across the room. "Is that why your trunk is packed? You have cleared off your desk, too."

"I will take this one trunk home this trip. The rest I will leave here for a while if that is all right?"

Mauro sat down again in gloomy disappointment, and the two were quiet for a time.

"I cannot imagine you as a married man," Mauro finally said.

"Why not? You have set an excellent example for me, Mauritius."

"You said your bride is not even in Venice yet. Stay the week and say your goodbyes at Radic's party, Fabian. What is your hurry?"

Fabian put on his favorite earrings while he told Mauro, "It is tempting, but I am afraid I will lose my nerve if I get too comfortable here again."

"When is the wedding?" Mauro asked more cheerfully for Fabian's sake.

"Maybe in September, around Stephan's wedding date, that way you can come to both celebrations. You need to show your wife all of Venice. She will love it. You can stay with my family while there."

"She'd like that, but Venice is so far for a pregnant woman to travel."

"It is not far at all by water," Fabian said. "Have your wife hit you over the head and sail you to Venice on one of your ships. I will not take no for an answer."

Mauro had made it to the island and back; maybe he could make it to Venice if he stayed in the cabin. "We will see," Mauro agreed with a smile.

"Bring Jero and Ruby, too," Fabian added cheerfully.

"I told you, Ruby is leaving us."

"Oh, shit. You did. I did not even consider what that meant. Is she going back to Greece for good, then?"

"She is leaving on Sunday. Everyone is quite unhappy over it, especially Jero."

Fabian pondered for a moment. "You said he was in Zadar."

Mauro looked down sheepishly and admitted, "Only because I sent him there. I did not want to give him much of a chance to worry and have a long goodbye."

"That is a tough break for him now that he has decided he loves her. He will recover with time."

Mauro nodded.

Fabian took his red hat from the peg, brushed the felt hastily, and then set it carefully over his smoothed hair.

Mauro scowled and said, "Are you going somewhere?"

"Oh, didn't I tell you? The men and I are going to the Green Goose to celebrate my demise. Are you game? A trip upstairs is optional," he added with a wink.

Mauro seemed to mull over the idea.

"Surely, your wife will finally trust you to come home undefiled."

Mauro followed Fabian to the door and replied, "I think she trusts me to behave, but Ruby and Patrik have not come back yet. I just asked Bem and Soren to go looking for them. They were in their chamber and said that they would."

Fabian blew out his candles, and the two walked into the torchlit hallway. He held the door for Mauro to go down the stairs.

"What was Patrik thinking, going out alone with her?" Fabian asked, finally sharing his friend's worry. "Should we ride out to find them?"

"Go for your drinks. Salar Nassim and I will ride out with a few more men if the four are not back in an hour or so."

They left the staircase and rounded the corner into the dining hall. The Carrera soldiers were there, mingling at the tables with a few Baric men.

"I am sure it will all turn out fine. Tomorrow you will have two less worries on your hands, Mauro. Come later for a celebratory glass. You know where to find us."

~ * ~

Resi had been alone in the sitting room when Mauro came back to the house from the Keep. After telling her about the search party, Mauro sent her upstairs to sit with the Venetian ladies while they all waited for Ruby's return. Mauro trusted Patrik to keep the girl safe, and he hoped they did not stray from the guarded roads. Why would they?

Mauro lit the candelabra on his desk and pulled the current account book from the shelf to keep his worries from overwhelming his thoughts. Re-adding the figures, Mauro admired Jero's steady hand. Jero never made a mistake. His thoughts went from his brother's servitude back to his missing ward when he heard Davor greet Ruby in the foyer. Mauro breathed a sigh of relief when he saw Ruby standing at the open study door.

"Davor said you were in here, Lord Baric."

"Ruby," he said, "come in."

Mauro was at his desk by the windows. He went to the door, and she let him take her hand. She had never been in the baron's study before.

Mauro discretely looked her over as he brought her closer to the light. She looked fine—a little dusty, and her hair was loose from her hat, but she seemed unharmed. Mauro watched for clues that she was hiding some other distress. He'd had hours to decide what he would say to her, but he abandoned his rehearsed speech and said simply, "Sit down, Ruby. Would you like a drink?"

She sat down on the cushioned chair next to his desk and accepted the glass of wine. "I am sorry to have worried you, Lord Baric," she said. "We had no idea we would be so late. I wanted to explain our delay."

Ruby took a sip from her glass and then said, "We were just going to ride through the farms, but then we met Cila, one of your tenants. I picked apricots with her, and she wanted me to meet her new husband. She had told me so much about him before. Well, we finally found him back at their cottage, and then they invited us to see their little farm and have a drink of their newly brewed ale. We didn't realize it was dark outside until we left them. We were almost back when we saw Bem and Soren on the main road, looking for us."

The baron's steady, unchanged expression revealed nothing, and so she asserted, "Patrik is not to blame, Lord Baric. I was the one who wanted to stay and have a look at their little house . . ."

Her voice trailed off.

Mauro dismissed her by saying, "You must be tired after such an exciting day, Ruby. On your way to your chamber, will you stop to talk to my wife? She is waiting for you. She might still be with the ladies in their room." Resi could tell Ruby the Venetians were leaving in the morning, he thought. Mauro did not want to voice any more distressful news today.

Ruby rose from her chair. She had expected to see anger in his piercing green eyes, disappointment at the very least, but they showed only fatigue in the flickering candlelight.

"I will talk to her, Lord Baric. Good night."

"Good night, Ruby."

Mauro sat pensively at the cluttered desk. He was in no hurry to follow her upstairs. He would give the two women time to talk, and Mauro would deal with Patrik in the morning. Their stories had better match.

Mauro put the ledgers away on their shelf and locked his study door. He needed some noise to drown out the thoughts spinning in his head.

In the foyer, Davor waited dutifully to be dismissed for the night.

"Davor," Mauro said.

The young valet turned his attention to his master. He was handsomely dressed in his green servant's waistcoat and matching breeches, but that would not do for an outing.

"Go change your clothes. Lord Fabian is going to be married, and we are missing his celebration at the Green Goose. I will meet you at the stables."

Davor had not been away from the castle since his sinful escapades in Rijeka. The young man grinned at the smiling baron, not able to suppress his excitement at the invitation. "Thank you, my lord," he cried and took the marble stairs, two at a time.

Mauro shook his head and chuckled at Davor's obvious delight. He was glad to see someone could easily unburden themselves this evening. Mauro then grabbed his cloak off the hook and walked out into the darkness to try to do the same.

Chapter 49

His head hurt as he lifted it to see his wife on the pillow next to him. She was shadowed in the dawning light.

"I didn't hear you come in last night," Resi said quietly.

Mauro rubbed his eyes with a groan. He had no memory of how he got back to the castle last night. His horse would have known the way in the dark. Perhaps Davor had helped him to his room.

Mauro focused on Resi's face; he knew that expression. She doubted him again.

"I, um . . . ." He cleared his dry throat and explained, "After I talked to Ruby, I joined the others for Fabian's send-off."

The first hour at the Green Goose was easy to recall—the brief discussion with Fabian alone at the corner booth and the many rowdy toasts of congratulations after that.

He remembered the trip home now and told Resi, "I was the first to leave. I rode back with Davor and the Carrera soldiers. Fabian told them if anyone were not fit to ride in the morning, they would walk to Venice."

Resi laughed softly at Fabian's threat. "He wouldn't follow through on that, would he?"

"He would," Mauro said with a chuckle.

Ah, but that hurt his head.

"Why are you still in your clothes, Mauro?"

He rubbed his temples to counter the ache there and answered, "I must have been in a hurry to get into bed with you."

She scowled at him in disbelief.

The room was brighter now, and Mauro noticed he was also wearing his buckled shoes. He pushed each one off with his toe, letting them fall noisily to the floor before he stretched out beside his wife. His head reeled again.

What were they toasting with last night? Mauro remembered now. Branislav had brought back a new spirit from a Dutch trader, and Andrea had purchased a small keg of it for her bar.

"Do you think Fabian will still leave today?" asked Resi.

"He was determined to when I last talked to him. Fabian has finally accepted his marriage as a necessary contract and said he will uphold his end of it."

"But it is only a contract to him. He won't be faithful to his bride, will he?"

Mauro read doubt in her expression. She was talking about their marriage again.

Mauro whispered to soothe her and his throbbing head, "Do not worry about Fabian's new wife, Resi. If she is Venetian, then her expectation of a husband's faithfulness will be low. But if she is anything like you, my dear, Fabian will fall in love with her and be eternally faithful."

Mauro then asked with a laugh, "What are you doing there?"

She had leaned over him, sniffing at his neck and torso. "I am smelling for another woman."

He did the same and took in her scent. "You are the only woman I smell here. Your perfume is delicious."

"Don't change the subject," she said suspiciously.

He pulled himself up next to her and breathed deeply again. "I must be hungry because you smell like Nela's cooking. What new concoction are you wearing?"

"We were tying herbs yesterday in the nursery, and I didn't take time to wash last night."

She giggled as he continued to explore her, despite his dizziness. He started at her neck, then nuzzled his way down one arm and then up along the other.

She had already forgotten she was supposed to be angry. "You have a nose like your dogs, Mauritius Baric."

"Mmm, yes, and this dog smells . . . oregano! Now basil, and here I smell dill. And Fennel."

Mauro sank lower under the covers. "This scent I especially adore," he said while playfully spreading her thighs.

She pressed back against the pillows and shut her eyes with pleasure. "What happened to keeping promises, Mauro?"

He came up from under the covers with a wicked smile. "I will behave. I am merely exploring."

He plopped back on the pillow, his head spinning from the brightness and rapid movement. The sun had risen above the mountain, and morning light filled their room now.

"We have four more months to go, Mauro," Resi said pitifully.

He stroked her unbound hair and pointed out, "Four months is not so long, my dear. We can enjoy each other without sinning."

"I wasn't thinking about that. I just realized it will be the first time we have no company," Resi mourned. "Stephan is gone, and Fabian is leaving. I will miss Lady Caterina and Lady Isabella. And then there's Ruby."

Resi sat up from her pillows and continued, "Ruby told me she talked to you in your study, Mauro. She was feeling better after her outing. Were you angry at her?"

"I was not angry, but I was worried."

"I wish you would have let them have their last week together. Why did you have to send him on your errand now?"

He wrapped his arm around her and said, "I told you, Jero was miserable, and Ruby would have been unhappy the entire week, too. It is better to cut the ties swiftly. It makes it less painful."

He began to stroke her temple the way she enjoyed, and she shut her eyes again.

"Since when are you an expert on love?" she whispered.

"Do you really believe what they have is love, Resi?" he asked thoughtfully. "A pretty, young stranger comes to live at the castle at a time when Jero is looking for a future wife. Of course, he would be attracted to her. Infatuated. But does he love her?"

"You believe Ruby is his choice by default?"

"I am not saying Jero and Ruby could not make a good match but, well, I do believe the timing was convenient. They are attracted to each other, but they will eventually be happy with someone else. We were all meant to fit with different partners, depending on the circumstances."

Resi could not agree. "Is this some special philosophy of yours, or do all men think like that, Mauro?"

He kissed her pouty frown to gain a truce. "Before you get too upset, let me try to explain."

"I'm listening."

"Jero and Ruby have barely begun courting. What they are feeling is infatuation mixed with, well, let us call it lust."

He pulled the tie of his wife's shift and stroked the top of her exposed bosom.

She held his stare, daring him. "I understand lust. Go on," she said.

"When the infatuation wears off and personalities are revealed, lovers usually find their desires were only superficial."

She frowned again. "Unless they find that it is love."

"That takes time, and sometimes it is better not to invest the time and be disappointed."

"We didn't invest any time," Resi asserted.

"Since our wedding, we have had time to truly know each other. Jero and Ruby have not gotten to that point yet. They can start over."

She looked into his eyes, soft in the morning light. "You said in the chapel that you loved me from the first day."

"I did, Resi, and I meant it. I loved those same things that Jero loves about Ruby: how pretty you were, dressed and undressed. I loved your laugh and your accented voice. If I am truthful, I may have wanted you more than I loved you. You captivated me, but I could leave you without aching for you. Now, though, you are a part of me. Our connection is felt deep in my being, and I yearn to see you each day."

"That is very romantic, Mauro."

"I never really found the words until just now, but that is how I feel about you, Resi. And in my heart, I believe Jero and Ruby will find that same love, but with other people."

Resi threw back her head. "Ruby loves Jero. She doesn't need to experiment like you, Mauro."

"Ruby is only nineteen, Resi, and this is her first taste of romance. She cannot know yet what love is."

"I was only nineteen when you sent for me, Mauro."

"And were you in love with me when you came here? No! You wanted me to break our contract so you could find love with someone else in Thessaloniki."

"But I fell in love with you."

"It is the same, my dear. Your fate changed when you came here, and you are happy now. Ruby's fate changed when the letter arrived. She will fall in love back at home, just like you did after coming here."

There was a knock on the door. The two exchanged puzzled glances, and Mauro got up to open it.

Verica was holding a pail of steaming water, and Aron was behind her with two more. "Lord Baric, sir, I did not know you were here," the maid said.

Mauro was glad for the interruption. He managed a smile and opened the door all the way to let them enter and go about their duties.

Davor stood a few feet away in the corridor, dressed for the day in his crisp valet's attire. "Can I assist you this morning, Lord Baric?" he asked.

The baron was still dressed in the clothes he wore when Davor helped him to bed. He walked closer and asked Davor quietly, "What happened last night?"

"I missed all the toasts, my lord, if that is what you mean." A smile crossed his lips when he added, "I went upstairs shortly after arriving, sir."

Mauro nodded knowingly and asked, "Are they loading the carriage?"

"They have just brought it around into the courtyard. The ladies are not done with their breakfast."

"And Lord Fabian? Is he up?"

"I have not been in the Keep this morning, sir. Should I find that out for you?"

"No. I will check on him myself. Have some breakfast sent up for me and my wife. I will not need your assistance beyond that this morning. You can help the grooms with the ladies' luggage."

Davor bowed dutifully and then hurried down the staircase.

Verica and Aron left the Baric's chamber, closing the door behind them. Resi was still sitting in bed.

Mauro poured some warm water into the washbasin to revive himself. He asked his wife, "Will you be all right today?"

"I won't cry over the ladies leaving if that is what you are worried about," she said convincingly. "Lady Caterina is glad to be going back to Venice to wait for Cyro and not be sent on to marry the Hungarian lord. Lady Isabella is unhappy, but she has made peace with her future, now that a husband has finally been arranged for her."

Resi watched Mauro splash his face and hair with the soapy water from the wide basin. After a moment, lost in her thoughts, she finally said, "I understand your point now, Mauro. It is just as you described. Both ladies were to be matched with a man in Hungary, and now all their circumstances have changed, for better or for worse. They have accepted their new futures with new matches. Lady Caterina is very happy with her unexpected outcome. In the end, I suppose it will work out for Ruby, too."

Mauro rubbed his head with the linen to shake off the last of his fogginess and smiled with satisfaction. "It always works out, my dear."

Chapter 50

The ladies said their formal goodbyes when they gathered by the carriage. Caterina was in tears when she told her final farewell to the Persian. Isabella watched them skeptically. For two people who were not intimately acquainted, they seemed especially heartbroken. Isabella would have many hours on the road home to discuss it all again with her friend.

Looking around, it seemed to Mauro that everyone had arrived. His valet hurried across the courtyard to his side. When Davor whispered his message to his master, Mauro covered his disappointment with his trained smile and then walked over to Caterina.

"Let me help you into the carriage, Caterina." He held out his hand to her, but she did not take it.

"Where is Fabian?" she fretted. "He said we must be ready before noon, and he himself is not even on time. He was supposed to ride along with us."

Isabella took Mauro's outstretched hand and stepped carefully up into the carriage while Caterina worried over her brother.

"Come along, Caterina dear," Isabella called out impatiently after she took her seat on one of the cushioned benches. She straightened the layers of her billowing gown and added, "It is better that we leave without him."

Isabella glanced out the open window in Bem's direction. He stood beside his three companions. She had not been emotional saying her farewell to him like Caterina had been with Salar Nassim. The Ethiopian was young and handsome, yes, but the game was over, and Isabella could leave her regrets within the castle walls. She had dallied with many men for entertainment, and her time with him had been just amusement, nothing more. She had convinced herself of that.

"Wait!" Caterina said as Mauro led her to the carriage.

She walked over to the baroness again and said, "I had nearly forgotten to tell you! Your little baby gown is finished, Lady Terese. I hope you will approve of the liberties I took with it. I left it in my room for you."

Resi hugged the small woman one last time and said, "I am certain I will love it."

The sound of horse hooves filled the courtyard and made the group turn toward the gate. It was Fabian and Vilim.

Vilim dismounted and leaned on the railing near the well. He pulled his hat down to shade his eyes.

Fabian tied his horse to the railing and walked gingerly toward the carriage. He looked around the small audience. It was how the Venetians had arrived—as a spectacle—and it seemed fitting that they would leave in the same manner.

Caterina cried with sisterly concern, "You look awful, Fabian! Where have you been this morning? What has happened to you?"

"You might better ask where he was last night," Isabella shouted from her seat inside the carriage.

Caterina's eyes widened with worry. "Are you just returning from your party?"

"It seems I am," he told her, squinting in the harsh sunlight.

Mauro said nothing but seemed glad to see his friend stagger home on his own.

"We almost left without you," Caterina scolded.

Fabian managed a chuckle. "You are leaving without me, Cat. I told you, I am taking the boat back."

She seemed ready to cry again. "I thought you were going in the carriage with us, and we would take you to the ferry harbor."

"You misunderstood, dear Sister. That was never my intention," he whispered to compensate for his throbbing head.

Caterina's lip quivered. "Well, Fabian. This is disappointing," she said.

Fabian took her gloved hand as she climbed into the carriage. He then nodded to Isabella, who turned away from him to look out the other window.

With the girls settled, Fabian walked up to the two Carrera drivers. They were at the ready on their high perch and looked to be sober and in good form for the start of the long journey home. The other three escorts were dressed as neatly as the drivers in their pale blue uniforms.

Fabian nodded his approval, and they mounted their readied horses and moved to the front of the carriage in response.

Fabian leaned into Caterina's open window. "Have a good journey, Sister. I will see you in Venice next week," he said before stepping back and out of the way.

The servant girls waved as the four horses began to pull the heavy carriage across the cobblestones and out through the gate. Then they were gone.

The crowd of well-wishers began to disperse, and Resi and Ruby went arm in arm into the house. Vilim still stood uneasily next to his horse, and Mauro went to assess his cousin's plight. Fabian did not join him but instead walked over to the four mercenaries.

"I wish I had been here earlier for the send-off," Fabian said in Bem's direction. "Did you find time for one last kiss?"

"I don't know what gives you that idea, Captain Carrera. One cannot have a last kiss if there was never a first kiss," Bem said coolly.

Fabian pressed him, "But you wanted to?"

"I want to do many things, but I know my limits."

"And your place?" Fabian insisted.

Bem's three companions listened to the verbal sparring without joining in, but Patrik took full advantage of Fabian's poor condition and taunted him, saying, "You seem disappointed, Captain Carrera. Bem kept a gentleman's promise, so there is no need to sharpen your blade today. Besides, what would a lady's man such as yourself do with a prick?"

Fabian said through clenched teeth, "I am surprised Lord Baric has not sent you away by now, Patrik."

Resi's brother stood within range of Fabian's fist and replied, "We came to a sort of accord while you were away. Mauro has a remarkable tolerance for flawed characters. You, Captain Carrera, should know that best of all."

Even in his wretched condition, Fabian still heard the insult in the Greek's remark. "You are generous with yourself, Patrik. It is your sister who smoothes your irregularities in the baron's eyes, but not in anyone else's."

"Ha! It was more likely my blood running onto his floor that changed Mauro's regard for me. Do you still want to fight me, Captain Carrera? I have quite recovered and could use some sport today."

"Well, I have not recovered from my sport last night. Like you said, I am a lady's man, and I did not get much sleep. I also had my fair share of drink and my head is about to burst open on its own without the help of your sword. Did you not drink with us last night? Oh, wait. Now I remember," he retaliated, "you were out sporting with your own maiden."

"There is no scandal to pin on me. We came back just after you left. I wouldn't have minded joining your celebration. I must say, though—it is a tribute to your drinking ability that you are standing with us right now. I heard someone brought out a cask of fresh rum. You should tell Andrea to keep it corked until your first child is christened. Without aging, that West Indies spirit is poison."

Fabian wobbled in his boots. He shut his eyes and remarked, "It is a little late for that news."

~*~

Mauro had gone with Davor to help Vilim to his room and left instructions to bring him spring water and dry bread. Coming back outside, Mauro saw Fabian was in close conversation with Patrik. He strode across the courtyard and interrupted their tense exchange.

"Patrik, we did not get to talk last night. I would like a private word with you," Mauro said as he approached.

"I was expecting you would," Patrik replied. "Do you mean right now?"

"Now would be good."

Mauro looked sternly from man to man, his message clear to everyone, and they began to disperse back to the Keep and stables.

Fabian remained. He put his hand on Mauro's shoulder for balance and said, "I still plan to leave with the afternoon boat. I will have Tin wake me in a few hours and come find you before I depart."

"You think you are up to it?" Mauro asked.

"I only have to recover enough for the horse ride to the village. I can sleep again on the boat."

Mauro grimly regarded his friend as he walked away, slowly following the others.

"Let's go somewhere else," Mauro said when he and Patrik were alone.

Patrik followed Mauro down the path from the sunny courtyard to a shaded bench next to the chapel. It was out of view for much of the grounds.

Mauro sat down and slumped back against the whitewashed building.

Patrik sat down beside him and asked, "Am I to be chastised?"

The baron watched the shadowed light stream through the branches of the oak that stretched out above them and gathered his thoughts.

"You should be grateful your friends found you yesterday instead of me," Mauro finally said.

Patrik defended his choice. "My concern yesterday was for Ruby. Yours was for Jero. I understand why you sent Jero away, but it was thoughtless, just the same."

"Thoughtless?" Mauro repeated with irritation. "I put much thought into it, and it was not an easy decision. It is better for her, and you know it."

"Do I? In Greece we do things differently, Mauro. We yell, we cry, we talk it through. I took her out riding and let her do all of that. We ran through rows of grapes like children, hiding from each other. And when Ruby could laugh again, I knew she could face her troubles."

Mauro said nothing, still staring up at the sky.

Patrik filled the silence. "I took care of her how I thought was best," he said. "I am sorry if you disagree, but her father gave her over to me in my letter. I do not need your permission."

Mauro finally turned to look at him, and there was anger in his piercing green eyes. "Ruby is still under my protection, letter or no letter. Your sister was worried sick that something had happened. Even if the road was safe, Ruby is an unmarried woman and you are an unmarried man. We have rules against such outings."

Patrik said point-blank, "We stayed on your roads and visited your farms. I thought we would not meet with danger there among your tenants. I kept her safe."

Mauro searched his face for the truth, and Patrik held his stare.

"Look, Mauro," he continued, "I have a special consideration for Ruby you don't know about. Two years ago, her father and mine sat me down and offered Ruby as my wife. I had been away soldiering, and my father wanted me at home, married and safe."

"And you did not want that arrangement?"

"You of all people might know the feeling of being forced into something you are not ready for."

Mauro nodded.

"I was restless, chasing my demons, and I told them no. I left shortly thereafter, back on the road with Salar Nassim and his company. Ruby doesn't even know her father made that offer."

"Are you having regrets?"

Patrik admitted, "I've always thought Ruby is a wonderful girl, but she deserves someone who is ready to marry. I am still restless, and my sister tells me I need to outgrow a few sinful habits. There might be a woman who can cure me, but I am not in any hurry to be cured."

The baron seemed unaffected by his brother-in-law's confession. He instead wanted to know, "Did you convince Ruby that her new husband will make her happy?"

Patrik explained, "She knows Nikko is a decent man. What I did not tell her is that he has little ambition, and they will lead a predictable life together. Now that Ruby has seen the world beyond the walls of Thessaloniki, she wants more than that. Nikko cannot offer her anything more."

Mauro listened, but his resolve was unyielding. "We all want more, Patrik, but it works out in the end with what we are given."

"Those are hollow words coming from you. You are a wealthy man, Mauro, with everything you could want. All Ruby wanted yesterday was to talk to Jero, and you took that away from her. It pained me to see her hurting like that."

Mauro had heard enough talk of love and relationships. He was through discussing what could not be changed. "You are a better friend than I gave you credit for," he declared, "but what is done is done. Jero will not be back until after you leave, and Ruby will eventually forget him."

"She knows that, Mauro," Patrik acknowledged, "but let her be sad about it. Can we agree on that?"

Patrik eagerly stood up to go. "I will not detain you further from your many duties. I personally have none, but my friends and I will find something to fill our day. Perhaps we will visit the village tavern and have a taste of this devil's water before the barkeeper pours it out. Good day, Mauro."

Patrik managed a smile and a curt bow to his brother-in-law, then walked away with an air of satisfaction.

Mauro remained seated on the bench in the quiet corner. He looked across the chapel garden to the grand entrance doors his grandfather had built. Had Lord Fredrik known such complications beyond the parties and spending sprees in his day? Mauro hoped not.

Suddenly restless again, Mauro rose and walked to the manor house, to the quiet of his study.

Chapter 51

Mauro sat in his open-collared shirt at his desk and looked at the uneaten lunch Davor had brought him earlier. He had no appetite.

With no sea breeze reaching within the tall castle walls, even the thick stone of the manor house could no longer keep out the penetrating afternoon heat.

To keep his mind occupied, Mauro skimmed through what Nestor and Jero had recorded the past week and then reviewed the manifests for the August and September shipments to decide when they might leave for Venice to attend his best friends' weddings.

A loud knock on the door disrupted his preoccupation.

Davor entered with Daniel at his side. He explained what Daniel had hastily told him in the foyer: "My Lord, Lord Dubovic is waiting outside the entrance to see you, sir, but he is in the company of eight armed soldiers. Simeon is the gatekeeper today, and he wants to be sure you would welcome them before he opens the way."

Mauro hesitated as he considered why his neighbor would arrive unannounced. "Do they look to be on their way somewhere, with full packs and saddlebags?"

Daniel replied, "Nnnot essss-pecially."

"The baron is eccentric," Mauro murmured to himself. "Alright, tell Simeon to let him and his men enter. Alberto can stable their horses out of the sun. Oh, and Daniel," Mauro added.

"Sssir?"

"Alert Simeon to put more men on the ramparts."

Daniel nodded and hurried out of the study.

Mauro stood up and began to button his damp shirt. His waistcoat was slung over a chairback near the door.

Davor brought it to him and said, "I will fetch your jacket and a cravat, sir."

"Have you seen my wife?"

Davor replied at the doorway, "The baroness and Lady Ruby just sat down to tea under the canopy. Will you want to join them with Lord Dubovic?"

"That is an excellent suggestion, Davor. I do not know what Lord Dubovic would be coming to tell me in person, but my wife can ease the unpleasantness of the meeting. Alert Nela we will need a few more platters of something, and then find Nestor—he will want to hear whatever news Dubovic has brought. But first, my jacket."

Davor bowed and left on the baron's errands.

In his two years as Baron of Baric Castle, Mauro had never had his neighbors casually dropping in, with the exception of Neven Leopold, perhaps. Something important was happening. Whatever it was, it already had the effect of clearing Mauro's mind of his other troubles.

Mauro took a swallow of wine as Davor entered the room with his arms full of necessary accessories. Lord Dubovic was known to be an elegant dresser, and Mauro's valet seemed to understand the need to highlight his master's status. He held out the baron's favorite taffeta jacket for him. Davor efficiently tied a colorful cravat and secured it with a pearl stickpin, and when he was done tugging the decorative lace in all the right places, Davor stepped back from his lord with a smile of approval.

Mauro was all business again when he said, "Now go warn the baroness we will be joining them in a few minutes."

~*~

Baron Dubovic stood near his horse at the stables in sleek leather riding attire, with tall boots and a matching black hat. The large plumes of ostrich feathers were the only ornamental extras to his masculine costume today. He looked fit for an older man and appeared much thinner without the layers of pleated taffeta breeches and lace collars he usually wore at their council meetings.

"Lord Baric!" The neighbor was the first to shout a greeting as Mauro strutted toward him. "I am happy to find you at home today. I hope my visit is not interrupting your schedule."

"You are most welcome, Lord Dubovic. We saw our visitors off today, and I did not schedule any other business. It is an opportune time."

"Excellent. I will not keep you long. I have only come to tell you of our sudden change in plans for the council meeting."

"You can tell me the new details over refreshments. My wife is on the terrace, and I was just about to join her," Mauro offered, waving beyond the courtyard to the manor house.

They walked briskly in silence, and Mauro tried to recall what the old plans had been. The council meeting was in three weeks, at the end of the month. Lord Raneri was to host the next meeting at his estate. It had been agreed to by the others who had attended the ball. Mauro hoped nothing tragic had happened in the short time since then.

Mauro saw his wife and Ruby sitting side by side at the marble table under the low summer canopy when the two men came up the terrace steps. The servants had laid out dishes piled with delicate sweets and savories in front of them. Davor was standing off to the side, holding a carafe that Mauro expected contained cold ale from the buttery. Mauro raised his brows at Davor, and his valet gave a nod of acknowledgment to the baron in answer—Nestor was on his way. Relieved by what his servants had achieved in the space of twenty minutes, Mauro took charge.

"Lord Dubovic, you remember my wife and her companion, Ruby Spiros?"

The women smiled enchantingly at the visitor, and Mauro smiled encouragingly back at them.

"Who could forget your lovely wife and her charming companion? Both made such an impression on everyone at your party."

He bowed over their politely offered hands.

"Very good to see you again, my lady," Dubovic said to each. He then sat down on the chair across from the baroness.

"Can I offer you a cool drink, Lord Dubovic?" Resi asked as hostess. Davor poured a mug of ale without further instruction.

The older baron took a large gulp, then turned to Mauro and said, "I will get right to it, Lord Baric."

Dubovic pulled out a scroll from his inside jacket pocket and handed it to Mauro. The visitor continued to explain, "The July meeting has been moved up to this Saturday. I apologize that you are the last to be informed, which is why I came in person. It took the entire week to settle on a date with everyone, but as you can see by the list, all the other regional lords will be in attendance. Since there will be a vote regarding the collection of tariffs on the trading routes that cross each barony, your attendance is required, Lord Baric."

Mauro opened the scroll. The parchment detailed that the meeting was indeed to occur at Lord Dubovic's castle at the end of the week. Mauro read through the list of names, which seemed complete.

Nestor stood at the doorway of the great hall, watching the scene. Lord Dubovic noticed and bellowed, "Good afternoon, Silvijo."

Nestor forced a pinched smile in place of his scowl and walked toward the group. He sat down next to Mauro.

"Nestor, our good neighbor has come to tell me of the change in dates for the council meeting. It has been moved up to this coming Saturday." Mauro handed his administrator the parchment.

Nestor adjusted his glasses on his nose to read the details. "This is short notice," he said flatly.

Dubovic shrugged. "Yes, well, it could not be helped. Baroness Raneri's father has taken gravely ill. They are leaving for his estate and are not sure when they will return." Lord Dubovic smiled distractedly to the ladies, who were listening while fanning themselves.

Nestor set the document down and asked, "Baron Raneri is personally attending his father-in-law?"

"Yes, Silvijo. Lord Grassi is admired, especially by his son-in-law. Lord Raneri wants to be by his side," Dubovic insisted. "We are accommodating him."

Mauro watched the two with curiosity. He saw the loathing that each could barely hold in check.

Nestor glared disapprovingly. "Where are the seals?" he asked.

Dubovic sighed dramatically and replied, "The original document is with the lords to the south. I penned this copy myself. As I told Lord Baric, Silvijo, we were making haste to finish the arrangements to accommodate everyone."

Mauro found fault with the hurried document. He told Lord Dubovic, "The date is inconvenient. My village is holding a celebration on Saturday. I cannot be in two places at once."

Dubovic took another drink and said, "Come for the vote, and you can be back to your party by dark."

Mauro considered the suggestion with a glance at Nestor.

"What is the occasion, Lord Baric?" Lord Dubovic asked.

"We are celebrating the baptism of Constable Radic's new child," Mauro told him.

"Ah! Has he finally had a son?"

Mauro noticed his wife's hurt expression. "No, we are celebrating a daughter. Constable Radic is well-liked and has many well-wishers. This was a good occasion to bring the villagers together for a communal party."

Lord Dubovic leaned in and quietly counseled, "Constables should have no friends, Lord Baric. A constable has the ear of the baron and should not have others whispering their wants in his own ear. That is why I change mine every few years so they do not become too familiar with the villagers and sympathize with their complaints."

"I appreciate your advice, Lord Dubovic, but just the same, the date of the council meeting puts me in a bit of a predicament. My constable is very eager to have me preside over the village feast since it is clear to him that I am in charge. Unfortunately, my steward is away on an errand until Sunday, and a second signature is also a requirement for the vote."

"Ah, but you have Silvijo to bring with you in your steward's place." Dubovic said directly to Nestor, "Your attention to detail is always welcome."

Mauro noticed his wife and Ruby looking beyond the table, and he turned to see what had caught their interest.

Fabian was walking toward the terrace from the courtyard path. He was dressed for travel in a plain linen doublet and leather breeches. Only his fashionable hat and silk ties that held up his matching red stockings gave away his wealth. As he came closer, Mauro could see he was freshly groomed, and a healthy color had returned to his tanned features. He was coming to say goodbye.

Sitting with his back to the courtyard, the visitor had not seen Fabian arrive. Baron Dubovic looked surprised when Mauro suddenly stood up.

"Excuse me, Lord Dubovic," Mauro said and waved his friend over to the table. Fabian could be counted on to take over a conversation, and Mauro was grateful for his friend's presence just now.

Fabian greeted the ladies first before turning to Mauro. "I did not mean to disrupt your party, Mauritius, but I have little time left to say my farewell."

"You remember Lord Dubovic, Fabian?"

The visiting baron stood up and greeted him, "Good day to you, Captain Carrera. I saw your father's carriage along the route. I thought you left with your sister."

"No, sir, I am not one to take carriage rides. But I am leaving today, just the same," acknowledged Fabian.

Dubovic remained standing and said to Mauro, "I have finished what I have come to say, Lord Baric. I will leave the copy of the new meeting details with you. Thank you for the refreshments."

He then turned to Fabian and said, "Have a safe return, Captain Carrera. I am sure Baron Baric will be at a loss without your soldiering skills. That makes two captains you have lost this month, am I right, Lord Baric?"

Fabian asserted, "Lord Baric has an excellent group of trained men to guard his land and castle walls. I am confident that there will be no breach in his continued safety after my departure."

Dubovic remarked, "As we all know, the problem lies outside the protected walls and tenant fields. I never travel public roads with less than six men, but I notice you venture out regularly with fewer escorts. There must be something in your spring water that gives your men their protective luck."

"Three skilled men on good horses is a lucky trio," Fabian countered. "You should need no more than that to venture out safely."

"I will take your word for it, Captain Carrera," the visitor replied politely.

He then turned to Resi and Ruby, who still sat attentively at the table. "Lady Baric, it has been a pleasure to see you and your companion again. Thank you for your hospitality."

The two women said a gracious goodbye to their guest, as they had learned from their Venetian friends.

Lord Dubovic continued to say, "Lord Baric, I hope you will consider the importance of your attendance this Saturday."

"I will consider it, Lord Dubovic." Mauro added, "Let me show you to your escorts."

"Do not bother yourself, Lord Baric. I know where they are waiting. Good day to you, sir. Captain Carrera. Silvijo," he said with a satisfied nod.

When the visitor was out of sight, Fabian took Mauro's arm and insisted, "What did he want?"

Mauro glanced at his wife, and Fabian dropped the question. He turned his attention back to the ladies and said, "My dear ladies, I must leave you now." His voice was laced with regret.

He stepped to Resi's side, took her hand in his gloved one, and kissed it, lingering to look at her pretty face. "I hope you will be able to travel to Venice later this summer, Lady Terese. It would be my honor to host the two of you."

Resi's weak smile turned downward when she replied, "I am looking forward to it, Fabian."

Fabian took Ruby's hand, making her cheeks flame when he kissed it. "I wish you a safe journey, Ruby, and much happiness in your marriage," he told her.

Her chin began to quiver. "Thank you, Lord Fabian. I wish the same for you," she managed to say.

There was an awkward silence, and Resi seemed to understand the men wanted to talk in private.

"If you will excuse us, Ruby and I have enjoyed far too much heat today. I think we will go indoors now."

She stood up, Ruby followed her lead, and the two left the terrace.

Mauro was grateful for her lie. She loved the hot weather and had told him so just yesterday.

"I, too, find the heat unbearable," Nestor added.

Mauro knew this to be the truth, and he waited for Nestor and Fabian to exchange their goodbyes before he sat back down at the table.

Fabian took Nestor's seat and poured himself a glass of ale from the crock Davor had left before he followed the others inside.

Mauro asked quietly, "Must you go today?"

"I have to, Mauritius. I cannot keep delaying my departure. It is torturing me."

"You look much better than you did a few hours ago."

Fabian held up his mug and toasted the air. "You know me—a little alcohol poisoning never slowed me down. Vilim is having a harder time, though. He made a mess, retching on the stairwell."

Mauro cringed at the description. "As long as he does recover. I am losing my guards right and left."

"Yes, and I do not like that such facts get noticed. What did the baron come to tell you, besides taunting you to find more protection?"

A scowl crossed Mauro's face when he explained, "The council meeting has been moved up to Saturday, the day of the village celebration. Dubovic came in person to tell me all the other lords have agreed to it." Mauro handed Fabian the rolled parchment.

Fabian read it through and shrugged when he set it back on the table. "Skip this one, then."

"I am obligated to attend. It says so right here," Mauro pointed out, tapping on the words on the parchment.

Mauro looked at the stiff writing on the paper. The list of names was a who's who of Croatian aristocracy.

"Why has the location been changed from Raneri Castle?" Fabian asked with sudden interest.

Mauro held Fabian's stare. "Dubovic said Lord Raneri is traveling to his dying father-in-law and cannot attend at all. The others want to move forward with the vote."

Fabian pondered the circumstances. After a moment, he said, "Either old Lord Grassi recovers, or he dies. In either case, I would wait until the funeral was scheduled before canceling my council obligations. We all know it can take months for a man to die."

"Morbid but true, Fabian. Baroness Raneri's father is quite prominent," Mauro maintained, "but that is not a good enough reason for Raneri to neglect his obligations at home, is it?"

Fabian shook his head and said, "I would send my wife to sit by her father's deathbed alone."

The sun had shifted, and they lost the shade of the canopy. Mauro took off his jacket in the heat and leaned back in his chair. "So, what shall I do, Fabian?" he asked.

"Won't Leopold be there? Ask him what he thinks."

Mauro chuckled to himself. "You always come up with the obvious, Fabian. Thank you! I will send a messenger to ask why I was the last to know, and why Neven has not suggested we ride there together."

Fabian took one last swallow from his mug and then stood up to leave. "I wish I could be here to counsel you more, but it is finally time I go, my friend. Oh, before I forget, my mother is sending you a belated wedding gift."

"Is she?"

"I told her I was given the task to bring a few bolts of fabric for your lady. She took it upon herself to select enough material for an entire autumn wardrobe. We could not take it with us on the horses, so it is being sent. You will have to hire a seamstress for your wife, after all."

"Your mother has probably included one in the trunk with the fabric," Mauro said.

"She probably has! My mother must be involved in everything," said Fabian.

Mauro laughed at Fabian's scowl. "You do not know how fortunate you are, Fabian. Your mother is a kind and lovely woman. Tell her thank you from me."

"Tell her yourself when you come to my wedding, Mauritius. Your wife must come too, even if she comes alone by sea and you the long way by land."

"I would not miss it. You are a good friend and best counselor, Fabian. I wanted to tell you, I will take your advice about Jero."

Fabian shook his head. "I have no idea what you are talking about, Mauro. Did I give you advice on Jero?"

"It is a shame you cannot remember the times you are most helpful."

"I do remember talking to Simeon last night. He is riding with me to the boat dock. He is going to the silversmith's to have his wife's ring melted down and rewrought for when Franja finally agrees to marry him. He said it did not feel right giving her the same ring," Fabian explained with a shrug.

"When we first met Simeon, he could talk about nothing else but his Elise."

"So memories do fade?"

"They do," Mauro affirmed. "You will meet your new bride and soon forget the missed chances."

"Yes, well . . ."

Mauro stood up to give his friend one last embrace. "We have done this before, Fabian. Have a safe crossing. Write to me when you are settled and tell me all the details of the new woman in your life. I will expect happy news."

"Misery also makes for good reading," Fabian said with a laugh, despite his evident melancholy.

"You will not be miserable, Fabian. Marriage will be good for you."

After one last embrace, the reluctant Venetian made his way briskly down the terrace steps and across the cobbled yard.

Alone under the canopy's shade, Mauro retrieved his jacket and glanced again at the open parchment on the table. He scanned the names on the list. At the bottom was S. Dubovic, scrolled in the neighbor's firm, sharp hand.

Then it hit him like a lost piece to a forgotten puzzle.

Sebastian Dubovic had courted Mauro's mother. Fabian had told him so at their last goodbye in the alley. But nobody at the castle remembered his visits.

Mauro anxiously rolled the scroll in his hands, thinking of what was to be done, now that he knew. He rushed into the great hall. "Davor!"

His valet came running from the foyer. "What is it, my lord?"

"Find Hugo for me," Mauro ordered.

"Hugo is with Jero and Teodor, my lord," Davor reminded him.

Mauro began to pace. Hugo was gone; Vilim was hungover in bed; Simeon had gone with Fabian to the village.

"Bring Eduard, then. Tell him I need a lucky trio."

"Right away, my lord."

Mauro went to his desk to write to his neighbor and closest ally. If anyone could set him at ease now, it was Neven Leopold. If not, Mauro would have to make another decision.

Ten minutes later, Mauro handed his sealed letter to his captain. "Eduard, I want the three men to ride to Leopold Castle and personally hand this letter to the baron. If Lord Leopold is not there, they are to find him. They are to wait for his answer and bring it back here as swiftly as possible."

"Is there something wrong, Mauro? Does this have to do with Baron Dubovic's visit?"

"I am double-checking some facts Dubovic told me. I will know better how to explain after I get Lord Leopold's reply."

"I will have the men ride with haste," Eduard promised.

"Yes, time is of the essence, Eduard. I have very little of it and much to learn."

~ * ~

It was decided that dinner would be served in the great hall. No breeze had made it from the Adriatic today, and by evening, the limestone pavers on the terrace were heated like an oven.

Resi and Ruby joined Nestor and Idita at the long table. The mercenaries would not be joining them. They had missed out on the celebrations at the Green Goose yesterday and had decided to have an outing there tonight. Only Davor attended the small party of four at dinner.

"Davor," Resi said loudly enough to gain his attention.

He came over to her side and stood by, waiting for her request. It wasn't a request she had, but a question.

"I have not seen my husband since he said goodbye to Fabian. Is he having his evening meal in the Keep?"

"He is in his study, my lady," Davor informed her dutifully.

Resi found this curious and looked to Nestor, who merely shrugged.

"He is eating alone in his study?" she asked further.

"No, Lady Baric, he is not eating there. He asked not to be disturbed, so I did not bring him a meal," Davor said. He stepped back to his station at the serving table.

Even if Mauro had confided in Davor why he did not want to be disturbed, Resi knew Davor would not tell her.

Ruby and Idita had overheard the quiet remarks, but they did not speculate on his reasons out loud. Each seemed somehow affected by the new stillness of the house, and they continued to eat their dinner in silence.

After dessert, the three women walked up the stairs together. Resi paused halfway up and looked back at the closed study door. She turned to go back down, but Idita took her hand to stop her.

"Your husband is fine, my lady," Idita said with certainty. "His father would do the same when he was troubled. Lord Lorenc would sometimes spend days alone, and then he would emerge from his study as though nothing had taken place. Mauro is very much like his father, even if he does not choose to believe it."

Resi was torn between going up the stairs quietly and going down to pound on the study door. "What troubles does Mauro have, Idita? He tells me nothing."

"I would not expect him to. He puts his troubles in a pot and watches them stew. Mauro has always been that way, Lady Baric. When he is ready to talk about it, he will."

Chapter 52

After Mauro sent the riders off with his message to Leopold Castle, he turned to the black trunk, sitting neglected in the corner of his study. It was the last of his mother's trunks, filled with her trinkets, accessories, and souvenirs. It also contained a chest of letters.

As a boy, Mauro had watched his mother at her writing table, penning correspondence in her flowing, feminine hand. She could spend hours on one letter, especially to her sister, and sometimes to his father when he had been away long enough to forgive him. She had written to Mauro, too, over the years. He knew what had been said in his letters. He braced himself for what he would find in these.

Mauro had cleared the long table of its scrolls and maps. He unpacked the trunk's contents and set aside the scarves and memorabilia that hid the solid wooden chest. Emptying this would change everything.

Lady Johanna had neatly tied the bundles of saved letters with ribbons and bits of twine. Some envelopes had dates on them. Mauro figured out the order of the others as he painstakingly set them out on the table. It seemed his mother had kept everything she had received in her years living at Baric Castle.

When the big trunk was empty and the stacks of parchment were in long rows in front of him, Mauro began to read each letter, note, and scrap of paper.

There were several sealed envelopes that Lady Johanna had written but, for her reasons, had never sent. He read these regretful pages first. It felt wrong as he opened each one, reading the private thoughts his mother had decided against sharing.

Still, he read all of them.

Then Mauro opened the correspondence his mother had received over the years and kept. He was fascinated, and miserable, learning how unfulfilled her life had been.

It was not all terrible news he read. Mauro gleaned that his mother must have written about happy events because others mentioned them, and they sent her messages of delight and encouragement in their letters. His Aunt Renate often wrote about Mauro and his life at Toth Castle. He was relieved that his aunt had not been critical of her nephew but had given her sister chatty news of his growth and progress over the years.

There were a few letters sent from his father while he was on his extended trips abroad. Lady Johanna had torn or crumpled many of his letters but then had smoothed out and refolded them with care. Mauro was strangely glad to read that his father's death had deeply affected his mother, despite their lack of love for each other. Lady Johanna had been his wife, and she had some feelings for him, after all.

When Mauro finally noticed that the sun had set and the rest of the study was dark, he lit more candles to help him finish his undertaking.

Sorting through the piles, Mauro picked up a letter about Jero again. On its pages, Lady Johanna never called him by his given name. She always referred to Jero as "the other boy" or "the bastard boy." It was clear how much his mother hated the boy his father had brought into the house. Mauro had spent most of his childhood in Jero's company, and she would have had to tolerate the "other boy" when the children were together. But not at night. Where did Jero sleep in those early years? Mauro could not conjure that memory.

Lady Johanna's dislike for his brother Mateo was less pervasive. Mauro remembered Mateo was not bothered by his mother's unwillingness to love him. He didn't need her love. Mateo had Idita as a mother figure, and the castle servants showered Mateo with attention. So did their father.

Mateo did not make it easy for his stepmother, either. He never called Lady Johanna "mother," as their father asked him to. He called her "Mauro's mother." And when she was not around, Mauro had heard him call her "Mauro's crazy mother."

Jero could not be as bold. Lord Lorenc had brought him into the house as a servant, and Mauro's mother treated him like one. Jero could not ignore her as easily as Mateo could. He was helpless if Lady Johanna decided to torment him with some unusual chore merely to spite her husband.

Mauro shut his eyes, and the memories rushed through him. He could see his father taking Jero harshly by the hand and pulling him away from his taskmaster-mother. At the time, Mauro had thought his father was reprimanding Jero for unnerving Lady Johanna, but now Mauro realized that his father had been protecting him instead.

Jero's secret existence had been torturous to both of his parents. Lord Lorenc had worked hard to keep the truth from everyone while Lady Johanna was consumed with her unhappiness over it. Mauro wished he had known some of this before, and he wished he had never known the rest of it at all.

The air was stale with candle smoke, and Mauro's tired eyes burned when he finally came to the letters he dreaded reading most. This correspondence had not come through the post since each folded paper had only "Lady

Johanna Baric" written on the front. His mother's name was penned in the same masculine hand as on the scroll Mauro had been given today.

Mauro was not ready to face the last clues of his mother's life. He went to the window and opened it for air. Looking into the shadowed garden didn't give him the clarity he had hoped for. His stomach churned with the realization that his mother might have taken a lover, and that lover was Sebastian Dubovic. After a deep breath of air, Mauro summoned his courage and went back to the table to find out the truth.

He had unpacked the folded parchments from Lord Dubovic in the order his mother had bundled them. Most were dated from the months before his father had died. Mauro read those first. Each was signed only with "S," but he knew who that "S" stood for.

The first letters were the longest and conveyed trivial emotions and what-ifs. Mauro read them all.

After Lord Lorenc's death, Dubovic's notes were sporadic and brief. Mauro reasoned the old baron might have come in person while Mauro was away during that time and only wrote to his mother when Mauro was at the castle.

He scanned each letter, moving papers around the table until he thought their stories flowed in the proper order. There was no way to be sure without all the dates.

When he was past what he thought had been the worst of them, Mauro held the next note in his trembling hand until the shock turned to numbness. There it was in black and white: his mother had conspired to kill his father.

Mauro reread the brief message. "S" would give Lady Johanna the poison, she would mix it into the wine, and then she would be a free woman.

But it had not worked. The men did not die from the poisoned wine but were recovering—and his mother was relieved! So was Mauro to read that about her.

The rest, Mauro could only guess at from Dubovic's notes to her. He read between the lines that his mother must have written about his father being ill in bed but not dead. Dubovic's following letter assured her that she would not have to grieve alone. "S" had sent for the surgeon.

Mauro could read no more. It was all too much to comprehend. There were still eight more notes to go, but he wanted to be ignorant again. His mother had agreed to murder. Not just his father's death, but his officers too.

Mauro crouched with his head in his hands. A jumble of thoughts twirled in his mind. Why didn't she leave the House of Baric and been rid of everyone if they made her so unhappy? His father would have been happier if she had, and he could still be alive today. He could have loved Mauro like Mauro needed to be loved by a father. Things could have been so different.

Having finally pieced together the last twenty-some years, Mauro felt the truth crushing him. He struggled to breathe. He needed to get out.

Mauro got up from the table, unlocked the door, and walked away from the painful letters. The foyer was dark, but he needed no candle to find his way in his house.

He went first to the empty kitchen. Franja would be there soon to begin her baking. She would tease the coals back to life in the fireplace. Had Jero slept here by the open hearth as a boy? Mauro now recalled Nela would leave the coals glowing in the winter for him to keep warm while Mauro slept under his plush feather comforter in the room he had shared with Mateo.

Mauro left the glow of the warm kitchen and went out into the garden. The late-night stars filled the sky, and Mauro inhaled the refreshing night air. Dawn was not far away.

Exhausted and not caring, Mauro wandered away from the manor house, down the path, until a door blocked his way. He opened it and felt the steam hit him. Yes, this was the perfect place to wash it all away.

Mauro had no candle, but the dark would do. His eyes were adjusted to the blackness now, and he followed the sound of water gurgling in the cool fountain. He dipped his hands in and took a drink.

Then he went through the arch and listened for the trickle of the hot tap replenishing the warm pool. He felt for the familiar bench, where he had found Patrik's letter, and where his wife had sat so timidly across from him the first time he had visited this place after the rainstorm. As he stripped off his clothes, Mauro tried to conjure the memory of the last time he was here with Resi, but his mind was blank.

The edge of the pool shimmered, and Mauro slipped naked into the warm water. The domed ceiling was beginning to glow with the first rays of morning, but he longed to keep the black as he sank to the bottom of the pool. The water was heavy, holding him down. Is this what it had been like for Mateo? Sinking, never rising, not breathing. Drowning.

Mateo was dead. His father and mother—both dead. Gone.

Mauro surfaced, gasping for breath, crying out for the deaths he could not change.

Mauro wailed with grief for the brother lost to the sea. He cried for all the wasted days he had felt alone and unimportant. He pounded the water in anger, for the brother shut out of his rightful place in this world.

Twelve years of tears flowed unchecked into the pool. Tears of pity for a mother who could not love the sons of the women her husband desperately missed. Tears of anguish for the father who could not bring himself to love one more wife.

The truth no longer scared Mauro. He would have a different life from his father's. He was surrounded by people who loved him if he could only open his heart to their joy. From today on, Mauro would be sure Resi knew how much she meant to him. He loved his brother and would tell him the truth at the next possible chance.

But first, Mauro would get his revenge and kill the man who had killed his father.

At peace now, Mauro could bear anything that was to come. He rose from the pool, dressed, and then stepped out into the dawning day.

~ * ~

Salar Nassim was on the tower roof, the only place of complete solitude he had found among the crowd of men living here. It was nearly sunrise, and the yellow of morning was beginning to consume the black of night. Torches illuminated the gatehouse, but the manor house was dark, except for a glow from the windows where the kitchen was coming to life. The rest of the walled compound was shrouded in shadows.

As Salar Nassim knelt on his carpet in prayer, he heard a cry in the distance. Some might have mistaken the faint howling for a wolf, but Salar Nassim knew this mournful lament from too many years on battlefields. It was not the wail of a dying man but the despair of a living one. Of a man whose friend had been full of grit only a few minutes before but now lay stiff and empty on the ground. Salar Nassim would never forget that sound. Soren had cried out for his dead brother with the same awful howl.

Curious, the Muslim rose from his mat and looked over the edge of the tower. Footsteps sounded on the ramparts. The shuffling of boots crossing the cobbled yard below him disappeared down a path into the garden. The Baric Watch had heard it, too, he thought.

When all was quiet again, Salar Nassim went back to his small carpet and finished his prayer before he rolled it up. Then he went down the tower stairs to his chamber to sleep another hour. News of death could wait, he thought. He would hear about it soon enough.

Chapter 53

Franja was measuring flour for the day's baking, and Nela was tying her apron at the doorway when the baron unexpectedly strode through. They curtsied to him before continuing with their tasks. The two found nothing unusual about their master's early arrival in the kitchen. They were used to the eccentric behavior of the Barics.

"I will take breakfast upstairs in my chamber," the baron told Cook without a greeting. Still, he smiled easily at her and Franja as he walked past and took a piece of toasted bread from the plate Ivana was carrying from the fire.

Meanwhile, Nestor had come down the stairs for his breakfast and found the study door open. He had looked in, but the room was empty. From the doorway, Nestor noticed Lady Johanna's black trunk in the center of the room. Strewn on the floor around it were silk scarves and pretty boxes.

He walked in for a closer look and saw the stacks of opened papers piled on the long table. Nestor browsed the table and recognized the handwriting of the Toth sisters on a row of parchments. He began to open one.

"Don't," Mauro said firmly from the doorway. He had the calm look of a man who had just recovered from a high fever, a man who knew he had made it through the worst of the sickness and would live.

Nestor put the envelope back on the pile.

Mauro shut the door behind him and then paced the long table.

Nestor followed the baron's eyes as Mauro scanned the bits of paper, parchment, and envelopes lying there, looking for one in particular.

"Tell me, Nestor," Mauro finally said, "did Dubovic have a dispute with my father around the time he died?"

Nestor sat down behind the desk and said thoughtfully, "They seemed to be on good terms for neighbors. Did you find something troublesome in one of these letters?"

Mauro leaned across the desktop and asserted, "I know Jero came from Dubovic's service, and I know about Sonja."

Nestor did not flinch despite the young baron breathing down on him. Instead, he adjusted his spectacles and met the baron's brilliant green eyes with his own.

"Your father paid more than a fair sum to Dubovic for Jero's contract," Nestor explained calmly. "He would have no ill-will against Lorenc for that."

"You said 'for that.' What other ill feelings would there be? It was clear to me yesterday that he and you do not share any admiration for each other."

"My opinion of Lord Dubovic had no effect on his relationship with your father. But your uncle, well, he has not been so generous with Baron Dubovic in the past."

Mauro took a step away from the desk. He had not considered his uncle's role in his troubles.

Nestor went on to explain, "Vladimir has rarely ruled in Dubovic's favor when handling regional disputes over the years. But then the old baron can be demanding and unreasonable."

Mauro asked, "What kind of disputes?"

"Nothing directed at the Barics. Most were with the Empire—tariff disagreements, war tributes, tax irregularities and the like."

Mauro walked to the window, where he absently watched the changing of his Guard taking place at the gatehouse. He pondered this twist, then asked, "Did my uncle rule against Dubovic intentionally?"

"I have not followed every dispute. I will say, though, that your uncle's rulings are rarely overturned in Venice. Dubovic, however, made it known he found Vladimir to be harsh in his judgment." Nestor watched Mauro at the window, still caught up in the spell of the moving soldiers.

"Wasn't there some trick written into the betrothal between Mateo and the Dubovic daughter?" Mauro asked. "That must have been another mark of injustice Dubovic held against my uncle."

Nestor chuckled unexpectedly and admitted, "I was the one who wrote the loophole into Mateo's marriage contract, not Vladimir, and I was very glad for it."

Mauro turned back to the room and asked, "Does the baron despise you for that?"

Nestor shrugged. "That was long ago, Mauro. His eldest daughter married well enough, in the end. Why this sudden interest in Dubovic's opinion of your family, though? Did he say something against the Barics during his visit?"

"Yesterday's visit? No. But my question to you is: why did you not tell me of his other visits?"

Nestor looked puzzled. "Mauro, the baron has been visiting on occasion for years," he said matter-of-factly.

"I mean recently, *secretively*, while the master of the house is away from home."

Nestor leaned back in his chair and sighed, his patience wearing thin. "It is far too early for interrogations, Mauro. I have yet to have my cup of coffee, and it is apparent that you have not yet been to bed. Go rest. We can go over this later."

"We will go over it now."

Nestor sat tall again and focused on his employer.

"As my estate administrator, Nestor, do you not know how often Baron Dubovic visited my home while I was away on campaigns?"

Nestor took a deep breath and let it out again. "I do not follow who comes and goes at your estate, or whether you are home at the time, Mauro. That is a question you should ask your scouts and gatekeepers."

Through clenched teeth, Mauro asked, "Do my scouts know if Lord Dubovic proposed marriage to my mother?"

"Marriage?" Nestor repeated. "Where did you hear this?"

"I read it." Mauro pointed to the table.

Nestor's eyes lingered on the papers. "Your mother was distressed after Lorenc's death. She was not herself," he said. "Did she accept his proposal?"

Mauro had searched for written clues in Dubovic's letters, but nothing spelled out that she had. "I am not certain. I do not have both sides of the correspondence. Do you think she was mad, Nestor? Did she go crazy before or after my father's death?"

Nestor leaned back again and studied Johanna's only child before he answered the awkward question. "You must understand, Mauro, Lady Johanna was difficult to please. We all tried hard to make her happy over the years, but I think we eventually gave up."

Mauro frowned.

"I am sorry if it is unpleasant to hear, but that is the truth of it," Nestor said.

"Not crazy then? Just a neglected, bitter woman?" Mauro asked coolly.

Realizing his failure to explain adequately, Nestor replied soothingly, "Lady Johanna was distraught after the funeral, and there was little we could do to comfort her. Idita and I decided such emotion was entirely natural after twenty-some years of marriage. Maybe she felt neglected, maybe she was bitter. But in answer to your question, Mauro, we never thought she was insane."

Mauro walked to the table. He picked up the last stack, then sifted through the papers until he found the page that he wanted.

Mauro handed Nestor the paper. "Would a sane person plot to kill her husband?"

Nestor's jaw dropped as he read the note. "Dear God," he mumbled.

"It is all there," Mauro cried. "She was the one who put the poison in the wine, like you suspected, but it was not enough. At least she seemed pleased that she had failed. Maybe she regretted it."

Nestor put the page down after reading it through. "Of course, she regretted it. Willful murder is a mortal sin. Your mother was a godly woman, Mauro, and would have believed she would burn in hell for eternity for such a crime."

"But she did not murder them, Nestor. They were recovering. Here, read the next note. Someone else had their hands on them to cause their deaths."

Nestor shook his head, trying to take it all in. "Why are you bent on solving this now, after two years?"

"Because I have found new pieces to the puzzle, and I must see it whole. You were my father's best friend, Nestor. I need your help piecing it all together."

"I am trying my best, Mauro." Nestor handed back the parchments, and Mauro set them back in their order on the table.

Mauro then took a seat next to his old advisor. Nestor's answer to the following question would determine what he would do next.

"Did my mother know about the emeralds?" Mauro asked point-blank.

"No."

His answer rang loud and certain, but then Nestor changed his mind as he thought the simple question through.

"Well, maybe," he clarified. "Your father never told your mother about the gems, but toward the end, he suspected she may have learned about them some other way."

Mauro attentively listened as Nestor explained, "As you know, Tomas was not only your father's master gem-cutter, but also an officer in his Guard. Lady Johanna had asked why Tomas stayed behind and did not go with the rest of the soldiers on campaigns. I was able to explain it away. But once, while Lorenc and his men were gone, Tomas sliced his hand while splitting a gemstone and Idita tended to him in the kitchen. Tomas later told me he saw your mother at the kitchen door. She may have overheard things said between him and Idita and later looked for the locked door in the cellar."

Mauro had one more question. "Tell me, how did Natalija come to be my mother's lady's maid? She fostered daughters of noblemen for years as her companions. Why suddenly choose a village girl in their place?"

Nestor thought about it. "I do not remember the exact circumstances, but I do remember that Natalija came to us the same summer your father died."

"I will ask her, then."

Satisfied, Mauro stood up and pushed the chair back to make room for his advisor to step away.

"This has been helpful, Nestor. Thank you," he said, opening the study door for them.

In the foyer, Nestor offered, "If I can be of more help to you, Mauro, I am at your service. Shall I take the key?"

"I'll keep this for now. There is no work for you in there this morning," Mauro told him, tucking the study room key into his pocket after locking the door. "If anyone asks where I am, I will be in my chamber. Sleeping. I am exhausted."

Nestor nodded and continued on his way to his breakfast.

Mauro climbed the stairs, two at a time. He saw several chambermaids coming and going from the room the Venetians had shared, but Natalija was not among the servants. It was just as well, Mauro thought. He was too tired to talk anymore this morning.

~*~

The Baric's chamber door was open, and Mauro entered to find his wife at their table with a platter of toast and ham and pastries in front of her. She was alone and dressed for the day in her brightly colored robes, loose and light, in anticipation of the continued heatwave.

"Good morning, my dear." He greeted her with a light kiss on her lips and then sat down as though nothing had transpired in the last twenty hours. He poured himself a cup of water and declared, "I have emptied my mother's trunk for Ruby to begin packing her things. The grooms will carry it upstairs later." He drank the water thirstily and began to fill his plate with the delicious-smelling food.

Resi had already eaten her fill. She set her napkin down next to her plate and contemplated her husband.

"Is that all you were doing yesterday?" she asked at last. "No one has seen you since yesterday afternoon."

Mauro had expected this question and had an answer ready. He put his fork down and managed a weak smile when he said, "It was thoughtless of me to not have Davor tell you I would be occupied well into the evening. Once I begin a project, I like to finish it. It was a daunting task to decide what to save and what to toss."

"Did one trunk take all night to sort? Where did you sleep after that?" she demanded to know.

He peeled a boiled egg and told her, "I did not sleep anywhere. I was up all night looking through everything. I was surprised at the memories my mother's collection brought back. I should have opened it a long time ago, but it is done now. A few of her things I will keep, but most were only useful to her."

It was the truth. The letters were of no use to anyone, and Mauro did not want to read them ever again.

Resi stared openly at her husband. "Are you feeling alright, Mauro?" Dark circles lined his eyes, and there was a dullness to their natural sparkle.

He reached across the small table and took her hand to calm her worry. "I really was up all night with my task. I think I will allow myself a little nap this morning."

She squeezed his hand. "Should I join you in bed?" There was a sparkle in her eyes.

"You could join me," he managed to say playfully, "but I will not last long, I am afraid."

He stood up and stretched. A few hours of sleep always set the world straight again. He removed his boots and waistcoat and then crawled under the covers and shut his eyes.

Resi followed him to the bed and looked him over. "Are you sure I should not call Idita? You look pale, Mauro."

He rolled over with a groan. "For the last time, I am not ill."

Resi sat on the side of the bed and stroked his soft hair. "What did you do after you emptied the trunk?" she asked.

He opened his eyes and said, "I came to breakfast."

She leaned in over him. "Then why do you smell like roses and not a sweaty man?"

"Ah yes, well, I took a bath in your perfumed water."

She cocked her head, ready to ask more questions, but he put his hand up to her lips. "I needed to think, and your bathhouse was the perfect place. We will talk more tonight, Resi. Let me sleep now."

Resi watched the lines in his face relax, and peace took over his expression. Idita had been right. She would learn what he wanted her to know when he was ready.

~*~

Resi closed the shutters to darken their room and then went to Ruby's chamber down the hall.

The door was open, and Ruby was sitting on the edge of her small bed tying her riding boots, dressed for an outing.

Resi sat down beside her. "I am so jealous of you, Ruby. Are you riding with Patricius again this morning?"

"I am just going to ride around the paddock before it gets too hot. Patricius might take me out riding later, when they are back from the practice fields."

"I wanted to tell you, Mauro emptied a trunk for you." Resi looked around the room. "Have you thought about what you will bring home?"

Ruby's eyes went to the pink billowing gown hanging inside the open wardrobe. "I'll only pack what I came with. I have no need for ball gowns as a merchant's wife."

"But you love that dress, Ruby. Take it with you for the memories it brings."

Ruby walked over to the wardrobe. "Do you think Nikko will like it? Venetian gowns are so different from ours, don't you think?"

"Greek men will find it just as beautiful as Venetian men do. You will convince Nikko it is for his enjoyment that you wear it, even if it is really for yours."

Ruby did not linger on that decision, but asked, "What should I pack with me? Patricius said I can only take what my horse can carry, and most of that will be food and my sleeping roll."

"Take soap! Enough to share," Resi said with a laugh.

Ruby nodded with a chuckle. "Traveling with four men will not give me much opportunity to bathe."

Resi looked at the pegs by the door. "Be sure to pack your cape. You will want it for a thunderstorm. The men may not stop for cover, and the cape will keep you dry on your horse."

"I will pack that, along with two changes of clothes and dry shoes. That should be enough for the journey. And my pot of soap," Ruby added with a wink.

Ruby continued chatting as she looked through the wardrobe drawers for other must-haves. When Resi didn't react, Ruby asked her quiet friend, "Is everything all right, Resi? Did you talk to your husband?"

Resi had been watching the guards in the courtyard below and turned back from the window. "What did you ask?"

"Have you seen your husband today?" Ruby repeated.

"Briefly. He had a little breakfast in our room and then crawled into bed. He said he stayed up all night unpacking his mother's trunk. I can't imagine it taking him all night. He is hiding something from me again."

"You have to trust him, Resi."

Resi shook her head with worry and sat down on the bed again. "He was in such a strange mood, Ruby, not at all himself."

"Maybe he saw a ghost in his mother's old trunk."

"If the ghost of Lady Johanna haunts this house, she is in her chamber, remember?"

"How could I not? Your mother-in-law's ghost made quite an impression on the Venetians!" exclaimed Ruby with a laugh.

"Lady Isabella is an unusual woman, isn't she? So frightened of the spirit world but fearless of the real one," Resi declared.

"I think she is very brave. I would like to be more like her."

"She told me once that she would have liked to be more like you, Ruby—innocent of the real world."

Ruby insisted, "I know what to expect in the real world now. I am not so innocent any longer."

Resi patted her friend's shoulder for encouragement. "Everyone always wants something they cannot have. Lady Isabella's life in Venice is far different from what yours will be in Thessaloniki. To be honest, I am glad to be here, somewhere in the middle of the two worlds."

"Will you come visit me soon?"

Resi promised her gloomy friend, "After the baby is born, we will come for a long visit." Then Resi hopped off the bed with forced energy. "Come on," she said. "Mauro won't let me get on a horse, but at least I can say hello to Ophelia so she doesn't think I am neglecting her."

The two walked arm in arm out into the hallway and down the stairs together.

"Poor Ophelia," Resi continued. "Once you are gone, I don't know who will take the time to ride her."

"Jero will ride her for you if you ask him," Ruby said decisively. She was able to say his name without becoming downhearted now.

"Yes, of course," Resi agreed. "I can always count on Jero."

Chapter 54

Mauro woke up with more questions than clarity about what he should do next. His short nap had unintentionally lasted all day, and the growling of his stomach told him he had missed at least one meal. He opened the door to see if Davor was waiting there, but the hallway was empty.

Mauro hastily dressed again and went downstairs. When he walked through the foyer, he encountered no one, so he decided to go find some food and more answers.

~*~

"Mauro! Where have you been hiding?" Vilim bellowed boisterously as the baron came across the dining room with his bowl of shellfish in his hand.

Mauro set his meal down on the crowded plank table next to his cousin. "Yes, well, I lost track of time reading about old family histories last night, and then I guess I overslept this morning." He dunked his bread into the buttery sauce and took a satisfying bite.

Simeon, who was sitting across from Vilim, joined the conversation. "Did you uncover more scandals about old Fredrik Baric?"

Vilim corrected Simeon, "Fredrik Baric was never caught in a scandal. It was said he could drink anyone under the table and negotiate a peace treaty, all on the same night. That sort of talent was respected in his day."

Simeon retorted, "Too bad you don't have any Baric blood in you, Vilim! You could have benefited from old Lord Fredrik's talent two nights ago. Everyone still respects you, even though you puked your guts out in our hallway."

Eduard laughed heartily next to Vilim. "Tin might not agree with that!"

Mauro grinned at his cousin and said consolingly, "I had almost forgotten your near-death arrival, Vilim. How are you? Feeling alright again?"

Vilim looked around the table of men—all had witnessed his moment of weakness. "No worries, Mauro, but I think I have finally learned my lesson about drinking games."

"Until the next bachelor party!" Eduard interjected to roars of agreement from the table. "Simeon might be next! What do you say, Simeon?"

Simeon shrugged sheepishly. They did not know he had already asked Franja his question, and she had turned him down.

Mauro interrupted the banter. "Simeon," he said, "can I talk to you a moment?" Mauro cocked his head toward the back of the room and began to walk away from the group.

"Don't you want your dinner, Mauro?" Vilim asked. The baron's full dish of steaming mussels was still next to him.

"I will be right there," Mauro hollered back, although he found he wasn't so hungry after all.

Mauro sat down at one of the card tables in the corner near the stairwell, and Simeon took the low stool across from him. "Now Mauro, if you are going to ask me about Franja—"

"No, Simeon," Mauro interrupted, "it is something else. I need you to jog my memory about the ambush."

"Which one?" Simeon said with a chuckle, still in a cheerful mood from the dinner banter.

"The last one," Mauro replied impatiently, "where my arm was sliced."

Simeon drummed his fingers on the table, recalling the details. "I helped the constable piece that one together. We had not yet crossed your northern border when it happened."

"So, we were on Dubovic's land?"

"Near the cliff, the spot that always gives his scouts trouble. Radic found out they are not policing that far south at all."

"Why not?" Mauro asked.

Simeon leaned forward precariously on his three-legged stool and asserted, "Because your neighbor owns a hell of a big piece of land, and the baron is too cheap to employ more scouts to protect it from bandits."

Mauro considered Simeon's choice of words. "Bandits, you say."

"Radic thought they had been bandits. Your men reported noticing there was no uniformity to the attackers—not in their dress or in their equipment. They were well-armed, but they looked like a ragtag group of men. Some didn't even have saddles for their horses."

Simeon then contemplated the baron across the small table. "Why are you asking about that now?"

Mauro absently rubbed the scar on his arm and explained, "It has come up again, and I need some answers."

Simeon nodded. "Then, let's put our heads together."

Mauro remarked, "We were not typical travelers that bandits would be waiting to rob, and they did not take any of our weapons or a riderless horse. Why do you think that is?"

The baron's serious tone began to affect Simeon, and he reflected just as earnestly. "It was either daring or desperate, considering our group was plainly armed. Still, we have been attacked by bandits a few times before."

"We have, but curiously my men have never been attacked when I was not with them."

"You make a good point, Mauro. None of the scouts have reported trouble in groups or even alone on that same stretch."

Mauro shifted uncomfortably on his seat. "Something has come up, Simeon. I am supposed to attend a council meeting at Dubovic Castle on Saturday."

"Saturday is the village party," Simeon reminded him.

"I know. But I would need a good excuse to miss this council vote, so I will have to attend. Fortunately, the meeting is early, and I could be back here by dusk for the party."

Simeon leaned in and said, "So you attend both. Is there something else in the way?"

Mauro stared across the dining hall at nothing in particular. "I have a bad feeling about it that I cannot shake," he replied at last.

Jolted by his friend's remark, Simeon sat up tall, eager to help. "You have good instincts, Mauro. Should I send for the constable?"

"If Radic had heard something, he would have come here to tell me already."

"Right," Simeon agreed. "Then you should confront the baron."

"The baron was just here innocently inviting me for Saturday. He seemed to have no malice toward me."

"But you had this bad feeling after his visit?" Simeon whispered across the table.

"Yes."

The two quietly reflected before Simeon suggested, "Don't go, then. It might be a setup."

"Setup or not, I have to go."

"Fully armed, of course?" Simeon said.

"I have written to Neven Leopold. We will go together, with our combined guardsmen." Then Mauro shrugged with self-doubt. "I might just be overthinking all of this, seeing problems that aren't there."

Simeon seemed to sense his commander's hesitation. "You have been under extra stress these past few weeks. Do you know the best way to relieve that sort of stress?" Simeon had a devilish grin on his bearded face.

Mauro raised his brows and warned, "Do not joke with me about my wife, Simeon. She came clean with God for her sins."

Simeon laughed out loud. "I wasn't thinking of women, Mauro. I meant a good game of dice would do the trick," he said with enthusiasm. "Let me go round up some players, all right?"

Mauro gave a nod. "All right, Simeon. I am up for a game or two."

~*~

While Mauro waited at the table, Salar Nassim and Bem passed Simeon in the stairwell.

Nassim whispered something to the African and then came over to Mauro's table alone. "Good evening, Lord Baric," he greeted him.

Mauro looked up from his thoughts. "Salar Nassim, good evening to you."

"May I sit down?" asked the Persian.

The two had not talked for several days, and Mauro thought this was opportune timing. The baron gestured to the empty stool Simeon had just occupied and said, "Please."

"Lord Baric, you know I am grateful for your hospitality," Salar Nassim began. "We have eaten like kings, and our horses are well-rested."

Mauro made light of it. "There is no need to thank me again. You are welcome guests, and I am happy to accommodate you."

"Yes, but I would like to know if there is anything I can do for you in return. I am at your service, Lord Baric."

The Persian held his stare, and Mauro sensed his words had more meaning behind them than empty compliments expected from a grateful guest.

Indeed, they did. Salar Nassim had overheard soldiers talking at breakfast. There had been no tragedy among the Barics that morning, no intruder or injury, but Salar Nassim was sure of what he had heard from the roof, and he had come to his own conclusion.

Mauro looked at him curiously. "What services are you offering, Salar Nassim? The war is over."

"The old one, yes, but there is always a fight to be fought. I have helped solve pesky troubles for men such as yourself, Lord Baric, if you are in need of a solution."

Mauro smiled despite his annoyance. Resi must have talked to Patrik about her worries yesterday. "Thank you for your concern, Salar Nassim. Despite what my wife might have told you, I have no troubles. There is no new fight."

"I have not talked to your wife, Lord Baric. But I will not disturb you further. I was just coming to have my evening meal. I see Bem has started without me."

Mauro looked across the room to where Bem was seated alone with a bowl of stew in front of him.

Salar Nassim got up to leave, and Mauro offered, "We are going to play some games in a bit. Come join us."

"With pleasure," Salar Nassim replied. A genuine smile made it to his raven eyes.

Mauro watched him go but had to laugh to himself. He would probably regret asking the talented gambler to join his game.

~*~

Mauro preferred cards over dice. He didn't play either very well since he never had the practice the others had. As their commander, Mauro had to ponder other strategies besides gaming ones.

Mauro felt in his pocket for his coin purse and gave it a jiggle. There was enough in it to lose a few rounds. After that, he would watch the others for the sport of it and enjoy some camaraderie. Simeon was right about one thing. Mauro already forgot what had troubled him so profoundly just a short time ago.

Simeon returned to the dining hall carrying a canvas bag of game pieces. "Shall we set up more tables, Mauro? I brought enough dice for a few games."

They pushed the two small plank tables together, and then two more.

Vilim came over carrying Mauro's neglected dinner. Mauro took the offered dish from him and dipped the fork in for a bite of the saucy mussels.

"Are you getting a dice game started?" Vilim asked.

"We are," Simeon replied, "and Mauro has agreed to play."

Vilim grinned and gave Mauro a friendly jab. "How much money do you have on you, Mauro? Should we let you go up to your treasury and grab another purse or two before we start?"

Mauro shot back, "Is that what you think of my playing skills, Vilim? I think I will pass on dice tonight. My coins last longer in card games."

"I will join you at your card table," Salar Nassim said from behind him.

Mauro turned and said, "Only if you promise not to use the tricks you so famously taught Fabian's sister."

"I can promise you that, but I cannot guarantee the same for my friends."

Bem came up next to Mauro and said, "I'd like to play some dice if there is room for one more?"

"Sit at our table," Vilim replied. "Where is your friend Soren? He took nearly every pot the last time I played with him."

"He and Patrik should be coming down any time now. We can warm up the dice before they get here," Bem replied.

Mauro, Salar Nassim, Eduard, and Milan filled the first table.

Milan was an exceptional player. He and the guardsmen would play a game nearly every evening in the Keep. He was happy to join the baron's table tonight.

Simeon, Bem, Vilim, and Daniel agreed on a dice game, and the occasional roar of disappointment or excitement drew out other players and spectators from the soldiers' sleeping chambers. Patrik and Soren heard the noise through the open doors of the stairwell and came down to join in the entertainment. Soon it was practically a party.

Mauro had drawn a winning card combination and was ready to reveal his hand when he noticed the others at his table were staring at the doorway. Mauro's scouts were coming in—the three riders had returned from Leopold Castle. Mauro dropped his cards and met them halfway across the room.

Bartol, his most senior scout, handed the baron a sealed letter, and Mauro hastily ripped it open to read his friend's answer.

Mauro looked up from the penned parchment and asked, "Lord Leopold was not at home, then?"

"No, my lord, but we were instructed how to find him. It wasn't a long ride into the forest," his scout replied.

"Did you run across any trouble on your journey?" Mauro wanted to know.

"None, sir." Then Bartol asked, "Did you get the news you were hoping for, Lord Baric?"

His scouts had ridden hard for this bit of information, and Mauro did not object to his curiosity.

"It is helpful news to me but not the answer I was hoping for. You did well returning so quickly. Thank you."

The baron went back to the card table and took a few coins from his pile there. It was enough to buy a few rounds of play for each rider.

"Have your meal and then relax and enjoy yourselves. You will have no duties tomorrow," the baron told the three scouts.

Eduard said, "Noted! Now, will you play your hand, Mauro?"

"Are you worried your luck will change?" Mauro asked with a chuckle.

Eduard tapped his cards nervously. "Luck can change quicker than you can spit in the wind. We have already placed our bets, Mauro. It is your call."

"Well, unless you switched my cards behind my back, I think I have finally won a round." Mauro threw a coin into the pile and showed his cards on the tabletop.

"That is a good hand, but not quite good enough, Lord Baric," Salar Nassim said with a sly smile. He turned his cards out for all to see.

Eduard dropped his cards with a groan.

Salar Nassim dragged the pile of coins to his stacks in front of him and began to add them to the neat rows.

Milan took the loose cards from the table and reshuffled them.

As Mauro watched Milan's swift movements, his mind went back to the questions he had asked Simeon. That's when he realized Milan could quickly answer the one nagging question that Simeon could not.

"Tell me, Milan. When you rode with my father's Guard, was there ever trouble at the bend, north of our border with Dubovic?"

The old soldier regarded the baron oddly. His question seemed to baffle the man.

"Trouble at the bend? Not that I recall, sir." After a thoughtful moment, Milan added, "Baron Dubovic did cut down the trees along the road to avoid trouble there. The cliffs still had some hiding spots, but without the extra cover, you could see horses waiting, and the bandits quit using that spot."

"That must have been twenty years ago for them to have grown so dense again," Mauro reflected.

"Twenty years sounds about right, sir." Milan continued, "Now that I think about it, your neighbor had trouble with robbers, indeed, but not along the north-south trade route. It was on the baron's own castle road. We were ambushed along there once. Your father had been called to a meeting of some sort. Even the soldiers in his traveling party were attacked."

"When was this, Milan?" Mauro asked.

"Also long ago, maybe fifteen years now, but I remember thinking it was strange that Lord Dubovic would leave his castle road unguarded."

Mauro turned to his other captain at the table. "Were you with them, Eduard?"

"Probably not," replied Eduard matter-of-factly while inspecting the new hand of cards Salar Nassim had dealt him. "If it was fifteen years ago, I would have been a new scout patrolling Baric roads. Why are you concerned with Dubovic's patrols, Mauro?"

"I am invited to Dubovic Castle on Saturday and I want to know if I should take a bigger escort."

Milan was the first to offer his opinion. "From what I understand, sir, you can expect few, if any, along that road. Dubovic takes most of his guardsmen with him when he travels, or they stay behind his walls to protect his estate. Your neighbor's troubles come from the squatters and other transients living in his hills and woods. His constable has no control over them."

Mauro put his question to the table. "Would these squatters and transients be warned to expect me coming down the road on Saturday? Or that I am known to travel with too few escorts?"

Eduard shook his head and played his card. "From what I have heard, Dubovic's squatters seek out unarmed folks with no escorts at all."

Salar Nassim had been listening to the conversation and asked, "Why the dilemma, Lord Baric? Why not just ride with more escorts as a precaution? You have the manpower."

Mauro had heard enough to come to a decision. He turned to Salar Nassim and said, "It sounds like I am asking a simple question with an obvious answer. In truth, it has to do with solving trouble beyond the number of escorts. My new problem is what you spoke of earlier, actually."

Salar Nassim nodded, catching the baron's reference to his earlier offer.

"As I said, Lord Baric, I am at your service."

"Could we meet in the morning to discuss it?" Mauro asked Salar Nassim.

"Gladly."

Eduard looked puzzled and asked his commander, "Will you want a larger entourage to escort you, Mauro? The village feast is on Saturday, and the men have been talking non-stop about the party since it was announced."

"No need to draw straws yet, Eduard. I will make my decision tomorrow."

Mauro tossed the rest of his coins into the pot and told his competitors, "It is inevitable these coins belong to one of you. Someone else can take my chair. I will see you all in the morning."

Eduard grinned and called Bartol over to be their fourth. He was an even worse player than the baron, so perhaps Eduard thought he had a chance to win back a few lire.

When Mauro opened the front manor house door, Davor stood by the staircase, waiting for the baron to dismiss him for the night.

The valet dutifully followed the baron up the stairs. On the landing, he asked, "Will you need me further tonight, my lord?"

"No, you may go to bed."

"Thank you, sir," Davor said as he went down the hallway.

"Oh, and Davor," Mauro called out. "The scouts have returned."

"Did you get the reply you wanted, my lord?"

"No, but Lord Leopold is sending a courier with his reply tomorrow. As soon as it arrives, you are to bring it to me. And I will need to meet with Natalija after lunch in my study. Can you tell her that?"

"I will tell her in the morning, sir. Good night, Lord Baric."

~*~

Mauro quietly opened his chamber, trying not to disturb his sleeping wife. He was surprised to find the candelabras in the room were still lit, and his wife was sitting on the edge of their bed, holding a white cloth in her lap.

She looked up.

Mauro shut the door and sat down on the chair to take off his boots and stockings. He unbuttoned his waistcoat and hung it on the chairback. His linen shirt clung to his skin from the heat of the evening, and he peeled it off.

He got up. Behind the screen, Mauro poured tepid water from a filled bucket into his basin to wash away the day's disappointments.

When her husband said nothing further, Resi came around the screen. "I somehow didn't expect you to sleep here tonight."

He reached out and touched her cheek. "I am sorry you worried, my dear. I lost track of time last night, is all."

"And tonight?"

"I had some things I needed to clarify with Simeon and Eduard."

He dipped his soapy hair into the clear water and dried it on a towel. He rubbed another soapy cloth across his neck, over his shoulders, and down his arms, then let the cool dampness evaporate in the warm air of their chamber.

Mauro looked over at his wife and asked, "What is your impression of Lord Dubovic?"

Resi seemed surprised by the question but gave it some thought as Mauro filled the second basin.

"He is a charming man," she reflected. "Mannered, elegantly dressed, like most of the noblemen I have met. I can tell he was an attractive man when he was younger."

"Do you have the sense that he is a dangerous man?" Mauro asked cautiously.

She shook her head. "No, not at all. He seems sincere and well-bred. He does not seem to be the soldiering type, though."

Mauro found her comment curious. All men were called to be soldiers, to either lead or to fight, sometimes both.

"What do you mean by soldiering type?" he asked her.

"Like you, Mauro. You are also elegant and well-bred, but there is a distinct difference between you and Lord Dubovic. It is something you possess. Since I trust you, danger would not the right word. You have more of an outward strength, a fortitude that the baron does not reveal."

Mauro was pleased by her explanation, but he did not talk of it further. He hastily continued his methodical routine behind the screen while Resi watched him in silence.

After a moment, she asked, "Why are you asking me about Baron Dubovic?"

He set his tin of paste down. "The baron came to summon me to the council meeting. It has been moved to Saturday."

"Yes, I was there, remember?"

"Yes, I know," he replied, deciding how much to reveal to his gentle wife. "There is something untrustworthy about the man," he finally said. "The invitation did not make sense to me."

"You are too suspicious, Mauro. I thought it was considerate of him to come in person. It must have been important that you not be left out."

"He must like me then, to be so attentive. Is that your opinion?" Mauro asked with a bite that did not go unnoticed.

"Where is this coming from, Mauro?" She looked hurt.

"I recently learned that Baron Dubovic could have been my new stepfather. But you knew that. Why did you keep this from me?"

Resi stepped back with alarm after their talk of danger. Mauro's voice held an explicit accusation, and she walked away to the open window for air.

"I, um, wasn't intentionally keeping anything from you, I promise."

From behind the screen, Mauro demanded, "What did he say to you at the ball?"

"Um, that he came to visit your mother after your father died. It sounded to me like they had formed a long friendship over the years as neighbors. He told me he was shocked when he learned your mother had passed so suddenly. At some point in our conversation, he said he had considered remarrying, and I assumed he meant your mother."

Mauro threw his towel on the ground and shouted, "Why do you know all this and I don't?"

She turned from the window. "I was going to bring it up, but I never had the chance. Should I have rushed to you at the ball and said, 'Lord Dubovic was at your house courting your mother'? I thought you would have known that already. You know everything that goes on here!" She was shouting now, too.

Mauro reached down and picked up the towel he had thrown. He wrung it out in frustration. She was right, of course.

Mauro came out into the room again and saw his wife's distressed expression. "I am sorry, Resi. Forgive me for losing my temper with you. It has been a trying day."

He went past her and sat on the bed, rubbing his temples to ease his growing headache. The little white gown Resi had been holding was on the coverlet next to him, and he picked it up.

He looked from it to his wife and then asked with a kind voice, "Did you sew this?"

"Lady Caterina did. It is wonderful, isn't it?" she said softly.

He touched the smooth cotton and emerald-colored stitching along the hem of the baby's dress. Caterina had embroidered sailboats, seashells, and towers in the likeness of the Keep, one after the other.

Mauro set it down carefully on the side table, thinking about the reason this all mattered to him. His anger was gone when he said, "Come here, Resi."

She came to the bed and stood in front of him.

"How is our little baby?" he asked.

He put his head on her belly, and she wrapped her arms around his shoulders, keeping him there against her. "I have not given you enough attention, Terese, and I hope you will forgive me."

She breathed in deeply. "There is nothing to forgive, Mauro. If you cannot tell me your troubles, then at least let me do what I can to unburden you."

He looked up at her, and she leaned down and kissed him tenderly on the mouth. With it, he knew she loved him, and she was his.

Mauro stood up and held her in his arms. "If I should die, Resi—"

"Shhh. Don't talk like that, Mauro. You are not leaving for battle."

Despite her anxious expression, he insisted, "If I should die, you cannot remarry. I could not bear to watch you from hell in another man's arms."

"You are the best man I know, Mauro. You will not end up in hell."

"I may not have time to ask God for forgiveness for the grave sin I have planned."

She managed a weak smile that he would worry again over this trivial sin.

He breathed in and out deeply as they held each other. God would forgive him for making love to his pregnant wife, but would God pardon him for plotting a man's murder?

He stepped back from his wife's embrace and lifted her nightgown over her head. He let it drop to the floor. Mauro did not ask her, and she did not protest. Instead, Resi unbuttoned his breeches, and he stepped out of them.

They stood there, not quite touching in the warm night air as if time had frozen them, each contemplating what this meant. Mauro's clear worry showed on his face. Resi could take some of those worries away, if only for a little while.

No words passed between them after that. Mauro laid her gently on the bed and blew out the candles. She let him love her the way he needed to that night, somberly in the quiet darkness, unburdening both of them.

His troubles were temporarily forgotten, but Mauro was spent from carrying their weight. He fell quickly into a dreamless sleep in his wife's arms.

Chapter 55

Mauro closed the study door behind him, and the four men found places to sit around the table. The opened letters were still stacked along its middle, but the mercenaries paid them no attention. They were looking toward the baron.

He sat at the end of the table, glancing from man to man, trying to decide how much he should reveal when explaining why he had asked them here.

"I have a problem," Mauro began, "and I cannot decide whether my problem is real or imaginary."

The men sat up with interest.

"I have been told all of my adult life that I am the last of my family line, the last Baric. I have hated that, and for the longest time I did not care whether I was or not. I care now." Mauro stood up and went to the window.

Salar Nassim counseled, "If you are troubled, Lord Baric, then your problem is real. What can we do to help you solve it?"

Mauro turned back to the four focused men. It had been the right choice to ask them for advice. He sat down at the table again and told them, "More attempts have been made to end my life within twenty miles of my home than in all the battles I have journeyed to. My neighbor, Baron Dubovic, wanted to marry my widowed mother. If she had no son, he could have convinced her to sign the estate over to her new husband. Unfortunately for him, my mother died before he could succeed in that profitable endeavor. Still, the assassination attempts continue."

"And you want to know why?" Bem asked.

"I know why," Mauro said. "All families have secrets, and I suspect my mother shared one important one with our neighbor."

"The one my father was punished for?" Patrik asked.

Mauro raised his brow, and Patrik knew the answer.

Salar Nassim interjected, "You said he'd invited you to his castle on Saturday."

"Yes, to stage an assassination, I fear."

Patrik scratched his head. "How does he intend to profit from your family secret, upon your death?" he asked. "Your mother is dead, there are no daughters or sons."

"I have a wife," Mauro said pointedly.

Patrik exclaimed, "He would marry my sister?"

The four men shifted uneasily.

"Your sister is a Baric now," Mauro reminded Patrik. "Upon my death, my uncle would give Resi time to consider her future and whether or not to remarry. During that time, she would be vulnerable to a corrupt neighbor, just like my mother was."

"Besides trying to murder you, what makes the man corrupt?" Soren asked.

Patrik asserted, "He is a baron of the Venetian Empire! What else do you need to know?"

The baron did not take offense at his brother-in-law's logic and clarified, "You have a point, Soren. Openly, the baron is an agreeable sort of man—a bejeweled gentleman who is pleasant to dine with and has a respectable reputation among my fellow council members. But I know he has deep financial troubles."

"How deep?" asked Salar Nassim.

"He hired my captain to steal his own merchant ship in open waters in order to sell it to pirates and take the insurance money as profit."

The men exchanged frowns.

"The Dubovic estate is three times the size of mine, and he cannot manage it, nor can he collect enough taxes from its tenants to pay the heavy debt he owes the Empire each year."

Bem interjected, "The Bible says money is the root of all evil, but the lack of it makes a man do treacherous acts."

"Desperate men are dangerous," Soren added.

Then Bem suggested the obvious, "If this man is planning to kill you on the road, Lord Baric, then you could just stay at home."

Salar Nassim disagreed. "Then there will be another attempt, Bem, and the next time Lord Baric will not have prior knowledge of the time and place."

The Persian turned to the baron and said, "I have an idea how to go about ending this threat."

Mauro smiled. "I was hoping you would."

The mercenaries seemed to unite as one in their thoughts.

"This lord is, or was, a wealthy man," Salar Nassim asserted.

"Wealth buys power," Bem added.

Mauro agreed.

"Like all powerful men, your neighbor does not want his hands soiled with unsavory deeds. So," Salar Nassim continued, "he will use his means to have others do his dirty work, like he did with your sea captain and the pirates."

"He would hire sellswords and mercenaries for an ambush," Patrik surmised.

"We have seen it before," Soren interjected.

"An ambush would have to overpower you and your escorts," Bem told the baron, "which means your neighbor must organize several armed men. If we could join these assassins and infiltrate their gang, then the odds would be in your favor, Lord Baric. You would outnumber them when we turn against the group during the attack."

"We?" Mauro asked skeptically.

"The baron would not use his own guardsmen that could be easily linked to him. The assassins would be strangers, like us," Salar Nassim assured him.

Patrik reasoned, "There are plenty of strangers that come through these territories looking to earn a quick income to help them on their way. This baron should be able to hire a good-sized group on short notice. They move on quietly after receiving their payment. We've been asked before."

Mauro was stunned at the idea. "You believe it is possible for you to join their group of sellswords? What if Dubovic's men already saw you in Solgrad and know your connection to me?"

"These drifters wouldn't have had a chance to encounter us in your village tavern, and we have been nowhere else during our stay here," Bem concluded.

"Unless your own men are involved," Patrik said ominously.

"I trust all my men," Mauro affirmed. "But it is already Thursday, and he might have already hired his gang of assassins."

Salar Nassim leaned in across the table and looked into the eyes of his own gang members. Each gave their commander a nod.

The Persian turned back to Mauro and said, "The only way for us to know for sure is to ask. Bem and Patrik are the best choices to send for a quick job like this. They can melt into any group of mercenaries."

Patrik suggested, "We should leave right away. Salar Nassim and Soren can meet up with us tomorrow to see if we've succeeded in being hired."

Mauro revealed his worry when he asked, "And if you do not succeed?"

"Then we will have a backup plan," Salar Nassim assured him.

The Persian stood up to leave, and the other three followed him to the door. He told the baron, "Once Bem and Patrik are on their way, you and I can discuss an alternative plan."

Mauro remained seated, staring at the rows of folded parchments on the table.

Salar Nassim looked at the baron with concern and asked, "Are we in agreement, Lord Baric?"

Mauro looked up at him and smiled. "We are in agreement. You said you were at my service, Salar Nassim. This is more than I could have expected in exchange for a few meals."

"That is the difference between mercenaries and soldiers, Lord Baric. We have a choice in who and what we fight for. Sometimes we even care who wins."

Patrik added, "I will always fight to protect my family. You are my family now."

"And we are family too, the four of us. We fight together," maintained Soren.

"Always," said Bem.

Mauro stood up and bowed out of respect for their friendship and their help. "I thank you all," he said.

~*~

Davor shut the front door behind the four men before Mauro called him over.

"Can you ask Cook to put together a sack of supplies for two riders? Nothing fancy, just some bread, cured ham and salted fish, maybe a few apples and a jug of ale."

"Yes, sir. And I told Natalija you wanted to see her, my lord." Davor cocked his head in the direction where the young maid stood in the shadow of the stairs. "She has been waiting, sir."

"Thank you, Davor."

Mauro took a few steps closer to the stairway. "Come here, Natalija."

She came away from her spot by the wall and slowly walked toward the baron.

"Davor was supposed to tell you to come to my study after lunch."

"He did, sir," she answered quietly.

Mauro had not set aside time for his discussion with her this morning. He sighed and said, "Since you are here, we will have our talk now."

Natalija solemnly followed the baron into the study.

"Shut the door, please," he said to her.

She did but remained by the door.

"Sit down," he said kindly.

She did as she was asked and sat down at the table. She had never been in the baron's study and looked around in awe.

Mauro cleared his throat to gain her attention again.

She spoke up before the baron could scold her, "I've tried my best to be a good maid in your house, your lordship. I tried to serve the ladies well, but they were very particular. I am sorry for any mistakes I have made. I will pack my bags right away, sir."

The baron began to smile and shake his head.

"Am I not being let go?" she dared to ask.

"No, Natalija, you have served the ladies and my family well, especially my mother. That is what I wanted to talk to you about. In private."

"Alright, Lord Baric."

His smile faded, and he looked sternly at her again. "There is a serious matter at hand, Natalija, and I need you to answer some questions. It is important that you not repeat our conversation to anyone, do you understand?"

"Yes, my lord," she replied with a matched seriousness.

"I want to talk to you first about my father."

"Oh, I don't think I can be of help, sir. I'd just come here in the summer, and I didn't see your father much. I only attended your mother. She kept me quite busy."

Mauro would start with this, then.

"Did she?" he asked. "What sort of tasks did my mother assign you?"

Natalija began thoughtfully, "Well, some days she was very particular about her attire, and she would try on several gowns before coming down for the day. Then I had to put them all correctly back, although she told me I did it wrong and—"

"Natalija." Mauro interrupted her. He would have to keep the girl focused on what he wanted to learn. "On those particular days that your mistress wanted to look especially well-dressed, did she have visitors?"

"Just the baron, sir. He would meet her on the small terrace, or in the sitting room," she replied.

"Which baron?" Mauro asked gently. "Not my father?"

"No, my lord. Baron Dubovic visited her. He is a very kind gentleman. He is the one who told my father Lady Baric was looking for a new lady's maid and I should apply for the position."

"Lord Dubovic did?" Mauro was surprised at this bit of information.

She perked up and answered, "Yes, he asked my father about us girls when he came to check on his orders. He ordered many supplies from the workshop that summer."

Something didn't make sense to Mauro. "Is there not a tanner closer to Lord Dubovic?"

Natalija nodded and explained, "The Orsino brothers have a tanning workshop in his village, sir. I know that because they are friends with my father and come to our house every so often. My father thinks he is a better tanner, so maybe they could not make what the baron wanted."

"Perhaps you are right," Mauro said to appease her, then continued with his central inquiry.

"Before my father's death, Natalija, did Lord Dubovic visit both my father and my mother?"

Natalija took an audible breath and released it. "That was a while ago, my lord. Let me think . . ."

Mauro patiently waited as she collected her thoughts.

"Not when I was with her, no," she finally said. "Lady Baric would have me wait by the door after I served their tea, and it was always just her ladyship and Lord Dubovic."

Mauro had more questions now than when the maid had first sat down. He asked her calmly, "What did they talk about?"

She shrugged and said, "Oh, I didn't listen in, Lord Baric. I was so nervous about the tea."

"You did see them together. Did they seem to be friends? Like Lady Caterina and I are friends, perhaps?"

"Well, um, it is hard for me to judge, sir."

"It is an easy question, and there is no wrong answer."

"If I think of it that way, well, I would say their friendship was more like Lady Isabella and you together, my lord. It is not that I took any special notice of you with your visitors, but the lady is so beautiful, and I was sometimes drawn to watch her on the terrace. Was that wrong of me, sir?"

"I believe she would not take offense to that, nor do I. But I am curious. What did you find different about Lady Isabella with me compared to Lady Caterina?"

"Well, my lord, she would take your hand or your arm, and you, um . . . you would walk very closely together, sir," she whispered, seemingly ashamed she had noticed their intimacy.

Mauro brushed it off. "Lady Isabella and I are old friends, and old friends walk together that way, Natalija. Did it seem that my mother and Baron Dubovic were also such old friends?" he asked. His outward calmness masked his nervousness to hear her reply.

"They seemed that way. Well, that is until you returned, Lord Baric. Then she would not see him when he called, and she no longer had me bring any letters."

"Letters? She had you post them in the village, instead of giving them to our courier?"

"I didn't post them, sir. I took them directly to the village surgeon at his apothecary."

She bit her lip when she saw the baron was surprised by this news.

"I thought that was strange, too," she quickly added, "and I wondered why her ladyship would write to the surgeon so often. I would pick up letters from him, too, before he moved."

Mauro wanted to know everything now. What to ask first?

"Was this Signor Sandrigo? What was he like? Were they friends?"

"Indeed, Sandrigo was his name, sir. He wasn't very friendly for a chemist, but he must have done a good business since he always seemed to be mixing something when I was there. He had a funny smell to him, and his shop smelled that way, too. Like when you open an old trunk."

"What did he say to you when you brought him a letter?"

"He didn't talk to me at all, sir. He just put it in his apron pocket and sometimes gave me one to take back to her ladyship."

"How did he come to replace Signor Martini?"

"That, I wouldn't know."

Natalija smiled again and added, "Signor Martini was a nice, old man. He would talk to me while mixing his recipes. My mother would send me on her errands to pick up a potion or powder from him when I lived there."

Mauro needed to keep her focused. "Was it Signor Sandrigo who came to heal my father and his officers?"

Natalija bent her head in sadness when recalling the event. "That was a terrible day, Lord Baric."

"I know it is hard for you, but I need to know what happened. Were you there?"

"I had to be there for my mistress, even though her ladyship was in quite a state. Everyone was frightened, really. We all thought it was the plague—many had suffered through that before. Your father and his men had been in agony all day, but her ladyship would not let Idita tend to them. Instead, she prayed over his lordship's bed through the night."

"Were they better after that?"

"I didn't see them, although I remember her ladyship saying they had lived through the night. She gave me a letter after that and told me to take it to the surgeon."

Mauro was afraid to hear the answer to his next question. "Was your mistress happy when she told you they had lived?"

"If I remember right, she looked quite empty, sort of drained of sadness or happiness. But I suppose I would look that way, too, having been up all night praying, sir."

"When you took her message, what did Signor Sandrigo do?"

Natalija answered slowly this time, "I, um . . . I don't know, sir. My mistress gave me leave to stay and visit my family after her errand. I didn't come back to the castle until the next morning, and then I had to help her dress all in black." Her lower lip quivered as she held back a sob.

"I am sorry to upset you, Natalija. Just one more question," he insisted. "Did you ever hear my mother talk of jewels with Lord Dubovic?"

Natalija took the edge of her apron and blotted her wet eyes while she pondered his unusual question. She sniffled and asked, "Like necklaces and rings, my lord?"

"Yes," he said encouragingly.

She wrung her hands as she thought hard to come up with an answer for the baron.

"I don't remember anything specific, my lord. The baroness did like to wear jewelry when Lord Dubovic visited, and he would compliment her, like gentlemen do, saying pretty words to praise her appearance. Is that what you meant, sir?"

Mauro nodded with relief. "That is exactly what I meant. Thank you, Natalija."

She sat taller in her chair after his praise.

"Before you go, I would like to reward you for your help. Is there something you would like? Perhaps a day off to visit your family?"

Mauro patiently waited as she considered his offer. Then an odd look of excitement grew on her young face.

"There is one thing that comes to mind, sir."

When she hesitated, Mauro prompted, "What is your request?"

"I hope you will not think it improper, sir, but seeing Soren leave your study just a while ago made me remember that he was going to tell me of his sailing adventures."

"Ah, yes. He will be leaving for good soon, did you know that?"

"I did hear that, my lord, which makes it all the more urgent to have your permission to meet with him, and maybe Marija too, and listen to his stories. We could sit on a bench near the fountain. That would be quite proper, wouldn't it, Lord Baric?"

She looked at him hopefully as he quickly made his decision.

"To make it even more proper, I will ask my wife to invite him this afternoon for tea with you and your sister. But do not tell Marija until I have talked to Soren since I am not sure of his plans today. The baroness will come get you if it all works out. How does that sound?"

Her expression lit up. "Wonderful. Thank you, Lord Baric."

She stood up and curtsied, and Mauro went to open the door for her.

"Remember, you are not to talk about why I asked to see you today."

"Yes, sir," she said, nodding nervously.

"But if you think of anything else about my mother's visitor, then come to me right away."

"I will, sir." Natalija curtsied a second time and then hurried down the corridor.

Davor was near the staircase holding a twill bag.

Mauro noticed it in his hand and asked, "Is that from Cook? I will take it to Patrik myself."

Davor handed him the sack and informed him, "Your muskets have just arrived, my lord. They were delivered to the armory while you were in your study, sir."

With all that had transpired in the last two days, Mauro had forgotten the shipment was coming. It also meant Jero had succeeded with the purchase. Even better, he had stayed on in Zadar.

"Excellent, I will check on the weapons myself."

Mauro looked in the food bag before going out the door. He took out the many little pastries and handed them back to Davor.

Davor held them precariously and explained to his master, "Cook was adamant that she could not let you eat only dry goods, sir."

"She is right," Mauro said with a chuckle, "but the food isn't for me, Davor. Patrik and Bem are leaving shortly, and it is for them on the road."

"Shouldn't Lady Ruby be going with them, sir?" Davor asked boldly.

"They have an errand to take care of first. They will be back in a few days to get her," Mauro divulged.

Davor nodded and walked back to the kitchen with his hands full of the little cakes.

Back in his study, Mauro hastily penned instructions for Patrick and Bem. His stomach growled, and he regretted not keeping one of the sugary pastries.

~*~

The crates of muskets had been unloaded, and the delivery men were heading back out the gate with their donkey cart when Mauro arrived at the armory. Two of his soldiers pried open the long crates, and Mauro leaned in to look over their shoulders.

As he did, he heard Patrik say, "We will be leaving now, Mauro."

Mauro gasped with surprise when he looked up. "What have you done to yourself?"

Patrik said, "I will take that as a compliment."

Mauro waved his two guards out. "Denis, Henrik. You can unpack these later."

The two soldiers put the muskets down and went out into the sunshine. Patrik and Mauro were alone in the diffused light of the armory.

"Let me have a look," Mauro said, walking around his brother-in-law.

Patrik was indeed a changed man from an hour ago. Soren had helped him cut his neatly trimmed beard to look as if it had been shaved without a looking glass. He had smoothed his hair with ash and grooming oil to make it straight and dark, then had bound it tightly with a thick leather cord. Lastly, Patrik had rolled in the hay in one of the stalls to soil his newly washed clothes.

"We need to look like we have been on the road for weeks. We are taking all of our gear with us, too."

"You smell like a horse, Patrik."

"That is the idea! How else to hide that we have been living in a baron's private chamber with running water and laundry service," Patrik said with a laugh. Then he finally noticed what Mauro was holding. "What do you have there?"

Mauro handed him the musket. "They are French."

Patrik gave a low whistle. "Beautiful."

"They are indeed. But what matters more is that they shoot straight."

Mauro held one up high and examined its aim. "I will show you how it is loaded and fired when you are back," Mauro promised.

"I'd like to try it."

Patrik handed the hefty weapon back to Mauro, who instead took hold of his hand.

"Your hands are too clean, Patrik."

Patrik examined his fingers as he had just examined the musket. "Shit, you are right. Your endless hot water gets a man too clean for his own good!"

To remedy that, the Greek looked around the neatly swept pavers of the armory for a seam of damp muck. He found some packed mud along the wall and began rubbing it under his nails. As he did, Patrik asked, "What is that pit for? Is it the kind of dungeon my father was locked in?"

Mauro joined him by the bar-covered hole in the floor of the armory.

"Has your father never talked about it?" Mauro asked cautiously.

"No."

"Well, he would have had a small room with a door, maybe with a window in it. The Toth's dungeon is completely underground. It would have been damp and dark, not pleasant like this."

Patrik looked down into the dirty hole with the bars over it. "This is pleasant?"

Mauro chuckled. "It is dry and light, at least," he said. "My soldiers walk by often, so you would not be neglected. You could yell obscenities up at them, and they would have to notice you."

"I am curious," Patrik said. "What criminals have been locked in this pit?"

Mauro replied, laughing, "I was probably the last one locked in this cell."

"You? What crime did you commit?" Patrik asked with a mischievous smile.

"My only crime then was being a little brother."

"I forgot you had a brother," Patrik said kindly.

Mauro was getting better at talking about Mateo and did not lose his sense of humor over it.

"Mateo liked to play pranks on me when I was young and gullible. This one time, he had convinced me to climb down inside the holding pit with him to see what it would be like to be a prisoner." Mauro chuckled at the memory and explained, "When we were both down there, Mateo quickly climbed out and pulled the ladder up after him."

"You said your guardsmen walk by often. How long did you spend in there?"

"In my case, I was out of luck, and Mateo knew it! You see, my father and most of his soldiers had ridden off the day before, and there was no reason for anyone else to come into the armory. When I did not show up for bedtime, Idita had the servants search the grounds for me, but no one thought to look in the pit until the next morning. It was a very long night for a little boy."

"What did your brother say in his defense?" asked Patrik with sincere interest.

"He found a way to blame it on Jero, I think! Poor Jero was always getting blamed for Mateo's follies."

Patrik seemed surprised and asked, "Jero lived with you when you were boys?"

"We grew up together," Mauro said. "He has been a servant here since he was a child, but was mostly a playmate for us until he was old enough to learn a job."

"Why didn't your brother like him?"

Mauro's expression lit up at the memory. "Mateo loved Jero. I am sure of that."

"But he blamed Jero for the mischief he caused."

Mauro explained, "It was in good fun. Everything Mateo did was meant to be amusing, and I think Jero forgave him for it. It was hard to stay angry at Mateo."

Patrik gave his new relation a long steady look. "I mean no offense, Mauro, but it is hard to believe you two were brothers. I mean, you don't come across as being so carefree."

Mauro laughed at Patrik's comment, despite the insult. "In our case, we were only half-brothers. His mother died quite young, and my father married my mother."

"Ah, that makes sense, then," Patrik said lightly.

Mauro thought it made sense, too. He had always thought Mateo's mother would have been a better one than his own. He heard himself saying, "My mother died just before Resi and I married."

Patrik nodded, knowing this, and then asked, "And Mateo? When did he die?"

Mauro took a deep breath and answered, "It was a long time ago. I was twelve, and he was fifteen."

"There you are, Patrik! Are you ready?"

Bem had come through the open armory doors with his boisterous interruption. He had also transformed his look to be plain and road-weary.

"Let me see your hands first," Patrik said to his friend.

Bem showed him that they were dirty again, even under the nails.

"Impressive," Patrik told his friend with a wink.

Mauro handed Bem the bag of provisions he had left by the door. "This is for you."

Bem examined the meager offerings inside. "It looks delicious," he said, chuckling.

"It is not meant to be a feast, merely something to have on your saddle, in case anyone snoops around your things. Do you have lire for lodgings and proper meals?"

Bem grinned and replied, "Thanks to your men, we have plenty of lire from our winnings."

All business again, Mauro pulled a folded parchment from his pocket and explained, "Here are the names of three inns and how to find them. The first on the list is probably your best bet."

Patrik read over the instructions and then put the parchment into his jacket pocket. "We will visit all of them, just in case."

"You do not have to do this for me," Mauro said earnestly.

Patrik was more cheerful than his brother-in-law when he said, "We don't mind, Mauro. We haven't had an adventure in a while. It will be fun to plot your murder."

"Be careful and do not get yourselves killed."

Bem stepped up. "Don't worry about us, Lord Baric. I trust Salar Nassim's plan. We will catch the man in his treachery, and you will watch him hang for his crimes soon enough."

Patrik added, "The plan is solid. Milan told us of a good meeting spot to check in with Nassim. He seems to know Dubovic's territory as well as your own. Did you know that?"

"I was told Milan was my father's best scout in his day. I trust that he gave you the right information for the right reason."

They left the cool enclosure of the armory and walked out into the sweltering midday sun.

Salar Nassim and Soren had brought the men's horses and handed off the reins. "We will meet you tomorrow. Be on time," Nassim said with a smile.

"Don't get too drunk and blow your cover," Soren warned Patrik with a friendly pat on the back.

"You do your part, and we will do ours," Patrik teased.

With that, Bem and Patrik mounted their horses and rode out the Baric gate.

Mauro had not told his soldiers of Bem and Patrik's undertaking, and the gatekeepers watched the two with curiosity as they left the compound with all their gear and bedrolls.

"Shall we finish going over the rest of the plans?" Salar Nassim asked the baron.

"Gladly, but there is one thing I need to organize first, and it has to do with Soren." Mauro held back his grin, finding the entire offer amusing.

"What can I help you with, Lord Baric?"

"My wife has invited you to tea, Soren. She wants you to share a few stories about your adventures as a sailor."

Soren looked stunned. "Tea with Terese?"

Salar Nassim cocked his head and said, "That is an invitation you should not pass up, Soren."

Mauro clarified, "Natalija told my wife you missed your storytelling opportunity before. Would you like to join Terese, Natalija, and her sister this afternoon on the terrace? Tea is optional."

"Well, Lord Baric, I told Natalija I would share my adventures with her. With your permission, I will make good on my promise. I thank Terese for her invitation."

"Good, I will tell the ladies to expect you. Perhaps during that same time, Salar Nassim and I could work out our alternative plan."

"Excellent. Send Tin for us when you are ready," Salar Nassim replied, and the two went back to the Keep.

With the morning matters settled, Mauro realized he was famished and went to see if there were still more pastries in the kitchen.

Chapter 56

In the three hours that passed between Mauro telling his wife that Soren was to come to tea and Soren's arrival, the news spread among the female house servants that the baroness had invited Natalija and Marija to sit with the handsome Dane.

Resi had, of course, invited Ruby to join them as well. Verica had no specific tasks that afternoon, and Resi had asked if she wanted to listen in, too. Verica had mentioned it to the other maids in the kitchen, and one by one, they asked the baroness if they might be allowed to hear the Dane's stories.

~*~

Resi and Ruby were sitting on the long sofa when Davor brought Soren into the sitting room.

Soren was relieved when he saw just these two women were there.

"Good afternoon, Terese. Hello, Ruby. I thought Natalija and her sister were joining us," he said, puzzled.

"They are," Resi told him sweetly. "The table has been set for us in the great hall. Shall we go over there?"

Soren agreed, not noticing the nervous glances Ruby and Resi exchanged.

Ruby opened the great hall door, and one could hear the chatter of many feminine voices coming from the large room.

Soren froze in panic at the entrance.

Resi turned to him and said encouragingly, "I am sorry to put you on the spot like this, Soren, but everyone loves to hear a good adventure story, especially when it is real. If you want to leave, I will understand."

He wanted to tell Terese he had changed his mind, but then he saw the crowd of young faces turn toward them at the door. They were smiling at him, welcoming him in. He was no longer the feared soldier. These women considered him their champion, not a threat.

Soren took a step forward and said, "I hope I will not disappoint the girls."

Resi linked his arm with hers. "I will show you where you can sit."

The maids were already seated. For this rare treat of joining their mistress, they had put on clean aprons and repinned their hair under their starched caps to look pretty for the foreign man. Plates of sliced cake and dishes of candied nuts and dried figs had been set out near two pots of tea.

Resi took the lead and poured the tea for Soren. The porcelain cup and saucer looked like a child's version in his large hands when he took it. Natalija was there with her sister, Marija, and Soren nodded to her with a smile as he settled in.

When everyone had been served their tea, Soren looked toward Natalija and asked, "Where should I start?"

She eagerly took his cue. "I was wondering about something you told me before, Soren." She paused to enjoy her friends' shocked expressions when she addressed him so informally. "If you are Danish," Natalija continued, "why did you sail on a Dutch ship? Or is that the same?"

He was grateful for her easy question to start his story. "It is not the same. The Danes are great seamen of the North, but the Dutch are great explorers to the far reaches of the oceans. My brother and I wanted an adventure, so we joined a trading ship that was to sail to the end of the world."

"How far is it to the end of the world, sir?" Marija asked timidly.

"The world actually has no end," Soren revealed.

The girls' stunned gasps and quick chatter seemed to say they did not believe him.

Soren explained, "If you keep sailing across the Atlantic Ocean, you will eventually meet up with new land. But if you go around that coastline and back into open water, you can sail all the way back to where you started. You need to know how the winds and weather work to get back, though, and the captain has maps to guide him."

The next inquisitor was Franja. "Where did your ship finally stop?"

"At a place called the West Indies. We had to cross a body of water so vast, that we did not see land for almost two months."

"You were on a ship for two months, sir?" Ivana asked in awe.

"We were on the ship longer than that. We first went to Africa," Soren told her, now becoming comfortable surrounded by the eager, feminine audience. "Three ships started the crossing together. My brother and I were on the one that carried a wealthy Dutch lord and his family. Our cargo hold was filled with furnishings and supplies he needed for his new home. The other two ships were filled with slaves."

"What did you need slaves for on the ocean?" Brigita wondered out loud.

"They brought some to work on the nobleman's new estate, and some would be sold to other landholders when we arrived at our destination. Many men are needed to work the fields in the New World. On these islands, they grow tobacco and miles of sugarcane, as far as the eye can see."

Louisa giggled to her friends. "Miles of sugar? That sounds delicious."

Soren overheard her comment and said, "It would be, but sugar cannot be eaten in the fields. It has to first be gleaned from the stalks, the way rye grains are beaten from their stalks to grind into flour. It takes shiploads of men to do all of that. They found those men in Africa, and they took them with us."

"What did you do for months on a ship, sir?" Verica ventured to ask.

"Well, for one thing, we had to keep her moving toward our destination. The captain and his first mate would constantly consult their maps and the stars. Being on an ocean isn't like looking out onto the Adriatic and seeing the islands on the horizon. There is nothing but waves and water for weeks at a time, and you can get stuck drifting if the wind stops or a storm blows you off course. We heard stories of ships that were torn apart by unimaginable waves and winds, and the sailors were never seen again."

"That sounds frightening. Were you ever afraid, Soren?" Natalija asked.

Around the table, the impressionable maids shook their heads with doubt the giant man could ever be afraid.

Soren smiled to himself and admitted to them, "I was, once or twice, like the time our captain expected to come to the island any day, and then those days turned into weeks. I did become afraid that we would never get to our destination."

"And did you, sir?" Louisa asked eagerly.

"Of course, he did," Brigita scolded, "or he would not be here to talk to us."

The girls all giggled in unison to concur.

"What sorts of people live in the New World, Soren?" Ruby asked next.

Soren thought for a moment. "The same as here, actually," he told her. "Sadly, most of the natives were killed by plagues that the first Spaniards brought to their world. The people on the islands now are from England, France, Holland, and Spain. And, of course, black men from West Africa work the farms that they call sugar plantations."

"Did you make sugar when you got there?" Louisa was curious to know.

Soren shook his head. "My brother and I worked on the ships at the port. Most ships arrived damaged in some way after the rough voyage," he explained to his captivated audience. "It takes many men and several weeks to repair a mast and mend the riggings and supports. Some masts are as tall as your baron's tower, and their many sails can push a ship at breathtaking speeds. Once, when we had finished repairing a ship for a French company, we helped them sail her to the next island. That short trip was harder to navigate than crossing the ocean because the route was lined with sharp coral."

The girls were impressed with his story about ships and sails, but Ranka wondered, "What is coral, sir?"

"Ah, well, coral is a sort of endless mass of underwater branches that grow together to make reefs as hard as rock and as sharp as an axe. Coral is of all colors imaginable, but its beauty brings danger. Since the water is so shallow everywhere there, you can never be sure if your ship will clear a coral reef. And if she doesn't, the reef can rip a hole in your planks and sink her."

"That does not sound like a nice place, sir," Brigita said. "I'm glad we don't have coral around our islands."

Soren reasoned, "Sailors here have had hundreds of years to map a course around your rocky islands. The West Indies is new and different from what sailors are used to navigating. The islands are mostly made of sand—sand so white you could image it might be snow. In Denmark, where I am from, there are great sandy shores, but nothing like the hot beaches that encircle the islands. Where there is no beach, there are rocky cliffs dotted with caves and sandy coves. Pirates like to use these hidden places to store their stolen goods."

The baroness had once read the maids a story about pirates. Natalija asked with excitement, "Did you meet any pirates, Soren?"

He chuckled and said, "Pirates look very much like other sailors when they are in the tavern, so I suppose I did. Despite the isolation of the West Indies, most islands have a busy port town with merchants and shops."

"Just like here," Marija interjected.

"Do they talk differently?" asked Natalija.

"Sometimes," Soren replied. "Some islands belong to the British, others to the Spanish or French. The Dutch have their islands, too. They are always fighting each other over who gets which."

Ivana leaned in and shyly asked, "How long did you stay in the New World, sir?"

"To be honest, I lost track of time while I was there. There are no winters to mark the change of the year. When we returned home, it was two years later," Soren told the group.

"Two years?" Verica repeated in surprise.

"We had a sense that it was time to go home, so we joined the crew of a merchant ship bringing tobacco back to Europe. We sailed directly to Marseille, which is a big port in the Kingdom of France. From there, my brother and I were hired on with a crew trading in the Mediterranean. We left that ship in Athens. That is where we met Salai Nassim."

"Where is your brother now?" Louisa asked.

Soren glanced over to Resi. He wanted someone else to talk for a while.

The baroness seemed to understand because she answered for him, "Soren lost his brother in a battle last year, Louisa."

"Was he older or younger than you?" Marija asked meekly.

Resi replied, "Soren and Niels were twins."

Their reaction was immediate. Adult twins were not common in those days after the prolonged war. The room resonated with the sounds of stiff skirts shifting and girls whispering to each other about how wonderful it would have been to see two Sorens.

"Did you look exactly alike, sir?" Ivana asked.

"We didn't think so," Soren replied. Then he turned to the baroness and asked, "You met Niels, Terese. Did we look just the same?"

Resi cocked her head and recalled, "There were a few differences in your personalities, and Niels talked quite a lot. Aside from that, I honestly could not tell the two of you apart." Resi then looked him over and said teasingly, "Except, well, perhaps Niels was a bit taller and maybe broader in the shoulders, wouldn't you say, Soren?"

Soren laughed, knowing Niels would have teased him just the same. "I wouldn't agree with that."

"Who was older?" Louisa wanted to know.

Ranka scoffed at her question. "Don't be silly, Louisa," she said. "Her ladyship said they were twins, remember?"

Louisa bowed her head and mumbled, "I forgot."

"One twin does have to be born first," Soren corrected Ranka. "My mother said Niels was first, and he always let it be known that he was my older brother."

"You must miss him, sir. Did you cry when he died?" Marija asked.

Natalija spoke up, "My little sister was mistakenly thinking that a man would cry as easily as she would."

The older maids shot Marija scolding looks for daring to ask such a question. Despite the reprimand, their questioning eyes turned back to Soren.

He thought quickly about what he might add. It was an innocent question from an innocent girl, and Soren decided she deserved to know the truth about losing a beloved brother.

"Well, Marija, my friend Patrik told me I cried when Niels died, but I don't remember doing that. I only remember being angry that he had left me. He died in October, just before an early winter set in. I cursed my brother that he had escaped our misery as we made our way through the bitter cold. At some point, though, I realized that Niels would have wanted to be with us and give us his warmth. I think that was when it finally became real to me, that Niels was truly dead and gone. I know I wept for him then."

The room was silent, but Soren was calm and at ease, finally saying the words out loud.

"Let me offer you some more tea, Soren," Resi said in an unsteady voice. Tears leaked from the corners of her eyes. Others dabbed their tears with their aprons.

"Um, Soren," Natalija said and sniffled, "are all the men where you come from so tall and fair?"

The room pulsated with nervous relief at her unusual question.

Even Soren found her question humorous and chuckled. "To be honest, I've never thought about it, Natalija. Many Danes do have golden hair, especially the children, although some have brown hair and dark eyes, like Southerners do. My father was tall and blond, and my mother too, so I guess I resemble them."

"Will you return to your home in the North?" Verica asked Soren.

"I do not expect I will, no. Instead, I think I would like to sail again to the West Indies," he admitted.

"Why would you go back across the ocean, sir, if the trip is so perilous?" asked Ranka.

"Because crossing the ocean is no more dangerous than anything else I have done. We will all die one day, and until then, we must live our lives," he said. He believed his own words this time.

Glancing over, Soren noticed that Salar Nassim and the baron were standing at the doorway to the great hall. He nodded to them.

Mauro walked in and interrupted the spell Soren had cast over the maids. "You have quite the enamored audience, Soren, but Nela will need their help in the kitchen soon. Girls, you may thank our guest for his stories."

There was a hum of mumbled thanks and curtsies in Soren's direction before the maids hastily filed out of the great hall through the servants' door in the back.

Resi and Ruby were still at the table with Soren.

Mauro walked over and kissed his wife on her cheek. He squeezed her hand to show his approval of her little tea party.

"Will you be at dinner tonight?" Resi asked quietly, looking up at him.

Mauro would disappoint her. "I have some important business to discuss with my captains, and I can do that best over a quick dinner in the Keep. I will see you after that." He released her hand and began to walk away.

"Lord Baric," Ruby blurted out, "where has Patrik gone to?"

Soren and Salar Nassim were already at the door. They stopped and looked to the baron for his answer.

A strained smile was on Mauro's lips when he said, "Why do you ask?"

"I saw them leave from my window. Their saddles were fully packed." Ruby held Mauro's stare and asked, "Why has Patrik left without me, Lord Baric?"

Mauro walked the few steps back to the table. "He has not left. Patrik volunteered to do an errand for me, and for that he needed his equipment."

Resi stood up to protest this news Mauro had been hiding.

Mauro told his wife directly, "He and Bem rode north on a quick errand. They will return with me when I come back from the council meeting on Saturday. That is all you need to know."

"That is all?" Resi repeated. "I doubt that."

Mauro met the challenge in her eyes, and then his features softened. "Your brother is doing me a favor, one that I could not ask of my own men. I assure you, Resi, he will be back on Saturday."

Ruby seemed to accept the baron's feeble explanation and did not insist on asking anything more. "Thank you, Lord Baric," she said, then hooked her arm in Resi's to make her leave with her. Ruby led her to the door, where Soren and Salar Nassim were waiting.

Resi stopped to thank Soren. Her smile was back when she said, "Thank you for being so generous to the maids. It was a real pleasure for us, you sharing your stories today, Soren."

"Thank you for inviting me, Terese," he replied with a bow, confident that he had gained much more from the storytelling than they had.

Chapter 57

Patrik and Bem paid for their lodging at the tavern in the first town they came to. Then, they rode on and took another room in the next village to the north. They spent time there, looking the inn's clientele over, and then rode on to the third place on Mauro's list.

Each village was less than an hour apart from the other, but they noticed a distinct difference in the second one. That is where the mercenaries decided to spend their afternoon and take a chance asking the fellow lodgers if they knew of anyone hiring for a quick job they could do.

~*~

Bem and Patrik worked the room, talking to anyone who would listen.

"Yeah, we need enough in our purse to make it to Prague and back again before winter," Patrik told the barkeeper, who was refilling his mug.

"Is that where you are from? Prague?" the old barman asked suspiciously.

Patrik laid the story on thick. "No, but I left my partner there. He was wounded and couldn't make the journey with me. I had to come get my friend here, but he has no money, either." He pointed over to Bem, who was at a table with two other men, playing a friendly game of dice. "Times are tough for mercenaries, now that they have called a truce."

Another man at the bar dragged his mug of ale along the counter and came to Patrik's side.

"So, you are a mercenary soldier, huh?" the stranger asked. "Killed lots of men, have you?" The stranger winked at the barkeeper, who chuckled in return.

"Who hasn't killed men? We just finished a fucking war, you idiot," Patrik practically shouted, then took a swig of his drink.

The men sitting at the two tables nearest the bar turned to glare at the commotion.

The stranger put his arm around Patrik's shoulder. "Hey, you don't have to get hostile, friend. Maybe I can help you." He looked over at the locals, who were still watching them at the bar, and lowered his voice when he asked, "How long are you here for?"

Patrik let the stinking man keep him close and played his part. "We don't plan to stay. We hate these Venetians. They patrol like they own the place," he complained quietly to his new friend.

The stranger laughed loudly as he told him, "They do own the place! We Croats just work for them."

Patrik hoped he wasn't wasting his time with this one drunken man, so he made sure his voice carried around the room again. "The best part about fighting is killing those stuck-up noblemen who think they rule the whole fucking world."

The stranger looked at the barkeeper and rocked on his stool, nodding his agreement.

He asked Patrik, "Are you and your friend staying here tonight?"

Patrik downed the last of his ale and answered with a shrug, "We rented a room. Why?"

"I will find you in the morning if I have more to say to you," he declared. Then the stranger slapped him on the back like an old buddy and rose from his perch at the bar.

"Yeah, sure," replied Patrik, sounding like it didn't matter, "see you around."

After the stranger left, Bem and Patrik saddled their horses and rode to the first and third taverns again. They tried to strike up interest with the same theatrics they had used earlier but had no success. They decided they would sleep at the second place, after all, and hoped for the right offer in the morning.

~ * ~

It had been another long, tedious day. Mauro met with his remaining officers and the mercenaries at the Keep's second-floor conference table. There they could talk confidentially. Mauro wanted his guardsmen to go on with their plans to attend the village party with the other Baric residents. They decided that Daniel would go tomorrow with Soren and Salar Nassim to the rendezvous spot with Patrik to learn whether he and Bem had been hired to kill Baron Baric. Mauro, Eduard, Simeon, and Vilim would play out the charade and ride to Dubovic Castle on Saturday morning. Either way, those five going ahead would protect the four riding to the council meeting.

When all the possible scenarios had been discussed, Mauro adjourned their meeting and went back to the quiet manor house. He began to climb the stairs but then changed his mind. He had caught Resi off guard earlier with the news that her brother had left until Saturday, and Mauro knew he needed to make that right with her. Still, there was one piece of unfinished business that plagued him.

Mauro stopped on the landing, making up his mind. He would go to Resi and explain it all after this last burden was behind him.

~*~

The foyer sconces glowed, and Mauro lit a candlestick from their flame and unlocked the study door. It was cooling off outside, but the air in the room was stale and stuffy.

Mauro opened the windows to let in the Adriatic breeze. Then he lit more candles and took one to the fireplace. The details of his mother's life were in neat piles on the table, and he would finally put her life to rest tonight.

Mauro started at the beginning of the rows and burned the papers one by one, the sealing wax on them sputtering and crackling in the hearth. He watched each ignite as though in a trance. When there was no trace left, he took the next stack of papers and did the same, one after the other.

Finally, Mauro came to the last pile of letters he had not found the courage to look at. What did it matter? Reading them would not bring him peace.

He held one over the flame but then set it down again. His hand shook. He must know the whole story until the last word, he decided right then. It might not bring him peace, but there would be an end to it.

Mauro opened the parchment he had just held over the fire. The broken seal did not give its sender away. It was merely a smear of wax to keep the message closed.

Determined now, Mauro returned to the nearly bare table and unfolded the remaining eight notes, finding their order and reading each word. A chill ran over him despite the muggy heat of the stagnant chamber.

They read:

My dearest, I will be away a fortnight. Upon my return, I will send for you. Yours in love, S.

Lovely Johanna, the plan will work and the estate will come to you. The boy will not suffer. It is better this way. Yours always, S.

My love, how I long to be with you again. The task is now in your hands. Come to me when you are done. Tenderly, S.

My darling! You were charming tonight as usual. No one suspects. Enclosed is the powder for his drink. Use it all to be sure. Send word. Your loving S.

Johanna, the boy stands in the way. Can you not see that? The powder will work for him. Do not fail me. In devotion, S.

I saw your son riding today. What is the delay, my darling? I will set up a different plan, so do not worry yourself. Your faithful S.

Johanna, my love, why would you change your mind? I will find a reason to send him away. We can let him live. Marry me, Johanna. It is what we have been wanting. Truly yours in love, S.

Johanna, I came to call on you today. They said you were ill and could not receive visitors. I will call again at the end of the week, and we can make our announcement. With loving admiration, S.

Mauro shook his head in disbelief. There it was. His mother was tormented in the end, but not by his father. Another man was to blame, and Mauro would get his revenge for both parents.

"Well, *S*, you fucking bastard," Mauro said to the empty room as he burned the first of the final notes. "My mother loved me more than you thought and loved you far less. We have a plan for you, too, Sebastian Dubovic."

The blue flames mesmerized him as Mauro dropped each parchment into the small fire. He wanted nothing more than for their wretched history to turn to ash so there would be nothing to remind him of his mother's breakdown.

When the fire flickered out, Mauro shut the grate, then the windows. Finally, he locked the door behind him. He was as empty as the table now, but he knew who could fill him.

He shuffled heavy-footed up the stairs and down the dark hall. Verica had left her door open for a chance at a breeze in the warm night. Mauro tiptoed past and closed his own door behind him with care. He did not wash or change or blow out his single candle. He slid into bed next to his sleeping wife and the child she carried. He said a rare prayer to God to keep his family safe from harm and then fell asleep, holding them tightly.

Chapter 58

It was daybreak. The baroness was still deep in her dreams when Verica came into her room to put away the clean garments she had retrieved from the laundry maids. The maid draped the silky fabric of one of the robes against her. She had once thought this type of dress impractical, with so many layers held together with sashes and ties, but Verica now admired the way her mistress could combine colors and textures to make her outfits new and beautiful.

Verica wished she could also don loose, flowing frocks on hot summer days such as these. She did not wear a corset, but it had begun to feel that way. Verica had blossomed since her uniform had been sewn earlier that year, and heavy fabric clung to her ribs in the humidity. With all that was going on, she dared not ask for a new dress for herself.

Standing in front of the looking glass, the maid was tugging at her bodice when she noticed the baroness's reflection looking back at her from the bed.

"Is your dress too tight, Verica? You aren't pregnant, too, are you?" Resi teased her. "How is Luka, anyway?"

Verica blushed when she admitted, "I have not even kissed Luka, my lady. Besides, Natalija thinks he is sweet on a village girl now." Feeling more miserable, Verica went back to her task of hanging the tunics in the wardrobe.

Resi saw the hurt look on her face. "You are far prettier than any village girl, Verica, and smarter, too. You can woo him back at the party."

"I don't know about that, Lady Baric. A village girl is easier to court for a village boy than a girl living at the castle."

"Are you so eager to court the village boys? I think of you as being too young to look at them that way. You are only sixteen."

Verica corrected her meekly, "I will be seventeen in November, my lady."

Resi studied her lady's maid as she went about her chore. "Maybe you will meet someone at the castle you like. One day, I expect to lose you to one of them."

"It will not be any time soon, my lady," Verica chirped back and then changed the subject. "What would you like to wear today, Lady Baric?"

The baroness did not try to cover her unhappiness like her servant had done. "I suppose it doesn't matter. I may not even leave my room today. There is no one to visit with."

"Lady Ruby is here. The baron is here," Verica said encouragingly.

"Is the baron here?"

Resi looked over at the pillow next to her. Someone had definitely slept there. The riding boots her husband had worn yesterday were in the corner, and his favorite shoes were gone. He had been here during the night—for a short time at least.

"I saw him myself this morning," Verica reported. "He was leaving to work with his men, something about some new weapons."

Resi threw up her hands. "Weapons, weapons, I am tired of all this fighting and plotting for more war. Can he not have a day without muskets and swords?" she moaned in self-pity. She pushed off the coverlet and got out of bed.

"I think war and fighting are his lordship's fate as a nobleman," Verica politely reminded her mistress.

"I am glad for your optimism, Verica," Resi told her. She went to the open window and leaned out. "The sun is already hot. I think I will take my bath now instead of this afternoon," she declared.

The baroness turned back to Verica with a smile and said, "You can bathe with me, if you like, and then you will be fresh and pretty to steal your Luka back tomorrow."

~ * ~

After their meeting last night, Vilim was skeptical of Mauro's farfetched plan. He told him so as they rode back together from the shooting fields.

"If Dubovic is indeed holding council, Mauro, then there will be other noblemen with their entourages taking that same route. No one will ambush us along the way. It is too well traveled and there would be too many witnesses," Vilim asserted.

"And I agreed with you, Vilim, but that other spot Milan spoke of—who would be coming and going along that stretch of road without an invitation? What if I am the only one invited?"

Vilim frowned in disagreement. He could not be convinced the old baron wanted Mauro dead. "Again, why would the baron ride all the way here to announce that the lords had agreed to the change? And in front of witnesses! There is no conspiracy here, Mauro."

"I told you already, Vilim. He wanted to have witnesses. And he needs a legitimate excuse for me to come."

Vilim did not know all that Mauro knew, and the neighbor's scheme still seemed all too clear. "He will host the council meeting, but perhaps the others have agreed to a different day," Mauro reasoned. "Dates get copied incorrectly all too often."

The horses trotted along side by side; the soldiers riding behind them were consumed in their own private conversations.

Vilim looked over at his troubled cousin and suggested, "You could send a courier and ask to confirm the date, and then Dubovic will have to come clean and answer correctly. That would solve all your worries."

Mauro stared ahead, sure of one thing: "I do not want him to come clean, Vilim. I want to snare him, to catch him at his own game."

"At least notify the authorities of your suspicion."

"What would I tell the Venetian authorities? If *you* think I am paranoid, so will they."

Vilim uncomfortably shifted on his saddle. He could not shake the thought that Mauro's suspicion had truly come from a place of paranoia.

"But if I have solid proof," Mauro continued to explain, "I can safely expose him. I cannot live my life looking over my shoulder, Vilim."

"I will gladly be at your side tomorrow," Vilim assured his cousin. "Still, I suspect you will be disappointed when we are *not* attacked along his castle road. We will either meet with a crowd of stuffy aristocrats for an afternoon of quibbling, or we will be turned away at the gate and then get roaring drunk at Radic's expense."

"At my expense, Vilim," Mauro reminded him with a chuckle.

Their horses packed together with their fellow soldiers as they approached the gate.

Mauro said in a hushed voice, "Promise me you will not question my theory any longer. My head is full of doubts already, Vilim, but I must do what feels right."

"I promise, Mauro. And whatever happens, your plan is indeed solid. I cannot imagine what could go wrong."

~ * ~

Bem and Patrik ate their breakfast in silence in the alehouse's dining room, keeping their heads low to show little interest in their surroundings, like men who plan to move on do.

A man with greasy, combed-over hair sat down at their table. "Are you the two going to Prague?" he inquired gruffly.

"Who are you?" Bem asked, being just as unfriendly as the stranger.

The greasy man glared at Bem and said, "I asked you a question."

"So did I." Bem held his inhospitable stare.

The man growled, "Buy me a drink."

Patrik was unflustered by the intruder. Wordlessly, he got up and went to the bar. He came back a minute later with a mug of ale and set it down in front of the stranger with a slosh.

Bem still stared at the man, playing a game of nerves. Bem seemed to be winning.

The man took a gulp from the mug, then said coolly, "I have room for two more in my gang."

"We don't want to join a gang," Patrik told him, appearing unimpressed with the offer. "We need to be on our way by Sunday."

"It is only a one-day job. It is better that you are on your way after it is done."

Bem sneered as he said, "Why us?"

The recruiter ignored Bem and told Patrik, "I hear you don't mind killing noblemen."

"News travels fast in a small place. Yeah, it is no loss to us. What kind of killing?"

"An ambush," the recruiter said. "The target travels with a small escort of two or three."

Patrik had been studying the man. His person was dirty and smelled foul, but his clothes were mended and orderly. He had the look of someone regularly employed. His was the job they wanted.

Bem and Patrik exchanged glances across the table.

"Day or night?" Bem asked, continuing with his menacing composure.

"Day." The man matched Bem's monotone.

"Three riders to hit?" Patrik repeated.

"They will be traveling along our landlord's castle road tomorrow near noon. The gang will jump them there. The job is to kill all of them. They must all go down."

Patrik asked the obvious question, "What about your lord's own Guard? Won't they be patrolling the road?"

The stranger took another drink and shook his head. "They will not be watching the road."

"So your lord is paying?" Bem asked.

The man sneered. "Does it matter?"

"No," Patrik replied. He took a swig of his drink and asked, "How much? We want to be paid up front."

The landlord's man scratched his stubble, considering their value to him. "Two gold coins total. I will pay you half when we meet, and the other half when the baron is dead."

Patrik made it known he was interested, but Bem played his role and icily asked, "A baron, huh? How many are in this gang of yours?"

This time, the recruiter answered Bem directly, "Enough to do the job. You and your partner make seven."

"Swords or pistols?" Patrik wanted to know.

"Swords. Can you handle one?"

The man had directed his question at the more likable Patrik, but Bem answered for him, "Do you want to test us?"

Bem's cold stare made for a believable assassin, and the man seemed to shudder in his seat. He shook it off and said, "No, I'll hear if you don't earn your money."

"We'll take the job," Patrik said.

The man stood up. "Meet me at the well tomorrow at full light. We will ride to the ambush spot and go over the plan from there."

"Agreed," Patrik said. He began to eat his breakfast again.

The man gave each a stern once-over and then left the table satisfied that they would do.

Bem went back to dunking his chunk of bread into his bowl of gravy, and the two said no more until they were back in their rented room above the bar.

~ * ~

"There is no reason to doubt our plan," Salar Nassim told the baron as he tightened the last strap on his saddle. "I have been on both sides—protecting clients from assassination and creating opportunities to assassinate their enemies." He patted his horse and stepped away. "I will admit what we are doing is risky. If Patrik and Bem were indeed hired, they will be instructed to kill all of you. The profit for these types of assassins is from looting the spoils of the job, and they will help themselves to whatever riches you have on your person. That is their motivation to see you dead."

Mauro looked down at his emerald ring. "Maybe I will leave a few things at home, just in case."

The Persian nodded in sympathy and continued to underscore the plan. "The three of us will be there to cover you and your captains. I will feel better after having spoken with Bem, but I cannot imagine the assassins will outnumber us once Patrik and Bem are fighting for you, and not against you."

"I am not worried," Mauro said confidently.

"Neither am I," Salar Nassim agreed. "My only worry comes tonight for Bem and Patrik. I trust they will be careful that they are not watched meeting us. If they are caught spying like this, they could be killed before the ambush."

Mauro liked the Persian's tactics and his easy manner. He understood why army generals had hired him so often for clandestine work. "It is not just their service you care about, Salar Nassim. You are like a father to your men."

"Like Soren said, we are a family. I have brought them together like brothers, and I feel responsible for them, as any father would."

They left the stables, and Mauro walked with Salar Nassim to the courtyard. Daniel and Soren were waiting for them, already on their horses.

Mauro quietly pointed out, "Daniel is not much of a talker, but he knows these hills and woods better than most."

Salar Nassim nodded to Daniel as he mounted his horse. "Then he's the man I need."

Mauro told the three riders, "Until tomorrow."

"Yes, Lord Baric. Until tomorrow," Salar Nassim assured him.

They turned their horses and rode out the gate.

~ * ~

Mauro was one step closer to ridding himself of the man who had been plaguing his family since before his return to Baric Castle. At this time tomorrow, he would be free from him. Mauro walked through the front door with those optimistic thoughts on his mind.

Meanwhile, Natalija had been standing in front of his study door. Her apron was wrinkled from all the twisting and folding she'd done to it while waiting for the baron to pass by. The maid spoke up as Mauro entered the foyer, "My lord, I have remembered something."

By the worried expression on her face, Mauro was certain it could not be good news. He glanced down the corridor to be sure they were alone. "Tell me, what is it?"

"I thought about it, sir, and Lord Dubovic did talk of jewelry," she whispered. "I remember, because he was usually so kind and soft-spoken when he met with my mistress. But on this occasion, he was scolding her."

"What harsh words did he say?"

"Well, sir, he asked where her emeralds were, like she had lost them, and he was angry," Natalija fretted.

The baron's expression was unreadable, so she explained further, "I helped her ladyship dress every day, my lord, and I knew she had many pretty jewels, but no emeralds. Your father had an emerald ring, and I noticed Count Toth wore one, too. You, my lord, and the baroness also wear emeralds on your hands. Baron Dubovic had many colorful rings on his fingers." She rambled on, "I thought maybe barons and baronesses are supposed to have a green gemstone, a sort of uniform to show their rank. I thought it was unkind of the baron to criticize your mother for not having one."

"Yes, Natalija," Mauro interrupted, "that was unkind of Lord Dubovic. When did he talk about her missing emeralds?"

"It was after the funeral Mass, sir. He came to visit her then. She was quite distraught talking to him."

"Now think hard, Natalija. What was my mother's reason for not wearing her emerald ring?"

Mauro held his breath.

"I remember her answer clearly now, sir. She said she did not know where the emeralds were. To be honest, I felt sorry for her ladyship to have misplaced such a beautiful jewel. Maybe she lost more than one."

Mauro breathed out. "You are right, Natalija. I believe she did. Thank you. You may go now."

The young maid curtsied to her master, then went off toward the kitchen, seemingly pleased with herself for having been helpful again.

Mauro stared at her whooshing skirts without seeing them. The emeralds were a blessing and a curse—that is what Nestor had warned Mauro the day he told him of the unique Baric fortune. It was proving to be true.

<h1 style="text-align:center">Chapter 59</h1>

Hugo and Teodor came bounding into the room they had rented above the alehouse in Zadar.

Teodor set his hat on the table and plopped down on his small bed across from Jero. "We are going for a swim," he announced.

Hugo added, "And after we've washed off this perfume from the French ladies, we will get some dinner and visit the Spanish girls across the street."

"Do you think they are different from the French girls?" Teodor asked.

Hugo sat down at the table with a big grin. "I do not know, but I am eager to find out." Then he said, "Come with us, Jero, just for laughs. You do not have to take a girl to bed. Teo doesn't."

Teodor sat up in his bed, insulted. "I would gladly take one to bed, but they cost too much, and my purse is nearly empty."

"Jero has the baron's money," Hugo pointed out. "He will give you some lire tonight, won't you, Jero?"

Teodor objected, "I cannot spend the baron's money. It is meant for our room and meals."

Hugo laughed at his reasoning. "Except, you already used some for drinks and cards."

"Well," Teodor said meekly, "I didn't think baron would mind that."

"Join us, Jero," Hugo said. "Teo will keep you company at the bar. It will do you good to move about."

Jero had not left the chamber since the first evening when they had explored Zadar together. Even with the excitement of the city's nightlife, Jero had not been able to shake his sorrowful mood.

But his shirt was clinging to him in their humid room under the lodging house roof, and a swim would be a refreshing relief. He considered Hugo's offer.

"Alright, a swim and dinner, but no Spanish girls," Jero said glumly.

Hugo went over to Jero's bed and sat down on the end of it. "We know you are heartsick, Jero, but you need to move forward, meet a girl. That is the only way to mend a broken heart."

He winked at Teodor to play along, but Teo only returned a puzzled look. Neither had ever had a steady sweetheart, let alone been heartbroken over one.

Hugo turned his sympathetic expression up a notch. "I am glad Mauro chose me for your companion. I have to admit, I have never enjoyed myself more. But, Jero, Mauro also told me to make sure you enjoyed yourself. You cannot merely sit in the room and let life pass you by."

Hugo and Teodor both gave Jero their best pathetic stare.

Jero knew what they were doing, and he appreciated their effort to break his melancholy. "I am sorry if I let you down," he replied. "I thought the baron was right at first—he said it would help me to get away from the castle and do something different. But it hasn't, and I cannot seem to motivate myself to enjoy anything, especially a pretty woman."

"You really love her, don't you?" Teo asked.

Jero lowered his head in defeat. "I do."

Hugo came closer to his side. "Look, Jero, I, um . . . I never told you this, but I tried to flirt with Ruby when I was assigned as her escort, but my charms somehow never worked with her. I think she had already set her sights on you from the beginning."

Hugo's confession did not change Jero's miserable mood. "It makes no difference now. Maybe she does love me, but she is still going to marry this Greek man and not me."

Hugo and Teodor exchanged shrugs across the room, perhaps deciding whether it might be best to let Jero sulk in the room after all.

Hugo finally offered, "I will tell the matron to send you some food if you like."

Jero got up and searched for his shoes. "I will tell her myself. I will join you for that swim."

Teo chattered as they waited for Jero, "You know, if I were you, Jero, I'd do what Cyro plans to do. Who knows if it will work but—go after her!"

Jero buckled his shoes and asked, "What do you mean? Follow her to Greece?"

Teo replied, "Don't follow her. Take her, Jero! And then marry her there!"

"What do you have to lose?" Hugo added with enthusiasm.

Jero found his hat and scoffed at the ridiculous suggestion. "I am the baron's steward. I cannot just leave my position and trot off to Greece."

Hugo grabbed his own hat. "I don't want to cause the baron any extra trouble," he said, "but you are a free man, aren't you? If you need to do this, I don't think the baron would stop you."

Jero pondered the idea more fully as they went to the door to leave.

"You could come back with her after you married her," Hugo reasoned.

Teodor agreed, "What is a few months' leave of absence for a lifetime of happiness? I am sure the baron will understand."

"Of course, he will understand." Jero smiled. "Maybe it is not too late. I still have time, right?"

"Right," Teo said.

Hugo opened the door. "After our swim, we can find some pretty ladies to celebrate your engagement."

"I cannot visit a brothel now. I just committed to marry Ruby."

"I would not expect you to," Hugo said, quickly backpedaling. "We will go to the tavern, then, and find two girls and five glasses to set the mood."

Jero stood at the threshold and considered what to do next. "We need to depart early to get to the party in time."

"Radic's party?" asked Teo. "Do you mean it, Jero? I wanted to go to Radic's party."

"We can leave first thing in the morning, Jero," Hugo agreed. "I'll just have two drinks and one girl. I promise."

~ * ~

The three riders didn't know which of the three places on Mauro's list Bem and Patrik would be lodged at, so one man went to each.

All the villages on Dubovic's land were along the seaside, so they had agreed with Bem before he left that he would fish from the main dock wherever he was staying at the beginning of sunset. Patrik was to stay behind in the tavern to keep their presence noticed.

Soren checked the first village they had ridden to, Salar Nassim remained at the second, and Daniel rode farther north to the third.

Bem was where he was supposed to be when Salar Nassim walked up the dock. There were other men fishing, trying their luck at the end of the day. Bem had a string and hook on a makeshift pole, and he had already caught two sizable fish.

Salar Nassim smiled to himself. Things must have gone well for Bem to already be waiting with a decent catch. "You've had luck today," Salar Nassim said, standing behind him, looking out over the sea.

Bem watched his line. "Did you want to buy one?" he asked, not paying the man behind him any undue attention.

"How many are there?" Salar Nassim asked as he took out his money pouch.

"Seven, if you count these two." Bem turned around and held up the fish.

Salar Nassim paid him a coin, and Bem handed over his catch.

"When will you fish again?" Nassim asked quietly.

"Tomorrow morning, at full sun. We will go to a new spot, but we don't know where. We will find out in the morning," Bem told his customer casually.

Salar Nassim pulled a muslin bag from the leather pack he carried on his shoulder and put the fish into it. When done, he asked, "What will you fish with?"

"Swords," Bem replied, barely audible.

Salar Nassim slung his burden back onto his shoulder and told him, "I will look for you tomorrow, then."

"I will be there."

Bem turned back to his pole, and Salar Nassim walked off with his dinner, back to his horse tied to the rail at the top of the pier. He strapped his pack onto his saddle and rode to the main highway. After a few miles, Salar Nassim turned off the road to a spot Daniel had picked out for them to camp. He settled his horse in for the night, began cleaning their meal, and waited for the other two to come back. The quarter moon did not give much light along the road for swift riding after the summer sun sank, so the wait felt exceptionally long.

Soren was the first to return. "You went fishing?" he asked his commander cheerfully.

"Bem caught these. I paid a fair price for them, too," he said with a chuckle.

Soren unsaddled his horse and put his gear next to the tree with Salar Nassim's. "Did they get in with the gang?" he asked.

"It seems they did. There will be seven of them."

Salar Nassim suddenly stopped talking and raised his hand when he heard a noise coming from the trees. But it was just Daniel returning. The Baric soldier came toward them and nodded a greeting as he tied up his horse.

Salar Nassim explained, "I was just telling Soren that Bem and Patrik were hired on, along with five others. They don't know the ambush site, but will be led there in the morning. Seven riders should be easy enough to follow."

Daniel pointed to the fish Salar Nassim had skewered on two sharpened sticks. "A go-good day's work d-dessserves a fa-fa-feast," said Daniel.

They were now used to his troubled speech and nodded back at Daniel good-naturedly.

Salar Nassim said, "How about you start the fire, Daniel. The baron's kitchen packed us a better dinner than our friends got. I think we will feast indeed."

~ * ~

Half-emptied platters cluttered the table by the cold hearth in the Barics' bedroom. Mauro had sent the servants away early for the night; the mess could wait until the morning.

Resi looked at Mauro across the room in the flickering candlelight. She had finished dressing for bed and sat in front of her grooming table, braiding her hair. "I am glad we had dinner together tonight, just the two of us."

"Ruby did not mind eating alone?" asked Mauro offhandedly while undressing. He took off his waistcoat and shirt. It felt good to let his skin breathe in the stuffy evening air.

"Ruby wasn't alone. She and Verica had their dinner together in her room, then Verica was going to help her finish her packing," she replied, tying off the end of her long braid.

Mauro sat on the chair and unbuckled his shoes, deciding whether to spoil their evening by mentioning what his wife would eventually discover.

He took a breath to calm his nerves and announced, "I want you to go to Radic's celebration without me tomorrow. I may not get to slip away so quickly from the meeting when it comes right down to it. Enjoy yourself at the party, Resi, and I will meet you in the village square as soon as I can."

He glanced over at her, hoping she would not argue. She did, of course.

"I don't want to be there without you, Mauro. I can wait here, and we can go together."

He watched her in the looking glass's reflection and tried to sound upbeat when he said, "You won't even miss me once you start talking to your friends. I will be there by sunset, at the latest."

After a moment, she unhappily agreed, "If that is what you want."

Mauro continued his evening routine, growing anxious about how he would tell her the rest of what she needed to hear before he left.

From behind the screen, he said, "It is known that there are unpatrolled places along the road to Dubovic Castle. If something were ever to happen to me, Jero is to tell you everything he knows, all right?"

"Why are you suddenly worried for your safety, Mauro? You are taking an escort, aren't you?"

Mauro stepped out from behind the screen, wiping his neck with a linen towel. "One always expects trouble," he said to her. "I was just thinking, we have never discussed the Baric business, and if something were to ever happen to me, you wouldn't know what would belong to you. Jero can disclose all the details."

"Jero knows, but I don't. Why do you have secrets from me, Mauro?" Resi asked with the same somber tone as he had used.

"The less you know, the safer you are."

He read in her face that it was a feeble answer, so he tried again, "Tell Jero that I said to show you the cellar and the crypt. The secrets are in there."

"Mauro, you are scaring me."

"Nothing will happen, my love. It is just . . . Jero knows everything about the castle, and one day you may need to know those things, too."

Resi protested, "But I have to wait until something *happens*? I wish you would share your secrets with me. You seem so burdened lately."

Mauro sat down on the bed, his folded hands heavy between his open legs. When he looked up again, he patted the bed next to him and said, "Come here, Resi, my dear. I will share a secret with you. It is something Jero does not know."

She did as he asked and sat down cautiously next to her husband. "Are you giving me my own secret to tell Jero if something happens to you?" she asked mockingly, not realizing the importance of what he was about to tell her.

"I suppose it is. I have been trying for more than a week to find a way to tell him this secret. It felt like there was never a good time. I should have made time for it." His voice finally wavered when he added, "It is important, Resi."

"Then tell me, Mauro."

Mauro stared at the polished planks, deciding how to explain the truth behind the complicated lie his father had fabricated for Jero. At last, he began, "You know my father was married once before he married my mother."

"To Margaret."

Mauro nodded. "Yes, Margaret. And I told you already that he was not there when she and their other children perished."

"You did." She bit her lower lip, bracing for something terrible.

"Well, after Margaret died, Mateo still needed a wet nurse. Idita found him one, and that woman stayed at the manor house to care for him. Her name was Sonja. She was the cooper's wife, and her husband and baby had died in those same weeks Margaret had. But Sonja had one more son a year later."

"Jero?" Resi said softly.

"Yes."

She knew now, and Mauro felt a weight fall from him. Resi took his hand in hers and held it in her lap until he finished telling her the story.

"I only learned this myself a few weeks ago. What I was told was that my father had fallen in love with Sonja and wanted to marry her. My aunt and uncle wanted him instead to marry my mother, who was a more fitting match for his position, and so they sent Sonja away while my father was gone with his soldiers. My father did not know she was pregnant with his child. At some point, Sonja went to live with her family and told them that Jero's father was a Croatian baron, but not which one. When she died suddenly, her relatives could not—or would not—support her child. Apparently, they sent letters to various baronies and sold Jero to the first baron who would claim him."

Resi shook her head in disbelief. "They sold their own blood into servitude? How old was Jero?"

Mauro shrugged. "He was three, maybe four. I am not sure. But what I do know is by the time my father tracked down where her relatives lived, Jero was gone. Against my mother's wishes, he never stopped searching for Jero. He finally found him in Baron Dubovic's service, and he bought him back."

"I don't understand. Why is Jero even a servant?"

"My mother did not want a bastard son in her house, and my uncle would not let my father legally claim Jero as his own. So, Jero was indentured and his true identity was kept hidden until my father could find a better solution. But he never did."

He turned to Resi. His eyes sparkled with tears when he said, "I know you never had a chance to meet my father, but Jero looks more like a Baric than I do."

Resi seemed both saddened and mystified by Mauro's story. "Would Jero not notice the resemblance? Did he never question his parentage?"

Mauro thought about how different their lives had been as they lived side by side in the same house. "Jero would not dare suggest he was anyone but who we told him he was. He was raised as a servant, taught to be obedient and not question his place in life."

"My head is reeling, Mauro. If I had found out a sister had been kept from me all these years within the same walls, I couldn't keep it a secret from her. You must tell Jero the truth."

"I will, Resi," he whispered.

He squeezed her hand for something solid to hold onto and said in a stronger voice, "I cannot give him the Baric name or a title, but I will give him everything else that should have been his. When he comes back, I will make all those wrongs right."

Resi dared to hope, "Jero could marry Ruby now."

"It is too late for that, my dear. Ruby has been given to another man."

"She doesn't want Nikko," Resi insisted.

"I cannot change everyone's destiny. Please, do not put one more problem on my shoulders, Resi."

Ruby's cause was lost, and Resi nodded in disappointment.

Still quiet and somber, Mauro said, "I feel better, knowing that you know and that you can tell Jero, if I cannot."

With a new sense of dread, Resi asked, "Who is riding with you tomorrow?"

Mauro hesitated. "Eduard, Simeon, and Vilim are my escorts."

Resi seemed to make a quick count of his soldiers in her mind. "Who will escort me to the party?"

Mauro rubbed his aching temples and replied, "I am sorry, I had not thought about that."

"Soren and Salar Nassim would enjoy the party. They could take me and Ruby in the wagon," she suggested.

"They have left to meet Patrik and Bem. I will figure out your escorts in the morning," Mauro said quickly.

"What is going on, Mauro? You have sent everyone away. How many secrets are you keeping from me tonight?"

He sidestepped her accusation and answered with a forced smile, "I know who will take you: Denis and Latif. They were my scouts, but I have promoted them to guardsmen. They are very trustworthy."

"Why not ask Daniel? He is trustworthy. Or has he gone, too?"

Mauro gave up trying to explain away the things he could not. "I am so tired, Resi. Can we go to bed now? I will arrange with Denis and Latif in the morning."

He kissed her on her forehead, feeling genuinely sorry he could not do more to ease her worries. It had to be like this.

He realized he was still half-dressed. "Crawl into bed without me," he said. "I will blow out the candles when I am done."

Mauro took the basin of dirty water from behind the screen and emptied it out the open window. He lingered there for a moment and looked out onto the hillside lit by bright stars that filled the night sky. Mauro could seal the mine, and the mountain would hide its secret forever. But could he keep the remaining earthly gems hidden and protected?

He went back to the grooming table and refilled the basin from the pail. He only had to get through Saturday, and then his world would be in order again, he thought.

He left his washed skin damp to cool him in the heat of the room and then joined his wife on top of the bedcover. She asked no more from Mauro before sleep took him, and he offered her no extra comfort in her unhappiness. They lay there together, their distractions keeping them apart.

~ * ~

Franja wouldn't have noticed the shadowed man sitting on the bench along the garden path if she had not been looking. She sat down next to him. "Why did you send Lazar to get me?"

"Why?" Simeon repeated. "Franja, I have not talked to you in days. I need to know why you are ignoring me."

"I am not ignoring you. I have my work and you have yours," she said from the end of the stone bench. "Summer is a busy time in the kitchen, you know that, Simeon."

"If you wanted to, you could have found time to see me, like we are meeting now."

"You have answered your own question, then."

Franja could not see his expression in the dim starlight, but she knew she had hurt him with her answer.

Simeon reached for her hand. "Franja, I love you. Why do you have this change of heart?"

This was not the conversation she wanted to have. "You are a wonderful man, Simeon, but—"

"No buts, Franja. I have a ring here in my pocket made for you, if you would be my wife. We could share a cottage and sit on our own bench under the stars like this. You could make your breads and cakes for the Barics, and I would serve the baron in his Guard, like we always have."

"And when the children come, Simeon, what then?" she asked.

"What then? Then we are blessed, Franja," he answered as he had before. "But why worry about that now? Be my wife, Franja. Make me a happy man."

Franja could not answer him tonight. Instead, she asked, "Will you go to Radic's party tomorrow?"

"I am a part of Lord Baric's escort, but we should back by sunset."

"Don't go to the party, then. Come back to the castle when you are done. It will be quiet here, and I will give you my answer. Goodbye, Simeon."

"Will you at least kiss me goodnight?"

She would grant him this much. She slid down the bench and kissed him softly on the lips. They stayed close in the dark. Then Simeon leaned in and kissed her more urgently but with a tenderness that kindled Franja's desire again.

Could she marry him, she wondered?

She pulled away. "I have to go. I will see you tomorrow evening." Franja walked down the dark path, back to her shared room in the hot attic.

Simeon watched her shadow disappear and went back to his chamber in the Keep.

Chapter 60

The greasy-haired man who had hired Bem and Patrik was named Franko. They met him and a group of rough-looking men by the village well.

"Fill up," Franko told the group of sellswords. "We will have a few hours' wait once we get there. I want to be settled long before our targets come through."

Patrik looked around at his new gang and the horses they rode. He and Bem looked the part of wanderers, but Patrik was aware that their steeds were in far better shape than they should be for riders who have been on the road steadily for weeks, but no one commented on it. Men like Patrik and Bem stole good horses when they could.

Their new companions were mostly Patrik's age: young enough to have not settled on a farm with a wife and child somewhere, yet old enough to have seen and done terrible things for survival. Two pairs, like Bem and Patrik, and a single mercenary were with Franko, filling their water pouches. They looked like the typical thugs for such a job. Patrik held no ill will toward any man trying to get ahead, but he didn't want to get friendly with the men he would have to kill to save his sister's husband.

After an hour of easy riding, Franko pointed out the spot where they would ambush the nobleman's party. The gang dismounted and began to unpack the extra armor and weapons they would use to bring the riders down.

Patrik noticed that the solitary man was strapping on a quiver of arrows. He was older than the others, maybe thirty, and was dressed from head to toe in well-worn leather garments. He looked like he knew what he was doing as he notched an arrow and stretched the bow to find the correct tension.

"You didn't say we'd be using bows, Franko," Patrik called over loudly.

Arrows made for an unfair fight for unsuspecting riders. Patrik was usually in favor of this, but not today. Mauro would indeed be hurt or killed before Bem and Patrik could defend him.

Getting no response from their commander, Patrik then directed his annoyance at the man in leather himself.

"Hey, put your quiver away! We are using swords for this job!"

"Shut up and mind your own business," the bowman told Patrik. "I can kill a dozen men with my bow before you have a chance to charge with your fucking sword."

Franko watched the two men, unmoved by their heated words. He would let them settle it.

"I know your type! When the ambush is over, you will strike us down with your bow for our cut of the booty," Patrik hollered.

The man hissed, "If you deserve it, Ottoman." He went on with his preparations, and Patrik strode to his horse.

Bem shook his head at his friend. The resolute grimace on Patrik's face meant trouble for both of them.

Patrik found what he was looking for and snarled, "You deserve this more." Patrik raised the loaded pistol at the stunned archer and pulled the trigger.

The bowman fell backward with a thud.

Bem let out an audible groan as the four recruits abandoned their preparations and surrounded Patrik, their swords held high.

Bem jumped to Patrik's side and drew his blade against the others.

"What the hell was that?" shouted Franko. "I said no pistols."

Patrik sprang onto a boulder. He was ready to make a spectacle of himself to save his and Bem's lives.

Waving his arms, Patrik said, "You heard him! The bowman said he could take down a dozen men before we were even ready with our swords. By my count, that includes you, me, your buddy—all of us. He would have taken the spoils from the bloated noblemen and left us for dead. I have heard this happened before," he cried. "I did you all a favor and saved you from an arrow to the back."

The other ruffians considered Patrik's explanation and agreed with his reasoning. They owed the dead man no allegiance and lowered their weapons.

Patrik and Bem breathed again when the four sellswords continued their preparations with little concern for the dead man lying in the road.

Franko paced in front of Patrik. "You really fucked that up. Now we only have six," their commander grumbled.

"If you stay, Franko, then we are seven again," said Bem as he strapped on his mail vest.

Franko kicked a stone in his path. It clattered against the rock-faced cliff in front of them.

"Can't you wield a sword, Franko?" one of the assassins asked their new commander.

The man's buddy added, "This will be child's play, Franko."

Franko unstrapped his weapon from his saddle and pointed it at Patrik. "You, get rid of the body and cover up that blood. The rest of you, hide your horses and let's get set up. We have wasted enough time."

Meanwhile, Daniel had heard the pistol shot in the forest while scouting for the sellswords. He ran through the trees in the direction of the shot. Peering through the underbrush, Daniel saw Bem walk two horses into the woods across the road. A little farther down, Patrik was dragging a body into a ditch. The Baric scout made a mental note of where they were along the castle road and went back to join Salar Nassim and Soren, who had been waiting a quarter mile up the road with the horses. Now they knew exactly where to position themselves.

~ * ~

Mauro wore his formal summer ensemble, a lace cravat, and fabric shoes. This attire was not his first choice for sword fighting, but he would play the charade fully to the end.

Standing at his desk, he removed two of his rings but left the inscribed one his father had given him on his finger. He set the inherited rings on a sheet of parchment and carefully sealed it with his green wax. On the envelope, he wrote, "For Jero." Mauro left the little package in the hidden compartment of the desk drawer—the one Jero had shown him. He then took one last look around the study before he locked it. Out of habit, Mauro tucked his key into his inside pocket.

Davor held the front door open for the baron, and Mauro turned to ask, "Do you plan to go to the party?"

Everyone had been given leave to attend, and Davor naturally assumed that included him. "I do plan on it, sir. Is that all right?"

"Yes, it is very right," Mauro said with a smile. "Just make sure the baroness leaves the party at a reasonable hour with her escorts. Latif and Denis are to stay near her and Lady Ruby. Give them a jab for me if you see them getting too drunk."

The valet chuckled. "With pleasure, sir." Then Davor asked, "Won't you escort your lady home yourself, Lord Baric?"

"That is my plan," Mauro quickly agreed, "but plans can change." He strode out the door before his valet had a chance to ask anything else.

The three Baric captains were readying their horses with Alberto's help in the stables when Mauro arrived.

"Will you be attending the party, Alberto?" Mauro asked.

"Me, sir? No. I have already given Radic my congratulations. I will stay behind and mind the stables with Geoff."

"Geoff isn't going?" Simeon asked with surprise. "The boy is almost a man now. When is he going to be let out to have some fun?"

Geoff, who had been buckling the strap of the baron's saddle, turned bright red with embarrassment.

Alberto had raised many grooms like sons, and he was not swayed that missing one party would compromise Geoff's burgeoning manhood. He told Simeon, "Tin has been given leave to go, and so has Josip. It is their time to meet some girls. That leaves only Milan and Lazar in the Keep, and me and Geoff in the stables, for when the guardsmen drag themselves back too full of ale to even slide off their saddles."

"I see your point," said Vilim with a chuckle.

Simeon rubbed Geoff's uncapped head and said, "Next time will be your turn, Geoff, and maybe by then you will know what to do with a girl when you dance with her."

Geoff ducked from under Simeon's fatherly grasp and slunk away from their good-natured teasing.

Once finished and ready, the men led their horses out into the morning sunshine, and Mauro took the reins from Alberto with a nod. The baron secured his sword on his saddle and turned to his escorts. "Shall we get this over with?"

The riders urged their horses along the cobbled yard and galloped out the open gate.

Chapter 61

After lunch had been put away, Nela excused the maids to change out of their servant uniforms and into something fancier for the party. There would be music and dancing, and people were coming from miles away to enjoy what had evolved into a rare communal celebration.

Radic had not intended for his daughter's baptismal party to be such a big event, but in the end, he didn't object either. The priest had blessed Elizabeta to attend, and Radic was looking forward to showing off his lovely young wife and their four little girls.

Village families were bringing food for the communal tables, and the Barics were no exception. Nela and Franja had already packed baskets of their specialty sweets and savories to be brought to the party in the baroness's wagon. The castle's donated hog was already roasting in a pit near the butcher's shop in the village square.

With the cooking and packing behind her, Nela sat on her stool and drank her afternoon cup of tea.

"Won't you be going to the festivities, Nela?" Franja asked as she hung up her apron on a peg by the door. "It would do you good to get out and socialize."

"You are one to talk, Franja. You've been sulking lately. Why don't you go to the village with the girls? They will be leaving shortly with the soldiers."

"I told you, Nela, I still feel a little under the weather this week. Besides, I think I have made my choice about Simeon. I asked him to meet me here, instead of at the party."

This was the news Nela was waiting to hear. "And what did you decide, Franja dear?"

Franja shook her head and put her finger to her lips. "That wouldn't be right to tell you before Simeon. You will have to wait until tomorrow."

Nela let out a laugh. "Lord help me, this is like one of Lady Baric's romance books. The story goes back and forth. You are keeping me in such suspense."

"I am glad I can be so entertaining," Franja said cheerfully.

Nela took her empty cup to the wash bucket and then walked to the door. "I am going to go put my feet up for a bit, but if you like, we can play some cards in the cellar later. It is nice and cool down there."

"I will come up with you and rest my swollen feet. If this heatwave doesn't pass soon, we will have to sleep in the cellar."

They left the kitchen and climbed the stairs to their quarters under the baking roof tiles.

~ * ~

"You look pretty, Ruby," Resi told her when Ruby came into the Baric's chamber.

"Davor just knocked on my door to say the wagon is ready." Ruby leaned against the bedpost, studying her friend in front of her looking glass. "Don't you think you should wear a Venetian gown to look your best today?"

Verica was fixing her mistress's hair and held the baroness's eyes with her own in the mirror.

Ruby looked from one face to the other in the reflection. "You aren't going, are you?"

Resi sighed as she tried to explain her decision, "I was just telling Verica that there is no sense in me going to the party yet. Mauro told me he wouldn't be there until this evening. That is still hours away."

"How will you get there later?" Ruby asked. "All the men will be gone to the village already."

"If you see my husband, you can tell him I am at the castle. Mauro will come get me and bring me back to the party. He won't mind." Resi didn't care if he minded or not. She could not enjoy herself without him today.

"I will wait with you here, then," said Ruby, and Verica nodded her agreement.

Resi shook her head. "You will do no such thing. Both of you go and have fun tonight. Dance a few dances, Ruby, say your goodbyes, but keep an eye on Verica and her handsome tanner," Resi teased her blushing maid.

Verica put the comb down and stepped back from the table. "If you don't mind, Lady Baric, I need to finish my own last touches in my room before we go."

"Of course, Verica. Have a wonderful time."

Verica curtsied to her mistress with a grin and hurried out the door.

Ruby went to shut it after her.

Resi remained in front of her looking glass, and Ruby went to stand behind her. She put her hands on Resi's shoulders and said, "Tell me what is really the matter."

Resi slumped in her chair. "Something is terribly wrong, Ruby. Couldn't you feel the tension this morning? Patrik and his friends are gone on some unexplained errand. Mauro's captains are going with him to this council meeting. Since when do the southern lords not stop here first to ride with Mauro? None of it makes any sense."

Resi drank the cup of water on her table and tried to calm her nerves.

"I didn't sense the same tension this morning. What exactly did your husband say to make you think that?" Ruby asked calmly.

Resi stood up and paced the room. "Strange things, odd comments," she jabbered. "He said if he dies, he doesn't want me to remarry. If something happens to him, Jero is to tell me all the Baric secrets."

Resi sat down on her bed and sniffed back tears of fear and frustration. "He has never spoken like that. This meeting is a ruse of some sort, and Mauro is voluntarily walking into trouble."

"At Baron Dubovic's castle? How can that be?"

Resi wiped her cheeks with her sleeve and took a deep breath to calm her thoughts. "I don't know, Ruby. There must be some other battle the men are riding to, instead, and are using this as a cover. Maybe there is trouble in Zadar. Maybe that is the real reason he sent Teodor and Hugo there earlier."

"Resi, you are getting all worked up over nothing," Ruby insisted. "I saw him leave. Your husband was wearing his finery, not his armor. He is not going into battle."

"You are right," Resi finally conceded.

"I have heard pregnant ladies have bouts of irrational thinking," Ruby cautiously declared. "Have you been sleeping well?"

"To be honest, I toss and turn all night. I must be on the brink of some breakdown. Perhaps I will try to nap while I wait for Mauro. I will not be at peace until he comes home."

The rest of the girls would be waiting outside by now, and Ruby would have to leave soon if she wanted to go with them.

"Do you want me to stay with you, Resi? I will, if you like."

"No. Knowing that I caused you to miss the party would make it all worse. Go and enjoy yourself. I will be fine after my nap."

"I will be watching out for the baron and tell him you are waiting here. Goodbye, Resi."

Ruby kissed her friend on the cheek and left to find Verica. She had left the chamber door open, and Resi could hear their footsteps pass by a few minutes later.

Curious to see who was left in the house, Resi went downstairs. The kitchen was empty and quiet. She thought Nela had said she would be staying at the castle, but perhaps she had changed her mind. No matter, Resi could help herself to something in the pantry if she got hungry.

Resi then went out onto the grand terrace. The cluster of colorfully clad maids had assembled near the gate to walk the mile together to the village. Soldiers were waiting on foot and horseback to accompany them, and Denis was helping Ruby onto the wagon's front bench. Resi didn't want to be noticed watching them, so she went back into the house and continued to the sitting room. Now would be the perfect time to get lost in a book, Resi thought, and searched the shelves.

An exciting adventure story would do her mood wonders. She left through the terrace door with a book in hand and made herself comfortable on a cushioned lounge chair under the grape arbor.

Chapter 62

Sebastian Dubovic had left his castle early that morning, mainly because he needed an alibi for why his soldiers did not come to his neighbor's rescue on his own castle road. Dubovic would stick to the story that it was an unfortunate error, that he had miscopied the date on the invitation, and his neighbor arrived on the wrong Saturday. How tragic it was that Baron Baric had not heeded his warning to travel with more soldiers, he would be sure to tell the officials. He himself had left Dubovic Castle with no less than eight guards accompanying him. These were still dangerous times.

Feeling confident in his plan, Lord Dubovic traveled to his seaside villa to wait for an update. It wasn't long before Dubovic's scouts sent a message, reporting that Baron Baric and his three escorts were seen heading north at a casual pace, dressed in ordinary clothes.

Good! The last thing Dubovic wanted was for the young lord to ride into his trap clad in mail and armor. Indeed, Lord Dubovic was pleased to the point of celebration as he thought how conveniently Radic's baptism plans matched his own plans. The entire Baric Guard would have been given leave to attend, and Baric Castle would be practically empty with Baron Baric and his household all gone. His idea was to join the village party in the afternoon under the guise of a neighborly well-wisher, and then Dubovic would follow Baroness Baric back to the castle when she returned home.

Lady Terese had flaunted her emerald ring at the ball. She would surely know about her husband's vast reserves. Lady Johanna had complained that her husband's modest living in the uncultured backwoods of the empire, keeping his true wealth secret, had deprived her of her entitled status in Venetian society. Lord Dubovic needed such wealth to maintain his own status, and he would have already had the treasure if Lady Johanna had told him where to look. The new Baroness Baric would show him tonight.

Dubovic was practically giddy over his cleverness. He treated himself to a leisurely lunch while his favorite boys played music and danced for him on the rooftop terrace overlooking the sparkling Adriatic.

~ * ~

Meanwhile, Jero and his two companions rode all day in the summer heat from Zadar, stopping only for short breaks to rest their horses. Jero was intent on making it back to the village before sunset, and Teodor and Hugo were happy to accommodate him.

As they approached Solgrad from the south, they could hear the hum of music and high-pitched laughter from a distance. They slowed their pace and trotted beside groups of people walking along the main route into town. After leaving their horses with the stable boy, they made their way through the narrow streets to the church square.

The sun was low in the sky but still plenty bright for Jero to find his beloved Ruby among the decorated tables and clusters of musicians surrounded by dancers. Hugo and Teodor spotted some friends and waved their goodbyes to Jero as he combed the crowded square, not seeing Ruby or the baroness. Finally, Jero came across Natalija, who held a horn of ale in the middle of some dancers. She was watching them dance with an odd, dreamy expression on her face.

"Hello, Jero," she chirped when he stopped in front of her. "Have you come to dance with me?"

"Where is Lady Ruby?" Jero asked urgently. His eyes scanned the faces of the partygoers.

Natalija took his hand and began to twirl back and forth in front of him. "Lady Ruby and Verica left. They didn't want to dance any longer," she said while swaying to the music.

Jero stopped searching the crowd and focused on the drunken Natalija. "And the baron? Where is he?" Jero asked, leaning in to hear her reply over the loud music.

"Which baron?" she wanted to know.

"Your baron, Natalija. Baron Baric," he clarified. "Where can I find him?"

"Oh, he didn't come to the party, Jero. At least I haven't seen him. His lordship went with his captains, I think. Everyone is gone. Where have you been, Jero?" She began to twirl again to the music.

Jero took a deep breath for patience. She still might be able to help him, so he raised his voice to be heard over the noise and asked, "Where is the baroness, Natalija? I do not see her."

Natalija cocked her head and frowned as she processed his question. "She didn't come, either," she finally replied.

Jero was caught off-guard by this news. The Barics were the village patrons. Why weren't they at their party? And the mercenaries?

Jero urged her to explain, "What do you mean by everyone? Did the mercenaries leave without Lady Ruby?"

"They all left, but Daniel went with them instead. Lady Ruby was very unhappy about it. And the baron left this morning to Lord Dubovic's castle. Davor said they would be back for the party. Why don't you dance with me, Jero? I thought you liked dancing?"

Nothing made any sense to Jero, and he asked, "Baron Dubovic invited all of them for today? And the baroness?"

Natalija closed her eyes and opened them wide again, as though the questions made her dizzy.

"I think so," she answered, "or maybe just the baron. Baron Baric likes meetings. I had a meeting with him, Jero. He brought me into his study and asked me many questions. I had never been in the baron's study before. It is very clean! Do you keep it clean for him?"

Jero might have found Natalija's remarks entertaining if the rest of what she said had not been so troubling. "Did Davor say this was a council meeting, Natalija?"

"I don't think so. He was very strange about it. The baron has been acting funny all week—staying up all night, then sleeping all day. Maybe he misses Lord Fabian. I miss Lord Fabian. He is so elegant and handsome, don't you think? You are handsome too, Jero. Do you want to dance with me?"

She stood in front of him with a questioning smile, tipping back and forth, too intoxicated to stay still.

Jero finally grinned at his friend and ended his useless interrogation. "I will later," he lied. "I have to talk to someone first."

"All right, Jero." She then disappeared into the dancing crowd to find a new partner.

Jero snaked his way through the boisterous villagers and found Hugo and Teodor at a makeshift table, helping themselves to the row of food that had been laid out.

Jero's stomach growled at the smell of the roasted pork, and he took a slice, along with a fist-sized mushroom pie from a platter.

"I am going back to the castle," Jero told Hugo before taking a big bite.

Hugo picked up a pastry from the same platter. "Did you find Lady Ruby?"

"Ruby has already left, and the baron has not shown up yet. Natalija said Lord Baric went to a meeting at Dubovic's castle today. It might have been a council meeting."

Hugo was usually a part of the baron's escort to the council meetings, and he perked up at this news. "Lord Raneri was to host the next meeting, but not for a few weeks," Hugo shouted in reply as a group of musicians encircled the men, strumming and singing a lively tune.

Jero hollered back, "Yes, well, plans change."

"Are you going back to the castle?" Teodor leaned in to ask as two village girls walked up to the table. One hooked her arm into Teo's and pulled him into the dance.

Hugo asked impatiently, "Do you need us to go with you, Jero?"

Jero could clearly see that Hugo wanted to stay with the young lady on his arm, so he asked no more of his companions. "It is a quick ride home, Hugo, and I know the way. Enjoy yourself," Jero replied with a friendly wave of goodbye.

Hugo hollered back, "Don't take no for an answer when you find Lady Ruby!"

~*~

Jero and his escorts had missed finding Ruby by only a few minutes and a few wrong turns through the crowd of well-wishers.

Denis and Latif had dutifully kept near Ruby's side while she chatted with friends and acquaintances at the gathering. Her escorts didn't argue when Ruby told them she and Verica were ready to leave after only an hour or so of mingling. Her abrupt departure suited their plans well. The young guardsmen could deliver Ruby and Verica safely to the castle and then ride back out to the village for unrestricted merriment with their friends.

The sun was at the horizon when Denis steered the Baric's wagon past the shooting field turn-off, the last bend in the castle road.

Latif trotted ahead of them on his horse and waved to the gatekeepers at the barred entrance. He didn't hear the rush of noise that shattered the rhythmic clomping of the wagon's steady horses.

Ruby took Verica's hand as the galloping riders were suddenly upon them as if from nowhere.

When the dust had settled and it became clear it was only their neighbor, Lord Dubovic with his escort, Ruby let out the breath she had been holding in.

Denis stopped the wagon, and Latif rode back to his side. Their happy-go-lucky expressions hardened as the black and red-clad soldiers lined up in front of them.

"I did not mean for you to stop," Lord Dubovic began to explain. "I was coming to return something to Lord Baric. We will follow you in."

"Lord Baric is at the village, sir," Denis informed the nobleman politely.

Dubovic seemed to consider the two Baric soldiers for a moment. Finally, he said with authority, "I was at the village, and Lord Baric is not there. So, if you will allow me, I would like to wait for his return."

Denis's quandary showed in his furrowed brow. It was not Denis's place to deny Lord Dubovic, but there was protocol, so he answered, "You may follow us in, sir, but your escorts will have to wait outside the gate."

"Wait outside your gate? Come, come, young man. Since when must my Guard wait outside our neighbor's walls? I was just here two days ago with this same escort, and we were welcomed then." Dubovic looked up at the ramparts with believable irritation and shouted, "Who is in charge here?"

Denis looked to Latif, the most senior soldier on duty that night. Begrudgingly, Latif rode over to the gatekeepers to confer with the guards there.

After a moment of consultation, the young recruits Adrijan and Neno turned the chain.

Lord Dubovic remained poised on his horse. A sly smile spread across his lips as they waited for the gate to open for them.

~*~

Alberto had been sitting on a bench outside the stables, smoking a pinch of tobacco after his evening meal. He saw the gate open and was surprised to see the eight Dubovic guardsmen ride into the courtyard behind the wagon carrying Ruby and Verica. He snuffed out his pipe and called into the stables for Geoff to come help with the horses.

Denis assisted Ruby down from the wagon, and then he lifted Verica off the bench seat with a friendly wink before setting her safely on the ground.

After leaving his horse with his men, Lord Dubovic said something to the departing women that would convince Ruby to hook her arm in his. Baron Dubovic led her away, toward the grand terrace, with Verica following beside her.

Alberto scowled as he watched the women walk away in the older baron's company. The stable master scanned the group for Baron Baric and his escort among the riders, but he saw only the red jackets of the Dubovic soldiers.

Holding the reins of the hitched horses, Denis waved to Alberto with an easy smile. Unfortunately, Denis had mistaken Alberto's wave for a greeting when he was, in fact, signaling his alarm. Denis turned too late to see what Alberto was pointing at: two of Dubovic's men had overpowered Latif, and four others charged the novice gatekeepers.

Witnessing this surprise attack, the two guards on the upper ramparts reached for their bows, but they were too late. The Dubovic soldiers had already loosened their arrows at them.

Denis stood alone in the courtyard, hopelessly outnumbered.

Sebastian Dubovic had warned his soldiers he wanted to be in and out of the Baric compound without leaving a mess. That meant no killing. But Dubovic's instructions did not forbid knocking Denis out and dragging him over the pavers to the gatehouse to be tied up with the others.

"Close the gate," Dubovic's Captain Marko ordered.

~*~

Geoff had been dozing in the straw when Alberto called him to come out and help Denis unhitch the horses. The boy stood paralyzed at the door as the chaos at the gate unfolded in front of him.

"Geoff," Alberto shouted, snapping him from his trance. "Follow me!"

The old horse master ran like a young man to the open armory doors, and Geoff sprinted from the stables after him.

"We need help!" cried Alberto. He stepped behind the studded door and pushed against it.

"Red and Black? Who are they?" Geoff asked. He, too, shoved against the solid oak with all he had.

"I've got this!" Alberto hissed. "Go get help, Geoff!"

"How?" cried Geoff. "The gate is shut!"

Alberto grunted with effort to secure the armory. "Through the well," he ordered the groom.

The heavy door moved, and Alberto lowered the iron pin into the paver.

Geoff seemed dazed. "The well? How do you know?" sputtered the boy as he pushed on the second door with Alberto.

"This is not the time, son. I heard you talking to Jero about your rocks. Take that same way out before they see you. Run to the constable, Geoff! I am counting on you!"

Geoff looked out from the armory, and his jaw dropped in dismay. Dubovic's men were overpowering the remaining Baric soldiers.

"Stay in the shadows, Geoff," was Alberto's last urgent demand.

Geoff took off running—around the back of the Keep, down the trail by the dog cages, up the servants' path behind the greenhouses, and finally to the kitchen entrance.

~*~

Alberto regretted not having Geoff's help. He was strong, but the iron-studded doors were meant to be closed by two men. Alberto shoved and heaved the second side until the hinge finally creaked, and the massive door moved. Just in time.

The Dubovic soldiers had imprisoned the remaining Baric guards in their gatehouse and now checked the grounds for other threats.

"Get the old man!" Captain Marko shouted from the ramparts. "At the tower doors! Stop him!"

Alberto set the second bolt into the stone floor mere moments before banging could be heard from the other side. He lowered the heavy iron bar into its place. A second set of massive doors within the armory were supposed to be secured next, but Alberto had no time. The upstairs entrance was unlocked.

Alberto grabbed a torch and scrambled up the spiral stairs to the dining hall, shouting, "Bolt the door, Milan!"

Milan came out of the common room, leaning on his cane, and called out, "What is all the yelling about?"

Panting, Alberto bent over with relief that he was not alone. "We are under attack," he explained. "Hurry, before they make it up the steps!"

The upstairs door into the Keep had two solid bars that could be lowered inside. Together, the men managed to slide those into place. A second iron gate was suspended outside, above the door to protect the vulnerable wood from axes.

Milan cursed that they had not kept the chain well-oiled, and the two struggled to move it.

"Lazar!" Milan called out.

His son ran into the dining hall, and Milan quickly explained the urgency.

Alberto left them to finish his task closing the second set of armory doors below.

When they had secured the entrance and no noise on the outside stairs could be heard, Milan ordered his son, "Close the shutters in the officers' chambers. And don't put your head out in case of arrows. I will be lighting the torches."

"The torches, Father?"

Lazar was only twelve and had never known the real purpose of the great iron cages on each corner of the tower roof.

"The flames will signal to the villagers that the castle is under siege."

"Let me help you, Father."

His father knew what to do, but he needed his son's assistance to get to the roof. Lazar put his arm around his father's waist to help him move more quickly up the flight of stairs.

Milan said to him at the second landing, "Quick, now. The shutters!" Then the lame man continued up the remaining flight of steps with the help of his cane.

Lazar went from room to room and closed the outside and inside shutters at each window. The first floor, where the common soldiers lived, had no windows to cover, but flaming arrows could reach the openings of the second-floor rooms where the officers resided, and the boy locked the heavy double panels against the threat.

In the chamber where the foreign visitors slept, Lazar paused to peer out of a small arrow slit built into the thick stone wall. The glowing rampart torches revealed the frightening reality. Lazar watched the unfamiliar red jackets running along the top of the wall. Two red soldiers settled in above the gate next to where the Baric guards lay slumped with arrows in their chests. Two more red-clad men stood by the barred entrance while four red soldiers ran toward the manor house and disappeared into the darkness by the terrace.

Lazar knew everyone from the Keep had gone to the village party. The manor house would be empty too, but, he wondered, why there was light coming from the lower windows of the great hall. No one should be there to light them.

~ * ~

Lord Dubovic had walked the two women into the great hall like he owned the place. The grand room was shrouded in shadows save for one corner sconce that had been left burning, and he lit the torches around the room from that.

Dubovic asked the captives, "Where is your mistress? Why did she not ride back with you from the party?" His voice was gruff, and he seemed agitated at the baroness's absence.

She was the one he wanted, not them.

In their fright, Ruby and Verica had not spoken to the nobleman as he led them into their home, and neither answered now.

Marko and three other guards came running through the terrace doorway breathing hard, unwittingly breaking the tension in the room. They waited by the door for further instructions.

Lord Dubovic asked again, "Where is your mistress?"

Ruby clutched Verica's hand for strength and answered the impatient guest, "Lady Baric is waiting for her husband, my lord. He was with you at your castle today. She is to meet him at the party, and they will come home together. I was not feeling well, so I came home early with my companion."

Ruby began trembling while she told her lie, but Dubovic did not notice as he paced in a circle around the women, considering Ruby's explanation. The baron had ordered his soldiers to mingle with the party-goers earlier, explicitly looking for Baroness Baric, and Dubovic was sure she was not in attendance.

"That is a pity your mistress did not ride back with you, my dear. She will be waiting all night. Her husband is dead," Dubovic said evenly.

The women held each other for support, and Verica began to cry at the shocking news.

Dubovic ignored them and called out, "Search the house."

Three of Dubovic's men ran out the double doors into the foyer. Their boots resonated on the stairs and down the otherwise silent corridor to the kitchen.

With the baron distracted, Ruby released Verica's hand and dashed across the great hall toward the terrace doors.

Marko needed only a few strides to catch up to Ruby in her long robes. He reached out and grabbed her arm. She reeled back onto the floor from the force of it.

Verica sobbed helplessly, frozen where Ruby had left her.

The rough soldier pulled Ruby to her feet.

Ruby fought him and cried, "We need to tell the constable about Lord Baric."

Marko slapped her hard across her face, and blood began to drip from her nose. Ruby stood tall and hissed, "Let go of me." She shook her arm free from his grip.

As if Verica no longer trusted her legs to support her, she sat down on the chair just a few feet behind her.

"Yes, sit down, ladies," Dubovic said with mock politeness.

Marko took Ruby by the folds of her sleeves and forced her onto the chair next to Verica.

"Tie that one to the armrest. I do not want to be bothered by her again," Baron Dubovic commanded his captain.

Then Sebastian Dubovic's mouth turned up into a smile when he told Ruby and Verica, "We will call your constable, but first I must speak to the baroness. Now, which one of you will tell me where she is?"

Chapter 63

Resi woke from her deep sleep on the lounging chair in the cool shade of the grapevines. It was twilight and unusually quiet. Perhaps no one had returned from the party yet, she thought.

The second thing Resi thought about as she stretched her aching limbs was how hungry she was. Nela would not be cooking tonight since most of the Baric household would gorge themselves on the vast offerings at the celebration. But there should be tasty plates of something in the pantry. Resi would help herself to an improvised dinner.

As fate, or luck, would have it, the baroness went in through the back kitchen door only a few minutes before the gate was opened to the incoming wagon and riders. She poured herself a cup of water from the crock on the servants' table. Sliced bread was on a plate there, and she took a piece with her into the pantry to see what delicious things she might find to go with the bread.

Resi tasted her way through the smoked ham and chunks of salted fish before deciding on the plate of chicken pâté. She was looking for a smaller dish when she heard the sound of the outside door slamming and quick footsteps coming into the room. Resi poked her head out of the pantry in time to see Geoff opening the cellar door.

"Where are you going in such a hurry?" she asked cheerfully.

Geoff shut the cellar door again and leaned against the wall to slow his racing heart. Naturally, he had not expected the baroness to be here, and he was still filled with fear from the ongoing attack in the courtyard.

She walked over to him with a chuckle. "Did I scare you, Geoff? You are as white as a ghost."

He seemed to gain control of his wits and urgently told her, "There is trouble, my lady. We are under attack!"

He opened the door to the cellar, pulled her in with him, and led her down the stairs.

"Attack? What are you talking about, Geoff?" she argued as he urged her along. "Where are we going?"

"Shhh. Keep quiet, my lady," he hissed through clenched teeth to keep himself from shouting. "We are going out the well."

They reached the bottom of the stairs and were doubly shocked to find Nela and Franja looking up at them from the small table they had set up next to the cool stone wall.

"Lady Baric? Geoff? What is the hurry?" Nela asked the startled intruders.

"What are you doing here?" a stunned Geoff replied.

"We are having our dinner," said Franja. "What are you doing down here with the baroness?"

Both Franja and Nela stood up and went to the baroness's side.

Obviously, Geoff had not expected this complication, but there was no time to waste defending his actions. He was just supposed to hurry through the tunnel and run to the village for help. Now he had to protect the three women, too.

"What am I doing?" he repeated angrily. "The castle is being attacked! Lord Dubovic's men have taken over. They came in with Lady Ruby and her wagon. Alberto locked down the tower and sent me to crawl out the well. They will be searching the rooms by now. It is only a matter of time before they find you here. Come on, we need to go!"

Nela and Franja looked bewildered, unable to comprehend what the boy was rambling on about, especially where they would be going from here.

The baroness knew exactly where he meant, and she urgently ordered, "Take them to the cave first, Geoff, then run like the wind. If Ruby is up there, I want to be with her."

"No, Lady Baric! You are in danger. Come to the cave with us."

Geoff started toward the pickling room, and the two servants followed him without question now.

He turned back and saw that the baroness held her ground. "They are here for no good purpose, my lady. I beg of you, come with me where you will be safe." He held out his hand to her.

"I know where I will be safe, Geoff," the baroness said confidently. "I am going to the wall. I will hide there and watch for Ruby."

"The wall?" Geoff questioned her foolishness. "You don't understand, Lady Baric. You will never get to the wall. They have outnumbered our guardsmen and are probably on the ramparts."

"Not the rampart wall, Geoff. The great hall wall. I will be careful."

She took his still outstretched hand and squeezed it, then turned to leave.

Geoff's expression fell to disappointment that he wouldn't be able to change his mistress's mind.

Nela knew the wall the baroness spoke of. "Yes, go, my lady. They will not be searching the servants' hall. Stay hidden, Lady Baric, and you will be safe."

She then turned to Geoff and added, "I don't know about this cave you are taking us to, but I know about the wall. Let her go. She will be all right."

Geoff looked one last time at the baroness and trusted Nela's words. Then the three hurried into the last room of the cellar and closed the door. Resi was alone again.

~ * ~

Jero was not far behind the Baric wagon that had brought Ruby and Verica home. Natalija had said Ruby had only left a short time before, and she had been right. Even though Jero had to walk to the edge of the village to get his horse, Bacchus made up for lost time, galloping swiftly up the castle road. The horse wanted to go home.

The last of the summer sun shone against the west walls of the Baric compound, and Jero could see the gate closing in the distance. He wondered why the soldiers on the rampart did not warn the gatekeepers that another rider was coming up the castle road so that the heavy gate would be kept open for him. Then he saw a figure in red walk along the wall above the entrance.

Something was wrong.

As Jero stared up at his home, wondering who was walking the wall, a flame ignited on the highest corner of the Keep. While he puzzled over how curious it was, another corner lit up, and soon after another, until four flames on the roof of the Baric tower burned in the approaching darkness. Even Jero, who was not a soldier, knew what this meant. He hurried to get his horse off the road before the red-clad soldiers patrolling the Baric wall noticed him.

Jero waited for his pounding heart to calm down while he stood in the black shadows of the pines. What was happening beyond the gate? Maybe he should ride to the village and call for help.

No, he decided, someone from the party would see the signal and come with the village men to defend against the intruders. If he left now for the village, it might be too late for his beloved Ruby. She was in there—her wagon had driven through, he was sure of it. If one of the Baric soldiers had lit the alarm, that meant no one was safe.

But Jero was alone, and the gate was compromised. What could he do but ride back for help? He had to think quickly.

Jero urged Bacchus along a trail that flanked the road, hoping the intruders had not left guards outside the walls. This trail was a shortcut to the shooting fields. There, he left Bacchus unhappily tied to the rail and took the narrow path around the back of the castle wall. The long sunset and the quarter moon gave enough light so he could find his way without difficulty until he came to the mountainside of the east wall. The path there was overgrown and deep in shadows, slowing Jero as he carefully made his way to the old well. He had not been there in years, but he recalled a barred opening in the ground. He searched where he expected the hole to be with his foot, kicking the underbrush until he felt hard metal.

Jero nearly jumped out of his skin!

The branches in front of him rose in the dim twilight, and two figures climbed out of the earth.

Jero heard the whispers of women and dared to call out, "Ruby, is that you?"

A muffled shriek of surprise came from the group, and Geoff answered, "Jero?"

Jero rushed the short distance to the castle servants and saw it was Cook who had climbed out with Geoff. Franja was close behind them, and Jero helped her step out of the grate and onto the solid ground.

Franja hugged him in relief, and Jero embraced her tightly in return.

He turned to Geoff and demanded, "What is wrong, Geoff? Who is attacking us? The tower signal is lit."

Geoff was a little more confident now that he was outside the walls and had met up with Jero. He explained what he knew, "Lord Dubovic and his soldiers came in through the gate after the wagon. Alberto secured the Keep and told me to go out through the well to get help. I met Nela and Franja in the cellar when I was escaping. I don't know any more than that."

"Yes, go for help! I left Bacchus tied to the post at the shooting fields. You can handle Bacchus, right?"

Geoff nodded that he could.

"First help Nela and Franja to the cave, Geoff. I am going to find Ruby. Do you know where she is?"

"I don't," Geoff replied. "I didn't see her, but I know she came in on the wagon. It all happened so quickly. I suppose she is with Baron Dubovic."

Then Geoff remembered one crucial detail. "We left Lady Baric in the house."

"What? You let her stay in there?" Jero groaned.

Geoff tried to make him understand. "She would not come with us. She said she wanted to find Ruby. She said she would look for her from the wall."

Nela put her arm on Jero's, and he turned to her in the dark. "You know how to get in, don't you?" Nela asked hopefully.

"The wall. Of course," Jero whispered. Jero had played there with Mauro when they were boys. You could see the entire great hall from the peepholes there. "I will find her, Nela."

Nela gave his arm a squeeze, and then the three set off toward the cave.

"Be careful, Jero," Franja added before they disappeared up the narrow path between the two tall pine trees.

Jero was careful climbing down the well. He pulled the grate over him before he made his way down the uneven steps into the tunnel. There was no light, but he trusted his memory that he just had to move forward, and at the end, there would be a door.

The narrow door was locked, but Jero was confident Geoff would have left a key on this side. He fumbled around on the sandy floor and found it under a rock at the edge of the threshold. He unlocked it and peered into the small pickling room. Candles were left lit, and Geoff had thought to shut the door to the cellar hallway.

So far, so good.

He cracked open the door to the main cellar. A torch had been left burning in the vast storage room. Jero wanted to keep to the dark, but he didn't want to extinguish the torch, either. In the end, he decided to risk being seen if someone were searching the cellar. For good measure, he unsheathed the knife on his belt and said a small prayer to God before venturing on.

Jero had never thought the cellar was as large as it felt right then, and it seemed to take him forever to creep along the shadowed wall to the stairs leading up to the kitchen.

Candle sconces there gave light from the bottom step to the kitchen door. This time, Jero decided to extinguish each flame as he tiptoed up the stairwell. He thought of Ruby and how frightened she must be. That gave him the courage to go up the dark steps, treading carefully with his leather soles on the hard marble. He prayed there would be no one on the other side of the door when he opened it.

Chapter 64

Resi quietly closed the door to the cellar after she ventured upstairs again. She looked around the empty kitchen and trembled with fear. The plates and crock she had used earlier lay shattered on the floor, and the stools around the massive table were overturned. Someone had been here.

Her wooden heels clattered with each step as she crept across the stone floor. Afraid of attracting attention, Resi took off her noisy slippers and then opened the door to the servants' hallway that connected the kitchen to the great hall.

With no candle, she probed her way along the wall until she felt the long crack that she knew was the hidden door. Resi found the latch above the panel. It worked. She pushed it open, then hurried in and closed it behind her. She was safe, and she took a minute to let it all sink in. She leaned against the wall and slid onto the floor like she had done before, when Mauro had shown her this secret viewing place.

Sitting there on the cold floor, Resi began to sob as the adrenaline waned. She wrapped her arms around her middle and thought of Mauro and his premonition that day. The baby moved and kicked.

She had forgotten she was not alone, and Resi would be brave for her little son. She wiped her tears with her flowing sleeves and took a deep breath, then went to the beam of light coming from the small peephole in the wall ahead of her. Looking out, Resi could see Ruby and Verica seated on the chairs by the hearth. Lord Dubovic paced behind them, and another man, dressed in a red military jacket, was leaning on the fireplace mantle. What did they want by holding her house hostage, Resi wondered?

The next peephole further down along the false wall also gave a view into the great room, but it let her see the far end and the entrance to the foyer. That door was open but guarded by another man in red. Two more red soldiers ran into the room and out of view.

Resi rushed back to the first peephole to see what they were doing. They had stopped in front of the baron. She put her ear to the hole and strained to hear what they were saying.

"The house appears empty, sir. The door across from us is locked. Should we break it down?" the soldier asked his commander.

"No, not yet. That is the baron's study. I know he always takes the key with him, so no one could be hiding in there. Did you check the cellar? The baroness might have heard us and fled down there."

Dubovic turned to Verica and asked, "Where is the cellar entrance, girl?"

Verica stared at the floor and did not answer until Marko pulled the pistol from his belt and put it to Ruby's head.

Ruby jolted from her trance but sat defiantly at his threat.

Verica choked back a sob with her friend's life in her hands. "It is the white door in the kitchen," she answered in a trembling voice, and Marko lowered his gun, laughing.

Inside her hidden room, Resi panicked. Now that she saw what was happening with her own eyes, she wanted to run away and join the others in the cave. At the same time, she was afraid for her friends and wanted to run to the great hall and help them.

At least she could get away from the awful vision. Resi leaned back against the wall and shut her eyes. That was when she heard the click of the latch.

"Mauro?" she whispered hopefully at the tall shadowed figure.

He shut the door and whispered back, "It is Jero."

Resi reached out in the dark. He found her hand and held it tightly.

"How did you know I was here? You just about scared me to death," she said, barely audible.

He stood close to her and whispered, "I met Geoff at the well opening, and Nela told me you were coming here." He let her hand go and went to look through a peephole.

Her panic was returning. "When did you get back? Where are the others?"

He turned back and said in a hushed voice, "There are no others. I was riding home alone when I saw the signal on the tower. We are under attack, Lady Terese. Geoff said Dubovic's men have taken the castle. What do you think they want?"

"They are looking for me, Jero. What should I do? Mauro went to a meeting at Dubovic Castle this morning even though he knew something bad would happen. I am scared. Why do they want me?"

He looked through another hole, hoping for answers, but found none. "I do not know what they could want with you, or Ruby and Verica. Do you know why Ruby is tied to her chair? She is bleeding."

Resi could not see the anger in Jero's face, but she could hear the danger in his voice. She tried to soothe him with her words. "They were sitting there when I came in here. Ruby is brave. She might have put up a fight."

If the soldiers fought a woman, they would not hesitate to kill one, too. Jero considered how long they might hold the two women like this if the baroness was not found.

"Geoff is on his way to get the constable," Jero told her, "but I cannot imagine Dubovic's men will open the gate for Radic and the others. Geoff will probably bring them around to the well."

"Lord Dubovic just sent his men to the cellar looking for me. What if he keeps a guard there? The tunnel will be useless."

Jero asserted, "I do not know how many men Dubovic brought, but he did not come with an army. There are only three or four here. There are two on the ramparts and probably two more at the gate. I did not see any others outside the wall when I walked around. Geoff is our only hope now. But if the alarm is not noticed, it will be hours before the party is over and the soldiers come back."

"Can we do something before then? Maybe we could sneak out to get the swords off the wall in the sitting room."

Jero scanned the great hall again. "That's no good, my lady. Already, one of the men is holding a pistol. If each soldier has one, we will be dead before we can fight them with swords."

Resi looked out another peephole. The captors seemed to be waiting impatiently for something to happen, too.

"We need pistols, then. Do you know how to shoot?" she asked Jero quietly. Resi certainly did not.

"Not pistols, no, but I can shoot a bow."

Saying this out loud gave Jero an idea. "Maybe there is a way to get one. The boys have been shooting rabbits in the garden. They leave their bows on a post by the kennels."

Resi pointed out the flaw in his idea. "If soldiers went into the cellar, they might still be in the kitchen, too. How will we get out of here?"

Jero chuckled to himself and told her, "I know every way in and out of this house, Lady Terese. We can easily get outside without going through the kitchen."

Jero took her two hands in his and said, "I think I have a plan, but I will need your help. Are you up to it, my lady?" He felt her nod. "There is another entrance to the buttery that comes into this corridor. We can go through there and slip out the small door in the wall by the fountain."

"Let's go before I lose my courage," she agreed quietly.

"Keep hold of my hand, Lady Terese, and we will be brave together."

Jero pulled the hinge, and the door sprung open just a crack. He lifted the latch, opened it a few inches farther, and looked out both ways. He guided her a few feet to a second door on the other side of the narrow hallway. From there, they went through a low corridor that Resi had never been in. It had a small window at the end that gave them some light.

Jero stopped and turned back to her, and Resi saw his expression was dark and focused. He was a Baric, she remembered, and at this moment, he looked very much like his brother.

He gave her a long look as though considering something.

"What is it?" she asked with concern.

"Your dress is too bright, my lady. The yellow and white are glowing in the dark. I do not wish to be improper, but, um, can you take some layers off?"

Resi looked down at her flowing tunic and robes and knew he was right. She could die at the hands of these men if they were seen, but she would not die of modesty saving herself.

Without further discussion, Resi removed her linen smock, the yellow embroidered overskirt, and her flowing white tunic until she stood in the sapphire blue shift that gathered tightly below her bosom and covered her down to her ankles.

Jero saw a dark apron on a peg that the men used to protect their clothes when moving the barrels of ale and said, "Here, madam." Jero handed her the oversized garment. "This will help a little."

She slipped it over her head and tied the apron high on her waist. It did cover her curves and darkened her figure. She had left her shoes in the kitchen, but walking barefooted outside was not going to be her complaint tonight.

They left the buttery and quickly crossed the fountain patio, keeping as best they could to the shadows of the garden path. Darkness hid the way around the greenhouses until they had to make a final dash through the open yard of the Keep. They hurried to the back of the tower and stopped at the kennels, where the dogs looked up at their masters with sleepy expressions.

"Here is the post I was talking about. The bows were hung here just the other day," Jero told her.

He had not bothered to keep his voice low, now that the tall tower would absorb their conversation, and no men patrolled the north wall.

"Maybe the boys left them leaning against the foundation." Resi felt along the granite stones for the missing bows while the dogs whimpered in their cages, wanting her to pet them.

A faint light glowed from the second floor above them. Someone had not closed those shutters.

Jero looked up and yelled hoarsely in vain, "Hey, up there?"

A boy's voice called back from the window, "Who goes there?"

Jero stepped back to see the window better. "Lazar, are you alone?" he yelled and whispered all at once.

"Jero?" Lazar called down in surprise.

Resi looked at Jero in excited relief. "This is good, isn't it?"

Jero nodded and quickly formed a plan. "Lazar," he shouted, "whose room is that?"

"Don't be angry, Jero. It is Lord Stephan's old room. It is empty now," Lazar told him defensively.

"It's fine, Lazar. I need you to go to Lord Fabian's room," Jero said urgently. "There is something he keeps there that I need you to throw down to me. Are you listening?"

"I am listening."

"Go and find his bow, the short one. Make sure it has a string and the arrows, then bring it here." Jero did not know if Fabian had packed his favorite weapon with him to Venice, but he was betting that he had left it here.

Resi took Jero's hand again while they waited an excruciating few minutes for Lazar to return.

"Got it," Lazar called down.

Jero looked up along the ramparts to be sure they were still alone on that side of the Keep before he said, "Now, let it drop."

"All of it?" Lazar asked.

The boy was right. There was a chance something would break on impact from the tall height. "I will only need three arrows and the bow. One at a time," Jero called up.

Resi tugged on his arm. "Only three?" she asked.

"I will be lucky to have time to shoot more than one," Jero replied.

Lazar dropped each arrow and then the bow, followed by the empty quiver.

Resi and Jero searched the dark ground and found them all. Nothing had broken, and the string was still with the bow.

The boy leaned out the window, and Jero gave him one last instruction, "Now, shut the shutters and go tell your father that you saw us. Do not open the tower doors for anyone but the baron or the constable. Tell your father not to open the doors for even me or the baroness—they might use us for no good purpose. Is that clear, Lazar? Promise me, now."

"Not for you or the baroness. I will tell him, Jero." Then Lazar shut the outside shutter.

"Good boy," Jero said quietly to himself. He then hurried to string the bow the same way Fabian had shown him in the woods. He'd had trouble bending the bow then, and he struggled again. Jero needed the torchlight from the corner where the dogs were, but he was afraid the hounds would give them away.

Resi whispered sweet words at their kennel doors to quiet them. It helped.

When Jero had finished readying his bow, he stood looking at the baroness with the dogs. "Lady Terese," he slowly said as if amazed he did not think of this before. "The dogs follow your command, don't they?"

"I suppose so. Do you want me to stay here and keep them quiet?"

"No, I want you to bring them."

He began searching for their leashes hung on the kennel walls.

She watched Jero's hopeful expression grow in the dim light as he explained what he wanted her to do.

If she could keep them quiet for the next few minutes, this would work, she thought.

Chapter 65

It had been an unfair fight. The five unaware assassins stood no chance against the practiced soldiers once Bem and Patrik turned on their ragtag group.

When Daniel, Soren, and Salar Nassim rode out from the cover of the trees where they had waited to counter the ambush, the tragic fate was sealed for Dubovic's overwhelmed mercenaries.

These desperate men, facing certain death, did not go down without a fight. With the tables suddenly turned on them, Dubovic's sellswords hacked and jabbed until their last breath.

Simeon mounted his horse to rejoin his scattered companions, leaving Franko for dead after Simeon's blade pierced his chest through the leather of his jacket.

But the gasping adversary was not yet dead. He struggled to pull his readied pistol from his sword belt, and, with his last gurgling breath, Franko shot at Simeon's moving horse.

The horse reared and fell from the stinging bullet in his haunch. Simeon landed hard on the rocky ground, and the wounded animal rolled onto him.

Eduard was the first to rush to Simeon's side. He knelt over his companion and cradled his bleeding head. "Come on, Simeon," he said, pleading in his ear. "Wake up for me now."

"Get the horse off him!" Bem yelled.

Patrik and Soren came to Bem's aid and pulled hard on Simeon's saddle, far enough for Vilim and Mauro to slide Simeon's leg free from the beast's weight.

Mauro took out his handkerchief and wiped the blood from Simeon's head. The trickle continued to run down his temple. He opened Simeon's waistcoat and felt his heart still beating.

"He is alive!" Mauro exclaimed.

"Look for broken bones before we move him," Eduard urged.

"His leg is broken. The bone is through," Salar Nassim said, pulling off his jacket to put pressure on the pulsing wound. He thought of Niels and their agony in the same situation not even a year ago. If they couldn't stop the bleeding from his crushed leg, there was little the men could do but wait for Simeon to die. Salar Nassim anxiously searched for Soren.

The Dane had not shirked and was already taking off his jacket to make a tourniquet. "Find me a strong stick or he'll bleed out!" Soren shouted over to Bem.

"I am going to put Baron Dubovic on a stick—a long, sharp one," cried Mauro. "Who will ride with me to the castle?"

Vilim said, "I will come."

"I will, too," said Patrik.

"Bem and I will come, too," Salar Nassim told the baron. "Soren and Daniel can stay with Simeon and keep pressure on the leg."

Eduard had wandered off, and Vilim spotted him, kicking Franko's dead body, again and again, in his grief. Vilim rushed over and pulled him away from the gruesome scene before Eduard could break his own leg in his fury.

Eduard was in no state to help with a raid on the neighboring castle, but he could help keep Simeon alive.

"Eduard," Salar Nassim called over, "there is a small stream just beyond those trees. Bring some cool water to help with the swelling on the back of Simeon's head."

Eduard nodded and walked silently away into the woods.

Mauro watched him go and then turned to the others and said, "Lord Dubovic will be surprised we made it on time to the meeting. Shall we finish this game?"

The five riders were at Dubovic's barred castle gate only minutes later. The gatekeepers were indeed surprised when the heavily armed visitors stopped in front of them.

One guard announced from behind the barrier, "Lord Dubovic did not leave word that he was expecting guests, sir. He is not due back until late."

"I am Baron Baric, and we are expected at your castle. Where was Lord Dubovic going that he would leave his invited guests waiting?"

The guard seemed to panic when he realized who the men were. "I think the baron is at a festival, my lord," he said. "Your festival, sir."

Mauro wanted to storm the gates and search the castle. "Open the way for us!" he shouted.

The gatekeeper was dumbfounded and disappeared from view.

Vilim said, "I believe he is telling the truth, Mauro. Dubovic is in Solgrad, gloating over his victory. Your premonition was right."

Mauro knew Dubovic was not merely gloating but was busy stealing what he had always wanted. Mauro and his soldiers were alive but not home to protect his castle. No one was.

"We have to go," Mauro said ominously.

He hastily turned his horse, and his companions followed him. They rode swiftly down the castle road, back to the others.

They arrived back, but nothing had changed. Simeon was lying lifeless on the ground, and Eduard bathed his brow with cool water from his water pouch.

Eduard looked up at the baron and said, "He still hasn't died, Mauro. Let's put him on my horse. I will carry him home."

The trip back would be a challenging ride for Eduard and possibly the death of Simeon, but they had no choice.

Mauro nodded his agreement, and Soren and Daniel carefully lifted Simeon onto Eduard's strong stallion. They tied him securely in front of the saddle to keep him from falling over, and then they covered him with the blanket from his dead horse.

Everyone agreed they would leave the lifeless bodies where they had fallen and let the authorities deal with them. They wanted to hurry back to the main highway, back to Solgrad.

~*~

The last rays of sunlight had faded over the Adriatic when Mauro's horse lumbered up the ridge that looked down over Solgrad. He could hear lively music thrumming in the distance and see circles of light glowing in the center of town. But what sent a chill through Mauro was the light to the east. Four of them. The castle was calling out to the men in the village and across the countryside. The tower signal could be seen for miles if the men weren't already surrounded by torchlight and drunk on ale.

His entourage looked up to where the baron was looking. No one had to repeat what the other was thinking. Whatever Dubovic had intended to do, it was happening now. They had to hurry.

Mauro rode up to Eduard. He lifted the blanket from Simeon's face and felt his forehead. It was burning up, a dangerous sign, but he wasn't ice cold.

"Eduard, Idita was going to the festival. Find her," he ordered.

Eduard nodded gravely.

"Daniel," Mauro called out to his other captain.

Daniel left the pack of riders and came to the baron's side.

"You go with Eduard. We will ride on." Mauro then held Daniel by the shoulder and whispered, "Tell Idita not to hesitate to take the leg."

Daniel could not mask his shocked expression. A man without a leg could never be a soldier again, could never ride, and could never do what Simeon took for granted each day. But the baron wanted his friend to live, and Daniel seemed to understand that. He gave a quick nod to his commander that he would follow his order.

~*~

There was no plan for what they would do when they came to the castle gates, and no one asked Mauro to give them one. Plans failed, and it had been a trying day. Something would come to them when they reached their destination. For now, the only thing the group of angry soldiers could do was to ride hard along the familiar road.

As fast as they were traveling up, a single rider was traveling down. Even in the dim starlight, Mauro knew this horse, and so did Janus, who sped up to greet his pal.

"Halt, Bacchus!" Mauro yelled out before they met the charging steed.

Geoff recognized the horses and his master's voice. The baron was here; all would be well.

The boy pulled with all his might against the reins of Fabian's stallion. "Whoa!" Geoff commanded.

Mauro held Bacchus's reins to keep the agitated horse steady alongside him. "We saw the signal," Mauro shouted over the sound of unhappy neighing.

"Lord Dubovic is holding the castle, my lord," Geoff panted. "He and his guards rode in when your men brought Lady Ruby back from the village. They fought them, sir, but your soldiers were overpowered. Alberto locked the Keep and must have lit the torches. I don't know what happened after that. I had already run to the kitchen and out the cellar."

"How do you have Bacchus?" Vilim asked him urgently. "Where is Jero?"

Geoff explained breathlessly, "I was bringing Nela and Franja to the cave. I met Jero on the path from the well. He was coming back from the village, but Hugo and Teodor stayed on at the party. Jero said he saw the torches being lit as he rode up, so he left his horse tied up and took the hidden way. He told me where to find Bacchus. Oh, and I told him where to find your wife, my lord. She stayed behind in the castle."

"My wife is in the castle?" Mauro cried with disbelief.

"She never went to the party, my lord. I think she was waiting for you. Please, don't blame me, sir. I tried to talk her out of it, but Nela said it would be alright."

The warriors grew agitated as the events became clear, and they were impatient to be on their way.

"Is my sister safe?" Patrik wanted to know.

"I was with her just a little while ago. She said she was going to check for Lady Ruby from the wall. I thought it was too dangerous to venture to the wall, but Jero said he knows how to find her," Geoff reported.

"Well done, Resi," Mauro said under his breath, knowing where she would be. "That is good news, Geoff. Jero will protect her there," Mauro assured him. "Go now! Find the constable and pass the word on to any soldiers you see along the way. We will come in through the well, like Jero did."

Mauro released his hold on Bacchus, and Geoff sped off toward the glowing village in the distance.

The baron told his companions, "Now we have a good plan."

Patrik scoffed in disbelief. "We go in through the well?"

"How is this possible, Mauro?" Vilim asked.

The others were just as skeptical.

Mauro hastily explained, "It is not the well in the courtyard, Vilim. It is an ancient well under the manor house, and it leads to a door in the cellar. My grandfather wanted an escape route, and I am grateful for his forethought. We will leave our horses by the grove. The element of surprise will be ours. They will never expect us to already be inside. I just hope Jero and Resi stay hidden in the wall."

Chapter 66

Resi and Jero stood in the shadows near the terrace glass doors. He nodded to her, and she nodded back that she was ready. They had already discussed their plan while they muzzled the two dogs back at the kennels.

Jero looked into the lit room at Ruby and Verica, waiting bravely for their fates to change. Captain Marko paced behind them. Jero had briefly met Marko when they camped on the neighbor's land on their return from Rijeka, just before the ball. Dubovic's captain and the other scouts had allowed the Baric riders to stay the night there. After they had left, Simeon told the group about the unpleasant encounters they'd had with the menacing man over the years.

Seeing the dried blood on Ruby's face made his own blood boil, and Jero remembered what Fabian had told him was most important about shooting—if you plan to kill a man, then do him a favor and kill him outright.

Jero hoped to get at least two shots with the bow before Dubovic's soldiers realized what was happening. Jero counted three other soldiers with Captain Marko in the great hall. One was at the foyer door, one at the hearth by the baron, and one just on the other side of the glass door where he and Resi stood, cloaked in darkness.

"Ready?" Jero whispered.

Resi took the muzzles off the dogs, and Jero kicked the door open, startling the guard standing there.

Then Resi gave the command to attack and released her grip on the dogs. They went for the closest victim.

It was Jero's move now. He quickly stepped onto the landing and shot one, two, three arrows from the quiver on his belt.

True to his mark, the first arrow struck Lord Dubovic's thigh, and the baron fell to the floor, wailing in pain. The second went straight into the heart of Ruby's tormentor, as Jero had intended. The third arrow hit the man standing next to the baron squarely in the neck, and he dropped to the floor, dead.

Jero had no more arrows for the remaining two men, but each dog had taken one man violently down. The brown and spotted dogs were gentle with the baroness, but they had been trained to attack. Once released, they went for the movements of the strangers.

During the chaos unfolding around them, Verica untied Ruby's bound arms, and the two women crouched in a corner of the room as the guards struggled against the attacking animals.

A mauling is terrible to witness. Resi shut the terrace doors to keep the noise from alerting the other soldiers guarding the gate outside. She accepted the brutality of her actions. These men would have killed her and her friends without a second thought. Resi showed them no mercy.

Jero nodded to the baroness that it was enough. She called the dogs off, and they trotted back to their master. She then hooked the leather straps onto their collars again and tied them to the marble column in the center of the room.

The captive women raced to embrace their heroes, but there was no time for rejoicing. They were not yet safe. The great hall had several entrances, and Jero hurried to the foyer door and barred it with the iron arm—one less entry to watch. Then he called out, "Go with Lady Baric. I will wait here for the constable."

Resi and Jero had decided earlier that the bathhouse was the best place to hide until they were rescued. The building could not be seen from the courtyard, and the only entrance could be bolted shut from the inside.

"Come with us, Jero," Ruby pleaded. "If the other soldiers find you alone, they will kill you. You have no more arrows."

He walked over to the baron, who had managed to prop himself against the stacked wood by the fireplace. Jero gripped the arrow sticking out from Dubovic's bleeding thigh and pulled it with a steady tug.

Dubovic blanched but did not yell out this time. He gritted his yellow teeth and held his abuser's hateful glare with his murderous one.

Jero stepped away and wiped the bloody shaft on his breeches. "I have one arrow now, and I will point it at the door," he said confidently. "Go, Ruby. I have come back to marry you. Be safe for me so I can."

"I won't let you die here alone," Ruby cried.

He smiled at her when he said, "No one else will die here tonight. Go. Please."

Resi tugged on Ruby's hand. "Jero is right. Come on. We will be safer away from here while we wait for the constable."

Verica and Resi left through the servants' hall, and Ruby finally followed them. They took the same hidden hallway through the buttery that she and Jero had taken earlier and followed the dark garden path to safety.

~ * ~

The red-clad soldiers patrolling the rampart above the main gate didn't notice Mauro and the others moving deliberately on the trail that flanked the castle's perimeter walls.

When they got to the east wall, Mauro found the iron cover to the well, and the six soldiers made it through the precarious entrance and down the dark, rocky tunnel with only minor stumbles.

A thin sliver of light came from under the cellar door as they approached it. Jero had locked the door, but Mauro knew to search for a key on the outside, too.

Vilim volunteered to go in first to ensure no one was guarding the cellar. It seemed like an eternity before he came back to tell them that all was clear.

After they made their way upstairs to the kitchen, the six decided to split up. Vilim paired with Bem and Soren with Salar Nassim. They would attack the Dubovic soldiers outside in twos. The intruders would have already searched the grounds and wouldn't expect a fight from inside the compound. Dubovic was most likely in the great hall, so Patrik and Mauro would surprise him and his men there. If Jero and Resi were indeed in the wall, they would see Mauro and Patrik from their hiding place and know they were safe.

Chapter 67

The two mauled men moaned a few minutes more and then lay silent in pools of blood on the stone floor. The baron was the only intruder left alive, and Jero had not thought about what he would do when he was alone with the vile man. Best ignore him, Jero decided, as he held his bow aimed at the closed terrace door.

Dubovic seemed to study him with amusement. "Relax, Jeronim," he said. "You are Jeronim the servant, are you not?"

Jero turned to the baron. No one had ever called him that. "My name is Jero. The constable is on his way," he added as if that would keep him quiet.

Dubovic tried to move and sucked in air from the stabbing pain. He said with a groan, "I welcome the constable. I am the one who has been attacked here."

"You attacked the castle. It will be obvious to everyone," Jero declared with disgust. He turned back to his watch.

Unbeknownst to Jero, Mauro and Patrik had come through the kitchen and opened the servants' door a crack at the other end of the great hall, enough to see the two men by the fireplace.

Mauro looked over and waved at Patrik to follow him in.

Patrik held his hand up to stop Mauro. He put his finger to his lips and his hand to his ear.

Mauro nodded that he understood Patrik's meaning. They would listen in for a moment to what was being said.

Across the room, by the fireplace, the older baron took a handkerchief from his jacket pocket and pressed it against his wounded thigh. He then answered Jero's accusation.

"I have a perfectly good reason for being here tonight. Still, the idiot magistrates in the capital will not question a baron's motives, or take a servant's word over mine."

Jero said nothing, focusing on the closed door, wishing help would arrive through it.

Lord Dubovic regarded him, then chuckled and said, "I had always wondered why Lorenc wanted you so badly, Jeronim. Why buy your freedom and then keep you as his servant?"

Jero held back the urge to spit on him.

The baron didn't seem to notice and went on to say, "Now that I have had a closer look at your unusual green eyes, I can plainly see the reason. You are Lorenc's bastard son, and your mother was his whore."

The man was hallucinating from the pain, Jero thought. Just a few more minutes, and Geoff would be here with the constable. He could ignore the man for that long.

Lord Dubovic restlessly shifted his weight onto his uninjured leg. He was wasting time and needed the servant to help him with his goal.

Patrik and Mauro watched and listened from the sidelines as Dubovic rambled on, "Did you know Lorenc sold his first son's marriage rights, along with a sizable purse of gold, just to get you back, Jeronim? I thought I had made quite a profit off you, but then the two Baric brothers tricked me."

Dubovic regarded Jero's puzzled expression and added, "Didn't you know that? Indeed, Lorenc paid a pretty price for your contract, considering you were the child of a whore. Perhaps he was touched in the head, like Lady Johanna. She was mad, but not too crazy to see I could help her out of her miserable marriage. I gave her the poison to put in his wine, you know."

Dubovic laughed at Jero's stunned expression. "Are you surprised, Jeronim? You are lucky she did not poison you."

"She can burn in hell," Jero said icily.

"Those are strong words from a servant, although that is what she said of you. I spent years courting her, listening to her complaints about you and Lorenc with one goal in mind." Dubovic shook his head and mumbled, "And then the bitch died, but I will have what I want without her help."

Jero walked away from the devious man and paced by the terrace door to keep from reaching out and strangling him.

"What do you want here?" Jero finally asked.

Dubovic said coolly, "I want the gemstones."

Jero shook his head in disbelief. Was this what all the mayhem was about?

The baron glared at him and said, "You are the young baron's steward, Jeronim, so I expect you know that I am talking about the emeralds."

"Emeralds?" Jero repeated numbly.

"Tell me where they are kept. Does your master keep them in his study? Is that why the door is always locked?"

Jero ran his fingers through his loosened hair. How could he shut the madman up?

"As his steward, I suppose you have a key," Dubovic continued. "Why don't you go unlock the door for me, and I can be on my way?"

Agitated, Jero paced again, stopping in front of the dead soldier with the arrow to the neck. His sword was lying next to his lifeless body, and Jero absently picked it up.

Baron Dubovic watched him guardedly from his place, slumped against the hearth.

Across the room, Mauro hovered in the doorway with Patrik. He seemed spellbound, watching the scene between the two unfold.

Both barons must have pondered the same question while Jero stared at the weapon in his hand: What will you do?

Dubovic tried again to win Jero's cooperation and regain the advantage back to him.

"I know what! You can come with me, Jero, and be my new steward. You will have only important responsibilities in my employment. I will not make you serve tea to the ladies, like the Barics do. Where is the pretty new Baroness Baric anyway?" Dubovic asked. "She may be of some use to me."

Jero pointed the sword at him. "You will leave her alone."

"Put the sword down, Jeronim. Who do you think the authorities will believe? It is my word against yours."

"They will believe Baron Baric when he comes to purge you from his house."

"Dear me, did I forget to tell you?" With a fake pout on his face, Dubovic told him, "Your baron is dead. I do not see how he could have survived this attack. So tragic."

Jero had been stalling, waiting for Mauro to rescue him from this nightmare, and he snapped. "He is not dead!"

"He is by now. And you, Jeronim, will be hanged for killing my men and holding me at blade-point."

Jero looked at the sword he held tight in his fist and recoiled.

"Dangerous things, swords. Best put it down, young man. You can let me go now, and I will explain our unfortunate misunderstanding to the constable." He pointed to the blood-soaked kerchief pressed to his thigh. "We can be friends, despite all of this. You help me find what I am looking for, and I will keep you from hanging."

Jero had heard enough.

"I will see you dead first."

Dubovic put his hand on the honed blade Jero held against his throat and said, "Look at you, playing the hero. You are no warrior. You do not have it in you."

Jero held the prisoner's stare and answered, "I disagree."

A fierce resolve washed over the gentle servant, and Dubovic's eyes widened in fear as he realized he had sealed his own doom.

From the other side of the room, listening in, Mauro and Patrik realized it, too. Mauro pulled the door open and sprinted across the expanse of the great hall.

"Jero, no!" Mauro cried out.

But Jero didn't hear his brother calling. He only heard Dubovic's plea wheezing as he pressed the blade into the intruder's throat.

Patrik caught up with Mauro at the hearth as they witnessed Jero sink the sword deeper. Then Jero collapsed to his knees on the stone floor, noticing nothing else but Dubovic's surprised expression frozen in time.

When Mauro knelt down beside him, Jero turned in alarm to face the new intruder. His panic melted away as he realized it wasn't Mauro's ghost he was looking at, but the real baron.

"Oh, God, what have I done?" Jero whispered.

Mauro found his voice and assured him, "It will be all right, Jero. It is never easy to kill a man."

Jero stared blankly, realizing his crime. "Killing him was easy," he whispered. "I wanted him dead. He wanted Lady Terese. The emeralds. He said he had killed you, Mauro, and he said Lord Lorenc was—" The impossible words were caught in his throat.

"I heard what Dubovic said, Jero. I heard the part about my father . . . our father." Mauro hung his head in anguish. "Oh, Jero, I am so sorry I did not tell you what I learned."

Patrik hastily asked, "Jero, where are Resi and Ruby?"

Jero jumped, surprised someone else had spoken. Then Jero remembered why he had killed the baron: to keep the women safe.

"Ruby was in here with Verica. Lady Terese was in the wall, Mauro. She handled the hounds brilliantly and—"

"Jero," Patrik interrupted softly, trying not to startle him again, "where are they now?"

"In the bathhouse. I told them not to open the door for anyone but me."

"They will know my voice," Patrik assured him gently. He turned to Mauro and said, "I'll go find them."

Mauro looked up from his misery and nodded. "Bring them here, Patrik. Tell them it is over."

Patrik hurried out the way they had come in, leaving the two brothers alone.

~*~

Jero averted his eyes in horror. "What is to become of me, Mauro? I have killed all these people. The baron is dead by my hands. I murdered him."

Mauro was unwavering in his brother's defense. "The baron held my house hostage, and he sent assassins to kill me today. His death would have come by hanging soon enough. You saved us the trouble of a tribunal."

"He talked about your father, Mauro," Jero whispered as though it pained him to say the words out loud.

There were no more secrets. Dubovic had made sure of that.

Mauro took Jero's trembling hand and said, "I think I have known my whole life we were supposed to be brothers, but I became sure of it only a few weeks ago. Forgive me for keeping it from you. I wanted to tell you right away, but I did not know how."

Jero began to cry and laugh all at once. "If I am supposed to be the older b-brother, why do I want to weep like a ch-child," he stuttered.

"No one is here but us, Jero, if you want to weep. This nightmare will end soon." Tears ran down Mauro's cheeks, and he wrapped his brother in his arms until Jero stopped shaking and found his voice again.

"I came back for Ruby, Mauro. I decided I would do what Cyro is doing and fight for her hand. I was going to ask Patrik if I could travel with them, to ask her father to consider me instead," Jero said, wiping the last of the tears with his dirty sleeve. "I was afraid to tell you I would be leaving, Mauro. But now it is over for me. I have murdered a nobleman."

"Do not despair, Jero. I heard Dubovic confess it all, and so did Patrik. You were defending the House of Baric and all that we love. This is your house, Jero. Remember that."

Jero stared back at him, wanting to believe it, but the shock of the last hour had finally set in, and he began to shiver uncontrollably. "I am s-s-so glad you are not dead, Mauro."

"So am I, Jero."

~*~

They both jumped as the terrace doors burst open and a roar of voices filled the air. Constable Radic led a group of soldiers and villagers, charging into the room; Bem and Vilim were with them. The two lounging dogs tied to the marble column came to life, barking and straining to get at the new intruders who looked around the great hall in bewilderment. Their foes already lay dead in bloody heaps across the room. Then they noticed the two living men huddled together at the hearth.

Mauro stayed focused on Jero in their last free moments. Cupping his brother's face in his hands, he said, "I will fix this, Jero. I will talk to the constable. I will tell him what happened."

Mauro helped Jero stand up and took him to the chair where Ruby had suffered her abuse only a short while ago. The rope was still tied to the armrest and dangled next to Jero as a reminder. Mauro took off his silk jacket and wrapped his shivering brother in it. He kissed Jero on his brow, like he would a child, and told him, "Stay here and wait for me."

Vilim came to Mauro's side. "What happened, Mauro?"

With surprising composure, Mauro told Vilim, "Jero killed the baron and saved my wife. Do not let anyone bother him until I come back."

Vilim looked over at the sword piercing Dubovic's bloodstained cravat and shuddered. He took off his own jacket and added it to Mauro's, wrapping it around the trembling figure. Following his orders, Vilim sat down on the armrest and quietly protected Jero from any questions the dozens of men filling the great hall tried to ask. It seemed that the entire village had come to fight for the Barics.

"Lord Baric, sir! It is a relief to see you! Did you kill all these men?" Constable Radic shouted over the noise.

"It would be easier to explain if I had, Radic, but it was Jero and my wife who slew them all."

Radic had not expected this answer, and it showed in his stunned reaction.

"In self-defense, Radic, and I have a half dozen witnesses who will say the same," Mauro proclaimed defiantly.

Radic scratched his beard while thinking of what was to be done. He was the sworn official in this matter.

"I don't doubt anything you have told me, Lord Baric, but you know the Republic's protocol. A baron has been killed here tonight. Your wife can stay with you, of course, if she was indeed involved, but I will have to take Jero with me until the Venetian authorities come. I am sorry, my lord," Constable Radic said.

Mauro looked over at his brother, sitting dazed among the room's commotion. "Jero stays here," he told his constable.

"Sir, you know I—"

"There has been another turn of events, Radic. My uncle is the regional authority, and he will understand my order, once he learns Jero is his nephew."

"Jero is a Baric?"

"I will not allow my brother to be arrested," Mauro said firmly.

"Well, sir, I will not argue that. You only have to look at the young man to guess it. Is there finally some proof about it?"

Mauro could hardly think about what proof there might be with the noise and disorder going on around him. Then the answer struck him. He had burned it. "You will have to take my word for now."

"I will," Radic assured him, leaning in to be heard over the din. "Jero is under arrest until the facts are all documented, but he may stay with you, my lord." The constable looked around and said, "We'll get started on this mess, sir, and get the bodies out. Too bad it had to be tonight of all nights. I am glad I was not too drunk to ride my horse."

"I believe Dubovic calculated that in his scheme."

"It seems the baron planned more than seizing your castle, sir. I heard you and your men were ambushed."

"Dubovic has wanted something from the Barics for many years, Radic, and I stood in his way. He did not manage to kill me today, but he admitted right here that he already committed murder in my house. He was the one who poisoned my father with the wine." Mauro hesitated a moment, then added, "He convinced my mother to help him."

The constable took a step back in shock. "He coerced her ladyship to do his murderous bidding? You know, sir, this bit of information makes the case all the more delicate. Perhaps you will want to discuss this with your uncle before I put the facts down on parchment."

Mauro had already decided these details had to remain private. "I will write to my uncle directly. He will know the next steps needed to register this crime."

Radic nodded gravely. "I will make a few notes now and have a good look around, if you will allow it, sir."

"I suppose you will need to talk to my wife."

"The baroness was a witness in the deaths of Dubovic and his men, my lord."

"Because of that, she has had quite a shock tonight, Radic. I would like to take her up to her room."

Radic offered, "I expect her ladyship will need much rest after such an ordeal. I will wait to hear from you, sir, instructing when to take Lady Baric's account of what happened. Shall we leave it at that, my lord?"

Mauro was grateful for the delay. "Thank you, Radic. I will send a messenger."

The constable bowed and turned from the baron, shouting orders to the others, "Light all available torches! We need more light in here!" His voice boomed above the noise. "And somebody take these barking dogs back outside!"

Mauro noticed Geoff among the procession of men coming and going in the great hall. He waved him over and said, "You have done well tonight, Geoff."

"Did Jero find the baroness, my lord?" the boy asked, not seeing the baron's wife in the chaos.

"Thanks to you, she is safe, Geoff. But I need you to do one more thing for me."

"Anything, sir," Geoff said eagerly, despite his outward exhaustion. The boy had already been through too much turmoil, but Mauro knew that Geoff alone could do this task without explanation.

"Someone needs to get Nela and Franja from the caves."

"Oh, they won't know they can come back, will they, sir? I will get them right now."

Mauro smiled at his enthusiasm and watched him hurry out the servants' door.

~*~

Patrik held his sister's hand as the two came in through the terrace doors. Resi ran the last few steps to her husband, and Mauro caught her in his arms.

"I thought I had lost you," Mauro whispered against her neck, kissing her there as he breathed her in.

"I almost thought the same," she told him through her tears of joy.

"You were so brave tonight, my love."

He stepped back and looked her over to be sure she was whole. "I am sorry I wasn't here to protect you."

"Jero protected me tonight. He was my champion, and so was Geoff."

"I met Geoff on the castle road," Mauro said. "He was the reason we knew how to find you. They boy was as courageous as my best soldiers. And Jero . . ." Mauro couldn't go on. Reliving his talk with Jero in his mind and seeing the familiar faces helping to bring order back to his house was too overwhelming.

Gazing out at the crowd, Mauro noticed Ruby at the foyer door. He saw her search the room until her eyes rested on Jero. She would help him recover, he thought.

"Is it really over now?" Resi asked as he held her close again.

"The constable will want to talk to you, to hear what happened, but that can wait until you have rested. Let me take you upstairs, Resi, my love."

Mauro guided her out of the noisy hall into the quiet foyer.

"Is Verica back in her room?" he asked as they climbed the steps.

"Ruby took her there a few moments ago. She is pretty shaken up."

When they reached the second floor, Mauro could see a candle was burning in Verica's room by the glow under her door. "I will send Geoff up to stay with her tonight," he said.

Resi nodded sleepily.

Mauro opened their chamber door, and they went in together. He guided Resi to the bed. "I will help you undress if you like."

He unwrapped the linen towel she had draped over her shoulders in the bathhouse. Mauro noticed for the first time that she wore a canvas apron over her pretty, silken shift. He loosened the long ties and took the grimy smock away.

She sat down on the bed and watched him as he looked through her trunk for her favorite sleeping shift, then brought it to her. Resi's eyes were drooping, and she was nearly asleep sitting on the edge of the mattress.

Mauro lifted the dirty undergarment over her head and helped her into her soft nightgown. He unpinned her hair and let it fall around her shoulders. He stroked her curls as she closed her eyes again.

"I am tired of fighting, Resi. For ten years, I have been killing men for the Empire. Today, I killed to avenge my father," he told her as he tied her silky locks back with a ribbon, marveling at how light her hair felt in his hands—soft and pretty, just like her. "Racing home, I thought only of you, alone here, and how afraid I was to lose you. I could not let you be taken from me, and I was helpless to stop it. But you are an amazing woman, Resi. You were not helpless without me. You fought for yourself and for us."

Resi listened with closed eyes, and tears leaked from their corners.

He smiled down at her and said, "You were the protector tonight, my darling, and you make me so proud."

He kissed her soft lips, and she opened her eyes.

"It has been a long, long day," he said. "Sleep now, my love. I will be back as soon as I can."

Resi got under the covers and held her hand outstretched to him. Mauro took it in his when she asked, "Will you stay with me for a while?"

"Yes, my dearest," he answered.

Within minutes, she was asleep, and Mauro reluctantly took himself away from her to go back downstairs.

Chapter 68

Jero sat hunched over in the chair by the hearth with Vilim by his side. Ruby held out a cup of water, and Jero absently accepted the drink without noticing who had offered it.

Vilim quietly left when Ruby knelt in front of Jero.

"You didn't die," she said after they were alone.

Hearing her voice, Jero looked up over the top of the mug he clung to, and the room came into focus once again. Ruby had washed the blood from her face and fixed her tangled hair. She looked unharmed, and Jero was relieved.

"I kept that part of my promise," he meekly replied. He set the cup down on the stone floor and began to unwrap the layers of jackets.

She stood up and took his hand in hers. "Will you walk me upstairs, Jero? I am going to get some sleep. You should, too."

Jero was stiff from sitting for so long. He let her lead him out the foyer door. It felt good to leave the bustling noise of the great hall behind, and they ambled up the stairs together.

Ruby broke the silence when they reached the top landing and continued down the corridor. "Resi told me how brave you were. How you came up with a plan to save us."

"I think I was only brave because of you, Ruby. I had to do something, anything, to free you."

They were in front of Ruby's chamber door. She grasped the handle but didn't turn it.

"You said you came back to marry me."

Jero leaned against the wall by the door and fought the urge to take her in his arms.

"I did say that, and I do intend to marry you, once I get your father's blessing. I want more than anything for you to be my wife, Ruby. I love you."

Jero felt light, almost dizzy, having said the words out loud. He stood in front of her, and his arm found its natural place around her waist. It was not how a man should touch a woman engaged to marry another, but Jero didn't care. He needed to hold her close.

"Ruby," he began.

She looked up at him, waiting.

"I am coming with you," he declared. "I will stay in Greece and live with you there if that is what it takes. But if it pleases you, I want to bring you back here, back to Baric Castle."

She rested her head against his chest in relief. "Oh, Jero, it would please me very much. I know when my father meets you, he will say yes, but I would like to come back. I have grown to love it here."

He stroked her soft hair draped over her slender shoulder. "Do you remember when we kissed by the lake?" he whispered in her ear as he breathed in her scent. "Do you remember what you said to me?" Jero knew every word she had said, but he wanted to hear it again.

She looked up and smiled. "I said, 'The next time you kiss me, you will have to marry me.'"

"May I?" Jero asked.

"Kiss me?"

"Marry you."

"Yes, Jero. Yes to both."

Jero had sat three days in the rented chamber in Zadar under the inn's hot roof, wondering if Ruby could even love him as much as he loved her. He finally believed that she did.

Ruby turned the handle, and her door swung open behind them.

Jero followed her in and shut it. He had killed a man tonight, but he would not do anything else to land in hell. He only needed to hold Ruby in his arms for a while.

~*~

A few minutes later, Jero opened her door and saw Mauro on the other side of the corridor coming from his own chamber, where he had left his wife sleeping.

Mauro waited for Jero at the top of the stairs. "I won't ask what you were doing." Mauro sounded like the baron again.

"I needed to be alone with her for a moment," Jero explained anyway.

"Do you love her?" Mauro needed to hear that he did.

"Now more than ever," Jero said.

They stood together at the top of the steps, and Mauro wondered, "How can you be sure, Jero?"

Jero looked off into the dark distance and told his brother, "When I walk into a room full of people, hers is the voice I hear first. She is the face I seek out. I go to sleep with her in my thoughts. And when I finally kissed her, it was unlike any other woman I have kissed. I know the difference between lust and lightning bolts. It feels right with Ruby."

Mauro knew that was exactly how he felt with Resi, and he was glad to hear it explained in words.

"I am happy for you, Jero. You should go to bed now with those thoughts, and you will sleep well."

"Do I get to stay here tonight, then? Does the constable not want to take me away?"

"I explained a few things to Radic. He will be back on Monday to talk to you and Resi. It is late, Jero. Get some sleep now."

Mauro started down the stairs.

"Mauro, wait."

Mauro walked the few steps back to his brother's side.

"There is something weighing on my mind, Mauro. Maybe you can help me."

"What is it, Jero?"

Jero took a breath and asked, "Do you think Lord Lorenc loved my mother?"

"Yes, I do," he said.

"Then she wasn't his whore?"

"Dubovic was just trying to taunt you, Jero. Your mother was no whore. I know that her name was Sonja, and she took care of Mateo after she lost her own baby and husband in the plague. She must have been a special woman if Father fell in love with her. Idita told me he would have married her, but Uncle Vladimir was against it. He had her sent away before either of them knew she was pregnant. When Father learned of it, he searched for you, Jero, and brought you home."

"I feel like I am in a dream, Mauro, but I am glad to finally know this. Thank you."

"It is the truth, and I am glad to tell you all I know. Now I must go back downstairs," Mauro said.

"I will come with you."

"You will not," Mauro asserted. "This will be my last order to you: Go get some sleep."

"And you, Mauro?" Jero challenged. "When will you sleep?"

"Well," said Mauro with a shrug, "that is the curse of being the master of the house."

"I am too tired to argue with you, but I don't expect this will be the last time you tell me what to do."

Mauro, who was already halfway down the stairs, looked over his shoulder and smiled. "You know me too well. Good night, Jero."

When Mauro returned to the great hall, he was glad to see it had been emptied while he was away. Men were mopping up the last pools of blood to spare the Baric maids the gruesome chore. The bodies had been taken to the courtyard and loaded onto a wagon to be returned to Dubovic Castle. Mauro didn't know who would be there to claim them, but he didn't care, either.

The house servants had come back to the castle with the villagers after the alarm had been sounded, but Radic had kept them out of the great hall.

Franja was the one exception Radic had made, and she came toward the baron when he entered the room.

"Lord Baric, sir, I have been asking where Simeon is, and no one can tell me. He rode out with you today is all I am certain of."

"He is with Eduard in the village," Mauro answered honestly.

"Oh, well, he had said he wasn't going to the party, but I guess he changed his mind. Thank you, my lord," she said with visible disappointment.

Mauro could not send her out without the whole truth. "I need to explain, Franja. Eduard took him there to find Idita. Simeon was hurt in an ambush, and it is bad. He hit his head and broke his leg. I heard he is at Radic's house."

Mauro instinctively put his arm around her shoulders, and Franja slumped against him. She would have fallen to the floor if he had let her go.

"I know he would not want you to worry, Franja. Simeon is a strong man, a survivor. Go get some sleep now," the baron said kindly. "I will have Idita come talk to you when she returns in the morning."

Mauro walked with her to the servants' entrance and felt her gather her strength. She nodded that she would be alright, and he released his grip. Franja walked solemnly away and out of sight down the corridor.

Mauro had one more person to find tonight.

"Get up, Geoff," ordered Mauro when he found him.

The boy was back in the great hall, crouched on his hands and knees with a bucket of water and a rag.

"Leave that to someone else. You have done too much tonight," Mauro said.

Geoff stood up stiffly and wiped his wet hands on his breeches. "I'm alright, my lord. I am not tired, and this needs to be done," he told his master.

"Your sister needs you, Geoff," the baron said.

Geoff seemed to panic. "What has happened to Verica?"

Mauro put his hands on the tall boy's shoulders and told him soothingly, "She is not hurt, Geoff, but she is not feeling well. She was with Lady Ruby here in the hall with Dubovic's men, the same men whose blood you just cleaned up. Stay with your sister tonight. She might need someone to talk to."

Geoff showed no reaction, and Mauro was worried as he waited for the boy's response.

Finally, the boy blinked, and tears began to fall as it all seemed to sink in. Geoff dropped his rag into the bucket of bloody water and said, "I didn't know that, my lord. Thank you, sir. I will take my leave now." Geoff walked out the foyer door.

Mauro was now all alone in the torchlit great hall. His eyes told him it was the same room as yesterday and last year, but in his mind, he knew it was not.

Exhausted, Mauro sat down on the upholstered chair Jero had just vacated and cradled his head in his hands. He wanted his house back to normal before he could rest. What was left to do tonight?

The chair next to him creaked with the weight of a new occupant. Mauro looked over to find Patrik sitting next to him.

The two sat in silence for a few moments, and then Patrik asked, "Will you jail me too, Mauro?"

Mauro laughed out loud at the unexpected question. "Do you want to be jailed, Patrik? You could just confess to our priest. I think that should absolve you. There is no need for a trial."

"I am not talking about killing the men today." His tired eyes focused on Mauro when he added, "I know your secret, don't I? The one you imprisoned my father for."

Mauro ran his fingers through his hair. "Ah, yes. That is a problem," he said calmly.

Their eyes met.

"Can you keep a secret, Patrik, like your father has all these years? Or will you double-cross me?" It was a real question, and Mauro wanted his answer.

Patrik seemed to consider the options. "In principle, I always double-cross aristocrats who have more than they deserve in life. But we are family, Mauro, and my family deserves all that life can offer. Your secret is safe with me."

Mauro's voice softened when he asked, "Did I thank you for your help today, Brother?"

The added word did not go unnoticed.

"You have been a little busy for that. Still, I need no 'thank you.' I will defend you any day. Brother."

Mauro nodded and smiled. "I need one more favor, though." Mauro leaned back in his chair and stretched his arms over his head, stalling while thinking of the best way to ask.

Patrik was dead tired and growing impatient. "Anything, Mauro. Just ask."

"Can you postpone your journey back home?"

Patrik leaned in and asked, "Is there more trouble?"

"Jero has it in his mind that he is going to Greece with you. He wants to ask Angelos Spiros to give Ruby to him and not this other man."

Patrik was the one who laughed this time. "Well, this will be interesting. Sure, why not! There is no need to postpone our departure, though. I think I can get the others to agree quickly enough."

Mauro sat up tall again. "Yes, but now that he is being charged with murder, Jero cannot simply leave until the authorities agree to release him. He will be exonerated as soon as my uncle can put his seal on it, but these things can take time. He needs to clear his name first, or they will consider him a fugitive."

Patrik considered this. "How much time does Jero need?"

Mauro shrugged. "I can send a courier tomorrow, and I am sure my uncle will make it a priority to hear his case. But it could take two weeks, maybe longer."

"Two weeks?" Patrik shook his head. "We need to leave sooner than that."

Mauro held his stare. "What about a week, then?"

Patrik took a deep breath and then blew it out in frustration. "I don't know. I will ask the others. Bem will not be happy, and Salar Nassim is already anxious to be on his way."

"That is all I ask of you. One week, and the rest we will leave to fate." Mauro stood up and stretched. "Come, I will walk you out. I need some air before I go to bed."

—·*·—

Mauro did not make it to bed before the dawn rose. He found Alberto and Milan and thanked them for their quick actions in lighting the alarm and holding the Keep. In the courtyard, Mauro learned that two of his soldiers had been killed in the first attack on the castle. He had their bodies laid out in the chapel for the night. Only then did he retire to his study to write an urgent letter to his uncle and two more letters calling in the favors he had been offered by Lord Carrera and Lord Valli for taking care of their daughters.

Rays of pink streaked the eastern sky as Mauro finally climbed the staircase again. Davor was coming down the servants' stairway to begin his duties, and Mauro waved him over. He handed him the three letters from his waistcoat pocket. Each was carefully addressed, and Mauro expected Davor would know how to expedite them.

"These must go out today," Mauro said.

The valet's handsome face was pale from the short night, and his eyes drooped, but he accepted his first duty of the day. He looked at the destinations written on the sealed parchments.

"It is Sunday, sir, and the boat does not run to Venice," Davor reminded him.

"Yes, so it is. Pay the extra price for a special crossing," the baron said. "The correspondence is urgent."

"Yes, of course, my lord. I will get right on it," Davor assured him. He started down the stairs.

"Will you go to Mass today?" Mauro asked over the baluster.

The baron gave Davor Sundays free to attend church and meet with his family, but Davor was loyal to his master.

"May I, sir? I can stay at the castle if you prefer."

"I insist you go, and when you see Father David, tell him that Jero and I will come tomorrow for our confessions." With so much at stake, Mauro reasoned that God might look more favorably on the House of Baric if he confessed his sins as soon as possible.

"Would you rather the priest come to the castle and hold confession here again, my lord?"

"No, I will take the sacrament at the church. I need to go to the village tomorrow to check on Simeon's condition. If he did not survive the night, then I will make arrangements with the priest when I see him."

"Of course, my lord."

"I am going to sleep now, Davor, and won't need your assistance beyond getting these letters out." Mauro opened the door to his shuttered chamber and closed out the world for the rest of the day.

Chapter 69

They didn't retrieve Simeon on Monday, and not even on Tuesday. The miserable heatwave had ended with an earth-shaking thunderstorm that washed the hillsides and flooded the cobbled streets for two solid days. The Barics and villagers stayed put in their houses and watched as the world cleaned itself from their windows.

When the sun shone on Wednesday and the wetness steamed away, it was a typical July day again, as though nothing had happened. But everything had changed for Jero in the House of Baric.

Word had spread fast about Jero's heroic role in saving the castle from the intruders and the dramatic death of Lord Dubovic, and everyone came to show him their gratitude. But word had also spread of his newly discovered parentage, and the congratulations were given with stiff bows and curtsies, not the usual warm hugs and handshakes the old Jero was accustomed to. Jero did not like being Mauro's new brother so far, and he took his troubles to the only one he thought could help him: Mauro.

Jero sat slumped on the chair next to Mauro's writing desk and complained, "Everyone is treating me differently. I cannot walk into a room and have a conversation with one person without the entire room coming to attention. I have always been a servant, Mauro. I do not want to be the master."

Mauro put his quill down and said, "If you think about it, Jero, you have always been a servant with special privileges, with access to the master of the house that the other servants do not have. And you have always had servants under you, too. Who washes your clothes, mends your shirts, cooks your food, lights your fire, and brings your water? Servants serving you have done all of that without question. Now there must be a distinction made. You are a Baric, Jero, and going forward, the servants will call you Lord Jero, like they call Fabian Lord Fabian. He does not have a title either, but it distinguishes his status here."

"But Fabian is not a bastard," Jero quietly reminded him.

Mauro knew the facts might contradict him, but he was firm in his opinion. "Father did not get a chance to marry your mother, but I believe he loved her. Bastard or not, you are Lorenc Baric's son, and you will be shown respect in this house."

Mauro stood up and walked away from his desk to the window. He spoke more sympathetically when he said, "How you choose to have your servants address you at your new home will be your business, Jero. Be friends with them if you choose, but it will make your life harder."

Jero understood the separation between a commander and his soldiers, a steward and his staff, and the Barics and everyone else. Jero had never imagined he would see what his world looked like from the top tier.

Mauro turned back to Jero and reminded him, "Try to remember that you are to call my wife Terese. If she offers that you call her Resi, I am not opposed to that."

"I must admit, I am having a hard time with it, Mauro. Your wife has always been *Lady* Terese to me."

"And she will be the first to tell you that she is not a lady," Mauro maintained. "It took Resi a long time to adjust to being a baroness and all the formalities that went with it. She has embraced her new life and so will you."

Jero pointed out, "But Terese has a legitimate title since marrying you. I will never be accepted into the bloodline. If your uncle did not allow it twenty-some years ago, why would he allow it now?"

"We will wait and hear what he will say in light of everything that has happened. Until then, Jero, this is how I will run my house." Mauro went back to his desk and picked up his quill.

With that, the conversation was ended, and Jero quietly left the room.

~ * ~

The four mercenaries agreed to give Jero a week to solve his legal problems. Patrik had managed this by convincing Salar Nassim that they needed Jero on the journey. He would be the sixth rider, and the Persian had always said that six was the luckiest number.

Patrik was pleased that he could arrange this for Ruby's sake, but he first had a few words of advice for Jero before sharing the good news with him, which he did the following day.

~*~

Several Baric residents and officers were whiling away the day in the great hall as the dramatic summer storm thundered outside. Some played music, others busied themselves with mending or reading to make the time pass, and Patrik and Jero were at the small table where Caterina had learned card cheating from Salar Nassim.

They were in the middle of a game when Patrik declared, "I am doing you a favor by telling you this, Jero."

Jero drew two cards and checked his luck with the other ones in his hand. "What do you have to tell me, Patrik?" He folded with nothing to play.

Patrik scooped up Jero's unlucky cards and shuffled the deck. "You realize Angelos Spiros is a protective father? He won't like that you are pursuing his daughter so openly without his blessing."

Jero picked up the new hand and sorted through the cards. "I do not think I am so obvious with my affection," he replied.

"That's because you cannot see what others can."

"I am sincere in my love for Ruby," Jero said.

"I am sure you are, but don't forget that you have disrupted plans that Ruby's father worked hard to negotiate. He may not like you at all because of that."

"We will talk to him, both of us."

"I have no doubt you will eventually sway him and marry his daughter. It helps that you are a rich man now," Patrik added. "But Father Spiros might make you wait—just for the sport of it."

A week ago, Patrik's warning would have given Jero debilitating doubt in himself, but today he said, "I will wait as long as it takes."

"Bravo, Jero. That is the right answer if you love Ruby. But let me give you a word of warning."

Jero set his cards down on the table.

Patrik met his eyes and said, "Ruby believes she will marry you, which is why I worry that she would not deny you whatever you asked. So, I am telling you, Jero: don't ask it."

The remark took Jero by surprise. "Is that what you think of me, Patrik?"

"What I think doesn't matter, Jero. I am just telling you that as far as we know, Ruby is still bound to Nikko. If she arrives home with a baby in her belly, her family will say you took advantage of another man's woman, and Ruby will be shamed for letting you."

Ruby's open affection had tempted Jero, but he insisted, "I would never do anything that would disgrace Ruby. You have my word."

Patrik collected the cards again. "I am glad we cleared that up, Jero," he replied. "And now for the terms."

"Terms for what?" Jero asked as he accepted the newly dealt cards.

"We have a long trip ahead of us, and you must agree to my terms if you are to come along."

Jero nodded.

"Good. I trust that you have some self-control, but just the same, Ruby will sleep at my side on the road, not at yours. And if we run into trouble, we know now that you can kill a man, and we will expect you to fight without hesitation. Lastly, you will not be given special treatment in our company. There are no lords among us."

"Yes, of course."

"If that is all acceptable, Jero, my friends and I will wait one week for you to clear your name."

Mauro had warned Jero that the mercenaries might not even agree to his request, and Jero thought about Patrik's terms as he studied his cards. Patrik had dealt him a good hand, and Jero looked up, smiling.

"I agree to all your terms, Patrik. Thank you for taking me along. I promise I won't be of any trouble."

Chapter 70

Eduard took it hard when Idita amputated Simeon's leg. In the noise and chaos of the Radic sitting room, Eduard pleaded that Simeon was a soldier and he would not want to live as a legless man. "Let him be," he begged Idita as she cleaned the borrowed saw.

Idita was firm with him. The leg was dead from being tied off, and Simeon was delirious with fever. She was not a surgeon, but after decades of doctoring, she had the knowledge of one.

"These are the baron's instructions, Eduard," she said. "He knows God has granted me the skill to save Simeon's life. God may still take him. It is He who will decide Simeon's fate, not you and not me."

Idita could not be dissuaded, so Eduard and Daniel had no choice but to assist her. They held Simeon down while the petite nurse competently sawed off the fractured bones above the knee, seared the flesh and arteries closed, and then sewed the skin to cover the open wound.

After the gut-wrenching surgery, Eduard agreed it was the only thing that could have saved his friend's life. It was in God's hands like she had said, and Eduard hoped God would be merciful.

After three feverish days recovering on a cot in the sitting room of the Radic home, Simeon was brought back to his chamber in the Keep. Idita had stayed by his side until she was sure Simeon would survive the wagon ride home.

Mauro had accompanied him during the ride from the village, but Simeon refused to look his way. Earlier, Simeon had asked Idita why she did not let him die, and she had told him the truth. Helpless and crippled now, Simeon could not forgive Mauro for condemning him to this existence.

The soldiers carefully carried their injured friend to his room on the officers' floor, and Mauro put Tin in charge of bringing Simeon what he needed while bedridden there.

Franja had tried several times to visit Simeon during his first days back. No one had kept her away, but Simeon did not want her to see him in this sorry state. He thought she was only visiting him out of pity, and he wanted no one's sympathy.

Eduard was the only one Simeon would talk to.

"Give him time. He will come around," Eduard told them all.

~*~

Mauro was powerless to help Simeon in his painful recovery, so he focused his worries on Jero's cause. He'd laid out Jero's story and all the known facts of his parentage to Lords Carrera and Valli. They were powerful politicians in Venice, and Mauro had asked them to bend the rules for him in his desperate letters. They had known his family for decades, and Mauro hoped they would see the truth in Jero's plight without presenting actual proof of his entitlement.

Two days later, a courier from Venice arrived at Baric Castle. Mauro tipped the man a silver coin and read through Lord Carrera's proposal. He took the stairs two at a time and knocked on Jero's door.

In his room, Jero was sorting through his possessions and feeling melancholy. The difficult task of packing had to be faced. No matter the outcome, he would be leaving the House of Baric sometime soon.

Jero looked up from his chore when Mauro came into his chamber with a beaming smile.

"Come ride with me," Mauro said.

"Now? Where do you want to go?"

"You will see."

Intrigued, Jero abandoned his chore, and the two brothers saddled their horses and rode south on the trade road. It was a fine day, and the warm wind blew their jacket tails behind them as they sped down the familiar route.

After a time, Mauro slowed his horse to a trot and broke the silence. "Do you feel cheated, Jero?" he asked unexpectedly.

Jero took a moment to think about it. "Being indentured?" he asked.

"You could have lived the life Mateo and I had if Father had not kept the truth from us."

"I guess I never expected to lead any different life from the one I had. But knowing what we know now, perhaps we were all cheated in some way."

"How could he have let it go on for so long, you serving us all these years?"

"Sons serve their fathers in many ways, and brothers serve brothers, too. Father was a generous man with a warm heart, Mauro. I am sorry you do not remember that."

Mauro pondered, "If only he had told me the truth."

"Would your younger self have accepted me as a brother?" Jero rightfully pointed out.

Mauro reflected, "I suppose not. But I do now, Jero. I could not have asked for a more loyal friend and truer brother."

They passed several travelers and merchants, and then they were alone on the highway once more.

Mauro slowed his horse again and said, "I have good news to tell you."

"I heard Davor announce the courier earlier. Did you get a reply to your letters?"

"Yes, the best reply I could have hoped for. Lord Carrera has much influence, but I never expected he could make such a promise."

"Am I to be accepted as a son, then?"

"You will be officially added to the Baric lineage, Jero. I am sorry to say that I will remain titleholder of the barony, even though you are older."

Jero chuckled with relief. "You were born to be the next baron, not I."

"I hoped you would understand," Mauro said as they rode on toward their destination. "It is only because your mother was never Father's wife. But your children will be in line after mine. They will be included in the Venetian aristocracy, and so will you, Jero."

"I would have been happy without any nobility, Mauro, you know that. I liked being the steward of Baric Castle. I would have been content to take Ruby as my wife and raise our family in Tomas's old cottage."

"But I would not have been happy, Jero. You saved my wife and everything that is dear to me. That is a debt I would like to repay."

"I need no reward, Mauro. You have done so much for me already."

"There is something of the Barics I would like you to have. It is not a reward for your heroics, because I was planning to give it to you before everything happened," Mauro said with a chuckle.

Their horses trotted along, past the salt flats and farther south on the highway. Jero looked over and saw how impatient Mauro was to tell him. "What have you been plotting?" he asked.

"I know you are a modest man, but you need a proper house, not a cottage. I am giving you my villa," Mauro proudly announced.

"Mauro, you can't be serious."

"It has been finalized, Jero. You are the new landlord of the old tenant farm and villa. Manage it well, and you will have a good income. Signor Bernardo will make the changes you suggested. As a matter of fact, the renovations should be done by the time you are back from Thessaloniki."

"I do not know what to say, Mauro. You know I am very fond of your villa house, even the way it is now. It will be more than perfect for me and Ruby. Thank you."

"I want you to have more, but Lord Carrera was very clear that the bulk of the estate must stay with the barony. I have the salt fields, the village, our river port, and all the farmlands to the northeast. Signor Rosso will officially split the property, and we can work out what to do with the emerald mine in private."

"It goes with the castle," Jero said with conviction. "Besides, it is used to keep the village prosperous."

Mauro agreed, "I would rather not have to spend any of the emeralds, but it does seem necessary from time to time. We will figure something out."

He stopped his horse at the overgrown entrance to a little-used side road. "I wanted to go down this way. The road is in better shape than this gate." Mauro jumped off his horse and moved the broken gate aside.

When he was back in his saddle, Mauro said, "Come on, I will race you," and he urged Janus to a full gallop.

In a quick reaction, Bacchus followed Janus down the narrow road, picking up speed as Jero clung to the reins in delight.

As the pines and shrubs passed by in a blur, they quickly approached the end of the hardened dirt road, side by side. Ahead of them was a small manor house with several outbuildings. The tiled roof was faded, and the plaster was cracked from the salt and sun.

Mauro dismounted and tied Janus to a rail post. The glistening sea was in full view in front of them.

"What is this place?" Jero asked, stopping beside him, catching his breath.

"Have you never been here?"

"No."

Of course, Jero would not have visited, Mauro realized. His father had closed this place up after the accident. The old stone house had a padlock on the weathered door. The windows had long ago been shuttered, and a few of those boards were broken. Mauro walked up to one and peered in. "This house was once a busy inn," he explained.

Jero followed him along the neglected walkway. "It looks like there has been no caretaker here for years."

"When Mateo was alive, Father would let us stay here on sweltering summer days. I wonder why he never let you come with us."

"Maybe he did not trust the three of us away together, out of his watch."

"With good reason," Mauro agreed with a chuckle. He strolled past their waiting horses tied near the inn's front entrance and continued toward the horizon. Mauro stopped when he reached the edge of the unkempt property. The Adriatic sparkled in front of him.

Jero caught up to him. "It is lovely here."

Mauro nodded. "I am going to have the inn repaired and let Ivanoslav Tomsic live here."

"Ivanoslav? I thought he went north after his illness."

Mauro thought about the last conversation he'd had with the younger Tomsic captain and explained, "The old captain wants to die looking out at the sea, Jero. Ivanoslav served the Barics for years and probably knows what we really exchange on our moonless deliveries with the Kokkinos ship. The father or the son could have turned us in for smuggling and earned a sizable reward for it, but they never did. And Barics have never thanked them for it."

"It is a prime piece of seashore, Mauro. Making the old captain a caretaker would be very charitable."

"To be honest, I am not naturally so charitable. Father David put the idea into my head. By doing this, I am fulfilling a penance for my sins of lust and greed," Mauro told him with a chuckle.

Jero raised his brows at his brother's confession. "I thought you did not care about going to heaven, Mauro."

"Saving my soul from burning in hell is not my worry, but completing this penance solves my concern for a suitable caretaker. I have thought about this place off and on recently. It has been neglected for too long."

Mauro pointed down at the narrow, rocky beach below and explained, "There is room to put a small pier there, once the path is fortified. It is a deep, little inlet. Maybe it can be profitable for fishing and the inn for lodging again."

It finally became clear to Jero where they were.

"Are these the diving cliffs, Mauro?"

Mauro looked beyond Jero, out to the sea. A scowl crossed his face when he remarked, "It is not as high as I remembered."

The two had been as close as brothers leading up to that fateful day. Still, Mauro had not confided in Jero about the accident.

"Will you finally tell me what happened here?" Jero urged. "You could have sneaked out and found me in the stables, Mauro. We could have talked about it then."

Mauro shut his eyes as the memories came flooding back.

"I almost did, but I could not risk leaving the room. It sounds foolish now, but I thought maybe it had been one of Mateo's pranks, and I wanted to be there when he crawled up the trellis and into our window."

"You were waiting for him the whole time?"

"Yes, I waited, wondering why he would choose to stay away, why he would leave me. I hated him for it. I cursed him. I missed him. I miss him still."

Jero looked into his brother's distant eyes and pleaded, "How did he die, Mauro? Tell me."

This was the reason Mauro had brought Jero there. Not to tell him about re-making the inn, but to finally unburden what had weighed on him all these years. Standing there, where the accident had happened, the locked-up feelings of despair and helplessness were more overwhelming than Mauro had anticipated. He took strength from Jero's steady hold and began to tell him everything.

"Grgur was the guard in charge of us that day. He was to take us home. There had been a terrible storm night before, but I remember it was already hot and muggy again when Grgur had us wait in our room while he got the wagon ready. None of the village boys had come back to swim that morning, but Mateo wanted to go in one more time. When it was clear Grgur was busy in the stables, we snuck away, and laughed that Grgur would have to search for us. We came here, to this very spot."

Jero looked over the edge into the sea. "I can see why you wanted to swim here. It looks inviting."

"It was not inviting on that day." Mauro recalled the black clouds that had backed up against the mountains to the east, so unlike this day's blue skies, and told Jero, "I told Mateo that the sea was too rough. It was foaming over the rocks, and we could not see the diving hole. He teased me and said the diving hole would not have floated away and that it would be an adventure to swim when the gods were angry." Mauro shook his head, remembering those words. "He was fearless, Jero, and foolish."

"What did he do?"

"Mateo stripped out of his breeches to keep them dry for the ride home. I was still wearing mine, not wanting to go in. Still, he put his hand on my shoulder to jump together, like we always did. I remember the happy grin on his face like it was yesterday. He yelled, 'One, two, three,' and then he tugged at me as he ran the few steps and leaped off with a gleeful shout. I felt ashamed for being afraid, and so I went to the edge to jump in after him. I expected to see him swimming in the water, calling up at me to jump, but there was no Mateo."

Mauro was there now, not with Jero, as he relived that terrible moment.

"I had never seen the sea churning like that. You could always see the bottom, but not on that day. If he had already climbed out, there was no place to hide. Just to be sure, I ran down the path and looked in the seagrass there. I climbed over the rocks and plunged in, searching for him. The water was frothy, and the salt stung my eyes, but I looked for him. The waves kept pushing me against the boulders, but somehow I managed to climb back out and onto the path. I ran back up to the ledge, expecting Mateo to be standing there, but I was still alone.

"Grgur rode up to me on his horse. They told me I was screaming Mateo's name, but I do not remember that. Grgur looked for him all over the narrow shoreline and by the rocks. We went back to the inn and checked all the rooms. I pointed out that Mateo had left his breeches on the sandy ledge, and we should go back for them. Grgur said we would leave them there for Mateo when he came back. But he knew Mateo was not coming back.

"Grgur then pulled me up onto his horse and rode with me to the castle. I had never seen Grgur panic before, and it frightened me. He left me by the front door, and I went up to our chamber and sat alone for what seemed like hours, because it was dark when Father finally came to my room. I remember he lit a candle and sat by my bed. He did not tell me if they had found Mateo, or anything else. He simply asked, 'Why did you not jump with him, Mauritius?'"

When Mauro did not go on, Jero asked quietly, "What did you tell him?"

Mauro looked angry for a moment, and then his expression softened, and he took a deep breath. "What could I tell Father? That I was too scared to jump? That I knew we should not be swimming in the sea when the gods were angry? That Mateo never listened to me? I said nothing." Mauro did not try to stop the tears as they dropped from the corners of his misty eyes. "I was just a little boy! I needed my father to tell me that everything would be all right, to say that he was glad I did not die, too! But he did not do any of that, Jero. He just picked up the candle and left again. And so I waited for Mateo to come back to me, but of course, he never did."

Jero felt the weight of Mauro's tale, and he wiped the tears off his own cheeks. "Accidents happen to boys all the time," he whispered. "Mateo was brash and impulsive. If he had lived, he would have turned that boyish recklessness into his strength."

"He thought he was immortal, Jero, like the gods of the underworld he liked to tell stories about." Mauro searched the water for Mateo's ghost and said, "For the longest time, I thought maybe he had managed it, to be with them, to be immortal. But he was just dead."

Mauro then shouted at the Adriatic, "Why do I get to be immortal, Mateo? Why did I live through it all?" A calmness came over Mauro when he told the sea, "War showed me how random death is, Mateo. So many young soldiers died in the blink of an eye, and for what purpose? They too had fathers and brothers who loved them, who missed them. And I get to live on with no more than a few scars?"

Mauro finally turned to look at Jero and saw that he was undressing. "What are you doing?" he asked.

"I am going to jump," Jero replied, unbuttoning his waistcoat.

"No, Jero! Please, I beg of you." The horror of it overwhelmed him.

Jero's shirt was off, and he was removing his shoes. He, too, was overcome with grief, but after hearing Mauro's story, Jero knew this was the right thing to do in light of it all.

"Jump with me," Jero said as he continued undressing. "Nothing will harm you today."

Mauro stood dazed at the thought of losing another brother to the sea. "Please, Jero! Do you not understand?"

Jero put his hand on Mauro's shoulder, searching for the brave man trapped behind the little boy's fear in Mauro's tearful eyes.

Mauro moaned, "We stood right here, together. I hesitated. I let him go."

"The sea took him, Mauro, and it would have taken you, too. You blame yourself after all these years, but you cannot change what happened. Nobody can."

Jero removed his belt and rolled off his stockings.

Mauro stammered, "Why are you tormenting me? Do not jump! Please!"

Jero didn't back down. He spoke to the twelve-year-old Mauro, "Mateo is not waiting, and Neptune does not want us. Jump with me, Mauro. I will prove it to you."

Mauro blinked back the last of his tears and gathered his courage. He took a deep breath and began to undo his doublet. He removed his shirt and kicked off his shoes. He managed to untie his stockings despite his trembling, the whole time looking at his brother for strength.

Jero stood with Mauro at the cliff's edge and put his arm around his brother's shoulder. Jero's hand rested over the tattoo of Mateo's small hand.

"On three," Jero said quickly, not giving Mauro a chance to change his mind. "One, two, three!"

Together, they ran the two steps and plunged into the azure pool below.

Mauro sank in the clear water, letting the sea drag him down, not caring which way was up. Then he opened his eyes to see the lagoon's rocky bottom, still far below his reach. Colorful fish swam in the depths over the smooth rocks, but no one was with them. No one was waiting to take him. He was safe.

Legs fluttered above Mauro, moving toward the surface. He followed them and came up from the quiet depths to the noise of sea birds and the surf on the rocks. He took a gulp of air and looked around at the open sea.

Jero swam up to Mauro's side, panting for a breath. The current had brought them a good way from the shore, and they swam back to the narrow, rocky beach, where they each found a smooth boulder to sit on in the hot sunshine.

"It all looks farther away when you are twelve," Mauro finally said, breaking their silence.

Jero looked up at the ledge above them. "Some things are easier at twelve," Jero replied. "I have to admit that, if you had not been by my side, I would have been a little scared to jump."

Mauro laughed at his honesty. "Were you pretending to be brave for me, then?"

Jero laughed along with him. "Did I fool you?"

"I do not believe you were fooling. You are far braver than you admit, Jero. Thank you for that."

Then Mauro got up and began to climb the path back to the top of the cliff. Jero followed him; their sodden breeches dripped seawater along the way. The brothers picked up their shirts where they had dropped them and shook out the sand. The light linen filled with air and billowed in the wind.

Mauro slipped his shirt on over his head. It clung to his wet skin. He looked over at Jero, who used his as a towel, and Mauro grinned at his practical nature.

"Did I ever tell you, Jero, that sometimes I thought Mateo liked you better than he liked me? He might have even told me so, once or twice."

Smiling back, Jero said, "I, too, have missed him all these years. When I was little, I used to pretend that you and Mateo were my brothers. I knew it was not true, but pretending was enough for me. It gave me comfort."

Mauro rubbed his left shoulder. "Idita gave me his hand to remind me that Mateo will always be with me. I think she knew I needed his comfort to help me move forward. Today, though, for the very first time, I feel that he would want me to let him go, that I can carry on without him." Peacefulness grew inside him. "Everything feels different now, but in a good way."

They took their time dressing, and when they were finished, Mauro asked, "Do you mind going back alone? I think I will stay here by myself for a while."

Jero nodded that he understood. He walked back to the horses by the inn and mounted Bacchus to leave. Jero turned his horse and called out, "How fast do you think Fabian's stallion can run?"

Jero had led a restrained life as a servant, but Mateo had not been the only Baric son who had a streak of recklessness.

"He is faster than Janus," Mauro yelled back, knowing what was on Jero's mind.

Jero smiled to himself as he recalled Janus was even faster than Blaze. He turned his horse and trotted up the short dirt road until he reached the trade route. Two miles of smooth road stretched out ahead of him before the castle turnoff, and Jero hoped there would not be many travelers in his way.

He patted Bacchus's neck and said to the horse, "I am ready if you are."

Chapter 71

Count Toth rode in the next day with the dark blue splendor of twenty mounted escorts by his side. Mauro's message had found his uncle at his castle, and he immediately made plans to assist his troubled nephew.

The Baric scouts had alerted Mauro that morning that his uncle's troops had been seen on the northern route, and the entire Baric household lined up in the courtyard to welcome the count and his entourage when they rode in through the gates.

The former Baric was in his stiff blue general's jacket to match his soldiers. He did not look bothered by the sweltering heat of the day, except to remove his leather riding gloves, tucking them into his sword belt.

Mauro stood rigid and composed beside his wife. He had unwittingly become his uncle's soldier again, even though Mauro wore his embroidered linen jacket and summer loafers.

Resi managed a low curtsy despite her protruding middle. They had never met, and the count's smiling green eyes remained on her until she looked up at him again.

Mauro's uncle politely bowed to acknowledge his new niece but addressed her husband instead. A man of efficiency, his greeting was formal and brief. "I have come as you requested, Mauritius. Shall we go inside?"

There were no hugs or handshakes, and Mauro's reply was just as formal: "After you, Uncle."

The count glanced back at the gathered crowd and then led the way to the front door.

Mauro imagined that his wife's first impression of his only true relation must have been disappointing, but he couldn't coddle her now. He squeezed her hand and managed a quick smile before following his uncle toward the house. As Mauro had earlier asked, Jero walked at his side.

Davor held the massive oak door open for the approaching noblemen. The valet looked to his master for unspoken instructions, and Mauro gave them with a clear nod.

"Jero will be joining us, if that is all right, Uncle," Mauro informed him as he unlocked his study door.

Vladimir looked from Mauro to Jero and nodded.

Once in the room, the former Baric took the seat at the head of the long table. He removed his hat and placed it on the chair beside him, then motioned for his nephews to sit across from each other.

Davor returned from the kitchen with the readied tray of food and mugs of cool ale. He placed a crock of water on the table and a bottle of wine with glasses next to it.

"What can I offer you, Uncle?" Mauro asked in a friendly tone.

Vladimir took a mug of ale from the tray, and then Davor left them to their privacy.

Mauro's uncle wasted no time in getting to the point. "This is quite a mess I have to sort out for you two. But what is done cannot be changed." He looked directly at Jero and said, "Murdering a nobleman is a high crime."

"It was self-defense," Mauro interjected, "and that is easy to prove. The man invaded my walls, held my people hostage, and killed two of my soldiers while I was fighting off his plotted ambush."

"Yes, yes." His uncle waved his hand in the air to calm his nephew. "I actually stopped in at your village and got the documents from your constable. I have not yet read the testimonies, but he claims that the stories prove Jero's innocence and that Dubovic's crimes caused his own death. It is clear enough to me and your witnesses that Jero had no choice but to defend against Dubovic's attack on your castle. I do not foresee the need for a trial."

Mauro and Jero exchanged relieved glances.

"It is the other claim from you that is more unsettling."

"That Dubovic poisoned my father?" Mauro asked, still agitated.

"Yes," the count said flatly. "We will remove the part about your mother conspiring with him. She is dead, and there is no reason to taint her good name by involving her now. If she had helped him, I believe she did not do it willingly. I will not hear any more about her role in this."

"Of course, Uncle. Thank you. I am relieved you can clear Jero's name so quickly. Just so you know, he will be leaving at the end of the week."

The count looked at Jero and asked, "To where?"

Jero cleared his throat nervously and answered, "I plan to go to Greece, my lord. I will marry there and return with my bride."

The count shook his head with amusement. "Another Greek bride? You two are full of surprises."

Vladimir took another drink from his mug and then directed his attention back to Mauro. "Today was the first time I have seen your wife, Mauritius. She looks quite charming. Are you still disappointed with the arrangement?"

Mauro smiled. He knew his uncle was only pointing out the obvious. "The arrangement has been more than acceptable, Uncle Vladimir. I hope you can stay long enough to get to know Terese a little better."

Vladimir seemed to relax his manner. He took another drink and said, "Unfortunately, I must leave for Venice in the morning. Your claim of Dubovic's involvement in your father's death is a delicate matter best argued in person. He has quite a dossier open with the authorities, you know."

Mauro's thoughts went to Dubovic's pirating scheme, and he mentioned, "I understand Dubovic had some fraudulent insurance claims."

"Among other things." Their uncle went on to explain, "Baron Dubovic has been in poor standing with the Republic and owes years in back taxes. He has two married daughters, but I do not think their husbands can afford to take on the outstanding sum the estate owes. Dubovic's siblings are all dead, and the distant relations are not wealthy enough to take back the estate, either. I will recommend splitting and selling the land to settle their family's enormous debt."

"I am sure there are enough new noblemen in Venice who will want to buy themselves a castle," Mauro said.

"My concern is only with the new nobleman here." Vladimir glanced over at Jero. "I am afraid I cannot help you with your request, Mauritius. It is out of my power to change those things now."

Mauro got up and went to his writing desk. He found the two envelopes he had received just yesterday from Venice.

"It is resolved, Uncle Vladimir," Mauro said. He presented his uncle with the documents, and the count read through the many stamped and endorsed papers.

Their uncle took an audible breath. He looked at his two nephews and said, "I am impressed, Mauritius. It seems you have more influence than I do in this matter. If you are sure that is what you want, I will not stand against it this time. I will let you make whatever concessions you think are appropriate."

Underneath his cool façade, Mauro's heart pounded with joy. "Jero and I have already discussed it, Uncle, and we are both satisfied with the terms I have decided on."

The count set the papers down again. "I see that you will remain baron, Mauritius, and I am glad for that. There was a reason, Jero, that you were not named Lorenc's son so many years ago. But facts change, and I can see, sitting across from you here, that you are indeed my nephew. You look so much like him, you could be his ghost. It will take some time for me to grow accustomed to that."

Jero nodded politely.

"I have one last question for you, Mauritius. It relates to the family secret. May I speak freely?"

"Jero knows everything, Uncle."

"Well then, you mentioned in your letter to me that Dubovic suspected there was some reward for all of his plotting, some fortune that the Barics possess, but he wanted. Did he know where your treasure is kept?"

"He asked Jero to tell him where the gemstones were hidden, so it does not seem like he did," Mauro replied. "The alcove in the tunnel has been a secret all these years, but we moved the gems from there. No one else knows about the mine at the end of the cave, except for those who always have. Right now, that is just us three and Nestor." And Resi and Patrik, but Mauro would not complicate the discussion with this new detail.

The count looked pleased. He leaned back in his chair and asked, "Do you know how the emeralds were first discovered?"

Mauro replied, "I heard my grandfather Fredrik had mined them."

"He did, but he was not the first. It was actually my grandfather, Jeronim Baric, who first discovered the emerald vein. If news of the find got out to Venice, the Barics would have been in danger of losing their land to the greedy Empire. So, Jeronim quietly mined enough for posterity and then sealed the cave. But my father, your grandfather Fredrik, wanted more. With his new emeralds, he built this manor house, then the church, and then he expanded the village square. He was the one who began regularly trading the gems as payment. Then Lorenc spent the last of the fortune to renovate the manor house again. He secretly mined more from the cave to replenish Jeronim's original coffers. There should still be a small fortune left for you."

"There is, Uncle. But if I were to spend it, I do not know whom I would even trust to mine the cave again."

"Trust no one. Seal the cave, Mauritius, and be satisfied with the jewels stored for your needs. The Empire pays you little mind with your salt trade and harvest sales. Keep it that way, and the Barics will survive. You are the future of Croatia, you and Jero and your sons."

The count paused to let his treasonous words sink in.

"I will try to give you some peace for as long as I can, but the truce with the Habsburgs is fragile. If there is a new battle, I may have to call upon you and your soldiers to fortify my army again, but only as a last resort. I would like to see the last two Barics replenish the House of Baric with sons rather than emeralds."

"If it can be managed, my soldiers and I will be grateful to remain at home for a while."

Vladimir Toth clapped his hands together as though they had sealed a treaty. "Now, I would like to have a private word with Jero," he said.

~*~

As Mauro left the room, Vladimir focused his attention on the tray in the middle of the table. He took a piece of cake with his jeweled fingers and bit into it. He had not eaten that morning, and Franja's pastries were a delight.

"Are you hungry?" he asked Jero.

"No, sir."

The count was poised and self-assured as he studied his new nephew. He took a second mouthful while Jero politely waited for him to finish.

Jero was no longer intimidated seated next to him. He had looked upon these stern Baric faces his whole life, and he knew how to read them. The count's eyes would give him away.

"I would understand if you hated me, Jero," his uncle declared abruptly. "My brother never forgave me for interfering. He went to great lengths to get you back and petitioned to have you legitimized as his son, second in line after Mateo. I could have signed off on his first petition, but it would have set Johanna over the edge. She was already unstable. Then after Mateo died, Lorenc said he wanted you to be able to carry on the Baric name. I denied Lorenc's petition a second time. I am sorry for that, Jero."

Jero listened to the weak apology and had his own script ready.

"I do not hate you, sir. I have seen how the rules work with the titled class, and I did not fit into your orderly world. I may have grown up on the fringe of the Baric family, but my father included me in it as well as he could. Mauro and I grew up as close as any brothers, even if we were told we were not. And if my father fought to legitimize me after my mother's death, then that is enough for me to feel wanted like a son. I can live with the fact that you cannot accept me, as you do Mauro, but I hope one day you will."

Vladimir looked at his nephew and tried not to see his brother in his place, pleading once more for Jero's cause.

"I know your father was proud of you, Jero. He would have also been proud of Mauritius for insisting you be named a Baric. Mauro did not have to do that, you know."

Jero struggled to remain composed. "I do know that, and I promise you I will not take advantage of Mauro's generosity."

That was all Vladimir needed to hear. "You will do well with your brother by your side," he said.

"Thank you, sir."

"I have watched you grow over the years, Jero, and I believe you are worthy of our family name. Going forward, you may call me your uncle."

Then Vladimir slipped a gold ring off his right hand and set it on the table before Jero. The heirloom jewel had two small emeralds flanking the Baric crest.

"This ring belonged to my grandfather, your namesake," his uncle said. "It is yours now. Wear it well, Jeronim Lorenc Baric, and know where you belong."

Jero blinked back the tears. He understood it could not have been an easy decision to part with it. He slid the ancient ring onto his finger and stared at it for a long moment. When he finally looked up, the count was smiling a rare smile.

"Thank you, Uncle."

Vladimir turned his attention back to the table. "I am going to sample each of these tempting delicacies," he said to his nephew. "Would you like a plate, Jero?"

Jero wondered if he would ever be able to switch the tone of a conversation as skillfully as the Baric men could.

"No thank you, Uncle. I will leave you to your meal, if that is alright." Jero stood up and went to the door to leave.

Vladimir called over, "Find Mauritius for me, will you, Jero? Tell him I am anxious to sign the inquiry papers for your unfortunate incident here."

"I will, Uncle."

"And, Jero?"

"Yes, sir?" Jero gave his new uncle his full attention, thinking this was important.

Vladimir held up a powdery square and said, "Tell Franja I will need a box of these cakes to take with me tomorrow. And ask Nela if we could have a dish of her special calamari for dinner tonight."

The count wasn't all business, after all.

Chapter 72

Nela was happy to accommodate their honored guest's special request, and she oversaw every detail that evening to be sure the meal was perfect.

Cook wasn't flustered like the other servants when Count Toth walked into the kitchen just before dinner to say hello to her. The count was once her little boy Vladimir, who had sat with her by the fire on cold winter mornings, eating his buttered toast and drinking warmed milk, while a teenage Nela rolled out the fresh dough for that day's baking. He had always liked coming to the kitchen for her cooking and her company.

Count Toth had not visited the castle since Lady Johanna's funeral. He looked around at the young faces busily working in the kitchen.

"How have you been, Nela?" he asked cheerfully. "Will you not finally come back with me and manage my kitchen now?"

"And leave my mistress with a new Baric baby on the way? This is where I am needed, my lord," Nela replied just as merrily.

He came to the table where she was working and lifted the lids of the various platters, releasing the savory smells.

"Tell me, Nela. Are you fond of the new baroness?"

Even though Lady Johanna had been his wife's sister, she could speak the truth to him. "Indeed, I am. Her ladyship is like a burst of fresh sea air into this old house, my lord."

"And my nephew, Nela? How is he since her arrival?"

"Well, they do say that the sea air has healing properties. The young baron has had much grief these last years, and I have been worried for him. But I think he is going to be fine. I have never seen him happier."

"I am glad to know that. Now, if you ever change your mind, Nela . . ."

He began to flirt again but was distracted by Ivana, who set another readied platter on the kitchen table to be taken out to the sideboard in the great hall. It was his calamari.

He nodded his thanks to his favorite cook and said, "I see the dinner preparations are complete. I will go and take my place in the other room."

Nela gave him a wink and said, "Yes, my lord, take your place. You can tell me later whether you were satisfied with our menu here at Baric Castle."

~*~

Nela had managed a delicious meal for Count Toth, his high-ranking officers, and the remaining guests. Everyone was indeed satisfied with the kitchen's numerous dishes that evening. Toasts were given between each course, especially for Jero and Ruby's potential wedding engagement and to the next generation of Barics. The group speculated about who might be granted the right to buy the Dubovic land and what sort of new neighbors the Barics would have. And then the conversation became more somber.

Count Toth was a man used to feasting with politicians and then doing their bidding on the battlefields, so the discussion expectedly turned to war and politics. The count reported on the current debates in the Senate and the new troubles the Empire had in keeping the Habsburgs appeased. Men brought these topics up when among other men, and Resi listened in with fascination.

Resi sat to one side of her new uncle, and Jero had been honored to be seated on the other side of him. She felt at ease with her engaging dinner partner. Lord Toth was surprisingly attentive and likable, very different from her first impression a few hours ago. It was apparent how influential the count had been to her husband during his years under his uncle's wing. Mauro had the same smooth mannerisms. She wished she had met the count's brother, Mauro's father. She was convinced now that Lord Lorenc would have been different from how she had imagined him.

Mauro sat to Resi's left, and her brother and Salar Nassim sat across from them. The men debated the best route to take when crossing the mountains back to Thessaloniki. Salar Nassim preferred to travel down the coast of Dalmatia and cut over mid-way to take the road through Skopje. Following the coast as far south as Tirana was his other choice, but Count Toth had heard some disturbing news of trouble at the Ottoman borders near Ragusa. They pondered the advantages of going the longer but safer route, directly east into Habsburg territory and then south from there, the way the mercenaries had arrived. They would think on it until morning.

What was decided that evening, though, was the two groups of dinner guests would leave tomorrow without delay. The count and his troop of escorts would head north to Venice, and the mercenaries south, taking Jero and Ruby.

With an early start planned, Ruby and Resi excused themselves to retire for the night.

The others did not linger much longer, and Lord Toth went to the Keep with Mauro and the mercenaries. Mauro had told his uncle about Simeon's injuries and the decision to amputate his leg. Simeon had served in the count's army for several years, and the count had asked to visit him.

After leaving his uncle at Simeon's door to go in alone, Mauro followed the four mercenaries into their chamber across the hall.

"Thank you again for taking Jero," Mauro told the four men. "I am indebted to you."

"All our debts are squared, Lord Baric. Jero will be no extra burden for us," Salar Nassim insisted.

Patrik then said what they were all thinking, "I can tell you are uneasy about our tentative plans after our talk at dinner. It is only a few weeks' ride, Mauro, and we know how to avoid Ottoman trouble. We will pick the best route, don't you worry."

"I trust that you will."

"Castor will bring the two back to meet your ship on his next voyage. It will all work out," Patrik said.

"I forget sometimes that the wars are over," Mauro said. "It will be an uneventful journey, I am sure."

They had not shut the chamber door, and Mauro noticed his uncle leaving Simeon's room. He went to the doorway.

Count Toth came over to his nephew's side and quietly said, "You might be right about Simeon, Mauritius."

"Did he talk to you, at least?" Mauro asked.

"He talked to me. But what concerns me is that he does not talk to you," his uncle said grimly.

The Toth soldiers were housed on the top floor of the Keep, and the count still needed to confirm their departure with them. Vladimir patted Mauro on the shoulder for comfort and told him, "I will see you at breakfast before we leave. Good night, Mauro."

"Good night, Uncle."

Lord Toth went up the winding staircase, and Mauro remained, staring at Simeon's closed door.

Soren came up behind him and asked, "May I talk to Simeon?"

Mauro was surprised by his request. He stepped aside for Soren to enter and sat down at the long table in the hallway. He would wait, although he did not know what for.

~*~

Simeon was sitting up on his rumpled bed, propped against his pillows, when Soren entered without a greeting. He took the chair from Simeon's table next to the wall and brought it to the bedside. Then Soren noticed the crutch leaning against the wall and brought that.

Simeon watched him. The Baric captains and the mercenaries had been on friendly terms this last week, but they were not friends.

"Someone made you a nice crutch," Soren said, examining the handywork. "Have you used it? You should try to move around to keep strong."

Simeon scowled at him. "How can I move around with no leg?"

"You have two arms and another sound leg. Here, try," Soren said, holding out the crutch.

"Have you not looked at me? I'm a cripple," Simeon grumbled back.

"Today, yes, but not forever," Soren told him. "Why don't you let your friends help you? You could lean on your new crutch to get to the toilet instead of someone cleaning you up in your bed. Isn't that more unpleasant?"

Simeon sank down on his pillows and wished the Dane would go away. "Why are you bothering me? I did not choose to be a worthless invalid."

Soren touched the blanket where Simeon's leg should have been and asked, "May I have a look?"

Simeon glared at him but nodded weakly.

Soren lifted the bed cover and untied the linen wrapping. After a moment, he said brightly, "Idita did a good job. It is a clean cut above the knee and well-stitched. I have seen men with much less leg who eventually got around fine."

"I have no leg. She left me a stump. What kind of a man can I be with that?"

"Idita did what she had to do. I couldn't help but notice that she didn't take your manhood with the leg."

Simeon scoffed. "A lot of good that will do me."

"Did you know your lady friend has come by every day asking for you? Why don't you let her in? I thought you were going to marry her?"

"Franja is only coming out of pity. She will be better off finding a new man, a whole one."

"I've heard that a one-legged man can still satisfy a woman," Soren said as he wrapped and covered Simeon's leg with care. "She would not keep trying to see you, if she didn't believe it to be so." Soren challenged him to find fault in this, but Simeon only held his stare.

"She feels sorry for me," Simeon finally said.

"Of course, she feels sorry for you, Simeon. Your leg was crushed by a horse, and you had a lump the size of an apple on your head—you were out cold for two days! Look, we all feel sorry for your pain, but that is different from pitying you." Soren held out the crutch again. "Why don't you try it? I will help you."

"Why don't you leave me alone?"

Simeon found the strength to roll away from him, moaning with the effort, but Soren was not ready to give up.

"Seeing you reminds me of my brother," Soren said to Simeon's back. "I miss him every day. I wish the tourniquet had worked for Niels, and we could have stopped his bleeding, like we stopped yours. I wish he were here again. He was the surgeon of our group, you know, and he would've taken your leg off to save your life, too. The baron said you won't see him, Simeon. You won't even talk to him. He was right to do what he did."

Simeon could not muster gratitude for Mauro's desperate order. "Mauro ruined my life," he said to the wall.

"His order saved your life."

"He had no right to make that choice for me," Simeon growled and pulled his blanket up higher.

"You have a point," Soren said to the blanket. "The baron should have asked you, but he couldn't just then, could he? You were dying."

Soren stood up to leave but paused when he noticed what was hanging from the pegs along the wall. He took down Simeon's sheathed knife, put the blade on the mattress, and then leaned the crutch next to it. He went to the door and opened it.

Simeon rolled over. A gasp of surprise, perhaps even fear, slipped from his lips.

Soren said from the doorway, "Your friends care about you and your happiness, Simeon. You have free choice to live your life, or not. No one will fault you for your decision." He pointed to the bed. "Choose one or choose the other, but get on with it."

Mauro still sat at the table in the hallway and saw what Soren had left his friend. Mauro's eyes met Simeon's across the expanse, and then Soren closed the door on them.

Mauro stood up in alarm. "Why would you do that, Soren?"

"Do what, Lord Baric?"

"Put a knife in the hands of a suicidal man!" Mauro shouted.

The others came out of their chambers and watched whether the argument would evolve further.

Mauro ignored them all and started to open Simeon's door, but Soren caught the baron's arm and held him back.

"He is not going to kill himself, Lord Baric," Soren hissed, not to be heard through the closed door. "He is a proud man who needs to figure out how to ask for help. He wants to live."

Mauro did not open the door, and Soren released the baron's arm.

"What if you are wrong, Soren?"

"Simeon could have gotten that knife himself at any time if he truly wanted to. He will make the right choice. You will see."

Chapter 73

It was a difficult day at Baric Castle. Count Toth and his entourage left after breakfast, as planned. The second group loaded their gear onto their horses shortly thereafter. The Baric servants lined up in the courtyard to say their final farewells to Jero, who had been with them his whole life, and to his future bride, Ruby, whom they had all grown so fond of. There was not a dry eye among them.

"We will return soon," Jero told each and every one he embraced. This was his true family, and he could no longer hold back his tears before he finally let the last handshake go and mounted Zeus.

Patrik tightened the last straps on his horse. His sister was at his side.

"Promise me you will stop fighting now," Resi pleaded.

"I am not foolish about war any longer. I have a purse full of silver and gold, and I can live off that for a long time. First, though, Soren and I promised Bem we would help him find his wife in Athens. After that, I think I might do what Soren wants."

"Go back to Thessaloniki?"

"He wants to sail to the New World, Resi."

Patrik had not told his sister about Soren's wish, and she felt weak in the knees and clung to his saddle. There were too many goodbyes for one morning.

"Then I will never see you again, dearest brother."

"It is not forever, Resi," he said as he took his sister in his arms. "Soren has already been to the end of the world and made it back unscathed. I need one more adventure, but I will be back. Papa will be proud that I will finally be a sailor, don't you think?"

"He would be prouder if you were a captain," she managed to joke through her sobs.

"Be happy for me, Resi. It is the first thing I have looked forward to in a long time." She still frowned at him, and he added, "Except seeing you again, dearest Terese. I am very glad we came. You have a good life here. Stay well and make lots of little barons."

He mounted his laden horse, and she took his hand one last time and said, "Write to me before you leave on this final voyage so I can worry about you, Patricius."

"I will, and when I return, I will lounge on your lovely terrace with my nieces and nephews on my lap and tell them all about the New World and the strange things I encountered there."

"I expect the next time I see you, they will be old enough to enjoy that."

Patrik leaned down and kissed his sister's hand, and she let go of him.

Ruby was ready to leave on Fatina, behind Patrik's horse. She looked anxious and happy and sad all at once.

Resi had slept in Ruby's room last night and knew she should not say any more to delay their parting. She gave Ruby one last squeeze, and then Resi stepped back to Mauro's side.

The six lucky riders gave a final wave to their hosts and family and then galloped off through the gate. Resi collapsed mournfully into her husband's embrace when they were out of sight, and Mauro held her until he felt her getting stronger under his grip. The servants had wandered back to their duties, but Verica had stayed with the couple, off to the side. Mauro motioned for her to come to him. He passed his wife off to her lady's maid and whispered, "They will be back, Resi, my love. Go rest now. I will come find you later."

~*~

Resi let Verica walk her back into the house and up the stairs. At least she still had her young maid for company. The chamber doors were open, and the servants were already busy cleaning Ruby's room and the guest room, where Count Toth had slept. The maids would leave Jero's chamber as it was for now. They could not accept that he, too, had left the House of Baric.

Back in her room, Resi could not think of one thing she wanted to do that day, so she crawled back into the bed that she had forsaken last night and gave in to her need to put her heartbreak out of her mind. She fell into a restless sleep.

~*~

Mauro tried to keep his mind busy that day. Nestor had gladly resumed his role as the Barics' steward, and the two began outlining the documents they would present to Signor Rosso to register Jero's new land ownership. That took the rest of the morning and into the lunch hour.

Mauro met with Vilim later that afternoon and heard his report on the day's field practice. The men had started working with the newly purchased muskets, but it was clear to Vilim that they would need individualized instruction. With Simeon bedridden and Fabian gone, Mauro would have to think about how he would proceed with the training. Those were his two captains who had real experience with gunpowder and firearms. He decided to leave these details until tomorrow.

At last, Mauro focused on the most troublesome problem: his wife's unhappiness. He wanted to treat her to something special tonight, something that might help her feel some joy again after the sad goodbyes to their loved ones. Mauro also needed his spirits lifted, and he came up with a simple plan. He went to the kitchen to arrange the details.

~*~

Mauro let Resi sleep as he went about his work, but he grew concerned when she was still in bed at the end of the day. "Resi, my dear, wake up. You have missed the whole day," he said, shaking her gently.

She opened her eyes and focused on her husband. "There was nothing to miss," she said, and then she shut her eyes again.

"I have something for you, something I want you to see," he whispered in her ear. "Get up now and come out with me."

The playful note in his voice stirred her curiosity. Resi sat up and saw he was dressed in his favorite summer jacket. She noticed he smelled of lavender soap and not of horses.

"Is it time for dinner?"

"Yes, it is, but I have something to show you first. I usually go there at sunrise, but sunset will do."

"Another secret, Mauro?"

"Not really a secret," he said soothingly, "it is just my favorite place to go at the castle."

Mauro had told Resi about his leap with Jero into the sea and the story of Mateo's drowning. He had told her about the family treasure and showed her where he had hidden it in the crypt. They had taken a torch into the tunnel, and Mauro had shown her where the emeralds had been cut and stored since his forefathers had begun mining them. She knew about the wall but didn't think she would ever want to go in there again; the memories were too difficult.

This last place must indeed be special, Resi thought. His offer of adventure convinced her to get up. She tried to smooth her wrinkled skirts, but they were hopelessly crumpled. "Should I change my dress?" she asked.

"Your dress is perfect," he said. "I guarantee this place will not be dusty or dark or cold, at least not this time of the year. Here, let me help you lace your shoes."

"Is it outside?"

Mauro could barely contain his excitement. "Yes and no, but we will need to walk quite a distance. And we must hurry."

She was eager now and followed him down the stairs. They left the manor house through the front door, and Mauro led her across the empty courtyard to the tower steps.

"I have seen the Keep, remember?" she told him.

"Not the place I want to show you," he replied, hurrying her up the outside steps.

Still holding her hand, Mauro led her in through the dining room doors. Soldiers were eating their meals and stood at attention when they saw the baroness come in.

Mauro did not attempt to explain her presence and hurried her past the curious men. He led her to a far set of stairs he had not shown her before. They continued up and up, to the top floor, out the doors, and up a second set of stairs to the open roof.

The sky was beginning to fade to brilliant ribbons of orange with soft pink edges as the sun sank into the sea and the mountains faded to blackness behind them, to the east. A few lights twinkled in the direction of the village below them, and stars grew visible in the sky above. The view was unobstructed for miles and miles out to the islands, over the orchards, and up the long road leaving the Baric lands.

Mauro sat on the stone parapet and pulled his wife onto his lap. Both were out of breath from their urgent climb to catch a glimpse of the setting sun.

"Oh, Mauro, the view is beautiful," Resi said, locked in his arms. "It had never occurred to me that one could come up here."

"I started coming here when I first returned after my father's death," he explained as he stared out to the west. "I needed to find a quiet place at end of the day to clear my head—there was so much to do and learn all at once. Then I found that sunrises were even better."

Sitting on his knee, she looked up at his contented expression and asked, "Is that what you do so early each morning?"

"Sometimes all I need is a few minutes to feel a part of it all. It is so distant, yet close at the same time." Mauro wrapped his arms around her and absently stroked her round middle. "What you see, from end to end, belongs to the Barics. Hundreds of people count on us to do the right thing for them. When I need to remind myself of that, I come up here. I wanted to share that with you. It is mine, but it is also yours."

He set her back on the solid pavers and walked her to the center of the vast stone roof. When they had rushed by, Resi had not noticed that a low table was set on a carpet there with scattered cushions. Groups of candles were all around the rug, and Mauro went to light them. There were covered platters to the side, with a bottle of wine and glasses.

"Are we dining here, Mauro?"

"Yes, we are celebrating, just you and I. We will toast to our friends' well-being as they start their journey to a new life. And we will toast to our own good fortune, my love. I am happy tonight to begin the rest of my life with you."

No servants would interrupt their solitary banquet, and there were no formalities to uphold—just two people content with the world for once, and with each other.

Resi and Mauro relaxed on their cushions and talked of everything and nothing. They shared their hopes and dreams for a bright future together. Everything would be easy again, they concluded. Everything would be right for them going forward.

~*~

In another part of the Empire, Mauro and Resi's friends were settling in around a campfire. It had been a long day but an easy ride on well-traveled roads. As the baron and baroness had hoped, Jero and Ruby were just as happy on their glorious first night away. The two could never imagine that anything could crush their hopes for a new life together. But alas, mere hope cannot protect the Barics and their friends from what is to come. They will have to rely on deeper strengths to get them through what is destined for the House of Baric.

~The End of Part Two~

AN AFTERWORD

Thank you again, dear reader, for choosing this book and taking a chance on a new author!

When I first drafted *The House of Baric,* the story ended here, with Mauro and Resi on the rooftop, realizing they were finally happy. The original ending didn't have the last paragraph about Jero's and Ruby's first night away. I thought I would leave it to your imagination to decide if Angelos agreed to let Jero marry his daughter or whether Bem found his wife, and all the other little unresolved endings written in the pages. Not to be all doom and gloom, but in my imagination, I saw trouble ahead, and I knew enough about their futures to be able to write a third book. Plus, Resi still needed to have her baby! So, whenever you are ready, *Part Three: Widows and Weddings* will answer these last questions and will be the final ending.

I reread *A Brother's Defense* during the 2021 pandemic, and even to me, the storyteller, this middle book seemed too long. I couldn't help but get out my red marker and trim a few hundred unneeded words in each chapter. Satisfied with this edition, I wanted to design a new cover for this updated book. Artvee.com was an inspirational resource for me this year. In their public domain collection, I found several paintings that blended nicely to depict one moment in time from a favorite chapter. The added sword on the inn's walkway was from my first edition and was meant to forewarn you of peril. (Did it work?) I will pin the original artwork on my page at Pinterest.com/JillianBald. All components of the book's design were used with permission.

To learn more about the author and her stories, please visit:
www.JillianBald.com

Books in This Trilogy:

The House of Baric Part One: Shields Down
The House of Baric Part Two: A Brother's Defense
The House of Baric Part Three: Widows and Weddings

9 781943 594160